THE CARDBOARD KINGDOM

BY CHAD SELL

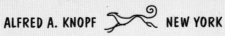

ALFRED A. KNOPF   NEW YORK

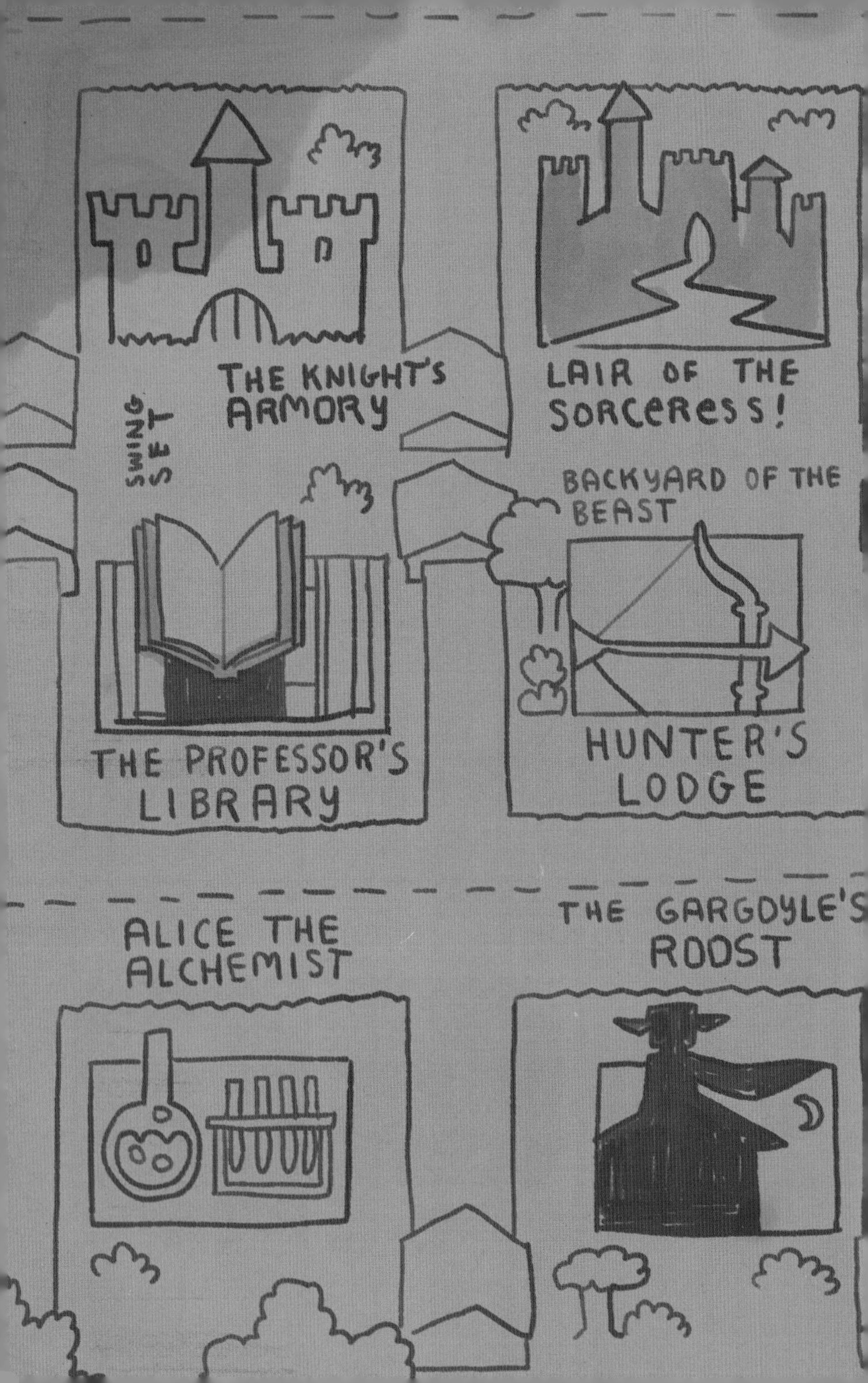
THE KNIGHT'S ARMORY
LAIR OF THE SORCERESS!
SWING SET
BACKYARD OF THE BEAST
THE PROFESSOR'S LIBRARY
HUNTER'S LODGE
ALICE THE ALCHEMIST
THE GARGOYLE'S ROOST

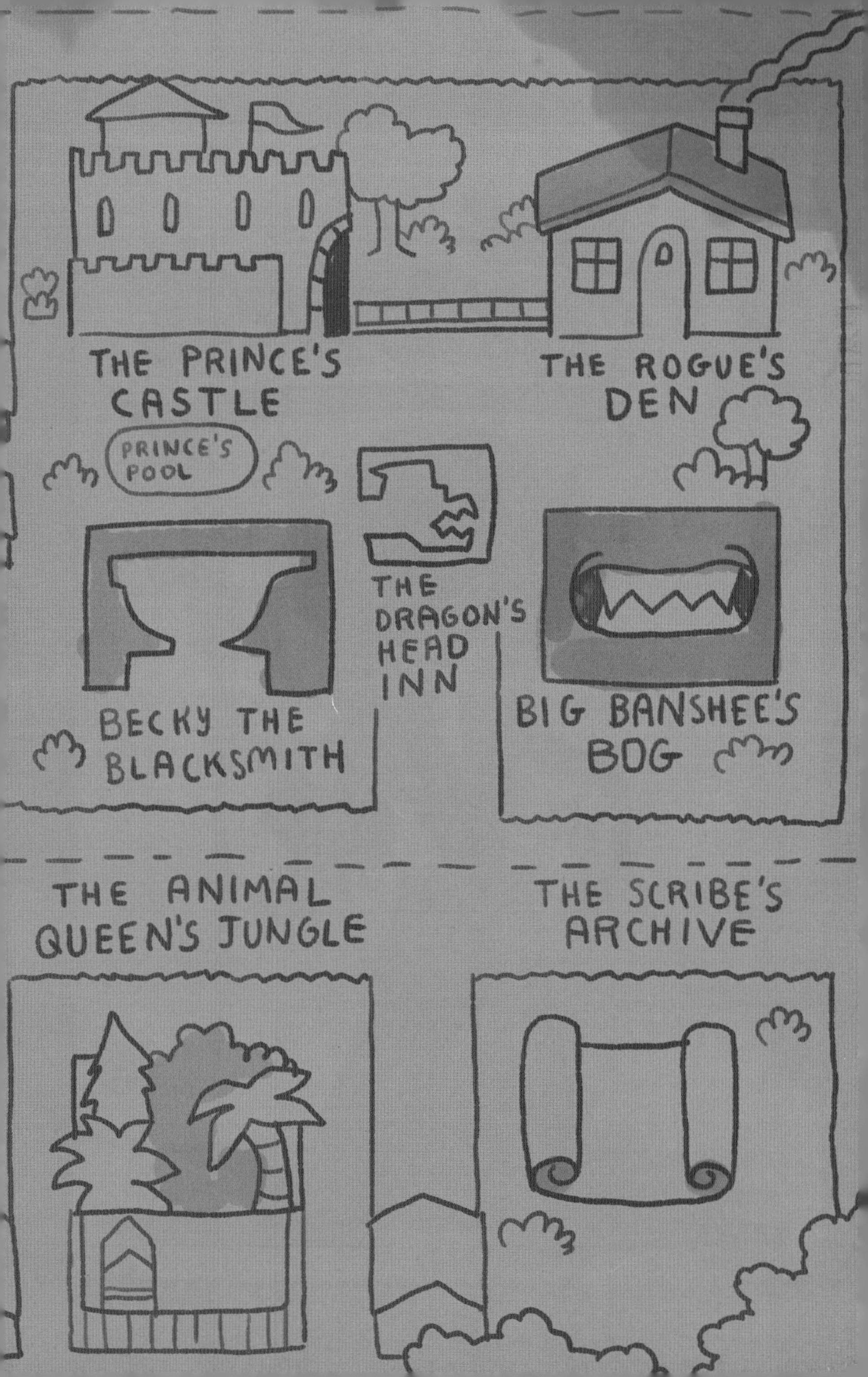
THE PRINCE'S CASTLE
PRINCE'S POOL
THE ROGUE'S DEN
THE DRAGON'S HEAD INN
BECKY THE BLACKSMITH
BIG BANSHEE'S BOG
THE ANIMAL QUEEN'S JUNGLE
THE SCRIBE'S ARCHIVE

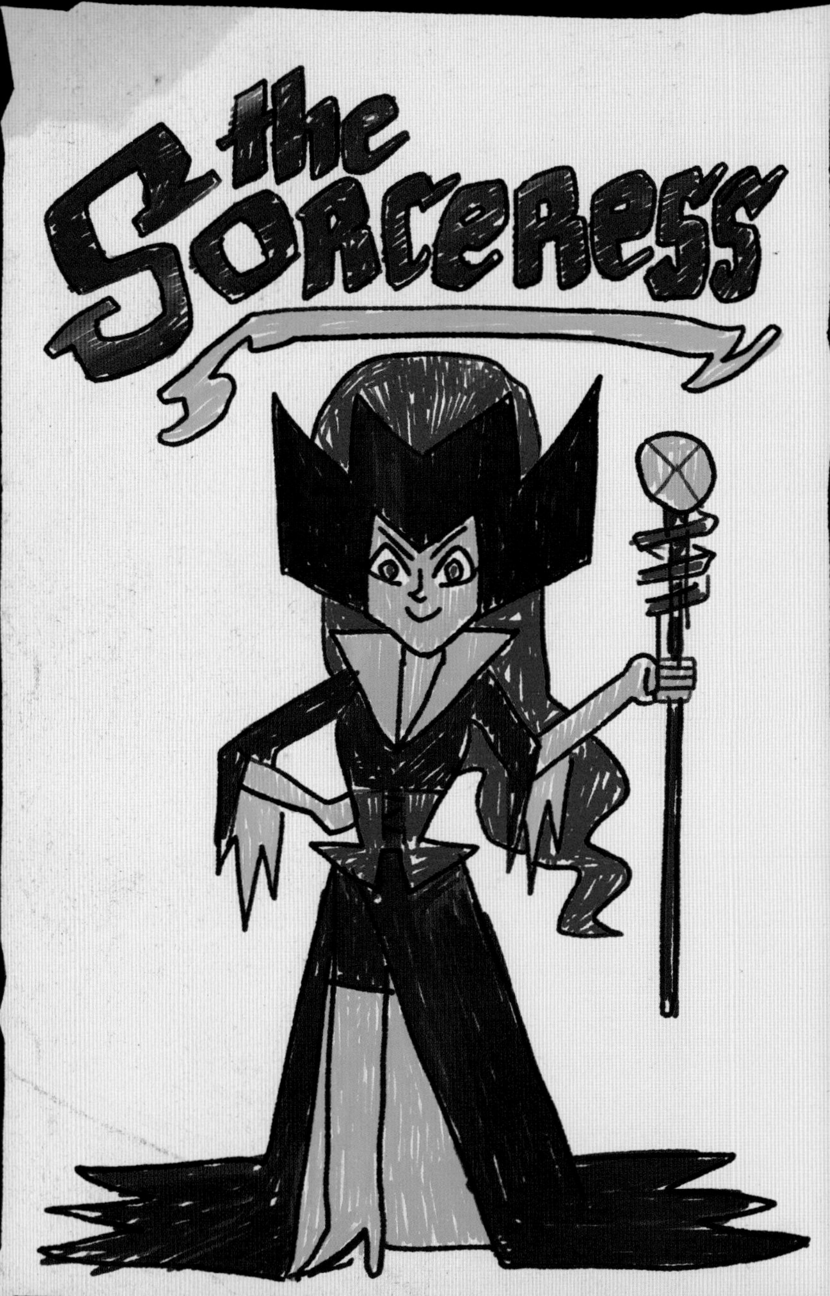
the Sorceress

BY JAY FULLER AND CHAD SELL

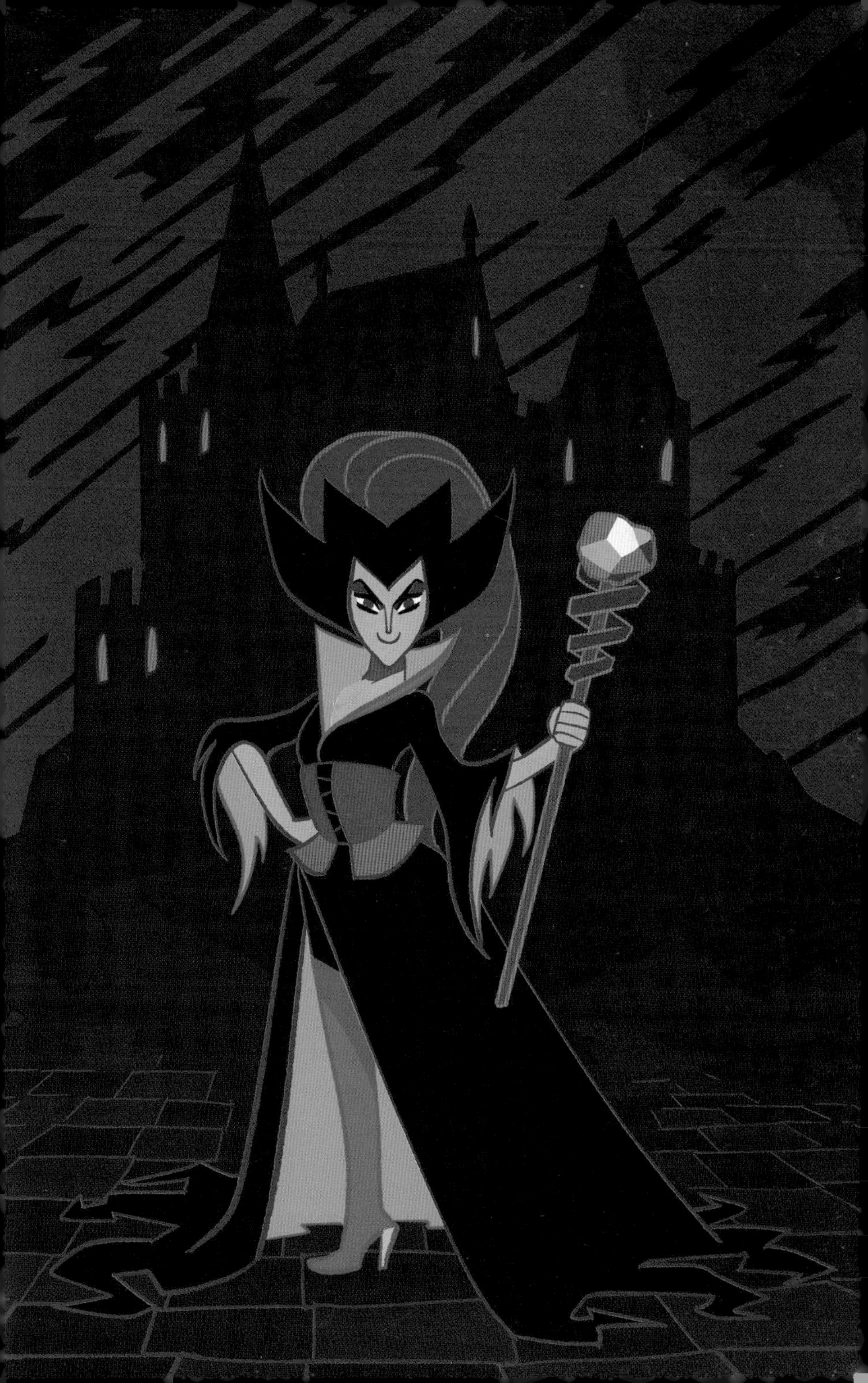

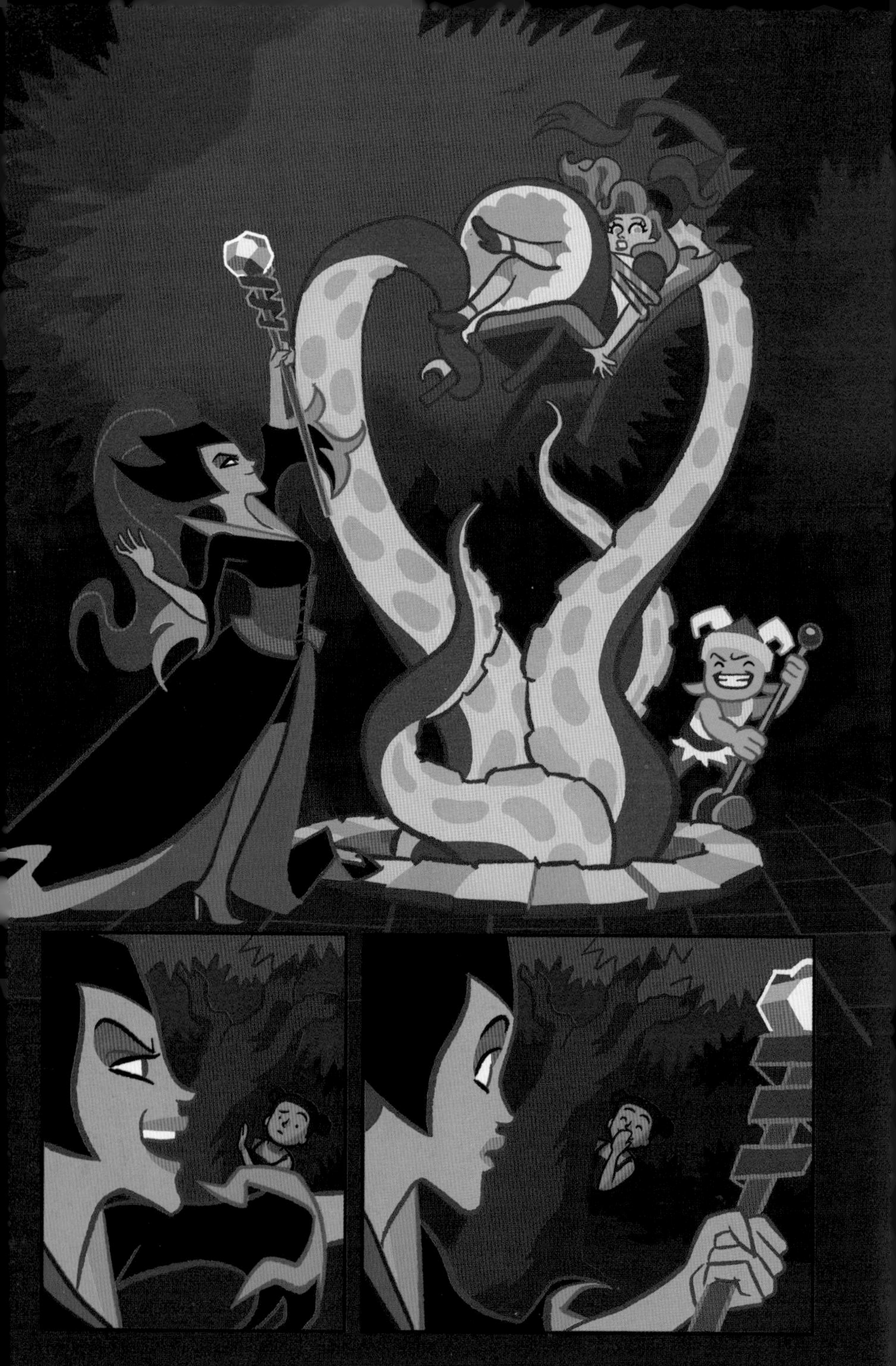

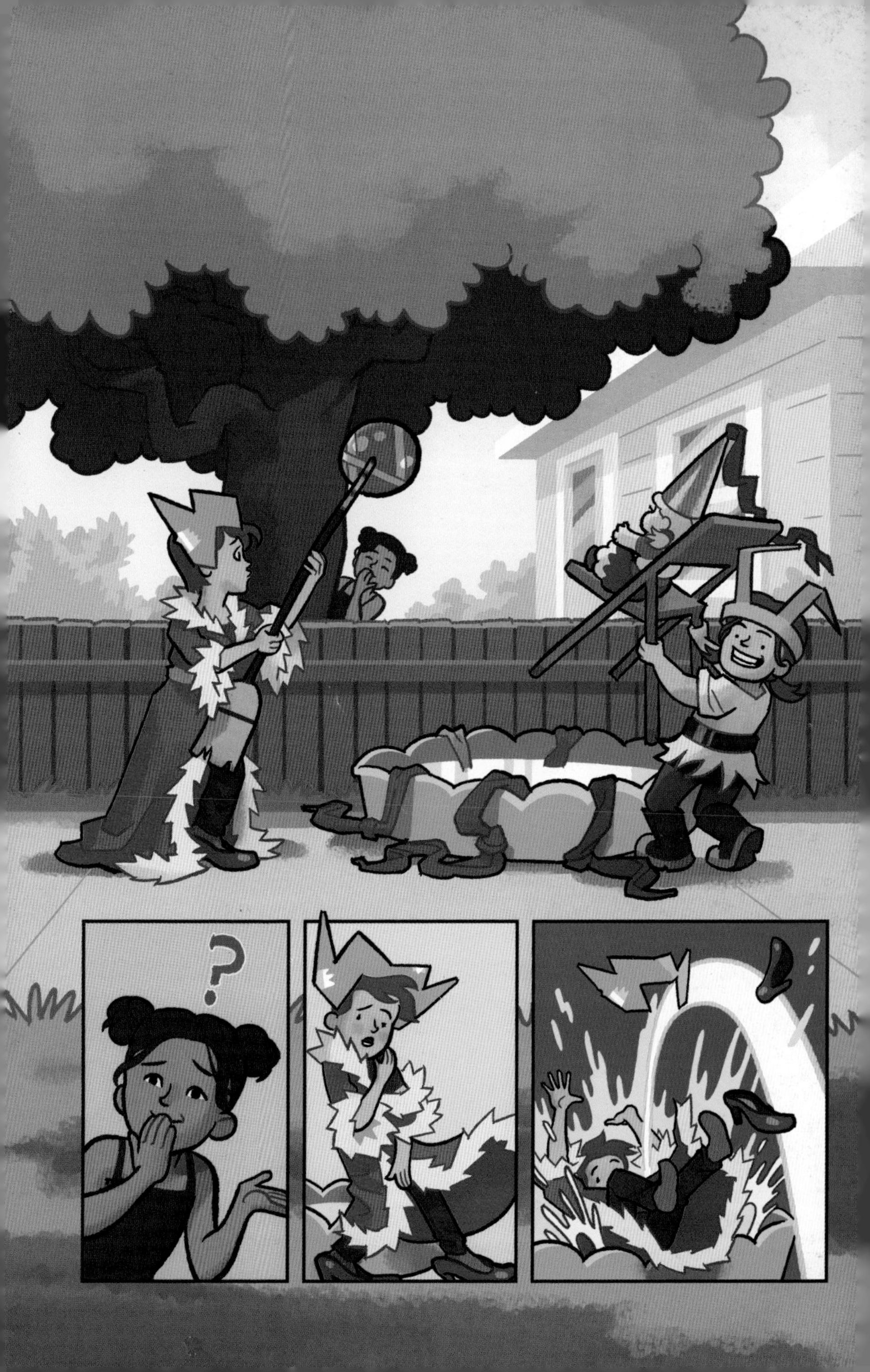

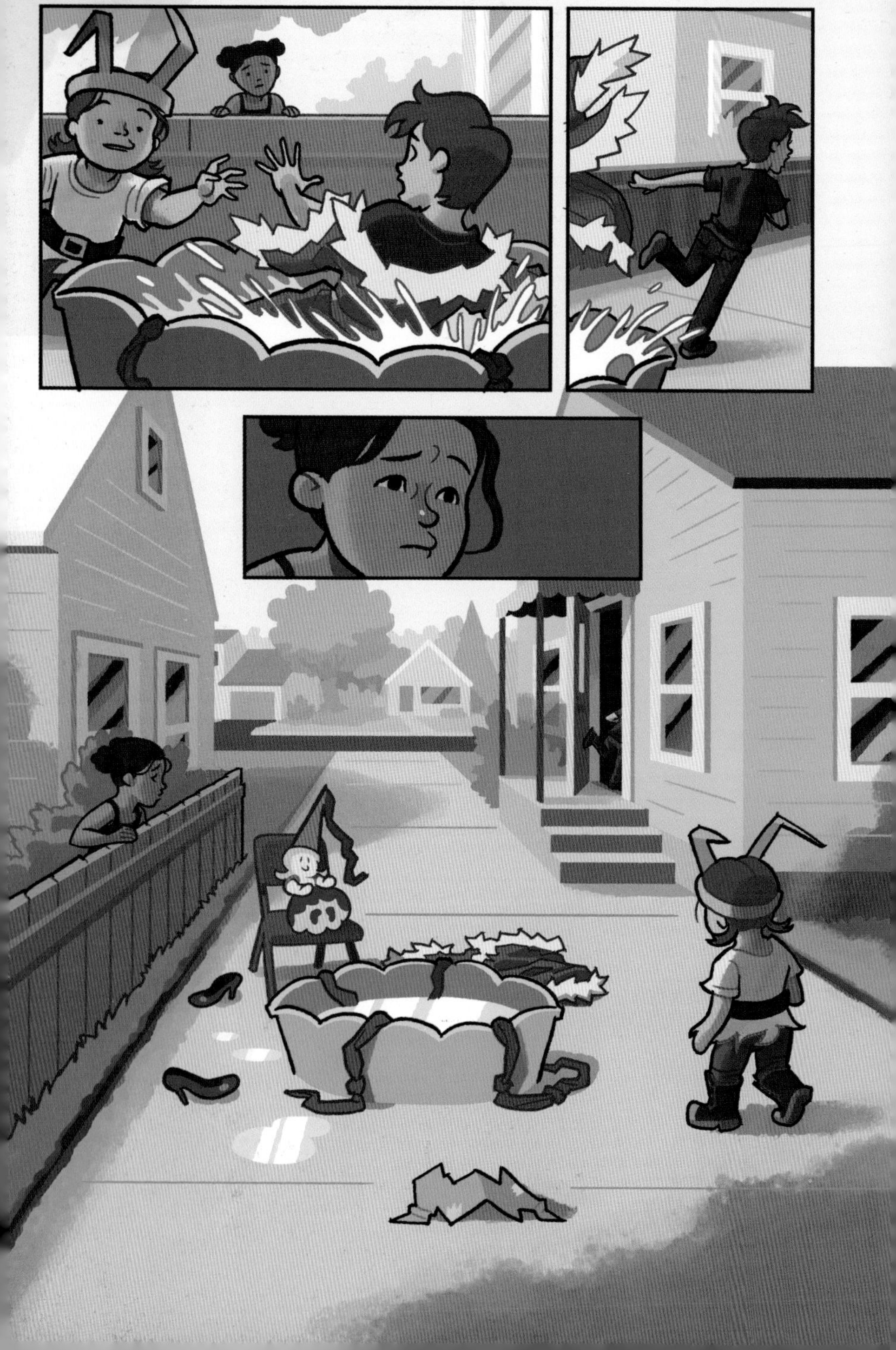

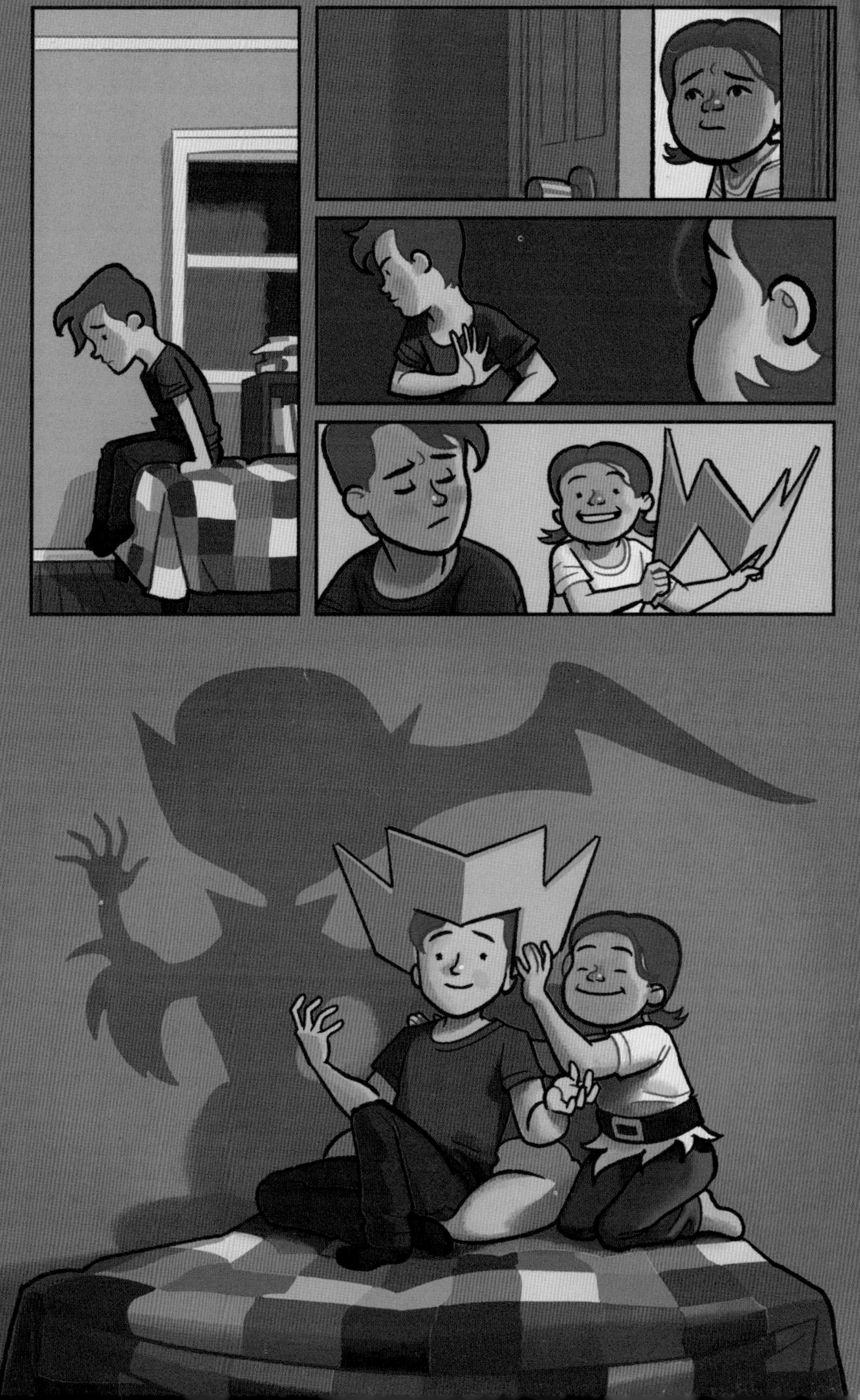

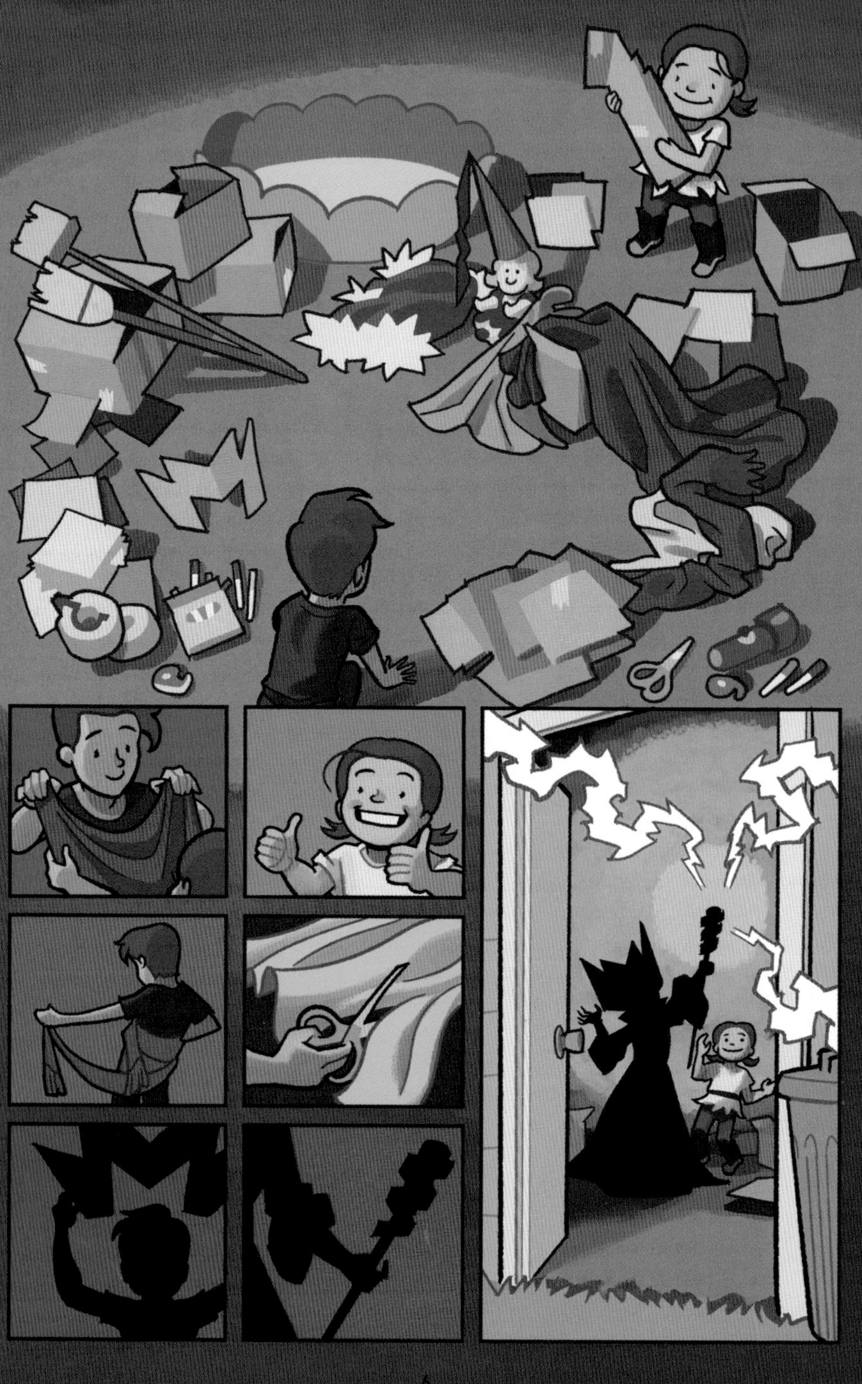

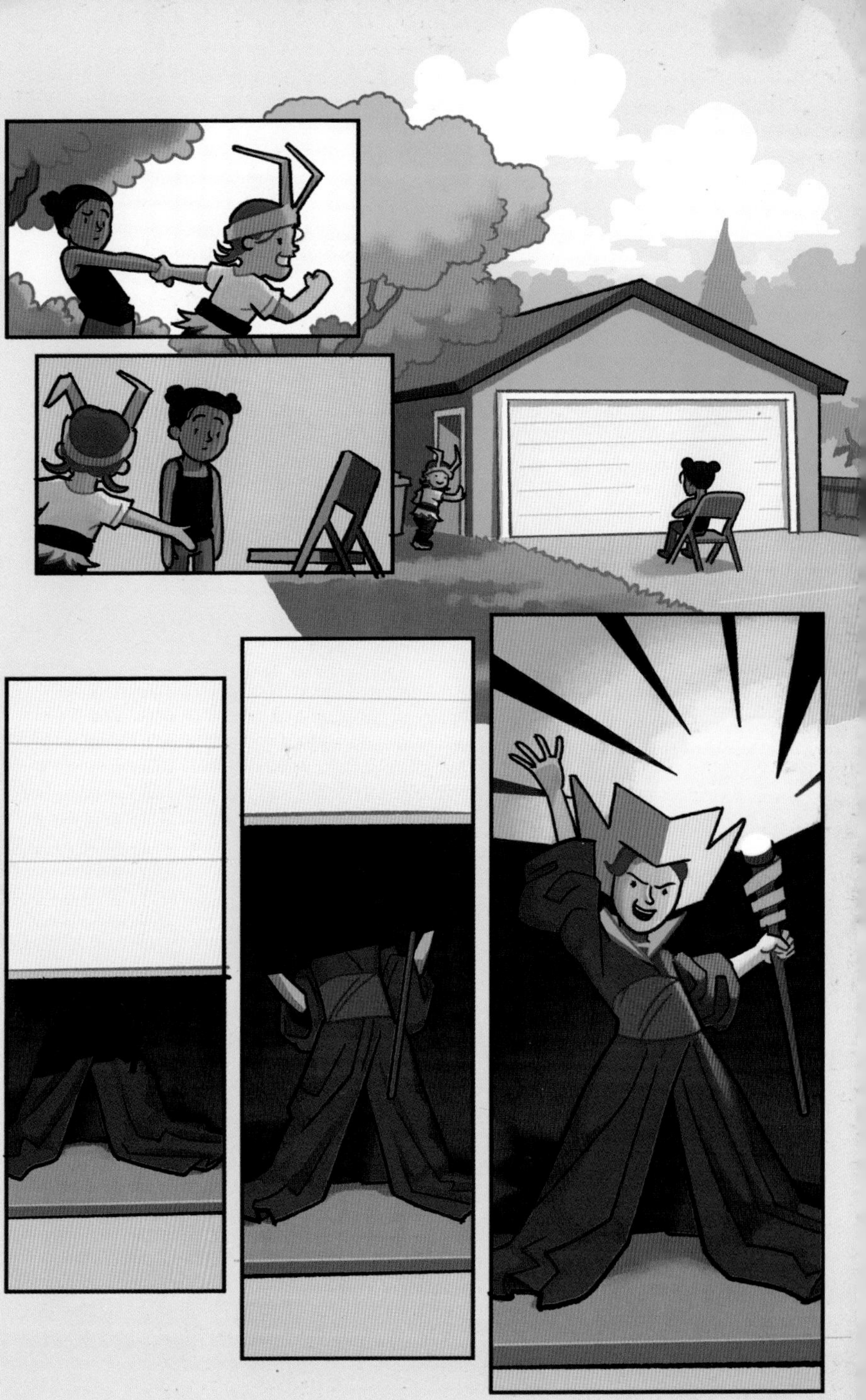

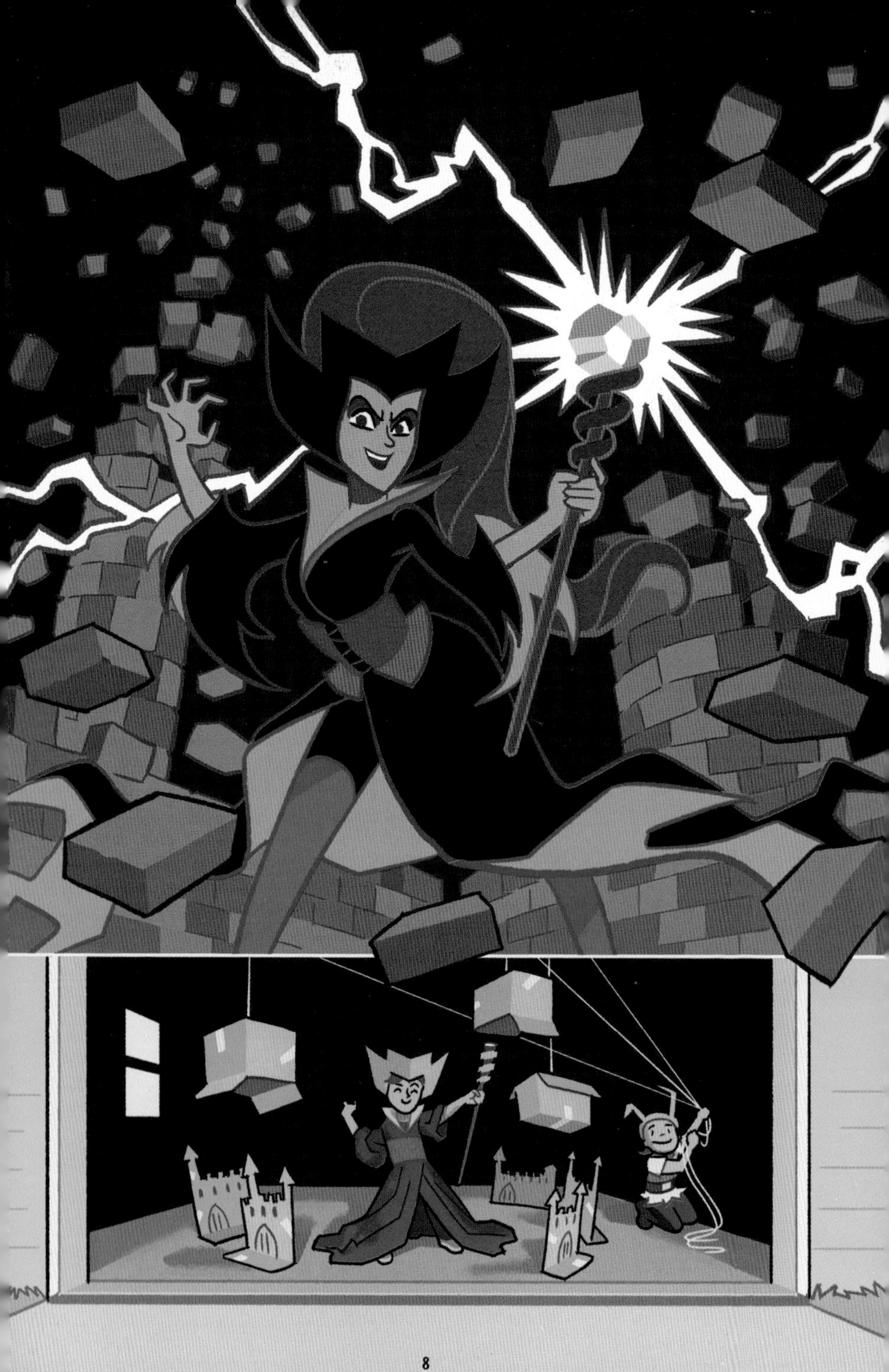

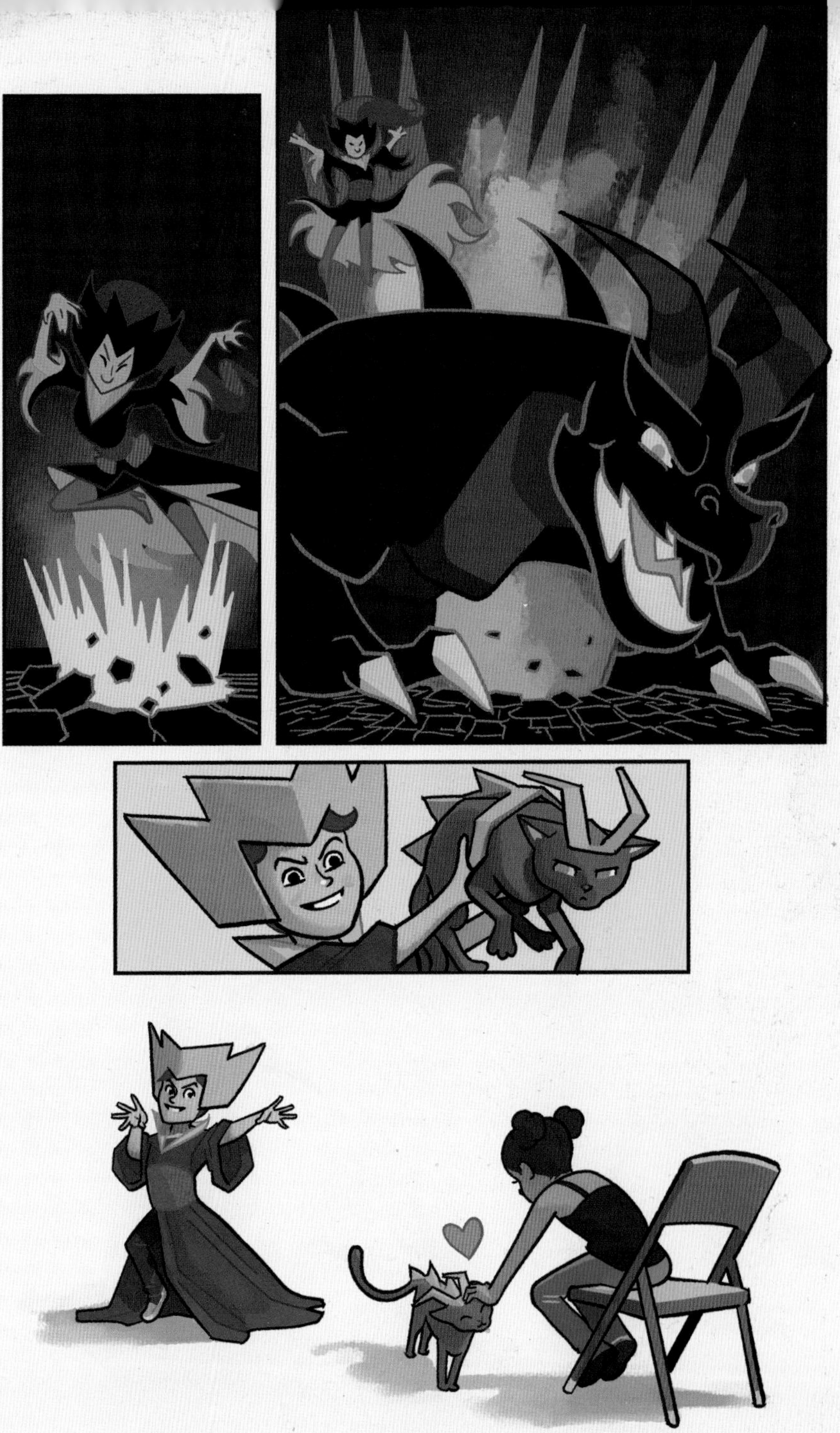

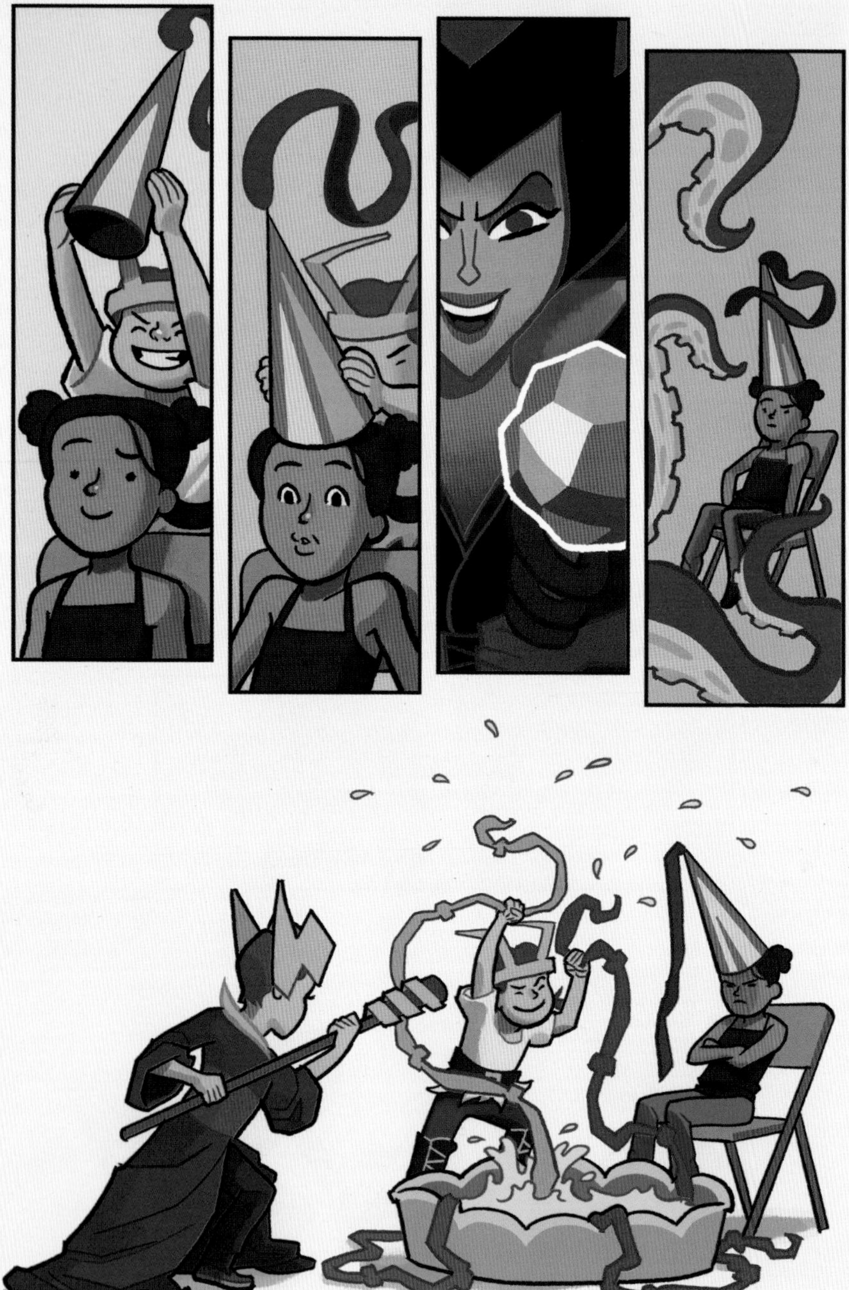

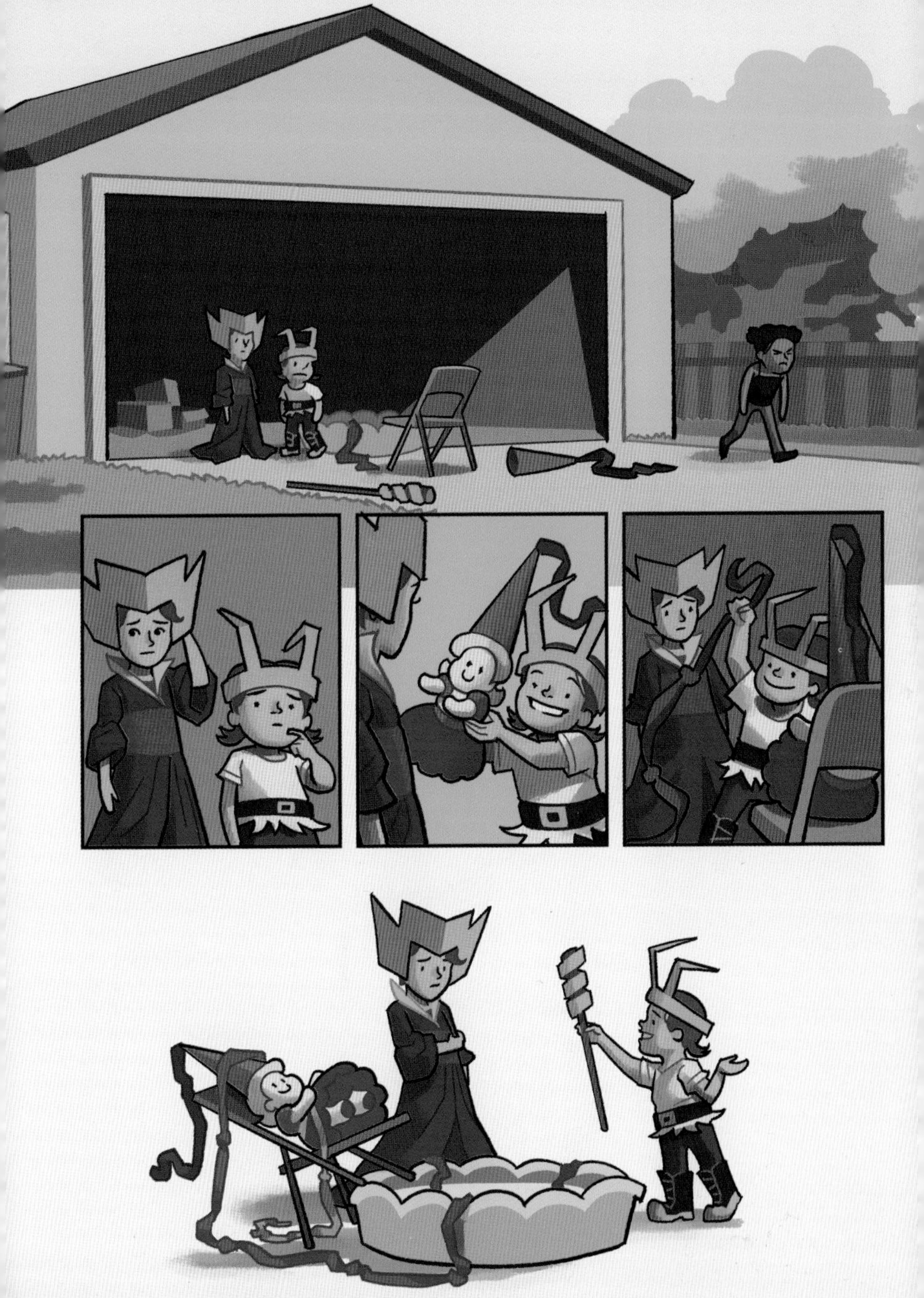

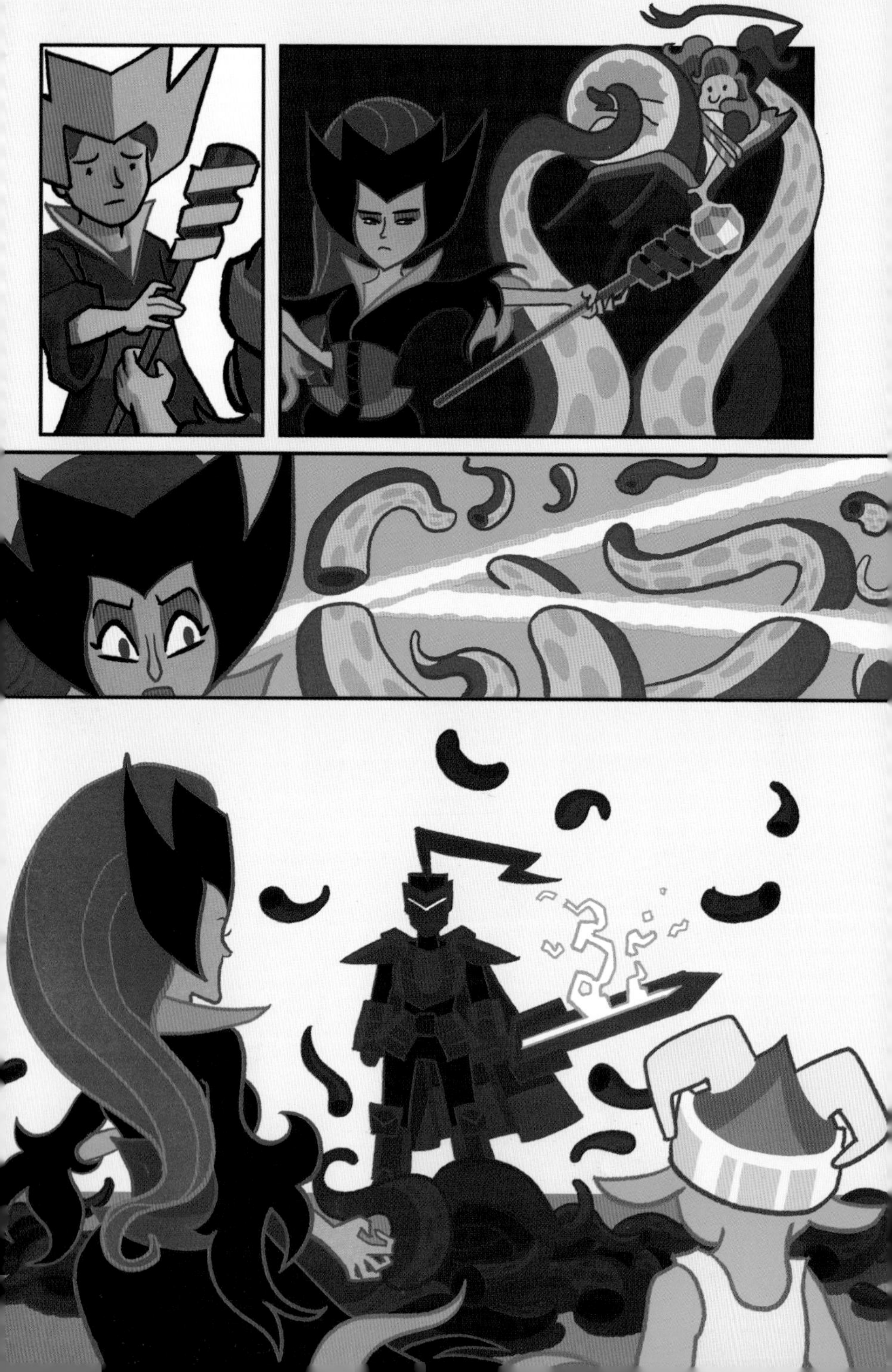

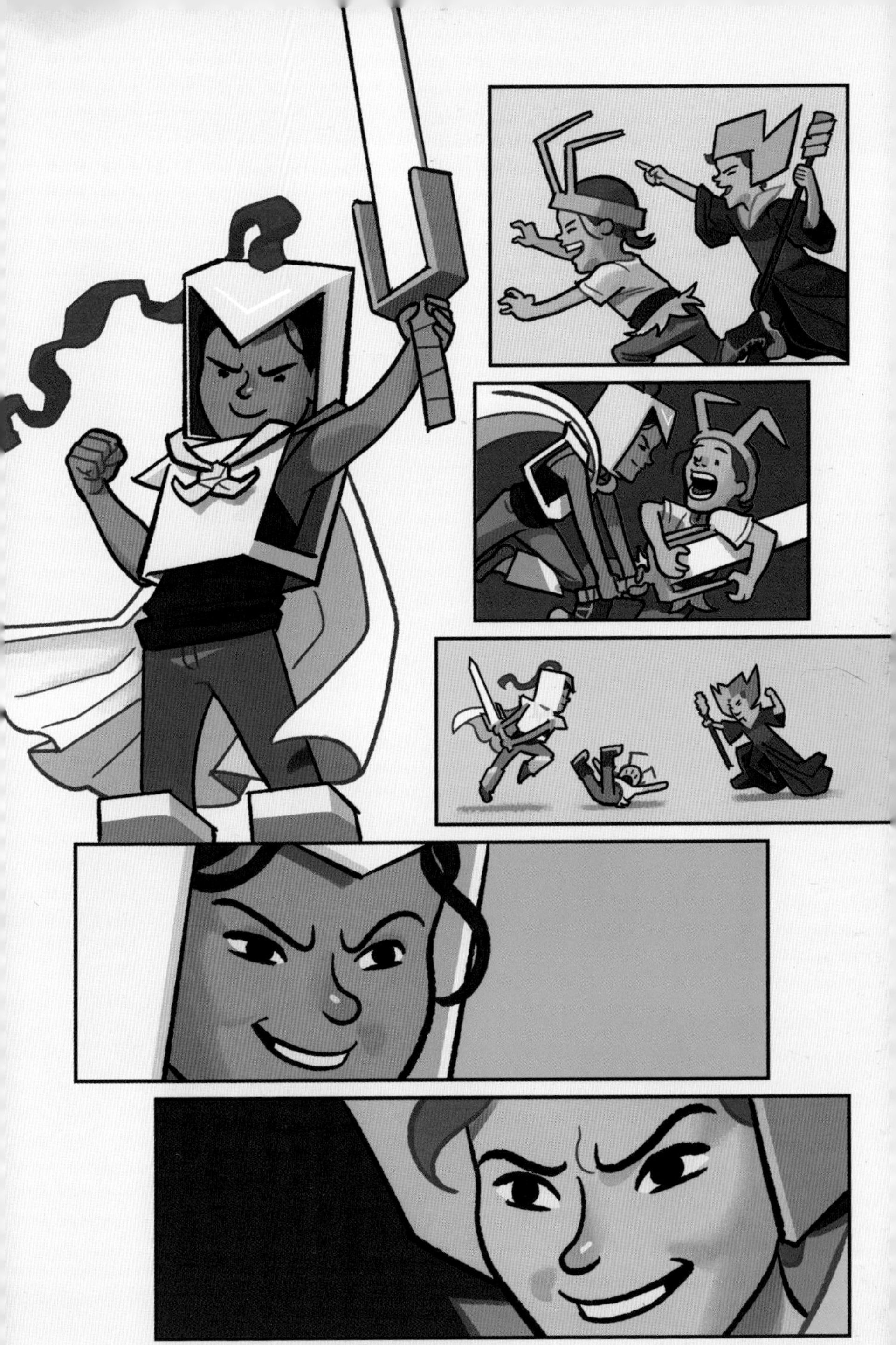

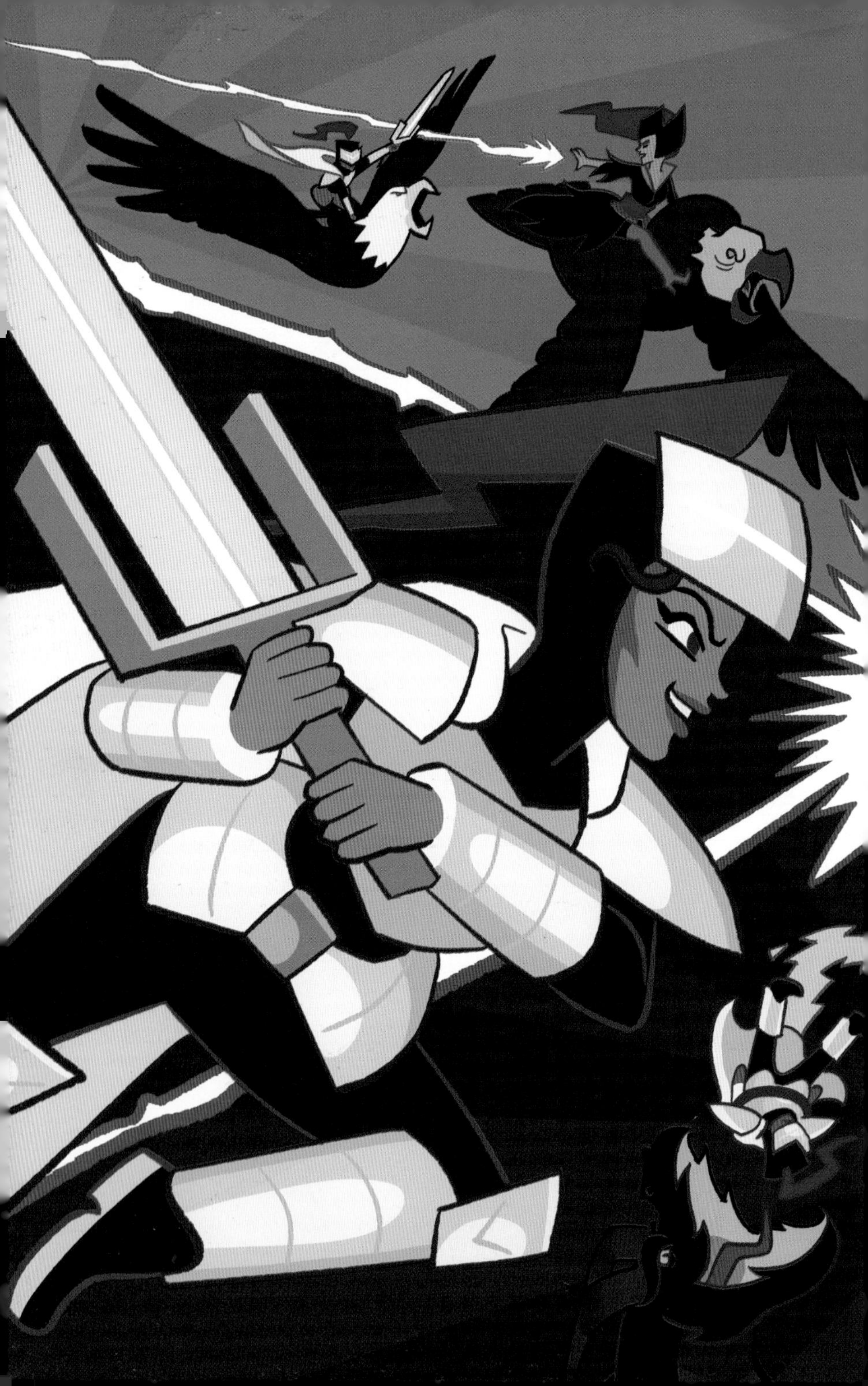

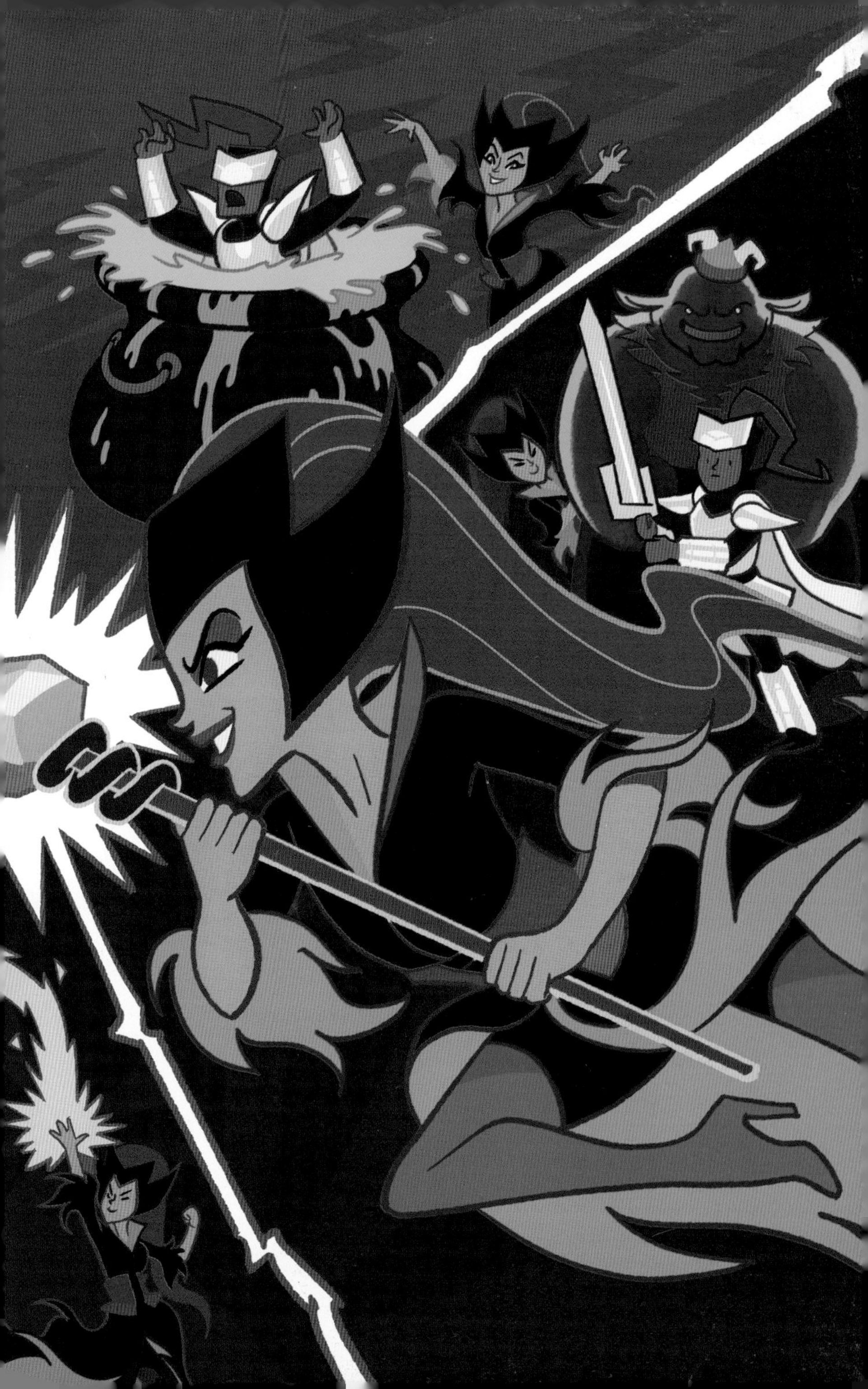

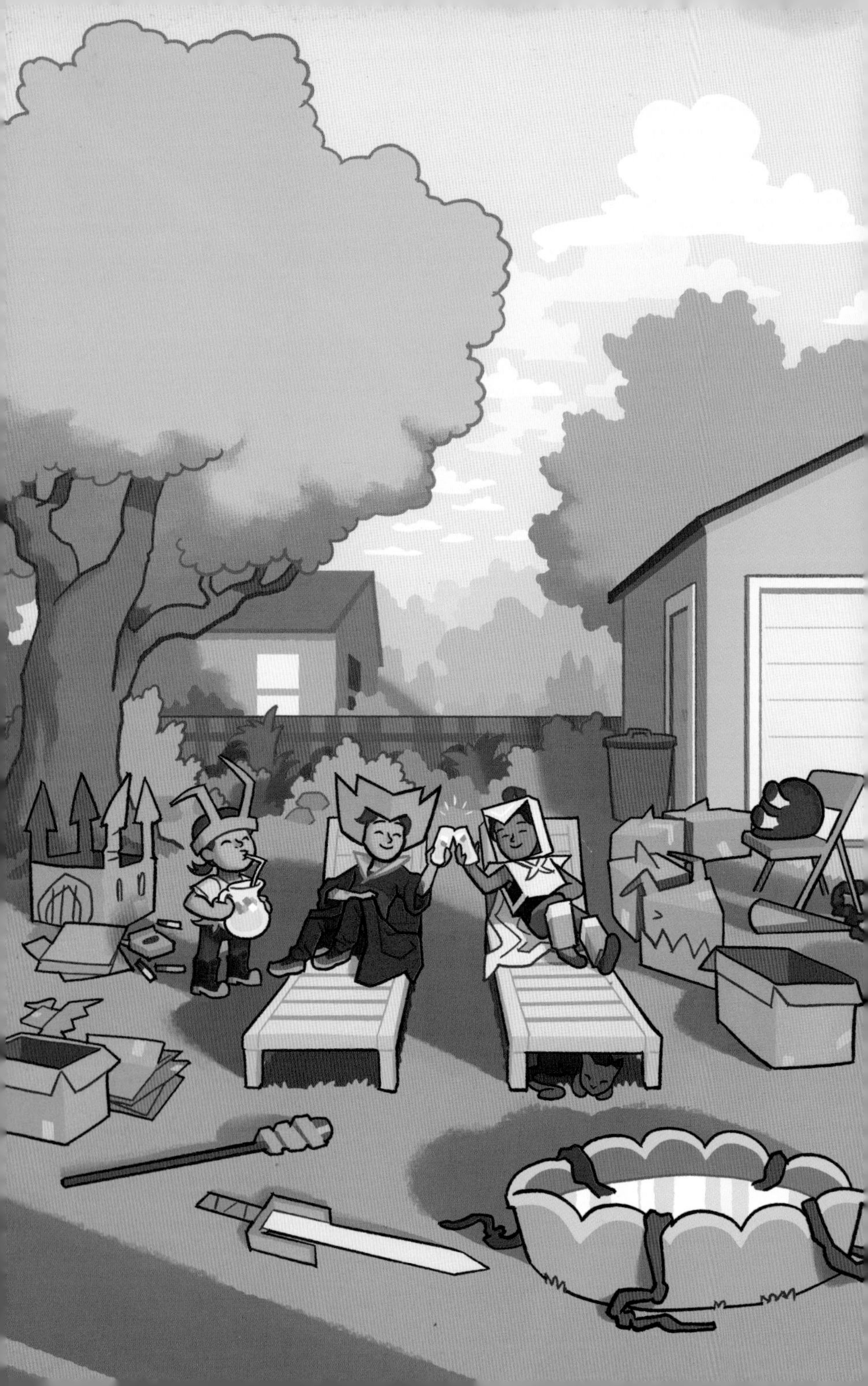

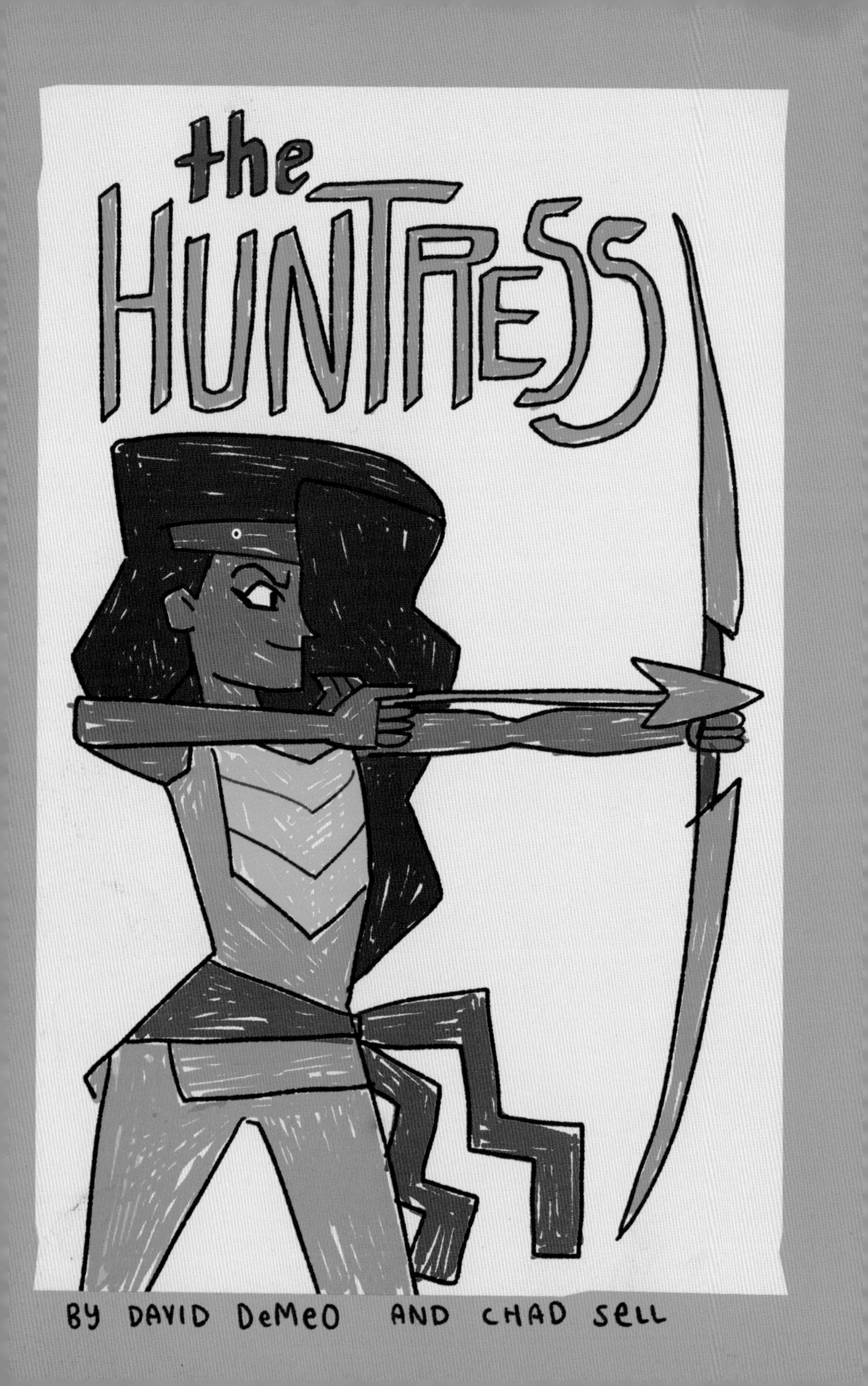
the HUNTRESS
BY DAVID DeMeO AND CHAD SELL

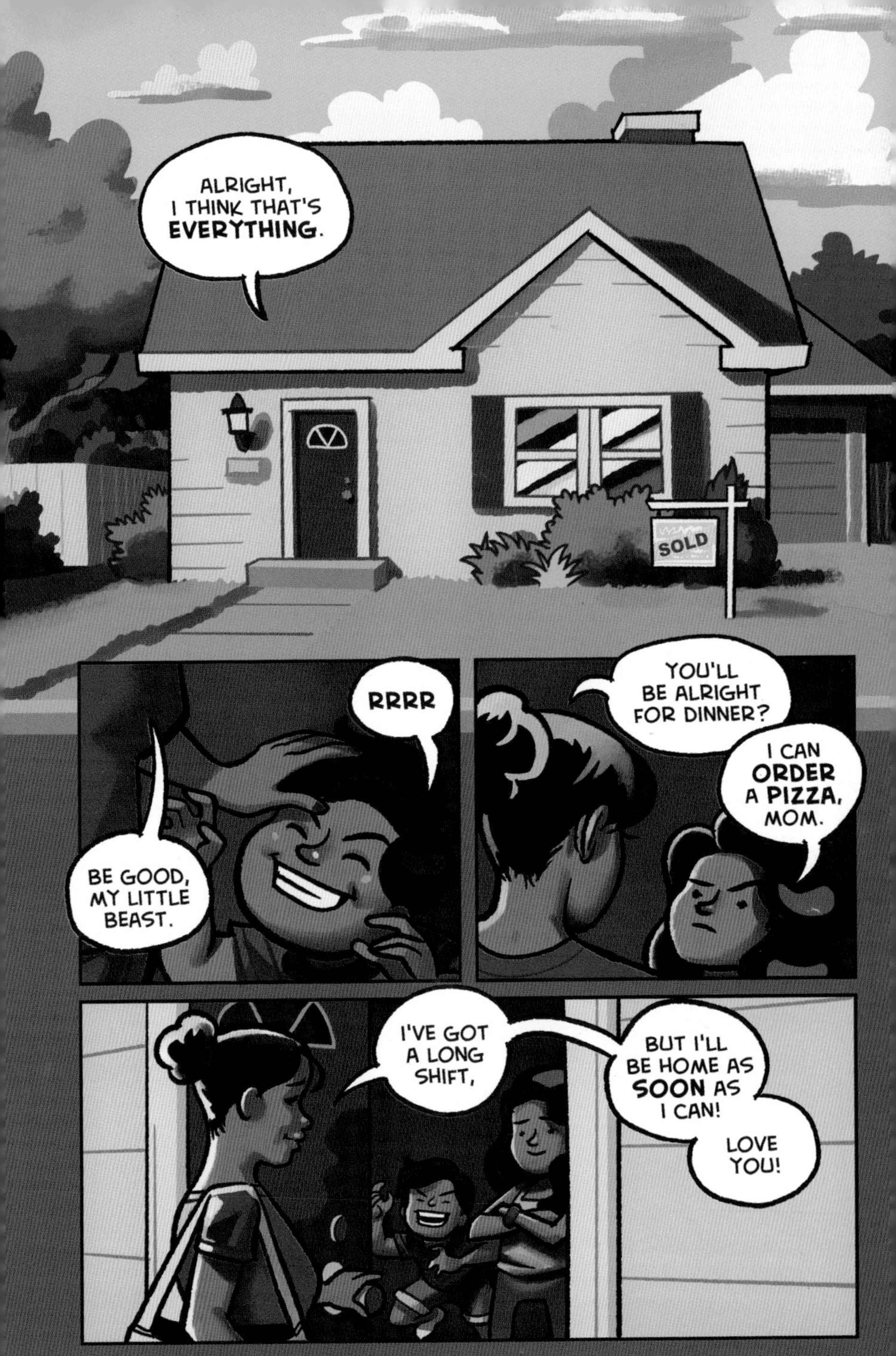

ALRIGHT, I THINK THAT'S **EVERYTHING**.
SOLD
RRRR
BE GOOD, MY LITTLE BEAST.
YOU'LL BE ALRIGHT FOR DINNER?
I CAN **ORDER** A **PIZZA**, MOM.
I'VE GOT A LONG SHIFT,
BUT I'LL BE HOME AS **SOON** AS I CAN!
LOVE YOU!

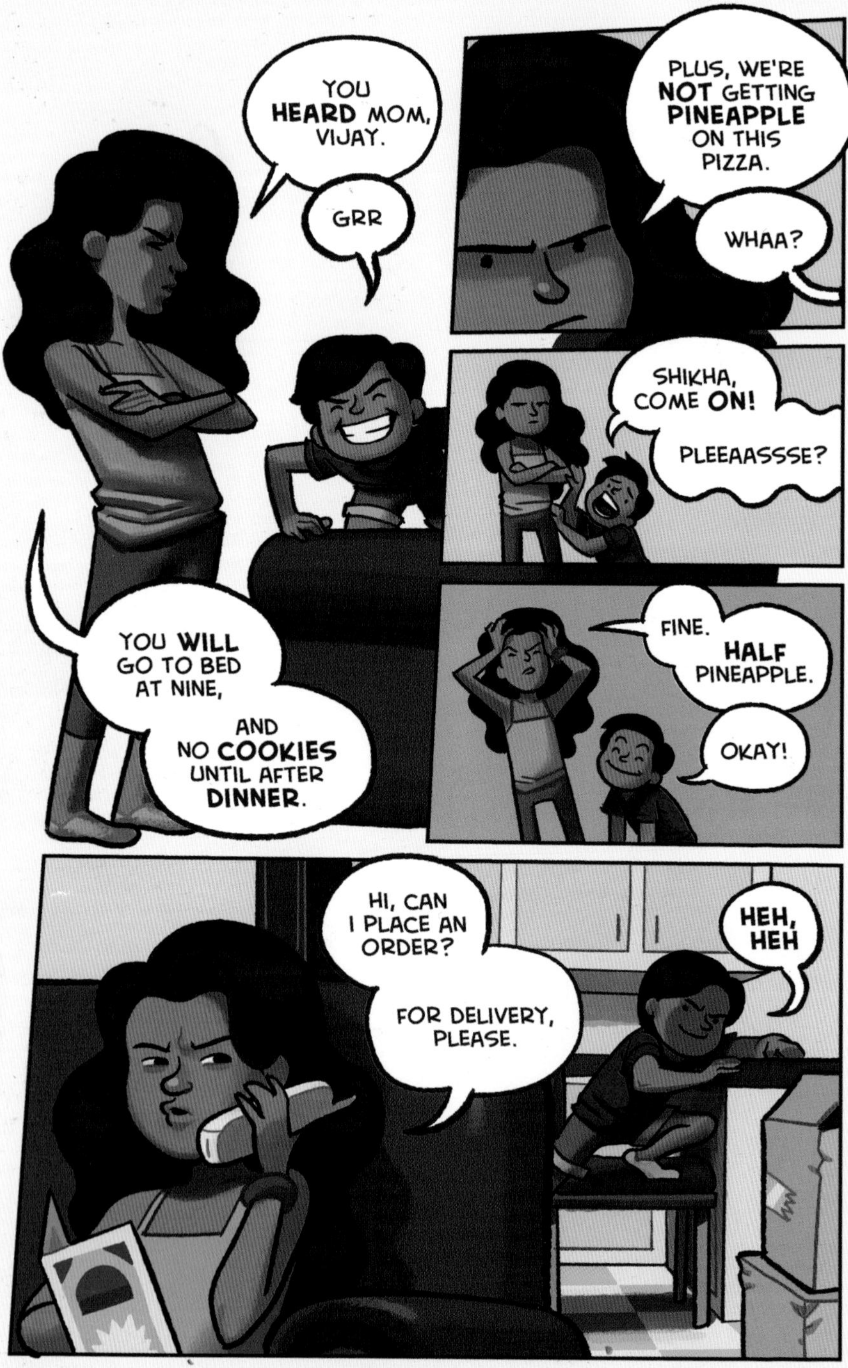
YOU HEARD MOM, VIJAY.
GRR
PLUS, WE'RE NOT GETTING PINEAPPLE ON THIS PIZZA.
WHAA?
SHIKHA, COME ON!
PLEEAASSSE?
YOU WILL GO TO BED AT NINE,
AND NO COOKIES UNTIL AFTER DINNER.
FINE.
HALF PINEAPPLE.
OKAY!
HI, CAN I PLACE AN ORDER?
FOR DELIVERY, PLEASE.
HEH, HEH

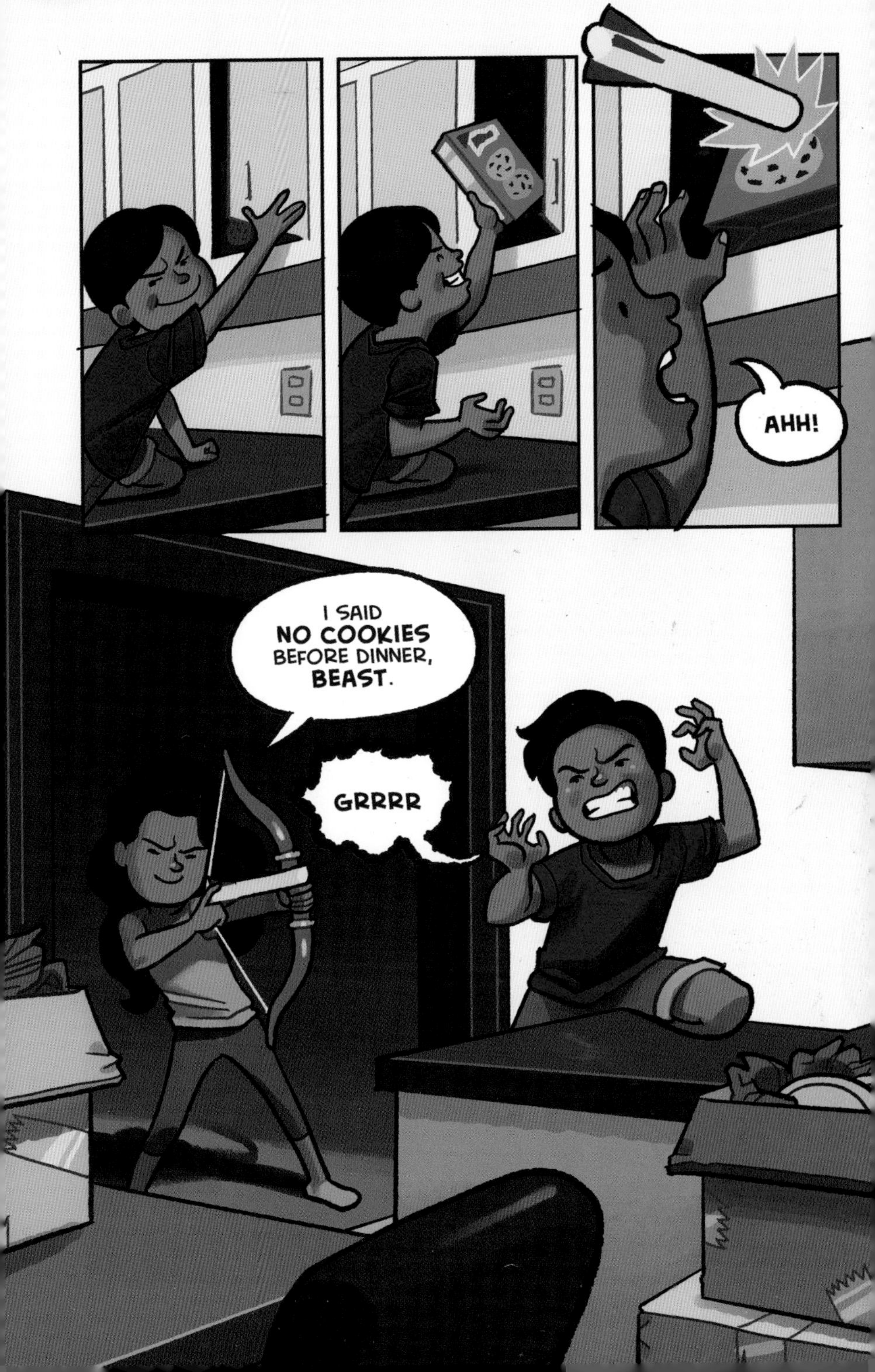
AHH!
I SAID NO COOKIES BEFORE DINNER, BEAST.
GRRRR

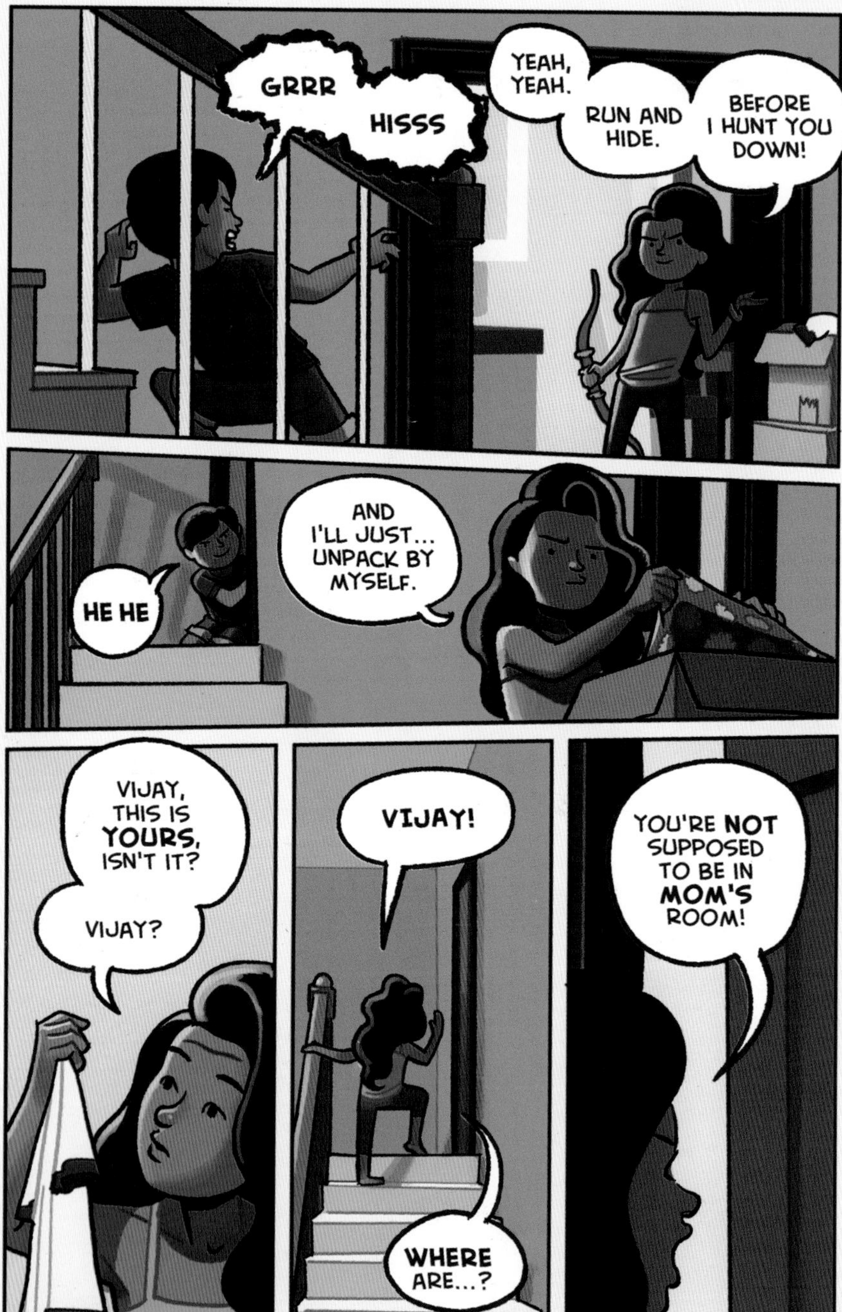
GRRR
HISSS
YEAH, YEAH.
RUN AND HIDE.
BEFORE I HUNT YOU DOWN!
HE HE
AND I'LL JUST... UNPACK BY MYSELF.
VIJAY, THIS IS YOURS, ISN'T IT?
VIJAY?
VIJAY!
WHERE ARE...?
YOU'RE NOT SUPPOSED TO BE IN MOM'S ROOM!

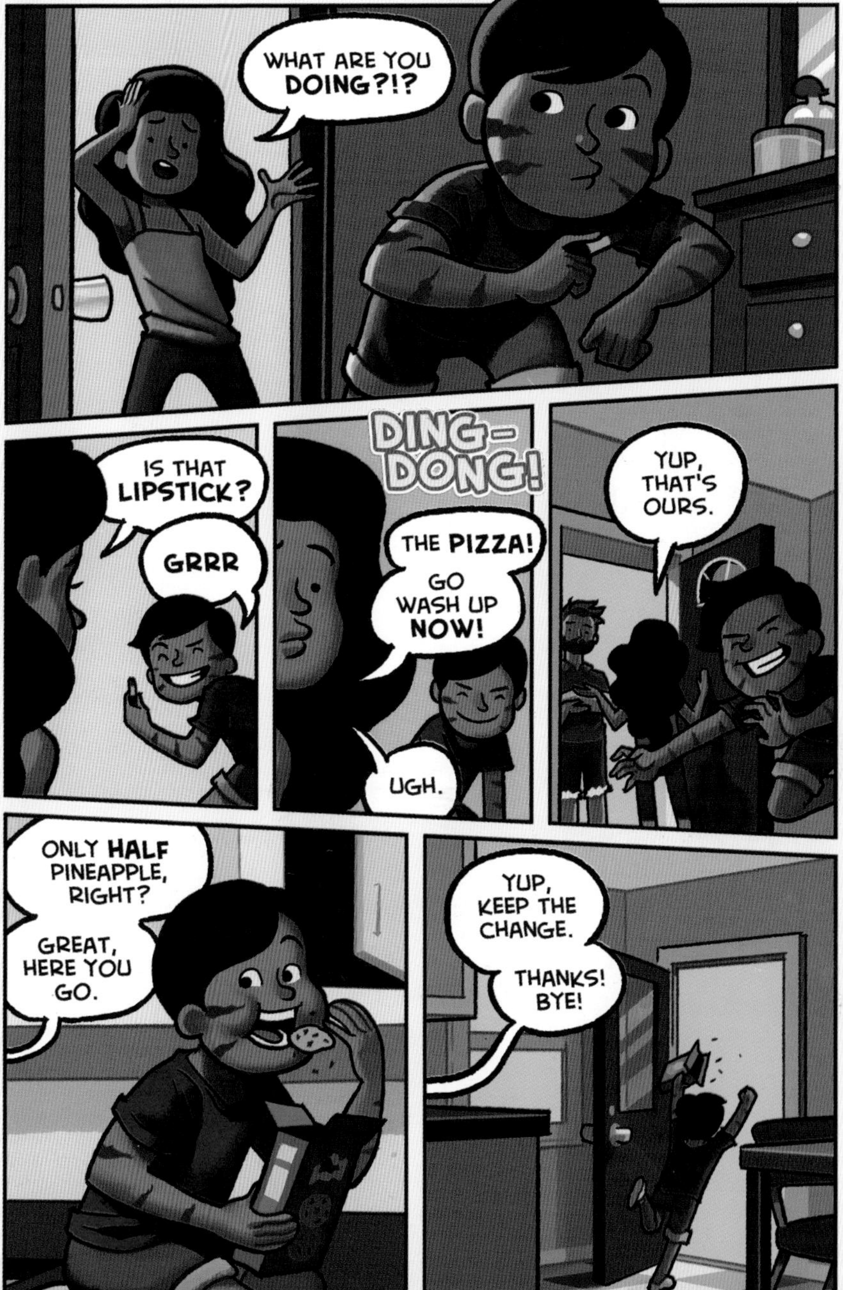
WHAT ARE YOU DOING?!?
IS THAT LIPSTICK?
GRRR
DING-DONG!
THE PIZZA!
GO WASH UP NOW!
UGH.
YUP, THAT'S OURS.
ONLY HALF PINEAPPLE, RIGHT?
GREAT, HERE YOU GO.
YUP, KEEP THE CHANGE.
THANKS! BYE!

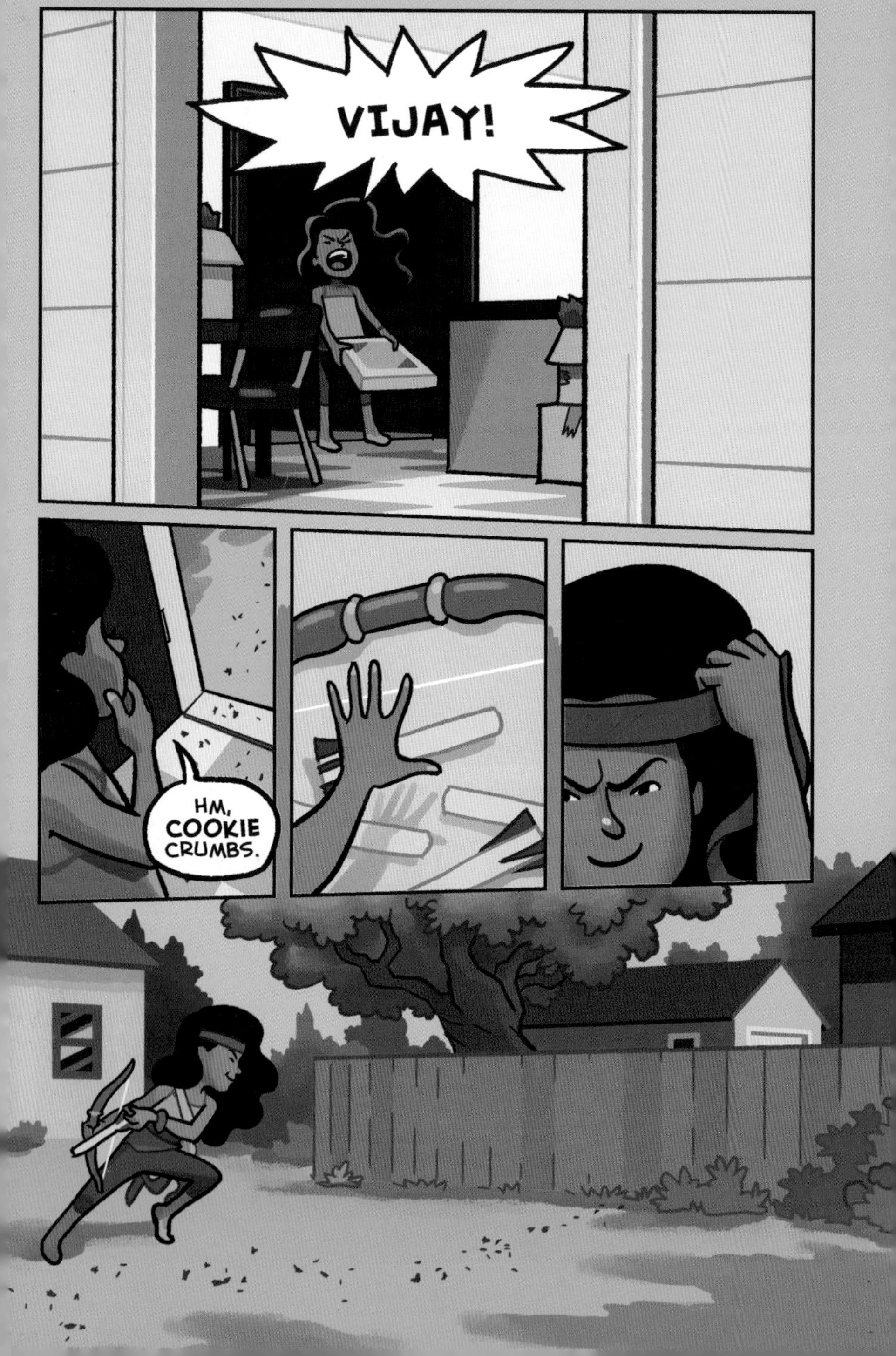
VIJAY!
HM, COOKIE CRUMBS.

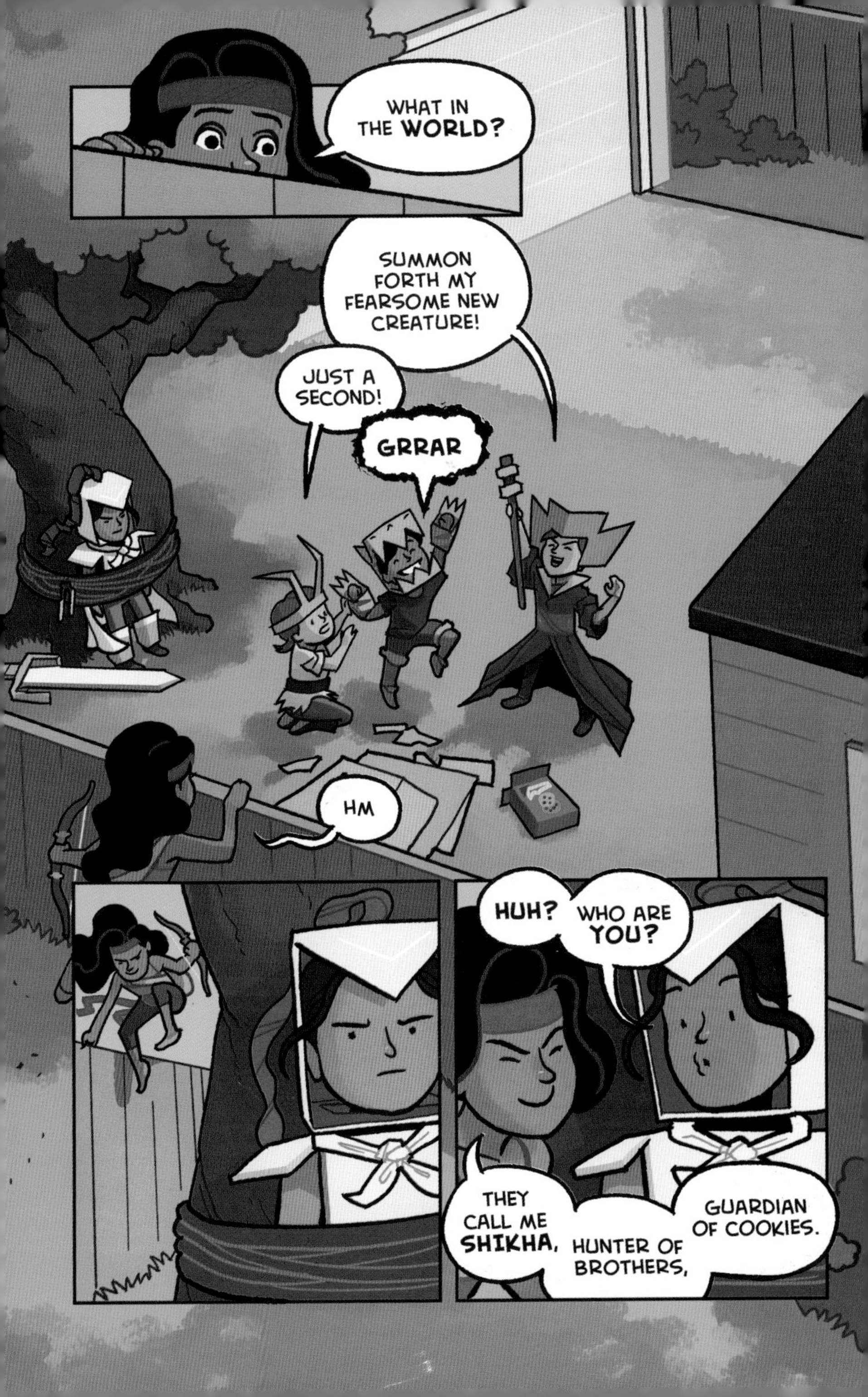
WHAT IN THE WORLD?
SUMMON FORTH MY FEARSOME NEW CREATURE!
JUST A SECOND!
GRRAR
HM
HUH?
WHO ARE YOU?
THEY CALL ME SHIKHA,
HUNTER OF BROTHERS,
GUARDIAN OF COOKIES.

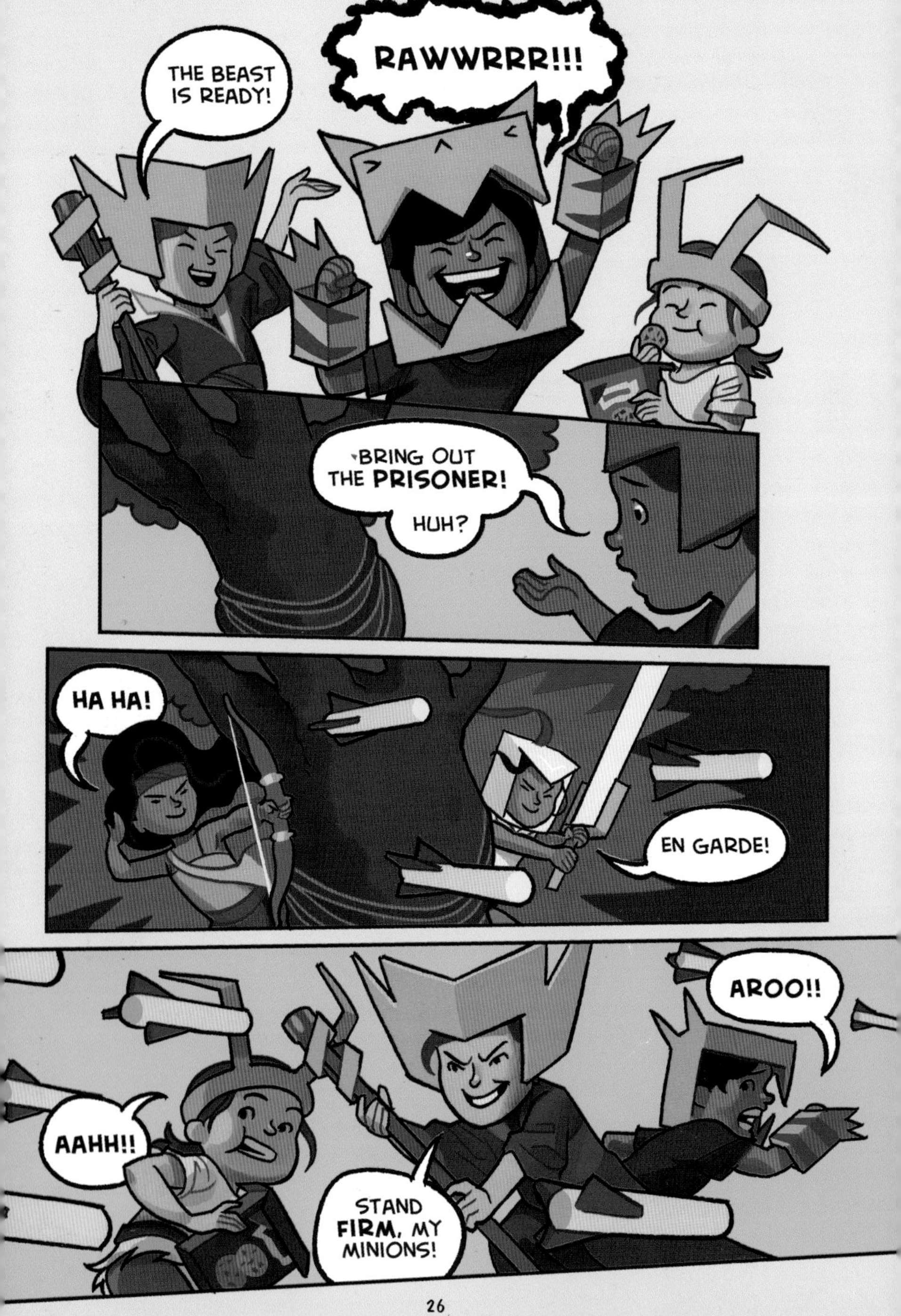
THE BEAST IS READY!
RAWWRRR!!!
BRING OUT THE PRISONER!
HUH?
HA HA!
EN GARDE!
AROO!!
AAHH!!
STAND FIRM, MY MINIONS!

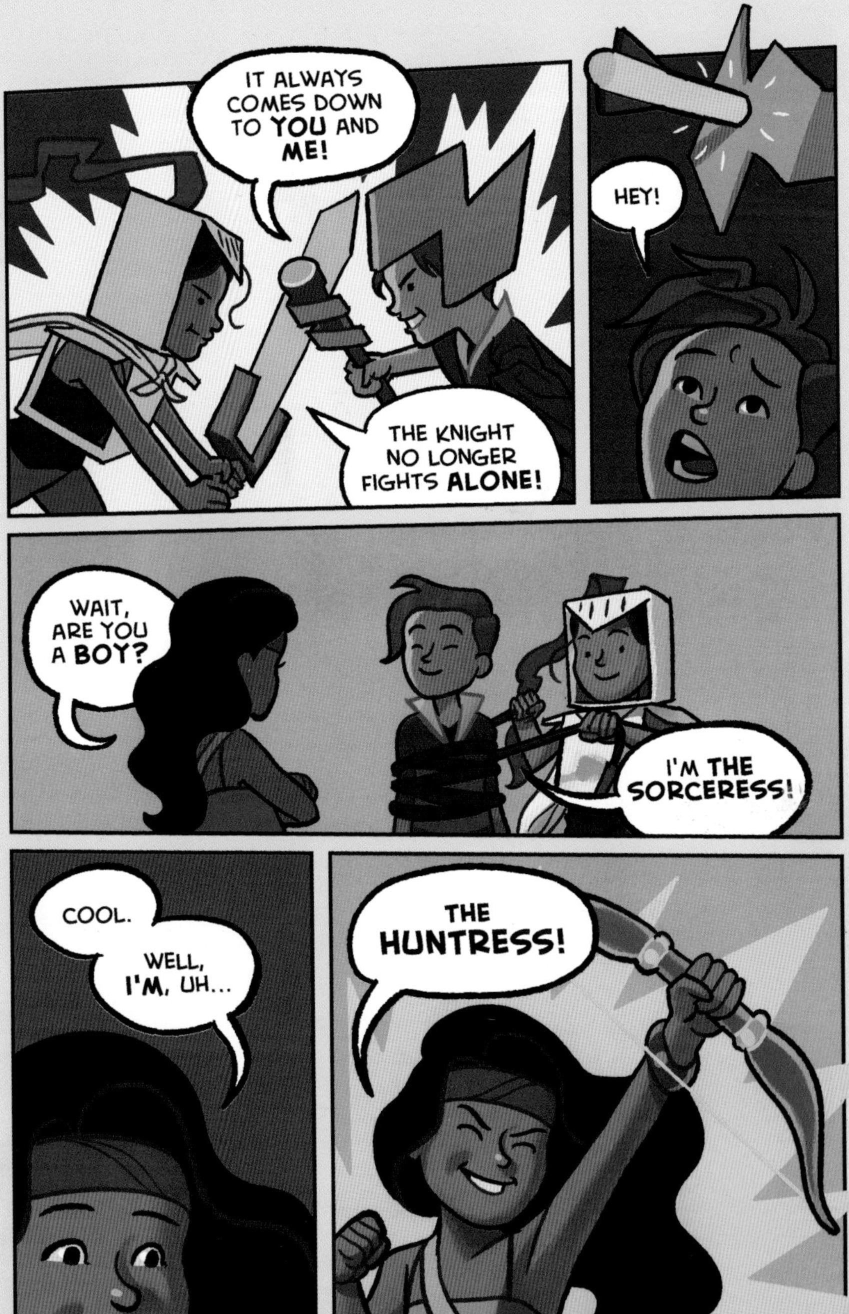
IT ALWAYS COMES DOWN TO **YOU** AND **ME!**
THE KNIGHT NO LONGER FIGHTS **ALONE!**
HEY!
WAIT, ARE YOU A **BOY?**
I'M **THE SORCERESS!**
COOL.
WELL, **I'M**, UH...
THE HUNTRESS!

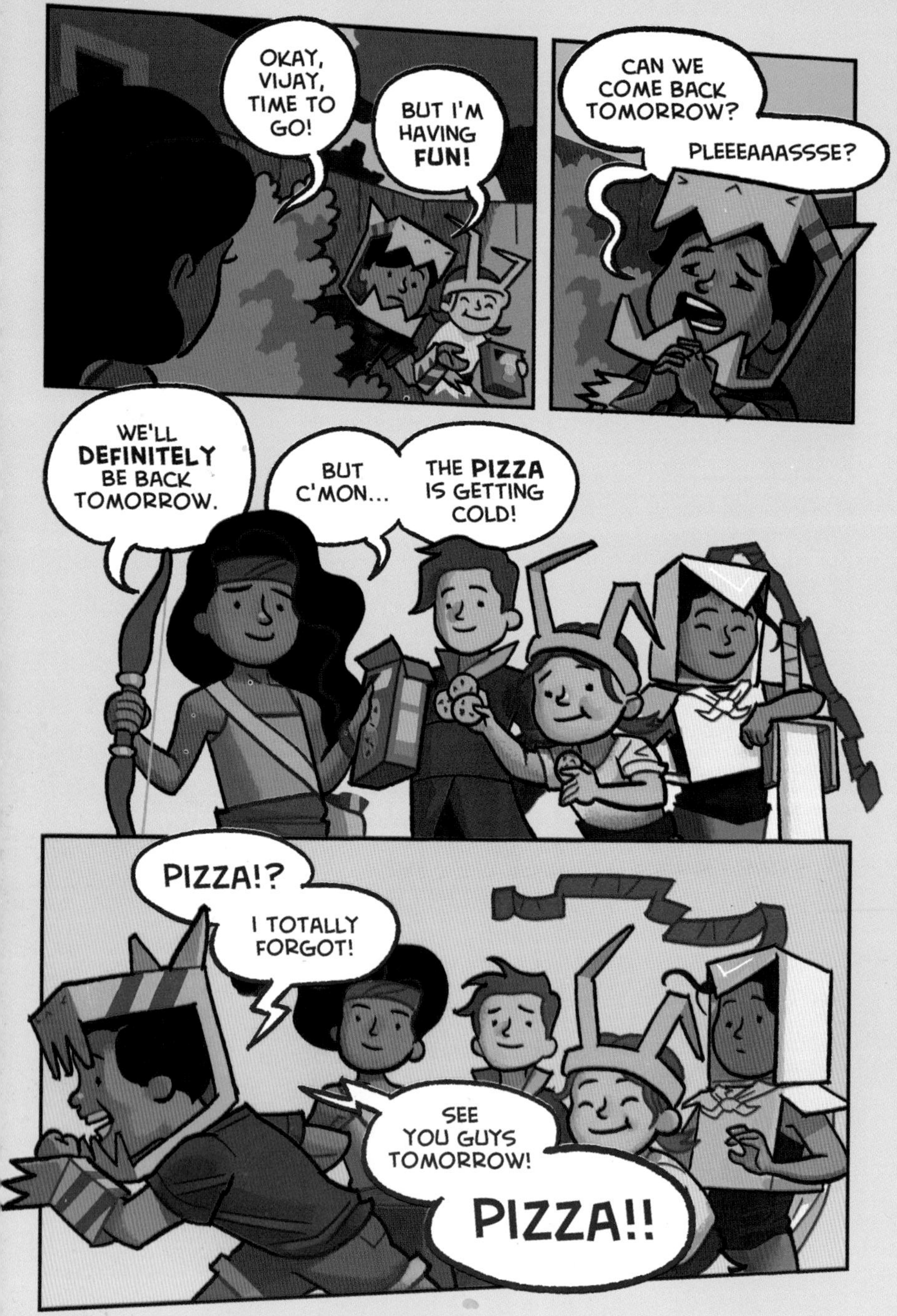
OKAY, VIJAY, TIME TO GO!
BUT I'M HAVING **FUN!**
CAN WE COME BACK TOMORROW?
PLEEEAAASSSE?
WE'LL **DEFINITELY** BE BACK TOMORROW.
BUT C'MON...
THE **PIZZA** IS GETTING COLD!
PIZZA!?
I TOTALLY FORGOT!
SEE YOU GUYS TOMORROW!
PIZZA!!

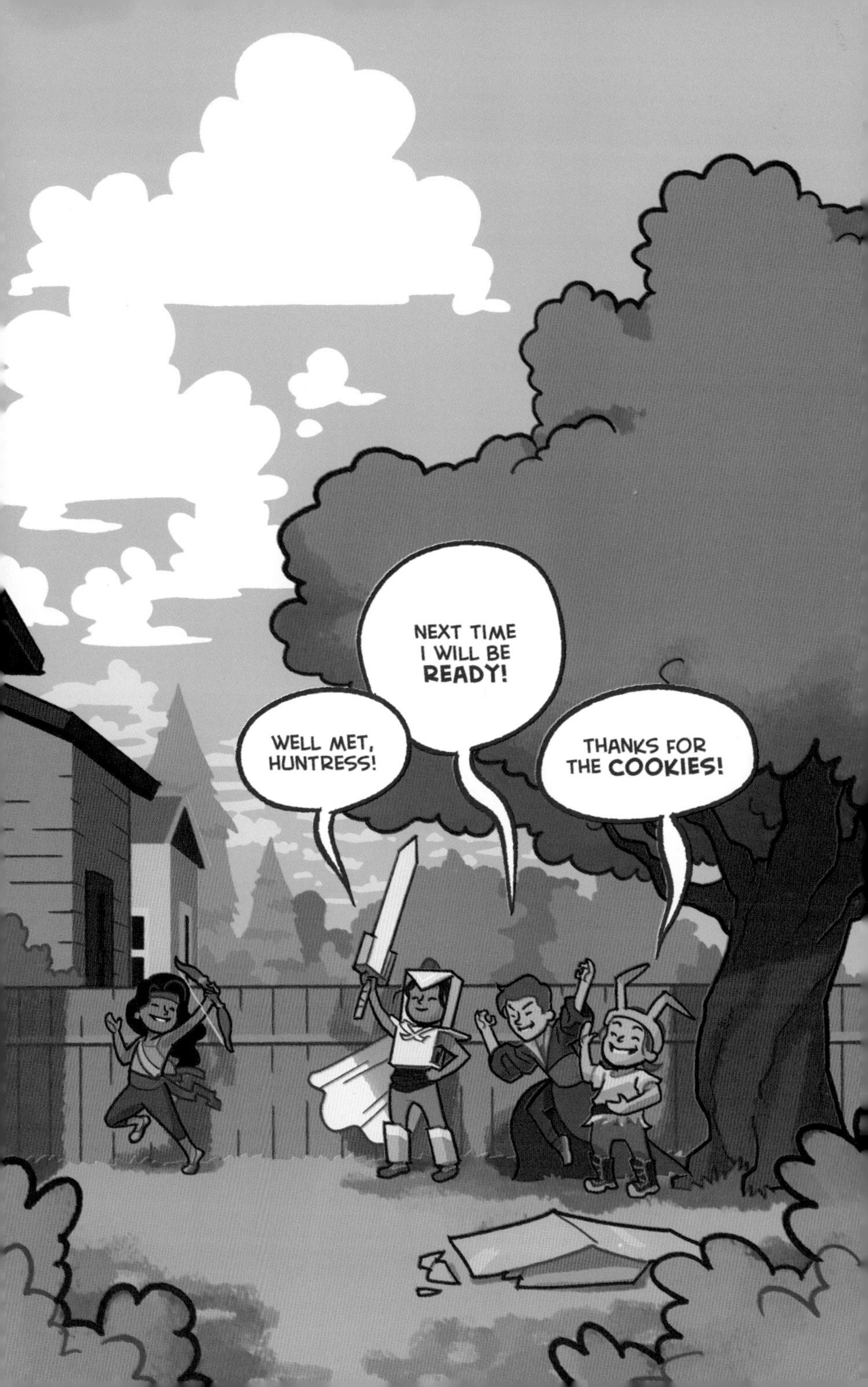
WELL MET, HUNTRESS!
NEXT TIME I WILL BE **READY!**
THANKS FOR THE **COOKIES!**

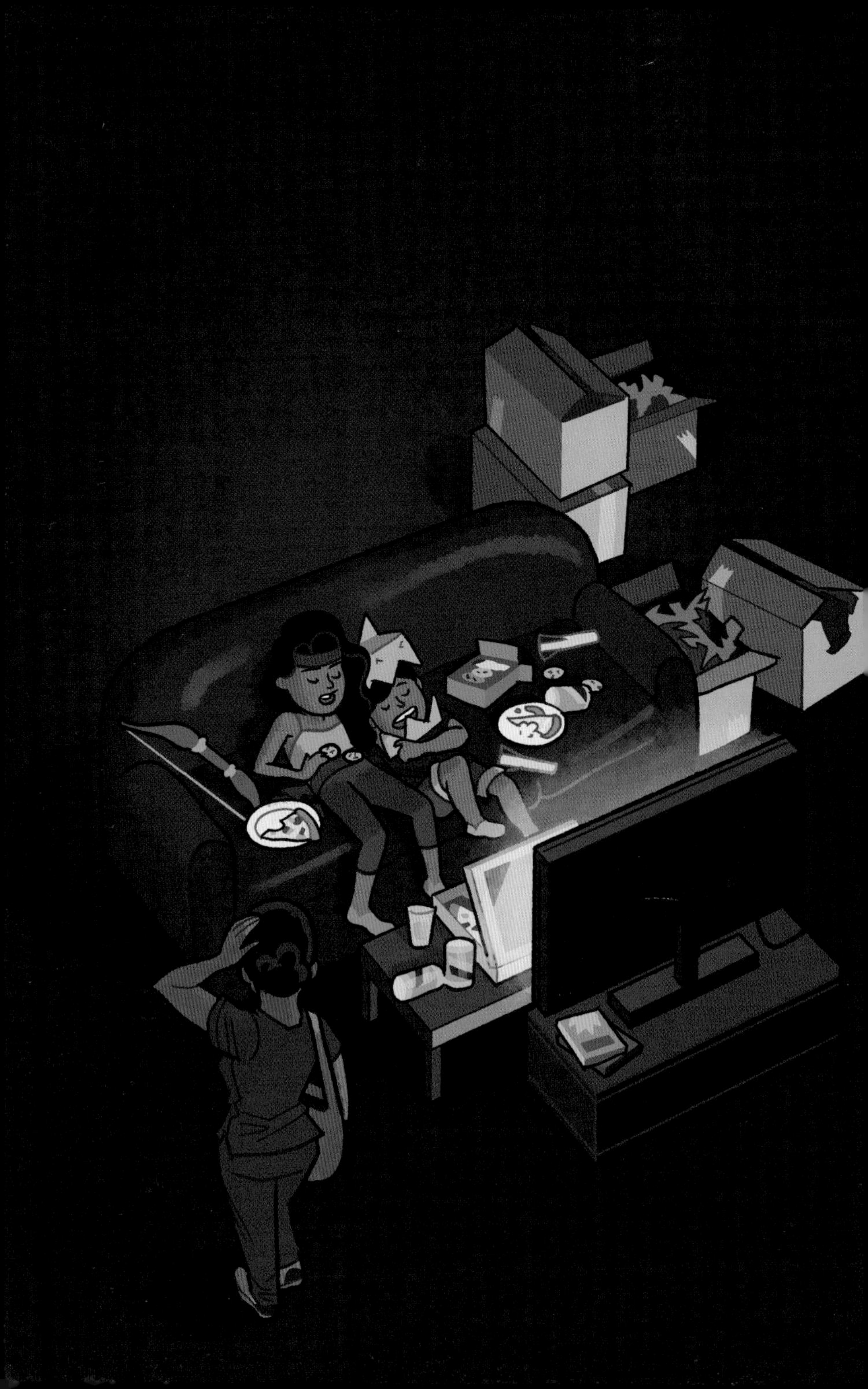

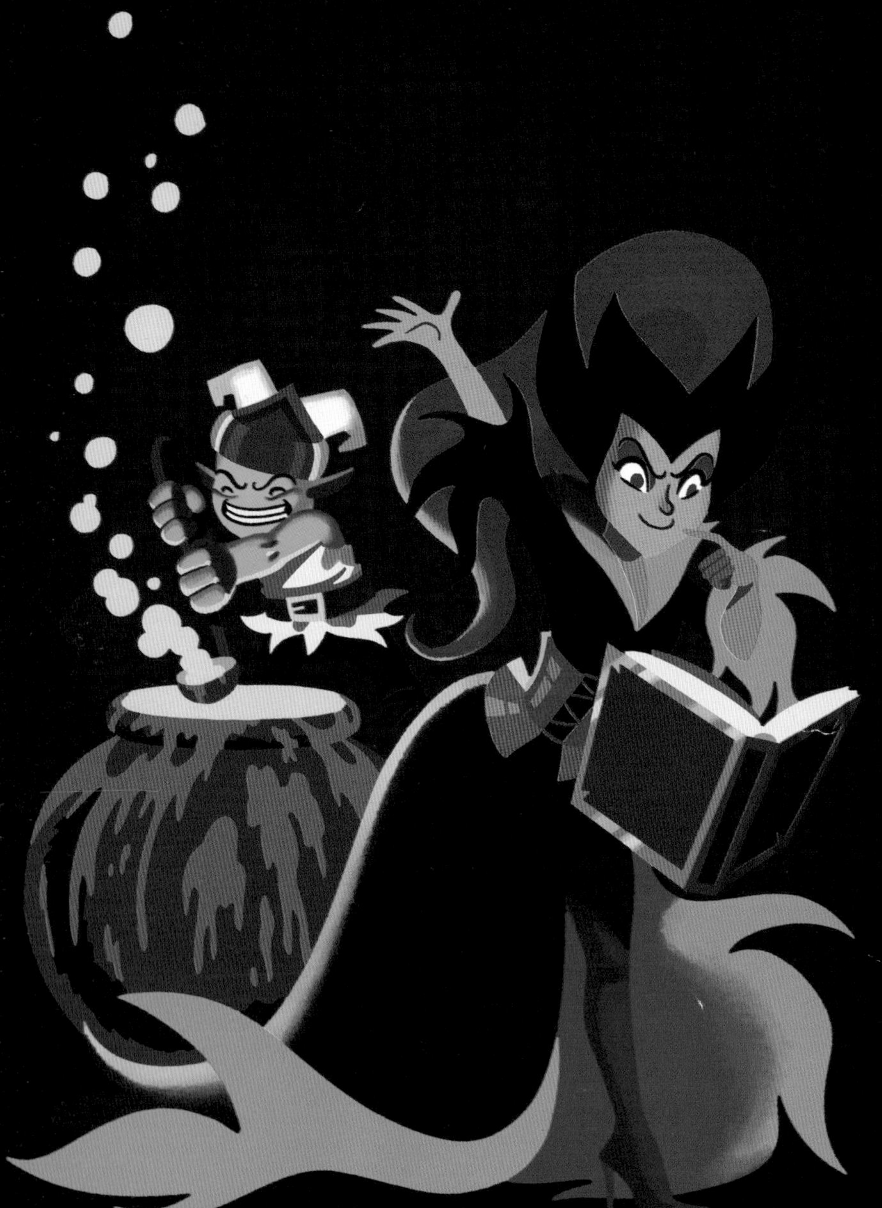

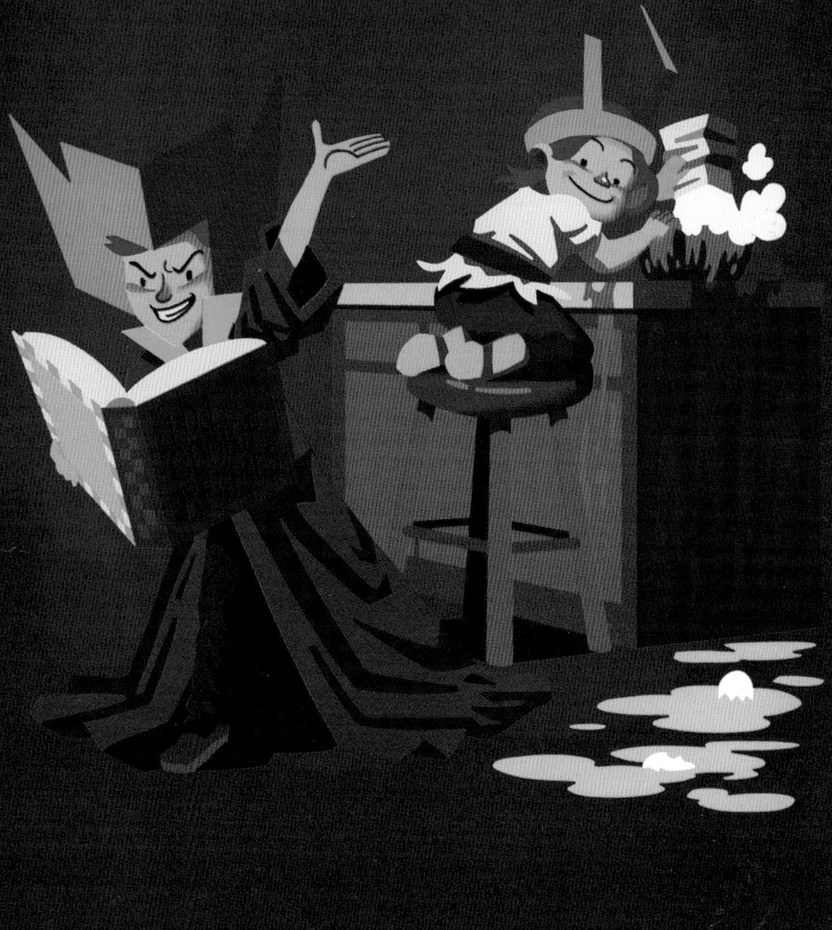

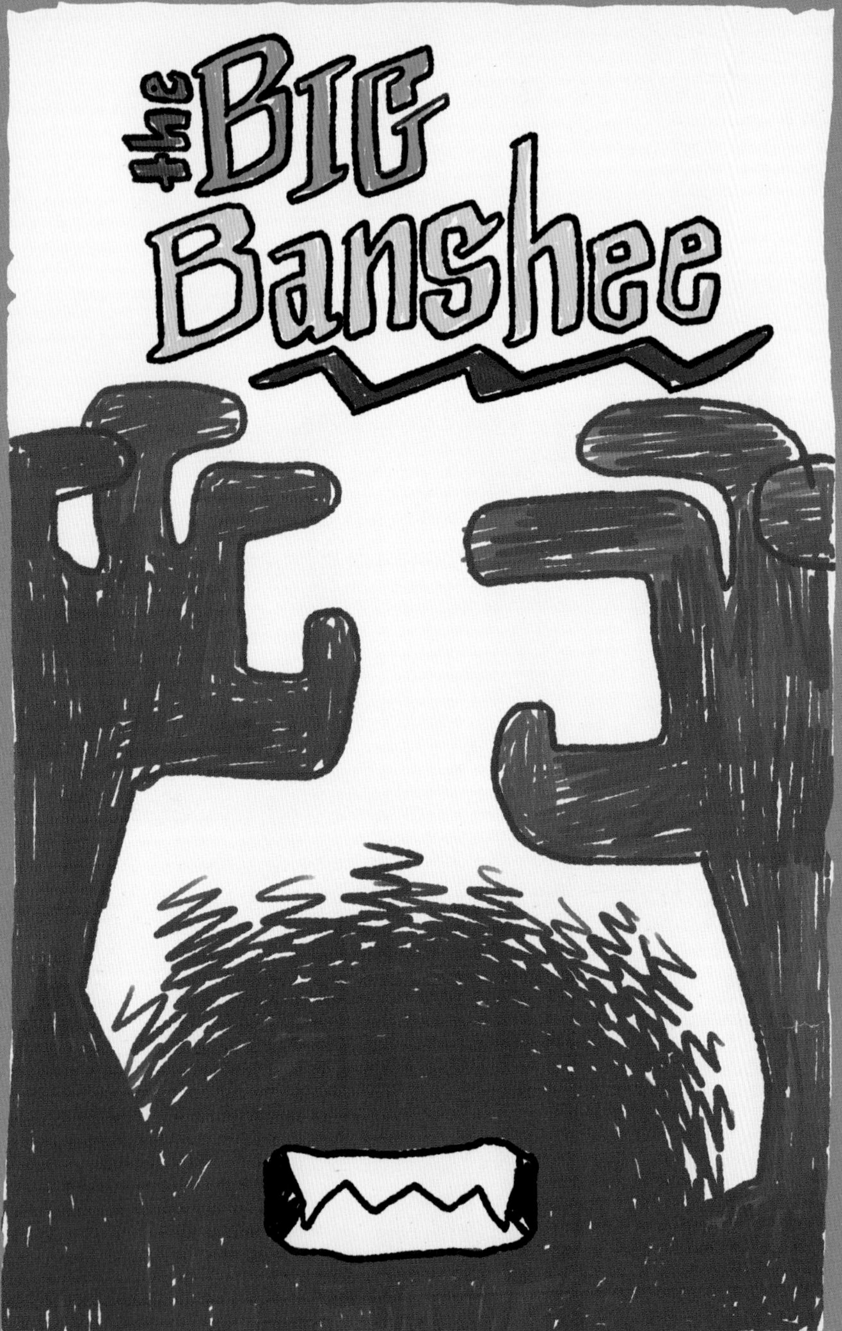

BY KATIE SCHENKEL AND CHAD SELL

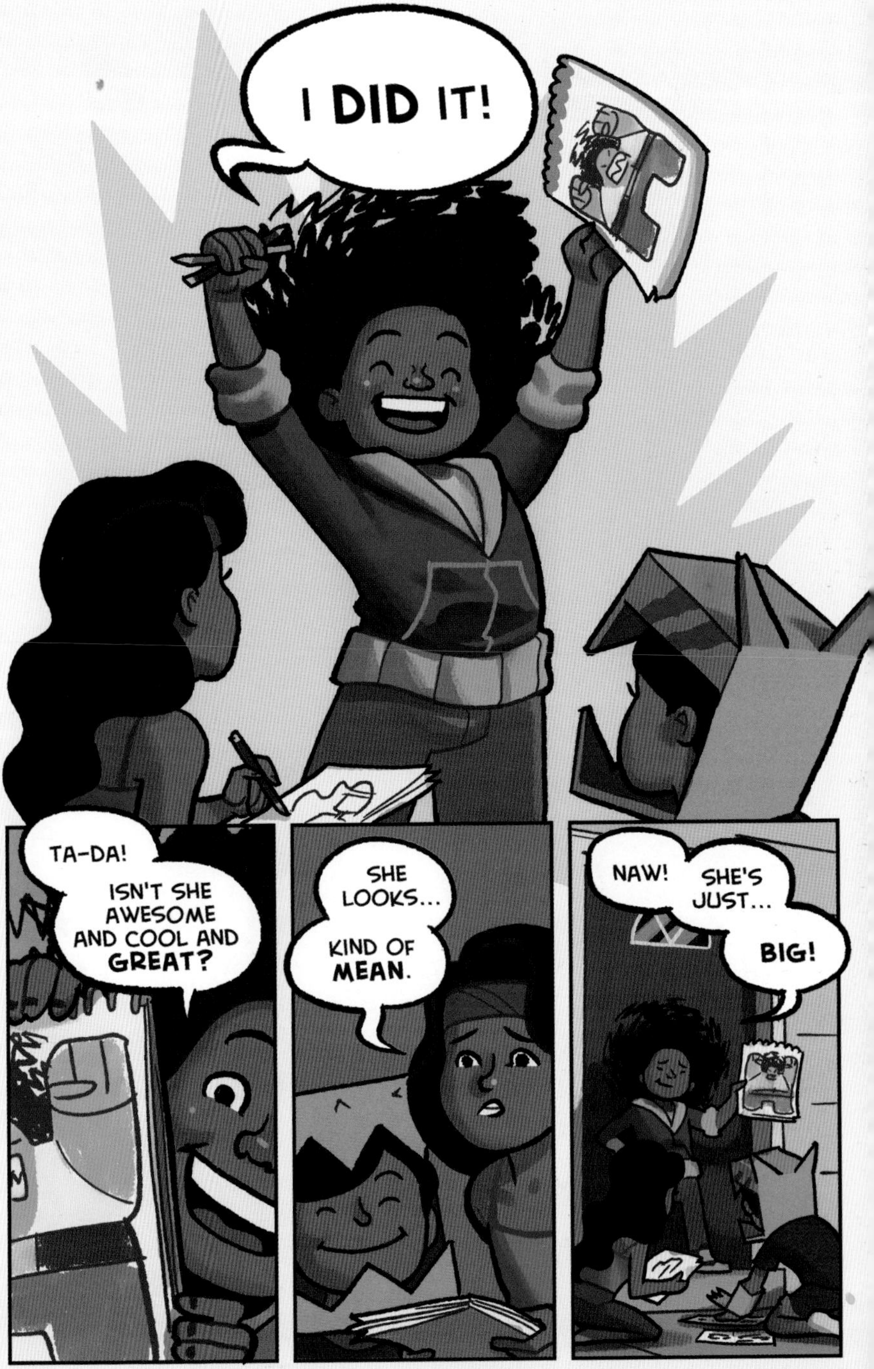
I DID IT!
TA-DA!
ISN'T SHE AWESOME AND COOL AND GREAT?
SHE LOOKS...
KIND OF MEAN.
NAW!
SHE'S JUST...
BIG!

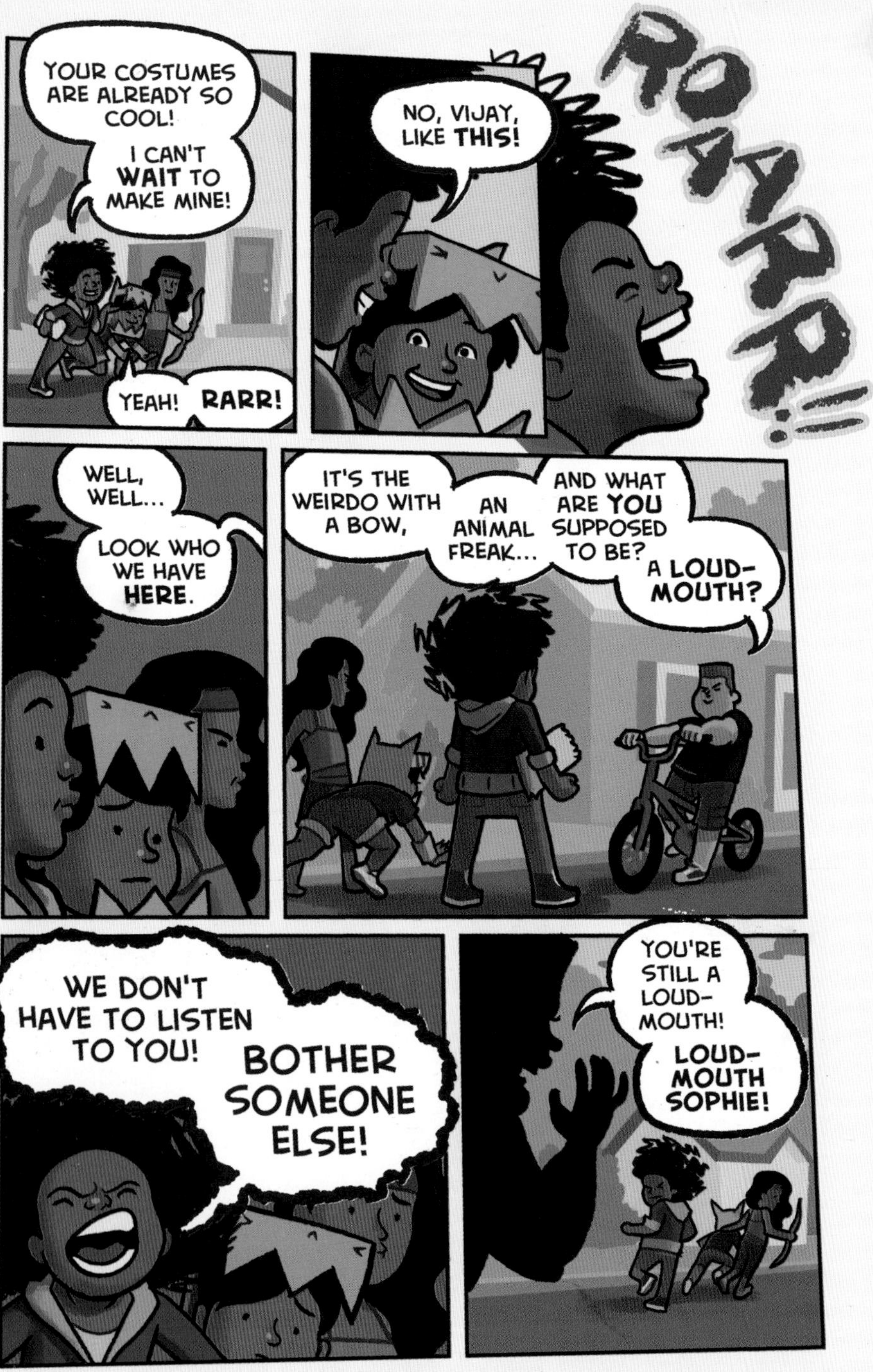
YOUR COSTUMES ARE ALREADY SO COOL!
I CAN'T WAIT TO MAKE MINE!
YEAH!
RARR!
NO, VIJAY, LIKE THIS!
ROAAAR!!!
WELL, WELL...
LOOK WHO WE HAVE HERE.
IT'S THE WEIRDO WITH A BOW,
AN ANIMAL FREAK...
AND WHAT ARE YOU SUPPOSED TO BE?
A LOUD-MOUTH?
WE DON'T HAVE TO LISTEN TO YOU!
BOTHER SOMEONE ELSE!
YOU'RE STILL A LOUD-MOUTH!
LOUD-MOUTH SOPHIE!

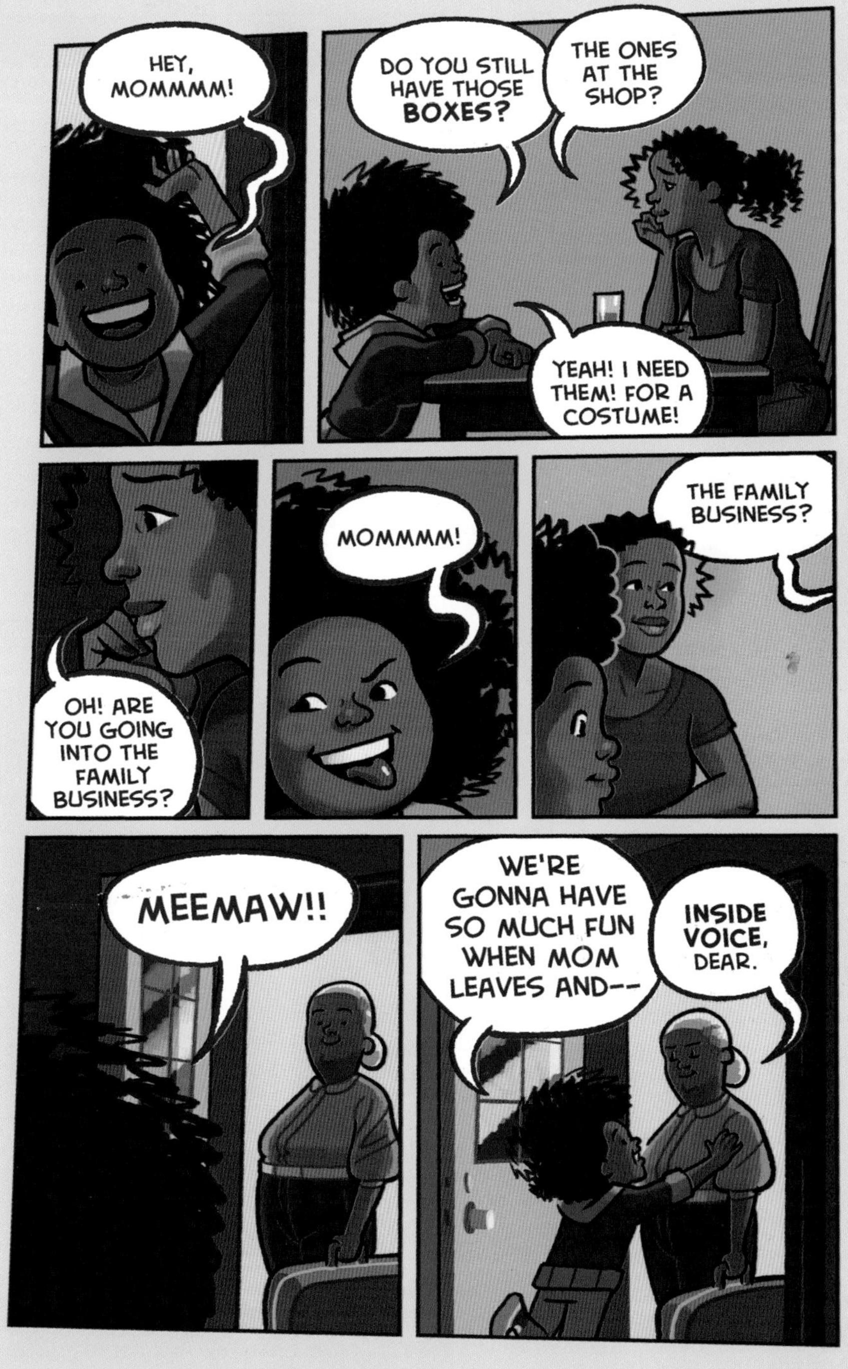
HEY, MOMMMM!
DO YOU STILL HAVE THOSE BOXES?
THE ONES AT THE SHOP?
YEAH! I NEED THEM! FOR A COSTUME!
OH! ARE YOU GOING INTO THE FAMILY BUSINESS?
MOMMMM!
THE FAMILY BUSINESS?
MEEMAW!!
WE'RE GONNA HAVE SO MUCH FUN WHEN MOM LEAVES AND--
INSIDE VOICE, DEAR.

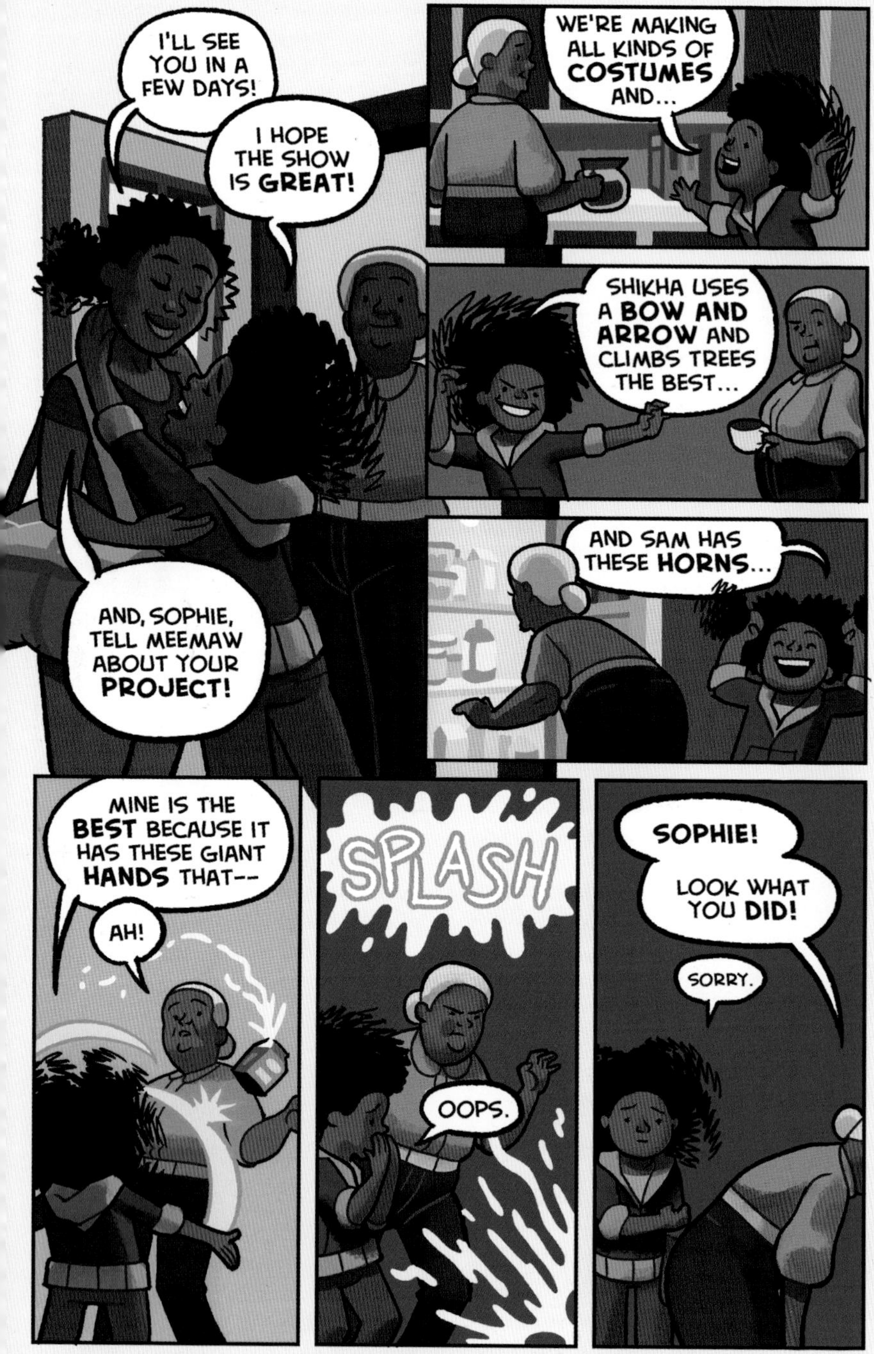
I'LL SEE YOU IN A FEW DAYS!
I HOPE THE SHOW IS GREAT!
WE'RE MAKING ALL KINDS OF COSTUMES AND...
SHIKHA USES A BOW AND ARROW AND CLIMBS TREES THE BEST...
AND SAM HAS THESE HORNS...
AND, SOPHIE, TELL MEEMAW ABOUT YOUR PROJECT!
MINE IS THE BEST BECAUSE IT HAS THESE GIANT HANDS THAT--
AH!
SPLASH
OOPS.
SOPHIE!
LOOK WHAT YOU DID!
SORRY.

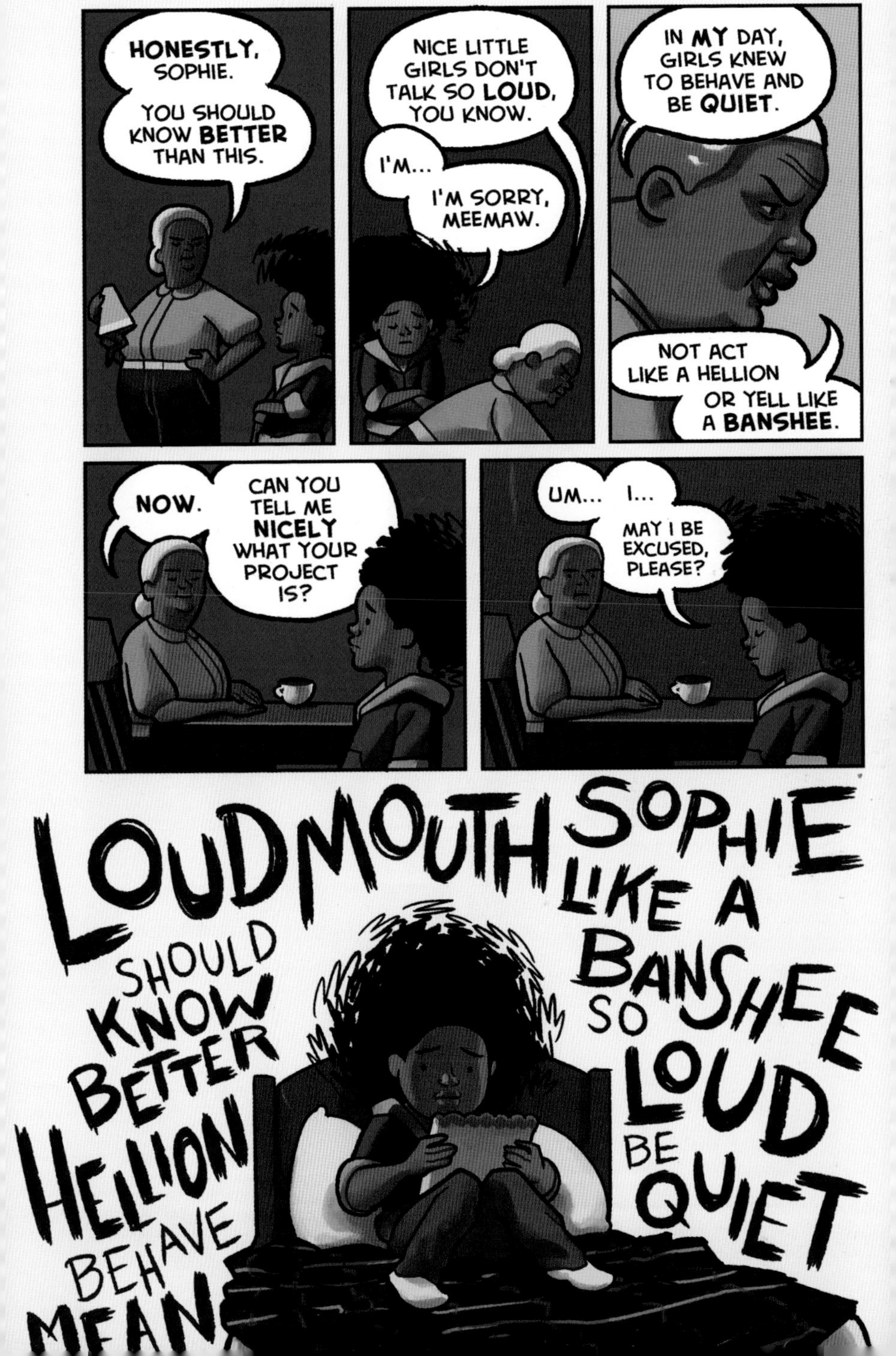
HONESTLY, SOPHIE.
YOU SHOULD KNOW BETTER THAN THIS.
NICE LITTLE GIRLS DON'T TALK SO LOUD, YOU KNOW.
I'M...
I'M SORRY, MEEMAW.
IN MY DAY, GIRLS KNEW TO BEHAVE AND BE QUIET.
NOT ACT LIKE A HELLION
OR YELL LIKE A BANSHEE.
NOW.
CAN YOU TELL ME NICELY WHAT YOUR PROJECT IS?
UM...
I...
MAY I BE EXCUSED, PLEASE?
LOUDMOUTH
SOPHIE
SHOULD KNOW BETTER
LIKE A BANSHEE
SO LOUD
HELLION
BEHAVE
BE QUIET
MEAN

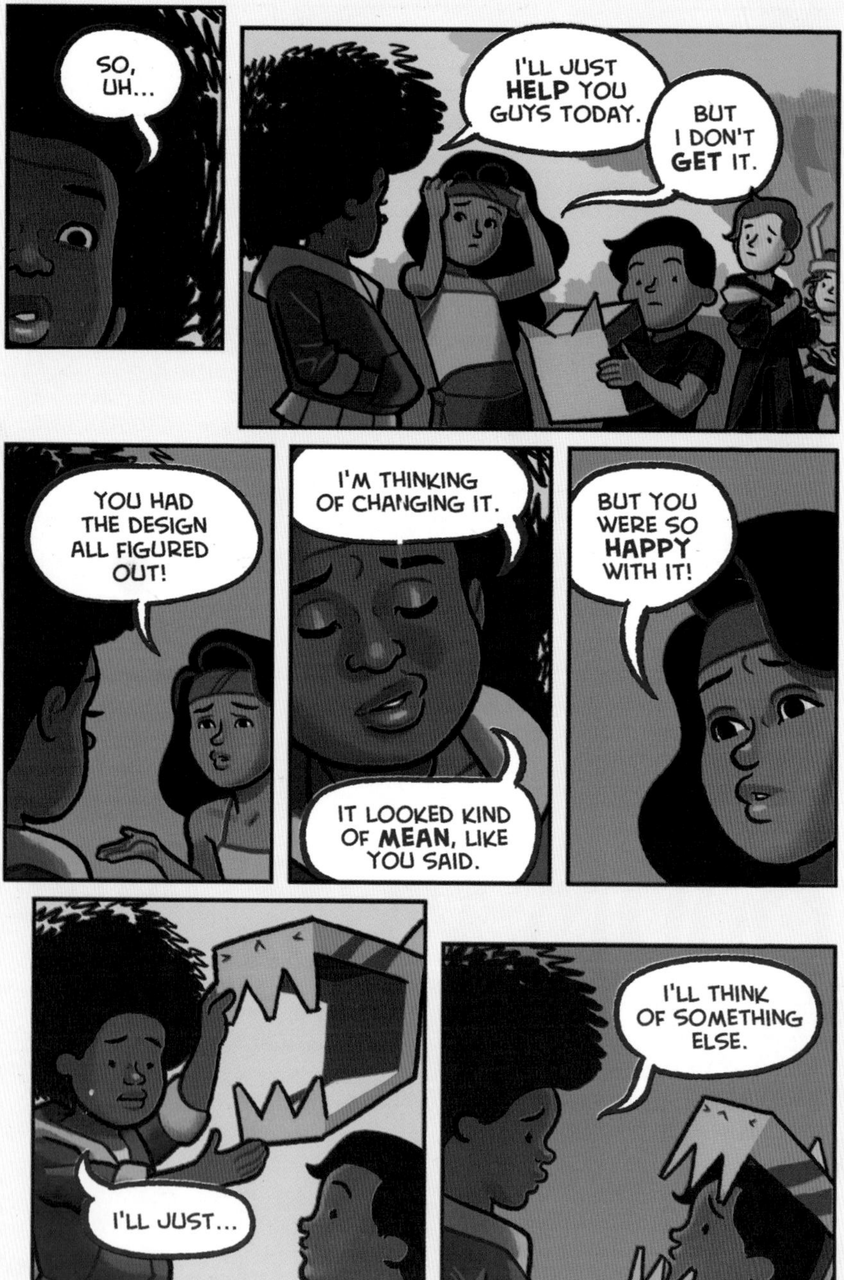
SO, UH...
I'LL JUST **HELP** YOU GUYS TODAY.
BUT I DON'T **GET** IT.
YOU HAD THE DESIGN ALL FIGURED OUT!
I'M THINKING OF CHANGING IT.
IT LOOKED KIND OF **MEAN**, LIKE YOU SAID.
BUT YOU WERE SO **HAPPY** WITH IT!
I'LL JUST...
I'LL THINK OF SOMETHING ELSE.

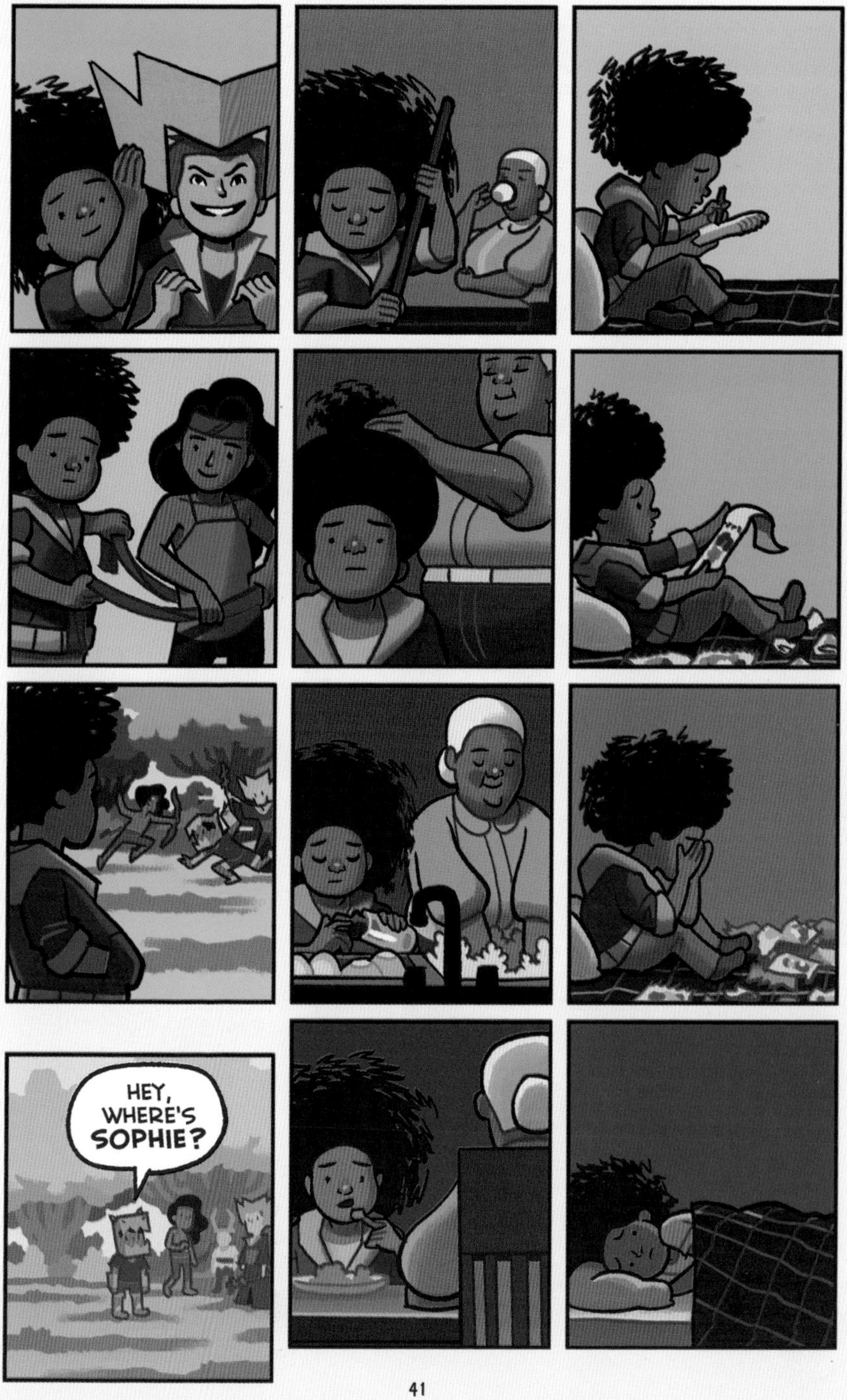
HEY, WHERE'S SOPHIE?

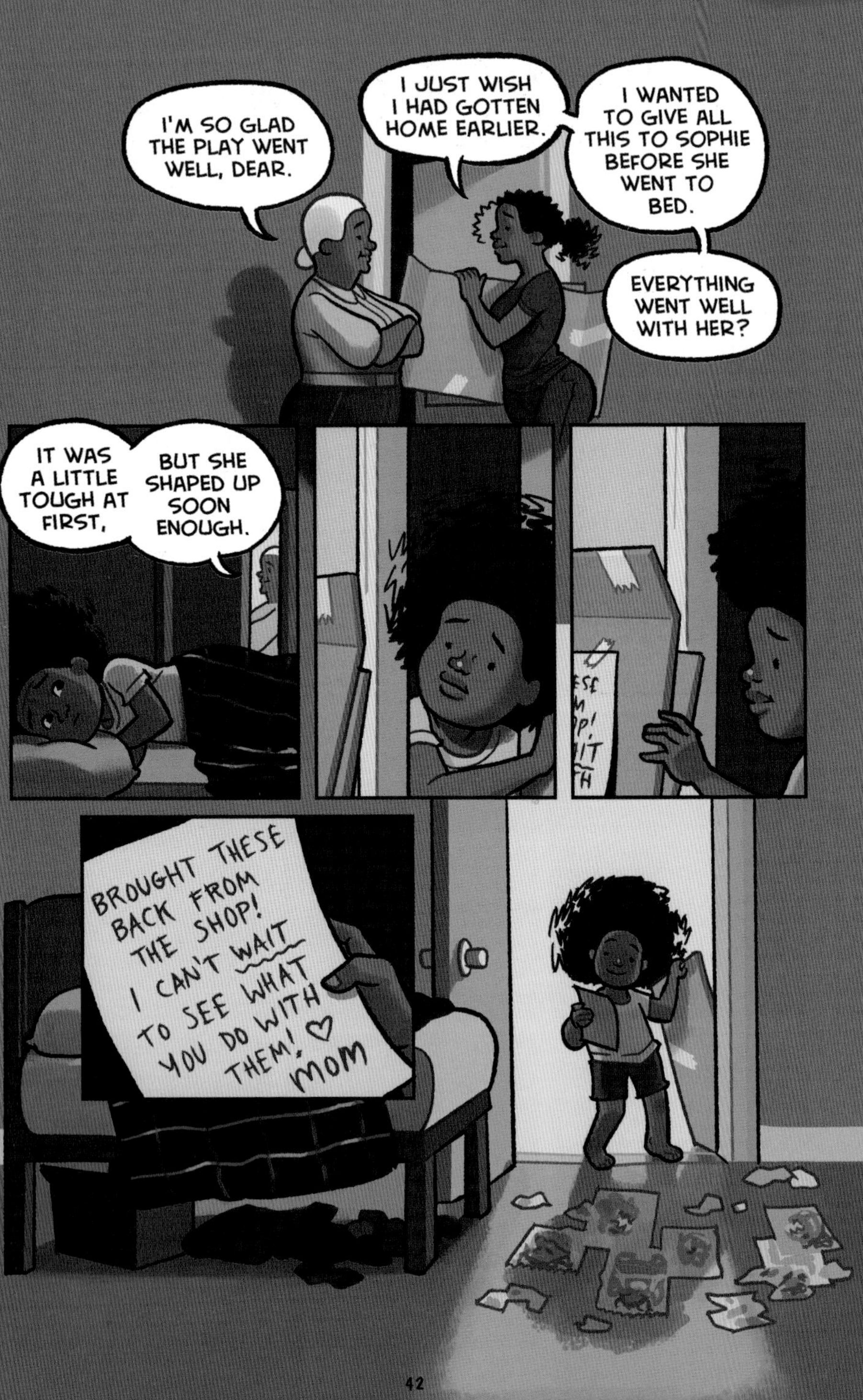

I'M SO GLAD THE PLAY WENT WELL, DEAR.
I JUST WISH I HAD GOTTEN HOME EARLIER.
I WANTED TO GIVE ALL THIS TO SOPHIE BEFORE SHE WENT TO BED.
EVERYTHING WENT WELL WITH HER?
IT WAS A LITTLE TOUGH AT FIRST,
BUT SHE SHAPED UP SOON ENOUGH.
BROUGHT THESE BACK FROM THE SHOP! I CAN'T WAIT TO SEE WHAT YOU DO WITH THEM! ♡ MOM

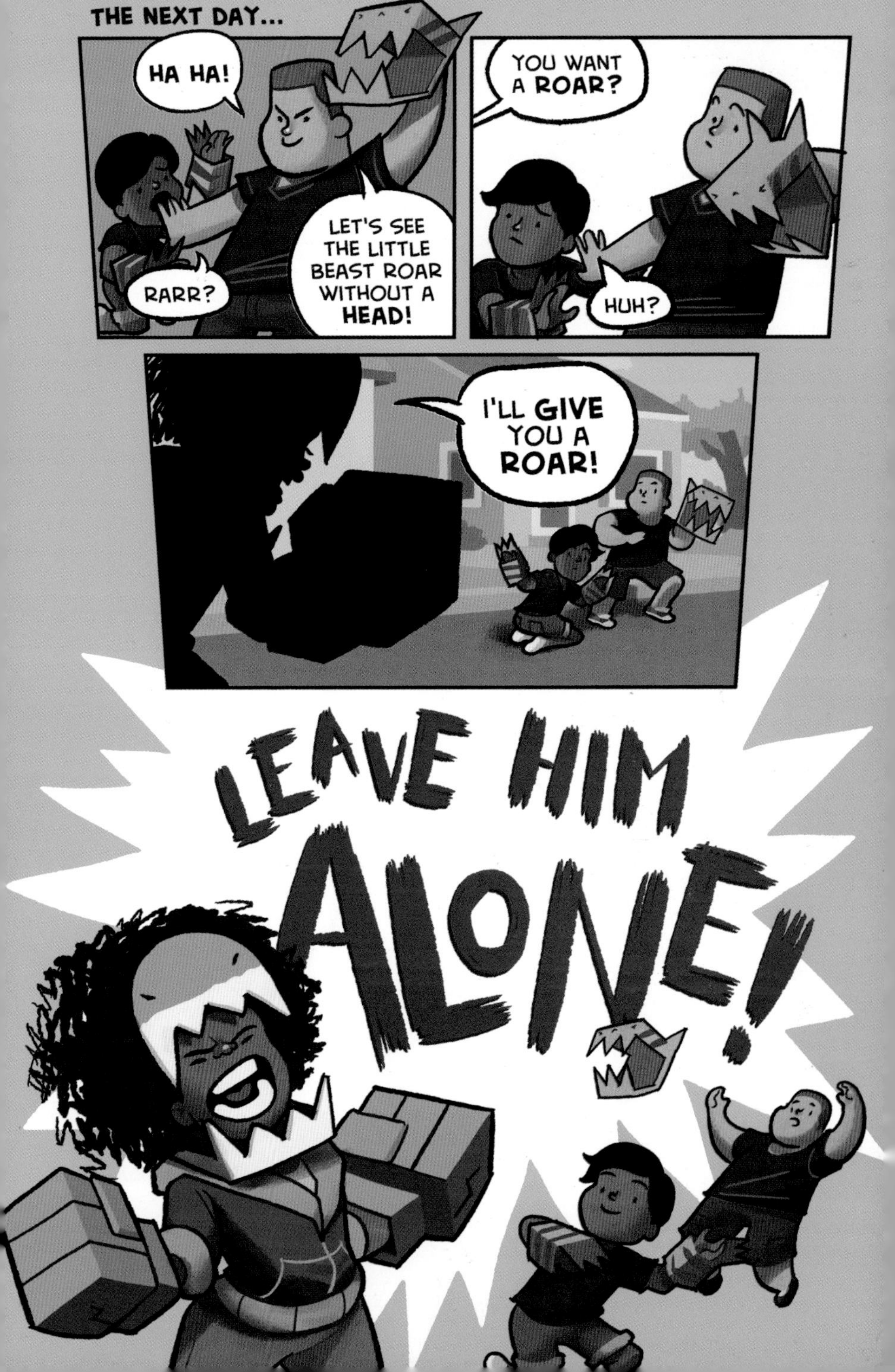
THE NEXT DAY...
HA HA!
RARR?
LET'S SEE THE LITTLE BEAST ROAR WITHOUT A **HEAD!**
YOU WANT A **ROAR?**
HUH?
I'LL **GIVE** YOU A **ROAR!**
LEAVE HIM ALONE!

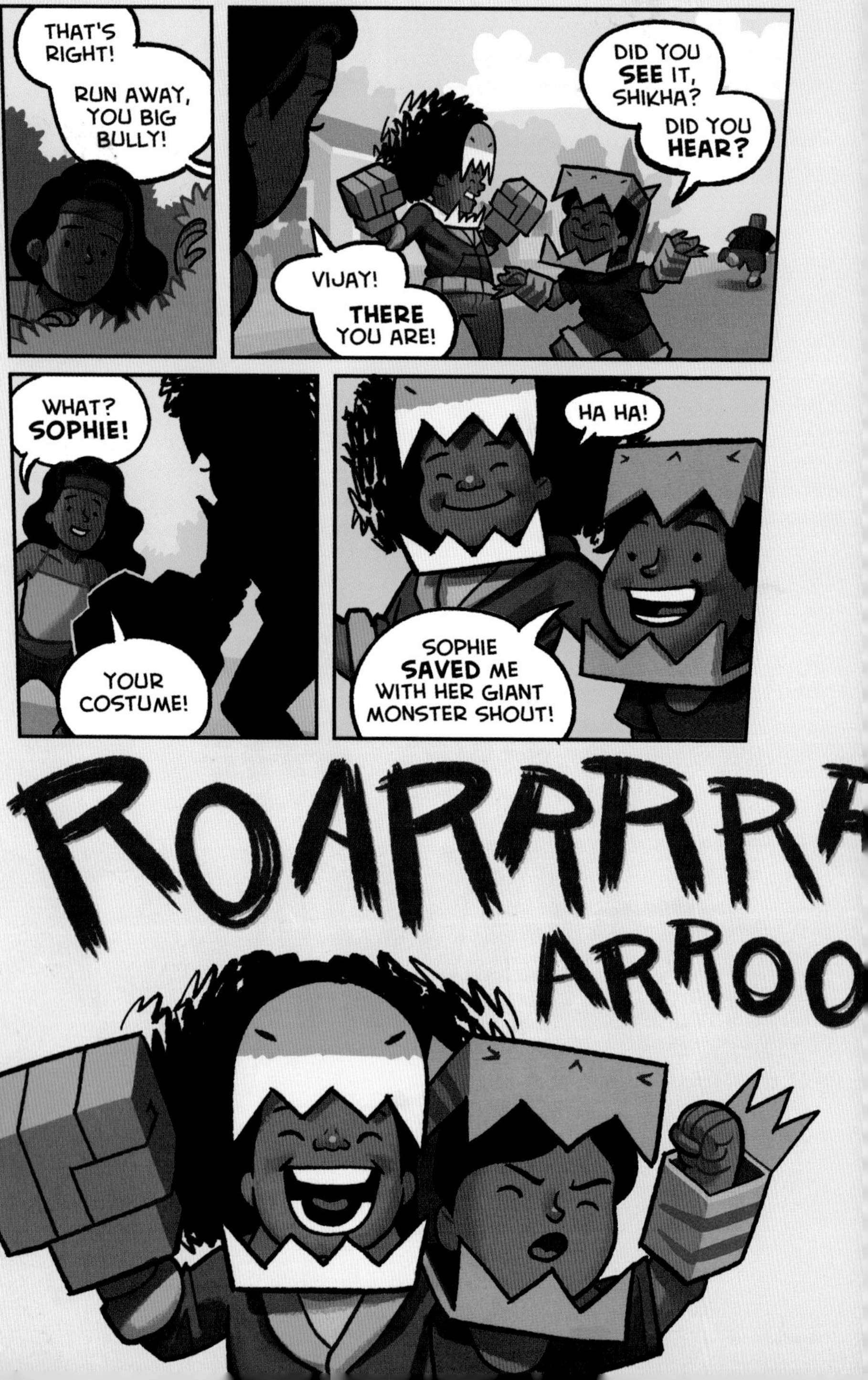

THAT'S RIGHT!
RUN AWAY, YOU BIG BULLY!
DID YOU SEE IT, SHIKHA?
DID YOU HEAR?
VIJAY!
THERE YOU ARE!
WHAT? SOPHIE!
YOUR COSTUME!
HA HA!
SOPHIE SAVED ME WITH HER GIANT MONSTER SHOUT!
ROARRRRR
ARROO

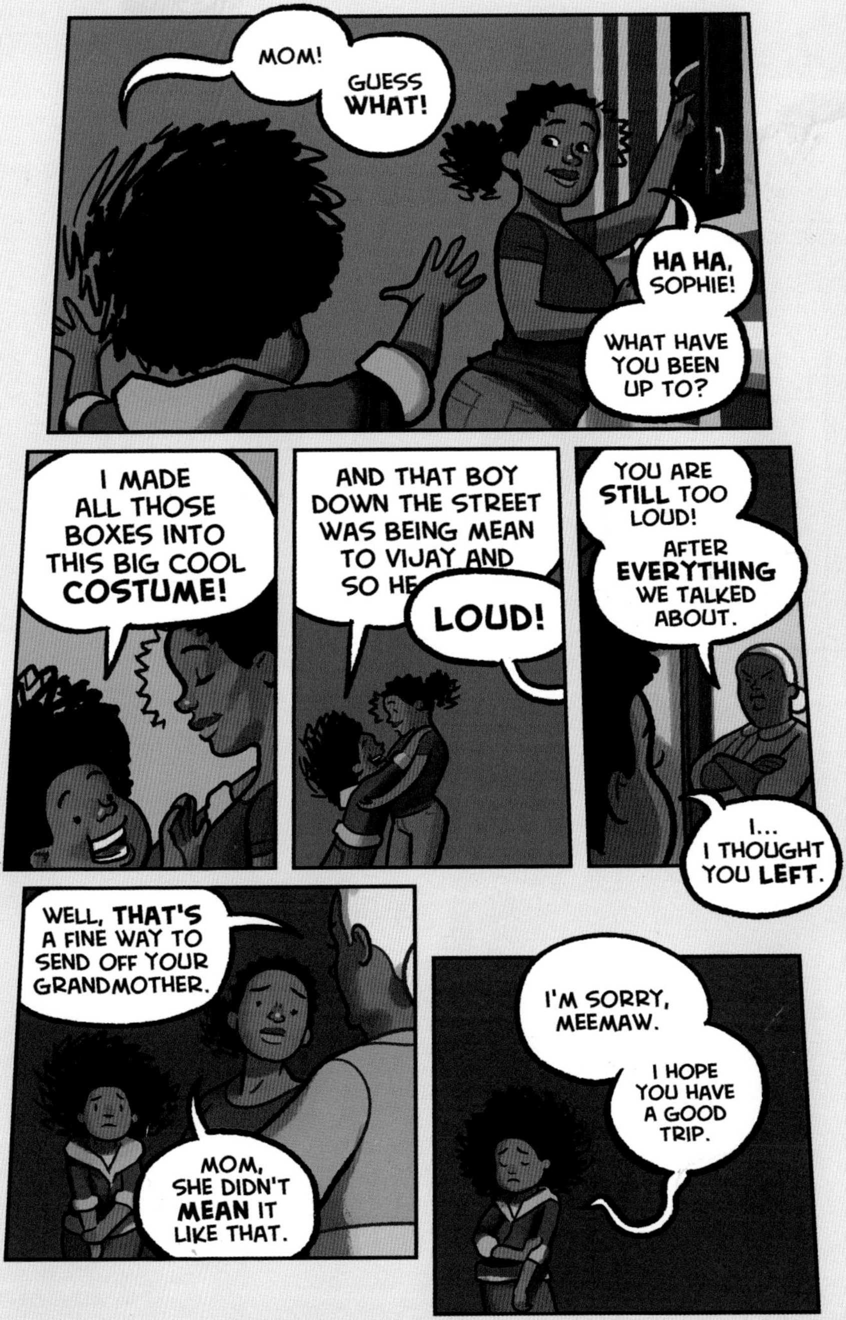
MOM!
GUESS WHAT!
HA HA, SOPHIE!
WHAT HAVE YOU BEEN UP TO?
I MADE ALL THOSE BOXES INTO THIS BIG COOL COSTUME!
AND THAT BOY DOWN THE STREET WAS BEING MEAN TO VIJAY AND SO HE
LOUD!
YOU ARE STILL TOO LOUD!
AFTER EVERYTHING WE TALKED ABOUT.
I... I THOUGHT YOU LEFT.
WELL, THAT'S A FINE WAY TO SEND OFF YOUR GRANDMOTHER.
MOM, SHE DIDN'T MEAN IT LIKE THAT.
I'M SORRY, MEEMAW.
I HOPE YOU HAVE A GOOD TRIP.

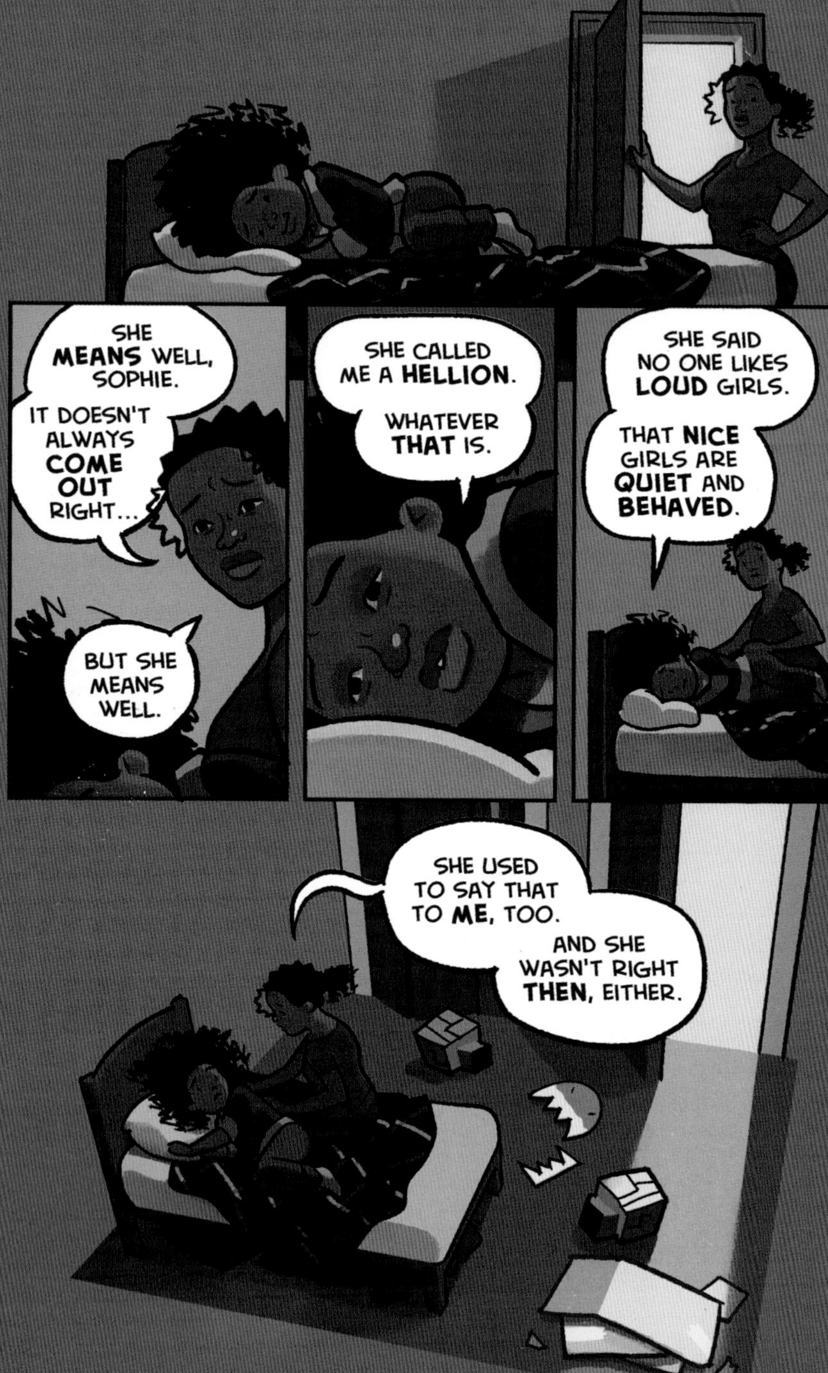
SHE MEANS WELL, SOPHIE.
IT DOESN'T ALWAYS COME OUT RIGHT...
BUT SHE MEANS WELL.
SHE CALLED ME A HELLION.
WHATEVER THAT IS.
SHE SAID NO ONE LIKES LOUD GIRLS.
THAT NICE GIRLS ARE QUIET AND BEHAVED.
SHE USED TO SAY THAT TO ME, TOO.
AND SHE WASN'T RIGHT THEN, EITHER.

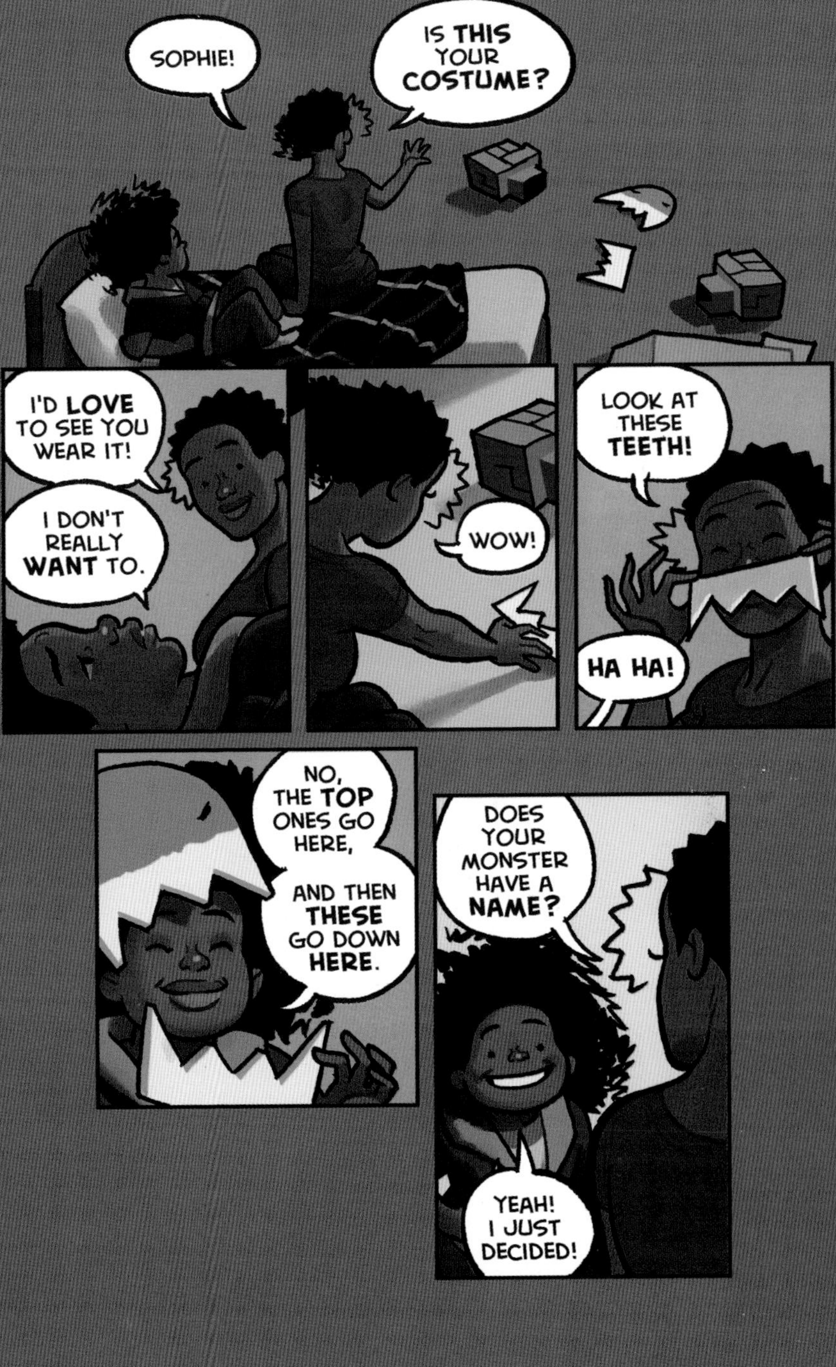
SOPHIE!
IS **THIS** YOUR **COSTUME?**
I'D **LOVE** TO SEE YOU WEAR IT!
I DON'T REALLY **WANT** TO.
WOW!
LOOK AT THESE **TEETH!**
HA HA!
NO, THE **TOP** ONES GO HERE,
AND THEN **THESE** GO DOWN **HERE**.
DOES YOUR MONSTER HAVE A **NAME?**
YEAH! I JUST DECIDED!

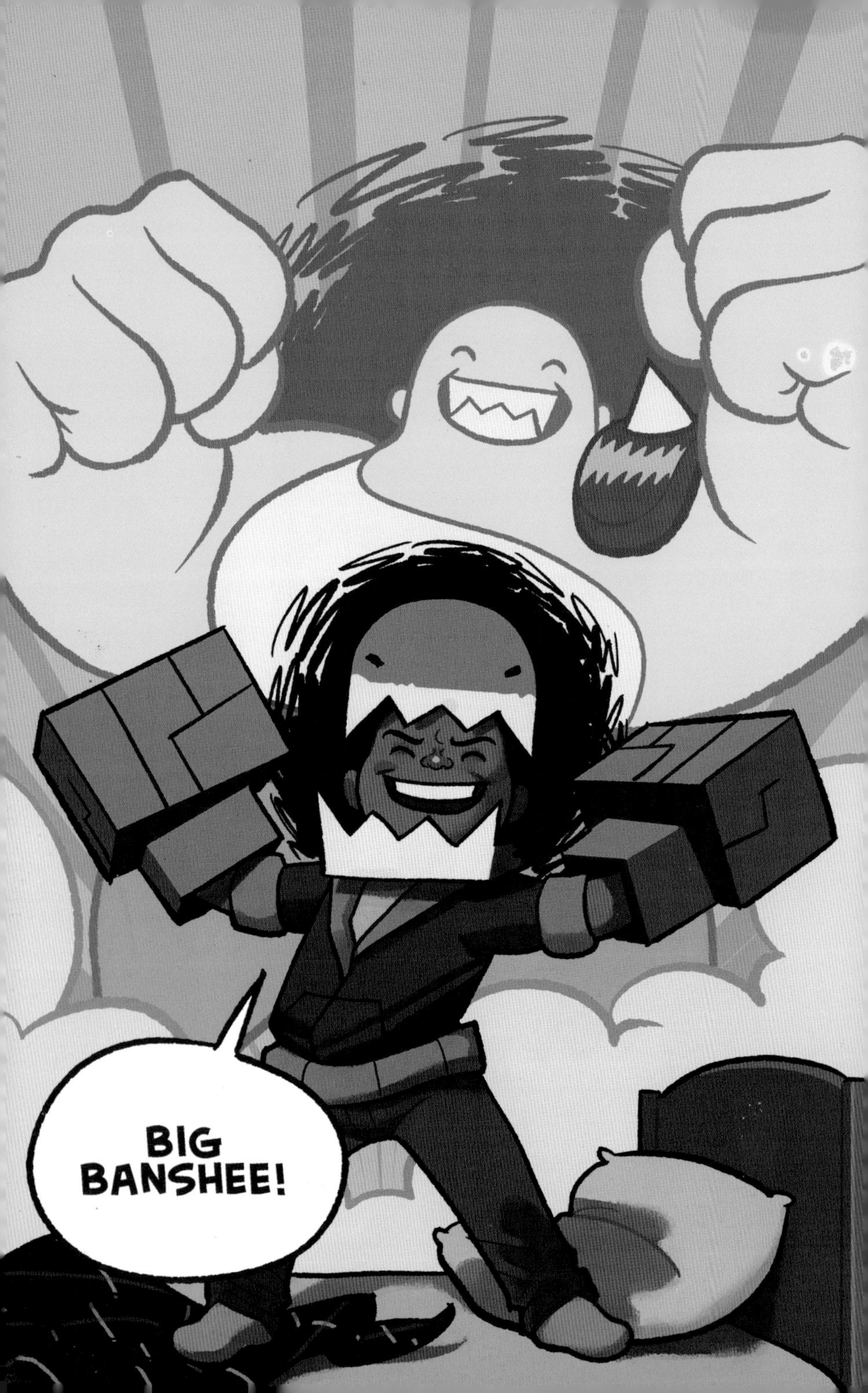
BIG BANSHEE!

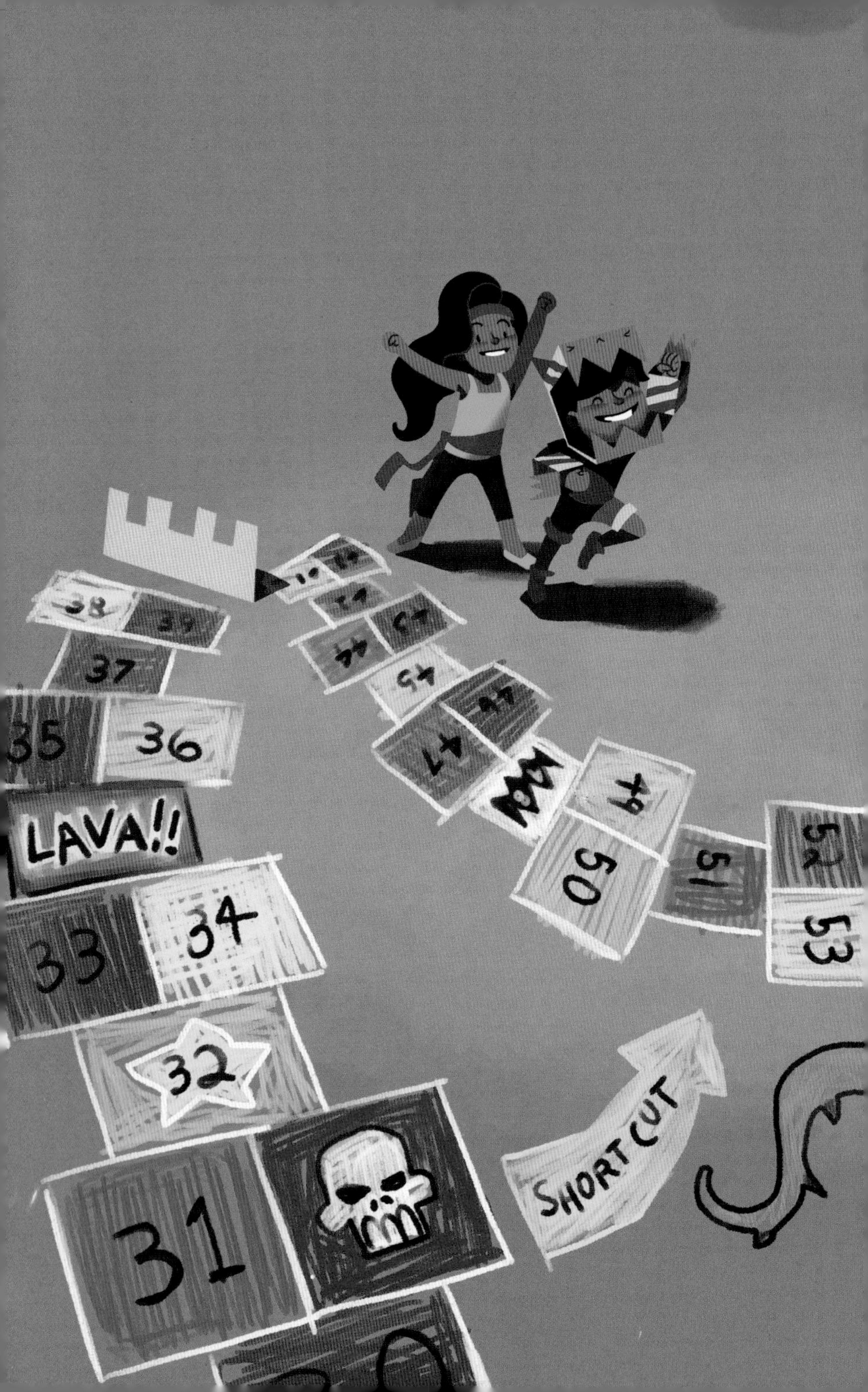
38
37
35
36
LAVA!!
33
34
32
31
SHORT CUT
47
50
51
53

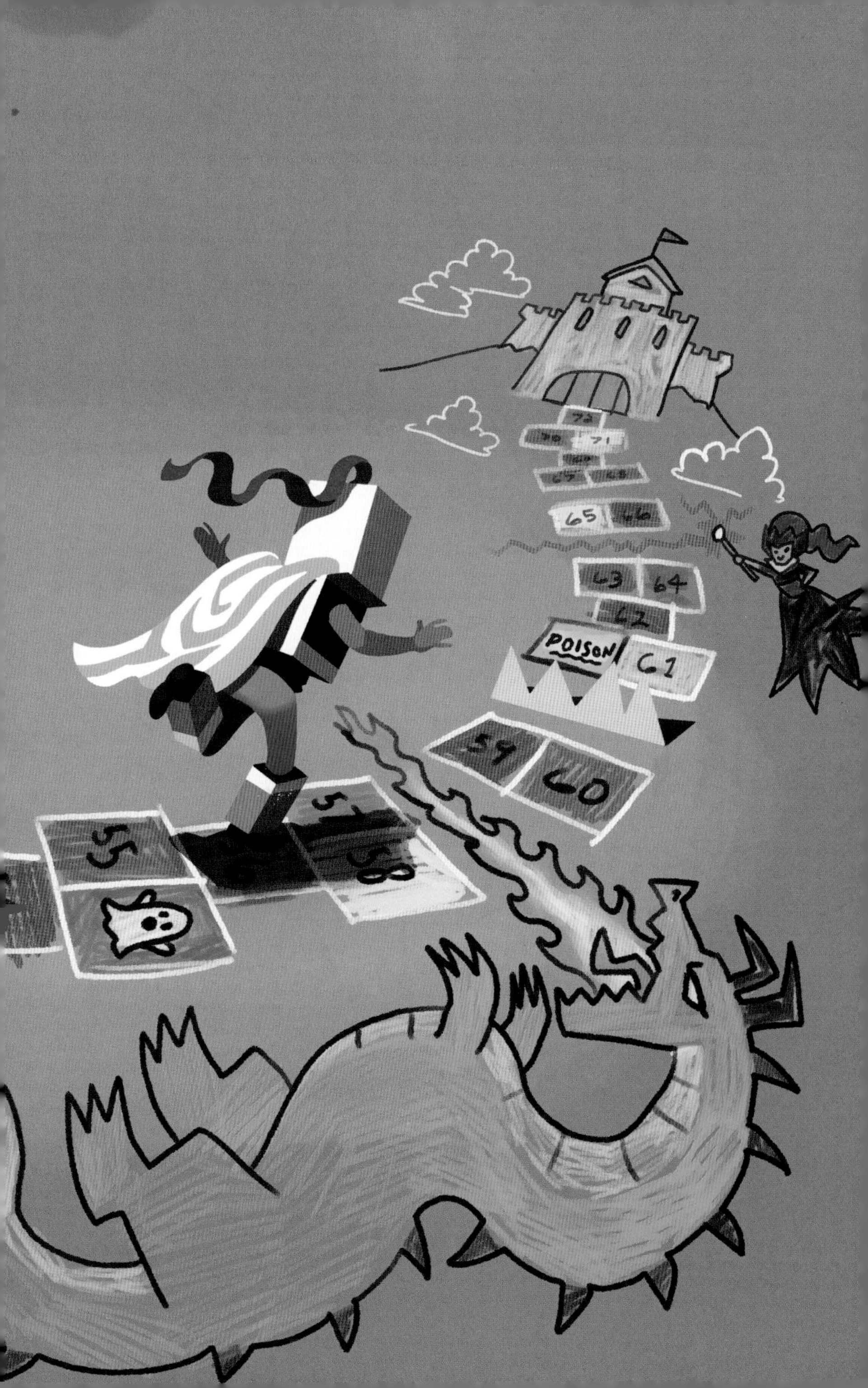

55
57
58
59
60
POISON
61
62
63
64
65

the Alchemist

AND THE

Blacksmith

BY KRIS MOORE AND CHAD SELL

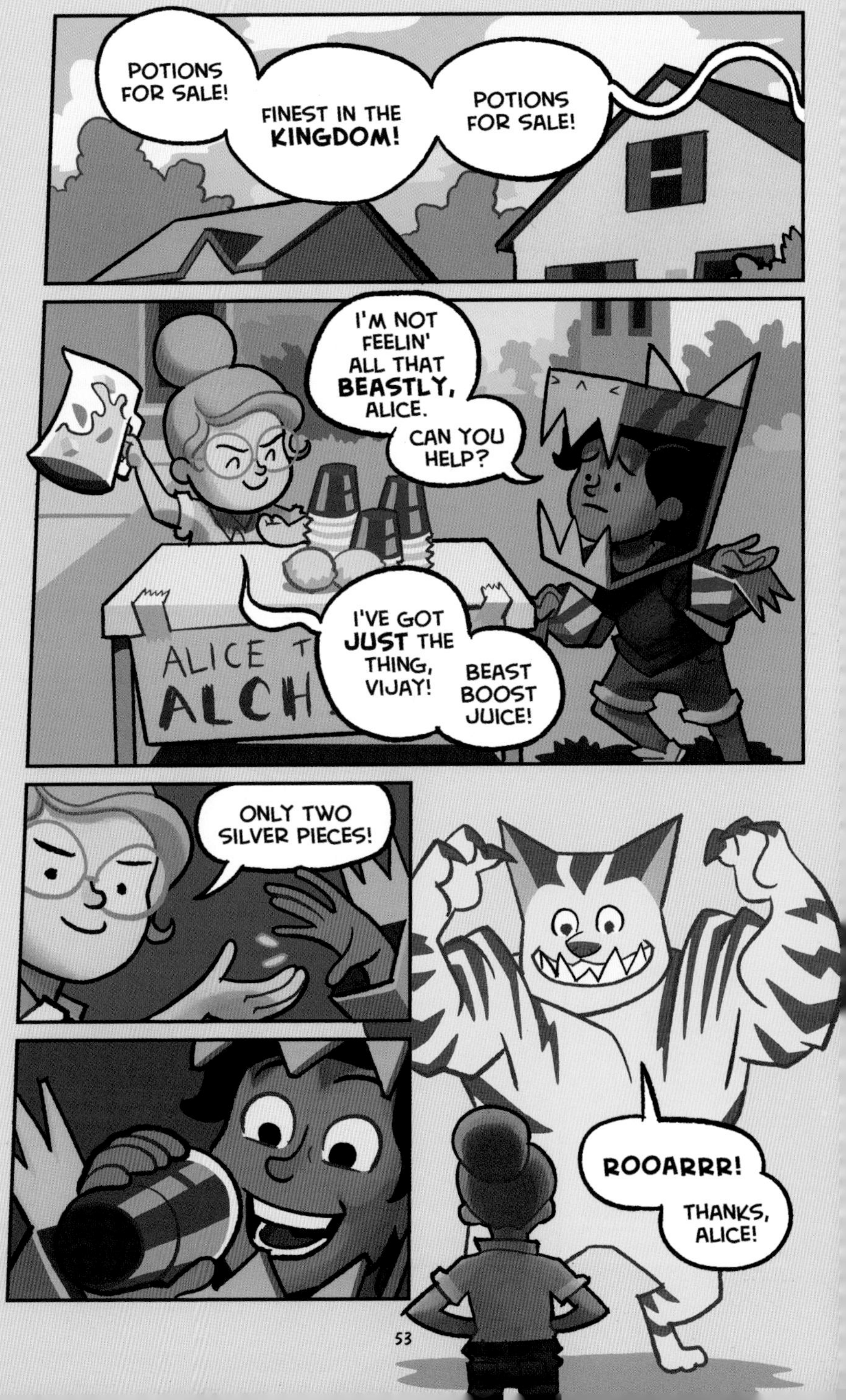
POTIONS FOR SALE!
FINEST IN THE KINGDOM!
POTIONS FOR SALE!
I'M NOT FEELIN' ALL THAT BEASTLY, ALICE.
CAN YOU HELP?
ALICE T
ALCH
I'VE GOT JUST THE THING, VIJAY!
BEAST BOOST JUICE!
ONLY TWO SILVER PIECES!
ROOARRR!
THANKS, ALICE!

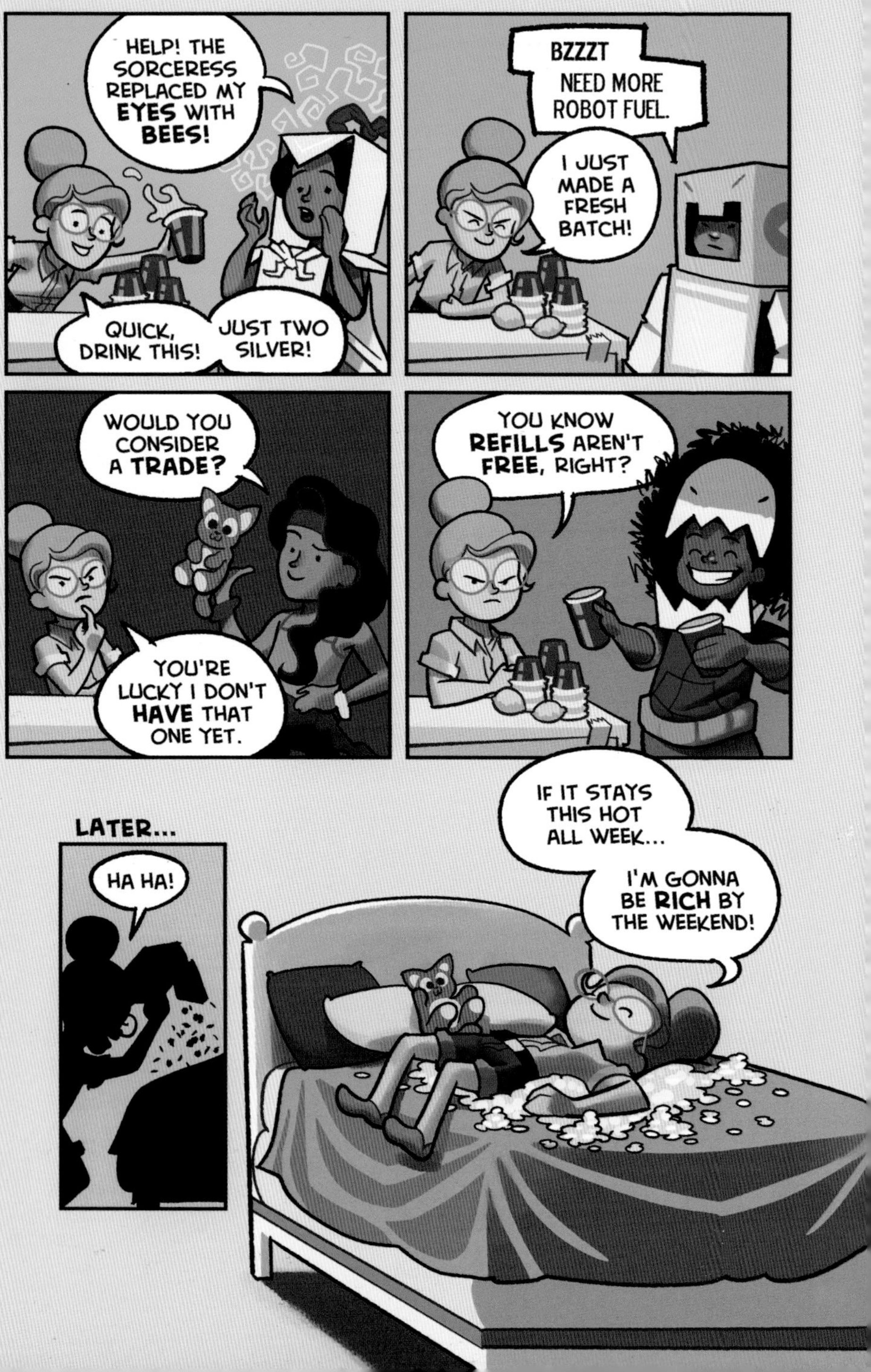
HELP! THE SORCERESS REPLACED MY EYES WITH BEES!
QUICK, DRINK THIS!
JUST TWO SILVER!
BZZZT
NEED MORE ROBOT FUEL.
I JUST MADE A FRESH BATCH!
WOULD YOU CONSIDER A TRADE?
YOU'RE LUCKY I DON'T HAVE THAT ONE YET.
YOU KNOW REFILLS AREN'T FREE, RIGHT?
LATER...
HA HA!
IF IT STAYS THIS HOT ALL WEEK...
I'M GONNA BE RICH BY THE WEEKEND!

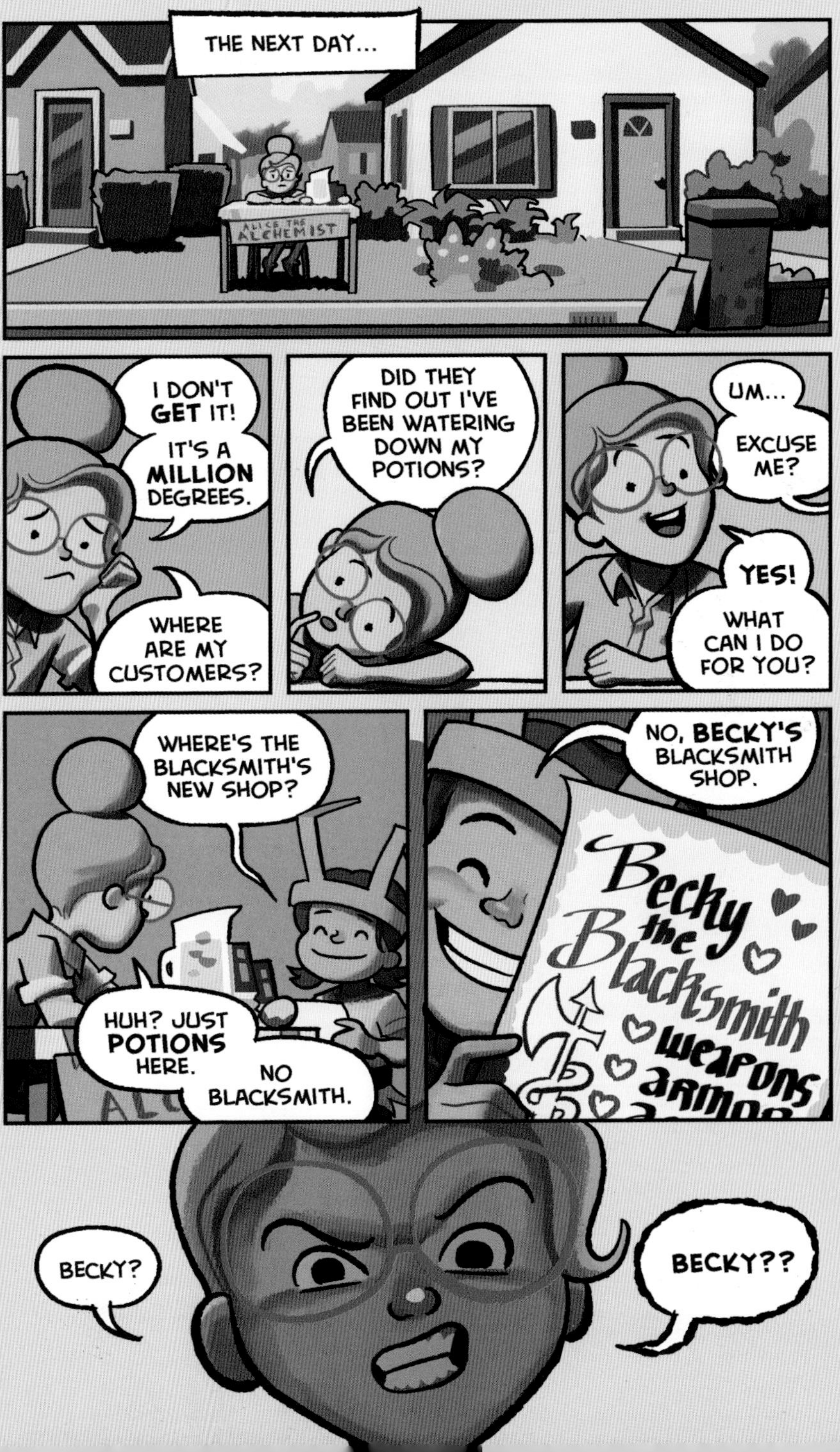
THE NEXT DAY...
ALICE THE ALCHEMIST
I DON'T **GET** IT!
IT'S A **MILLION** DEGREES.
WHERE ARE MY CUSTOMERS?
DID THEY FIND OUT I'VE BEEN WATERING DOWN MY POTIONS?
UM...
EXCUSE ME?
YES!
WHAT CAN I DO FOR YOU?
WHERE'S THE BLACKSMITH'S NEW SHOP?
HUH? JUST **POTIONS** HERE.
NO BLACKSMITH.
NO, **BECKY'S** BLACKSMITH SHOP.
Becky the Blacksmith
weapons
BECKY?
BECKY??

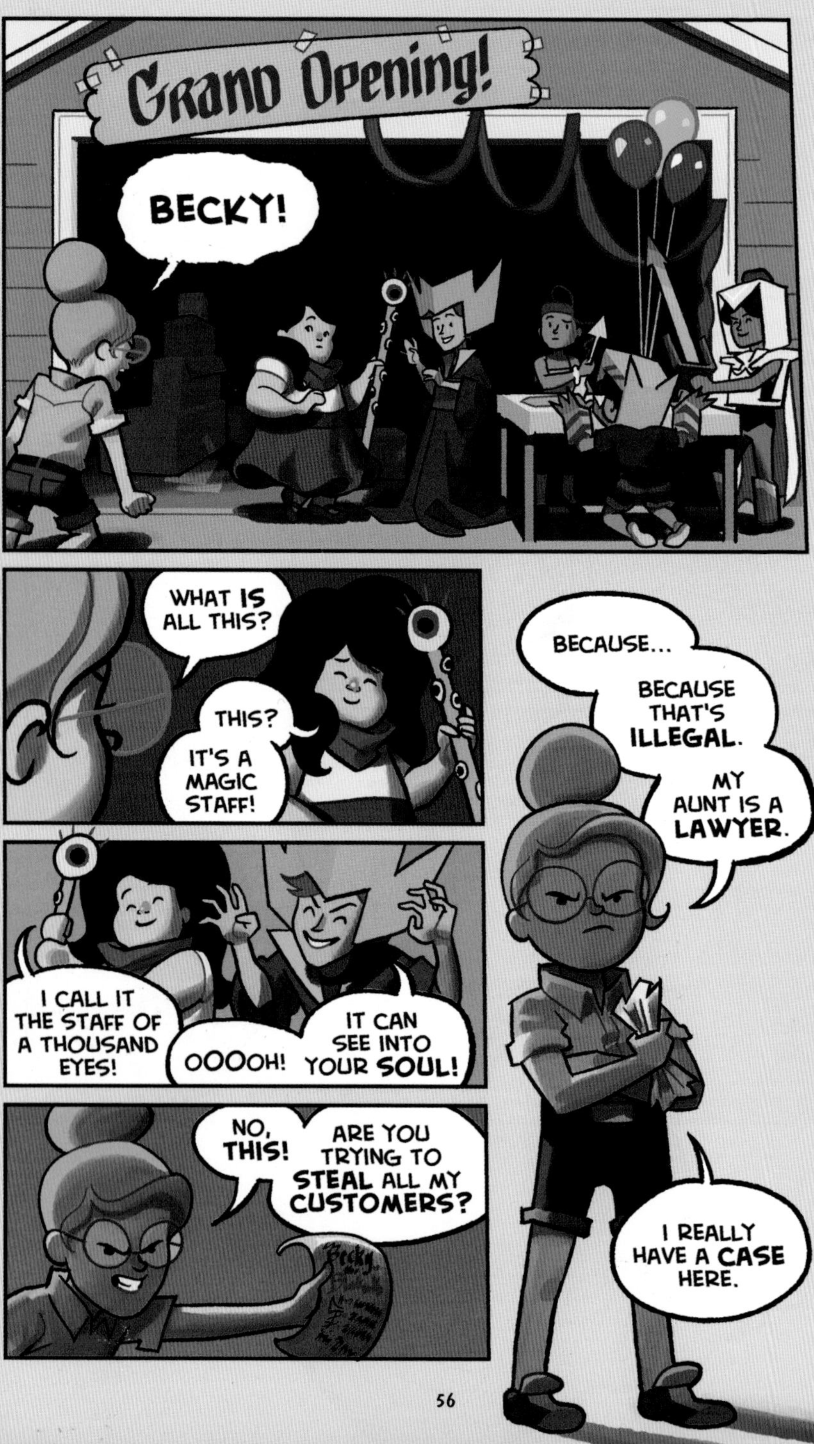
Grand Opening!
BECKY!
WHAT IS ALL THIS?
THIS?
IT'S A MAGIC STAFF!
I CALL IT THE STAFF OF A THOUSAND EYES!
OOOOH!
IT CAN SEE INTO YOUR SOUL!
NO, THIS!
ARE YOU TRYING TO STEAL ALL MY CUSTOMERS?
BECAUSE...
BECAUSE THAT'S ILLEGAL.
MY AUNT IS A LAWYER.
I REALLY HAVE A CASE HERE.

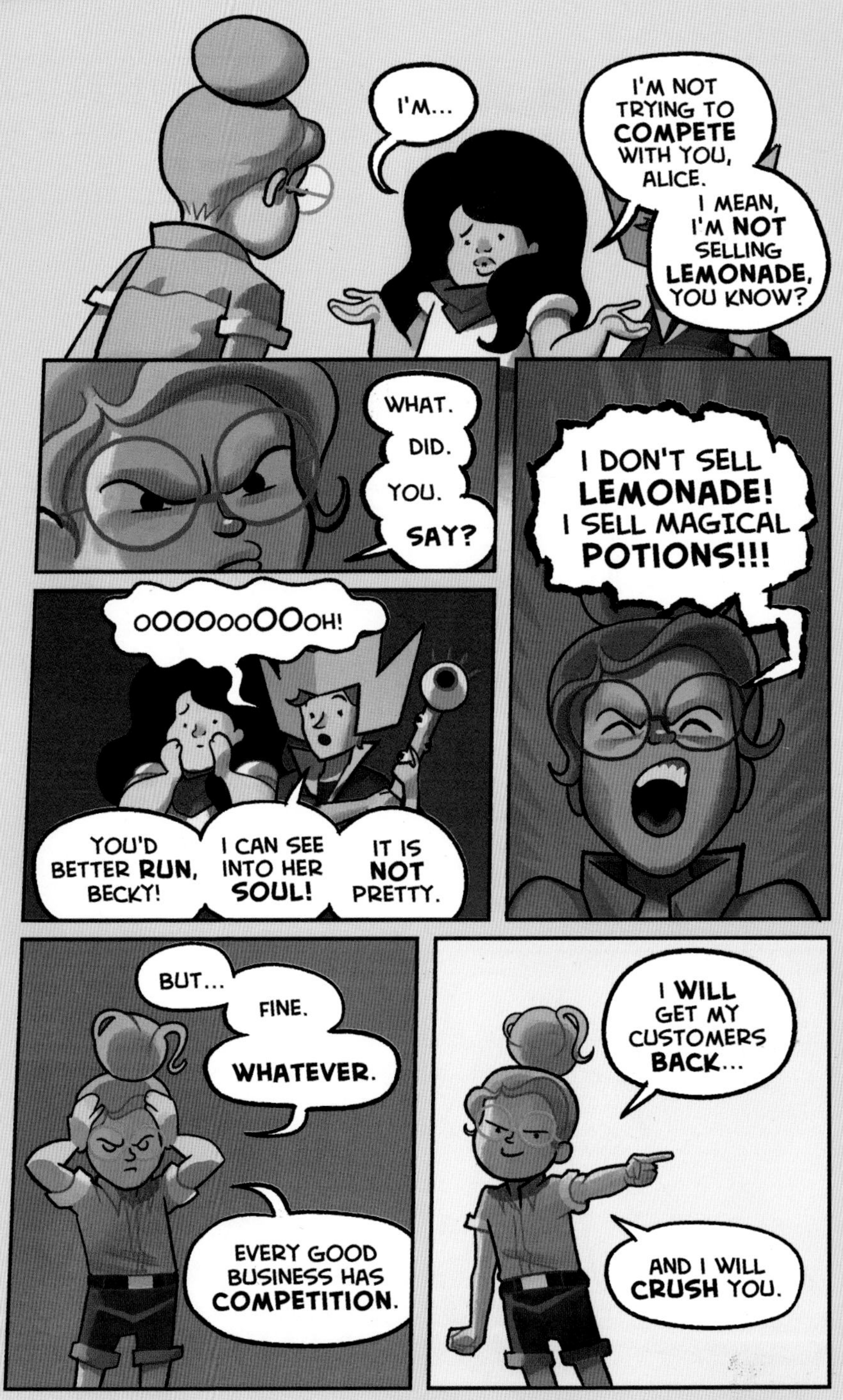
I'M...
I'M NOT TRYING TO COMPETE WITH YOU, ALICE.
I MEAN, I'M NOT SELLING LEMONADE, YOU KNOW?
WHAT.
DID.
YOU.
SAY?
I DON'T SELL LEMONADE! I SELL MAGICAL POTIONS!!!
OOOOOOOOOOH!
YOU'D BETTER RUN, BECKY!
I CAN SEE INTO HER SOUL!
IT IS NOT PRETTY.
BUT...
FINE.
WHATEVER.
EVERY GOOD BUSINESS HAS COMPETITION.
I WILL GET MY CUSTOMERS BACK...
AND I WILL CRUSH YOU.

LATER THAT DAY...

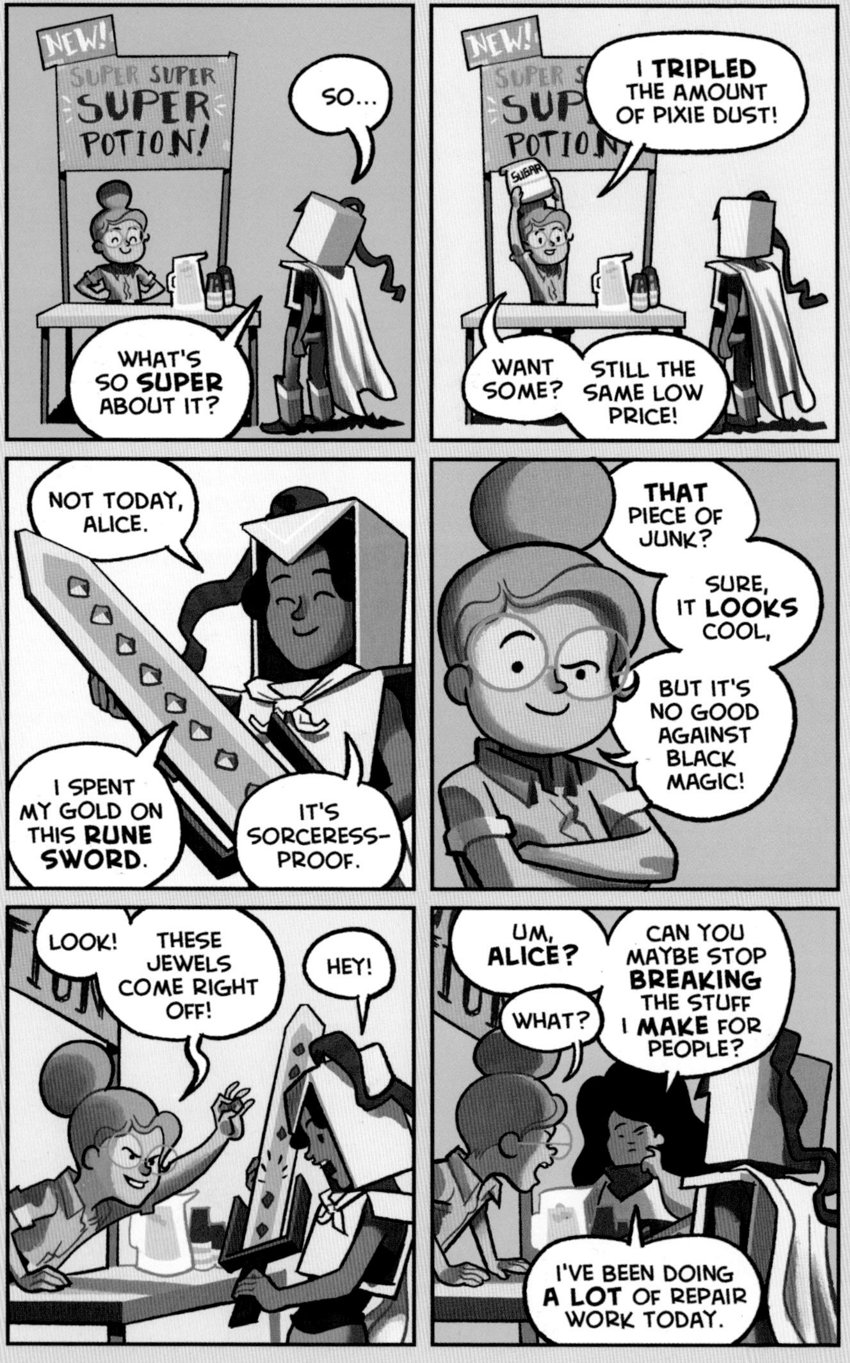
NEW!
SUPER SUPER SUPER POTION!
SO...
WHAT'S SO SUPER ABOUT IT?
NEW!
SUGAR
I TRIPLED THE AMOUNT OF PIXIE DUST!
WANT SOME?
STILL THE SAME LOW PRICE!
NOT TODAY, ALICE.
I SPENT MY GOLD ON THIS RUNE SWORD.
IT'S SORCERESS-PROOF.
THAT PIECE OF JUNK?
SURE, IT LOOKS COOL,
BUT IT'S NO GOOD AGAINST BLACK MAGIC!
LOOK!
THESE JEWELS COME RIGHT OFF!
HEY!
UM, ALICE?
WHAT?
CAN YOU MAYBE STOP BREAKING THE STUFF I MAKE FOR PEOPLE?
I'VE BEEN DOING A LOT OF REPAIR WORK TODAY.

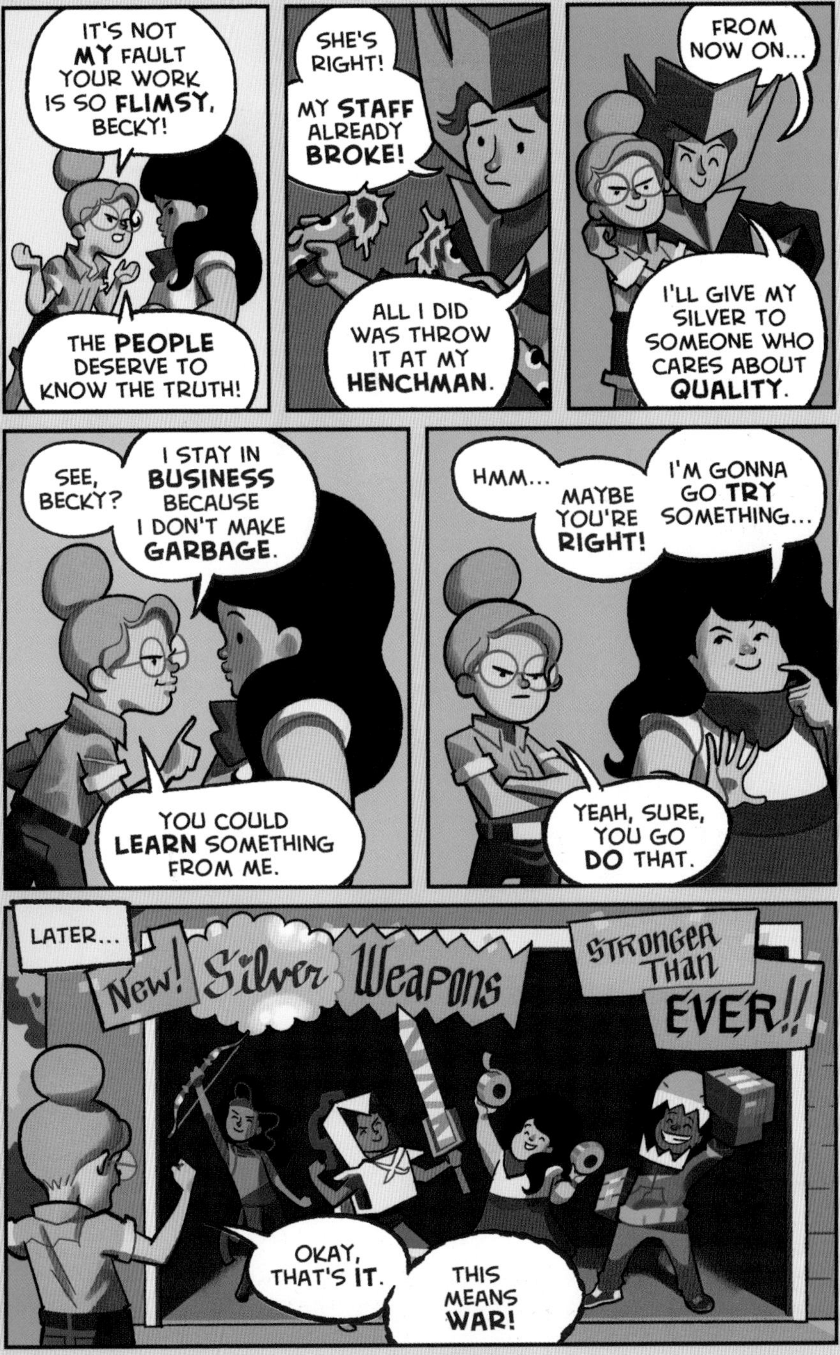
IT'S NOT MY FAULT YOUR WORK IS SO FLIMSY, BECKY!
THE PEOPLE DESERVE TO KNOW THE TRUTH!
SHE'S RIGHT!
MY STAFF ALREADY BROKE!
ALL I DID WAS THROW IT AT MY HENCHMAN.
FROM NOW ON...
I'LL GIVE MY SILVER TO SOMEONE WHO CARES ABOUT QUALITY.
SEE, BECKY?
I STAY IN BUSINESS BECAUSE I DON'T MAKE GARBAGE.
YOU COULD LEARN SOMETHING FROM ME.
HMM...
MAYBE YOU'RE RIGHT!
I'M GONNA GO TRY SOMETHING...
YEAH, SURE, YOU GO DO THAT.
LATER...
New! Silver Weapons
STRONGER THAN EVER!!
OKAY, THAT'S IT.
THIS MEANS WAR!

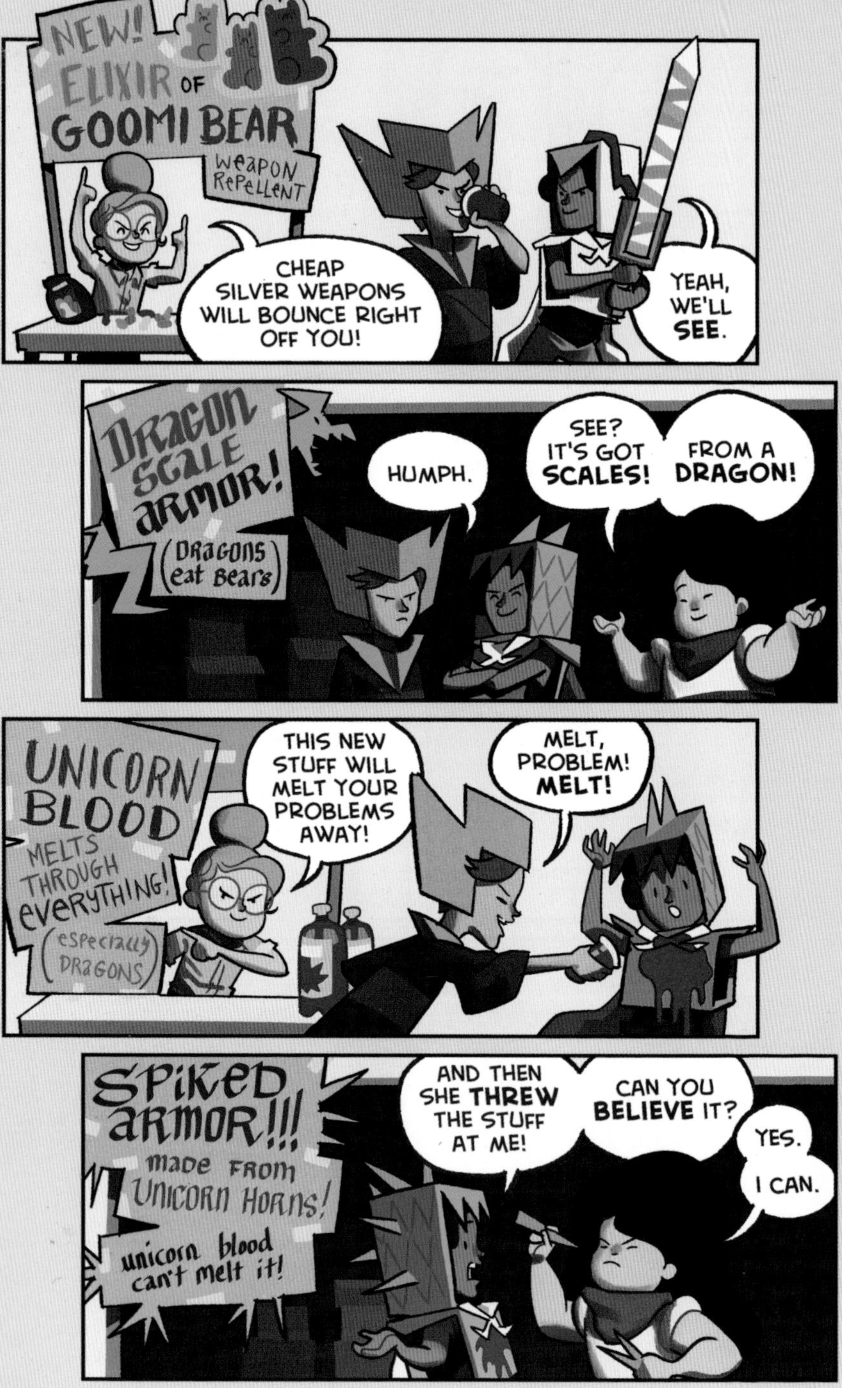
NEW!! ELIXIR OF GOOMI BEAR
WEAPON REPELLENT
CHEAP SILVER WEAPONS WILL BOUNCE RIGHT OFF YOU!
YEAH, WE'LL **SEE**.
DRAGON SCALE ARMOR!
(DRAGONS eat Bears)
HUMPH.
SEE? IT'S GOT **SCALES!**
FROM A **DRAGON!**
UNICORN BLOOD
MELTS THROUGH EVERYTHING!
(especially DRAGONS)
THIS NEW STUFF WILL MELT YOUR PROBLEMS AWAY!
MELT, PROBLEM! **MELT!**
SPIKED ARMOR!!!
made FROM UNICORN HORNS!
unicorn blood can't melt it!
AND THEN SHE **THREW** THE STUFF AT ME!
CAN YOU **BELIEVE** IT?
YES.
I CAN.

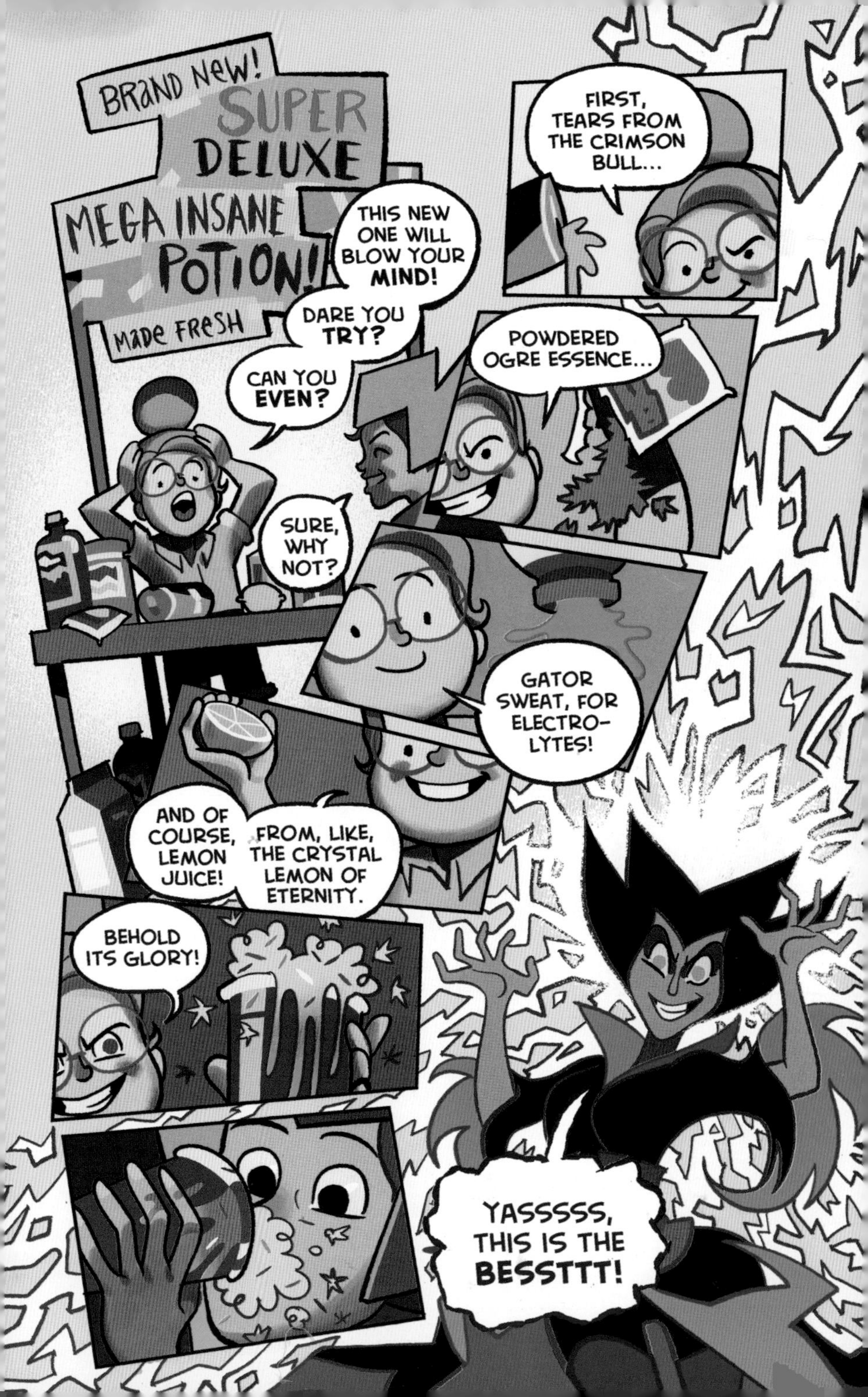
BRAND NEW! SUPER DELUXE MEGA INSANE POTION!
MADE FRESH
THIS NEW ONE WILL BLOW YOUR MIND!
DARE YOU TRY?
CAN YOU EVEN?
FIRST, TEARS FROM THE CRIMSON BULL...
POWDERED OGRE ESSENCE...
SURE, WHY NOT?
GATOR SWEAT, FOR ELECTRO-LYTES!
AND OF COURSE, LEMON JUICE!
FROM, LIKE, THE CRYSTAL LEMON OF ETERNITY.
BEHOLD ITS GLORY!
YASSSSS, THIS IS THE BESSTTT!

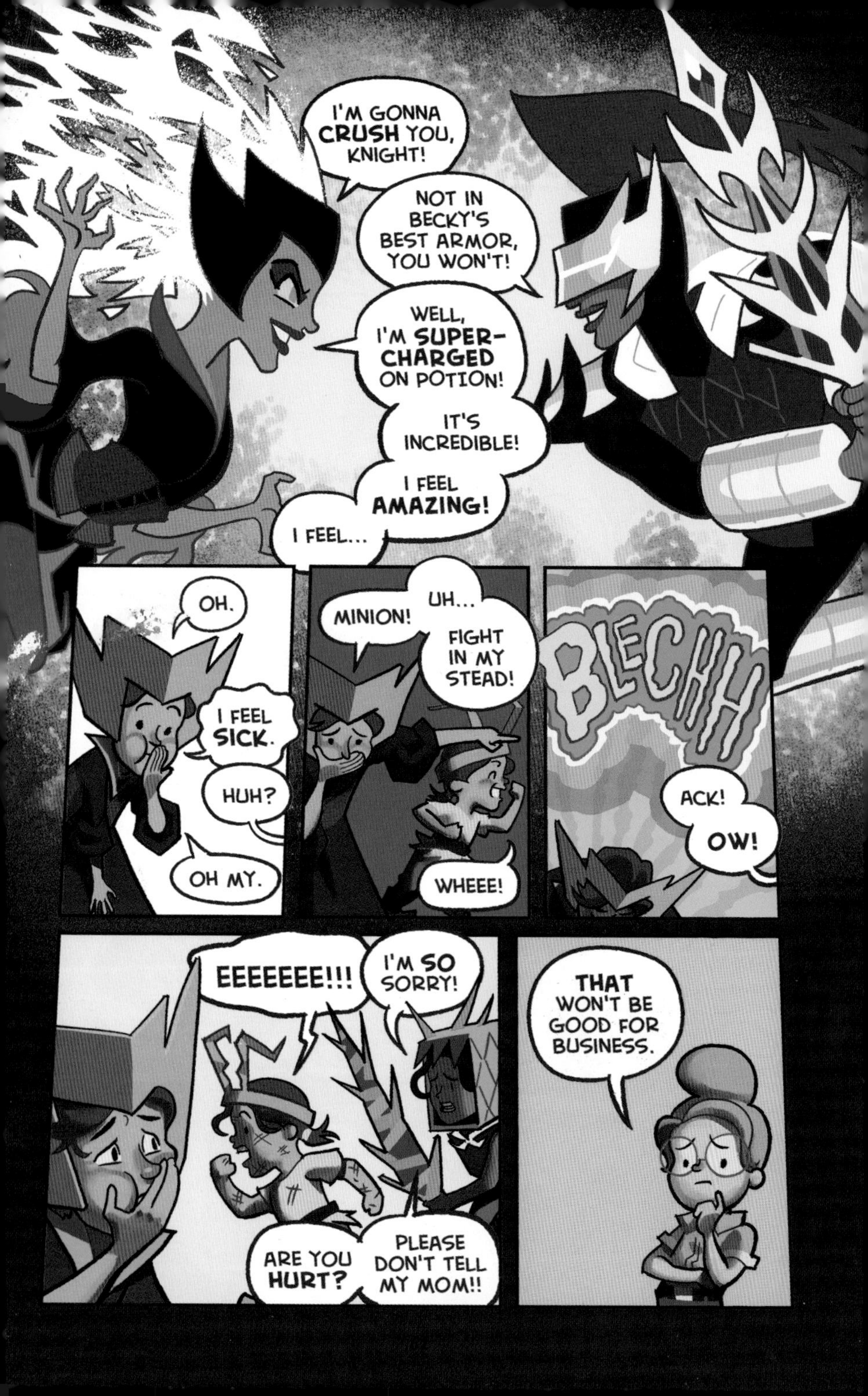
I'M GONNA CRUSH YOU, KNIGHT!
NOT IN BECKY'S BEST ARMOR, YOU WON'T!
WELL, I'M SUPER-CHARGED ON POTION!
IT'S INCREDIBLE!
I FEEL AMAZING!
I FEEL...
OH.
I FEEL SICK.
HUH?
OH MY.
MINION!
UH...
FIGHT IN MY STEAD!
WHEEE!
BLECHH
ACK!
OW!
EEEEEEE!!!
I'M SO SORRY!
ARE YOU HURT?
PLEASE DON'T TELL MY MOM!!
THAT WON'T BE GOOD FOR BUSINESS.

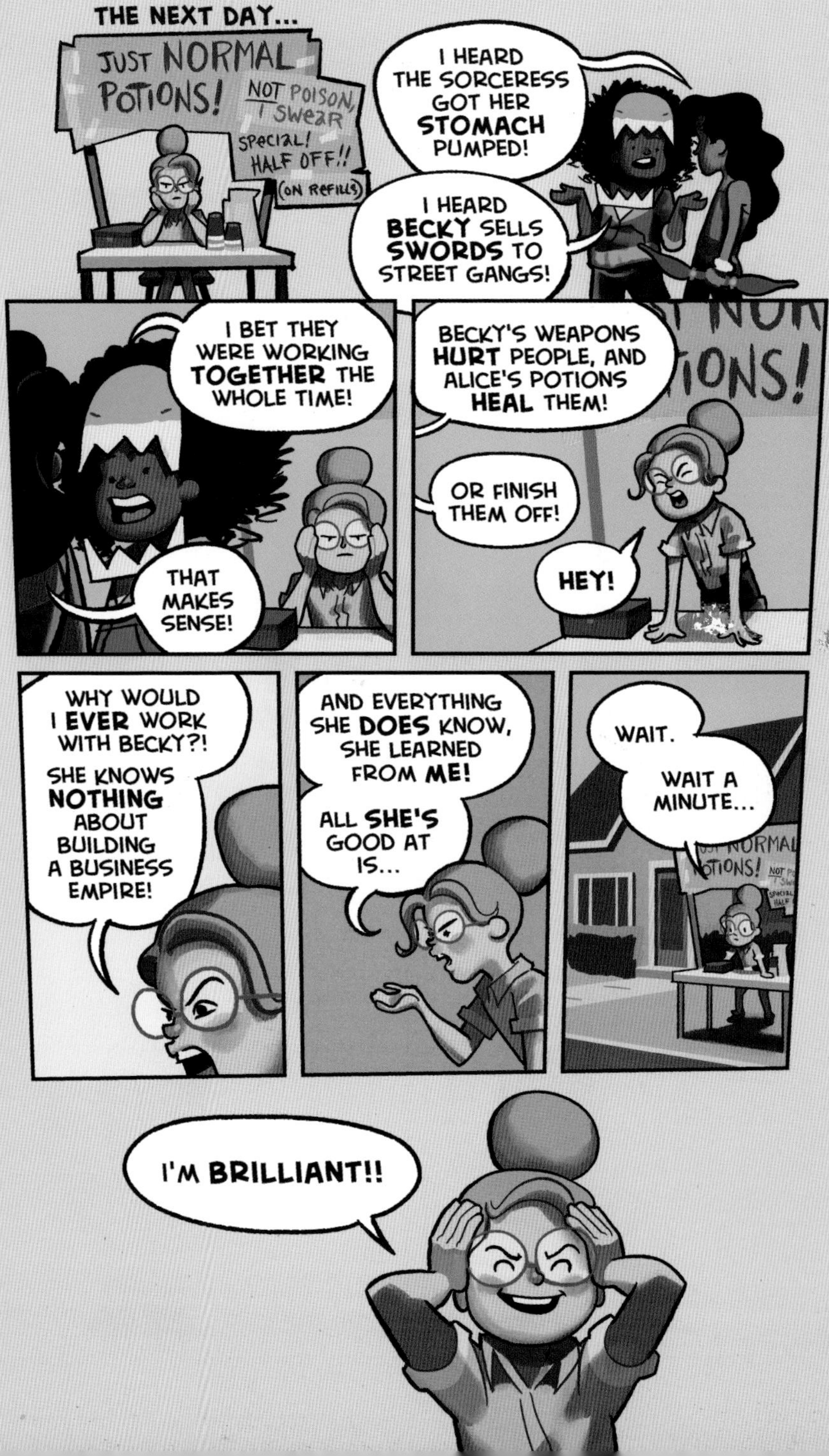
THE NEXT DAY...
JUST NORMAL POTIONS!
NOT POISON, I SWEAR
SPECIAL! HALF OFF!!
(ON REFILLS)
I HEARD THE SORCERESS GOT HER STOMACH PUMPED!
I HEARD BECKY SELLS SWORDS TO STREET GANGS!
I BET THEY WERE WORKING TOGETHER THE WHOLE TIME!
THAT MAKES SENSE!
BECKY'S WEAPONS HURT PEOPLE, AND ALICE'S POTIONS HEAL THEM!
OR FINISH THEM OFF!
HEY!
WHY WOULD I EVER WORK WITH BECKY?!
SHE KNOWS NOTHING ABOUT BUILDING A BUSINESS EMPIRE!
AND EVERYTHING SHE DOES KNOW, SHE LEARNED FROM ME!
ALL SHE'S GOOD AT IS...
WAIT.
WAIT A MINUTE...
I'M BRILLIANT!!

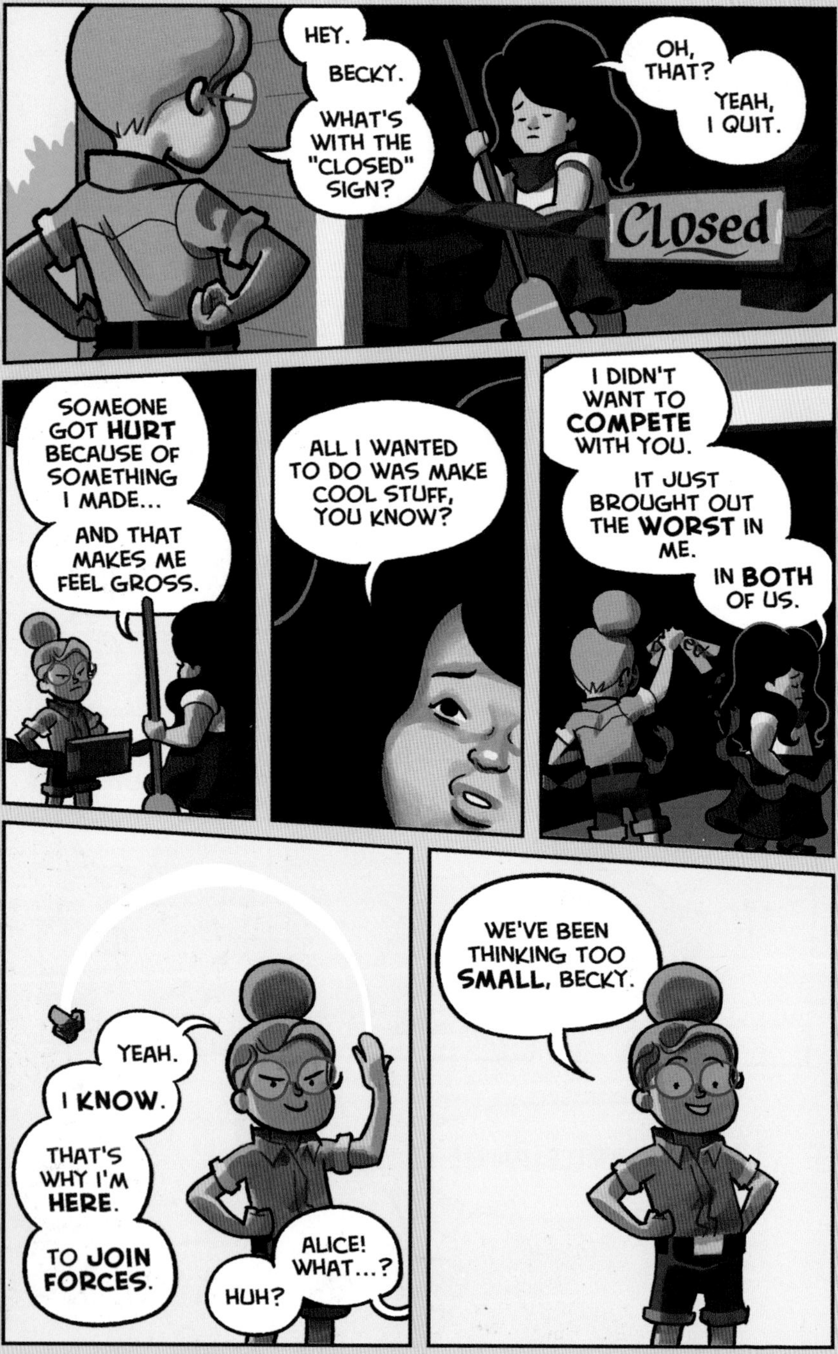
HEY.
BECKY.
WHAT'S WITH THE "CLOSED" SIGN?
OH, THAT?
YEAH, I QUIT.
Closed
SOMEONE GOT HURT BECAUSE OF SOMETHING I MADE...
AND THAT MAKES ME FEEL GROSS.
ALL I WANTED TO DO WAS MAKE COOL STUFF, YOU KNOW?
I DIDN'T WANT TO COMPETE WITH YOU.
IT JUST BROUGHT OUT THE WORST IN ME.
IN BOTH OF US.
YEAH.
I KNOW.
THAT'S WHY I'M HERE.
TO JOIN FORCES.
ALICE! WHAT...?
HUH?
WE'VE BEEN THINKING TOO SMALL, BECKY.

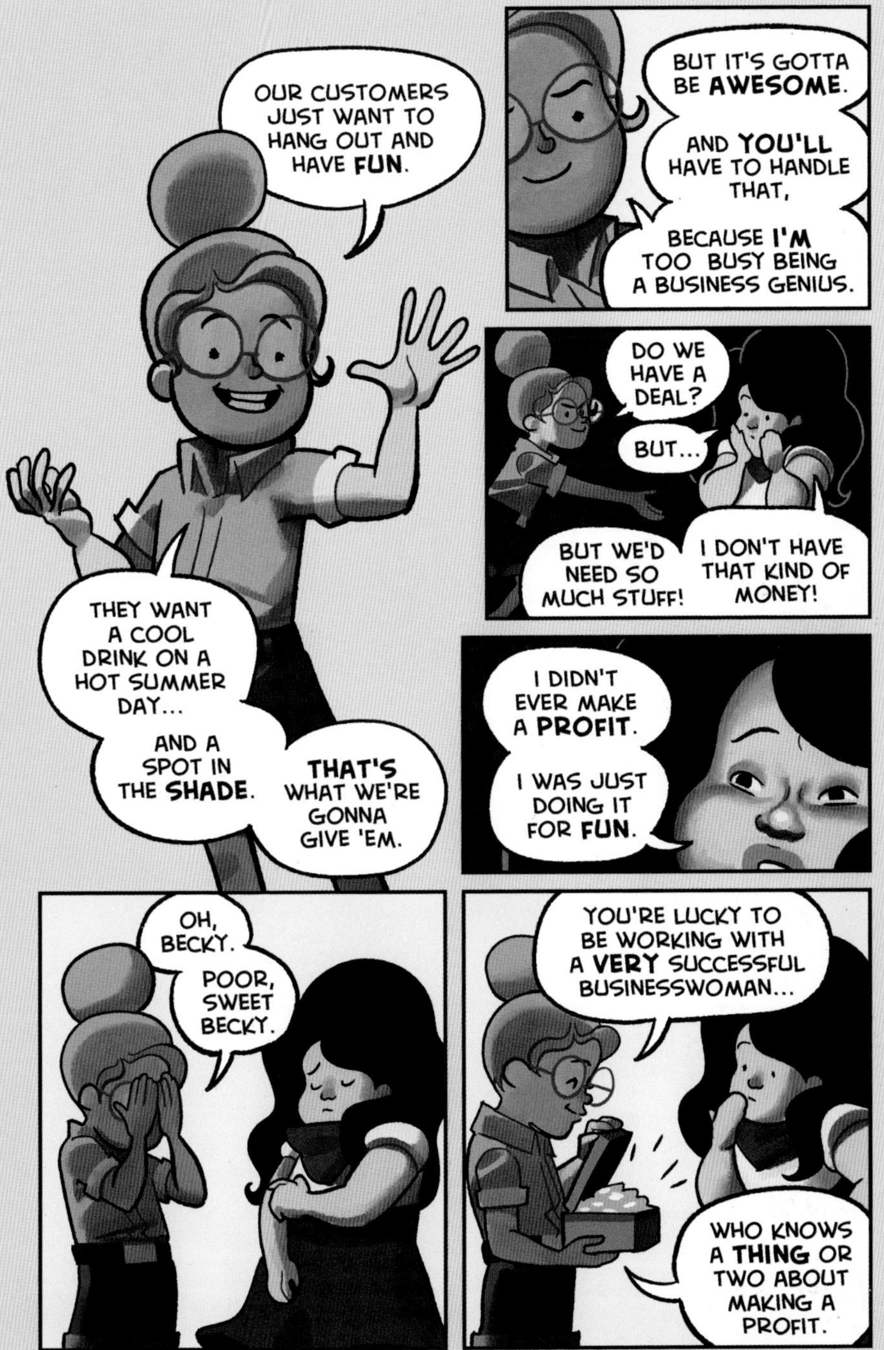
OUR CUSTOMERS JUST WANT TO HANG OUT AND HAVE FUN.
THEY WANT A COOL DRINK ON A HOT SUMMER DAY...
AND A SPOT IN THE SHADE.
THAT'S WHAT WE'RE GONNA GIVE 'EM.
BUT IT'S GOTTA BE AWESOME.
AND YOU'LL HAVE TO HANDLE THAT,
BECAUSE I'M TOO BUSY BEING A BUSINESS GENIUS.
DO WE HAVE A DEAL?
BUT...
BUT WE'D NEED SO MUCH STUFF!
I DON'T HAVE THAT KIND OF MONEY!
I DIDN'T EVER MAKE A PROFIT.
I WAS JUST DOING IT FOR FUN.
OH, BECKY.
POOR, SWEET BECKY.
YOU'RE LUCKY TO BE WORKING WITH A VERY SUCCESSFUL BUSINESSWOMAN...
WHO KNOWS A THING OR TWO ABOUT MAKING A PROFIT.

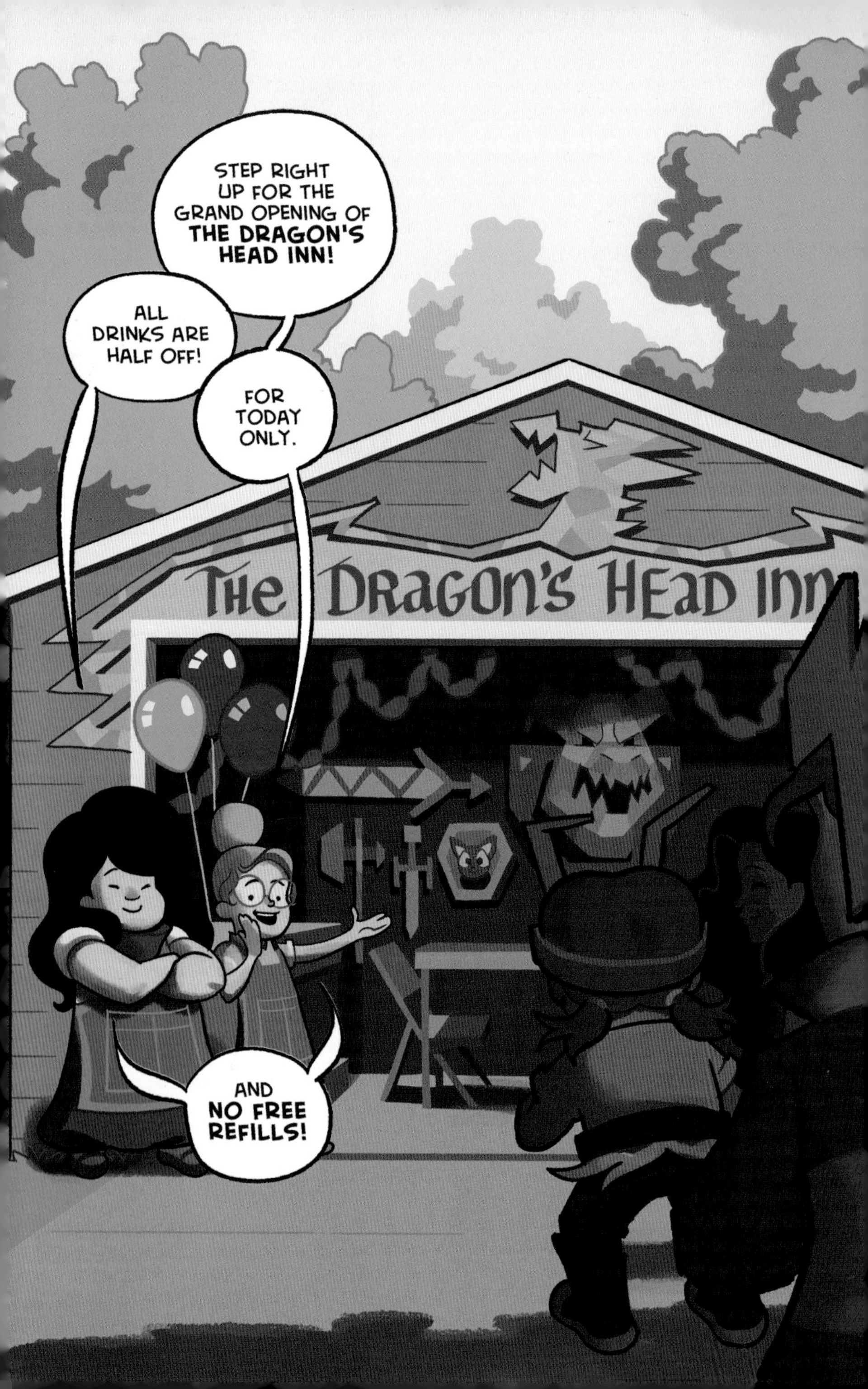
STEP RIGHT UP FOR THE GRAND OPENING OF **THE DRAGON'S HEAD INN!**
ALL DRINKS ARE HALF OFF!
FOR TODAY ONLY.
THE DRAGON'S HEAD INN
AND **NO FREE REFILLS!**

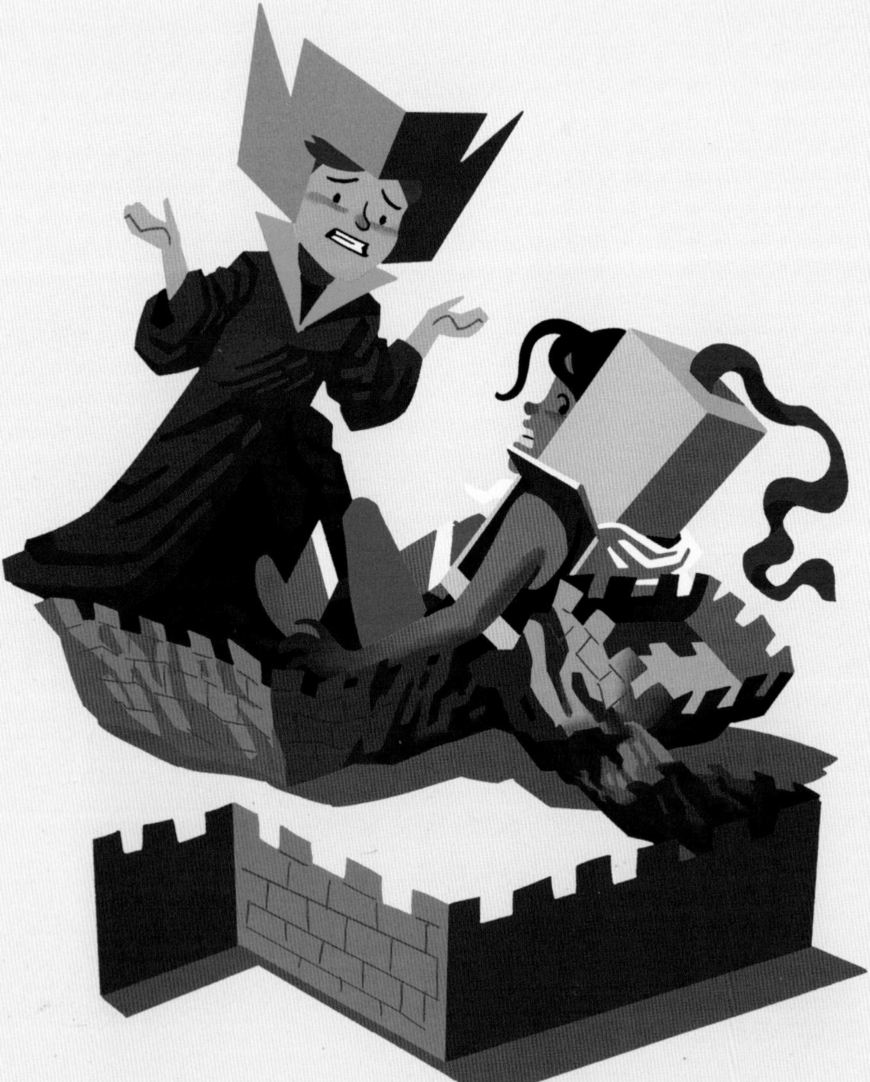

the Prince

BY MANUEL BETANCOURT AND CHAD SELL

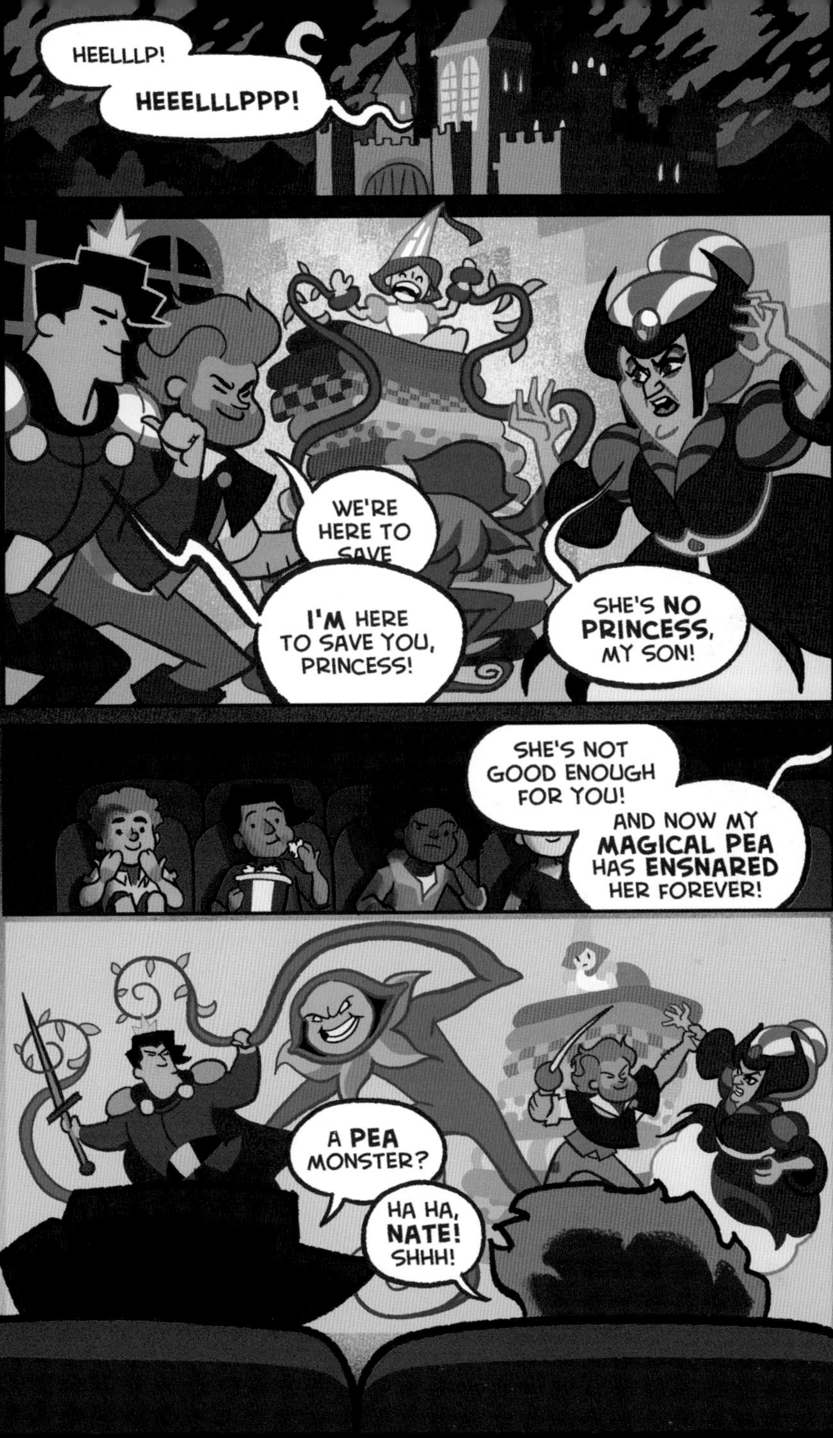
HEELLLP!
HEEELLLPPP!
WE'RE HERE TO SAVE
I'M HERE TO SAVE YOU, PRINCESS!
SHE'S NO PRINCESS, MY SON!
SHE'S NOT GOOD ENOUGH FOR YOU!
AND NOW MY MAGICAL PEA HAS ENSNARED HER FOREVER!
A PEA MONSTER?
HA HA, NATE! SHHH!

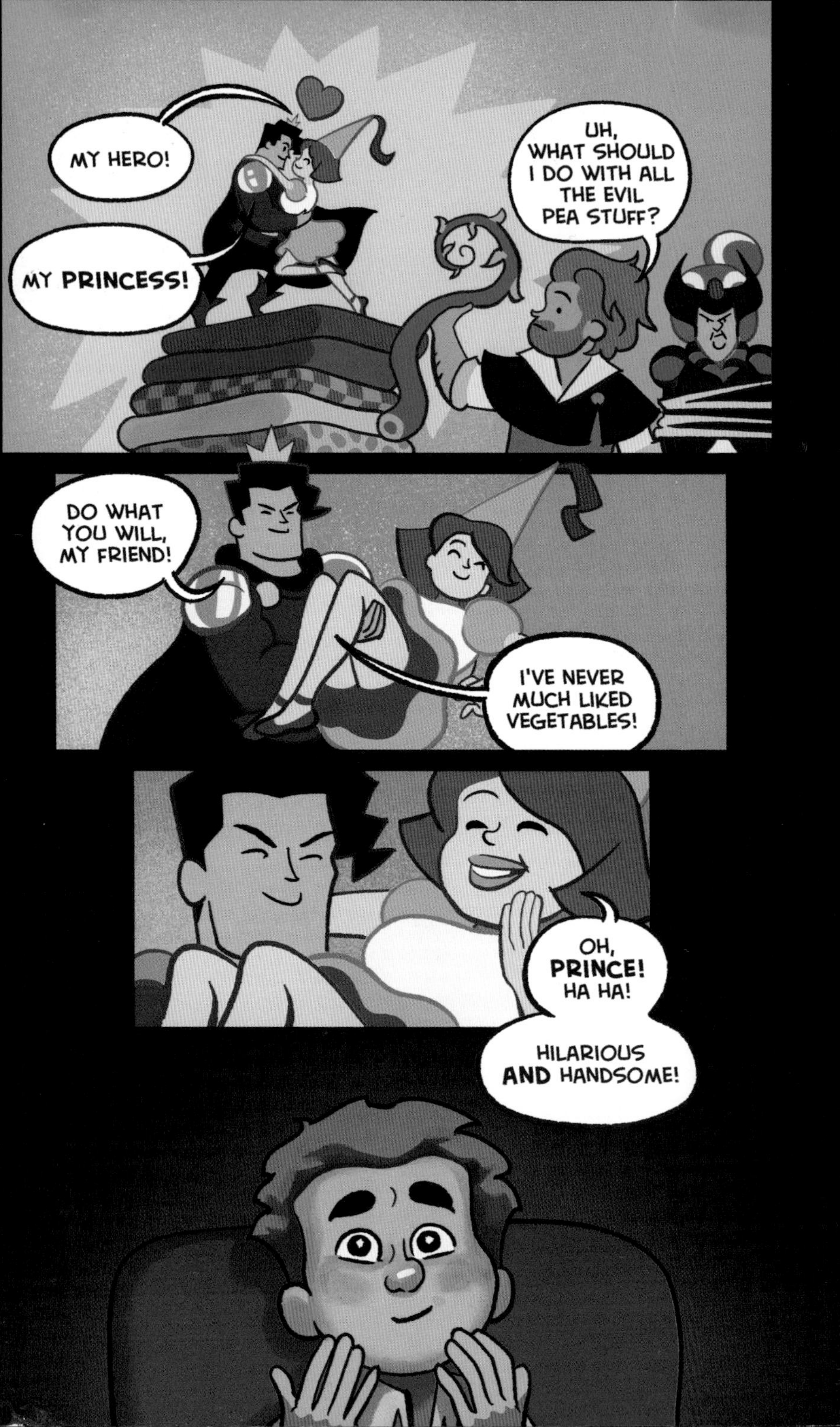
MY HERO!
MY PRINCESS!
UH, WHAT SHOULD I DO WITH ALL THE EVIL PEA STUFF?
DO WHAT YOU WILL, MY FRIEND!
I'VE NEVER MUCH LIKED VEGETABLES!
OH, PRINCE! HA HA!
HILARIOUS AND HANDSOME!

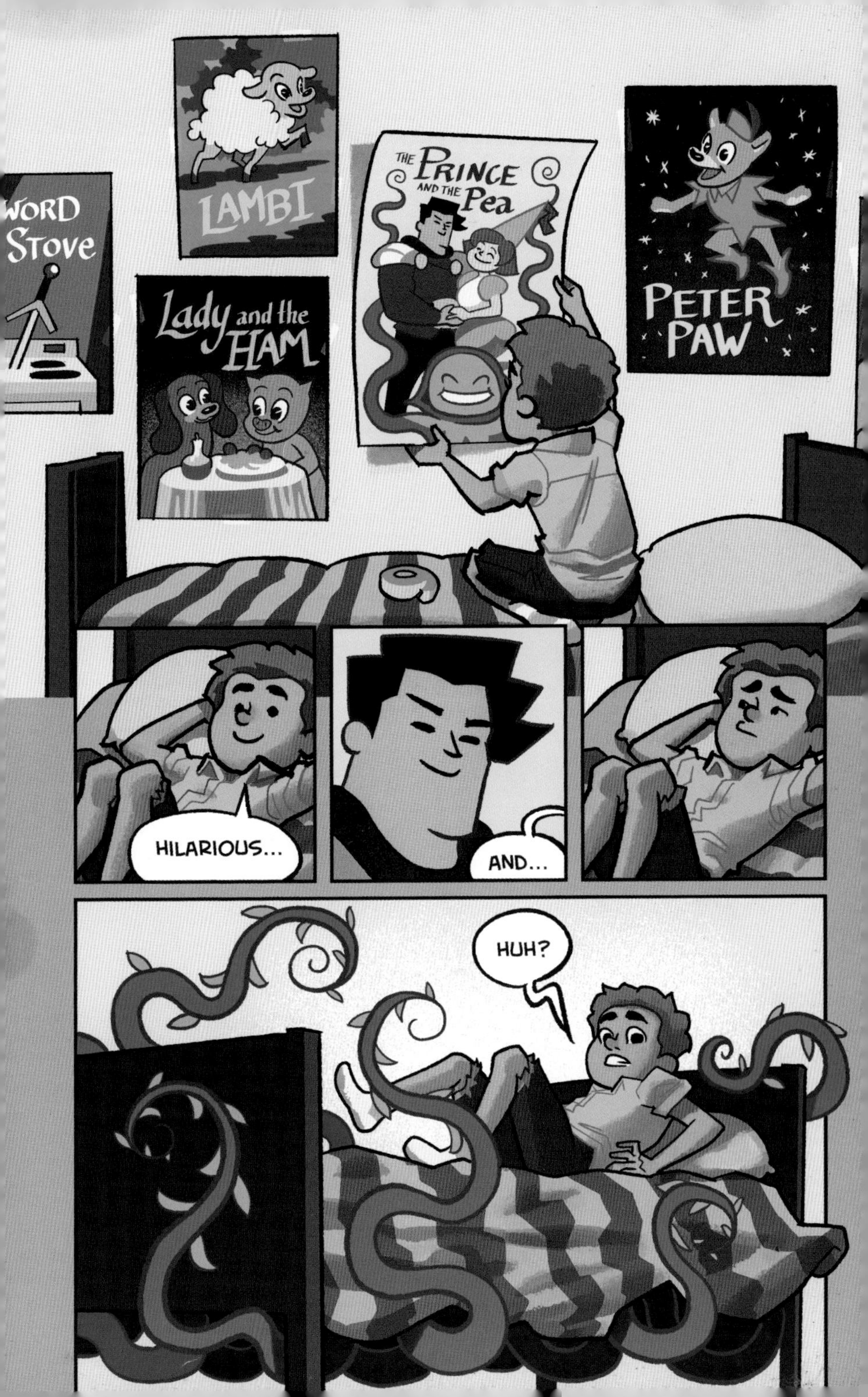
WORD
STOVE
LAMBI
THE PRINCE AND THE Pea
PETER PAW
Lady and the HAM
HILARIOUS...
AND...
HUH?

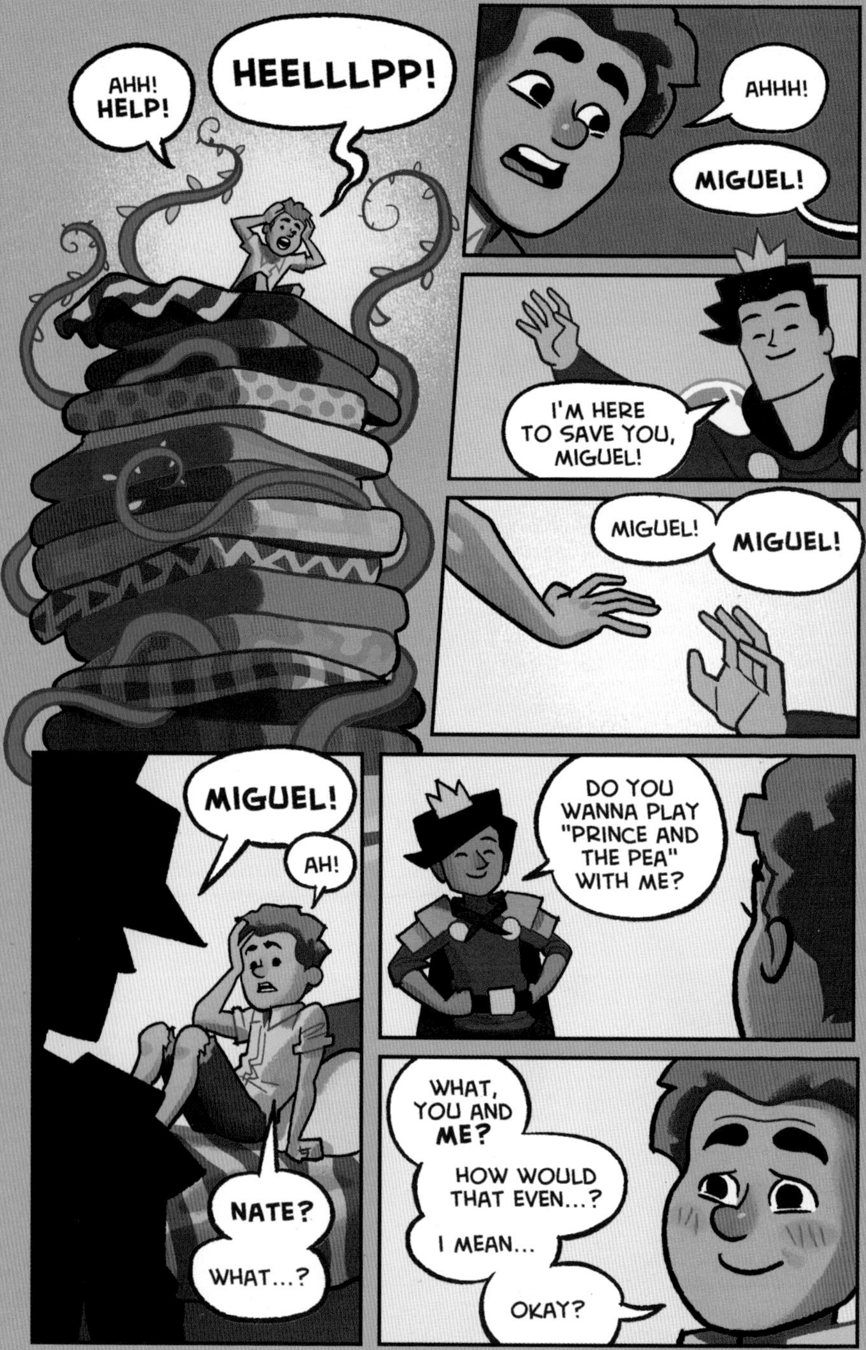
AHH! HELP!
HEELLLPP!
AHHH!
MIGUEL!
I'M HERE TO SAVE YOU, MIGUEL!
MIGUEL!
MIGUEL!
MIGUEL!
AH!
NATE?
WHAT...?
DO YOU WANNA PLAY "PRINCE AND THE PEA" WITH ME?
WHAT, YOU AND ME?
HOW WOULD THAT EVEN...?
I MEAN...
OKAY?

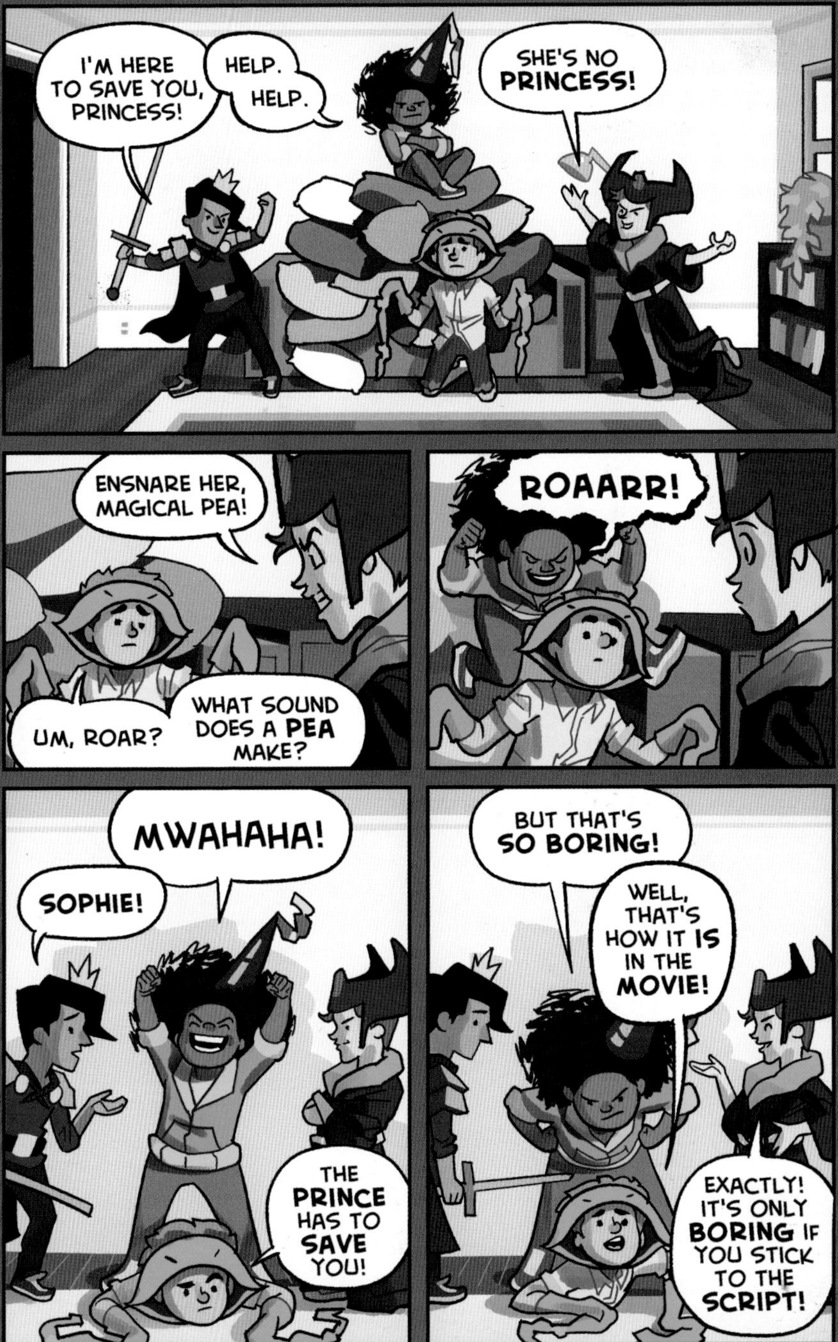
I'M HERE TO SAVE YOU, PRINCESS!
HELP. HELP.
SHE'S NO PRINCESS!
ENSNARE HER, MAGICAL PEA!
UM, ROAR?
WHAT SOUND DOES A PEA MAKE?
ROAARR!
SOPHIE!
MWAHAHA!
THE PRINCE HAS TO SAVE YOU!
BUT THAT'S SO BORING!
WELL, THAT'S HOW IT IS IN THE MOVIE!
EXACTLY! IT'S ONLY BORING IF YOU STICK TO THE SCRIPT!

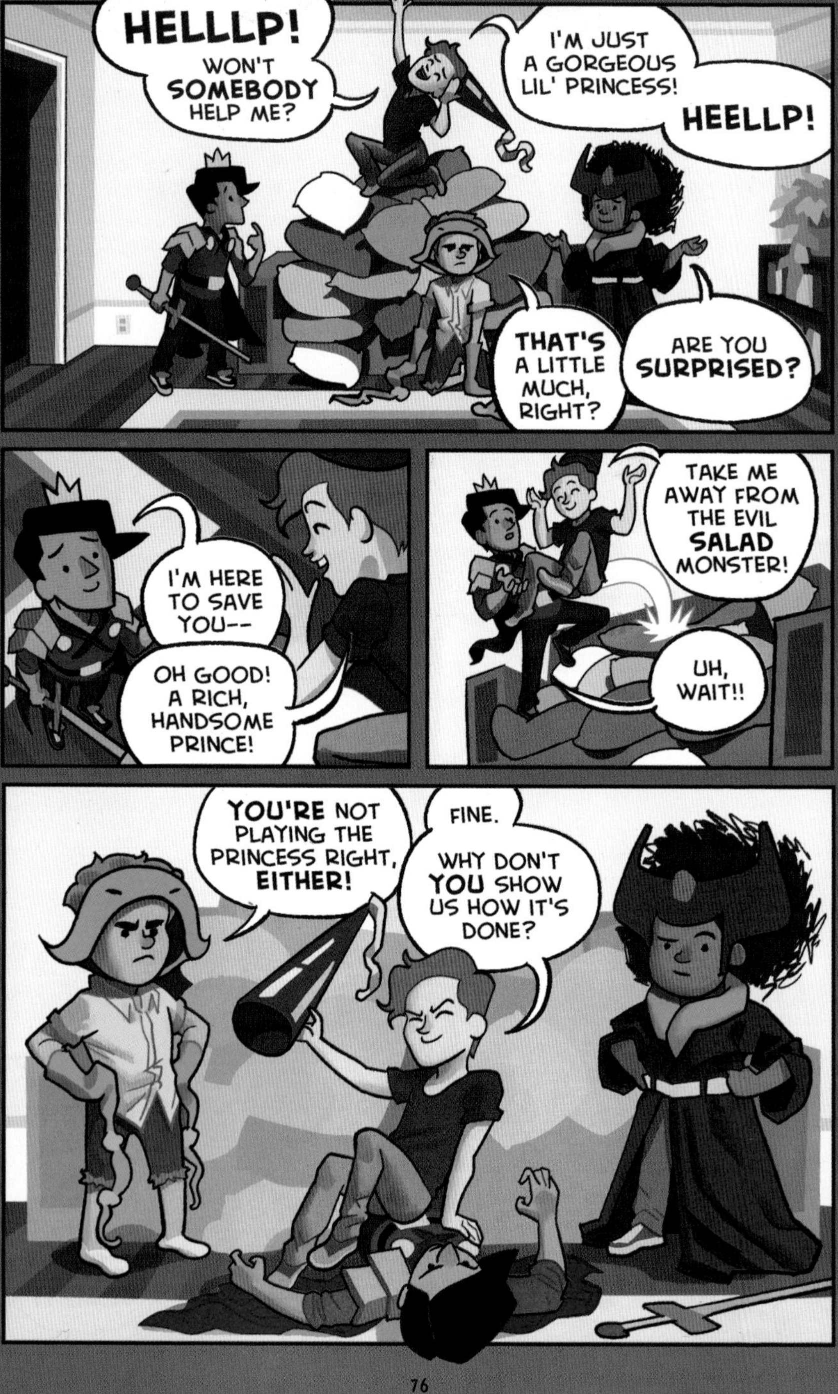
HELLLP! WON'T SOMEBODY HELP ME?
I'M JUST A GORGEOUS LIL' PRINCESS! HEELLP!
THAT'S A LITTLE MUCH, RIGHT?
ARE YOU SURPRISED?
I'M HERE TO SAVE YOU--
OH GOOD! A RICH, HANDSOME PRINCE!
TAKE ME AWAY FROM THE EVIL SALAD MONSTER!
UH, WAIT!!
YOU'RE NOT PLAYING THE PRINCESS RIGHT, EITHER!
FINE.
WHY DON'T YOU SHOW US HOW IT'S DONE?

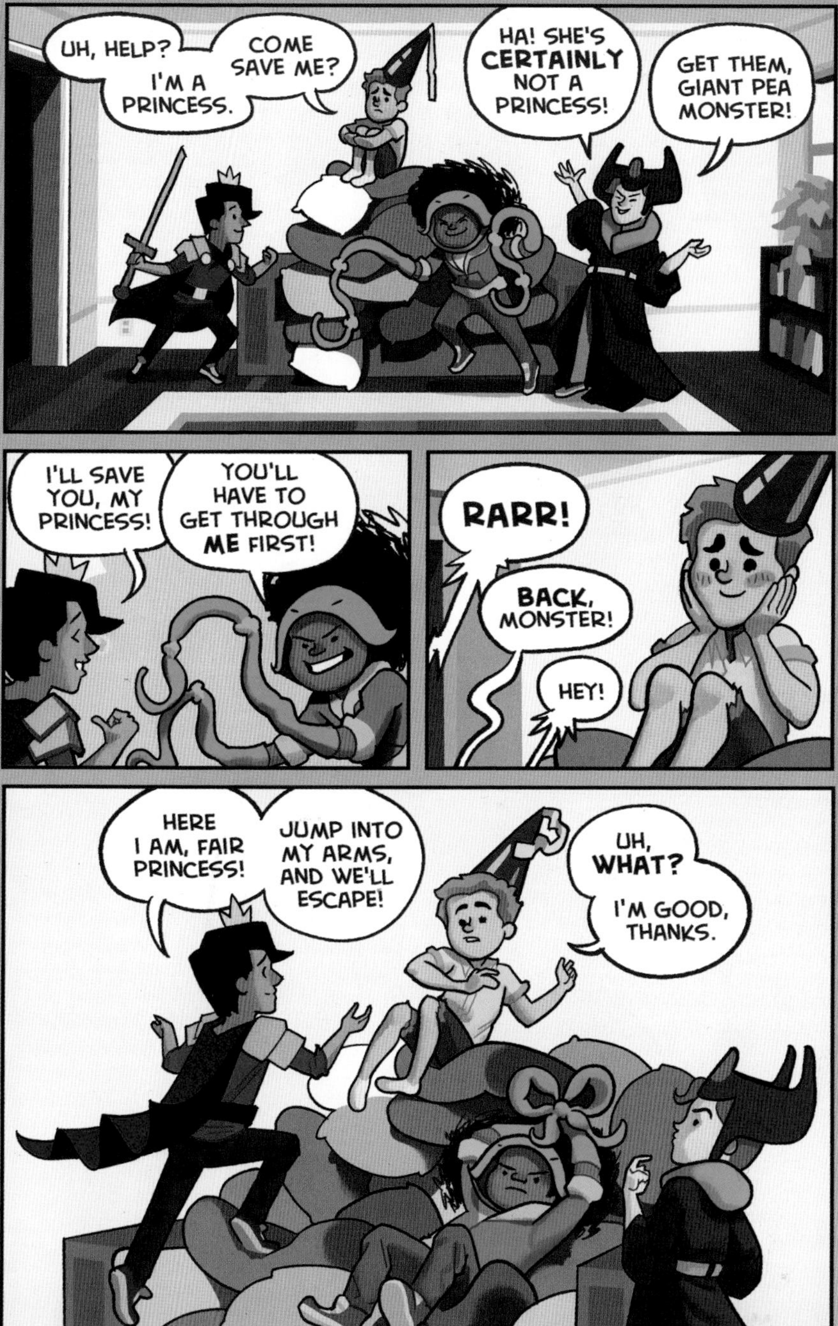
UH, HELP? I'M A PRINCESS.
COME SAVE ME?
HA! SHE'S **CERTAINLY** NOT A PRINCESS!
GET THEM, GIANT PEA MONSTER!
I'LL SAVE YOU, MY PRINCESS!
YOU'LL HAVE TO GET THROUGH **ME** FIRST!
RARR!
BACK, MONSTER!
HEY!
HERE I AM, FAIR PRINCESS!
JUMP INTO MY ARMS, AND WE'LL ESCAPE!
UH, **WHAT?**
I'M GOOD, THANKS.

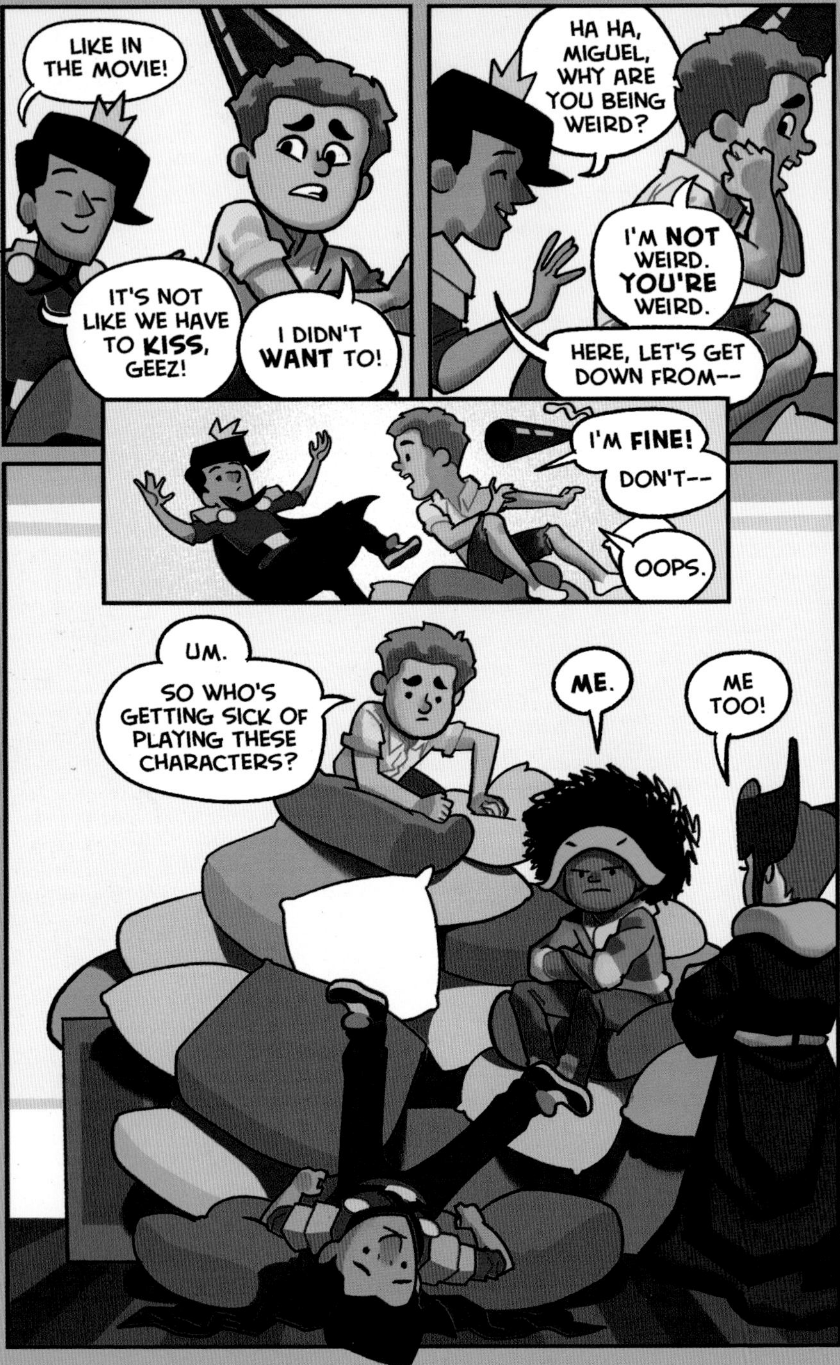
LIKE IN THE MOVIE!
IT'S NOT LIKE WE HAVE TO **KISS**, GEEZ!
I DIDN'T **WANT** TO!
HA HA, MIGUEL, WHY ARE YOU BEING WEIRD?
I'M **NOT** WEIRD. **YOU'RE** WEIRD.
HERE, LET'S GET DOWN FROM--
I'M **FINE!**
DON'T--
OOPS.
UM.
SO WHO'S GETTING SICK OF PLAYING THESE CHARACTERS?
ME.
ME TOO!

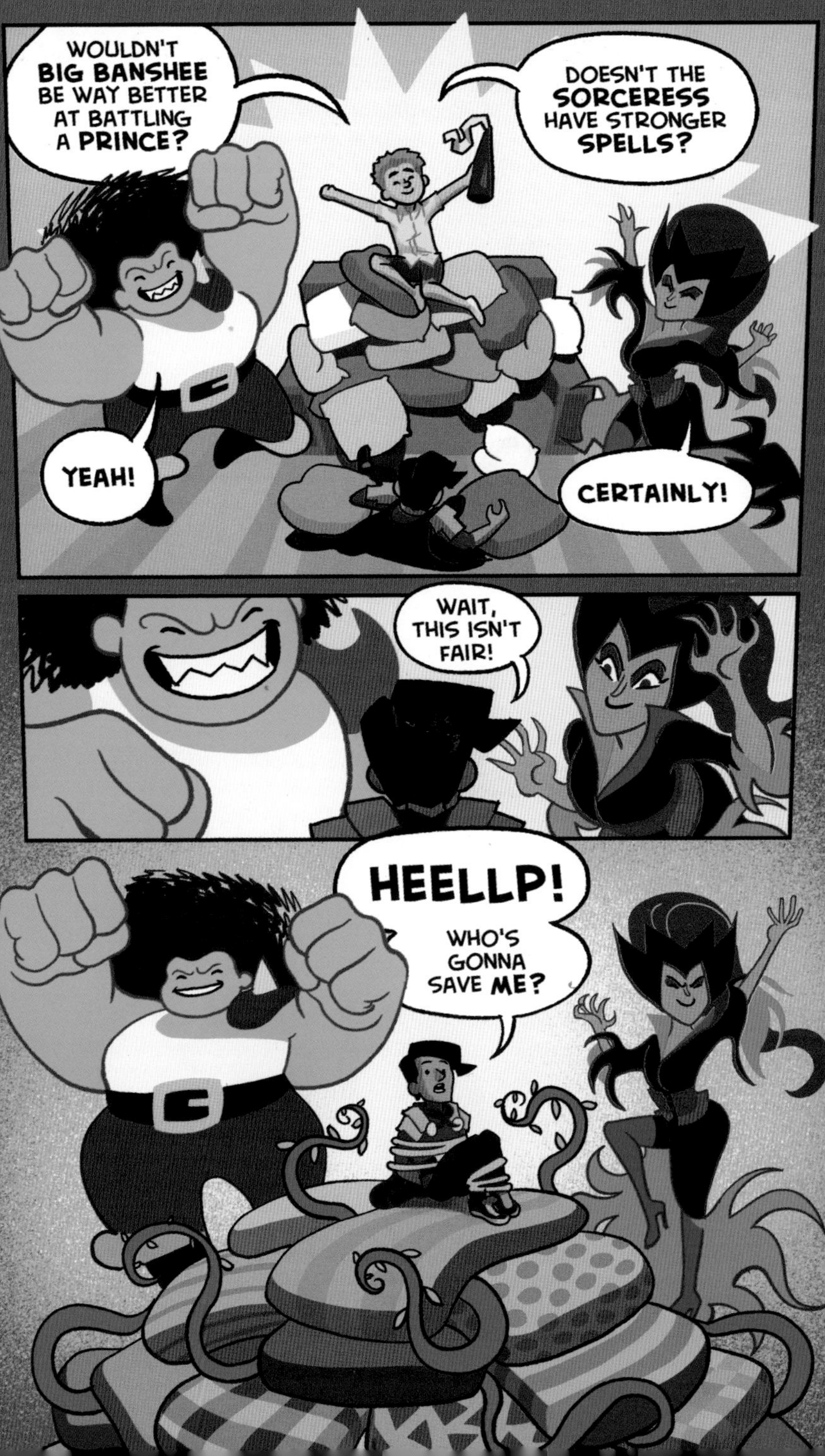
WOULDN'T BIG BANSHEE BE WAY BETTER AT BATTLING A PRINCE?
DOESN'T THE SORCERESS HAVE STRONGER SPELLS?
YEAH!
CERTAINLY!
WAIT, THIS ISN'T FAIR!
HEELLP!
WHO'S GONNA SAVE ME?

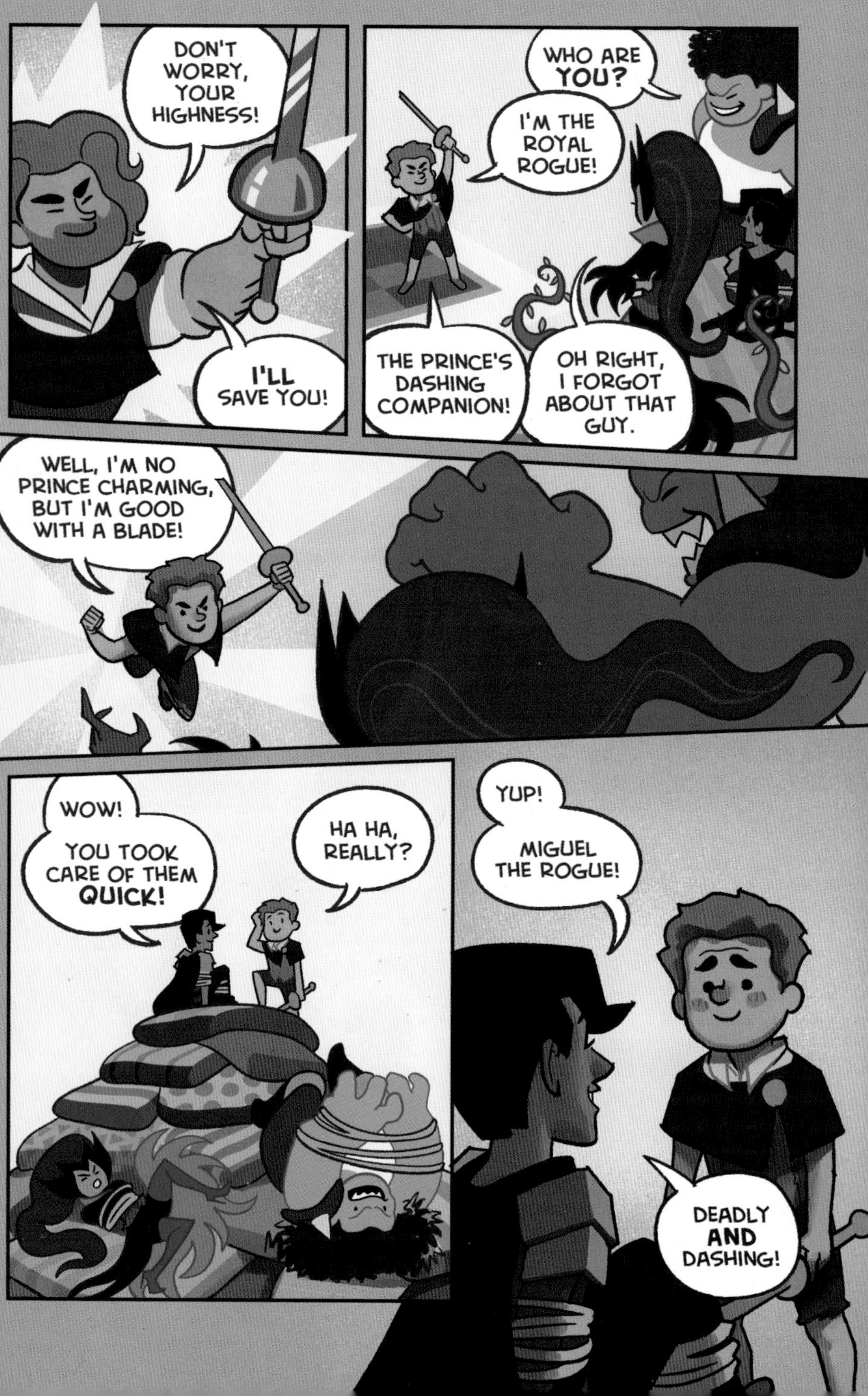
DON'T WORRY, YOUR HIGHNESS!
I'LL SAVE YOU!
WHO ARE YOU?
I'M THE ROYAL ROGUE!
THE PRINCE'S DASHING COMPANION!
OH RIGHT, I FORGOT ABOUT THAT GUY.
WELL, I'M NO PRINCE CHARMING, BUT I'M GOOD WITH A BLADE!
WOW!
YOU TOOK CARE OF THEM QUICK!
HA HA, REALLY?
YUP!
MIGUEL THE ROGUE!
DEADLY AND DASHING!

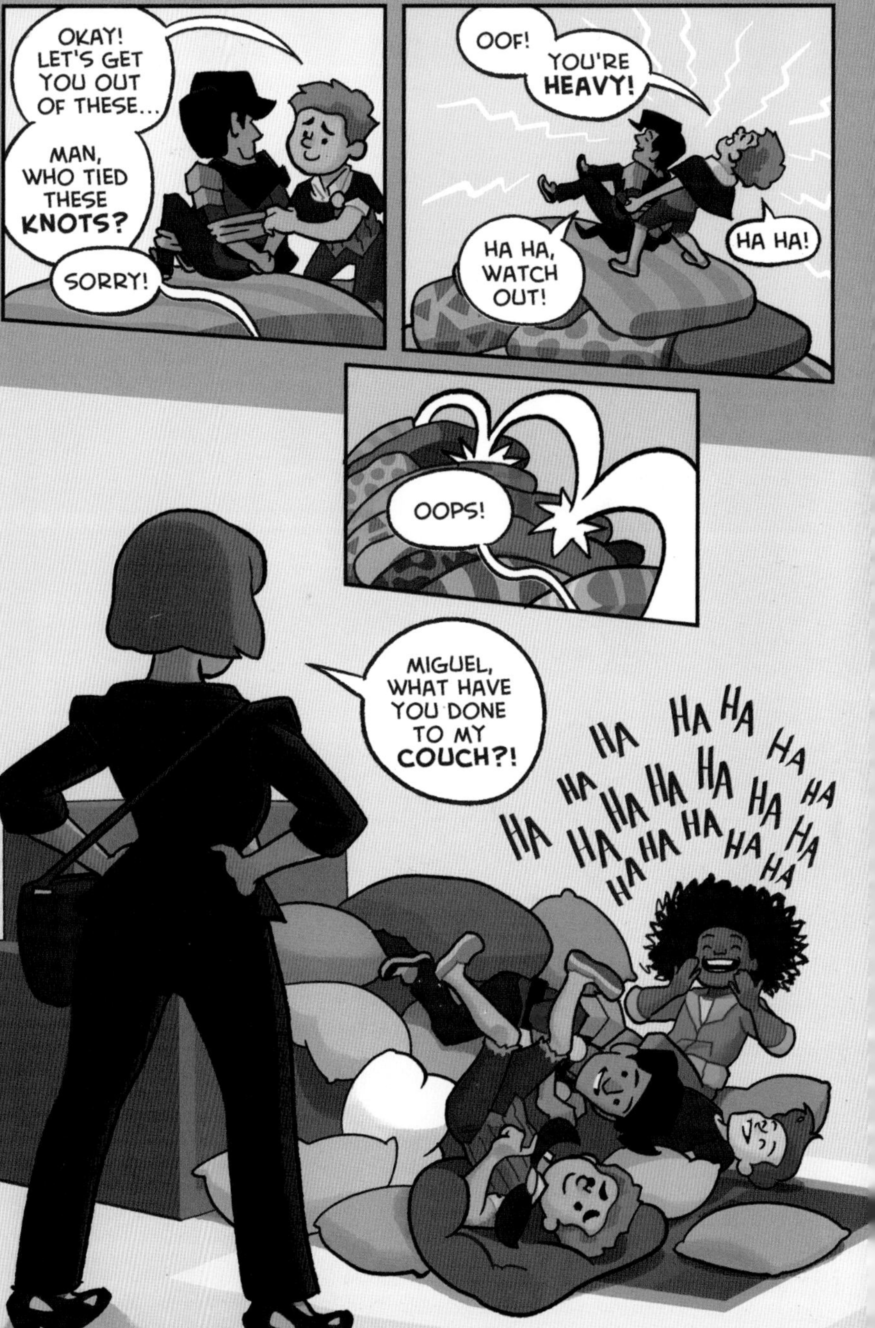
OKAY! LET'S GET YOU OUT OF THESE...
MAN, WHO TIED THESE KNOTS?
SORRY!
OOF!
YOU'RE HEAVY!
HA HA, WATCH OUT!
HA HA!
OOPS!
MIGUEL, WHAT HAVE YOU DONE TO MY COUCH?!
HA HA HA HA
HA HA HA HA HA HA HA
HA HA HA HA HA HA HA
HA HA HA HA

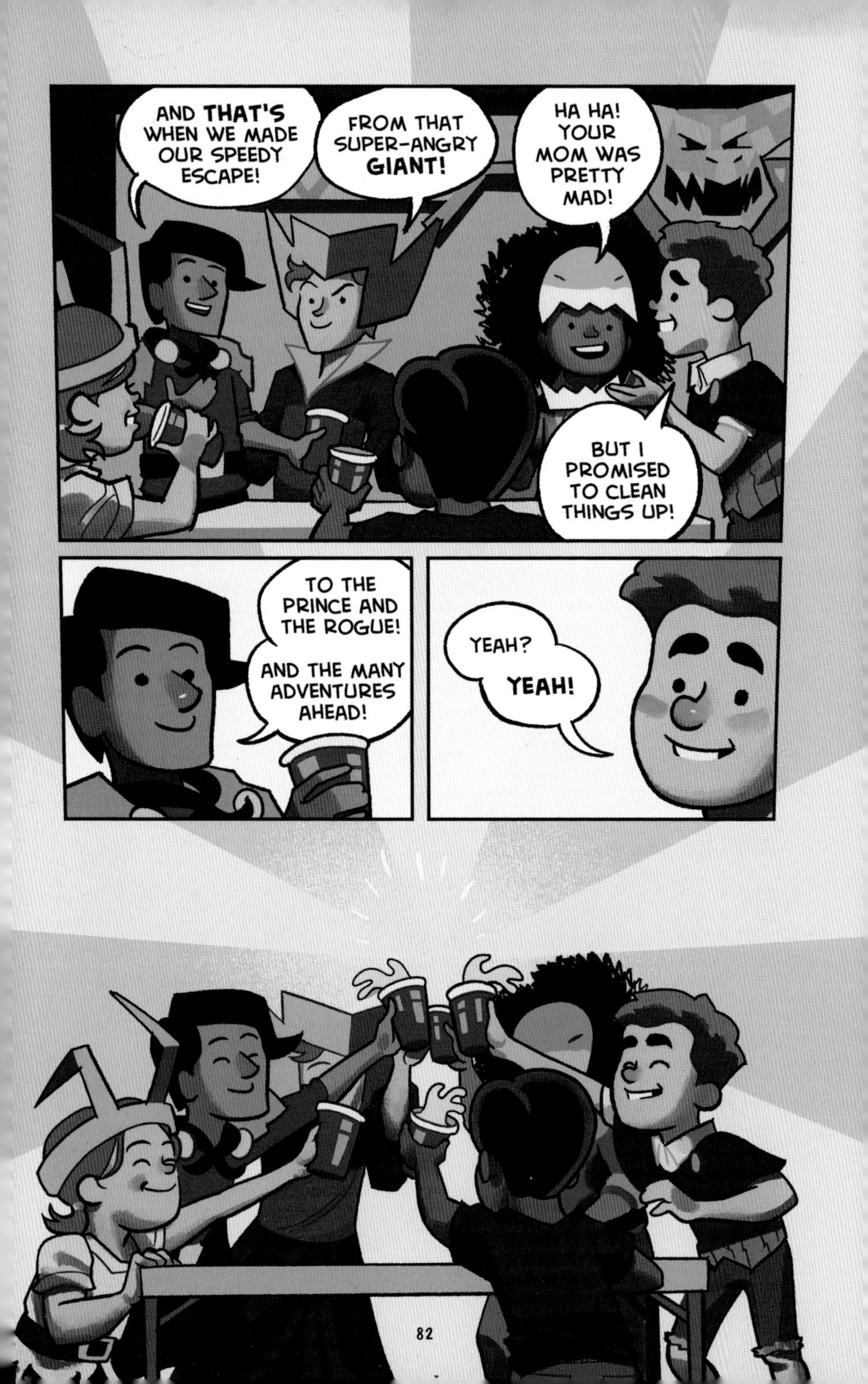
AND THAT'S WHEN WE MADE OUR SPEEDY ESCAPE!
FROM THAT SUPER-ANGRY GIANT!
HA HA! YOUR MOM WAS PRETTY MAD!
BUT I PROMISED TO CLEAN THINGS UP!
TO THE PRINCE AND THE ROGUE!
AND THE MANY ADVENTURES AHEAD!
YEAH?
YEAH!

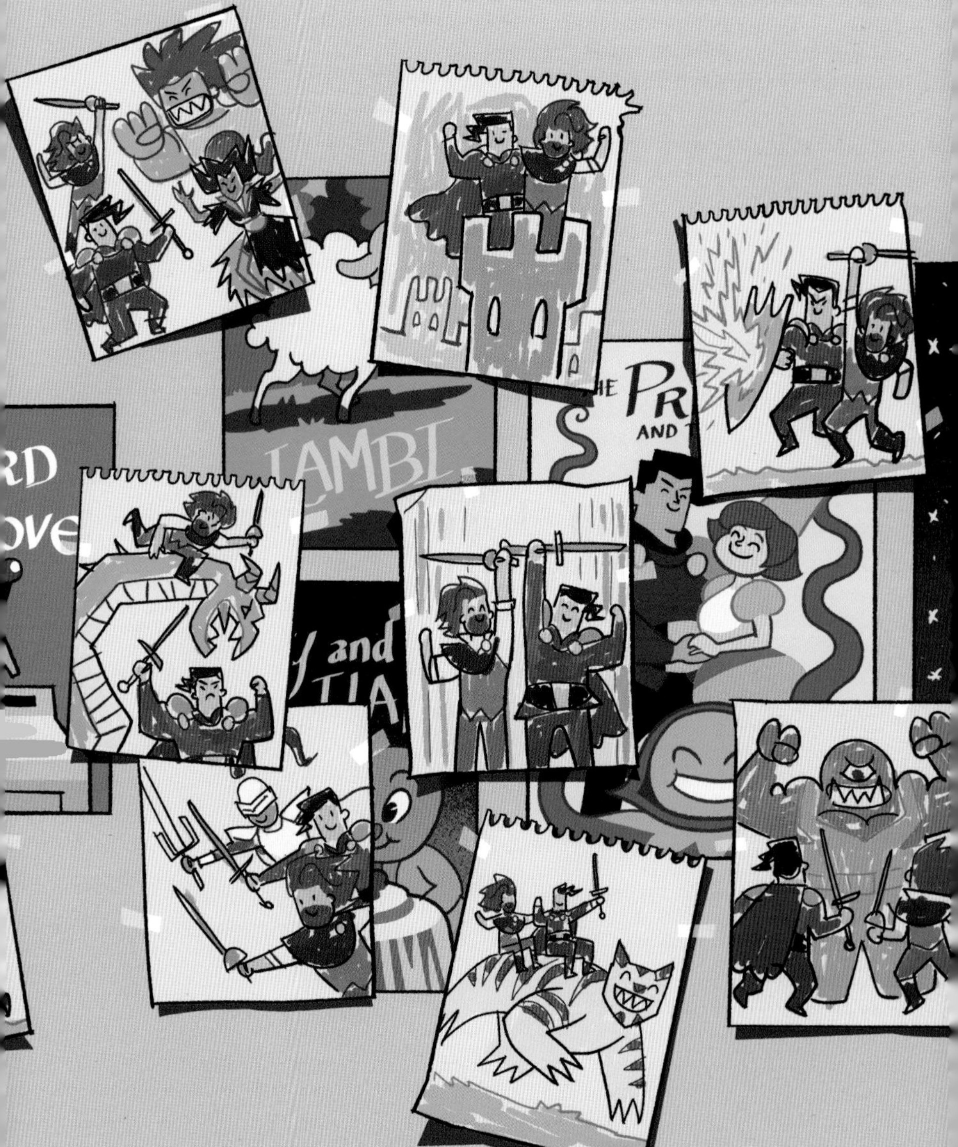
RD
ove
LAMBI
HE PR
and
TIA

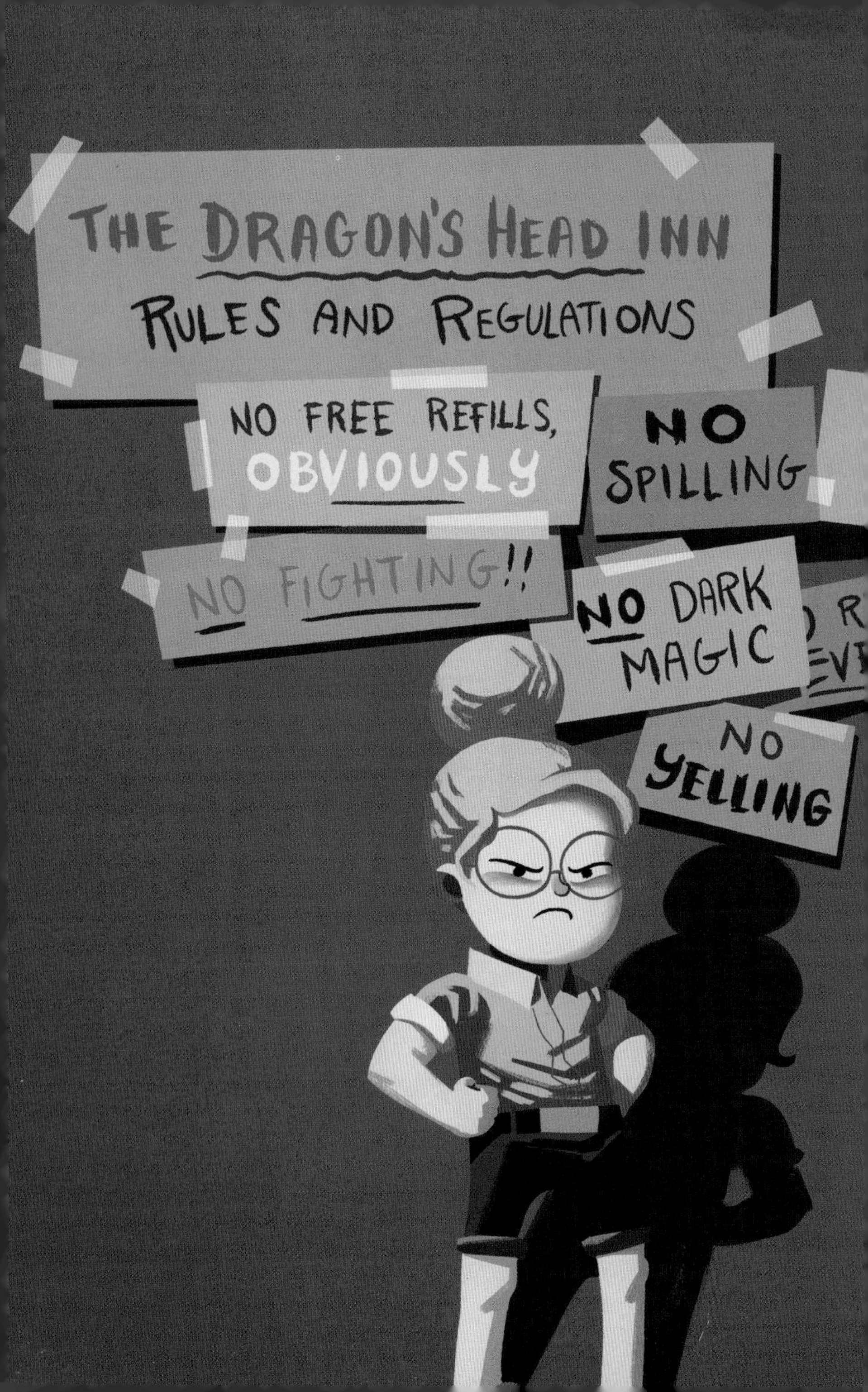
THE DRAGON'S HEAD INN
RULES AND REGULATIONS
NO FREE REFILLS, OBVIOUSLY
NO SPILLING
NO FIGHTING!!
NO DARK MAGIC
NO YELLING

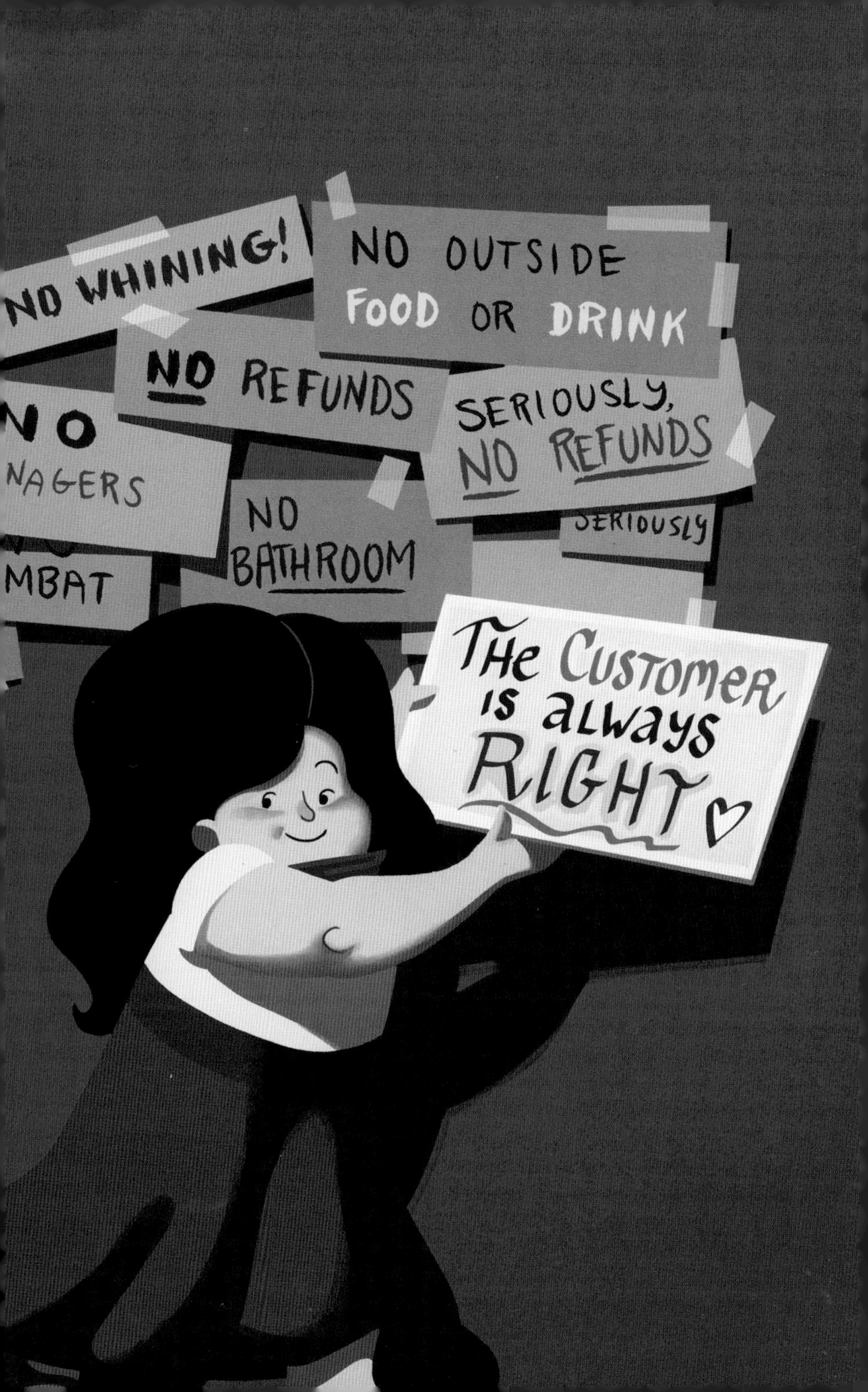
NO WHINING!
NO OUTSIDE FOOD OR DRINK
NO REFUNDS
SERIOUSLY, NO REFUNDS
NO BATHROOM
SERIOUSLY
The Customer is always RIGHT

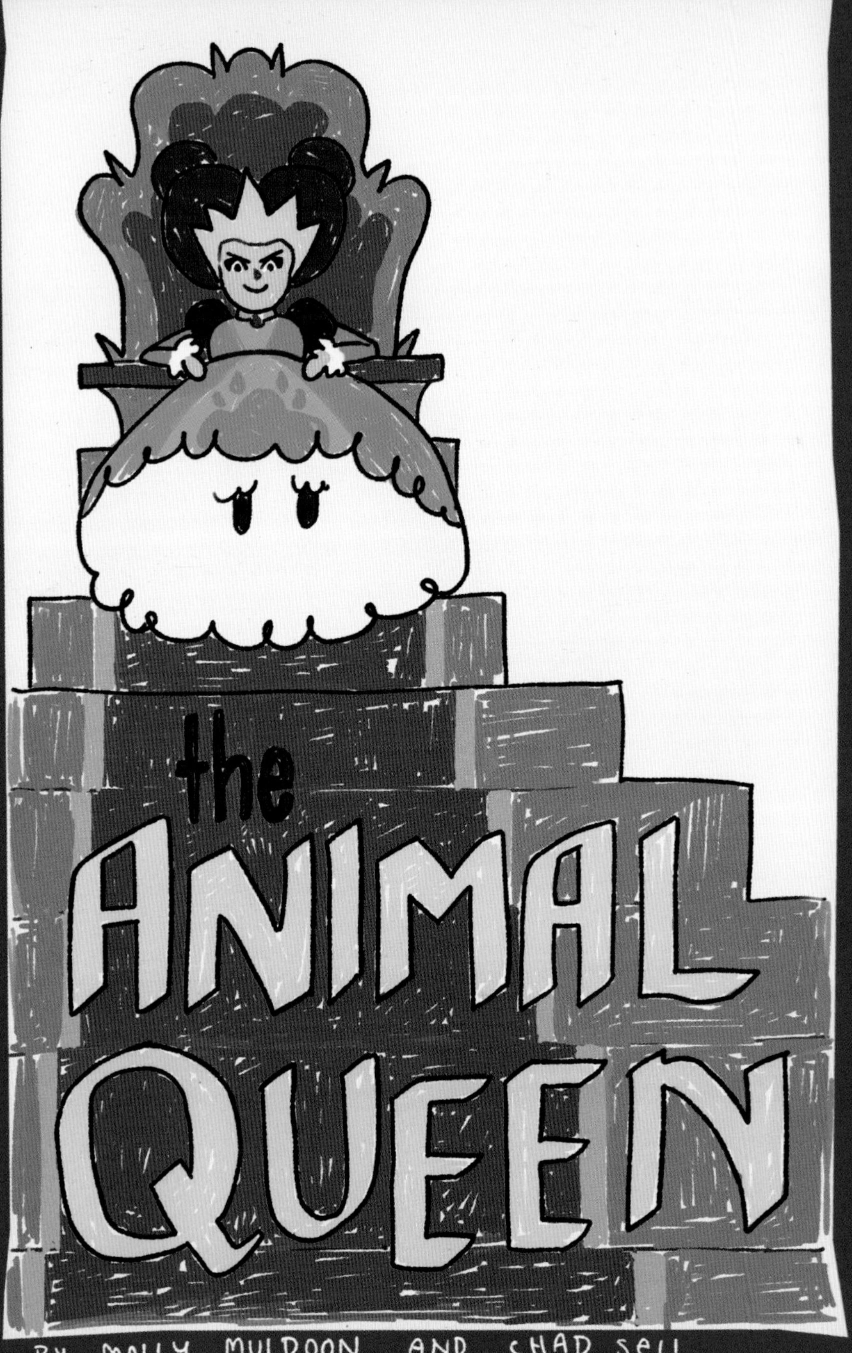
the
ANIMAL
QUEEN

BY MOLLY MULDOON AND CHAD SELL

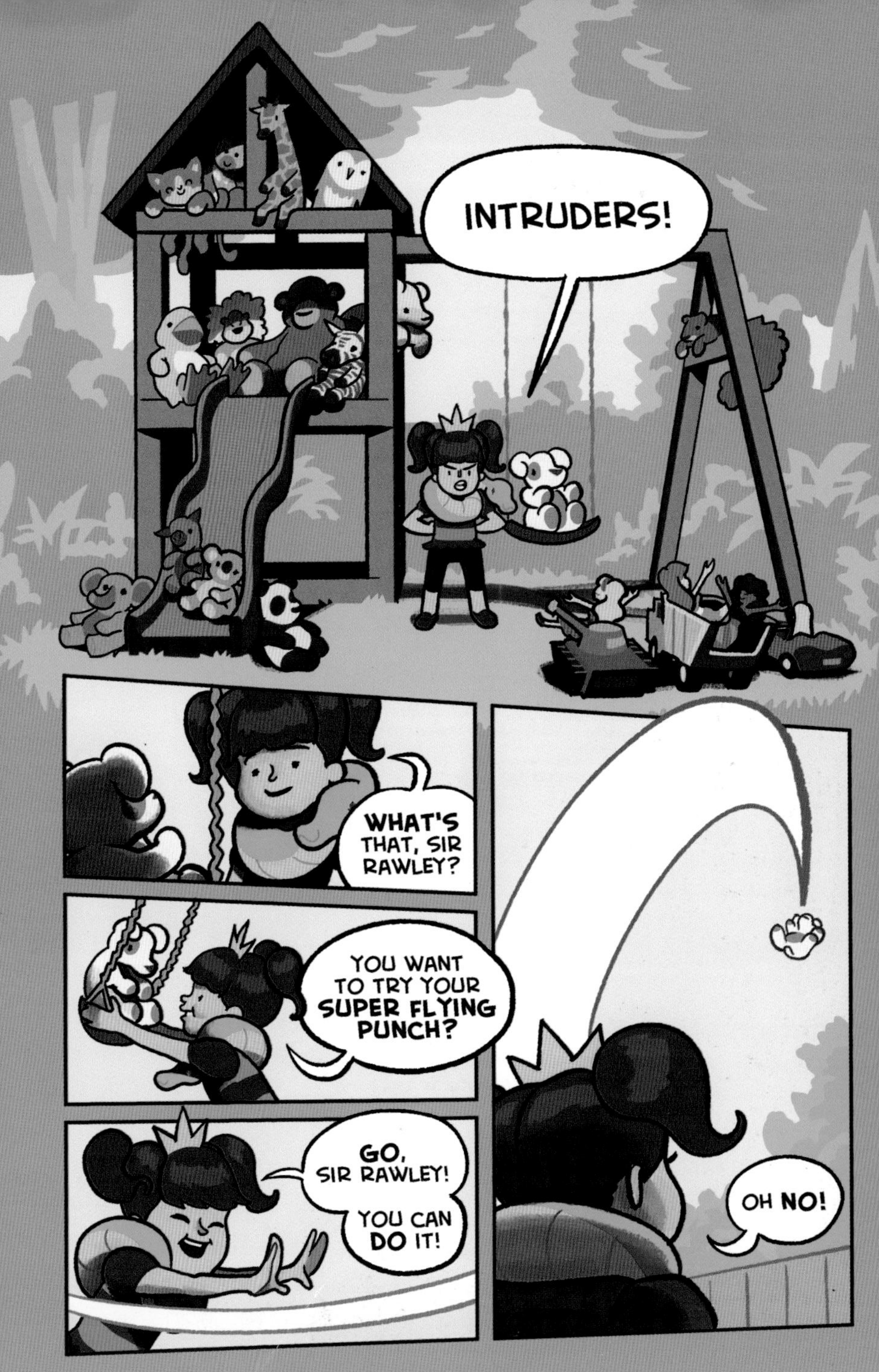
INTRUDERS!
WHAT'S THAT, SIR RAWLEY?
YOU WANT TO TRY YOUR SUPER FLYING PUNCH?
GO, SIR RAWLEY!
YOU CAN DO IT!
OH NO!

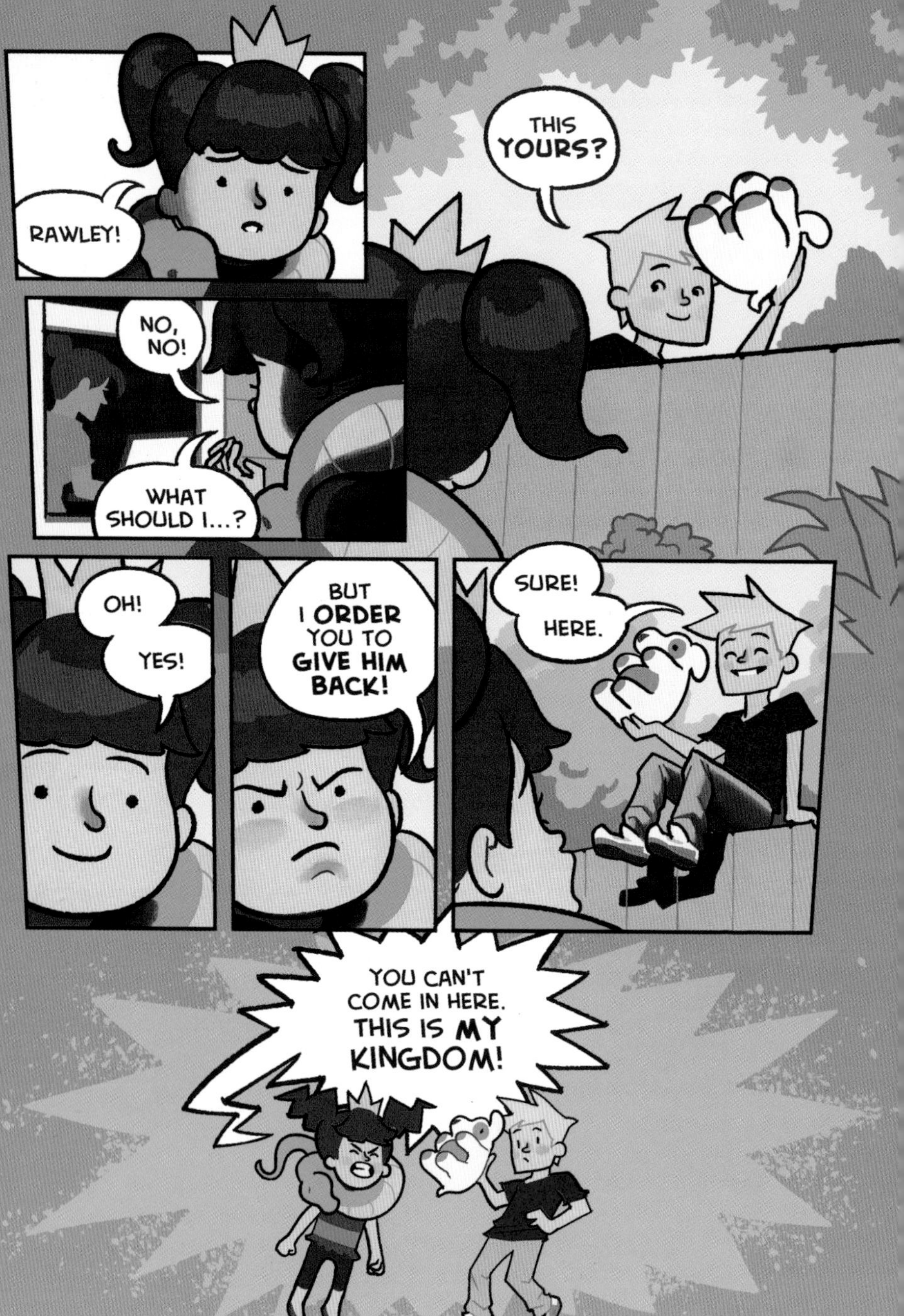
RAWLEY!
THIS YOURS?
NO, NO!
WHAT SHOULD I...?
OH!
YES!
BUT I ORDER YOU TO GIVE HIM BACK!
SURE!
HERE.
YOU CAN'T COME IN HERE. THIS IS MY KINGDOM!

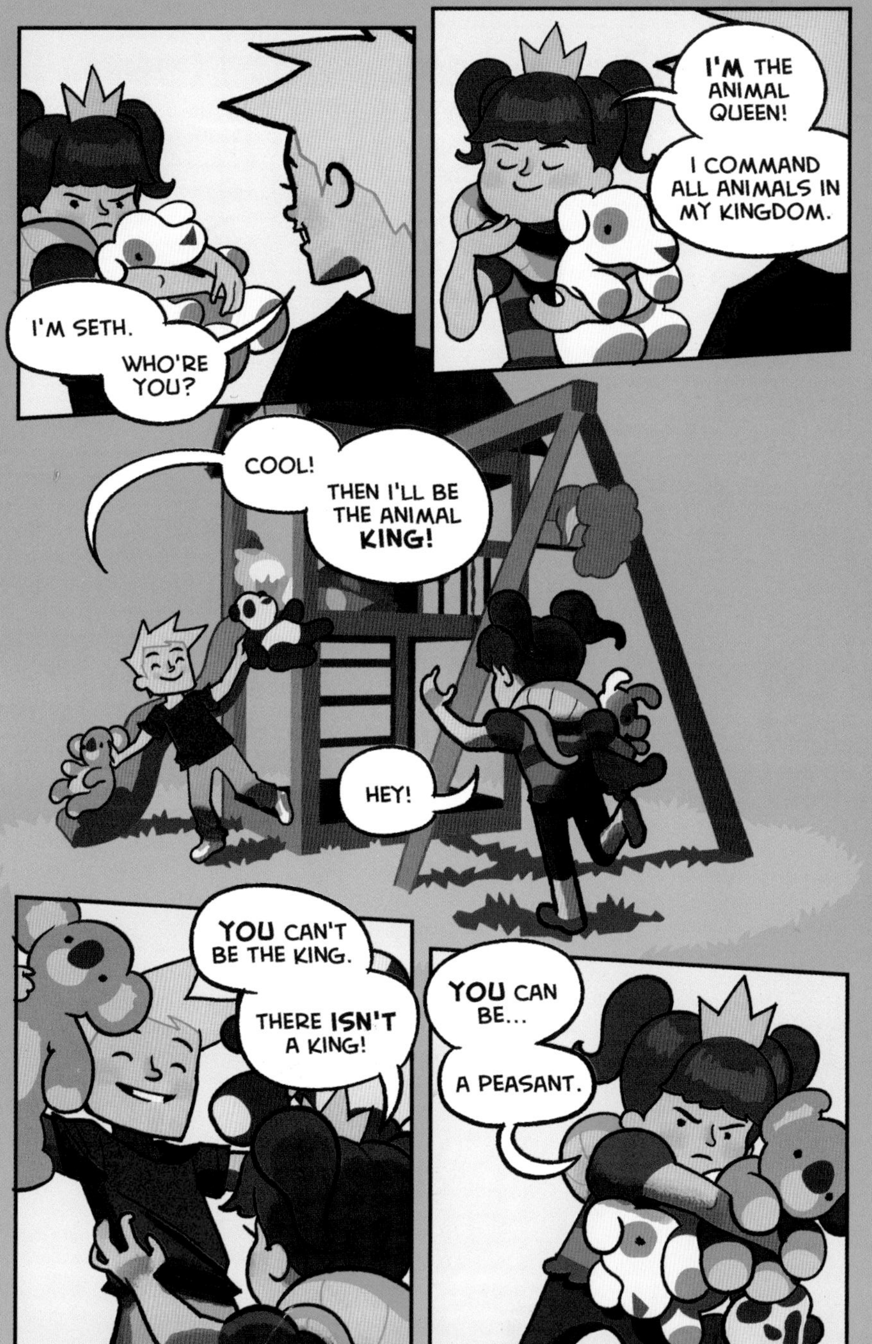
I'M SETH.
WHO'RE YOU?
I'M THE ANIMAL QUEEN!
I COMMAND ALL ANIMALS IN MY KINGDOM.
COOL!
THEN I'LL BE THE ANIMAL KING!
HEY!
YOU CAN'T BE THE KING.
THERE ISN'T A KING!
YOU CAN BE...
A PEASANT.

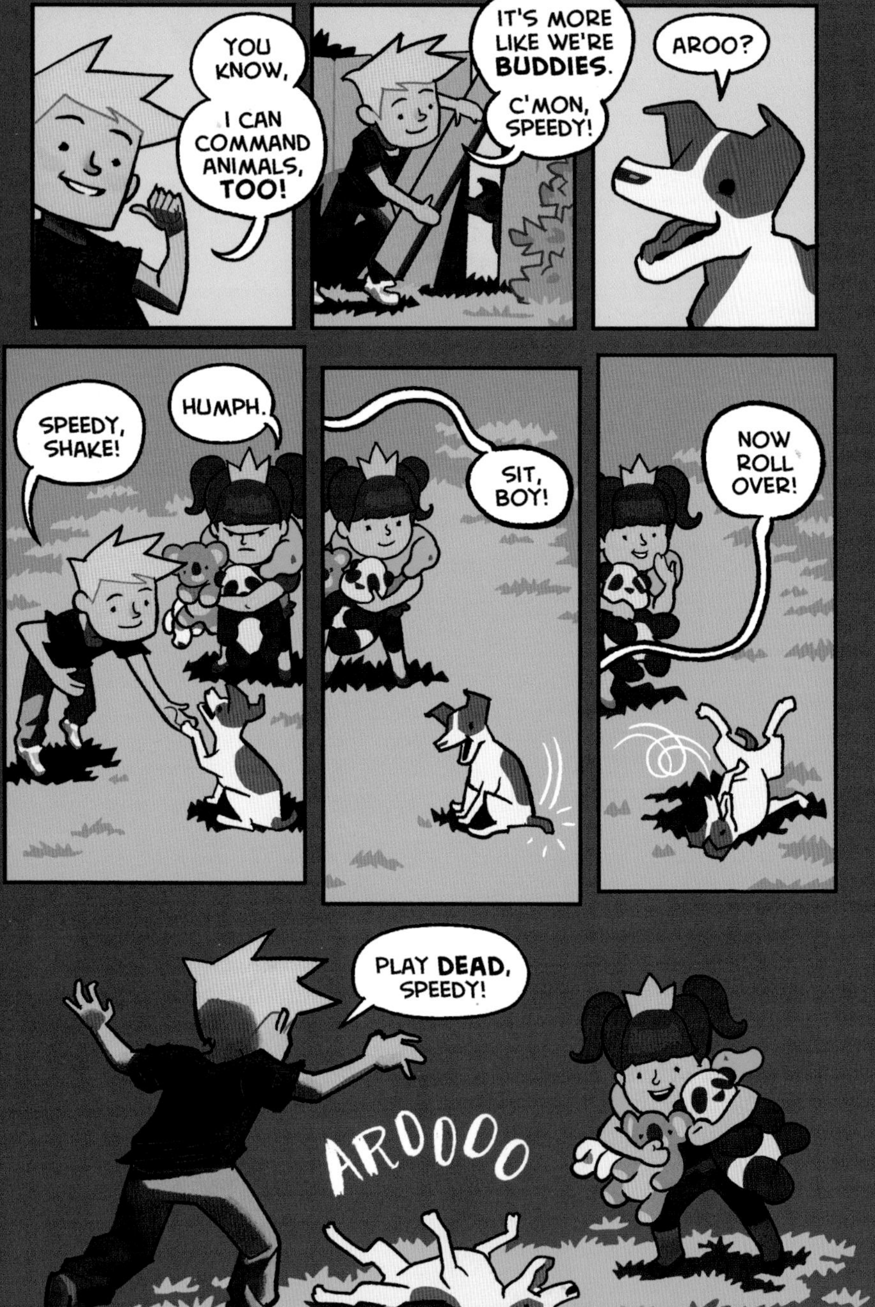
YOU KNOW,
I CAN COMMAND ANIMALS, TOO!
IT'S MORE LIKE WE'RE BUDDIES.
C'MON, SPEEDY!
AROO?
SPEEDY, SHAKE!
HUMPH.
SIT, BOY!
NOW ROLL OVER!
PLAY DEAD, SPEEDY!
AROOOO

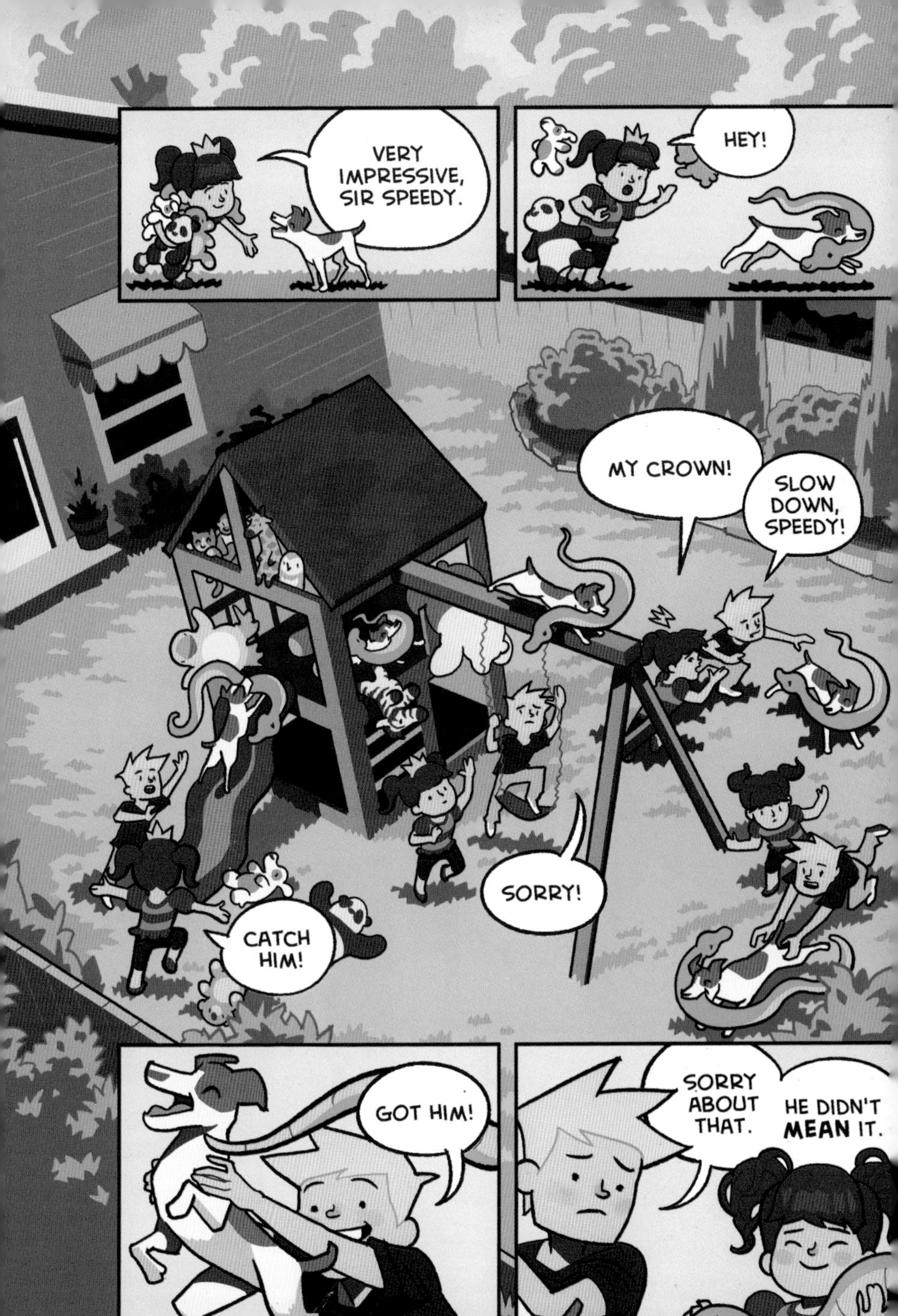
VERY IMPRESSIVE, SIR SPEEDY.
HEY!
MY CROWN!
SLOW DOWN, SPEEDY!
CATCH HIM!
SORRY!
GOT HIM!
SORRY ABOUT THAT.
HE DIDN'T **MEAN** IT.

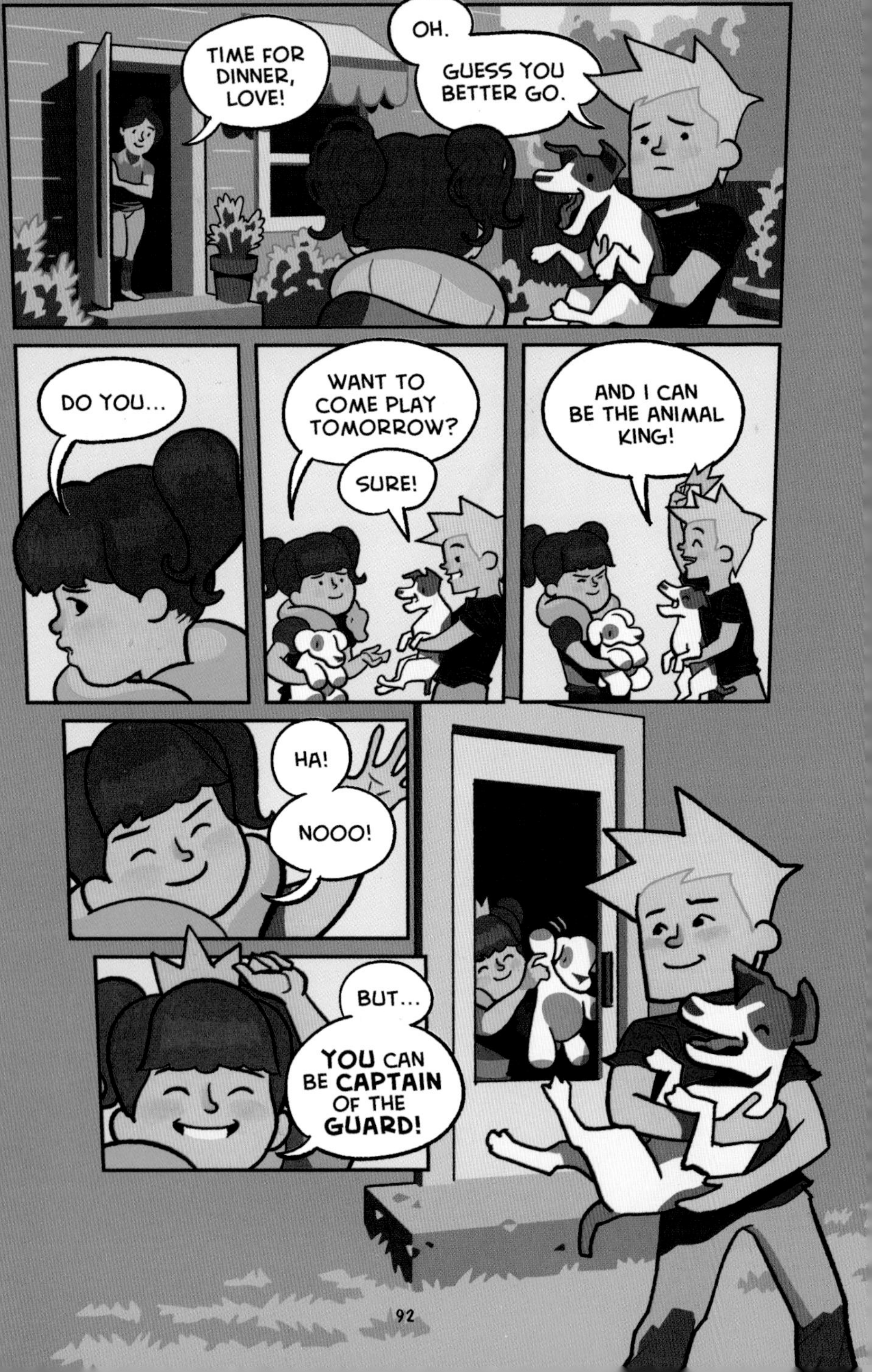
TIME FOR DINNER, LOVE!
OH.
GUESS YOU BETTER GO.
DO YOU...
WANT TO COME PLAY TOMORROW?
SURE!
AND I CAN BE THE ANIMAL KING!
HA!
NOOO!
BUT...
YOU CAN BE CAPTAIN OF THE GUARD!

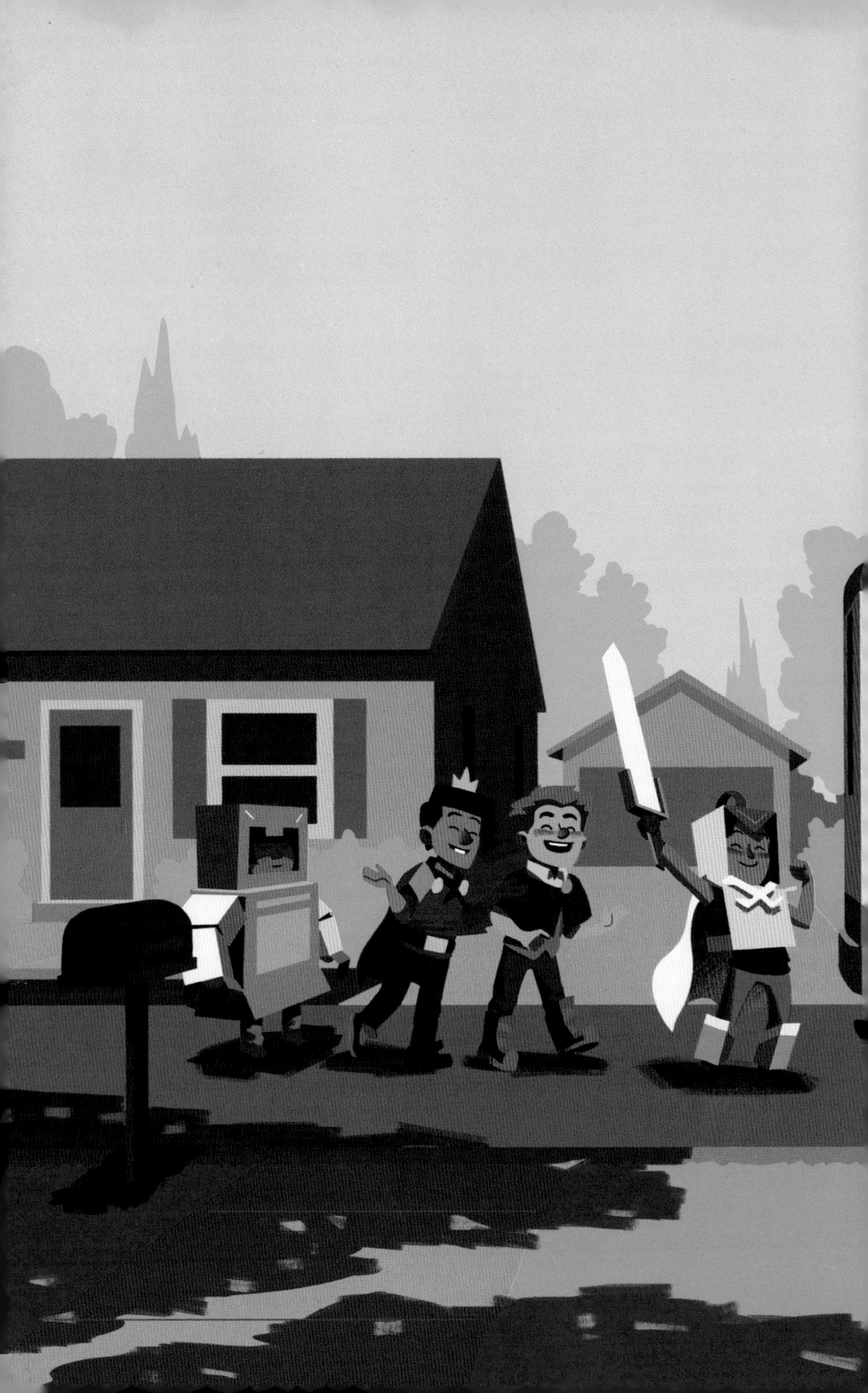

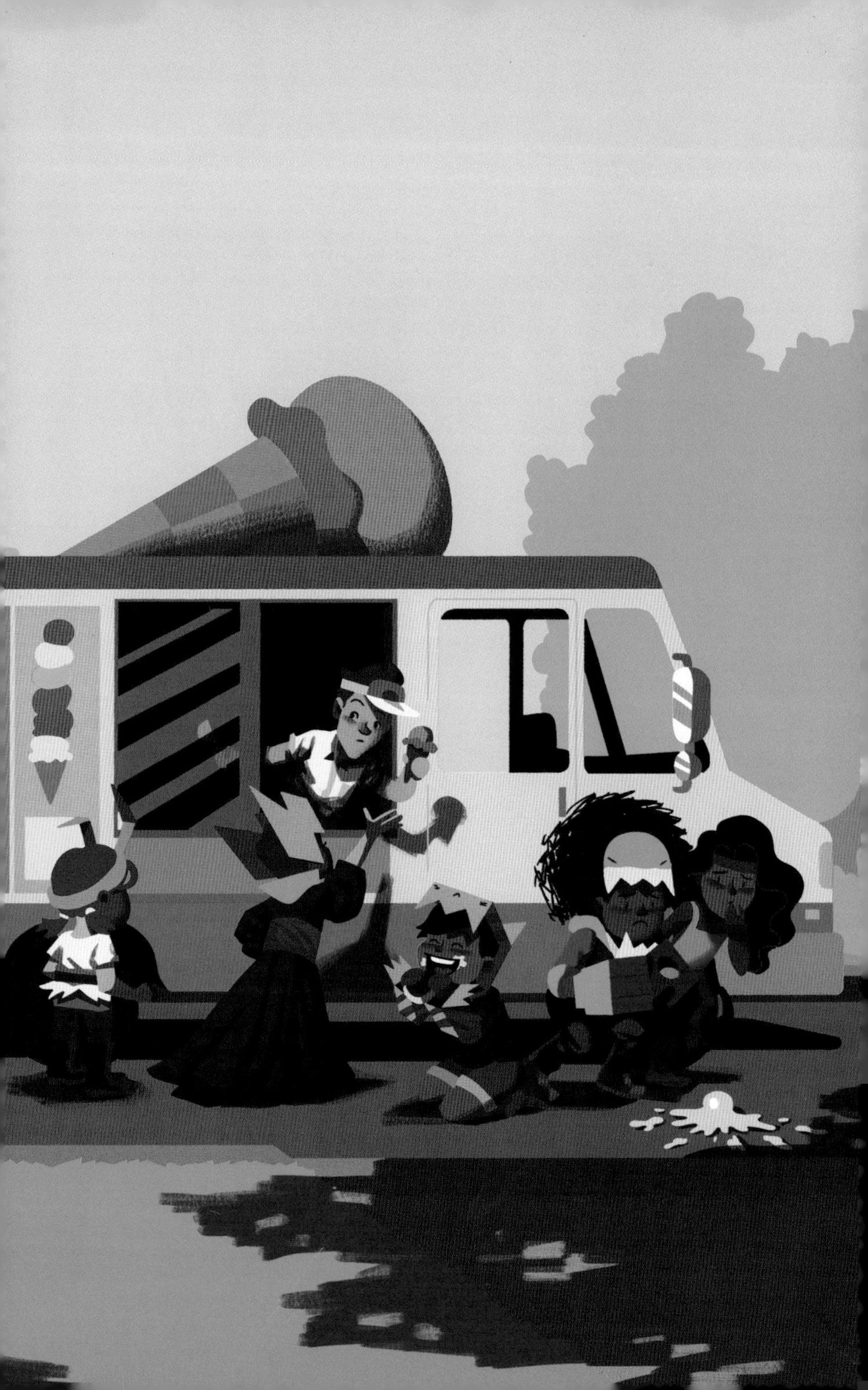

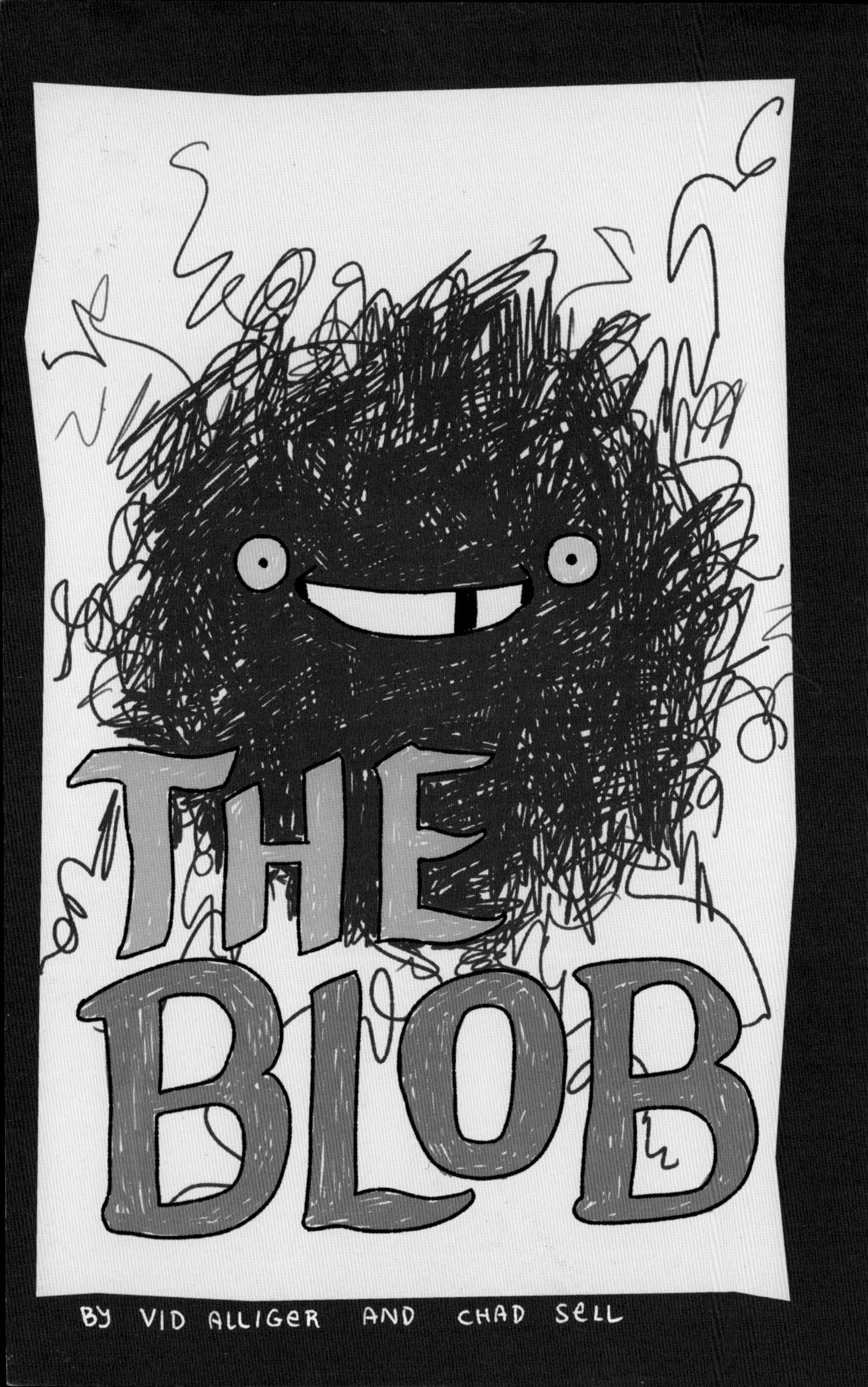
THE BLOB
BY VID ALLIGER AND CHAD SELL

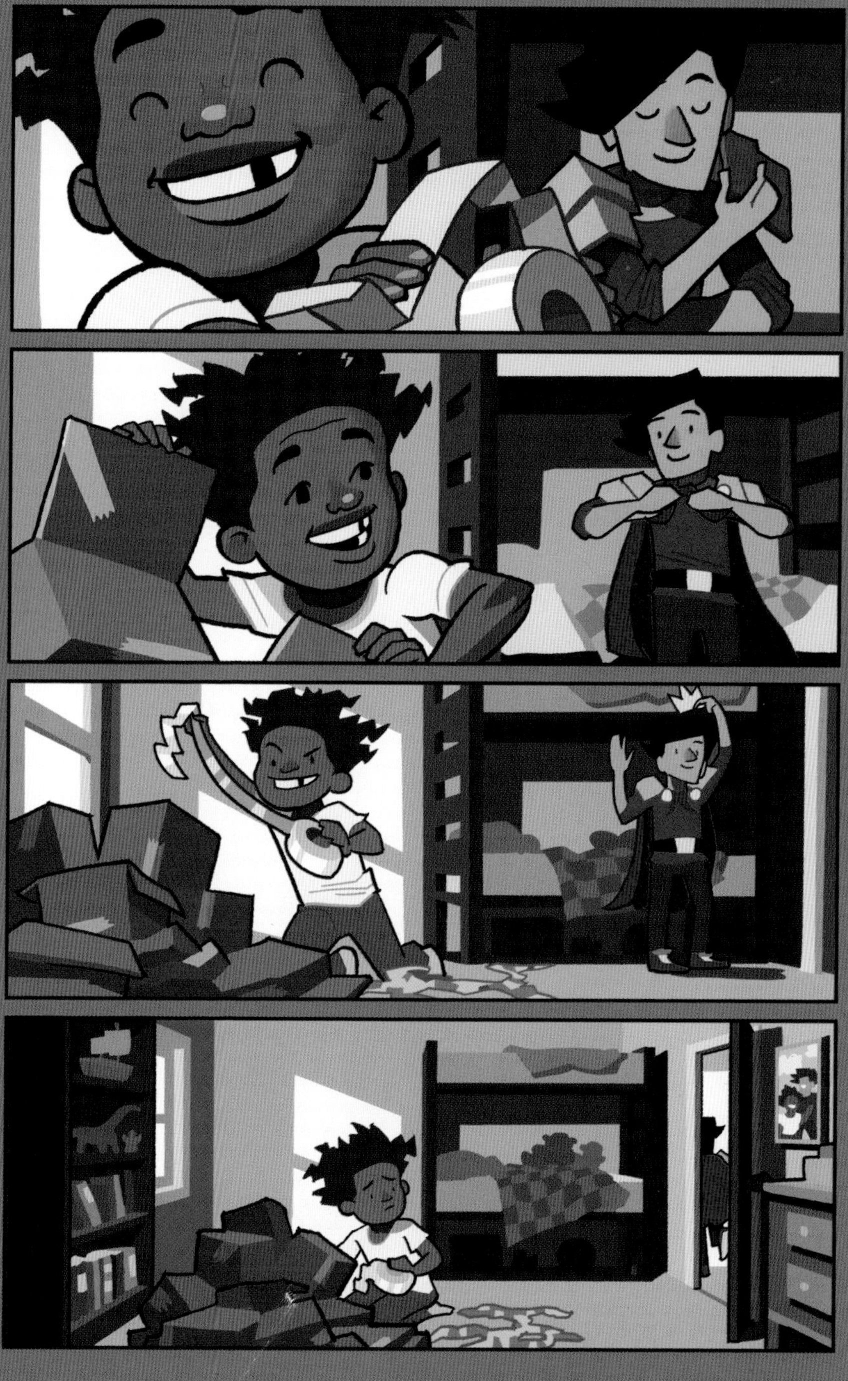

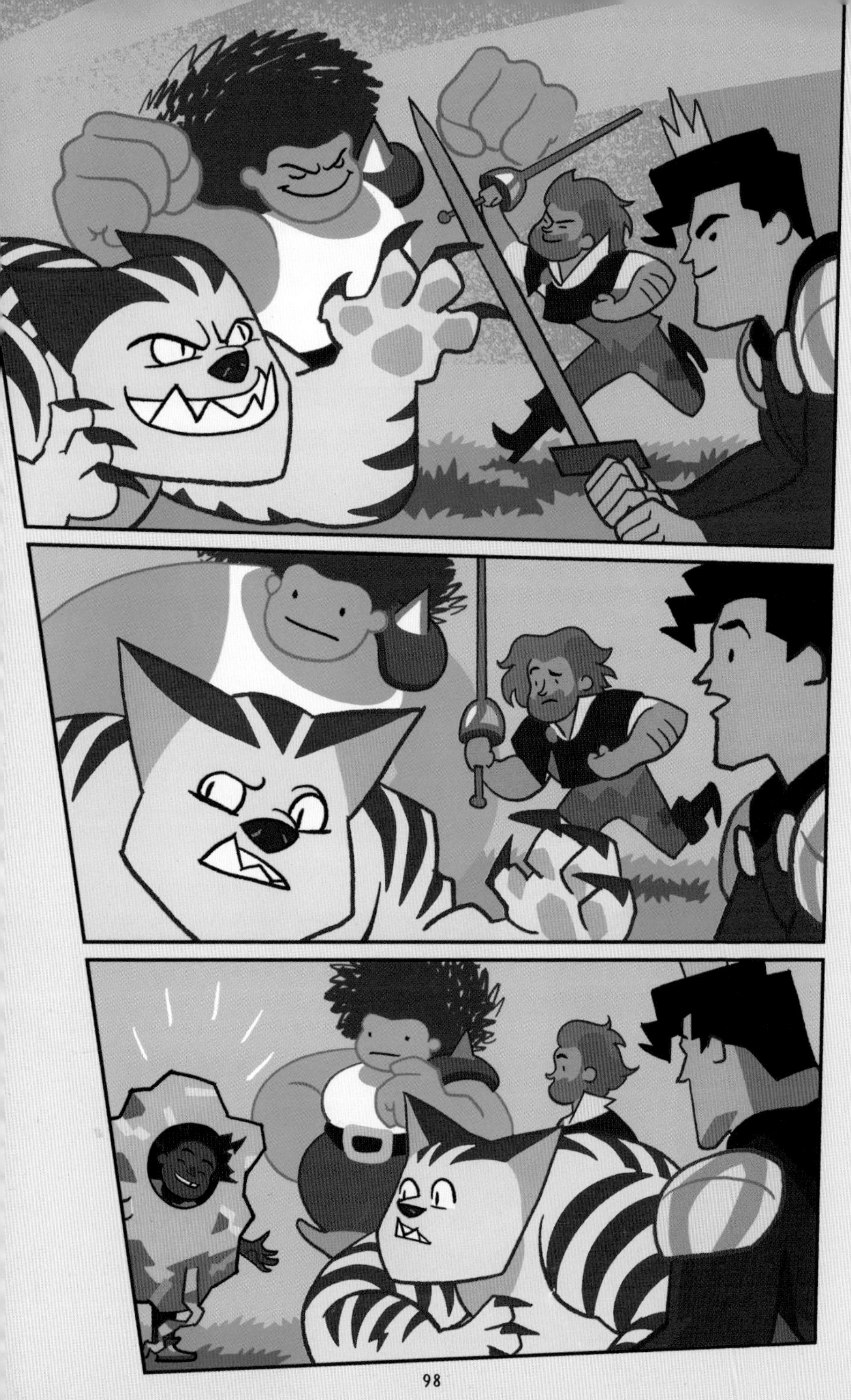

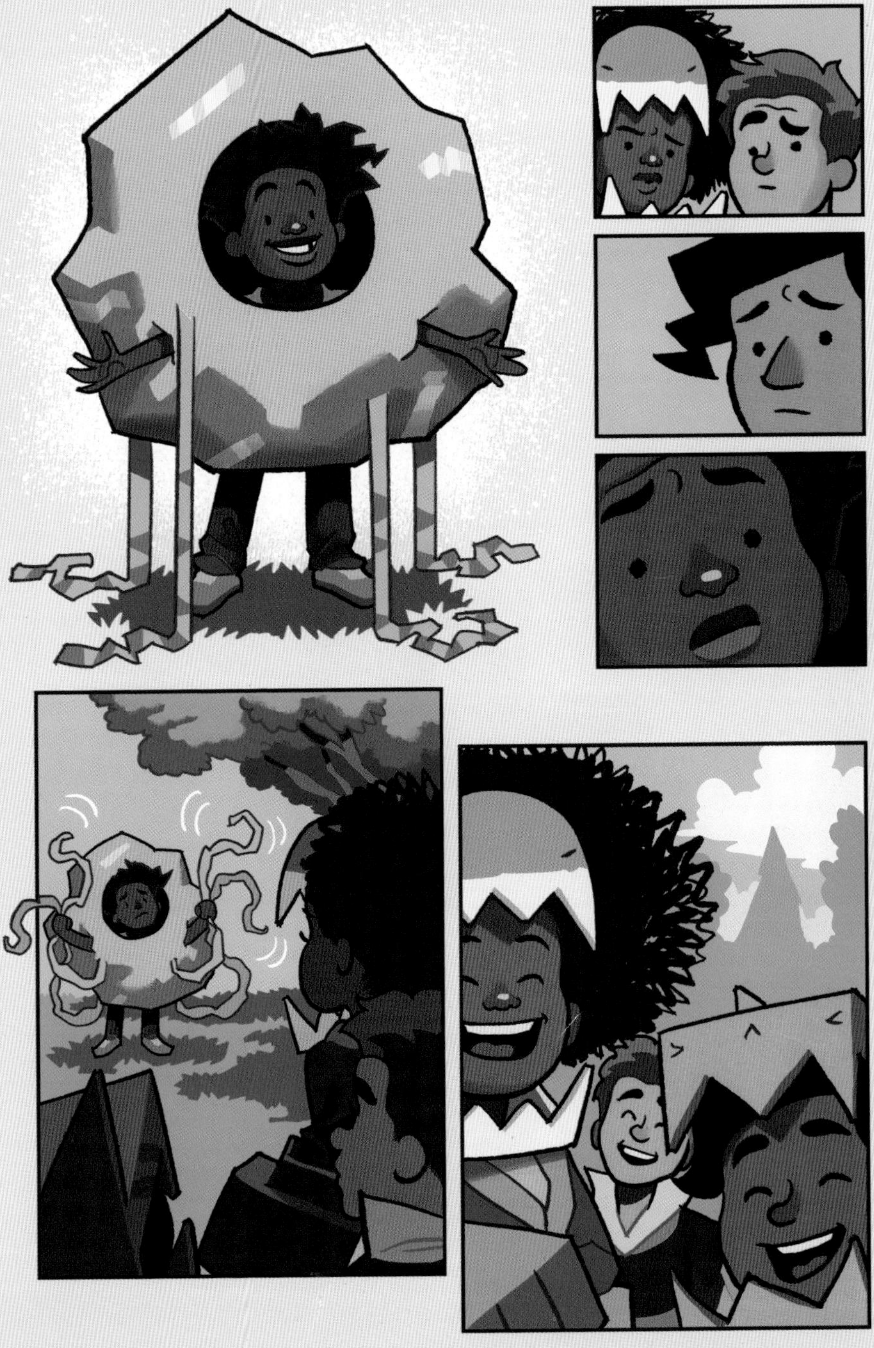

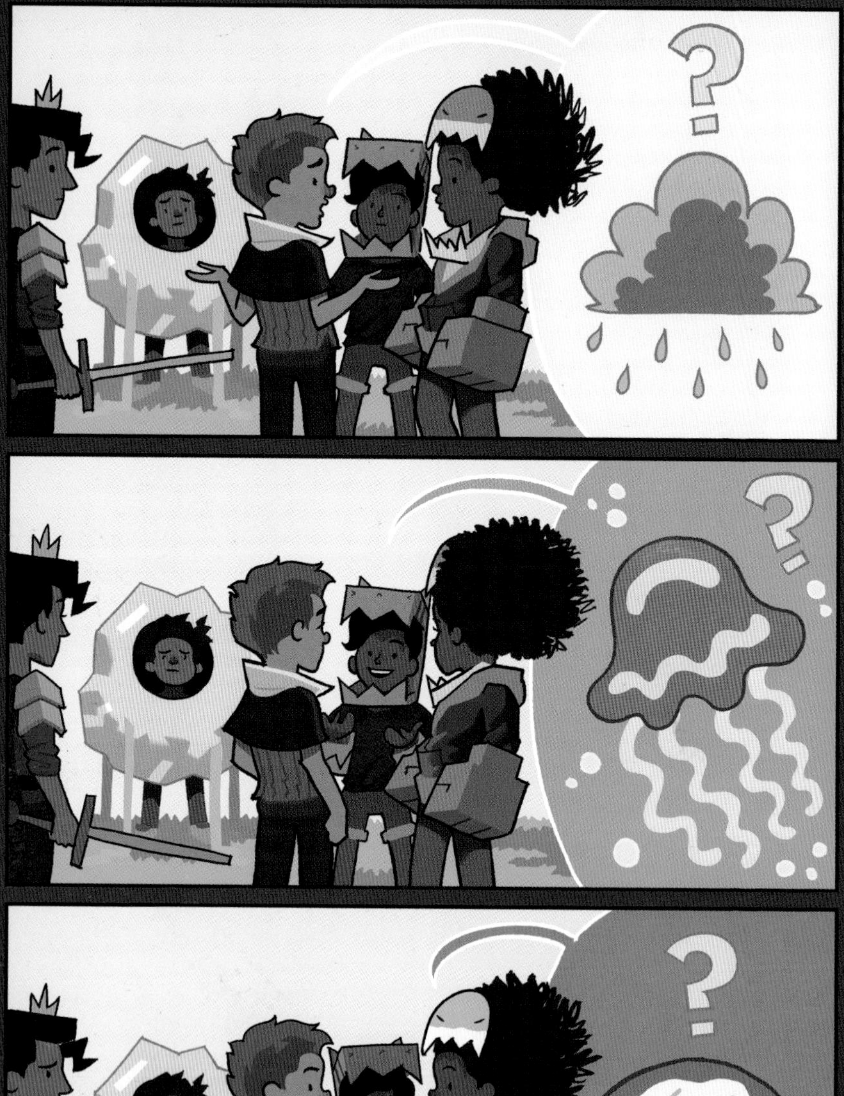
?
?
?

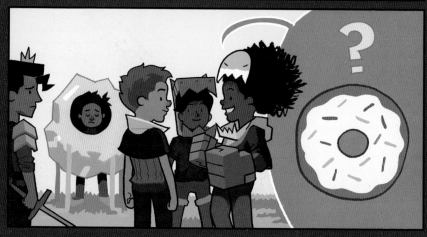

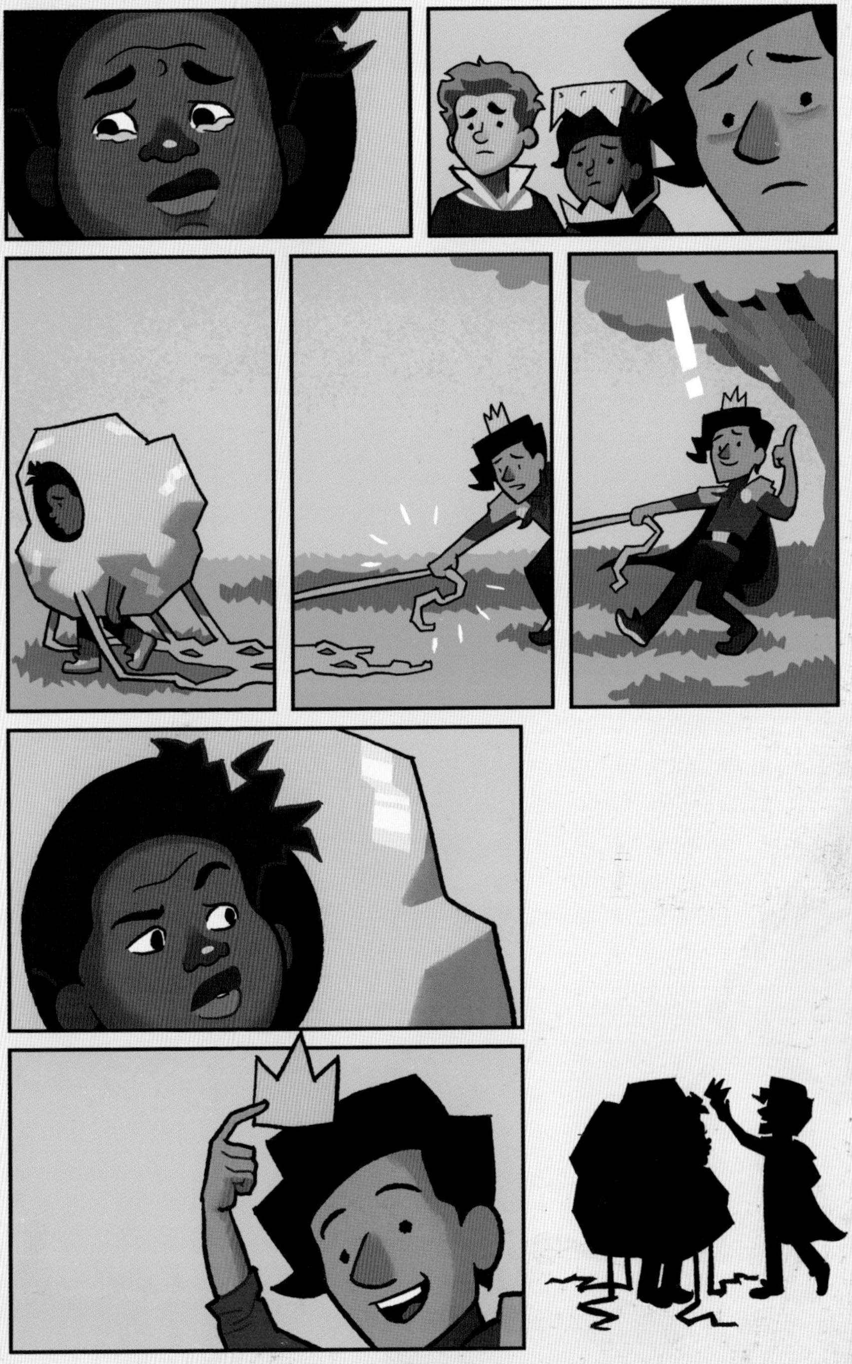
!

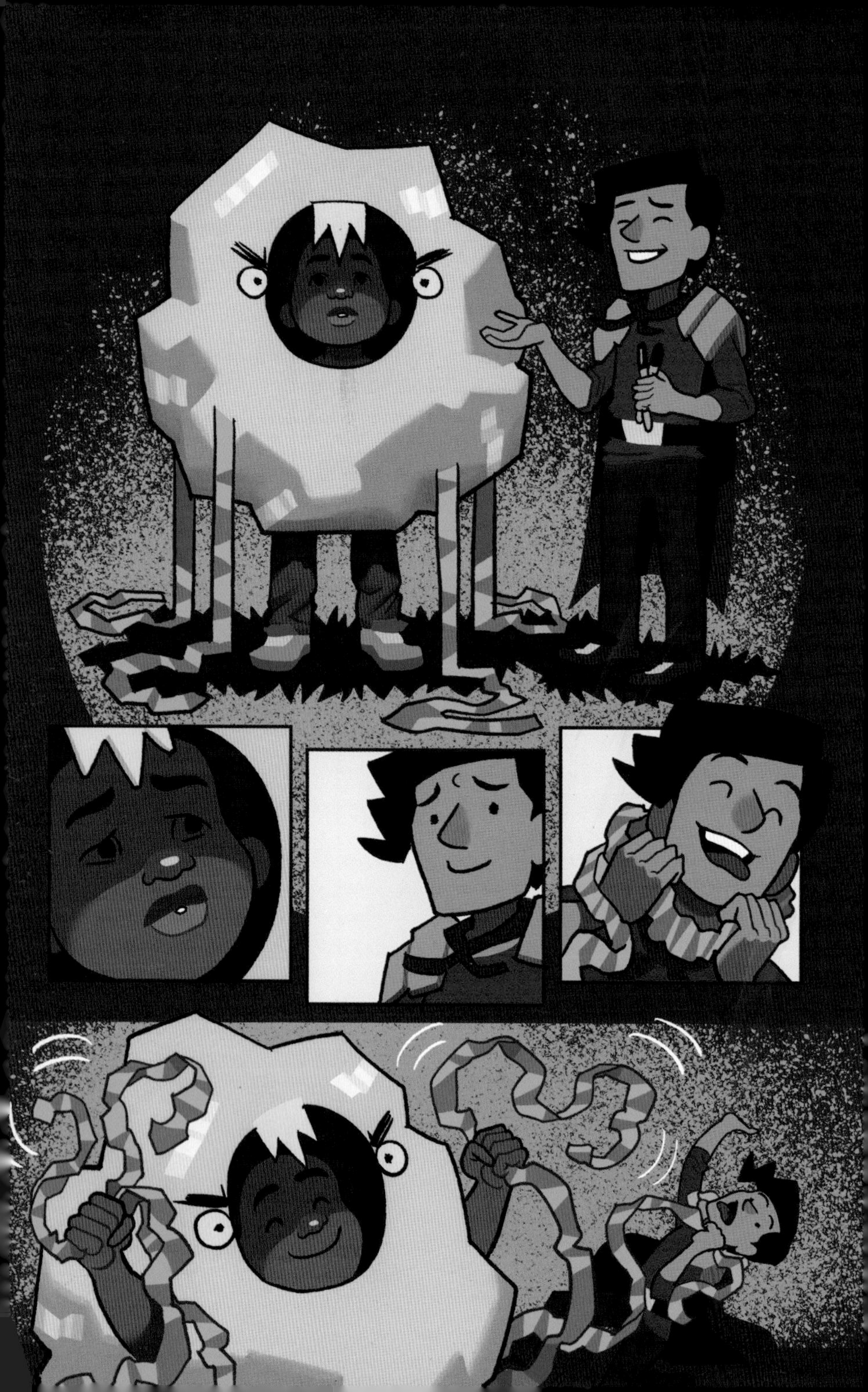

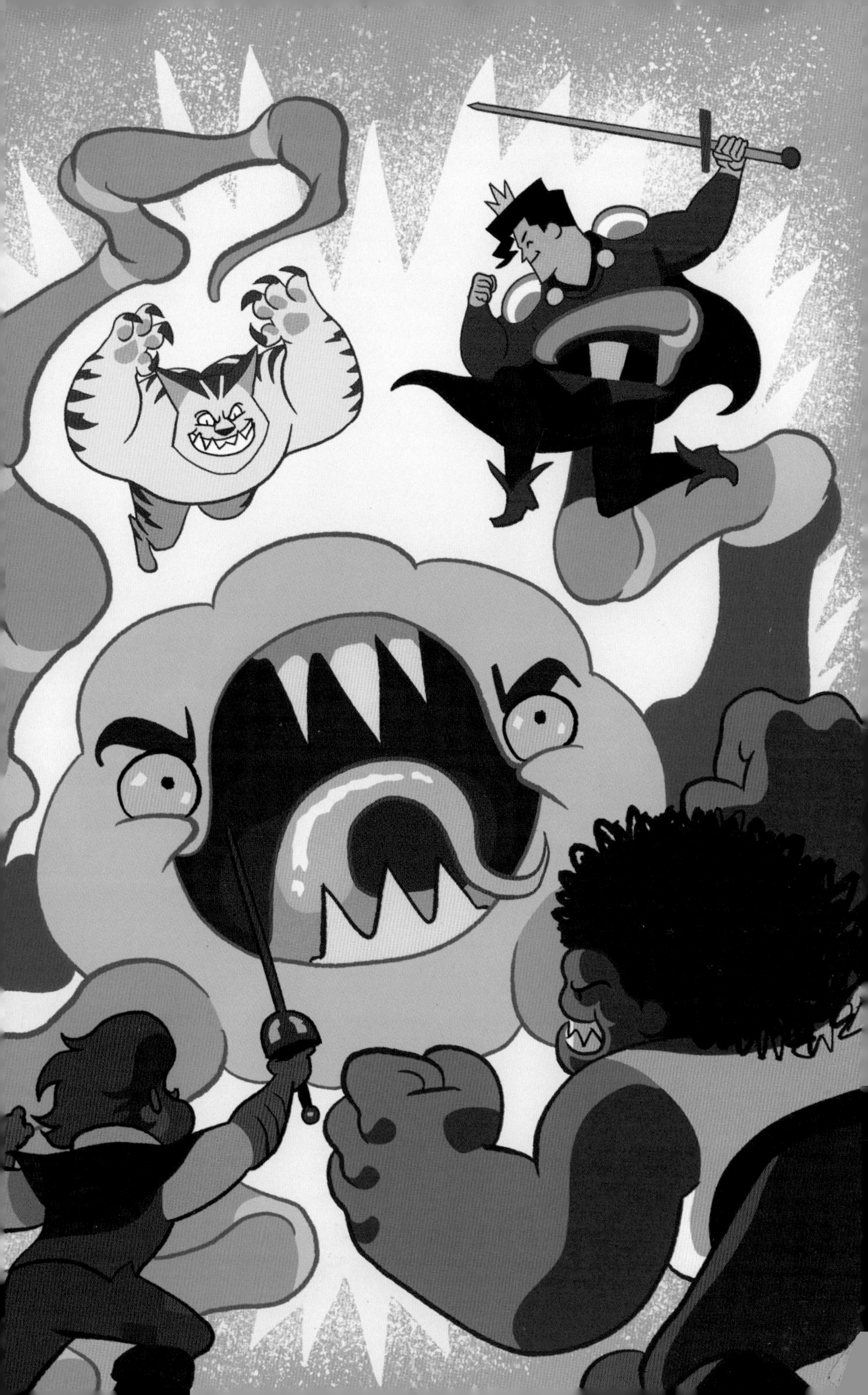

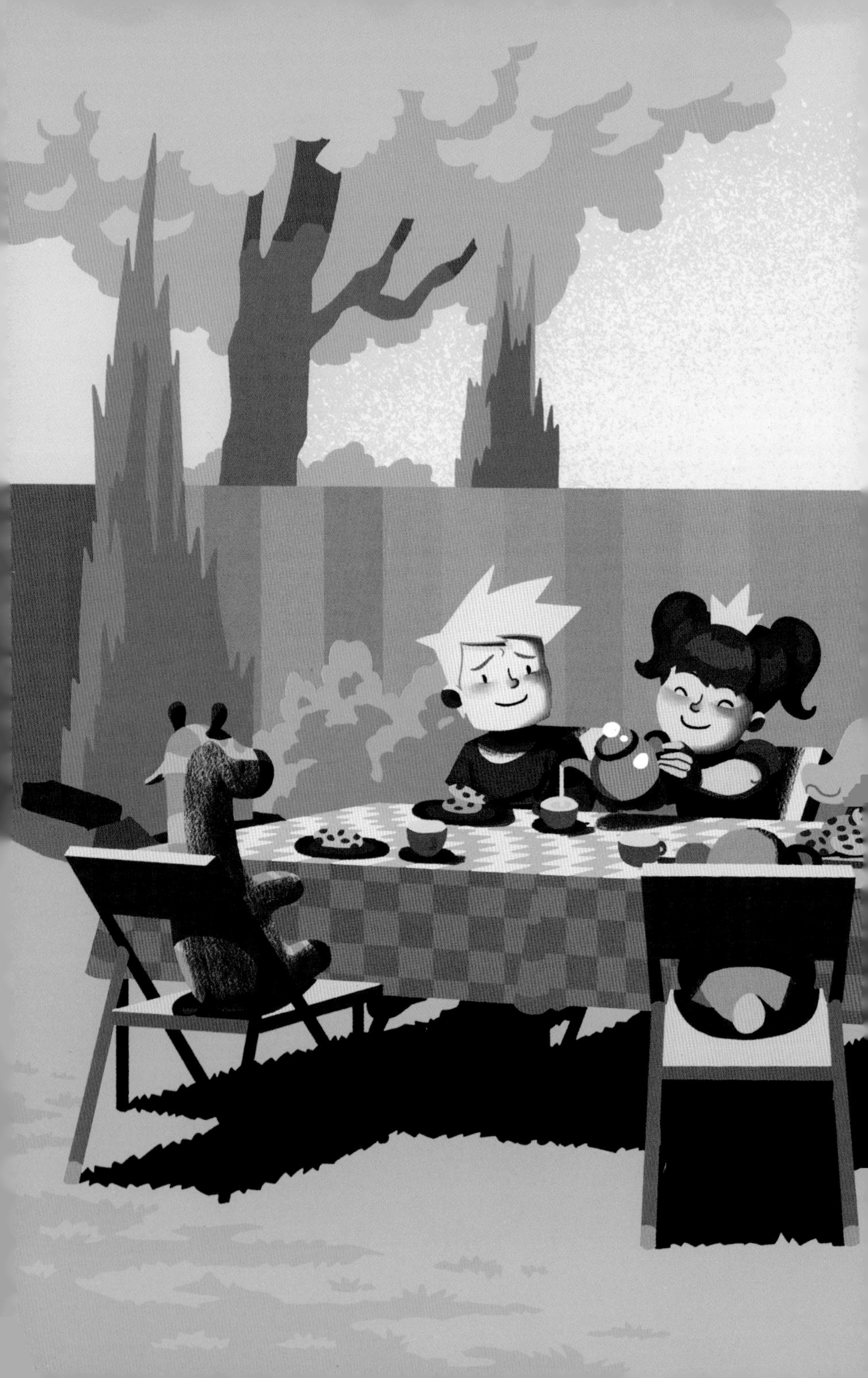

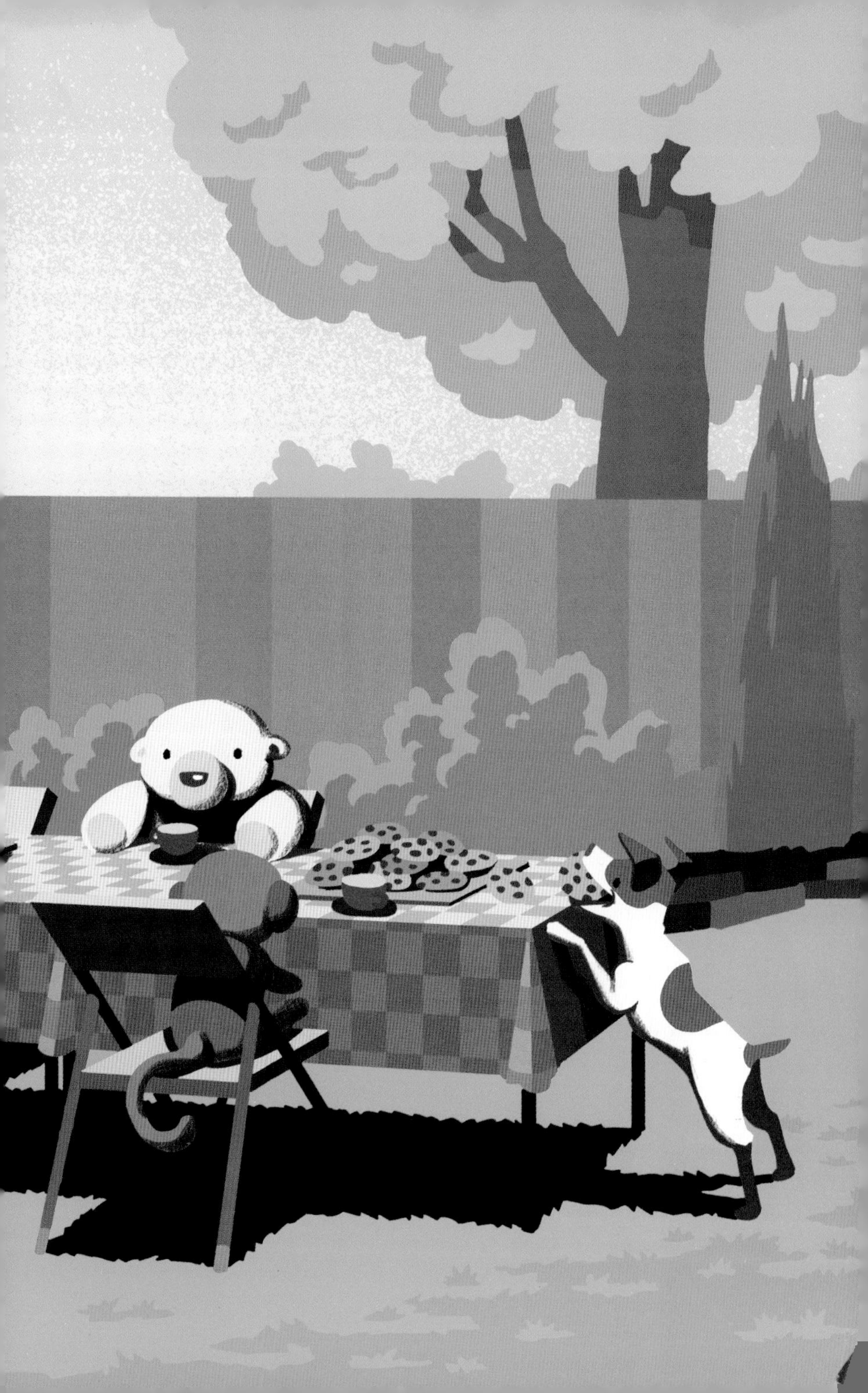

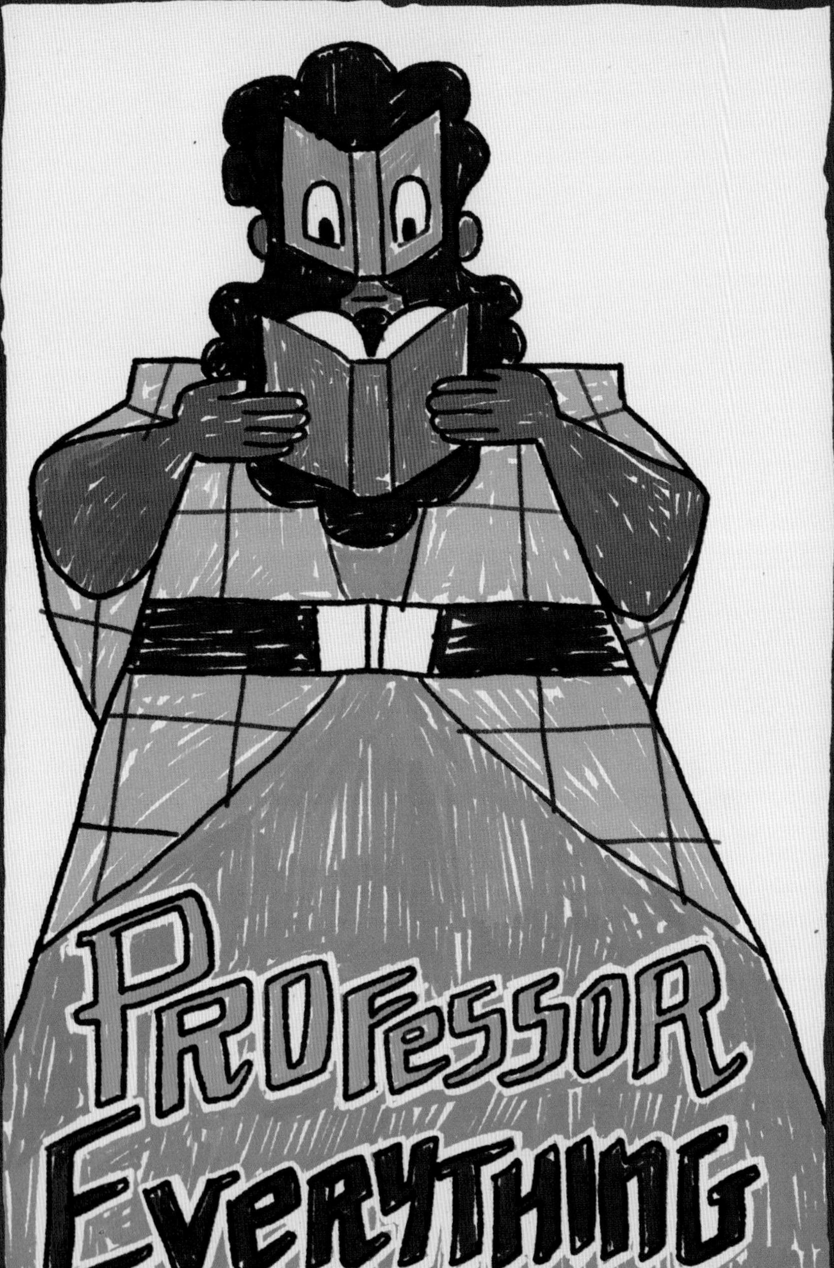
PROFESSOR
EVERYTHING

BY CLOUD JACOBS AND CHAD SELL

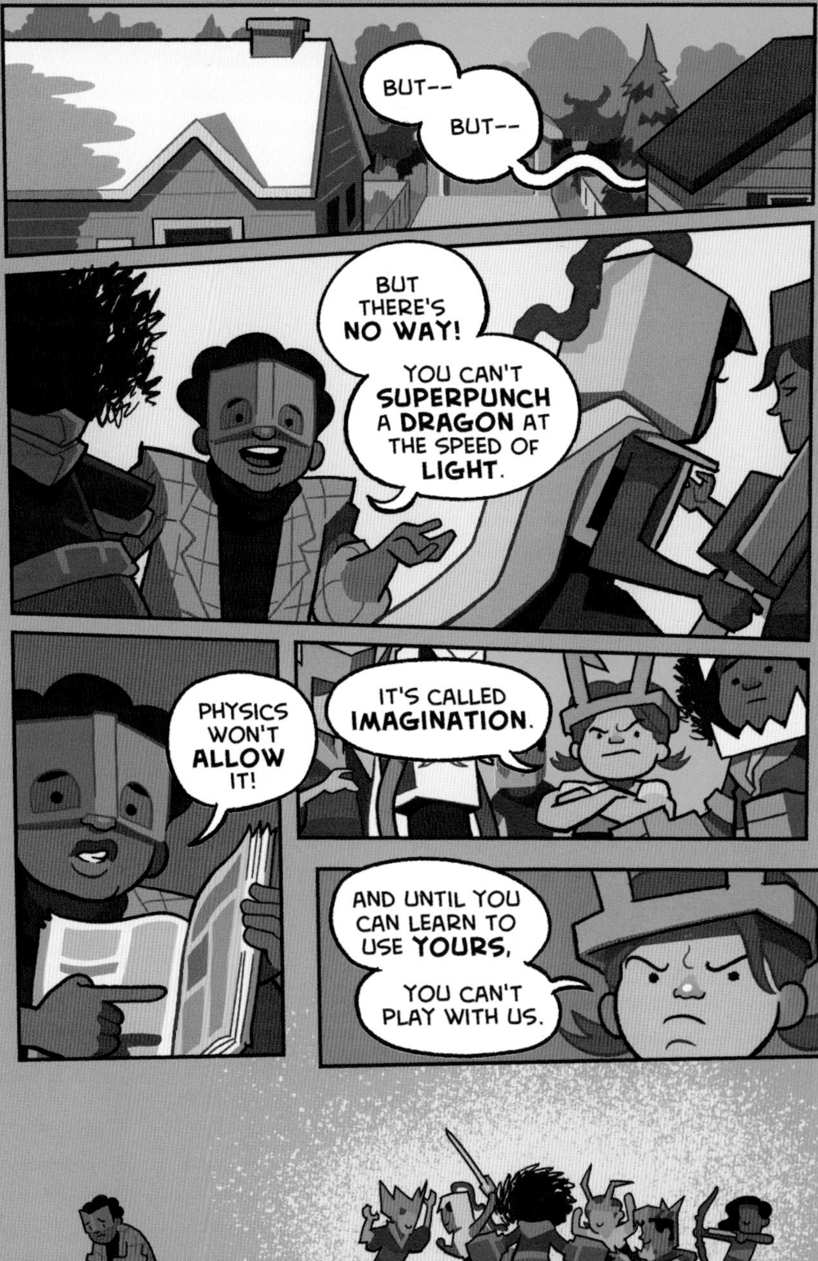
BUT--
BUT--
BUT THERE'S NO WAY!
YOU CAN'T SUPERPUNCH A DRAGON AT THE SPEED OF LIGHT.
PHYSICS WON'T ALLOW IT!
IT'S CALLED IMAGINATION.
AND UNTIL YOU CAN LEARN TO USE YOURS,
YOU CAN'T PLAY WITH US.

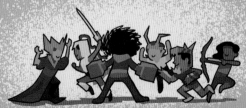

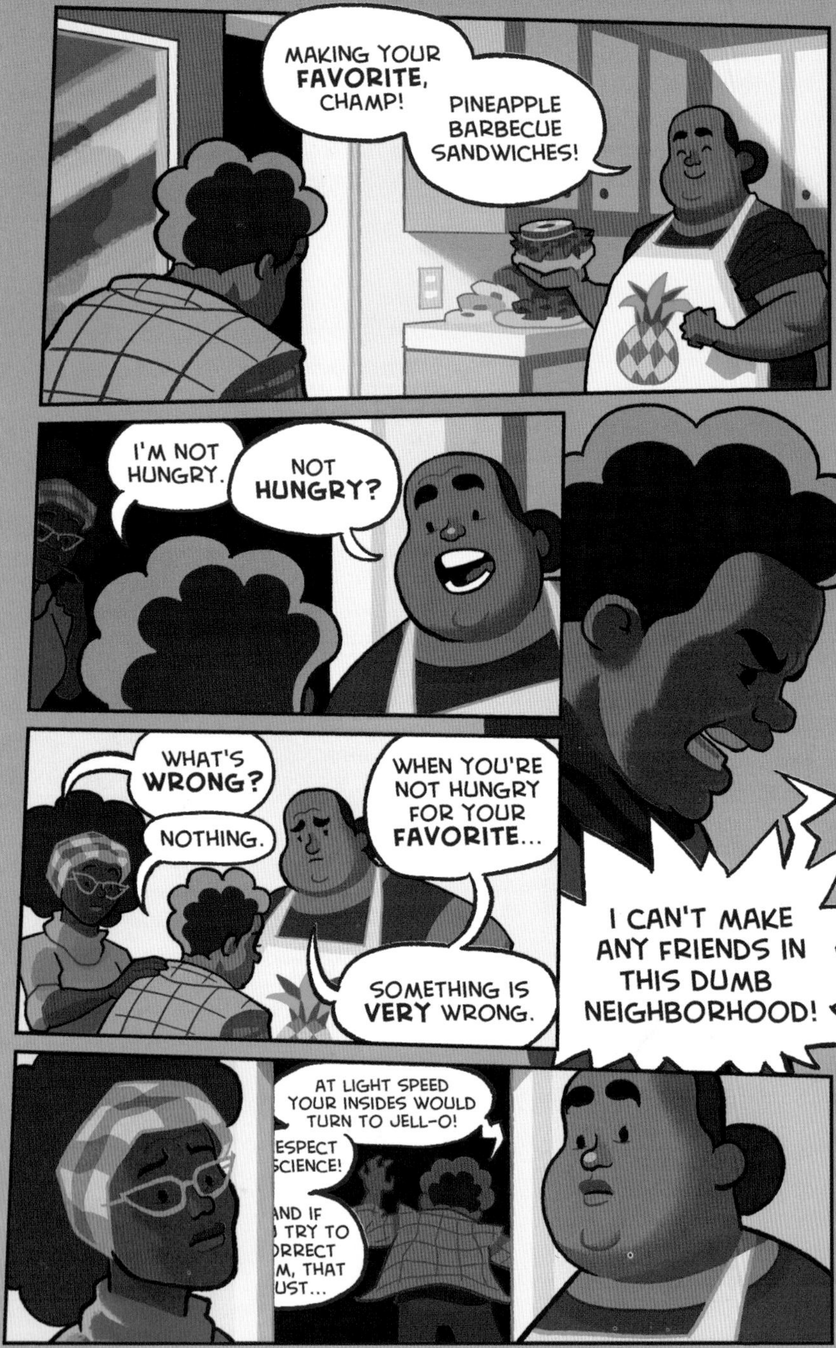
MAKING YOUR **FAVORITE,** CHAMP!
PINEAPPLE BARBECUE SANDWICHES!
I'M NOT HUNGRY.
NOT **HUNGRY?**
WHAT'S **WRONG?**
NOTHING.
WHEN YOU'RE NOT HUNGRY FOR YOUR **FAVORITE**...
SOMETHING IS **VERY** WRONG.
I CAN'T MAKE ANY FRIENDS IN THIS DUMB NEIGHBORHOOD!
AT LIGHT SPEED YOUR INSIDES WOULD TURN TO JELL-O!
ESPECT SCIENCE!
AND IF TRY TO ORRECT M, THAT UST...

SIGH...

HUH?

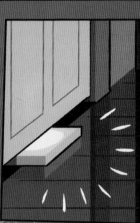

How to Make FRIENDS

TIP #1: SMILE!

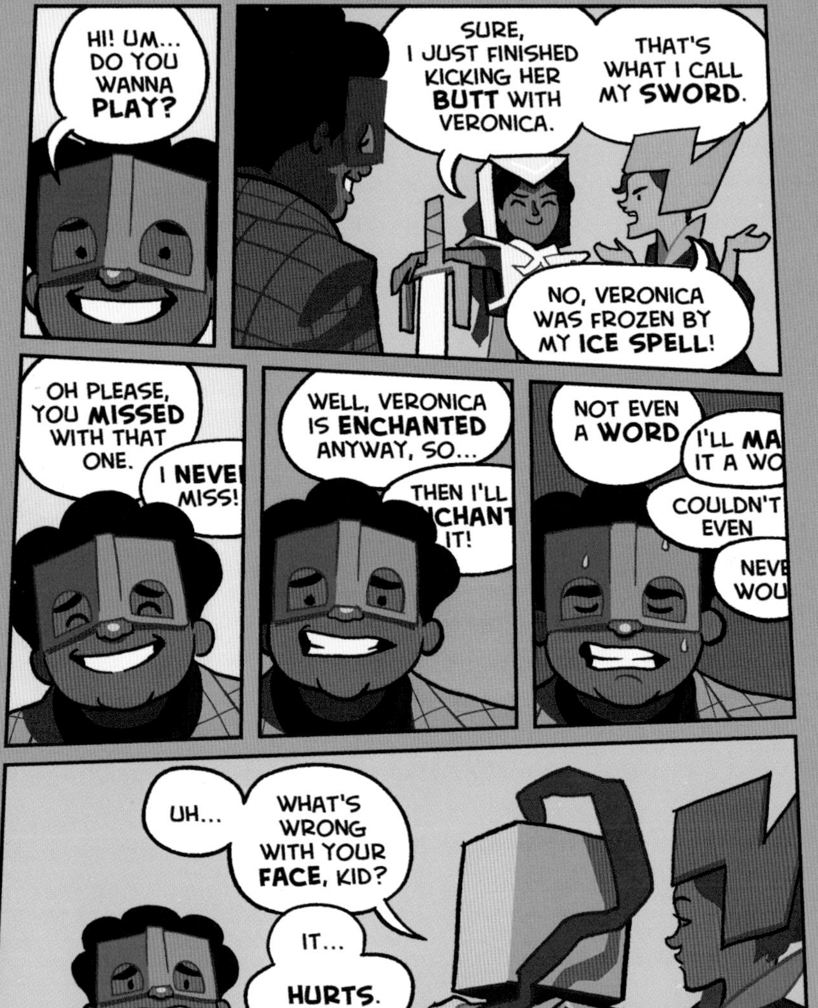
HI! UM... DO YOU WANNA PLAY?
SURE, I JUST FINISHED KICKING HER BUTT WITH VERONICA.
THAT'S WHAT I CALL MY SWORD.
NO, VERONICA WAS FROZEN BY MY ICE SPELL!
OH PLEASE, YOU MISSED WITH THAT ONE.
I NEVE MISS!
WELL, VERONICA IS ENCHANTED ANYWAY, SO...
THEN I'LL CHANT IT!
NOT EVEN A WORD
I'LL MA IT A WO
COULDN'T EVEN
NEVE WOU
UH...
WHAT'S WRONG WITH YOUR FACE, KID?
IT... HURTS.

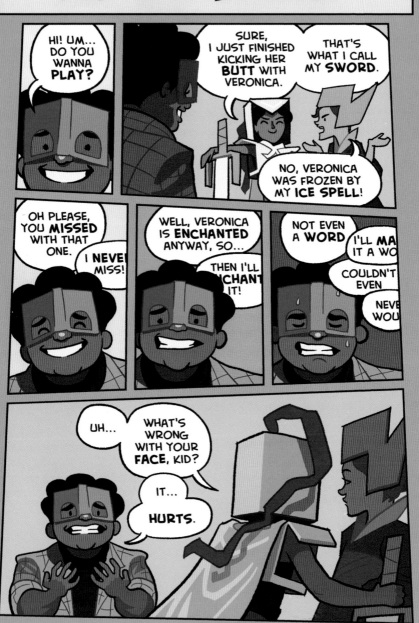

TIP #2: ASK SOMEONE ABOUT THEIR DAY!

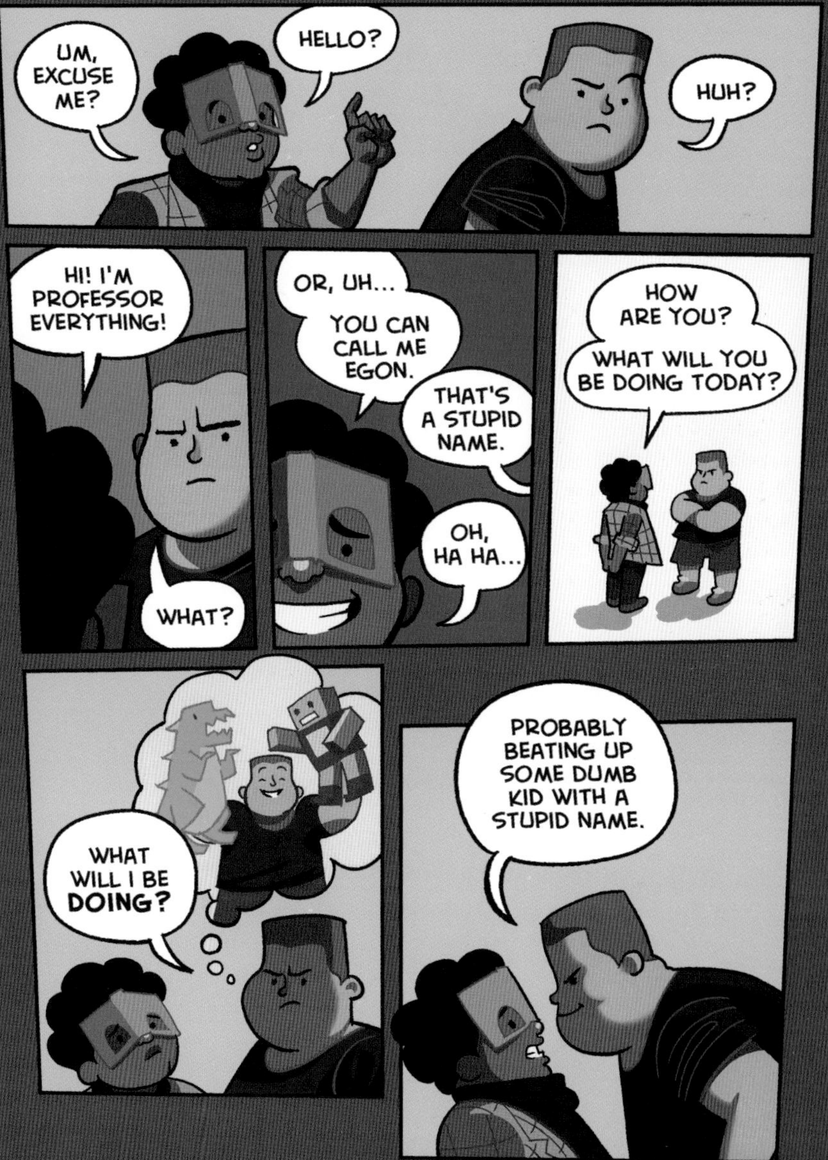
UM, EXCUSE ME?
HELLO?
HUH?
HI! I'M PROFESSOR EVERYTHING!
WHAT?
OR, UH...
YOU CAN CALL ME EGON.
THAT'S A STUPID NAME.
OH, HA HA...
HOW ARE YOU?
WHAT WILL YOU BE DOING TODAY?
WHAT WILL I BE DOING?
PROBABLY BEATING UP SOME DUMB KID WITH A STUPID NAME.

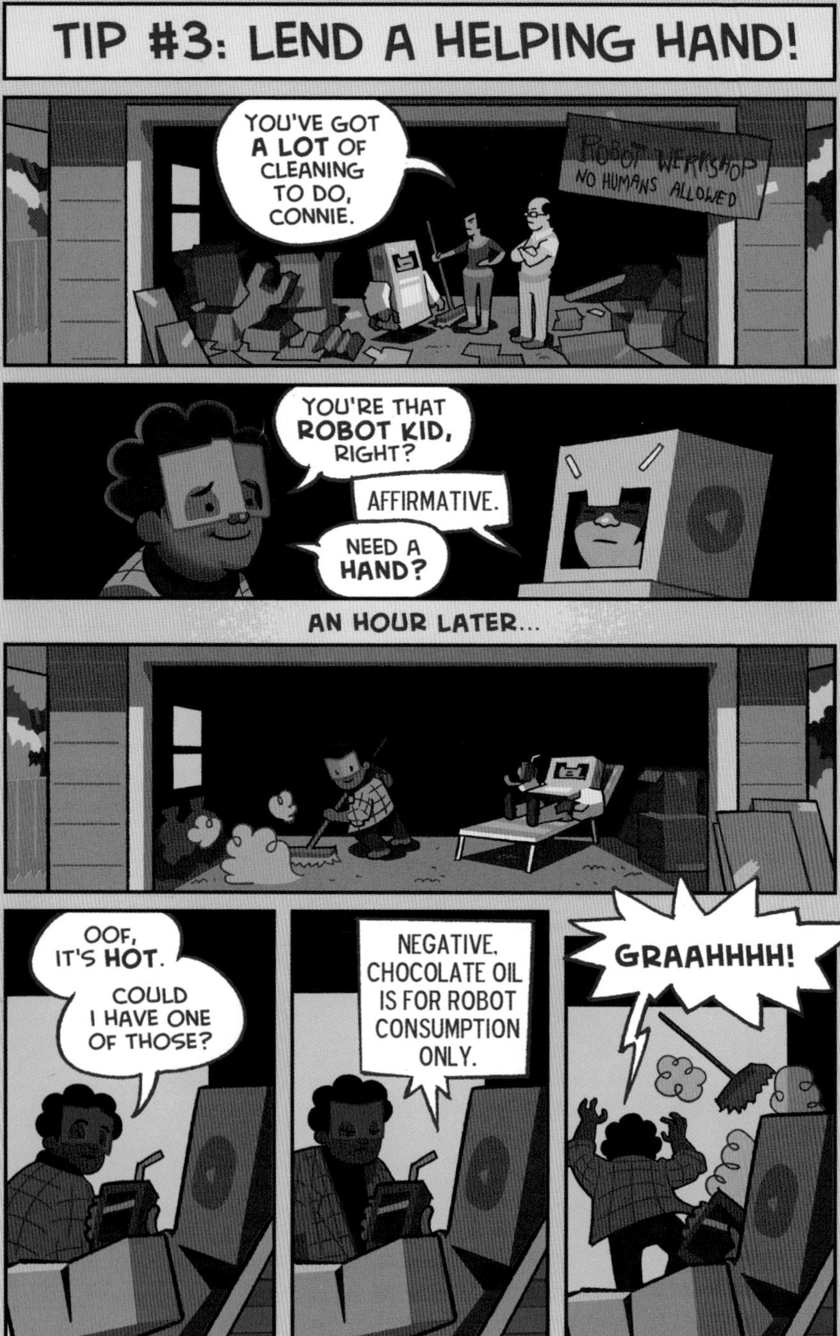
TIP #3: LEND A HELPING HAND!
YOU'VE GOT A LOT OF CLEANING TO DO, CONNIE.
ROBOT WORKSHOP NO HUMANS ALLOWED
YOU'RE THAT ROBOT KID, RIGHT?
AFFIRMATIVE.
NEED A HAND?
AN HOUR LATER...
OOF, IT'S HOT.
COULD I HAVE ONE OF THOSE?
NEGATIVE. CHOCOLATE OIL IS FOR ROBOT CONSUMPTION ONLY.
GRAAHHHH!

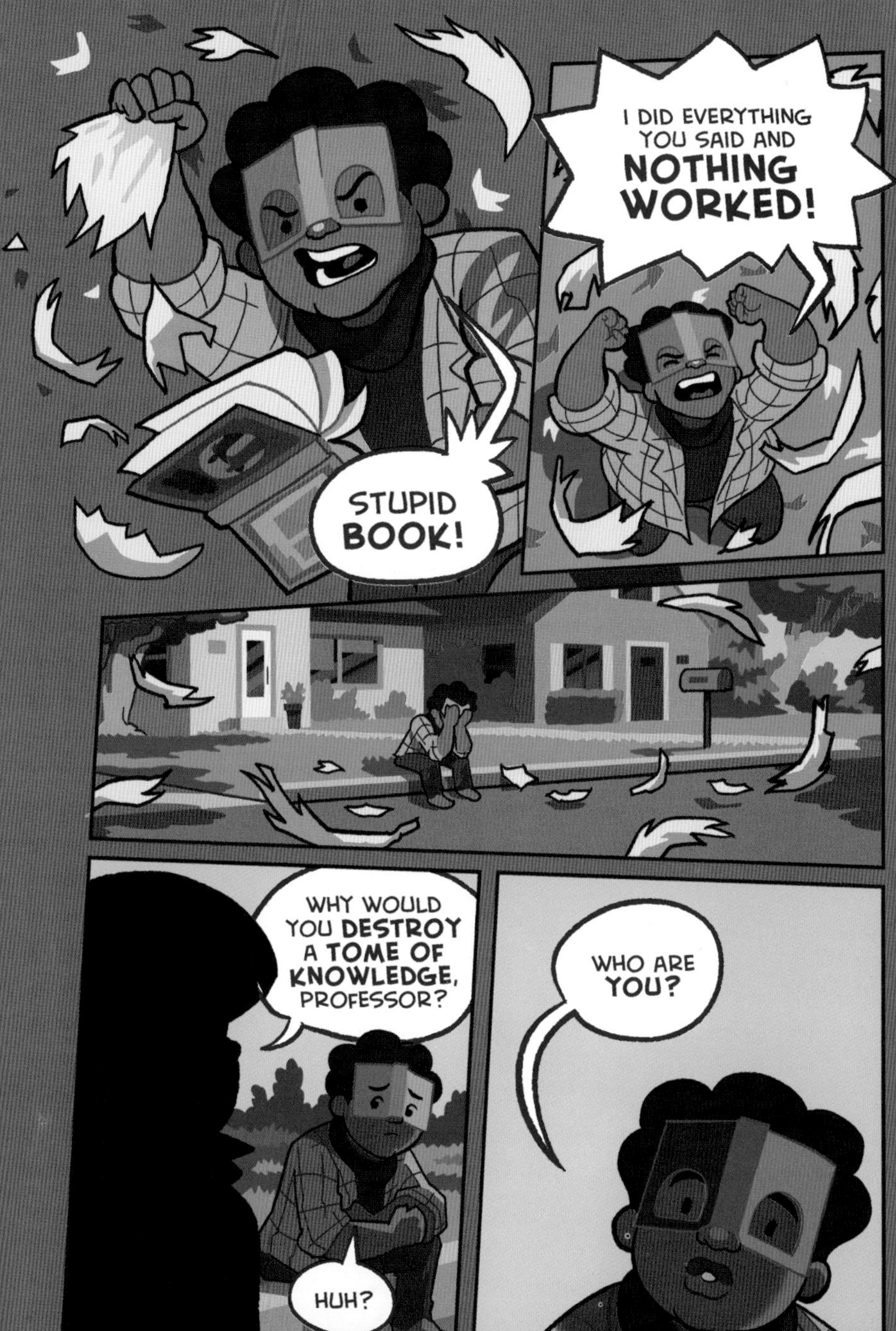
STUPID BOOK!
I DID EVERYTHING YOU SAID AND NOTHING WORKED!
WHY WOULD YOU DESTROY A TOME OF KNOWLEDGE, PROFESSOR?
HUH?
WHO ARE YOU?

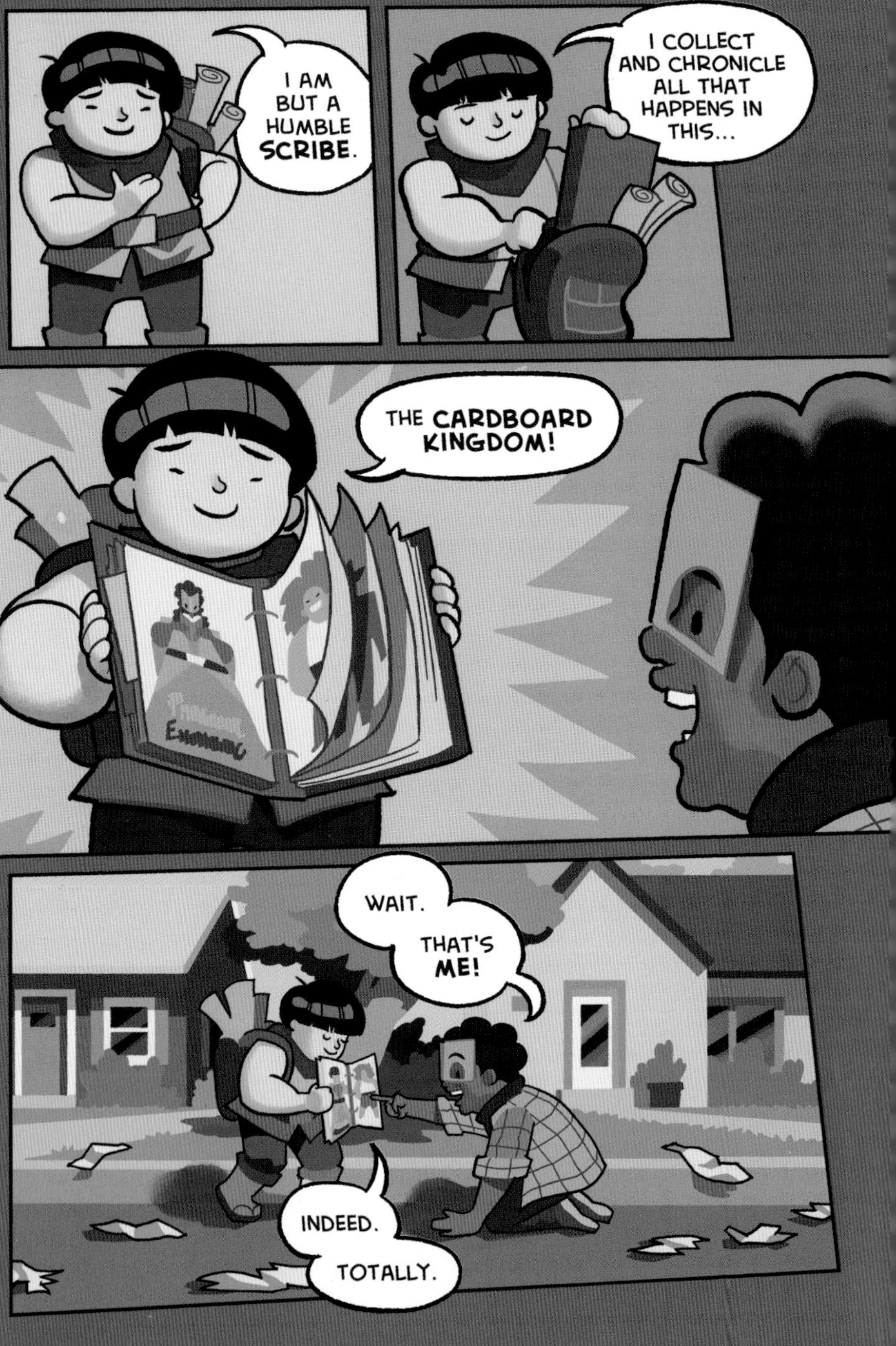
I AM BUT A HUMBLE SCRIBE.
I COLLECT AND CHRONICLE ALL THAT HAPPENS IN THIS...
THE CARDBOARD KINGDOM!
WAIT.
THAT'S ME!
INDEED.
TOTALLY.

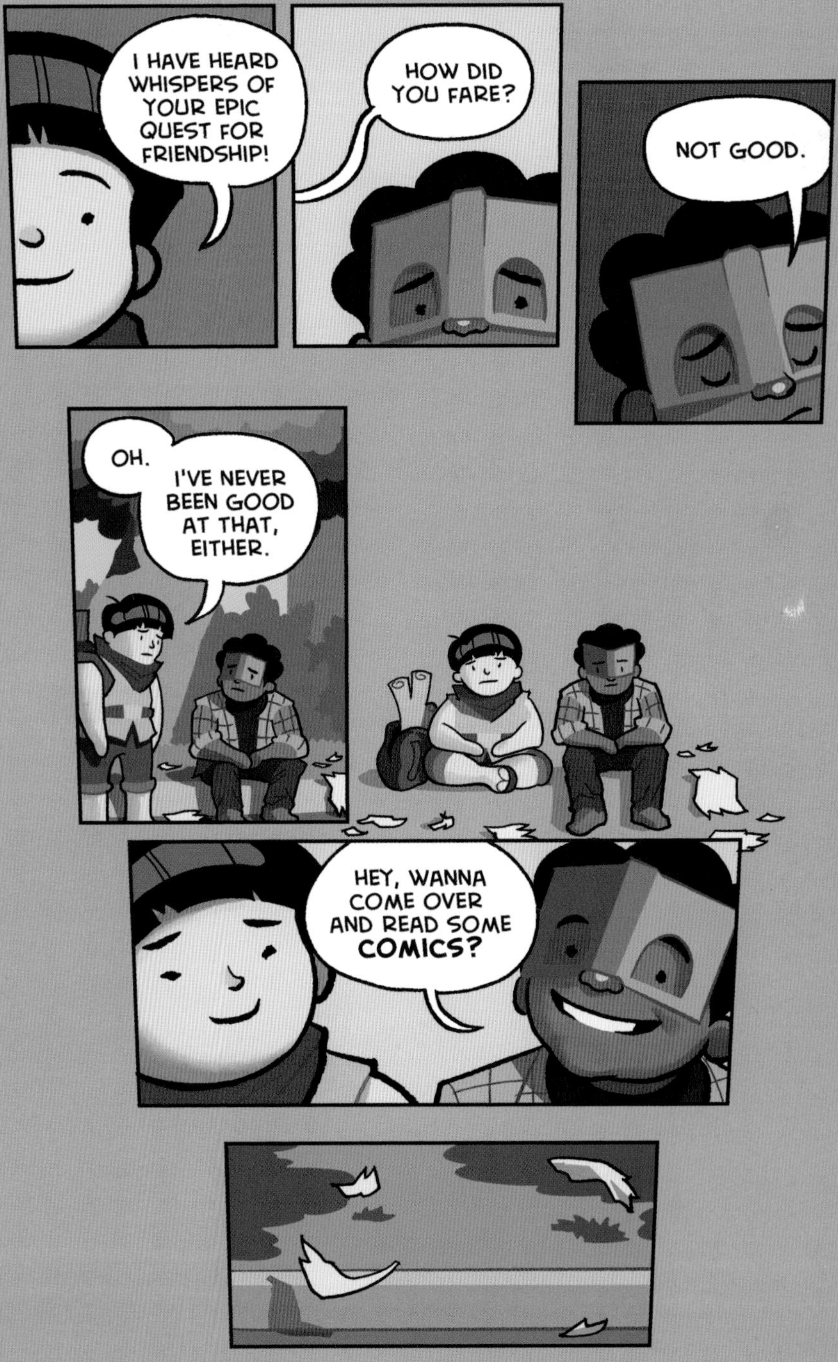
I HAVE HEARD WHISPERS OF YOUR EPIC QUEST FOR FRIENDSHIP!
HOW DID YOU FARE?
NOT GOOD.
OH.
I'VE NEVER BEEN GOOD AT THAT, EITHER.
HEY, WANNA COME OVER AND READ SOME COMICS?

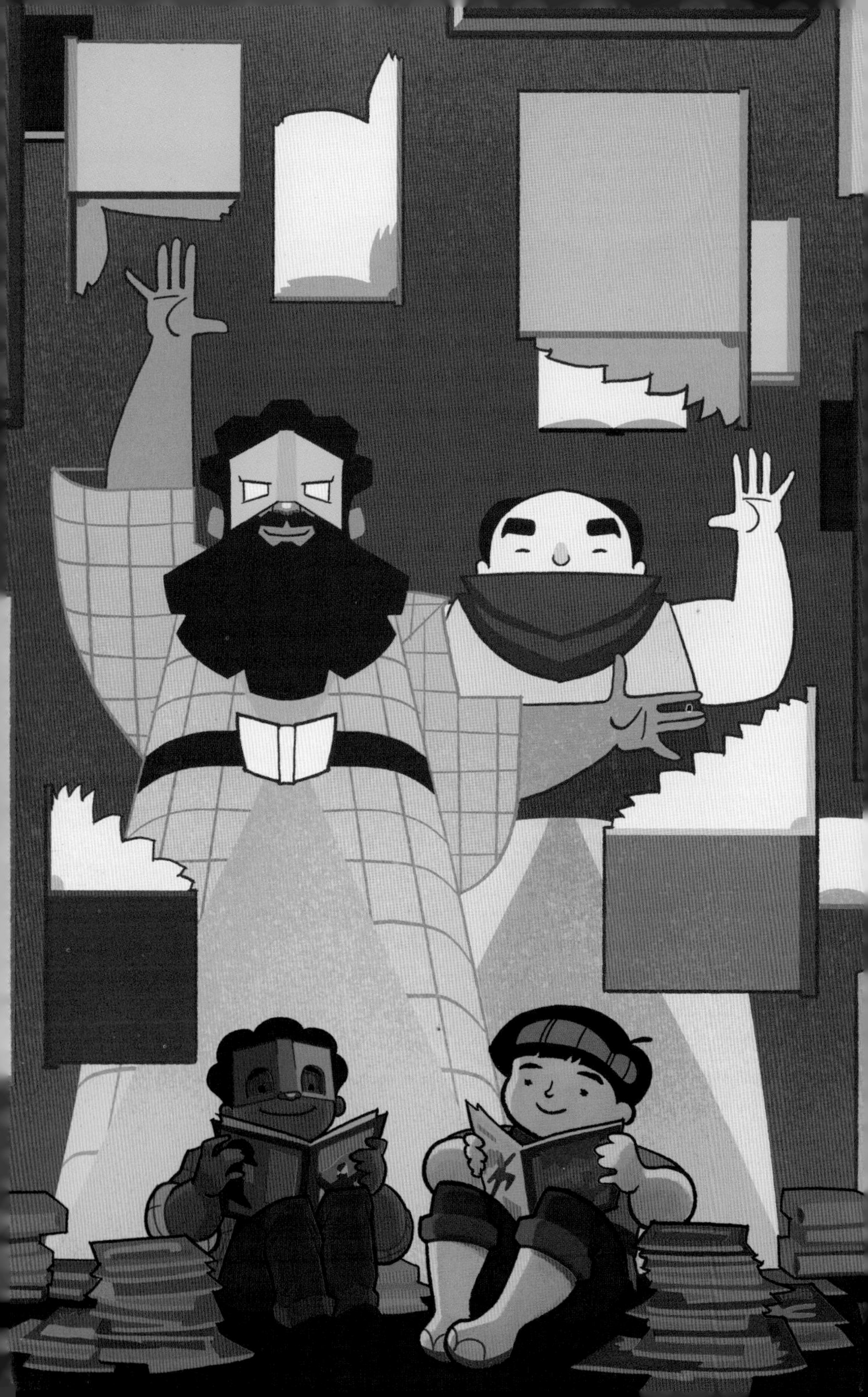

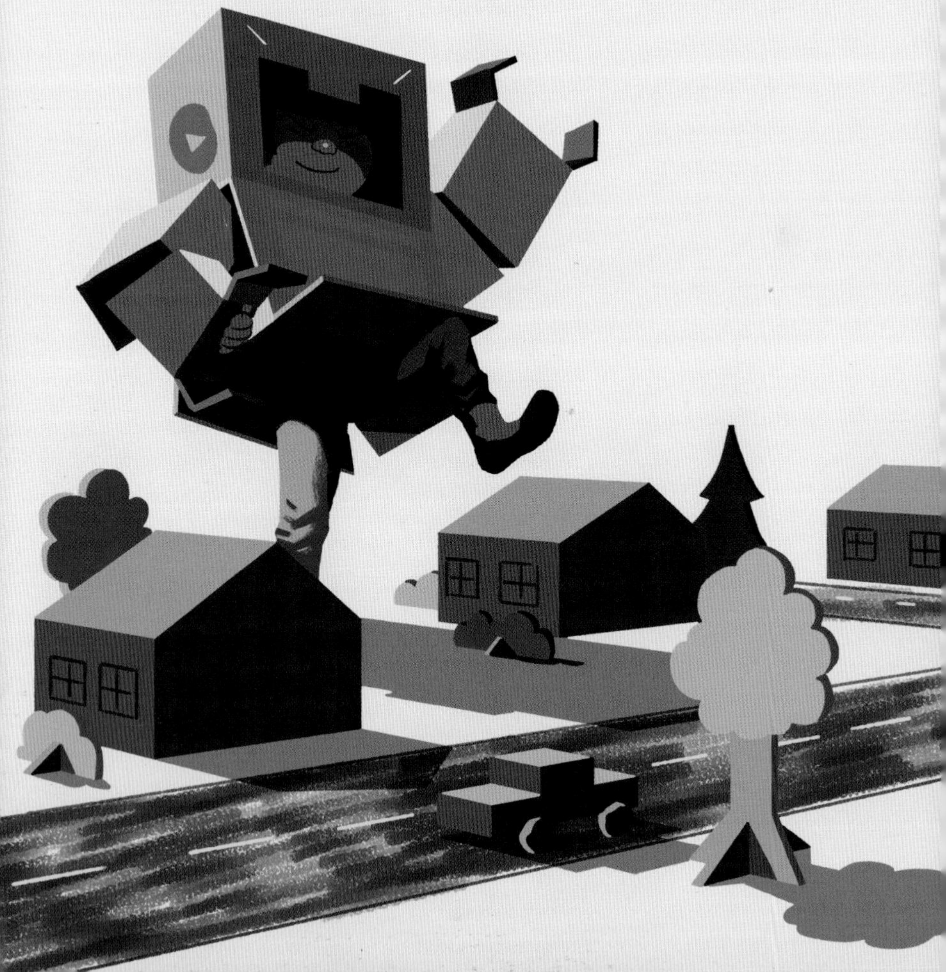

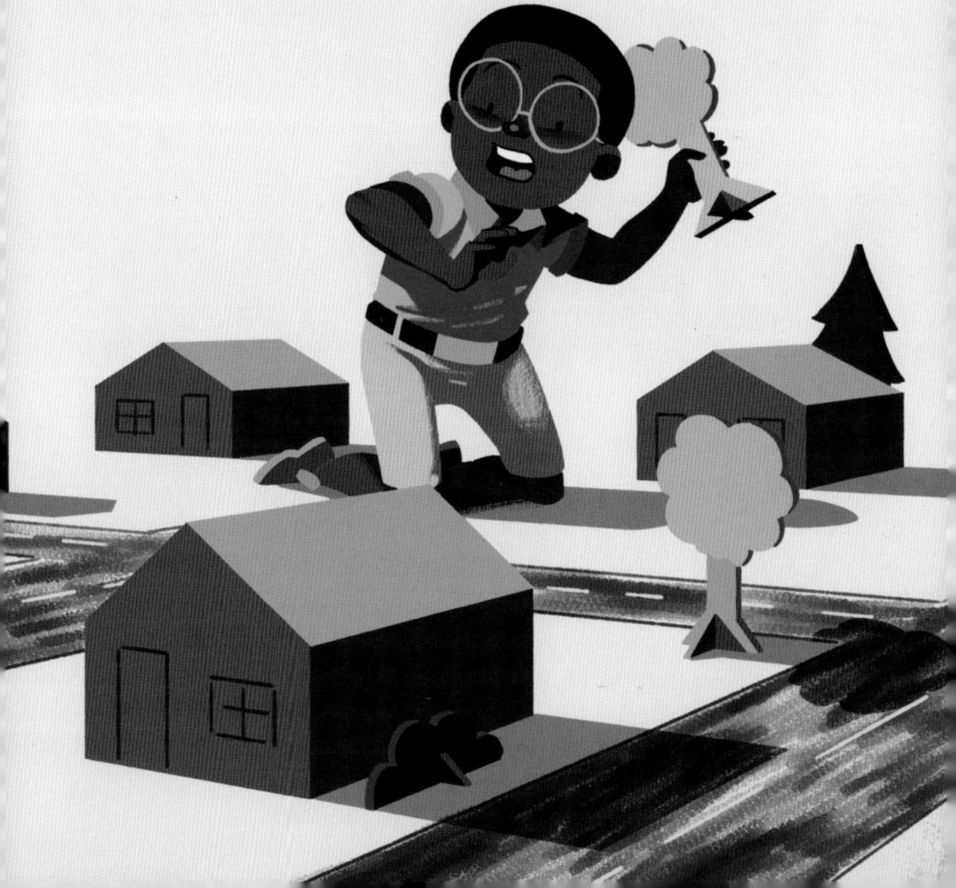

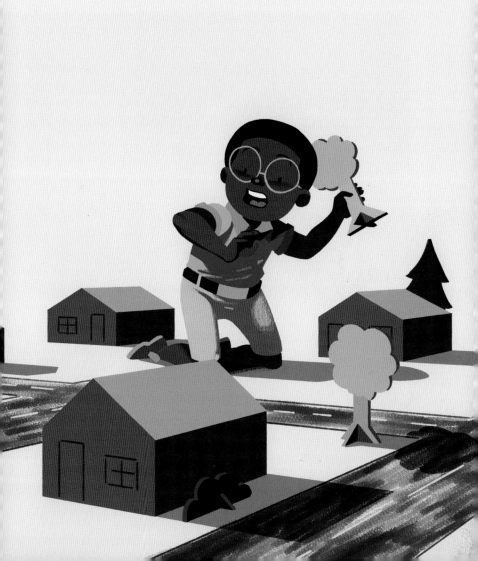

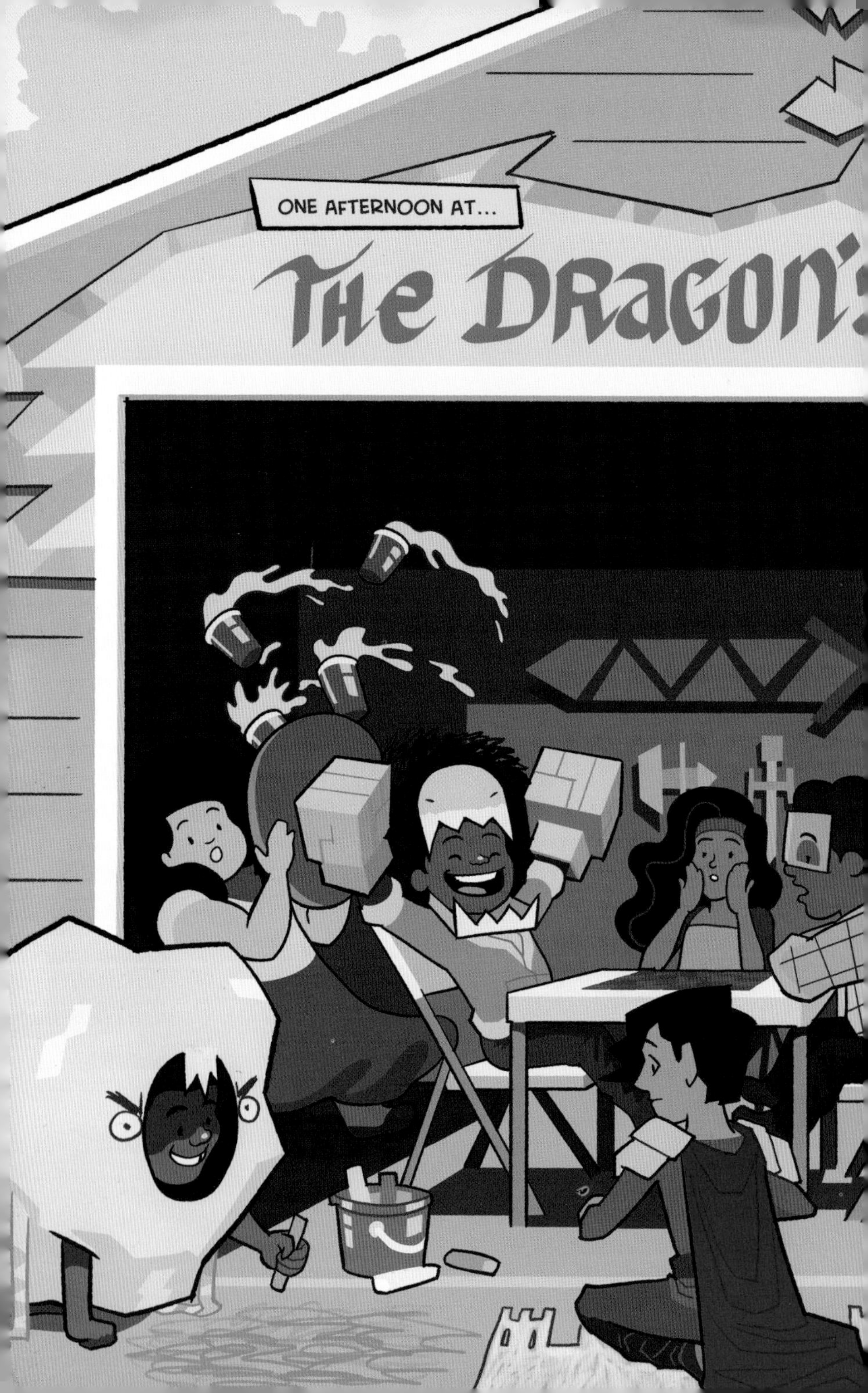
ONE AFTERNOON AT...
THE DRAGON'S

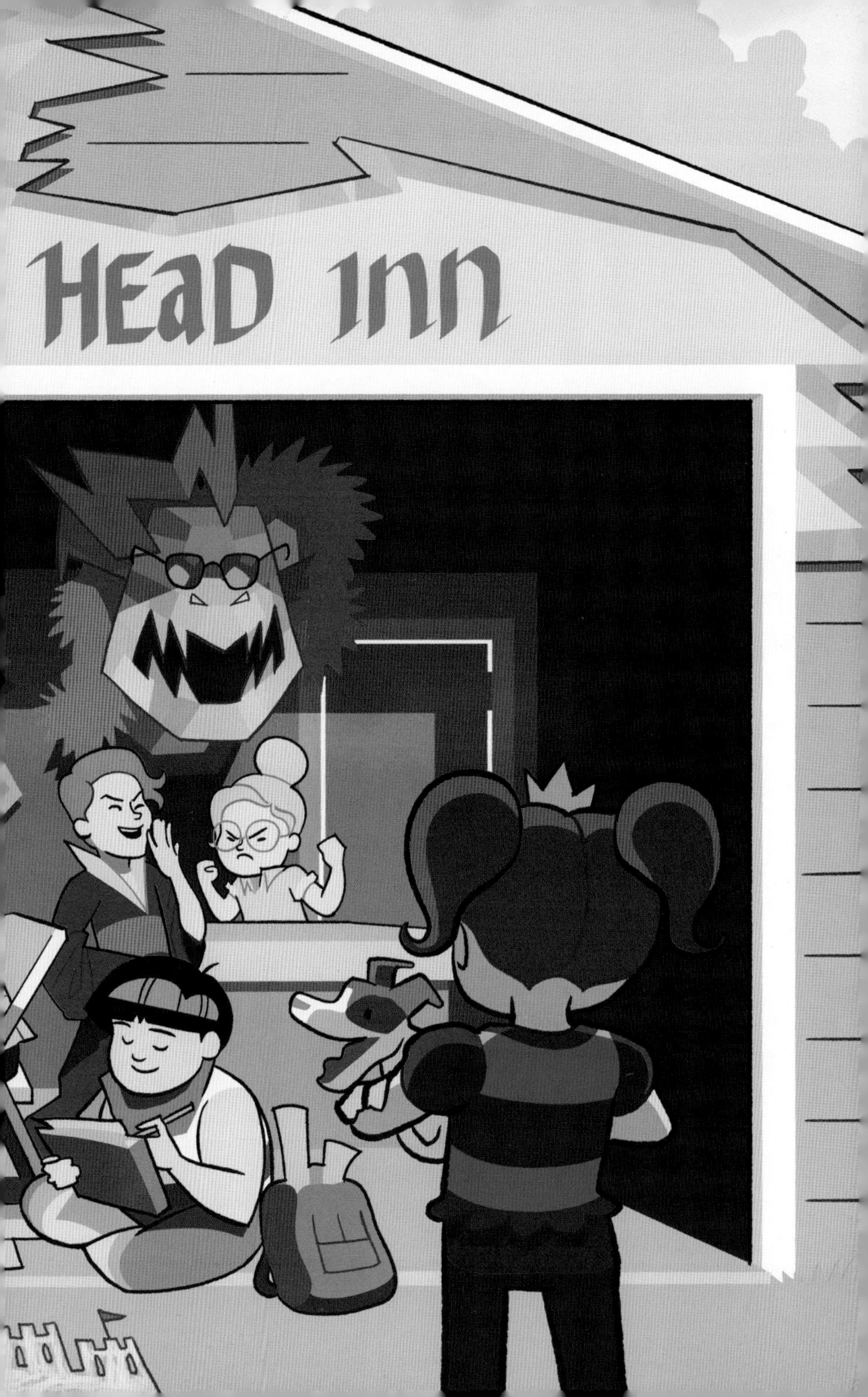
HEAD INN

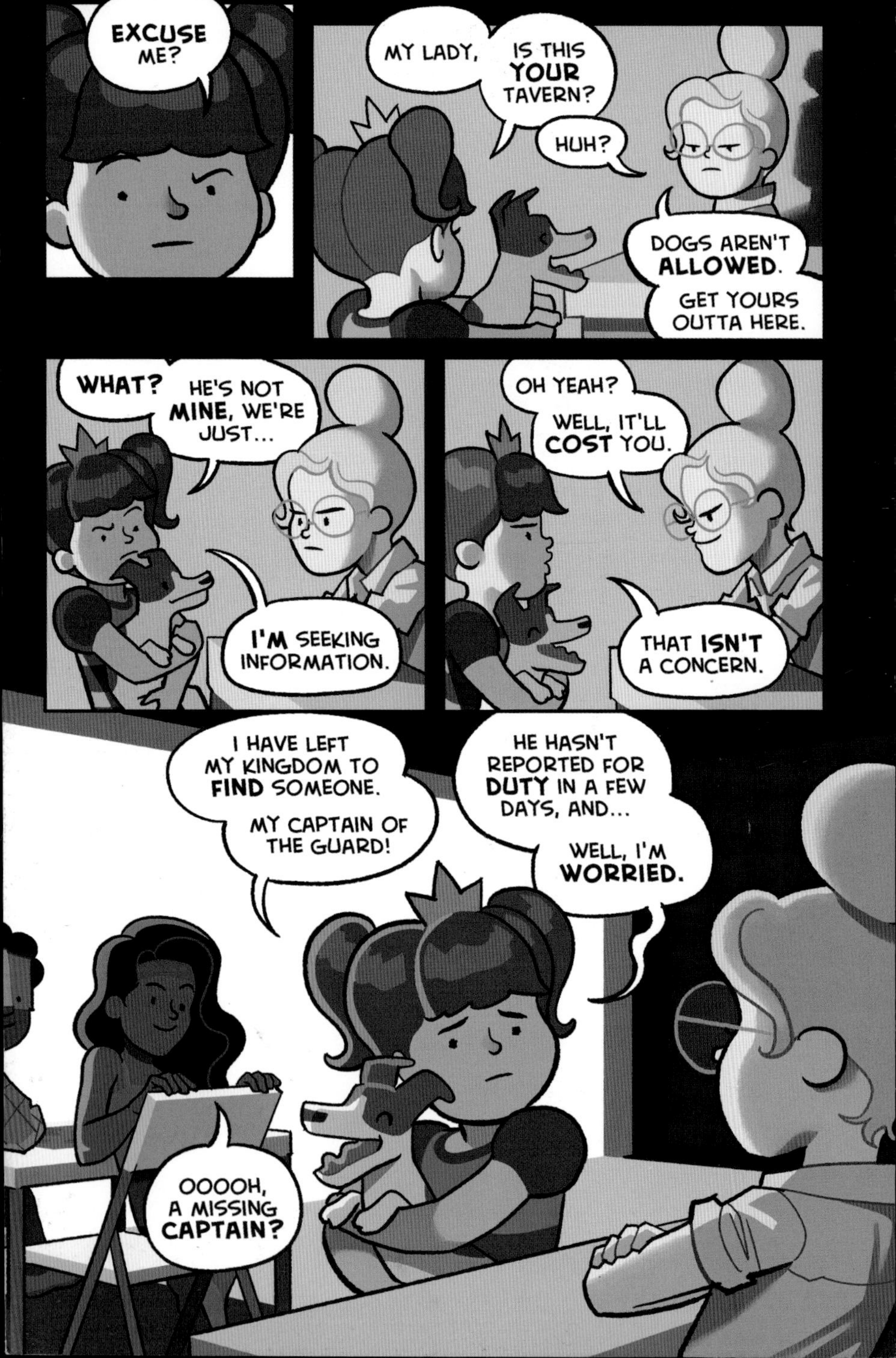
EXCUSE ME?
MY LADY,
IS THIS YOUR TAVERN?
HUH?
DOGS AREN'T ALLOWED.
GET YOURS OUTTA HERE.
WHAT?
HE'S NOT MINE, WE'RE JUST...
I'M SEEKING INFORMATION.
OH YEAH?
WELL, IT'LL COST YOU.
THAT ISN'T A CONCERN.
I HAVE LEFT MY KINGDOM TO FIND SOMEONE.
MY CAPTAIN OF THE GUARD!
HE HASN'T REPORTED FOR DUTY IN A FEW DAYS, AND...
WELL, I'M WORRIED.
OOOOH, A MISSING CAPTAIN?

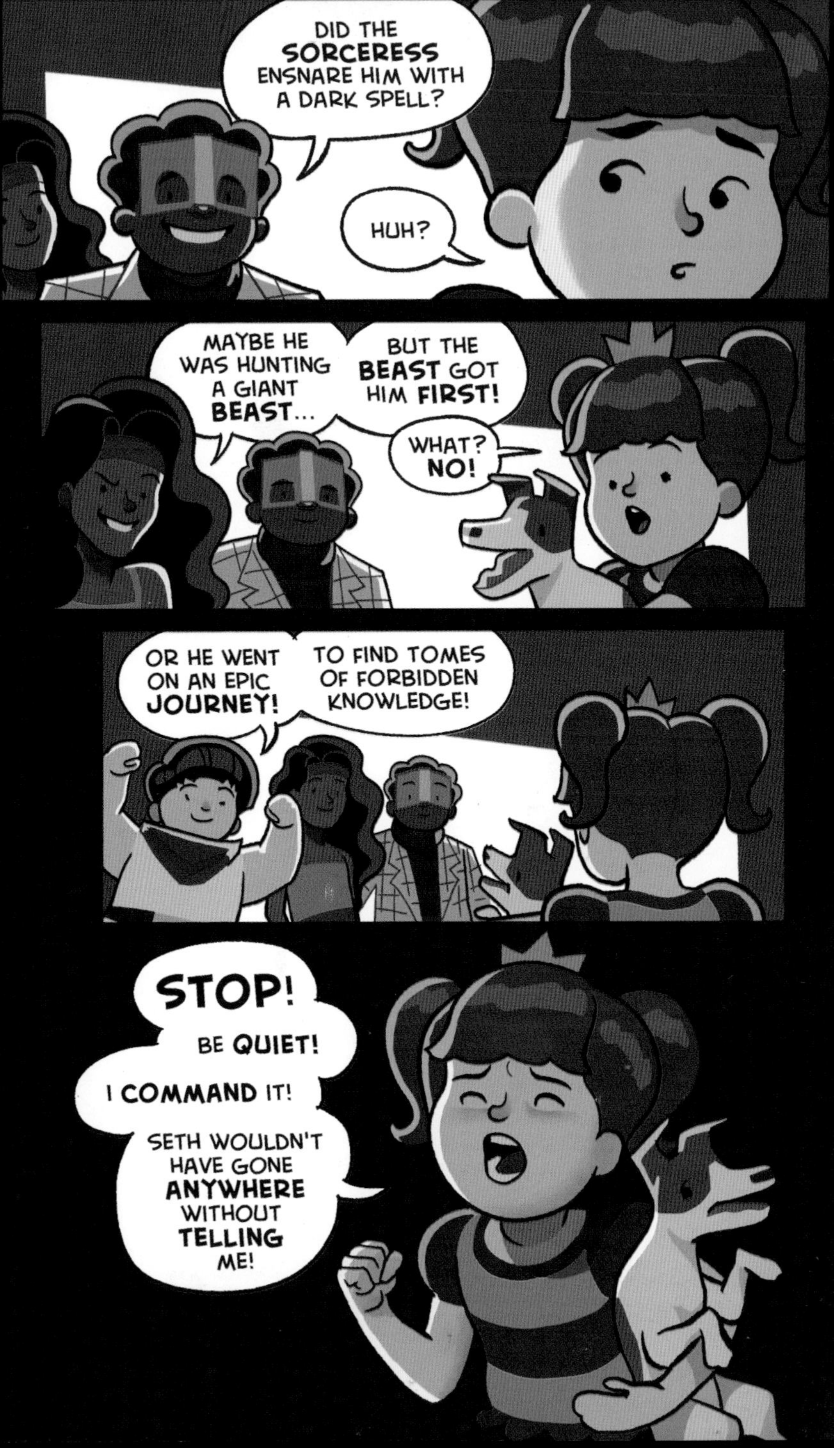
DID THE SORCERESS ENSNARE HIM WITH A DARK SPELL?
HUH?
MAYBE HE WAS HUNTING A GIANT BEAST...
BUT THE BEAST GOT HIM FIRST!
WHAT? NO!
OR HE WENT ON AN EPIC JOURNEY!
TO FIND TOMES OF FORBIDDEN KNOWLEDGE!
STOP!
BE QUIET!
I COMMAND IT!
SETH WOULDN'T HAVE GONE ANYWHERE WITHOUT TELLING ME!

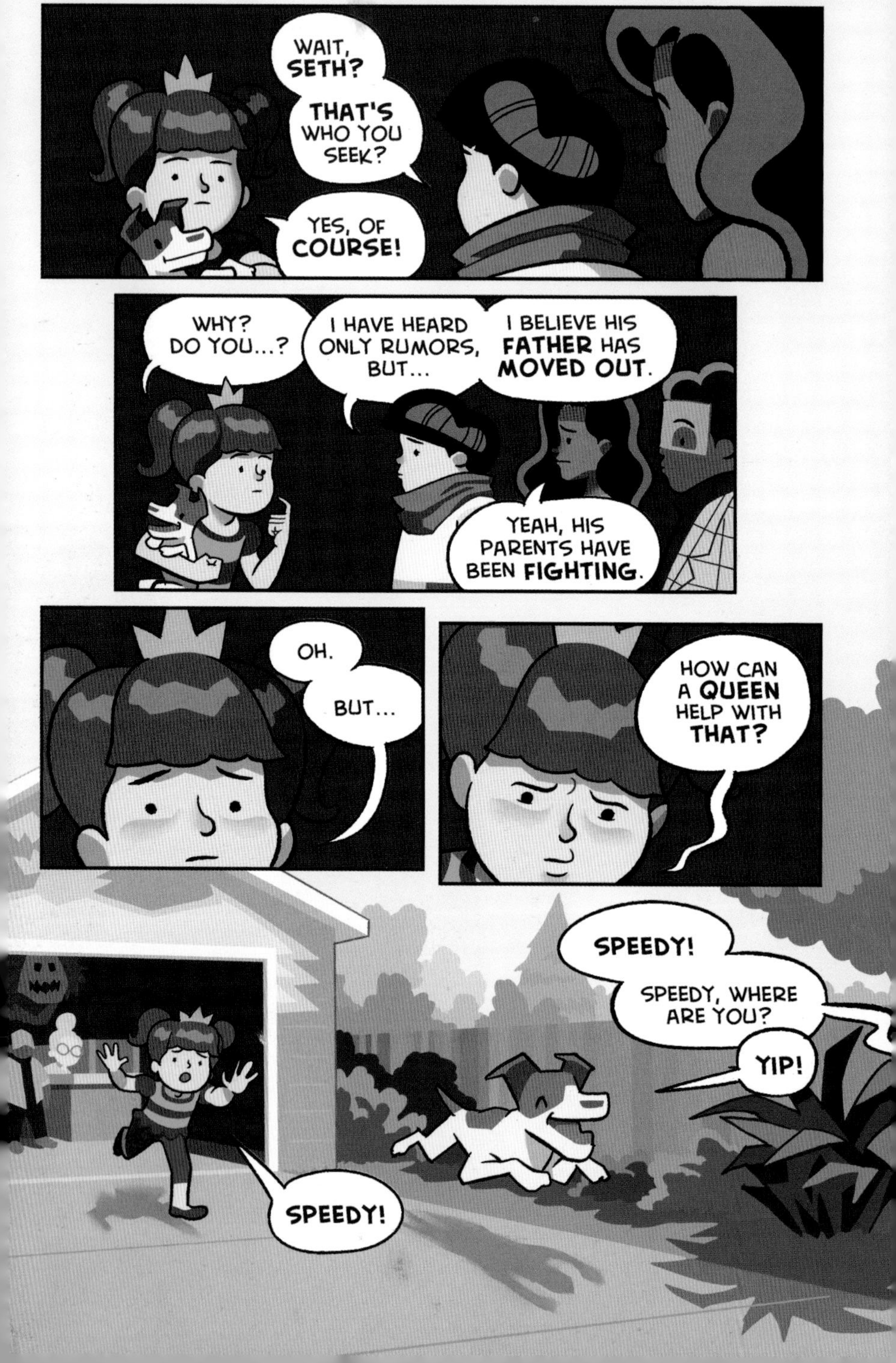
WAIT, SETH?
THAT'S WHO YOU SEEK?
YES, OF COURSE!
WHY? DO YOU...?
I HAVE HEARD ONLY RUMORS, BUT...
I BELIEVE HIS FATHER HAS MOVED OUT.
YEAH, HIS PARENTS HAVE BEEN FIGHTING.
OH.
BUT...
HOW CAN A QUEEN HELP WITH THAT?
SPEEDY!
SPEEDY, WHERE ARE YOU?
YIP!
SPEEDY!

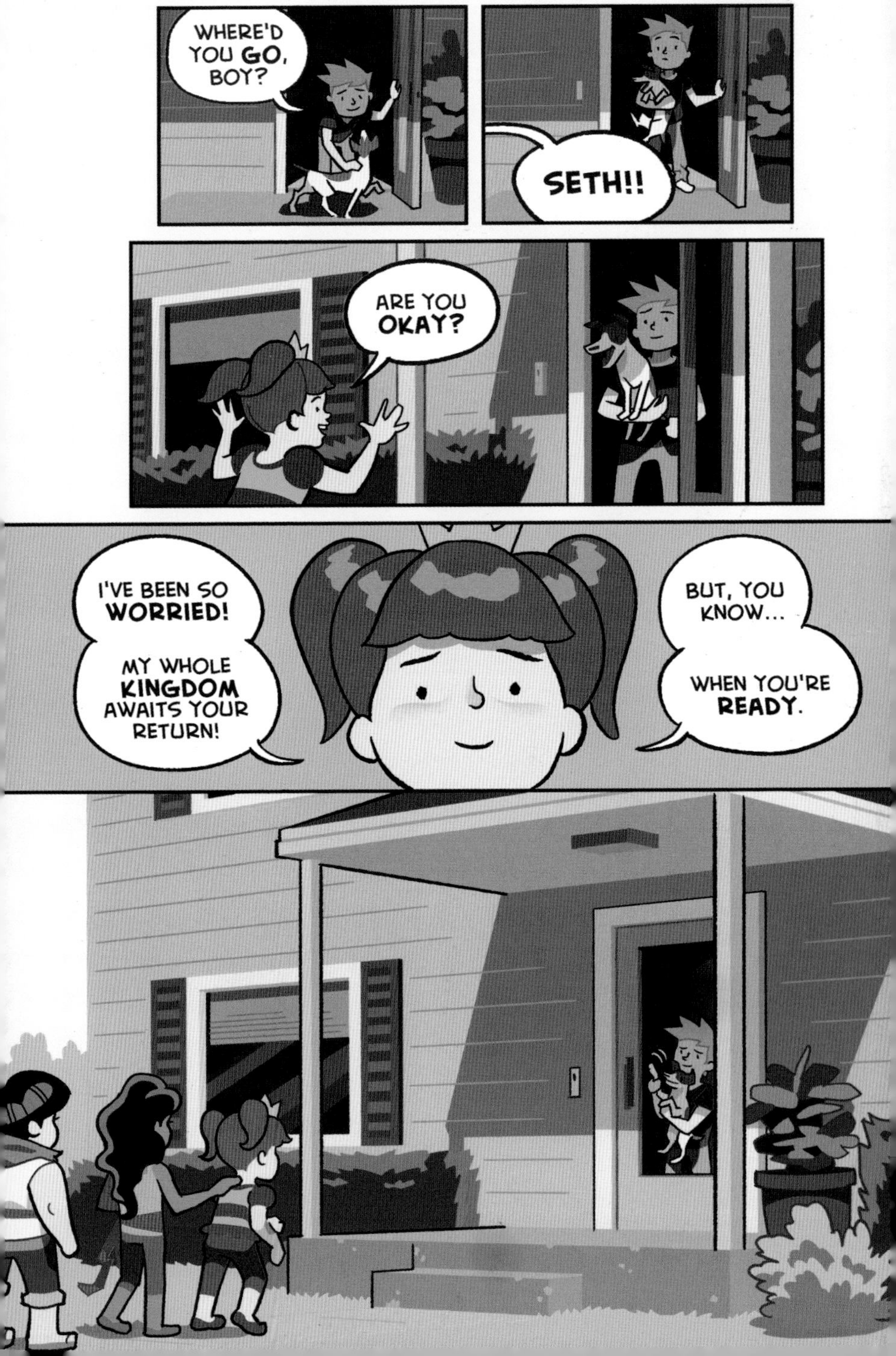
WHERE'D YOU GO, BOY?
SETH!!
ARE YOU OKAY?
I'VE BEEN SO WORRIED!
MY WHOLE KINGDOM AWAITS YOUR RETURN!
BUT, YOU KNOW...
WHEN YOU'RE READY.

THE
GARGOYLE

BY MICHAEL COLE AND CHAD SELL

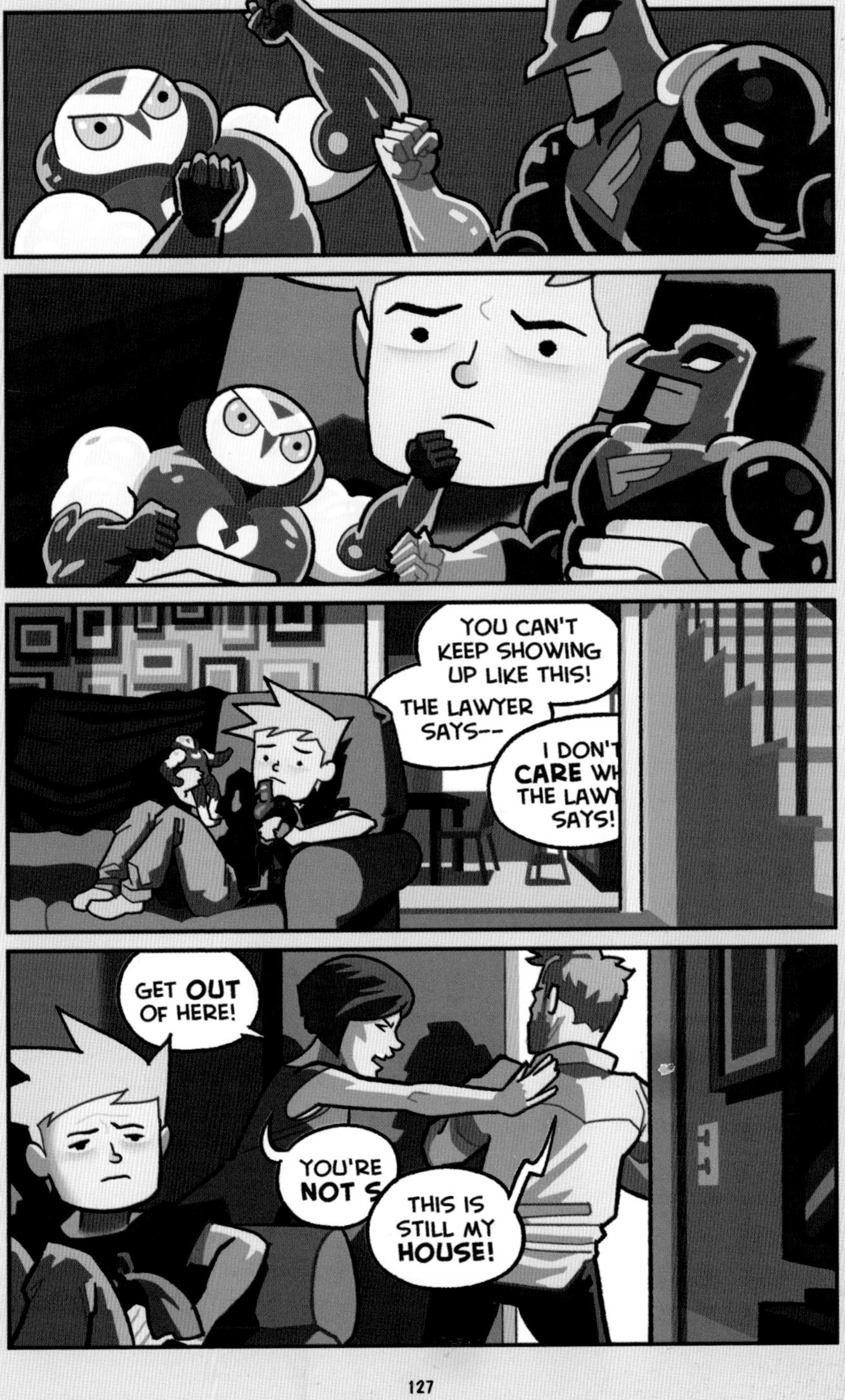
YOU CAN'T KEEP SHOWING UP LIKE THIS!
THE LAWYER SAYS--
I DON'T CARE WH THE LAWY SAYS!
GET OUT OF HERE!
YOU'RE NOT S
THIS IS STILL MY HOUSE!

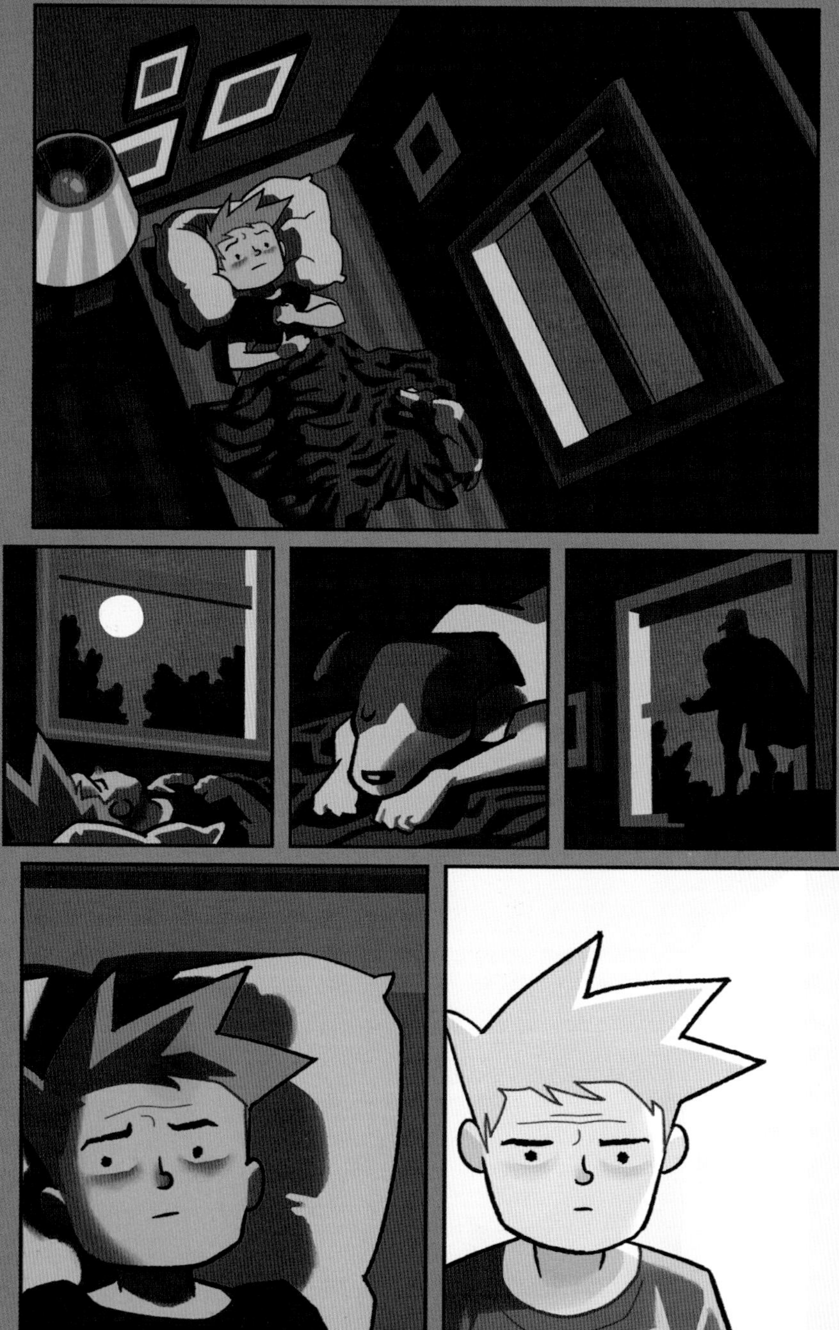

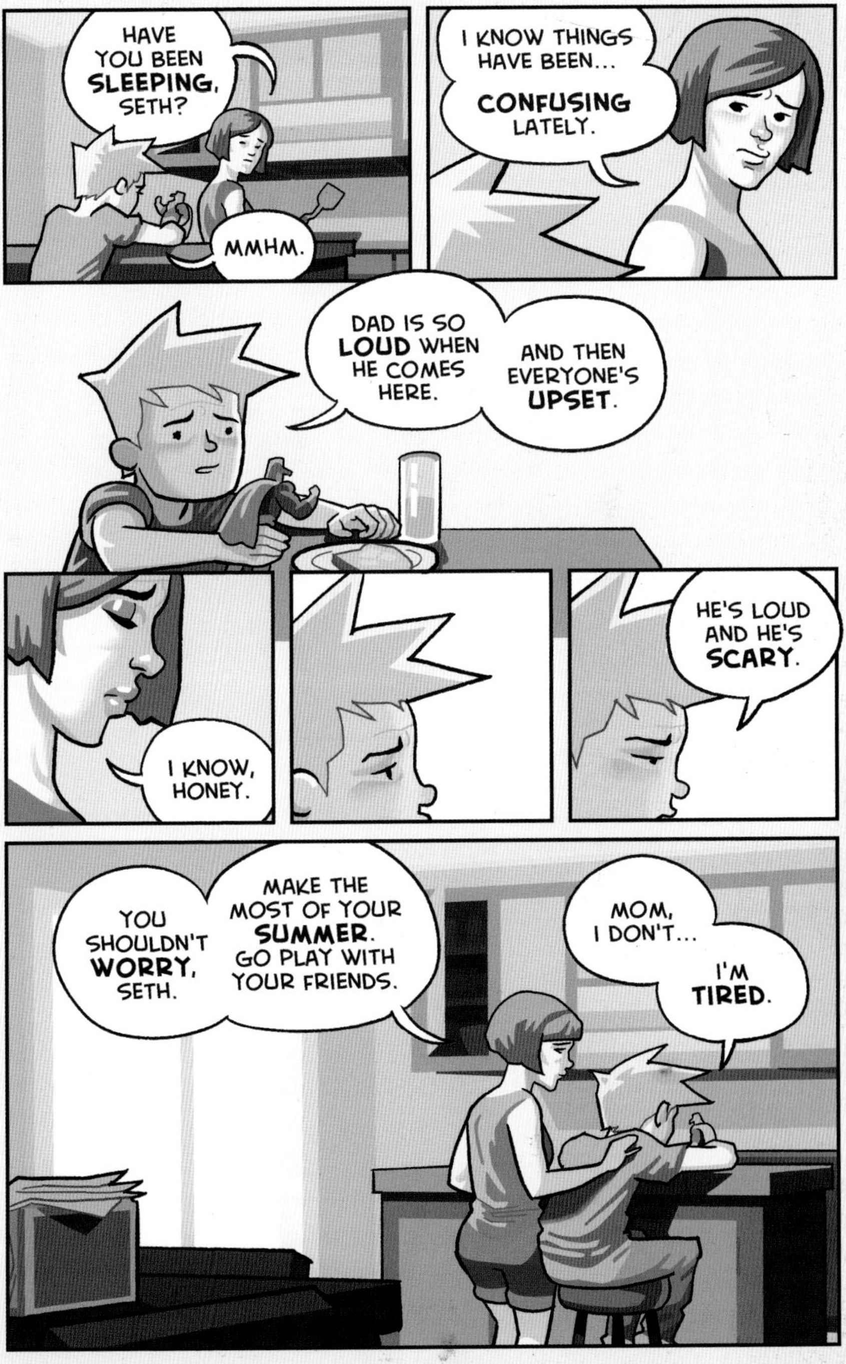
HAVE YOU BEEN SLEEPING, SETH?
MMHM.
I KNOW THINGS HAVE BEEN...
CONFUSING LATELY.
DAD IS SO LOUD WHEN HE COMES HERE.
AND THEN EVERYONE'S UPSET.
I KNOW, HONEY.
HE'S LOUD AND HE'S SCARY.
YOU SHOULDN'T WORRY, SETH.
MAKE THE MOST OF YOUR SUMMER. GO PLAY WITH YOUR FRIENDS.
MOM, I DON'T...
I'M TIRED.

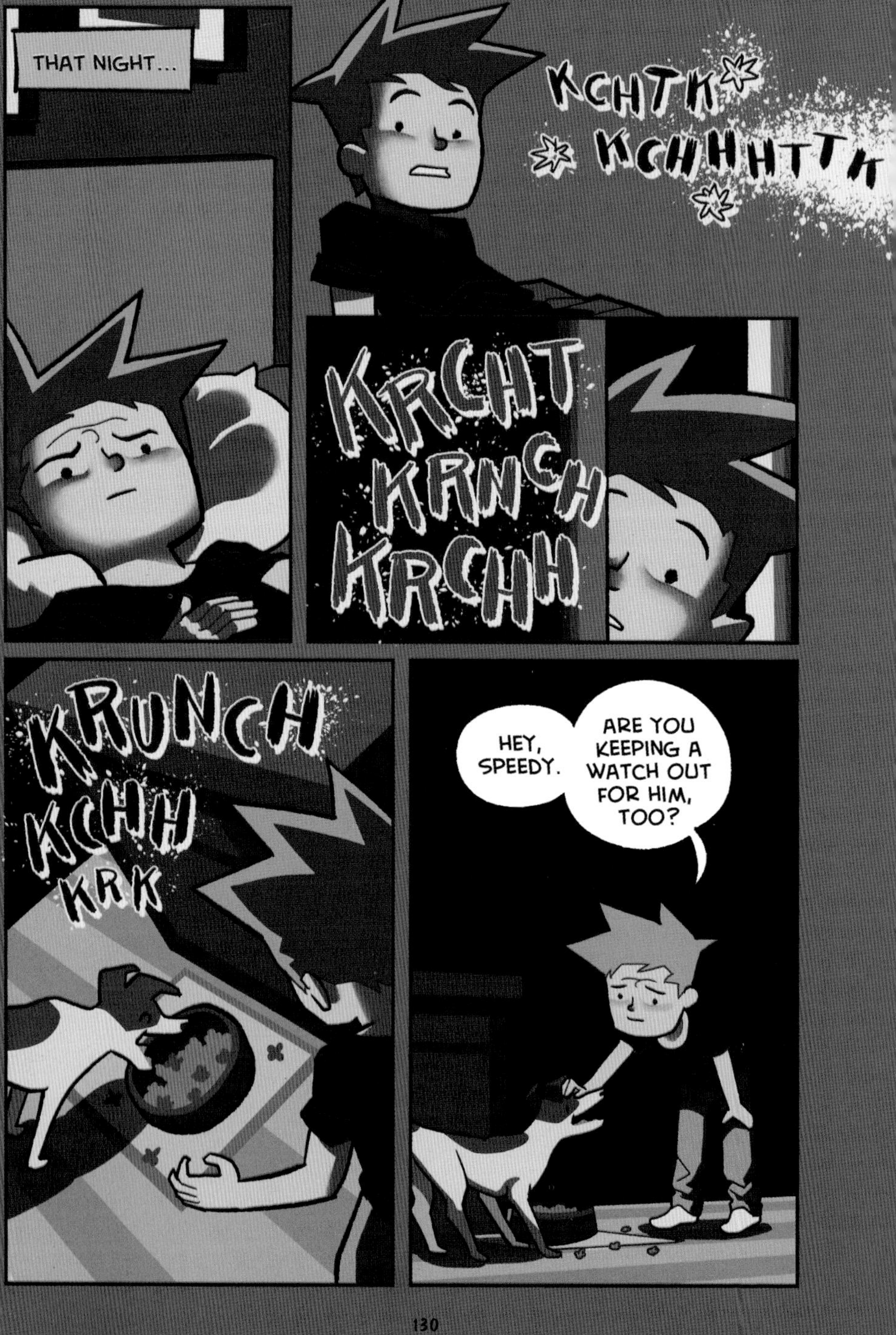
THAT NIGHT...
KCHTK
KCHHHTTK
KRCHT
KRNCH
KRCHH
KRUNCH
KCHH
KRK
HEY, SPEEDY.
ARE YOU KEEPING A WATCH OUT FOR HIM, TOO?

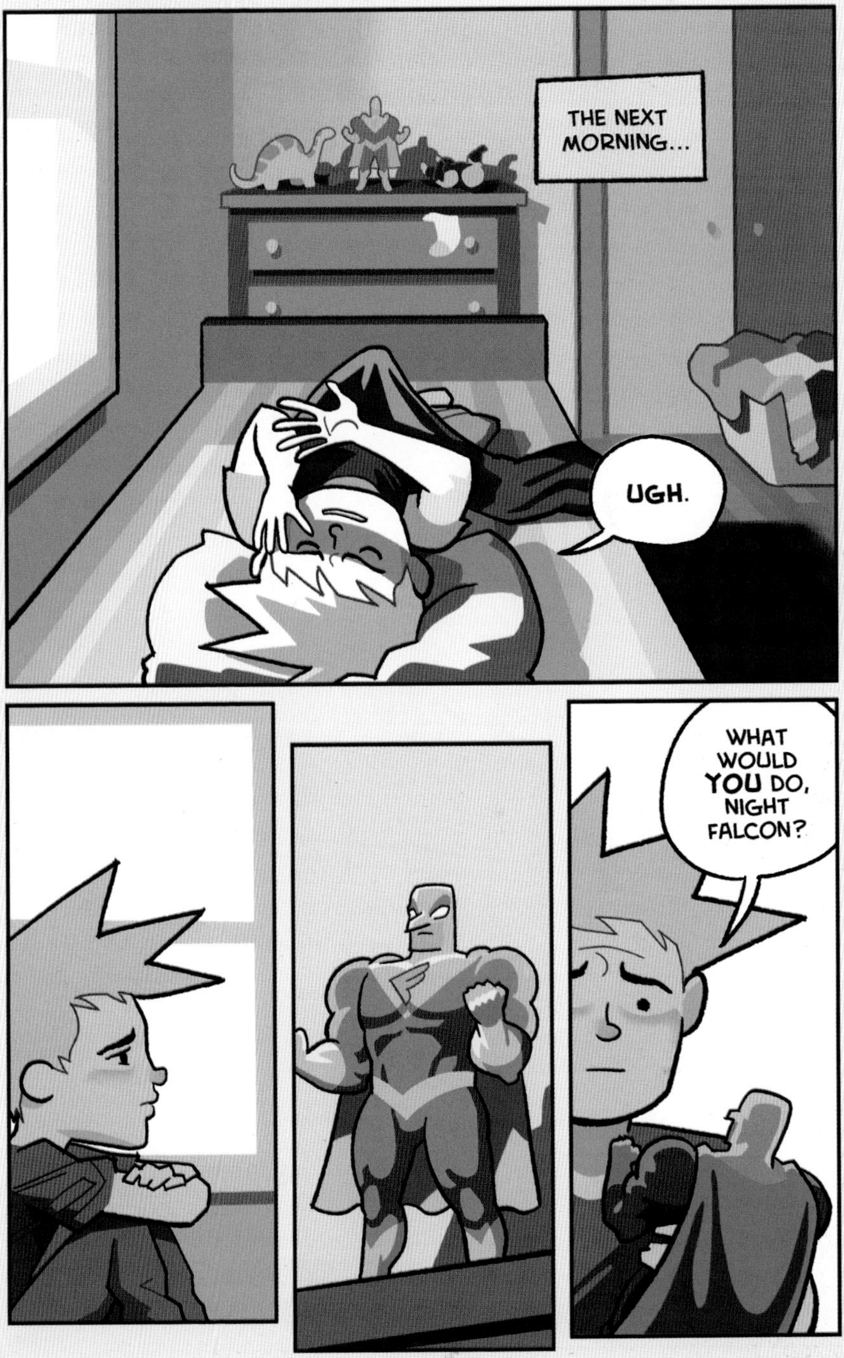
THE NEXT MORNING...
UGH.
WHAT WOULD YOU DO, NIGHT FALCON?

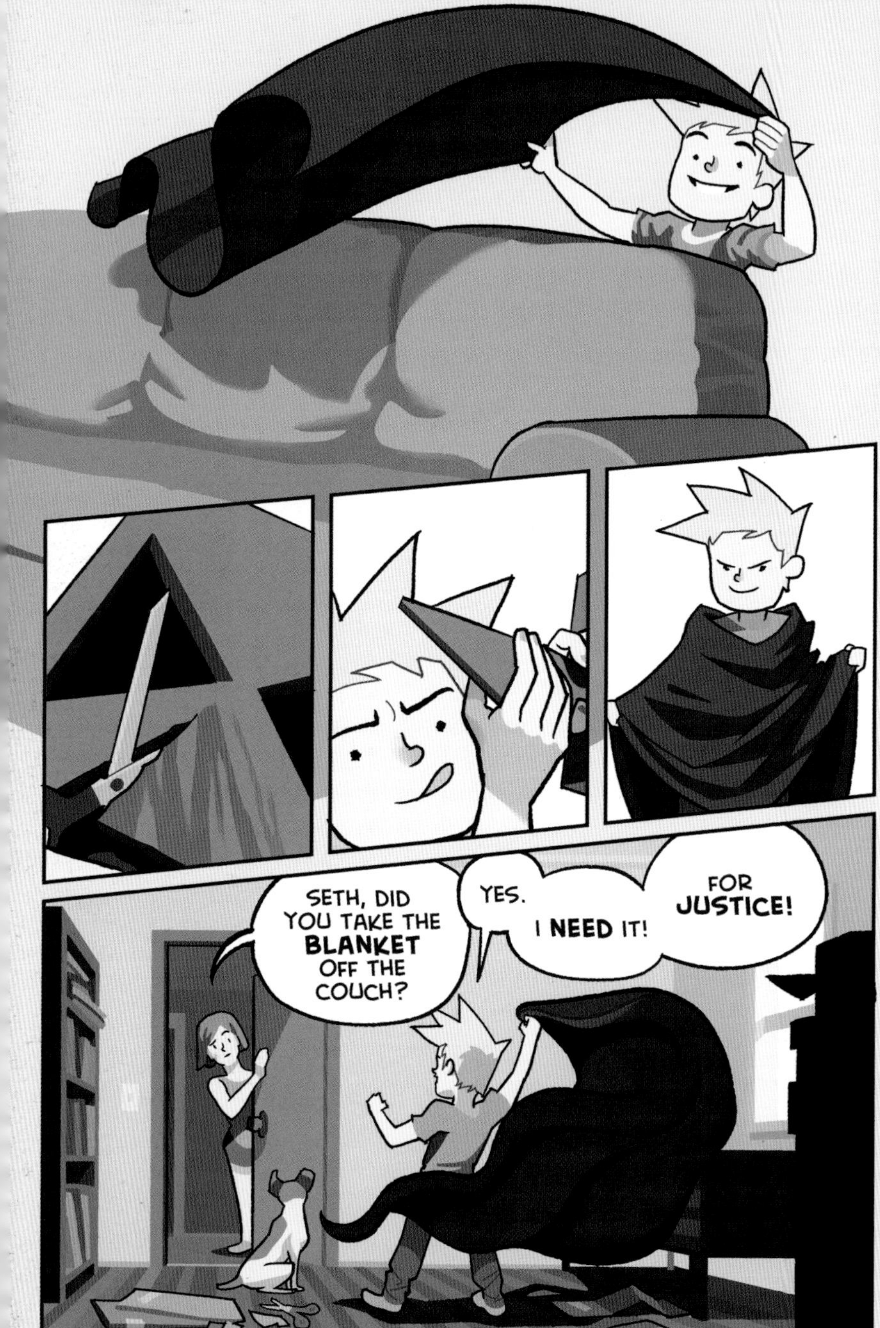
SETH, DID YOU TAKE THE **BLANKET** OFF THE COUCH?
YES.
I **NEED** IT!
FOR **JUSTICE!**

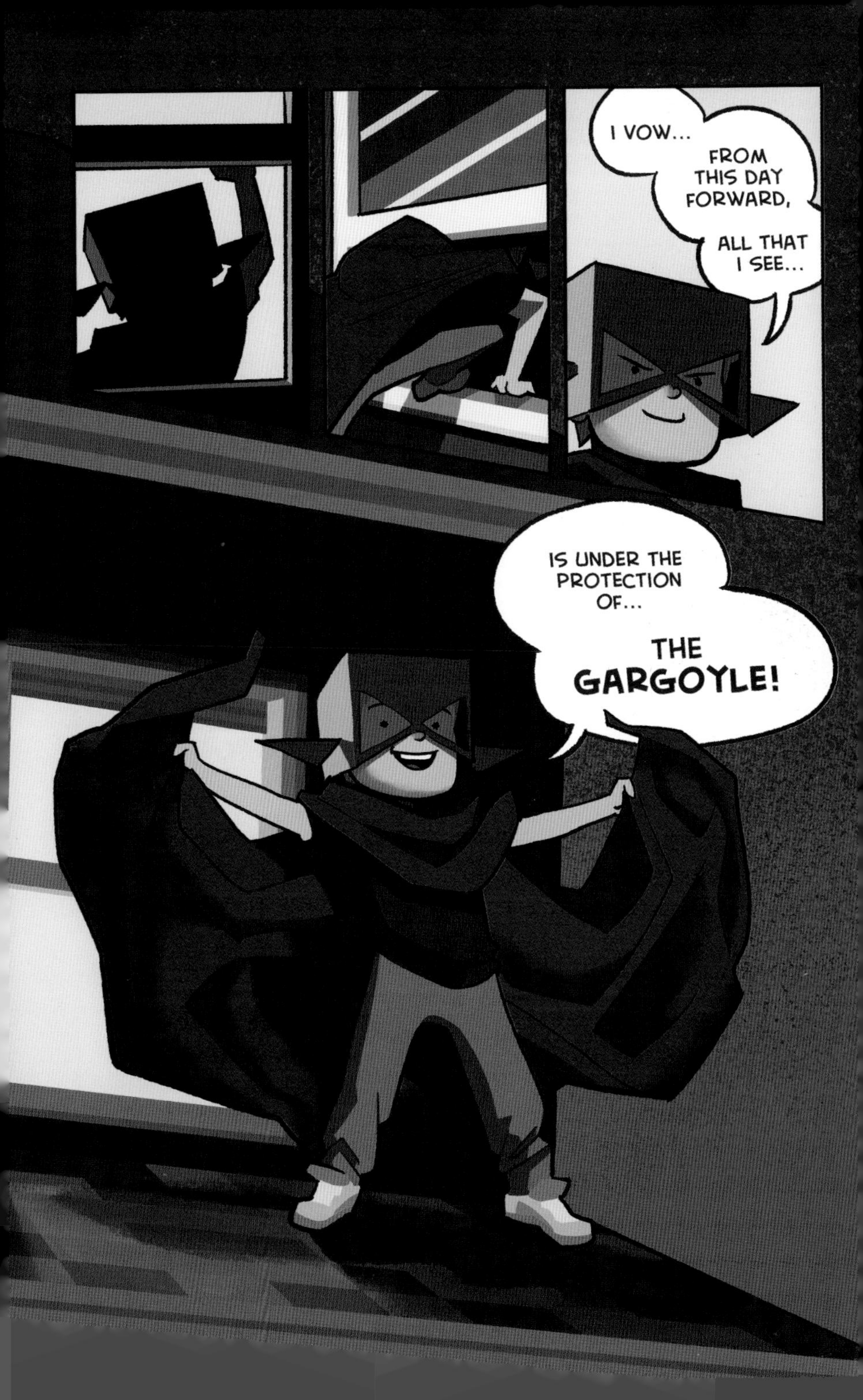
I VOW...
FROM THIS DAY FORWARD,
ALL THAT I SEE...
IS UNDER THE PROTECTION OF...
THE GARGOYLE!

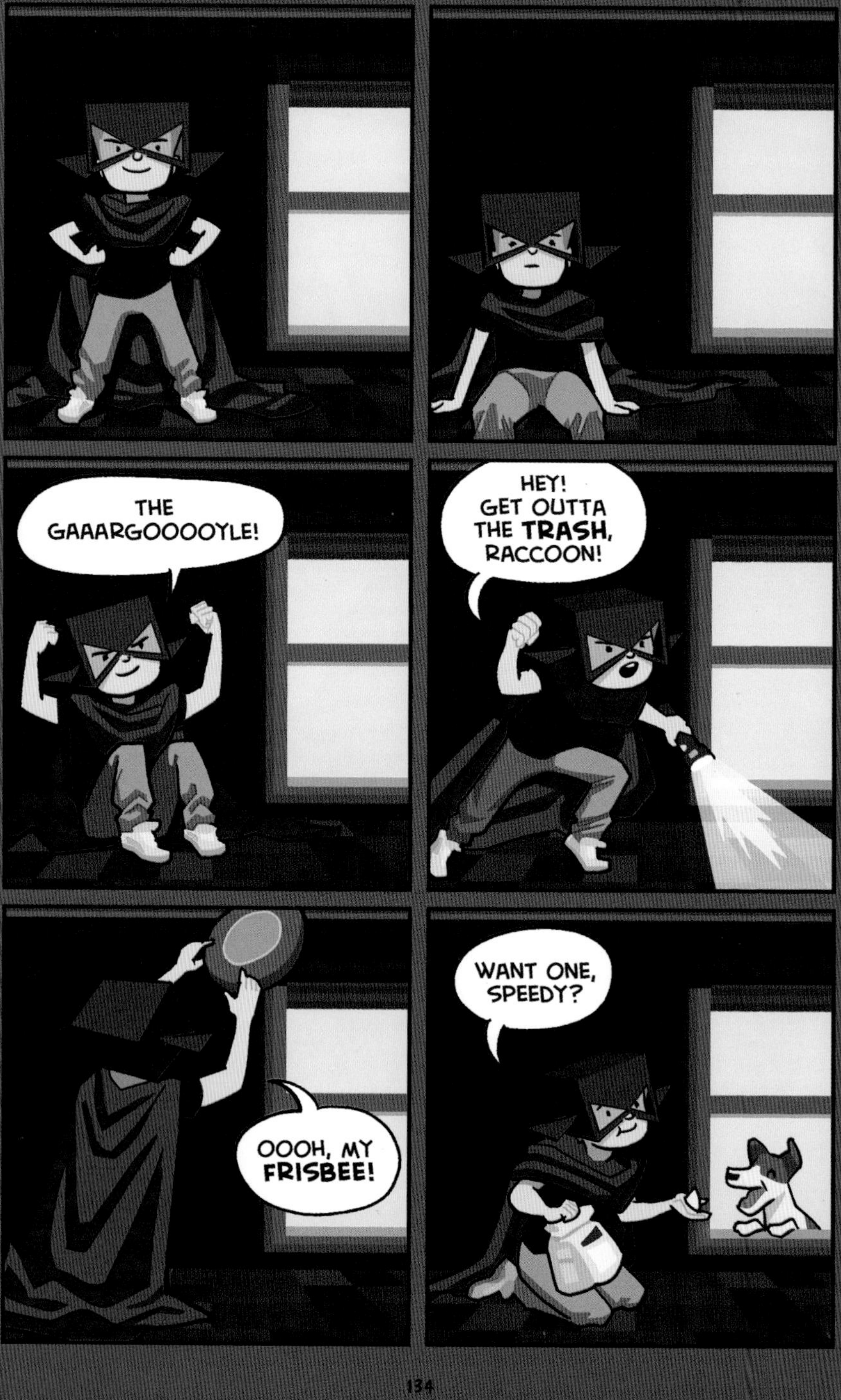
THE GAAARGOOOOYLE!
HEY! GET OUTTA THE **TRASH**, RACCOON!
OOOH, MY **FRISBEE**!
WANT ONE, SPEEDY?

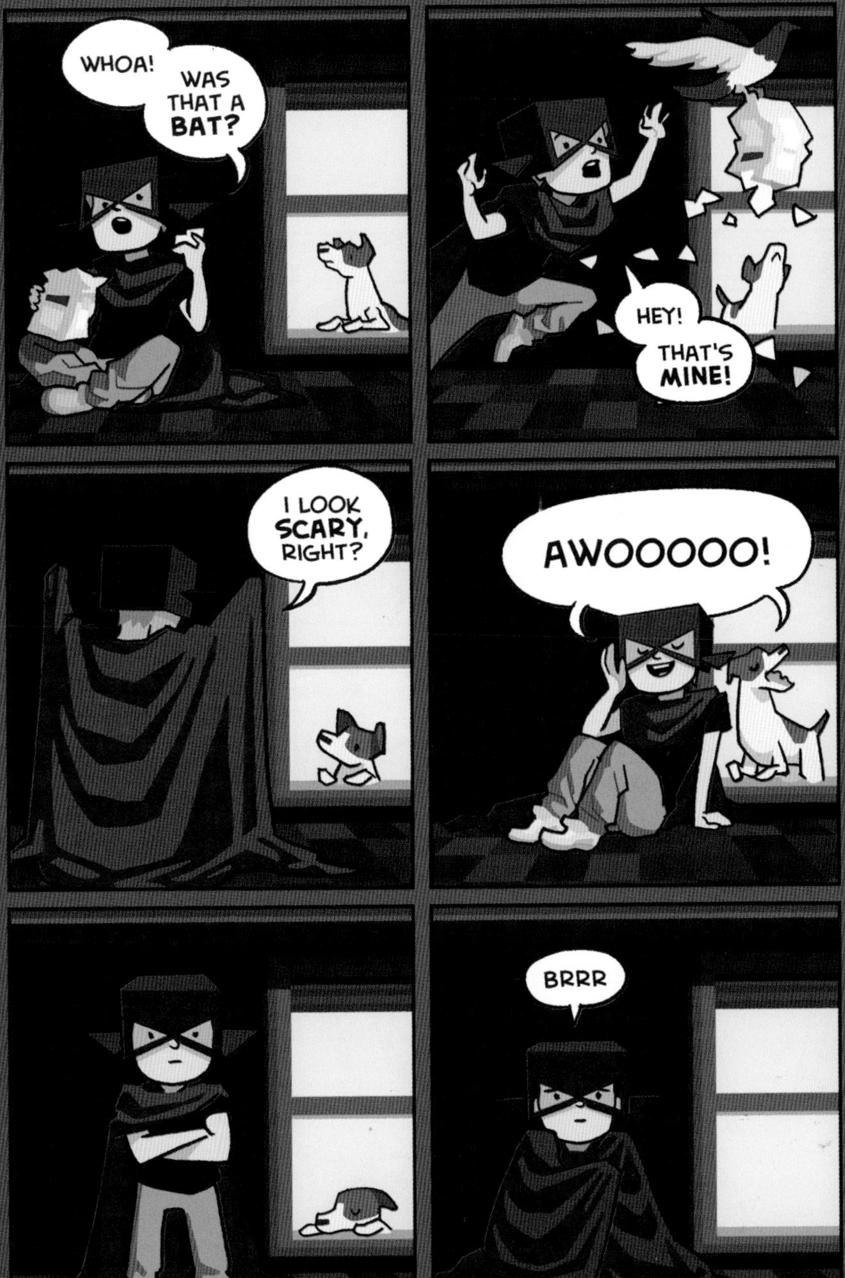
WHOA!
WAS THAT A BAT?
HEY!
THAT'S MINE!
I LOOK SCARY, RIGHT?
AWOOOOO!
BRRR

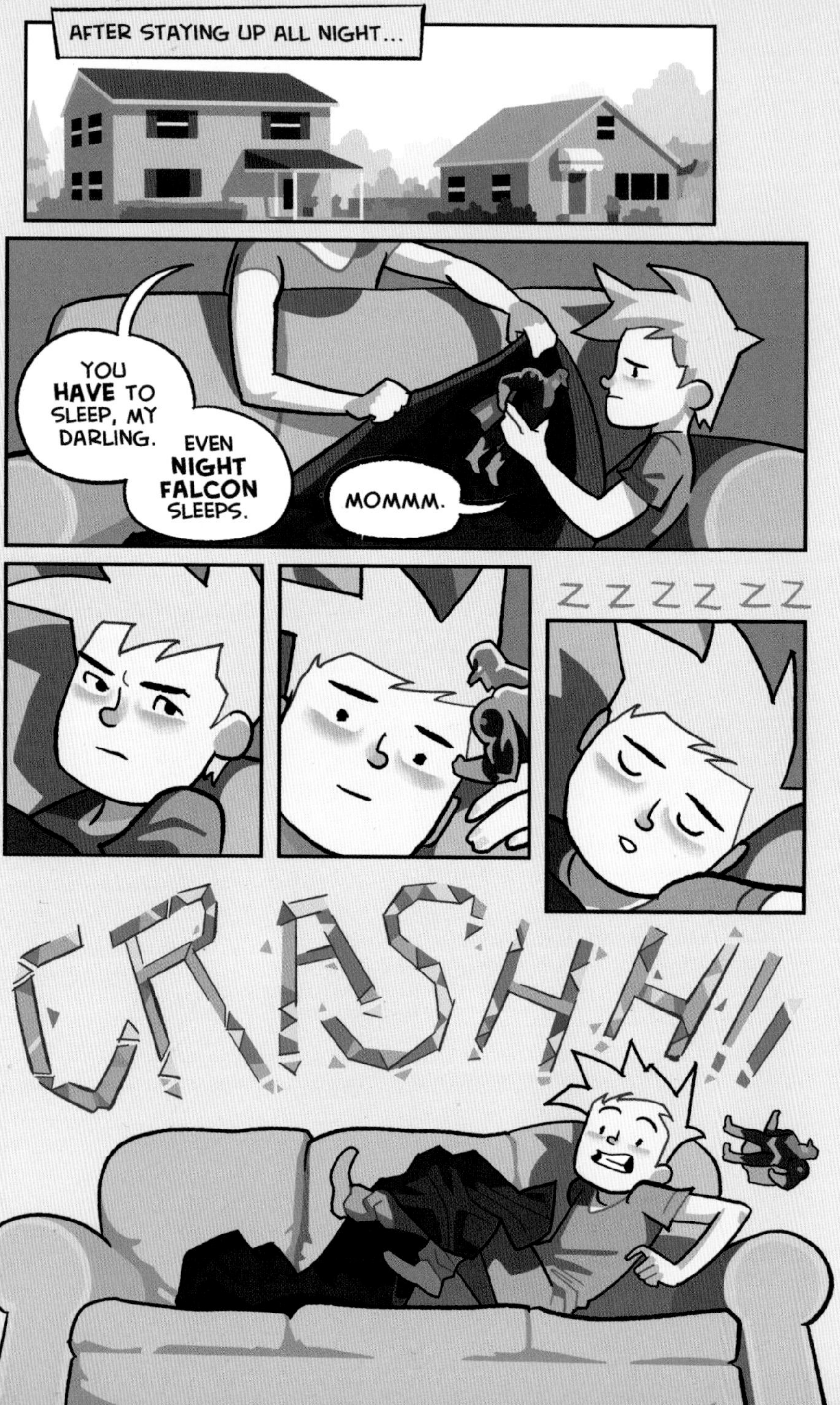
AFTER STAYING UP ALL NIGHT...
YOU **HAVE** TO SLEEP, MY DARLING.
EVEN **NIGHT FALCON** SLEEPS.
MOMMM.
ZZZZZZ
CRASH!!

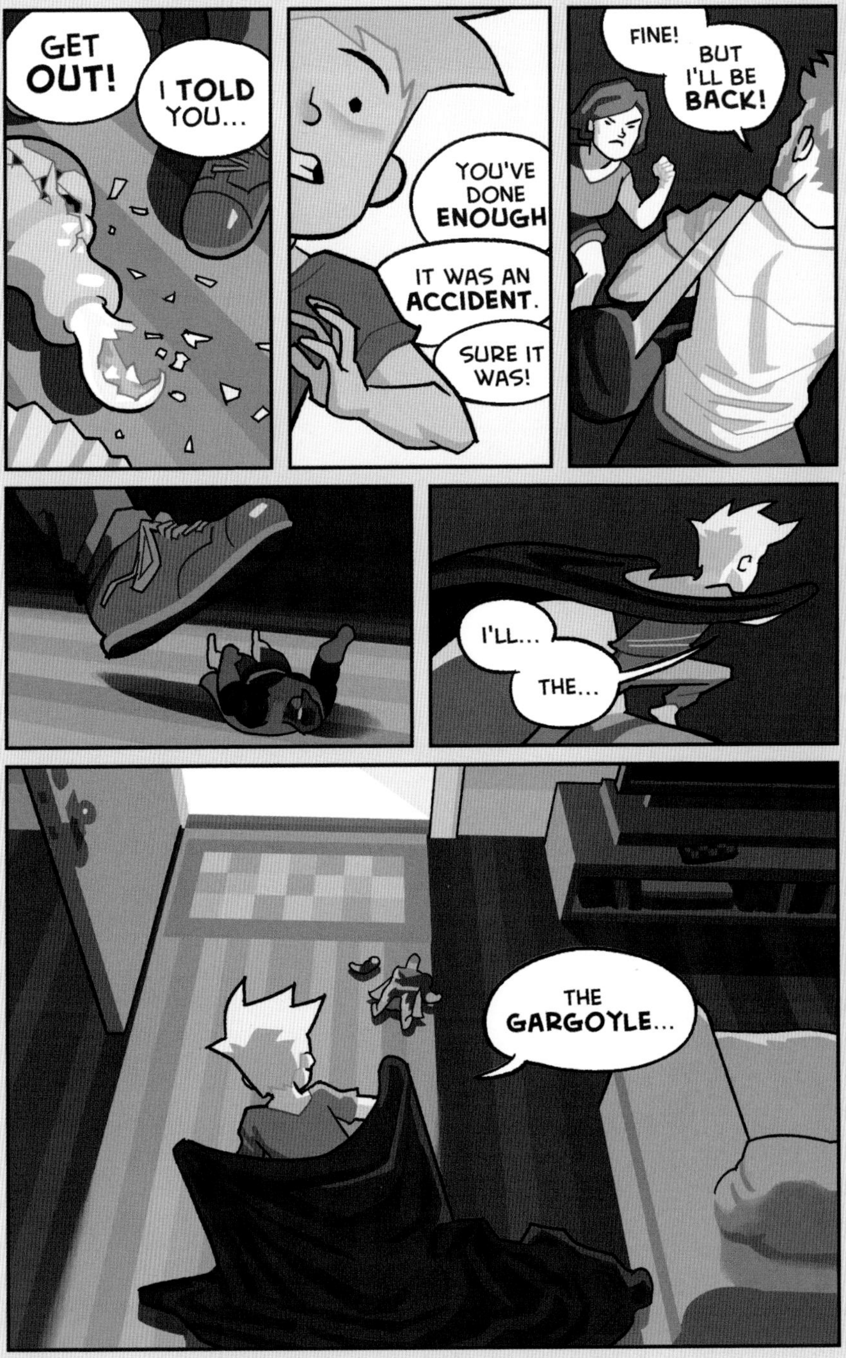
GET OUT!
I TOLD YOU...
YOU'VE DONE ENOUGH
IT WAS AN ACCIDENT.
SURE IT WAS!
FINE! BUT I'LL BE BACK!
I'LL...
THE...
THE GARGOYLE...

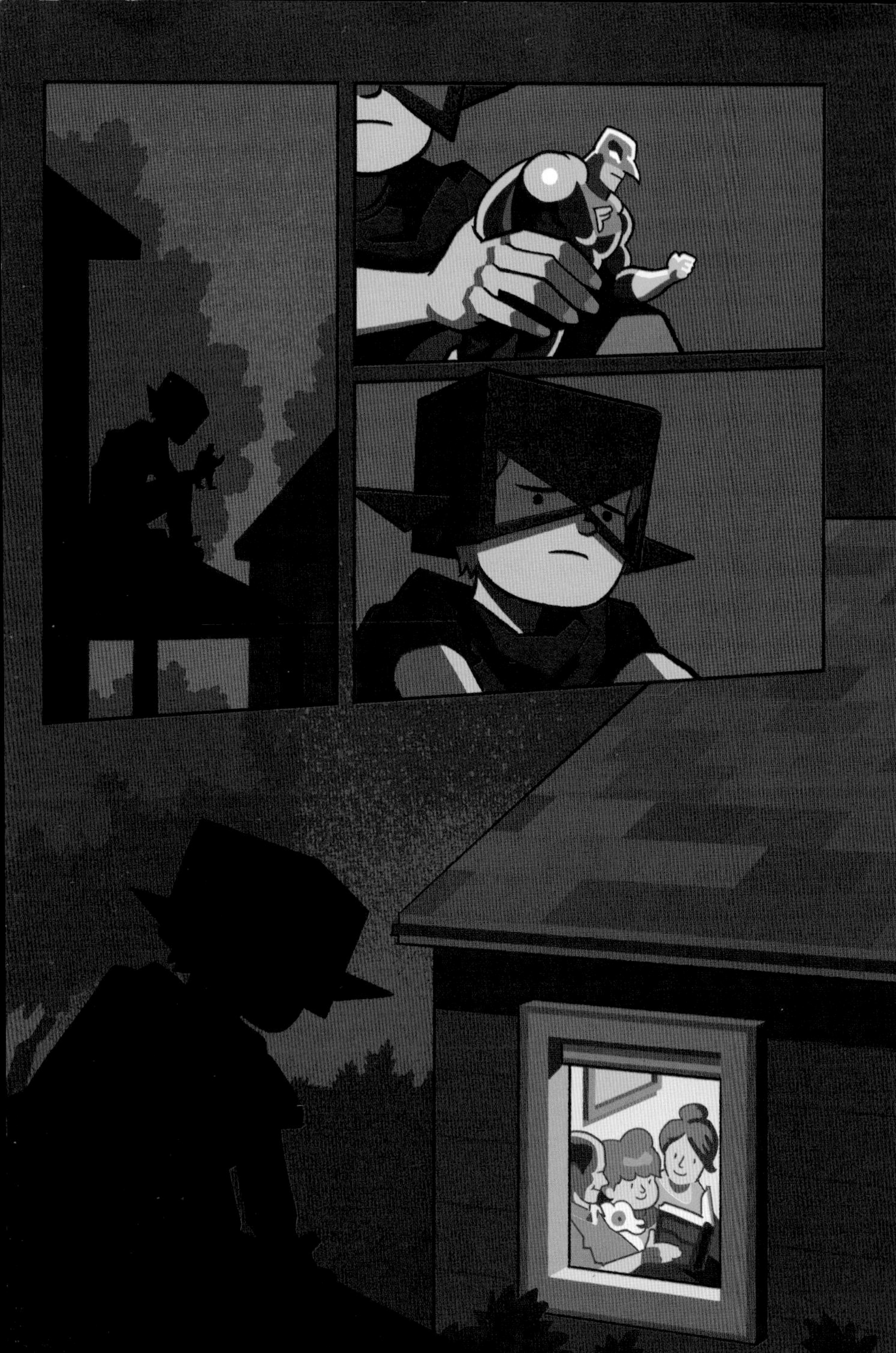

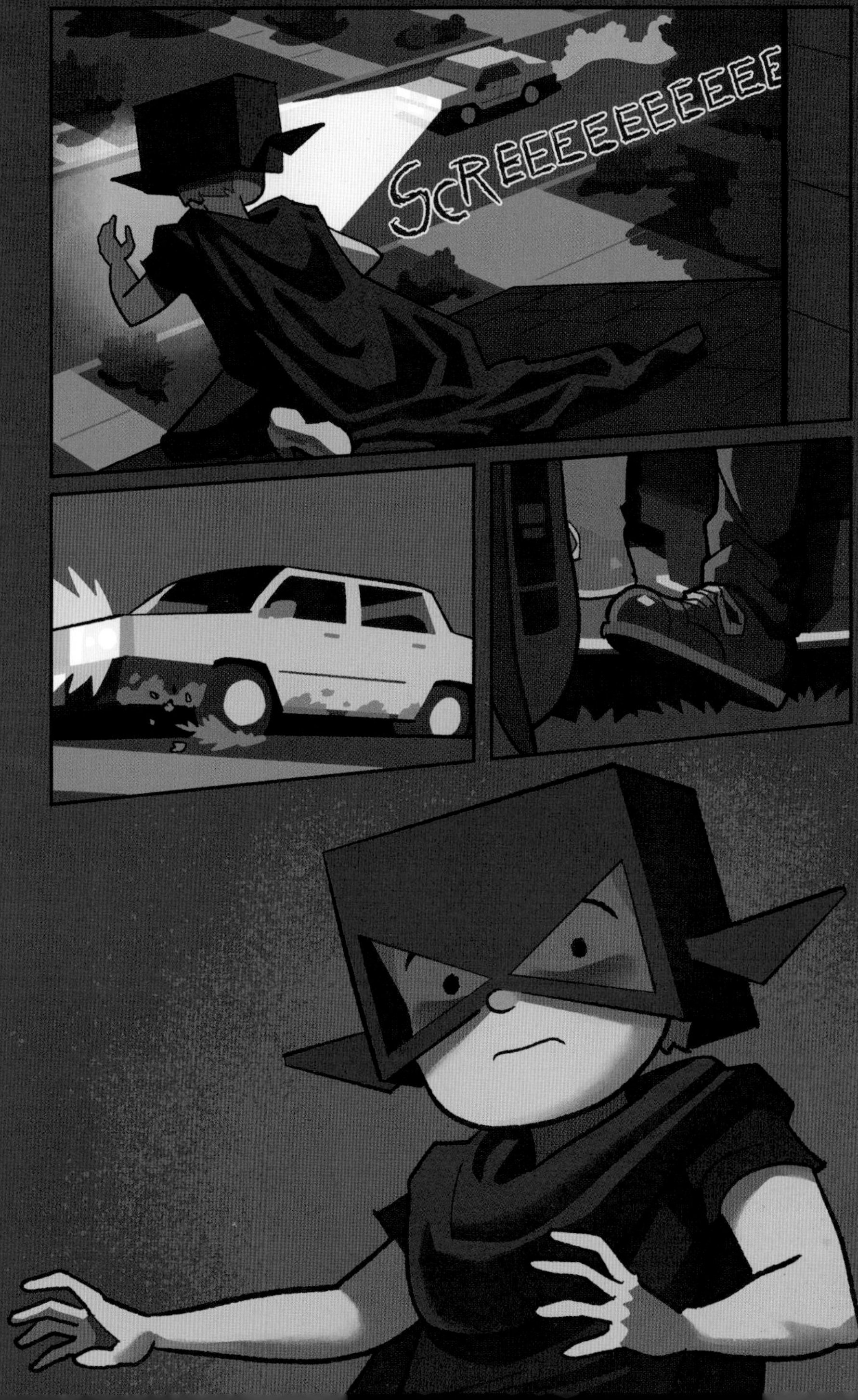
SCREEEEEEEEEEEE

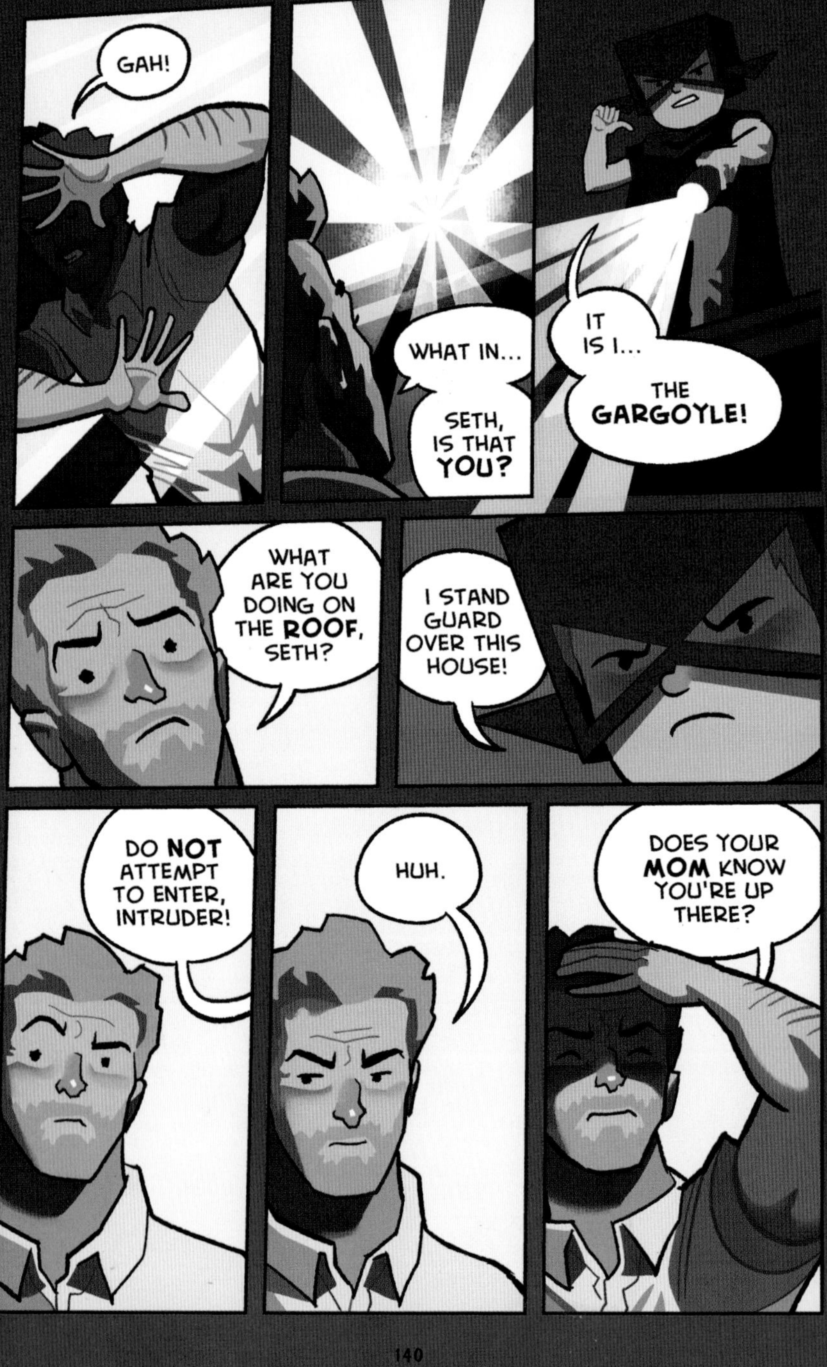
GAH!
WHAT IN...
SETH, IS THAT YOU?
IT IS I...
THE GARGOYLE!
WHAT ARE YOU DOING ON THE ROOF, SETH?
I STAND GUARD OVER THIS HOUSE!
DO NOT ATTEMPT TO ENTER, INTRUDER!
HUH.
DOES YOUR MOM KNOW YOU'RE UP THERE?

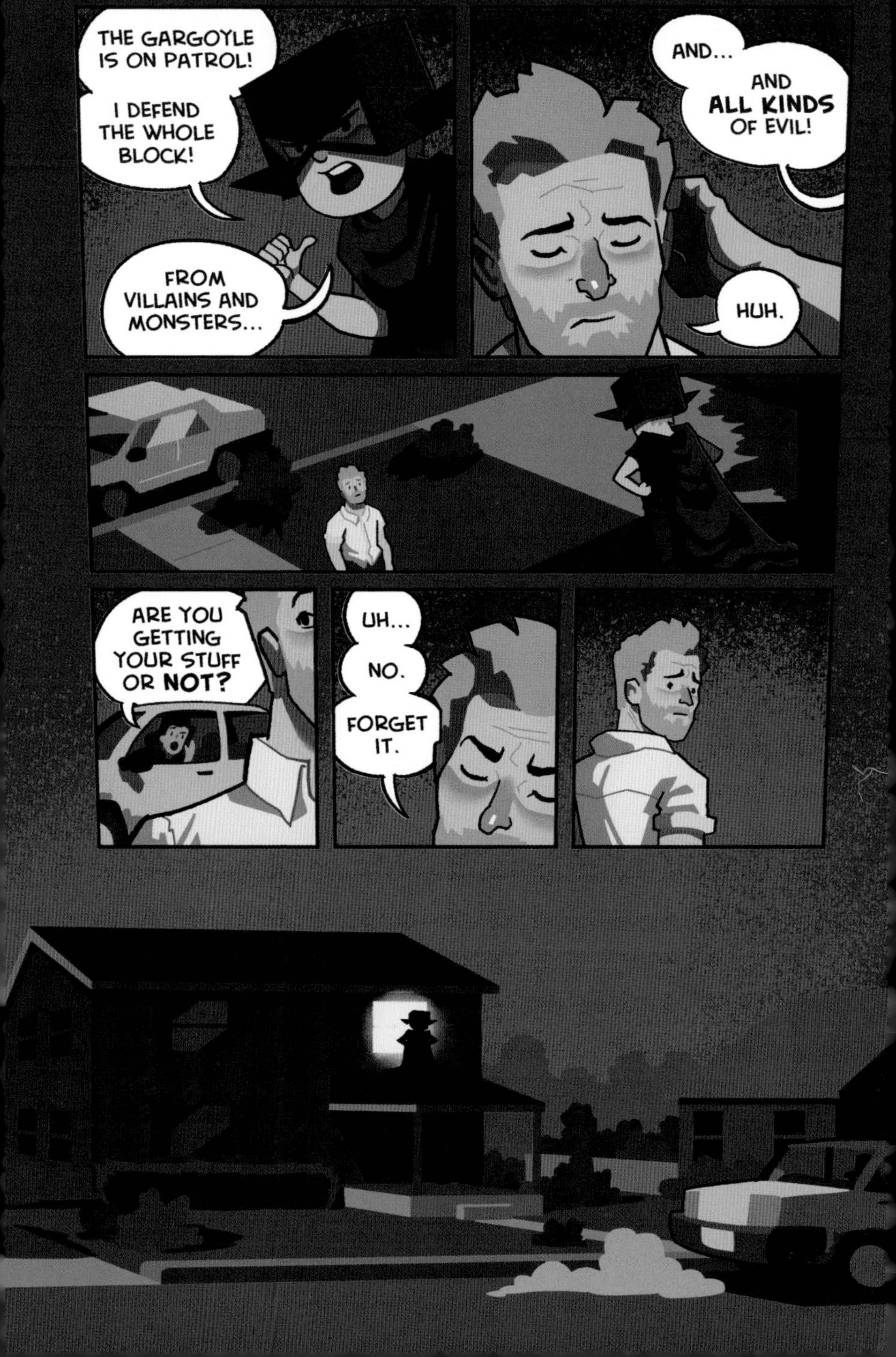
THE GARGOYLE IS ON PATROL!
I DEFEND THE WHOLE BLOCK!
FROM VILLAINS AND MONSTERS...
AND...
AND **ALL KINDS** OF EVIL!
HUH.
ARE YOU GETTING YOUR STUFF OR **NOT?**
UH...
NO.
FORGET IT.

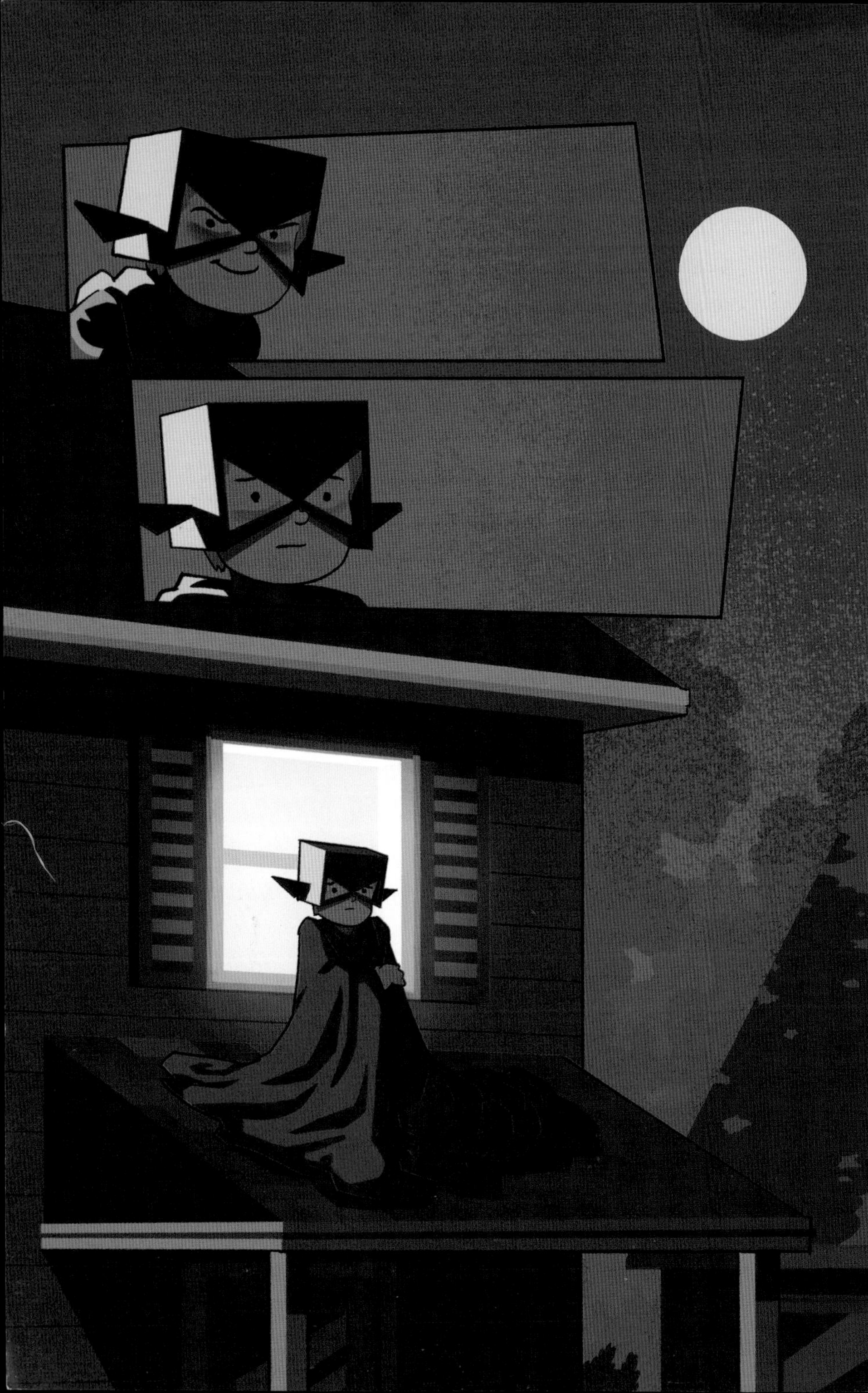

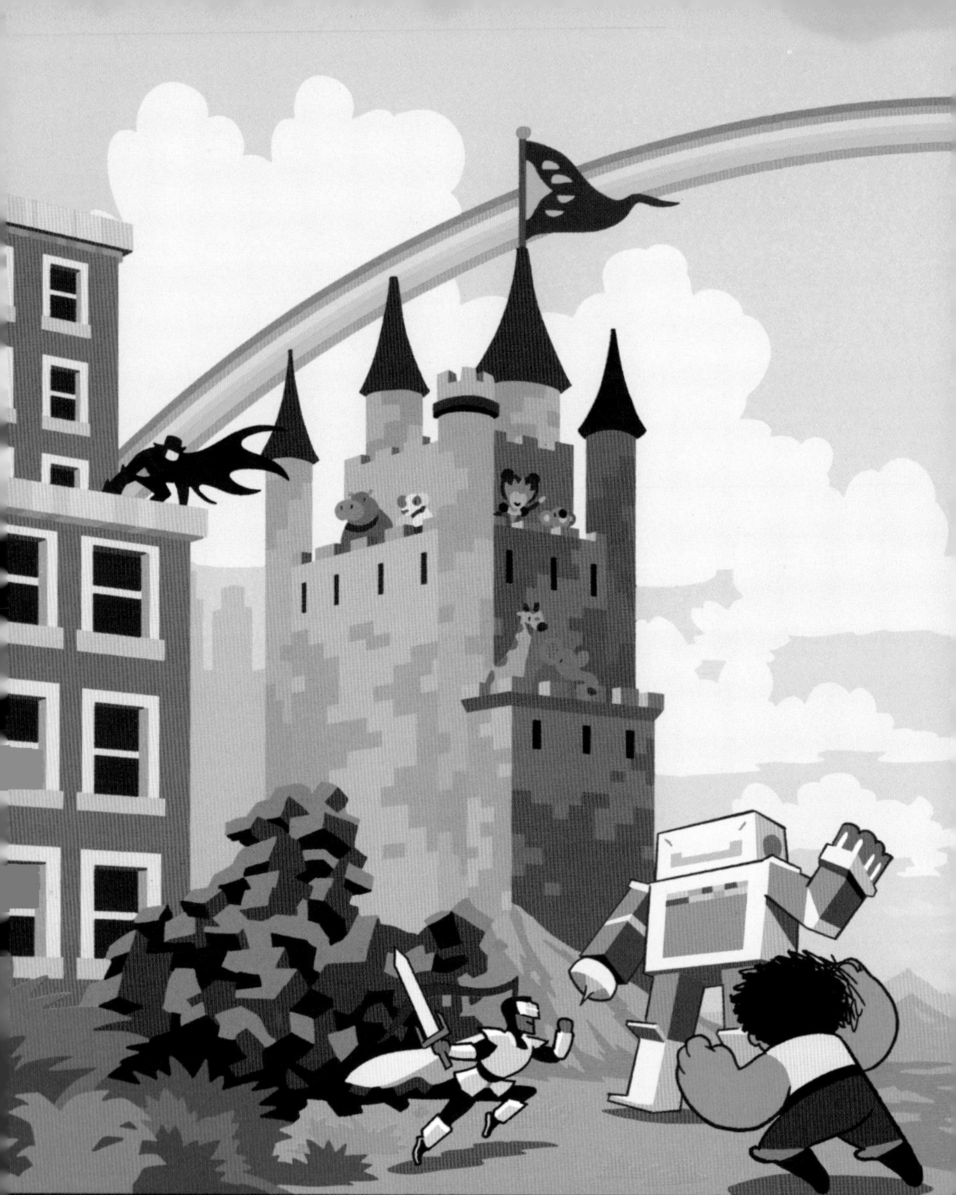

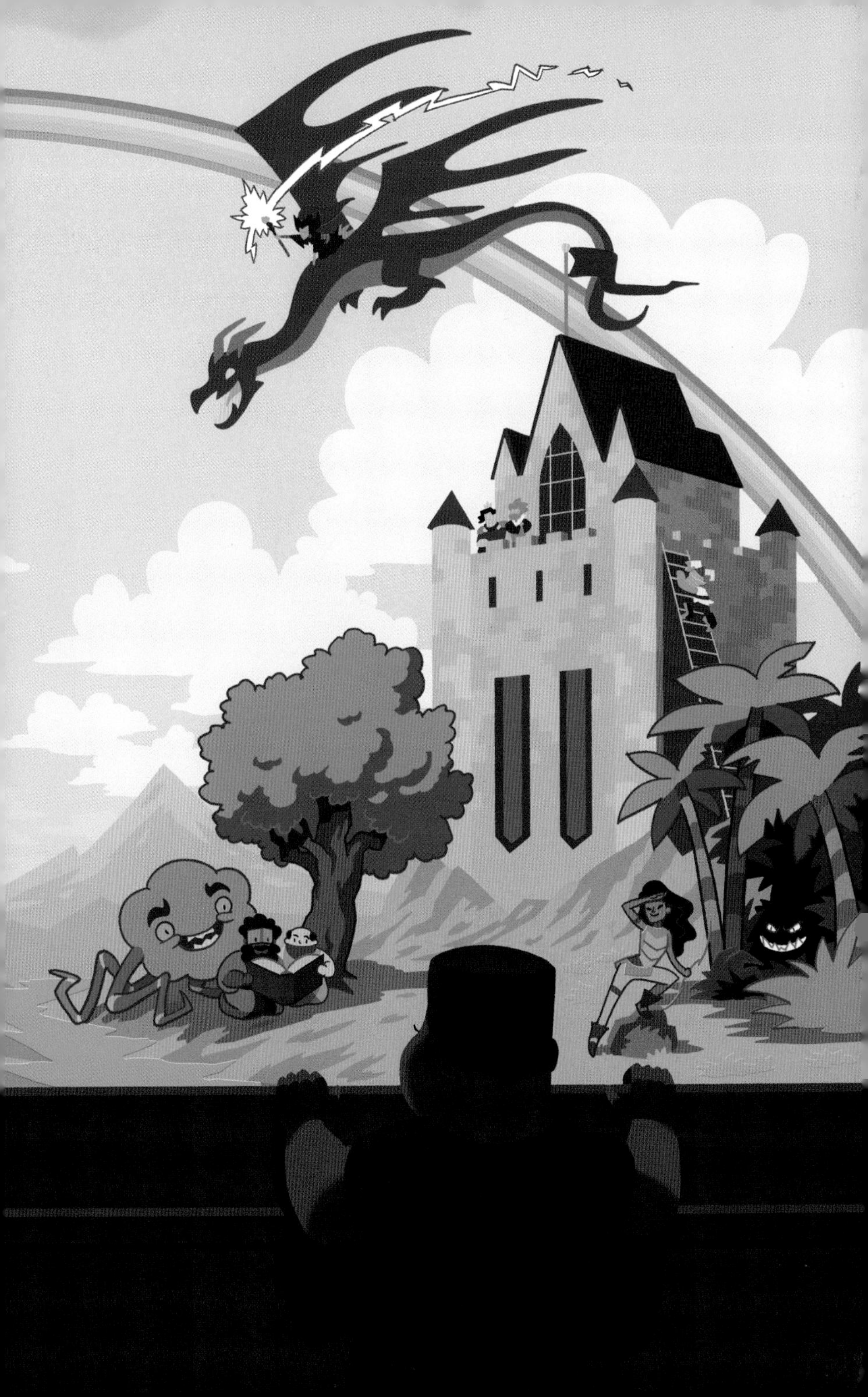

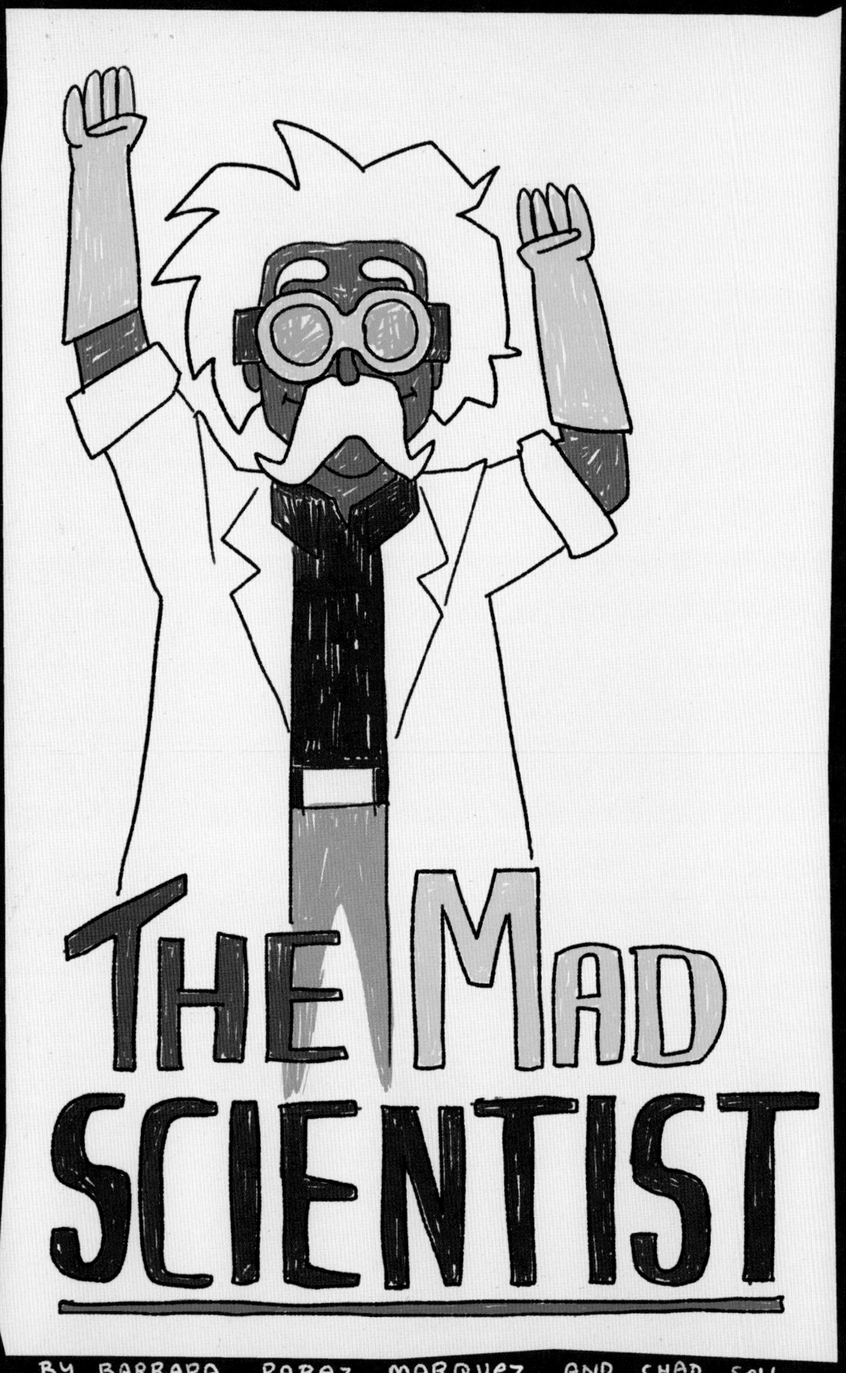
THE MAD
SCIENTIST

BY BARBARA PEREZ MARQUEZ AND CHAD SELL

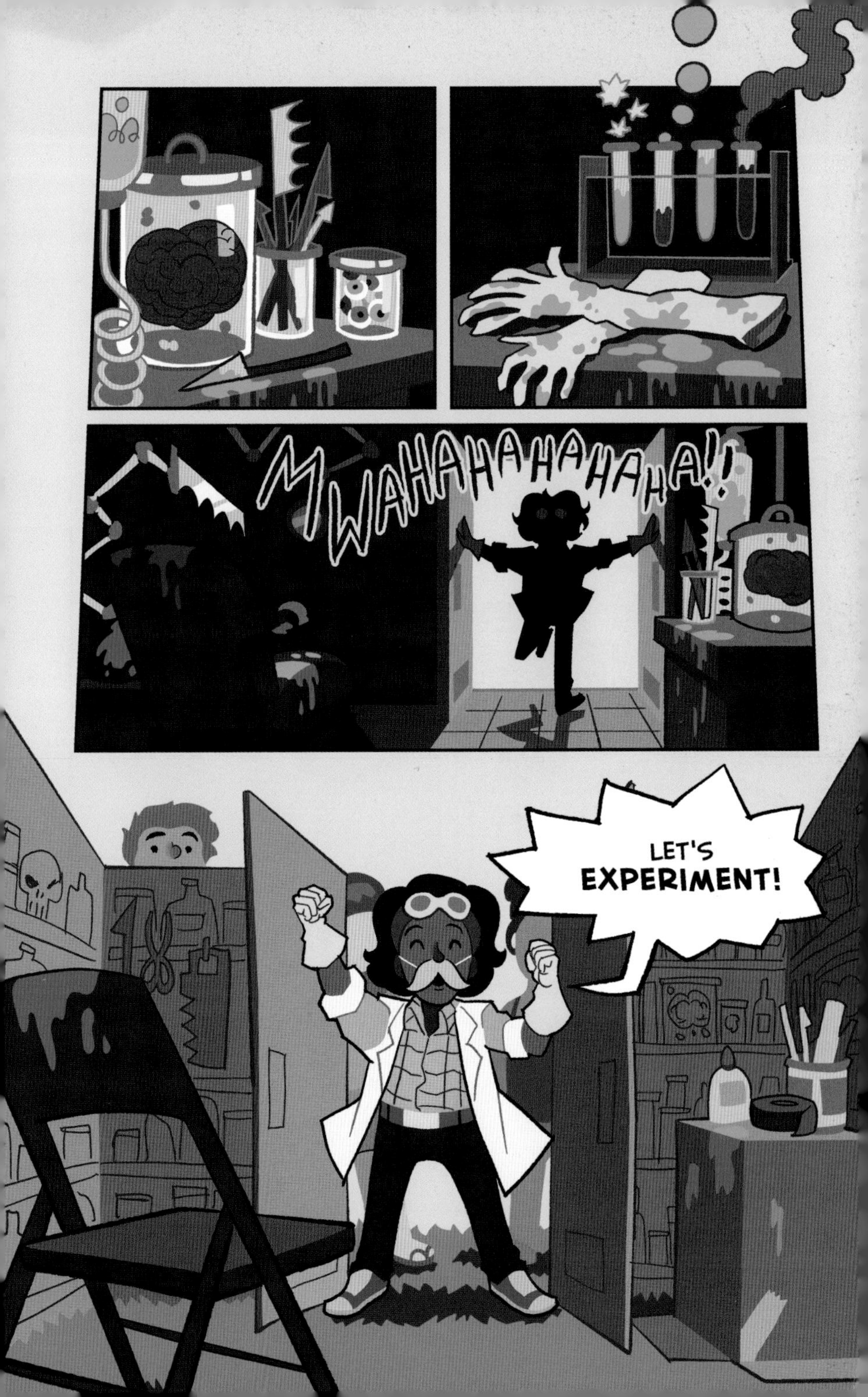
MWAHAHAHAHAHA!!
LET'S EXPERIMENT!

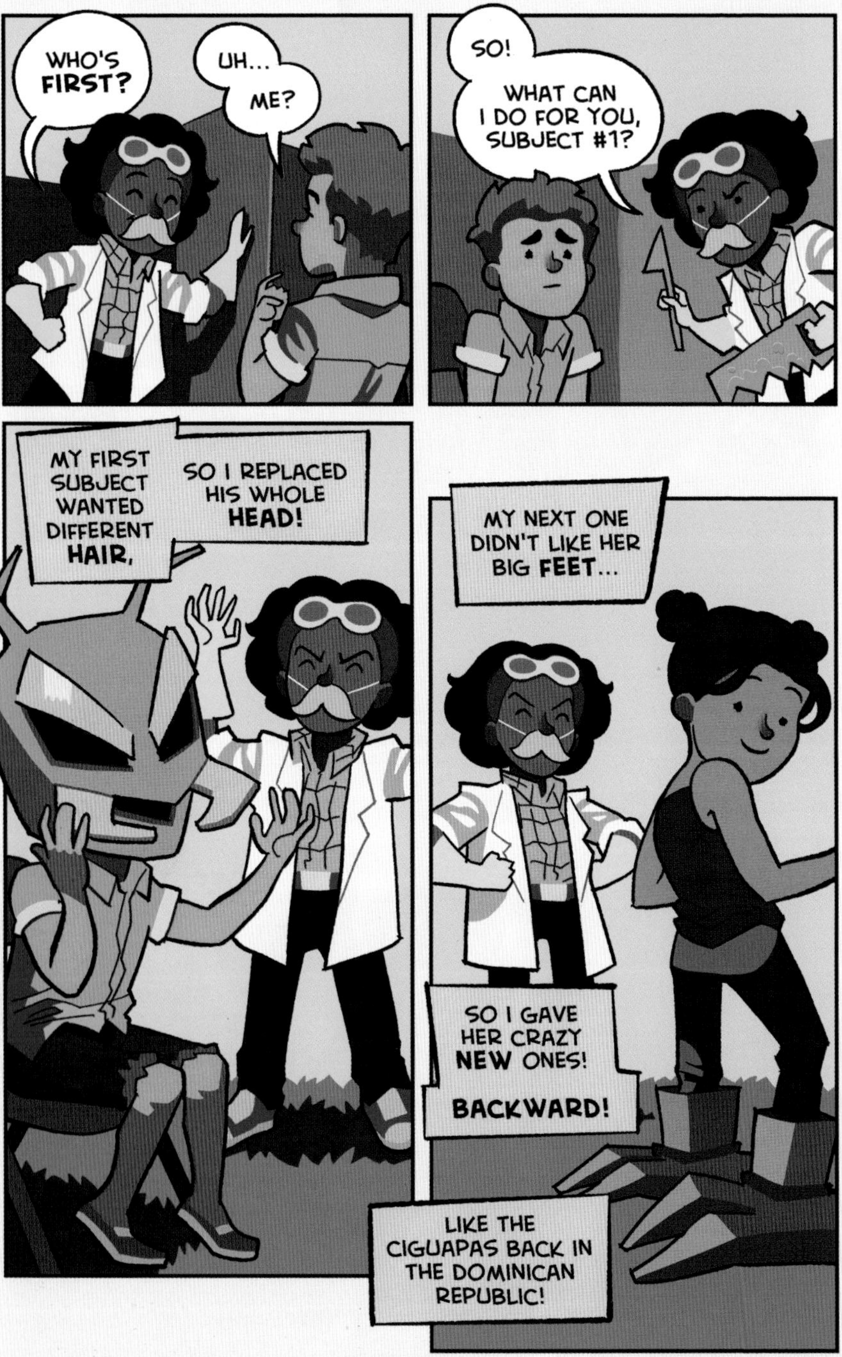

WHO'S **FIRST?**
UH... ME?
SO! WHAT CAN I DO FOR YOU, SUBJECT #1?
MY FIRST SUBJECT WANTED DIFFERENT **HAIR,**
SO I REPLACED HIS WHOLE **HEAD!**
MY NEXT ONE DIDN'T LIKE HER BIG **FEET...**
SO I GAVE HER CRAZY **NEW** ONES!
BACKWARD!
LIKE THE CIGUAPAS BACK IN THE DOMINICAN REPUBLIC!

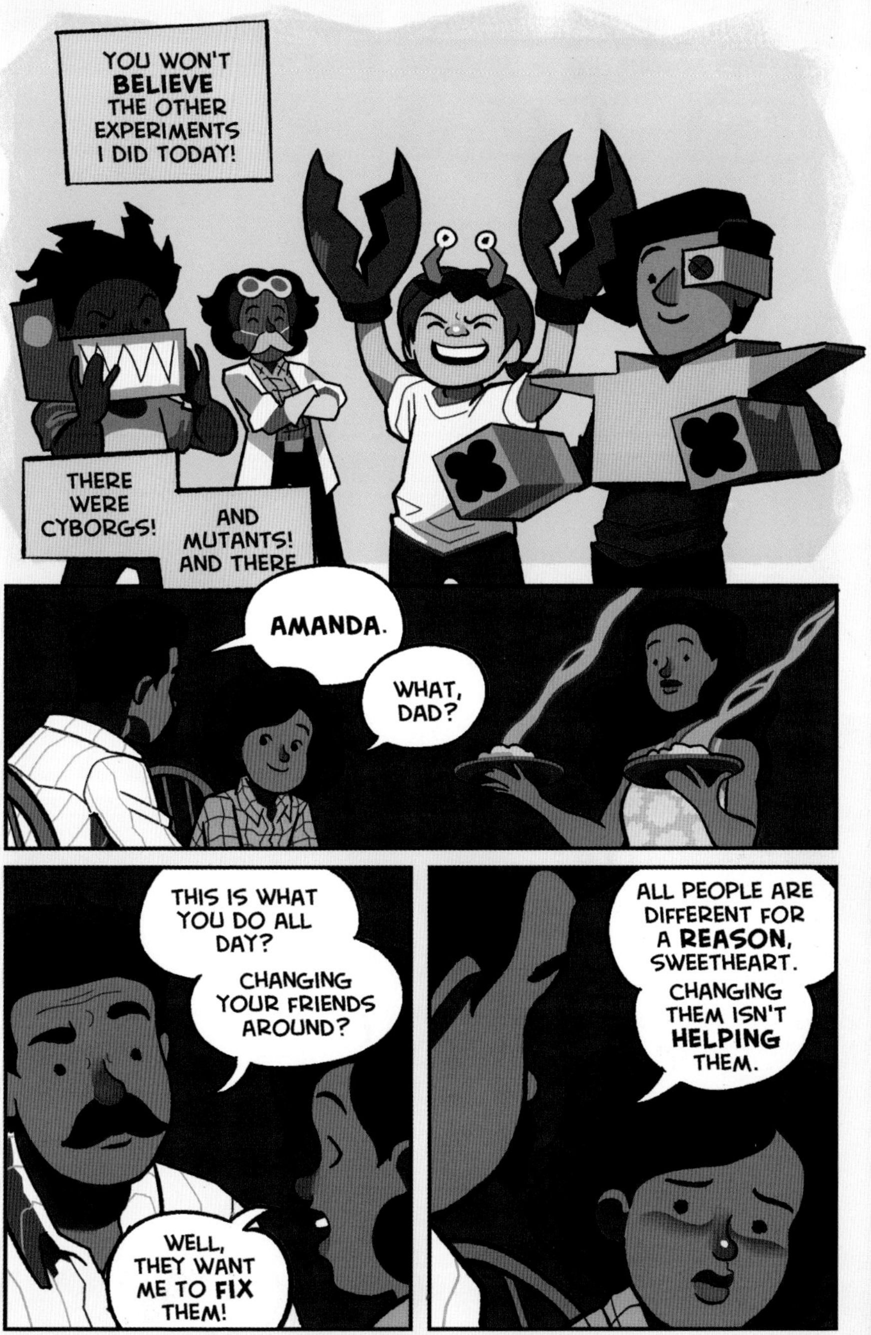
YOU WON'T **BELIEVE** THE OTHER EXPERIMENTS I DID TODAY!
THERE WERE CYBORGS!
AND MUTANTS! AND THERE
AMANDA.
WHAT, DAD?
THIS IS WHAT YOU DO ALL DAY?
CHANGING YOUR FRIENDS AROUND?
WELL, THEY WANT ME TO **FIX** THEM!
ALL PEOPLE ARE DIFFERENT FOR A **REASON**, SWEETHEART.
CHANGING THEM ISN'T **HELPING** THEM.

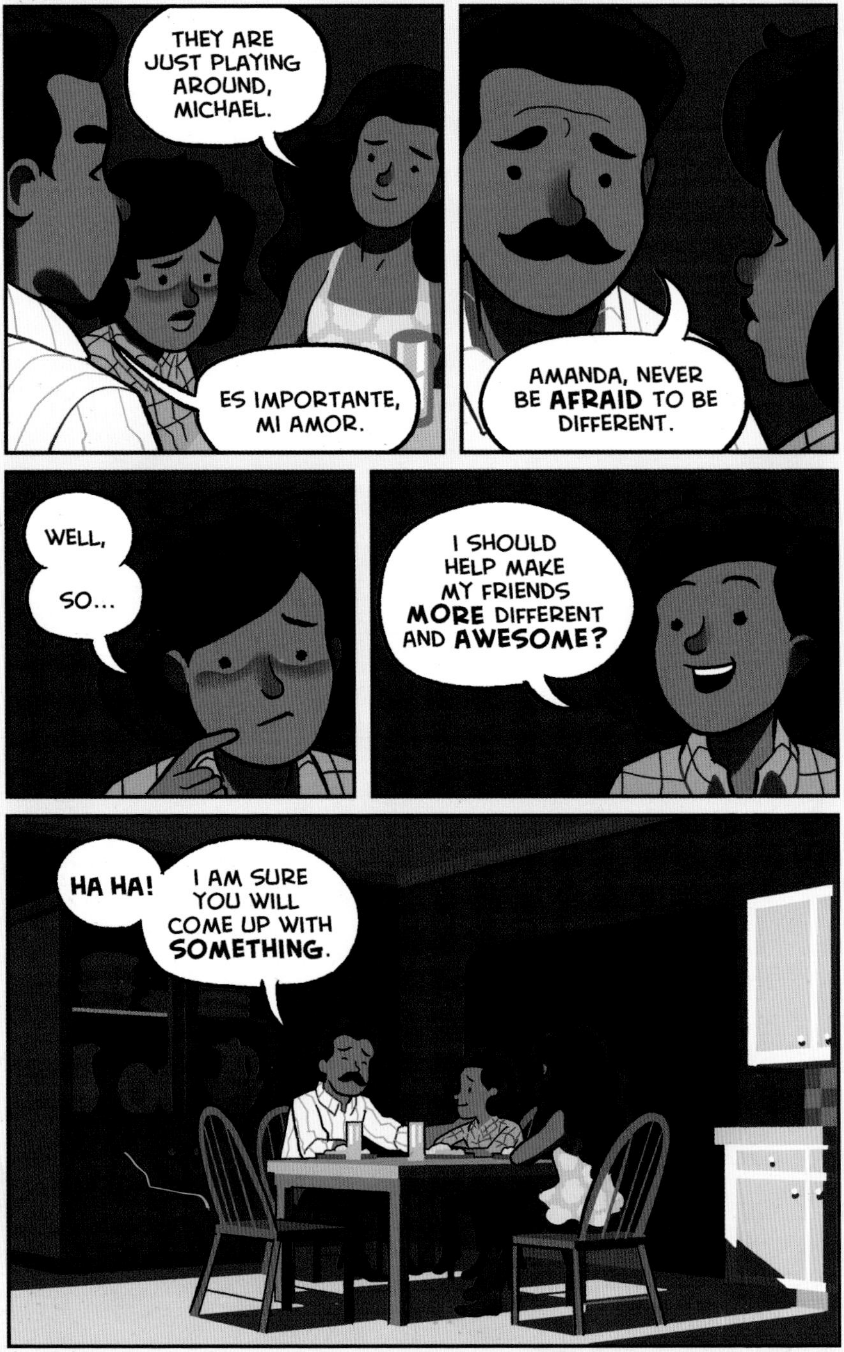
THEY ARE JUST PLAYING AROUND, MICHAEL.
ES IMPORTANTE, MI AMOR.
AMANDA, NEVER BE AFRAID TO BE DIFFERENT.
WELL,
SO...
I SHOULD HELP MAKE MY FRIENDS MORE DIFFERENT AND AWESOME?
HA HA!
I AM SURE YOU WILL COME UP WITH SOMETHING.

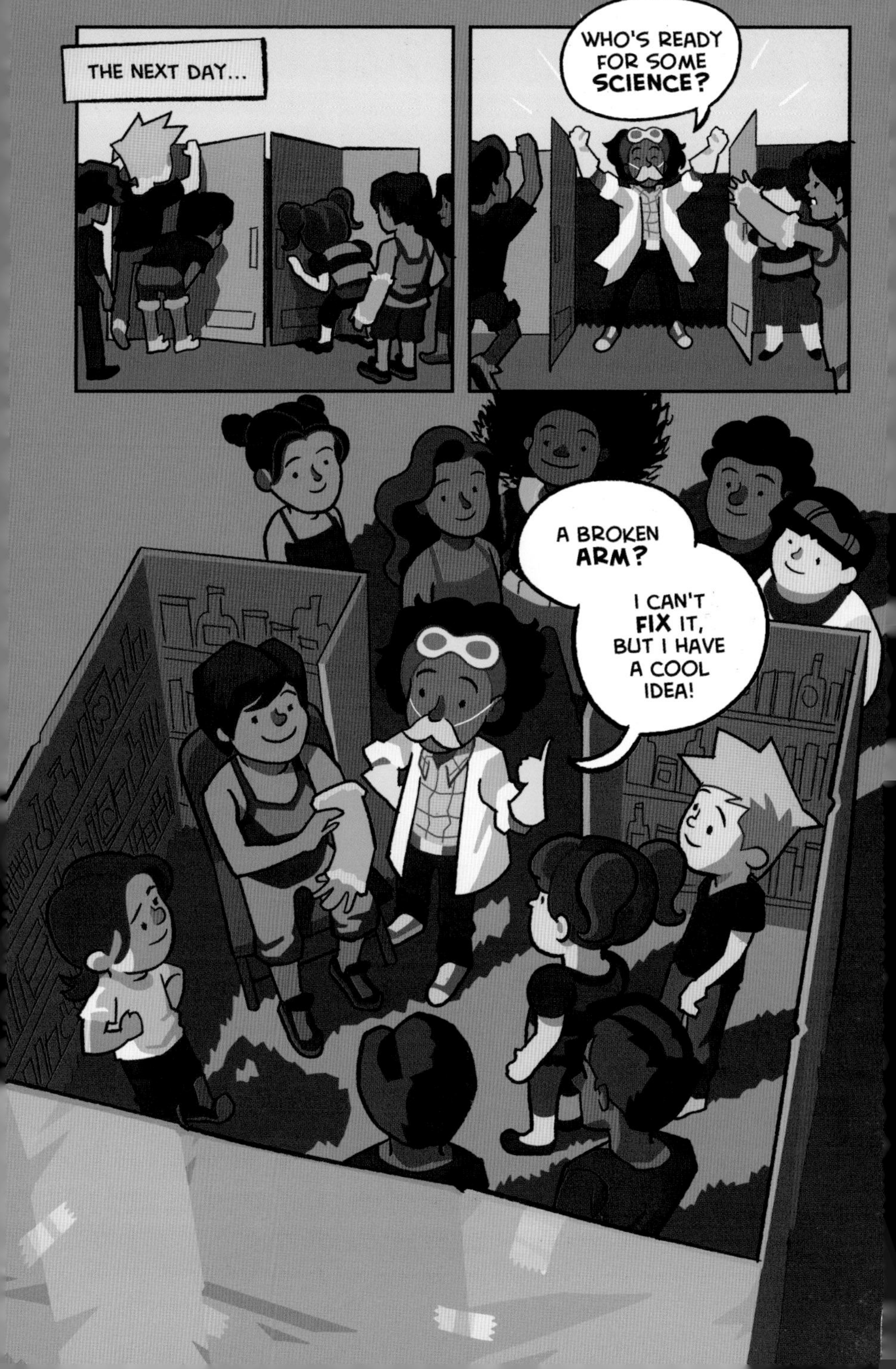
THE NEXT DAY...
WHO'S READY FOR SOME SCIENCE?
A BROKEN ARM?
I CAN'T FIX IT, BUT I HAVE A COOL IDEA!

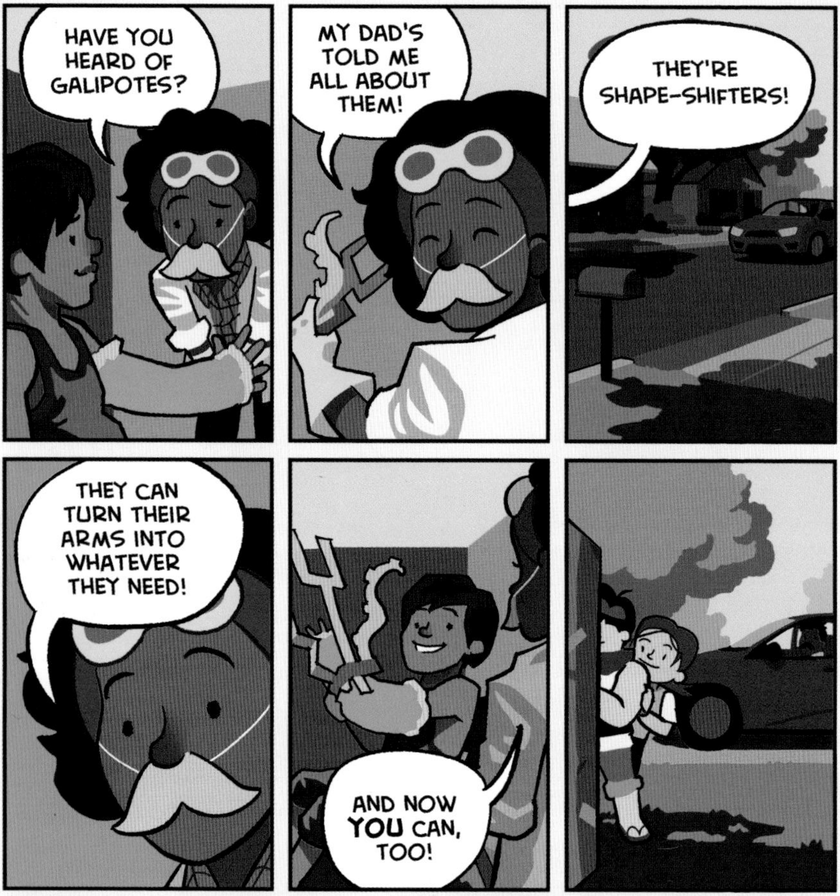
HAVE YOU HEARD OF GALIPOTES?
MY DAD'S TOLD ME ALL ABOUT THEM!
THEY'RE SHAPE-SHIFTERS!
THEY CAN TURN THEIR ARMS INTO WHATEVER THEY NEED!
AND NOW YOU CAN, TOO!
THINK THAT WILL WORK?
YEAH!
THIS IS SO COOL!
HOW DO YOU SAY IT?
GALLOP... LILY?

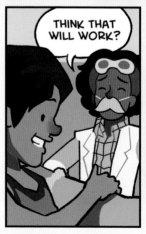

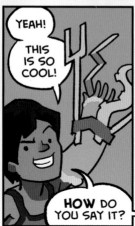

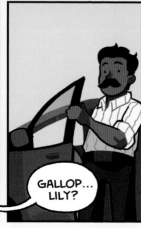

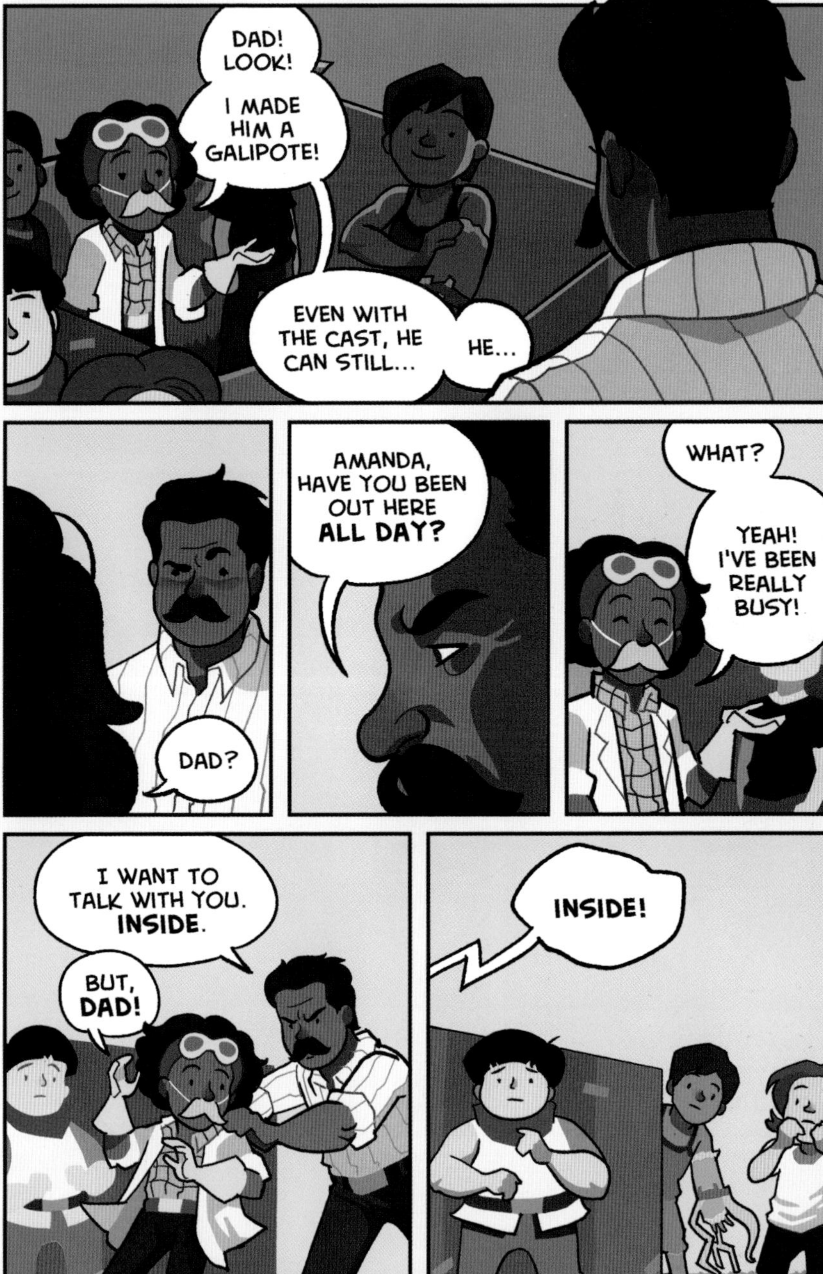
DAD! LOOK!
I MADE HIM A GALIPOTE!
EVEN WITH THE CAST, HE CAN STILL...
HE...
DAD?
AMANDA, HAVE YOU BEEN OUT HERE **ALL DAY?**
WHAT?
YEAH! I'VE BEEN REALLY BUSY!
I WANT TO TALK WITH YOU. **INSIDE**.
BUT, **DAD!**
INSIDE!

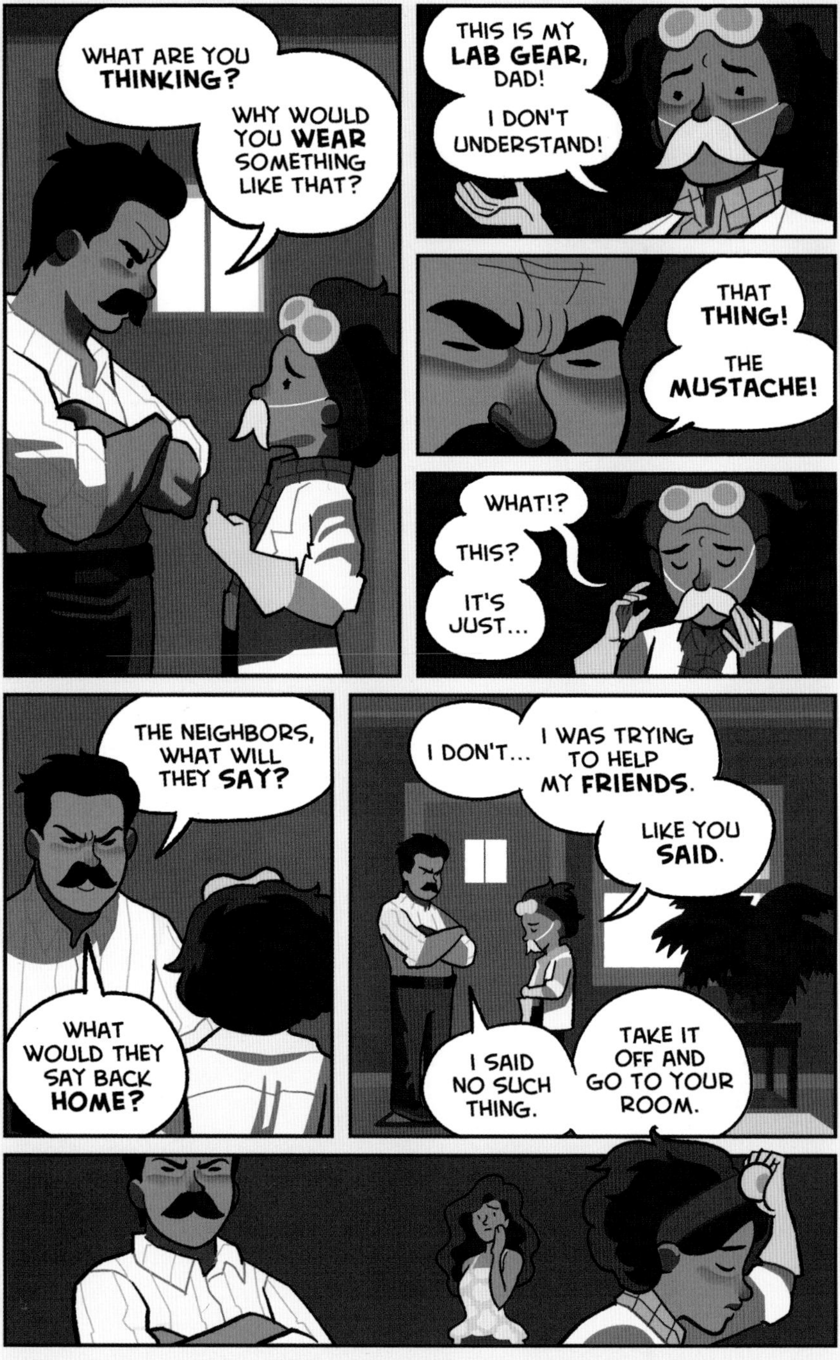
WHAT ARE YOU THINKING?
WHY WOULD YOU WEAR SOMETHING LIKE THAT?
THIS IS MY LAB GEAR, DAD!
I DON'T UNDERSTAND!
THAT THING!
THE MUSTACHE!
WHAT!?
THIS?
IT'S JUST...
THE NEIGHBORS, WHAT WILL THEY SAY?
WHAT WOULD THEY SAY BACK HOME?
I DON'T...
I WAS TRYING TO HELP MY FRIENDS.
LIKE YOU SAID.
I SAID NO SUCH THING.
TAKE IT OFF AND GO TO YOUR ROOM.

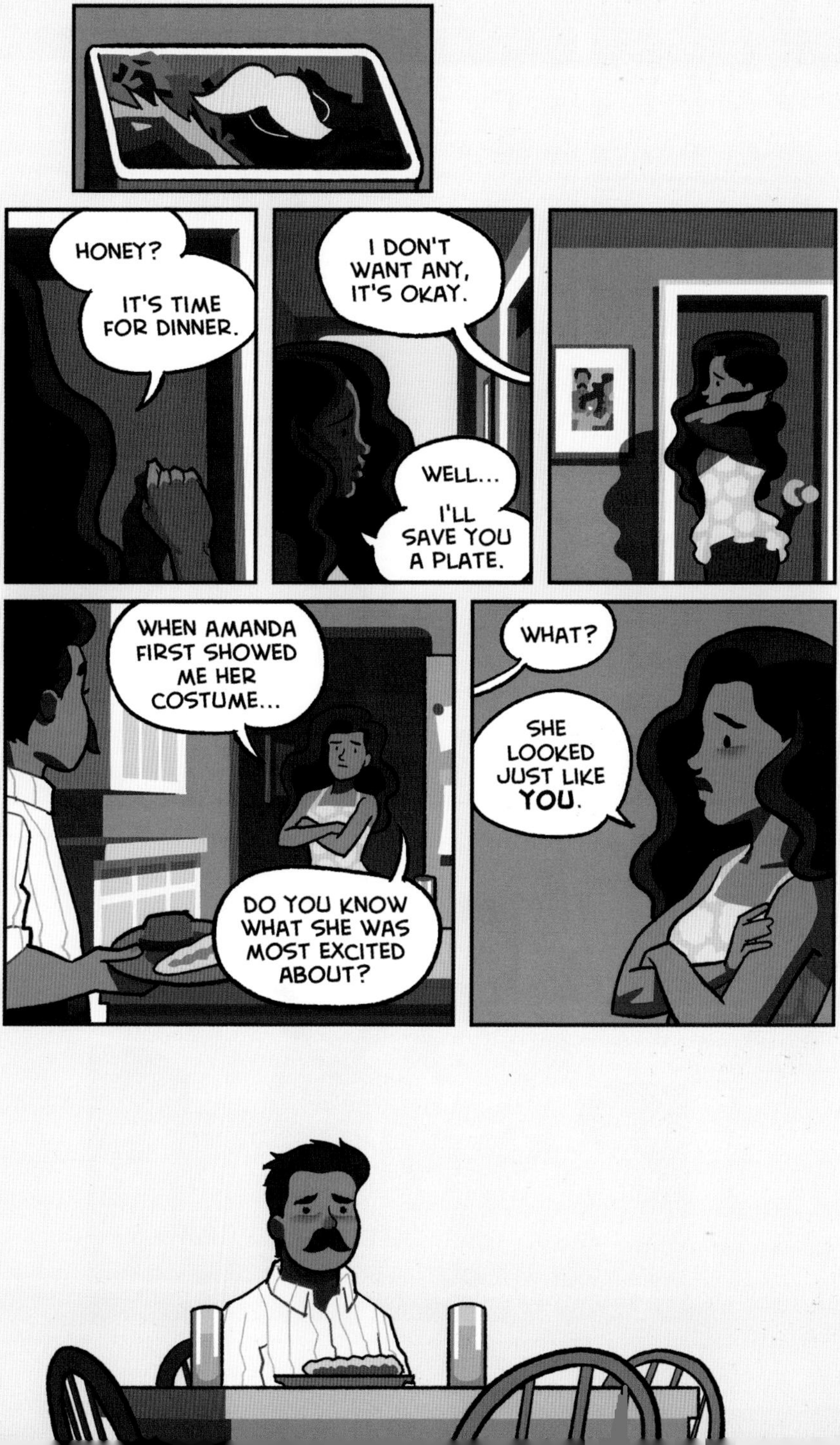
HONEY?
IT'S TIME FOR DINNER.
I DON'T WANT ANY, IT'S OKAY.
WELL...
I'LL SAVE YOU A PLATE.
WHEN AMANDA FIRST SHOWED ME HER COSTUME...
DO YOU KNOW WHAT SHE WAS MOST EXCITED ABOUT?
WHAT?
SHE LOOKED JUST LIKE **YOU**.

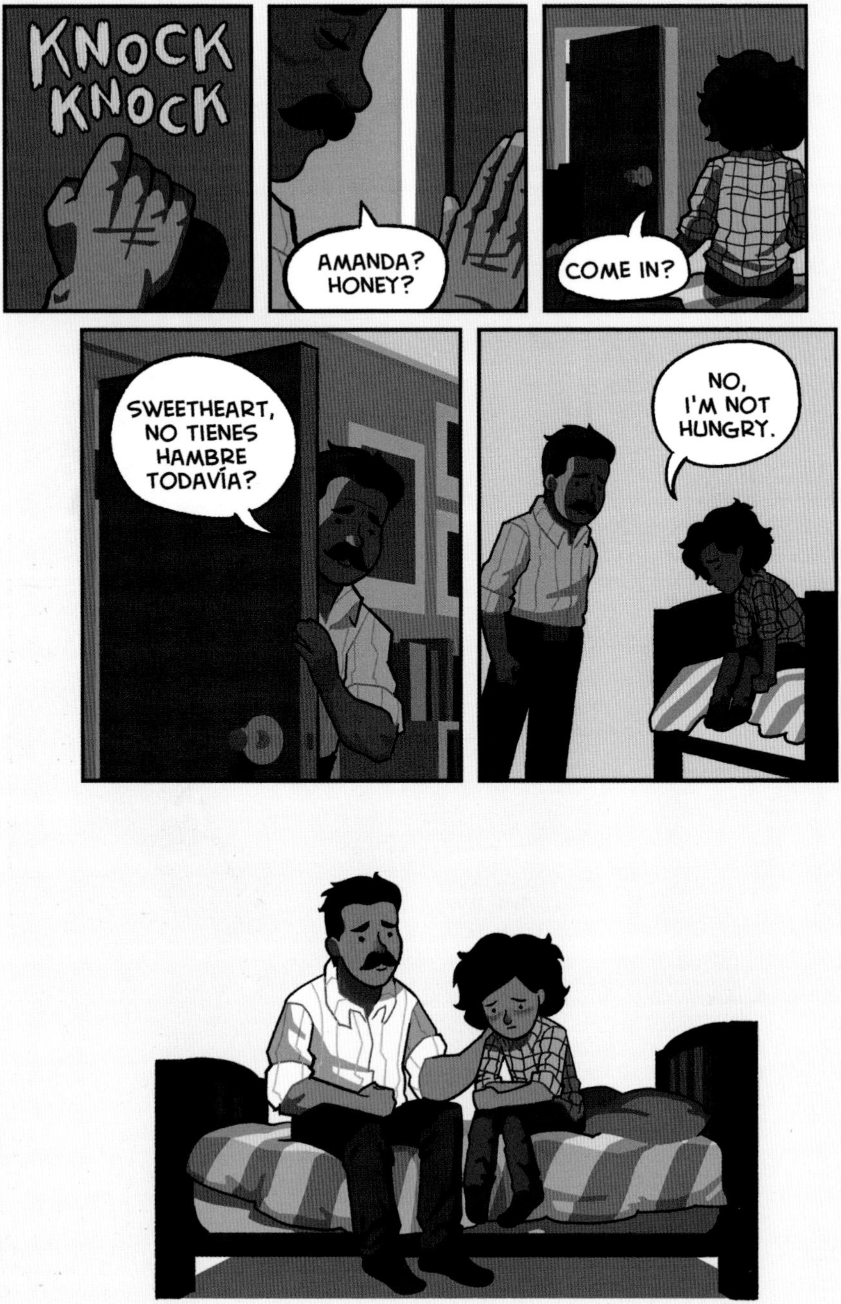
KNOCK KNOCK
AMANDA? HONEY?
COME IN?
SWEETHEART, NO TIENES HAMBRE TODAVÍA?
NO, I'M NOT HUNGRY.

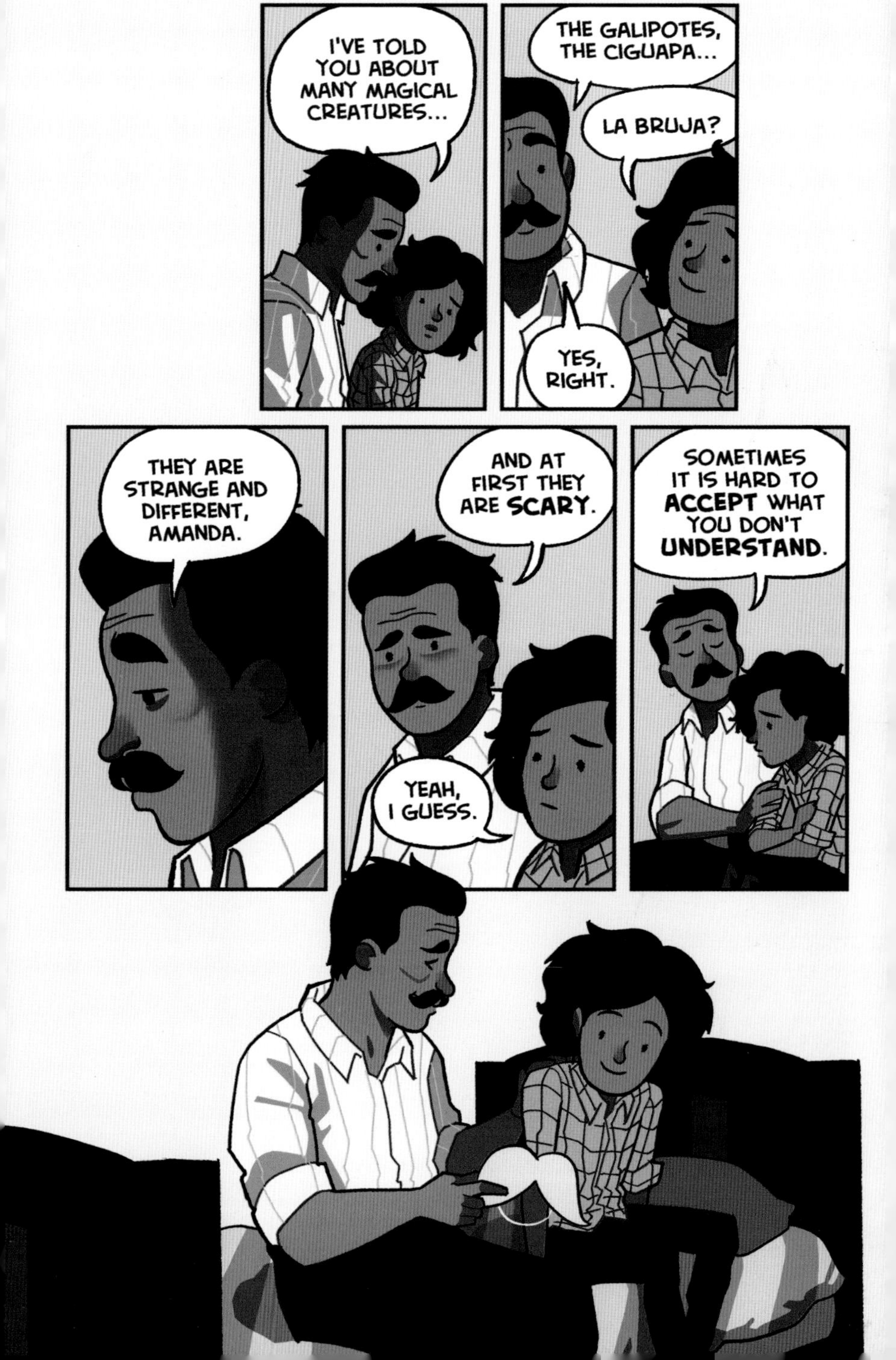
I'VE TOLD YOU ABOUT MANY MAGICAL CREATURES...
THE GALIPOTES, THE CIGUAPA...
LA BRUJA?
YES, RIGHT.
THEY ARE STRANGE AND DIFFERENT, AMANDA.
AND AT FIRST THEY ARE SCARY.
YEAH, I GUESS.
SOMETIMES IT IS HARD TO ACCEPT WHAT YOU DON'T UNDERSTAND.

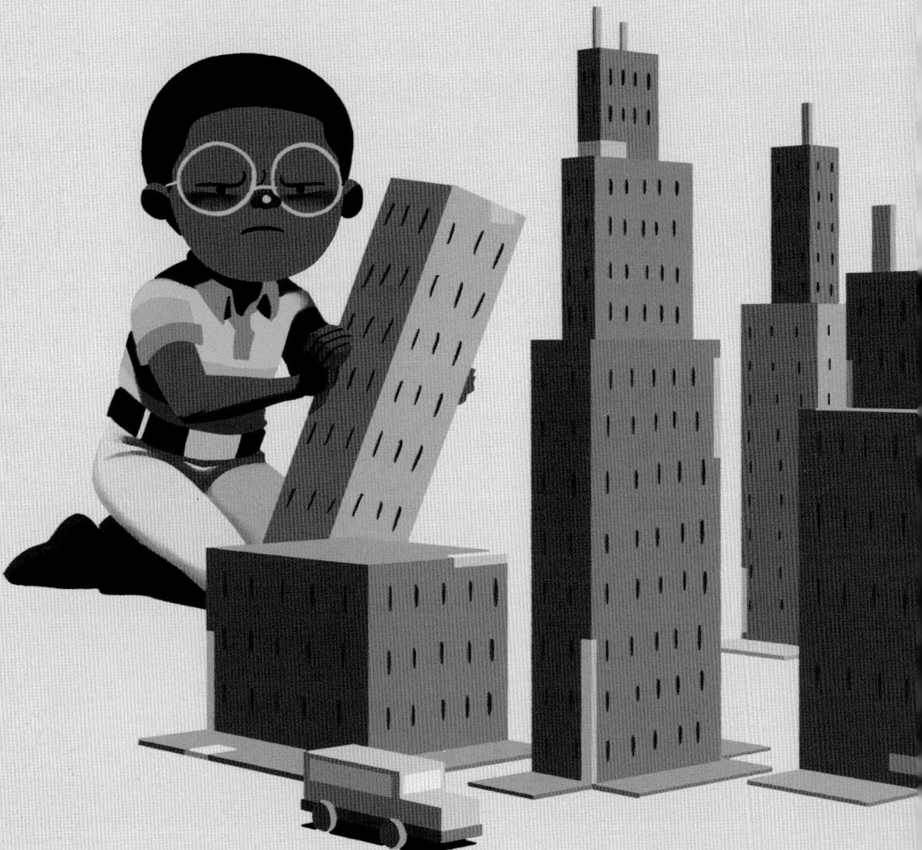

the ROBOT

BY VID ALLIGER AND CHAD SELL

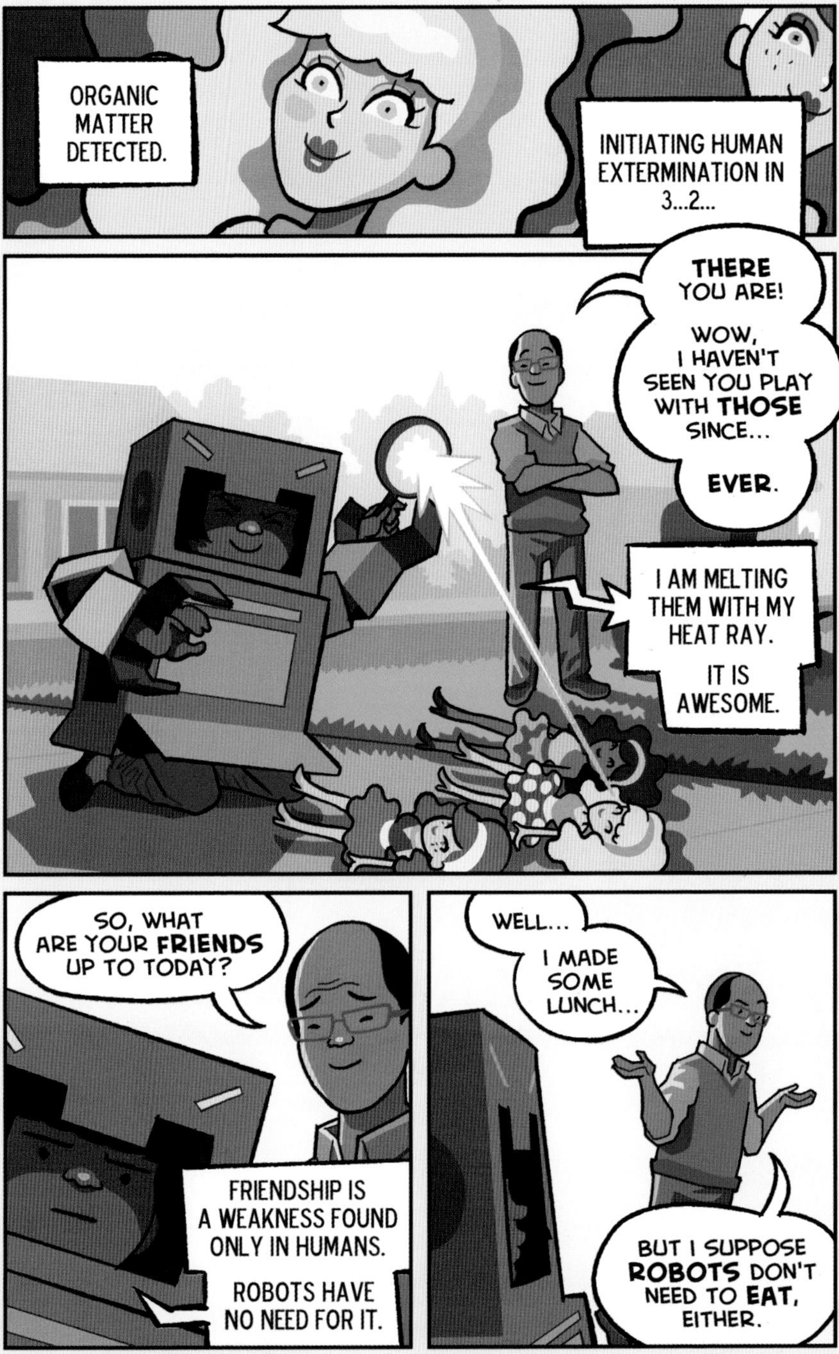
ORGANIC MATTER DETECTED.
INITIATING HUMAN EXTERMINATION IN 3...2...
THERE YOU ARE!
WOW, I HAVEN'T SEEN YOU PLAY WITH THOSE SINCE...
EVER.
I AM MELTING THEM WITH MY HEAT RAY.
IT IS AWESOME.
SO, WHAT ARE YOUR FRIENDS UP TO TODAY?
FRIENDSHIP IS A WEAKNESS FOUND ONLY IN HUMANS.
ROBOTS HAVE NO NEED FOR IT.
WELL...
I MADE SOME LUNCH...
BUT I SUPPOSE ROBOTS DON'T NEED TO EAT, EITHER.

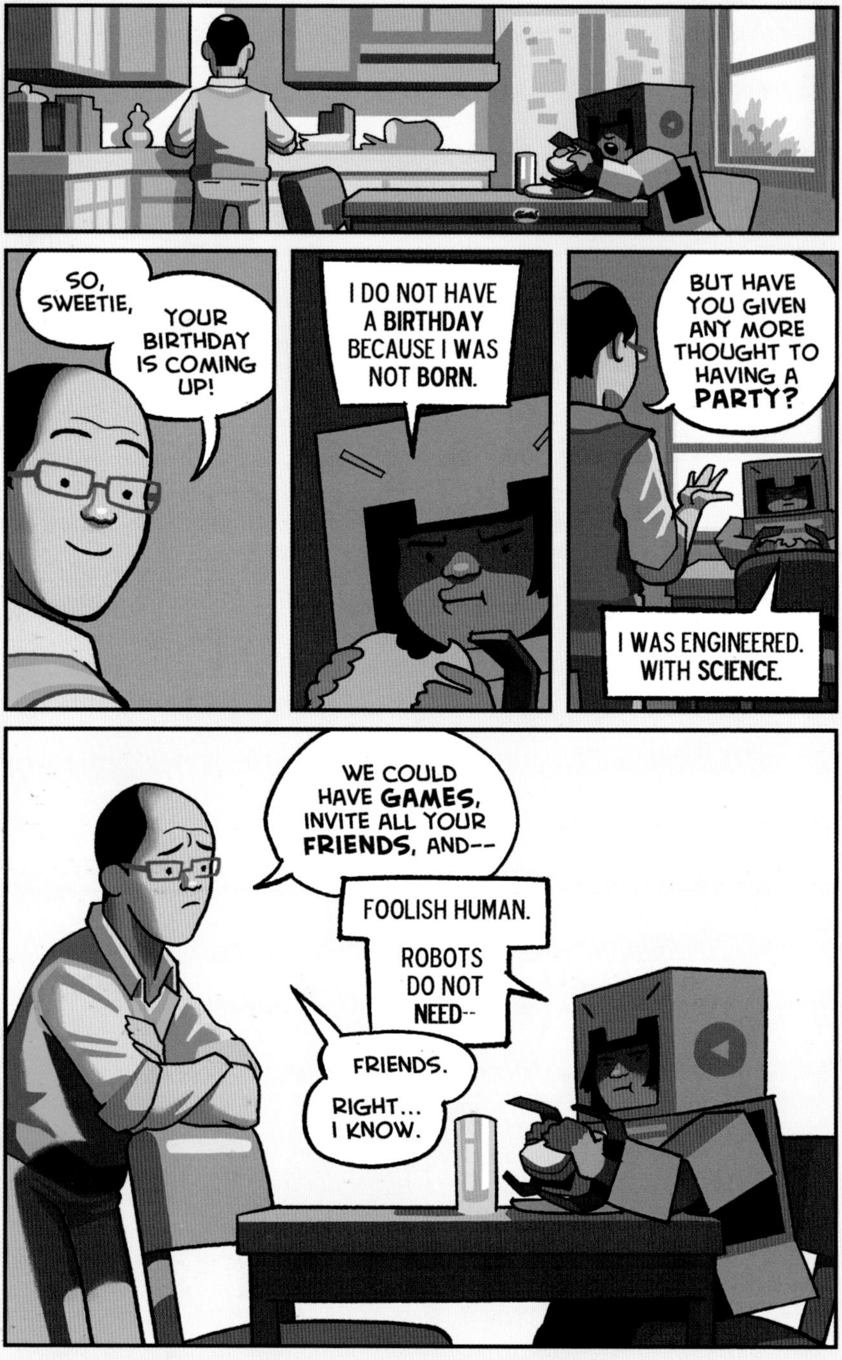
SO, SWEETIE, YOUR BIRTHDAY IS COMING UP!
I DO NOT HAVE A BIRTHDAY BECAUSE I WAS NOT BORN.
BUT HAVE YOU GIVEN ANY MORE THOUGHT TO HAVING A PARTY?
I WAS ENGINEERED. WITH SCIENCE.
WE COULD HAVE GAMES, INVITE ALL YOUR FRIENDS, AND--
FOOLISH HUMAN.
ROBOTS DO NOT NEED--
FRIENDS.
RIGHT... I KNOW.

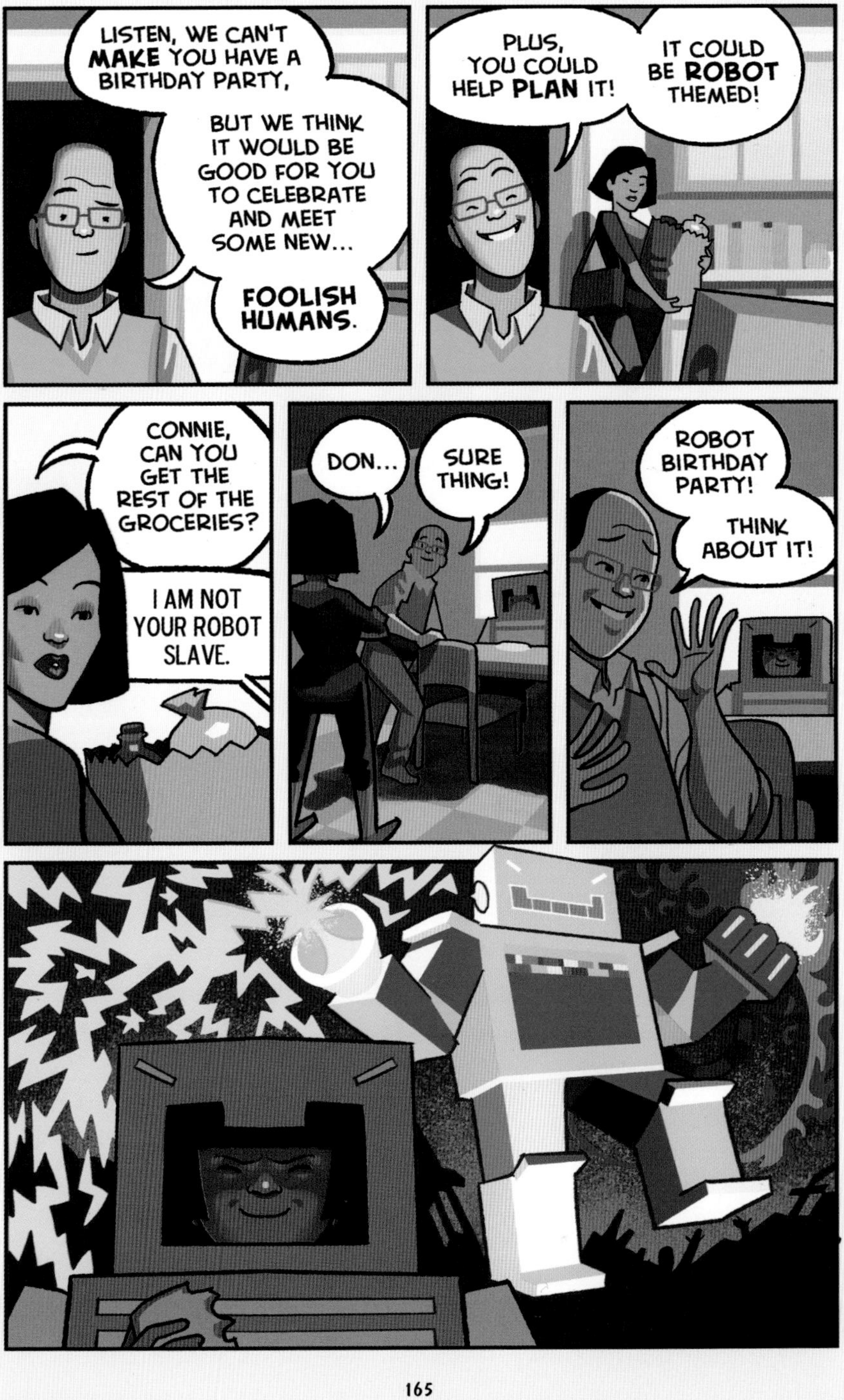
LISTEN, WE CAN'T **MAKE** YOU HAVE A BIRTHDAY PARTY,
BUT WE THINK IT WOULD BE GOOD FOR YOU TO CELEBRATE AND MEET SOME NEW...
FOOLISH HUMANS.
PLUS, YOU COULD HELP **PLAN** IT!
IT COULD BE **ROBOT** THEMED!
CONNIE, CAN YOU GET THE REST OF THE GROCERIES?
I AM NOT YOUR ROBOT SLAVE.
DON...
SURE THING!
ROBOT BIRTHDAY PARTY!
THINK ABOUT IT!

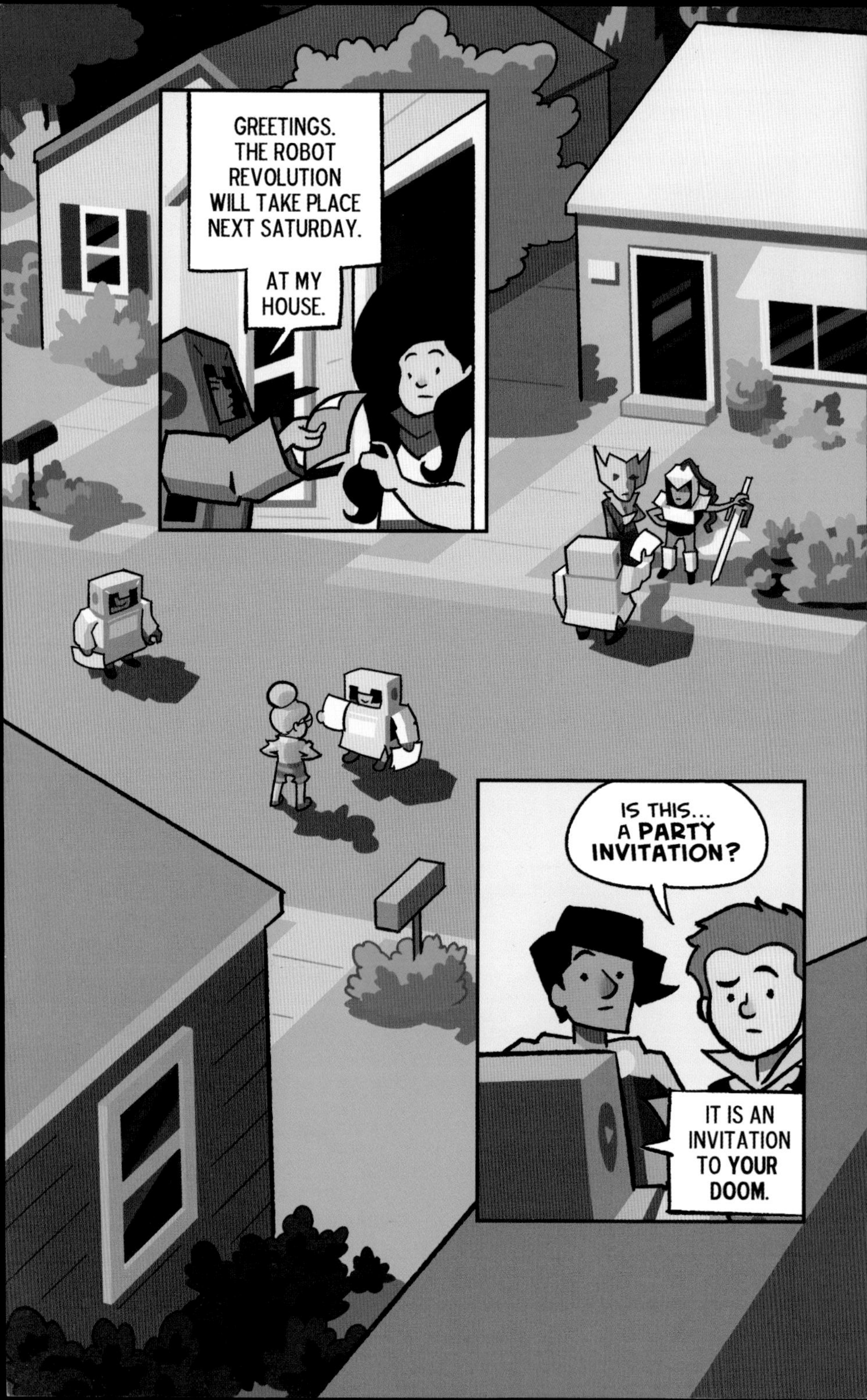

GREETINGS. THE ROBOT REVOLUTION WILL TAKE PLACE NEXT SATURDAY.
AT MY HOUSE.
IS THIS... A **PARTY** INVITATION?
IT IS AN INVITATION TO **YOUR** DOOM.

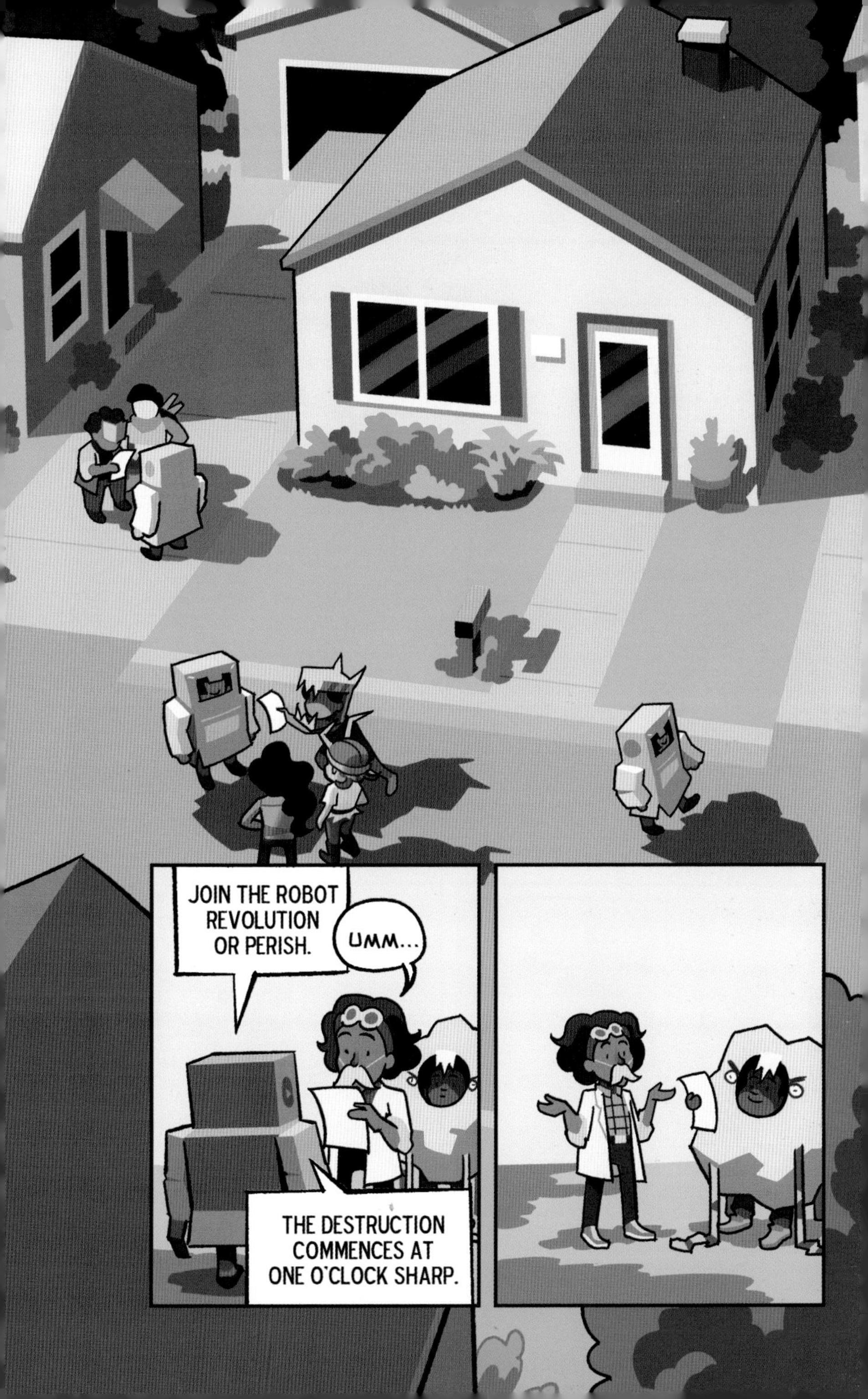
JOIN THE ROBOT REVOLUTION OR PERISH.
UMM...
THE DESTRUCTION COMMENCES AT ONE O'CLOCK SHARP.

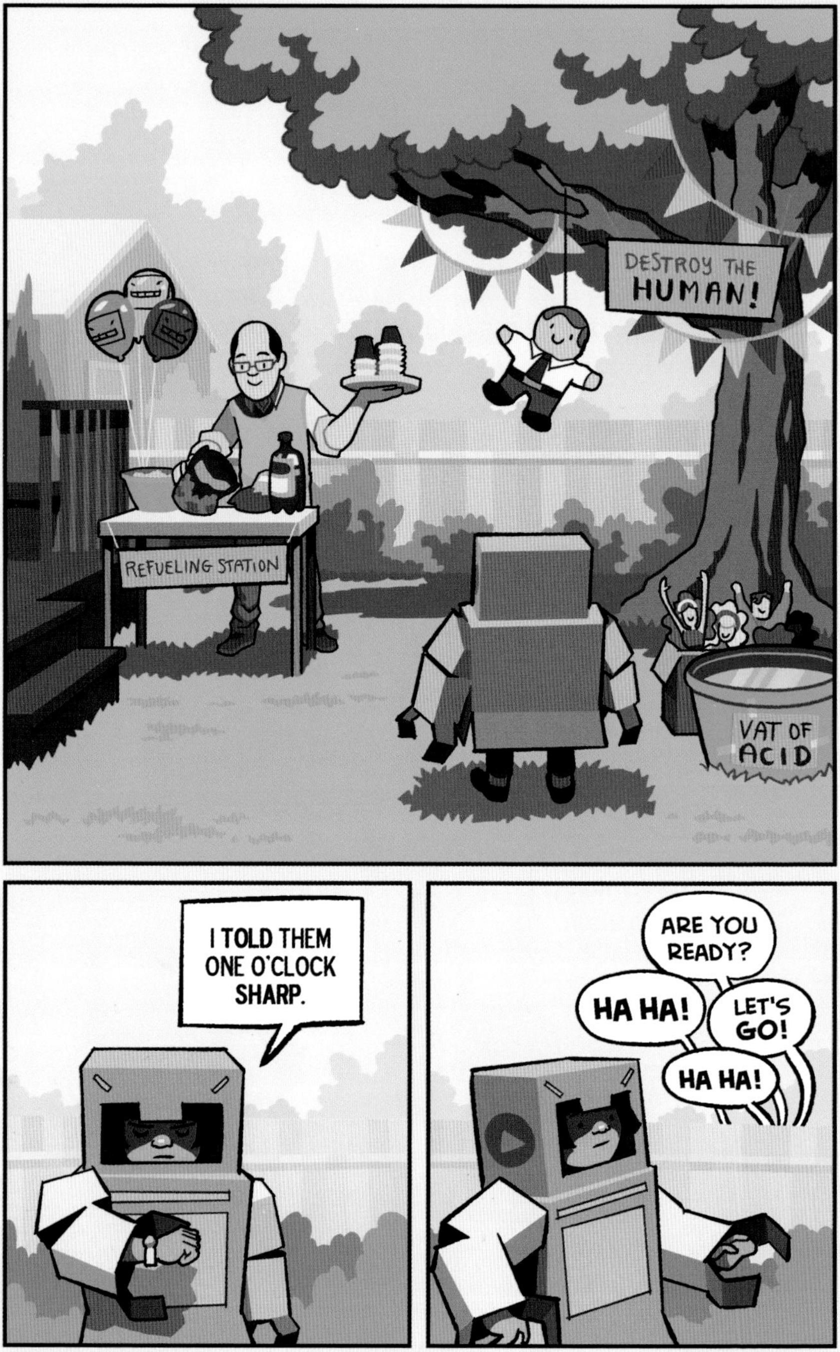
DESTROY THE HUMAN!
REFUELING STATION
VAT OF ACID
I TOLD THEM ONE O'CLOCK SHARP.
ARE YOU READY?
HA HA!
LET'S GO!
HA HA!

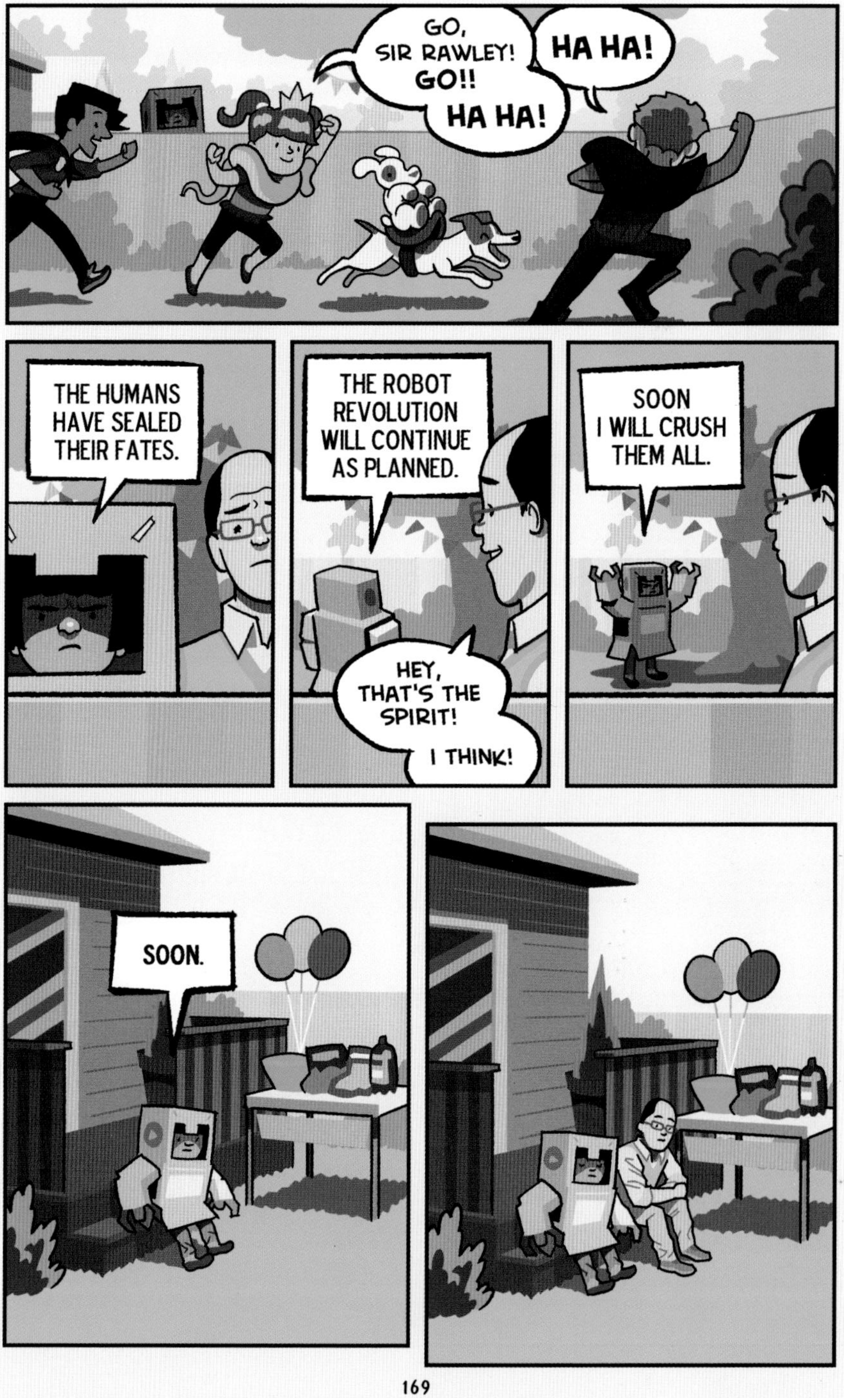
GO, SIR RAWLEY! GO!!
HA HA!
HA HA!
THE HUMANS HAVE SEALED THEIR FATES.
THE ROBOT REVOLUTION WILL CONTINUE AS PLANNED.
HEY, THAT'S THE SPIRIT!
I THINK!
SOON I WILL CRUSH THEM ALL.
SOON.

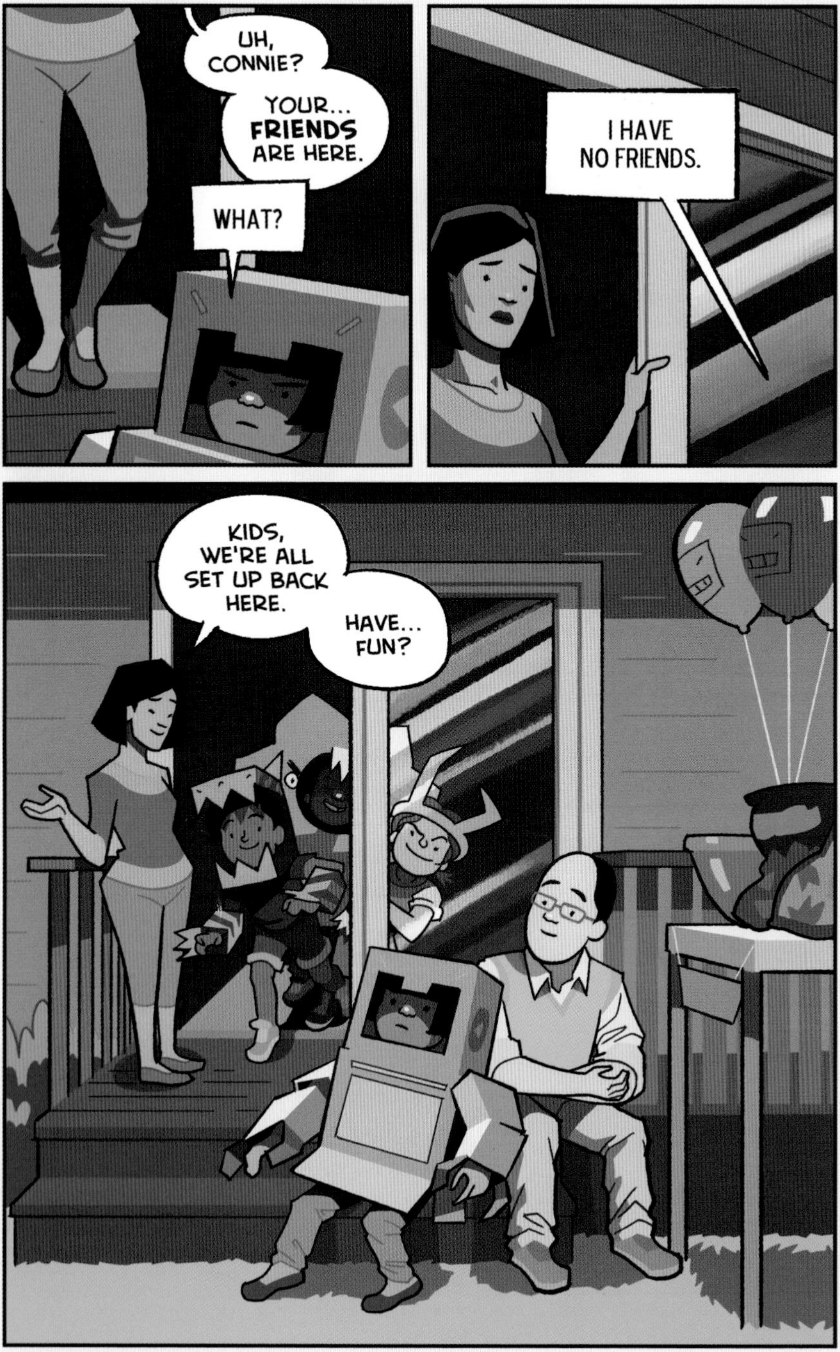
UH, CONNIE?
YOUR... FRIENDS ARE HERE.
WHAT?
I HAVE NO FRIENDS.
KIDS, WE'RE ALL SET UP BACK HERE.
HAVE... FUN?

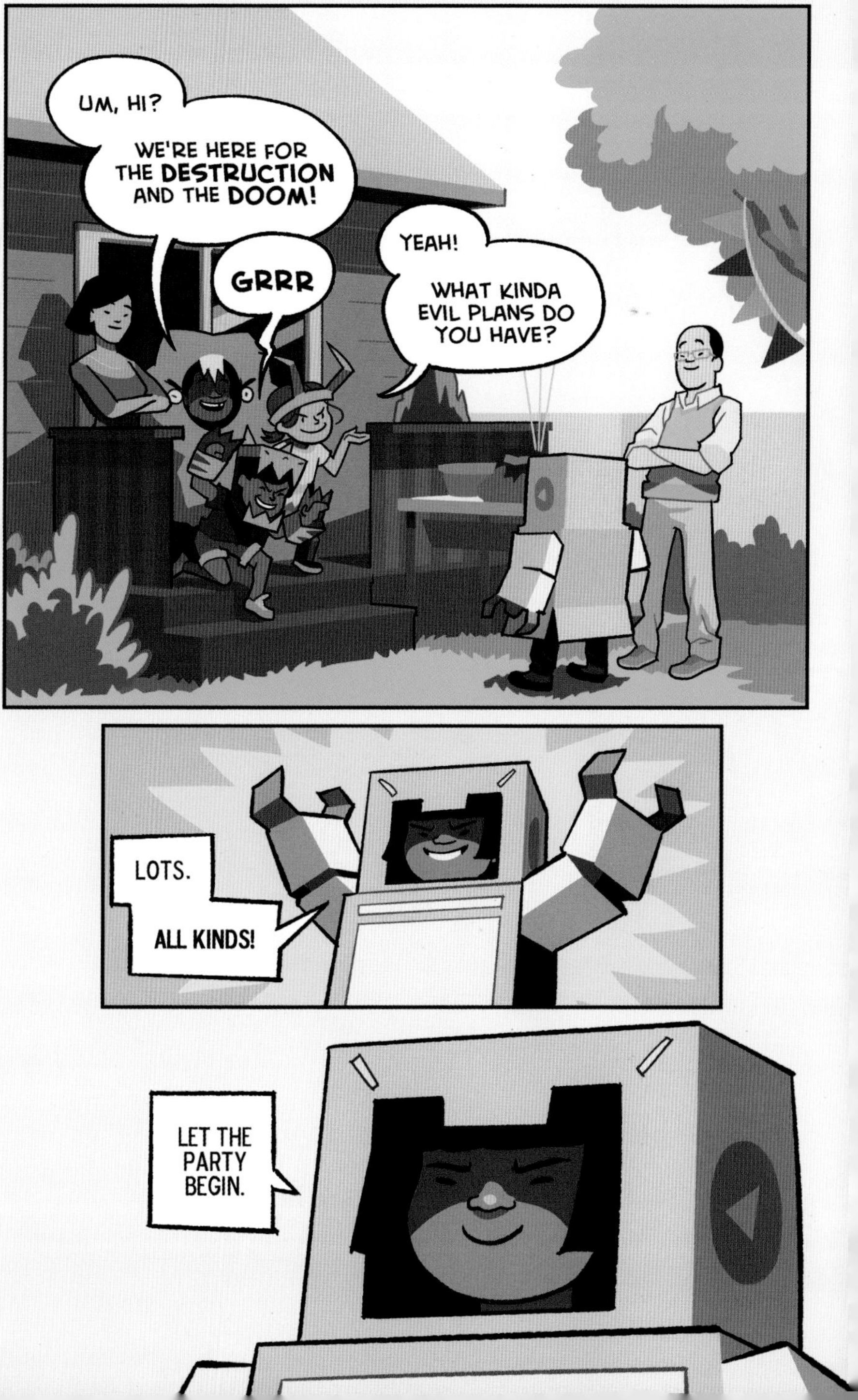
UM, HI?
WE'RE HERE FOR THE **DESTRUCTION** AND THE **DOOM**!
GRRR
YEAH!
WHAT KINDA EVIL PLANS DO YOU HAVE?
LOTS.
ALL KINDS!
LET THE PARTY BEGIN.

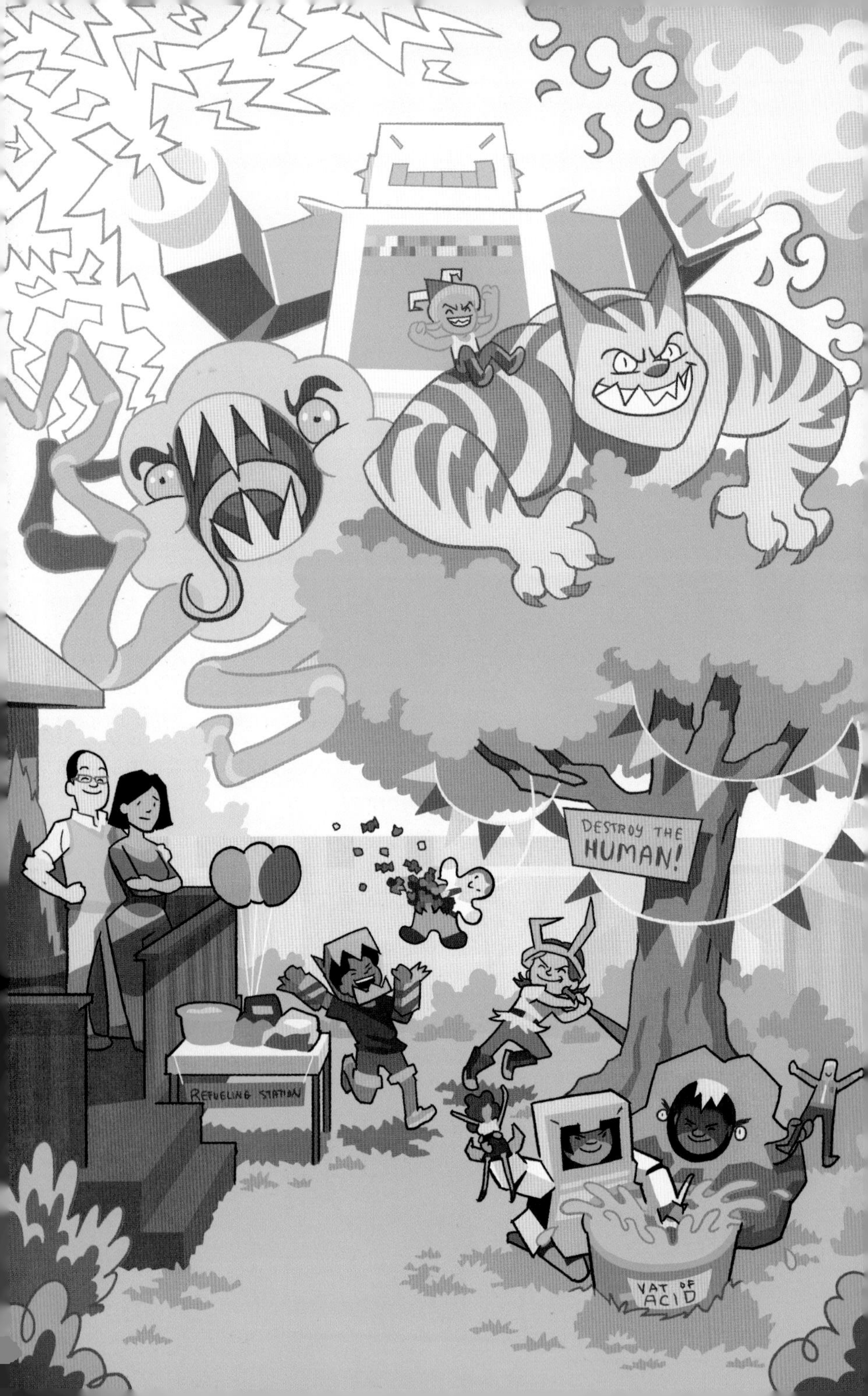
DESTROY THE HUMAN!
REFUELING STATION
VAT OF ACID

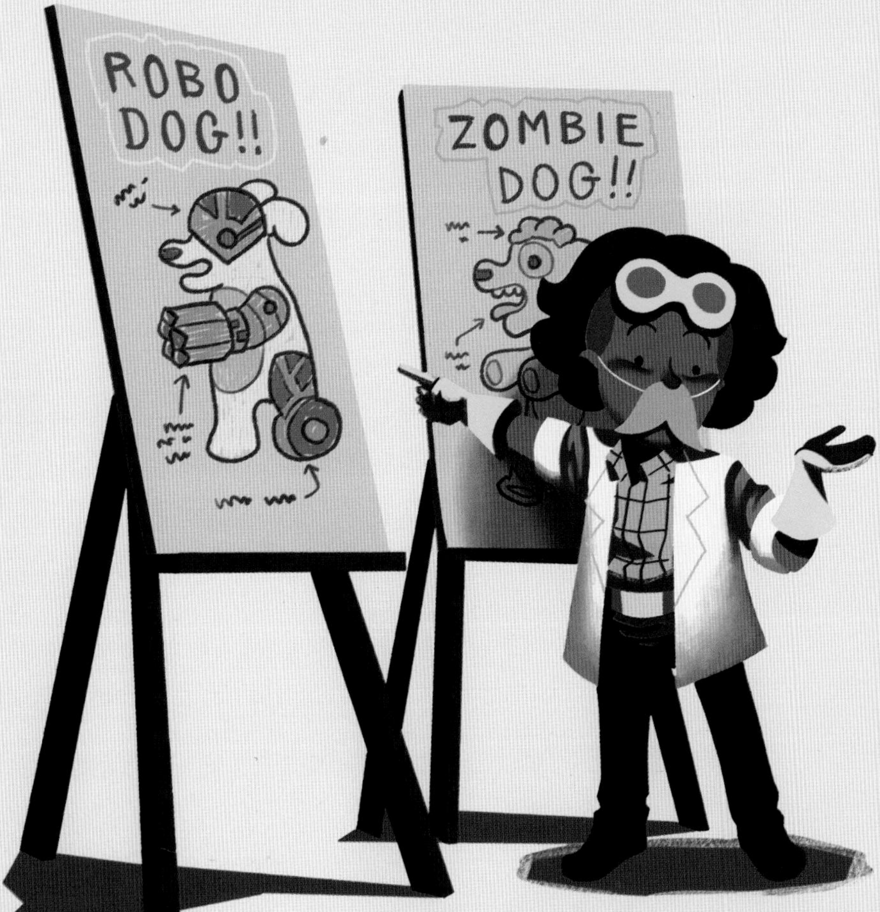
ROBO DOG!!
ZOMBIE DOG!!

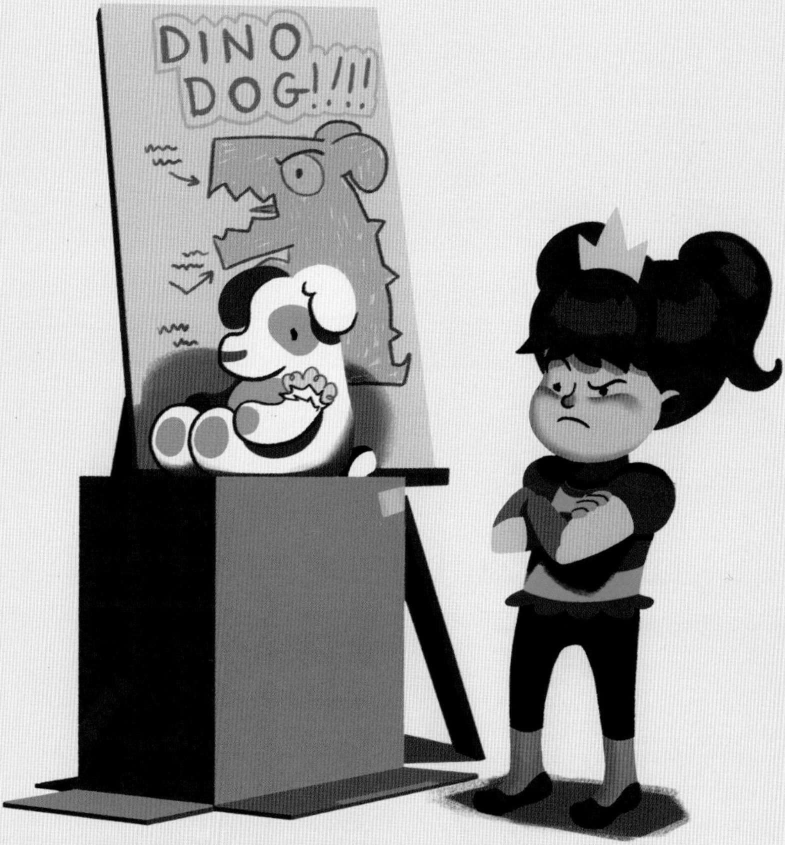
DINO DOG!!!!

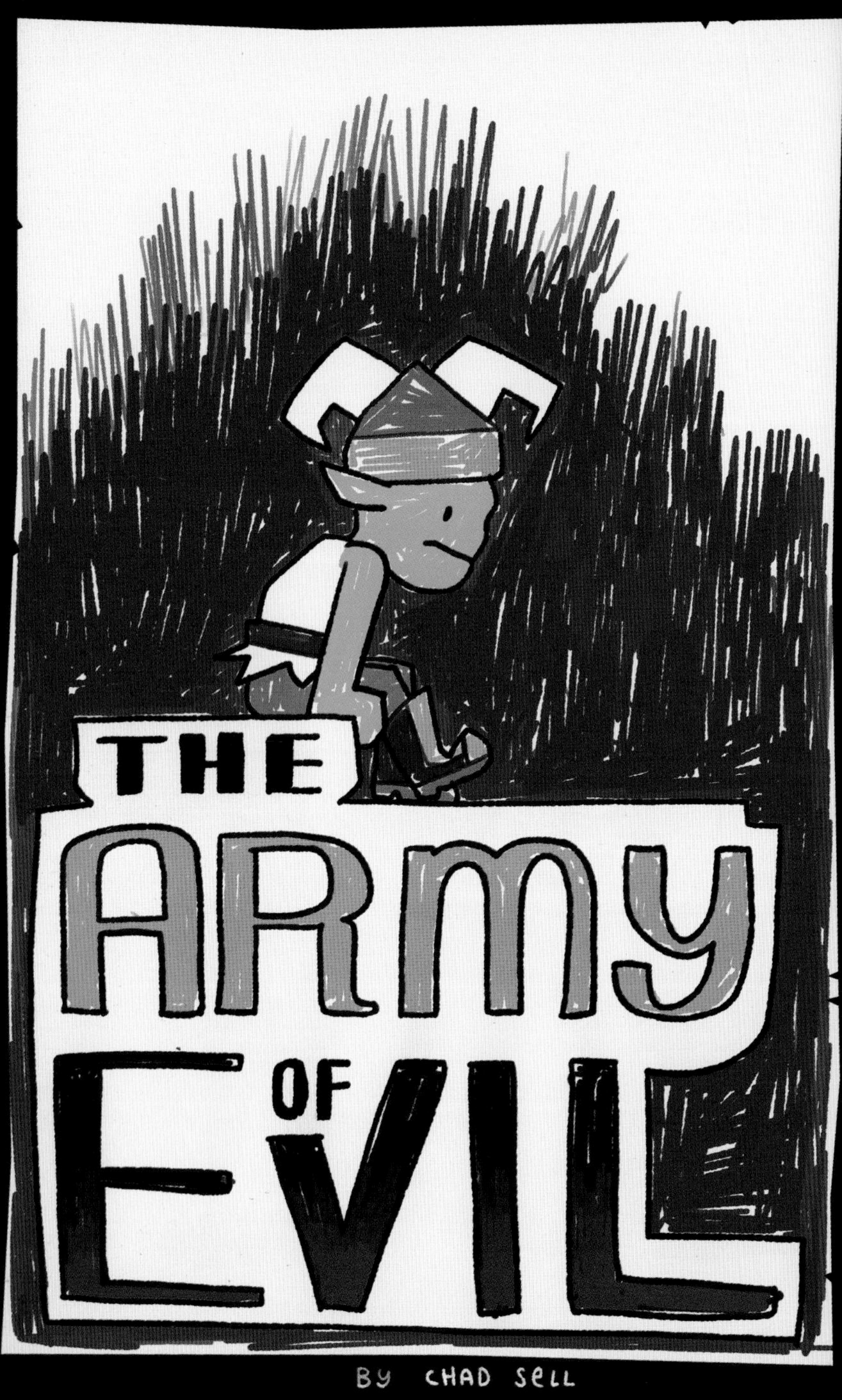
THE
ARMY
OF
EVIL
BY CHAD SELL

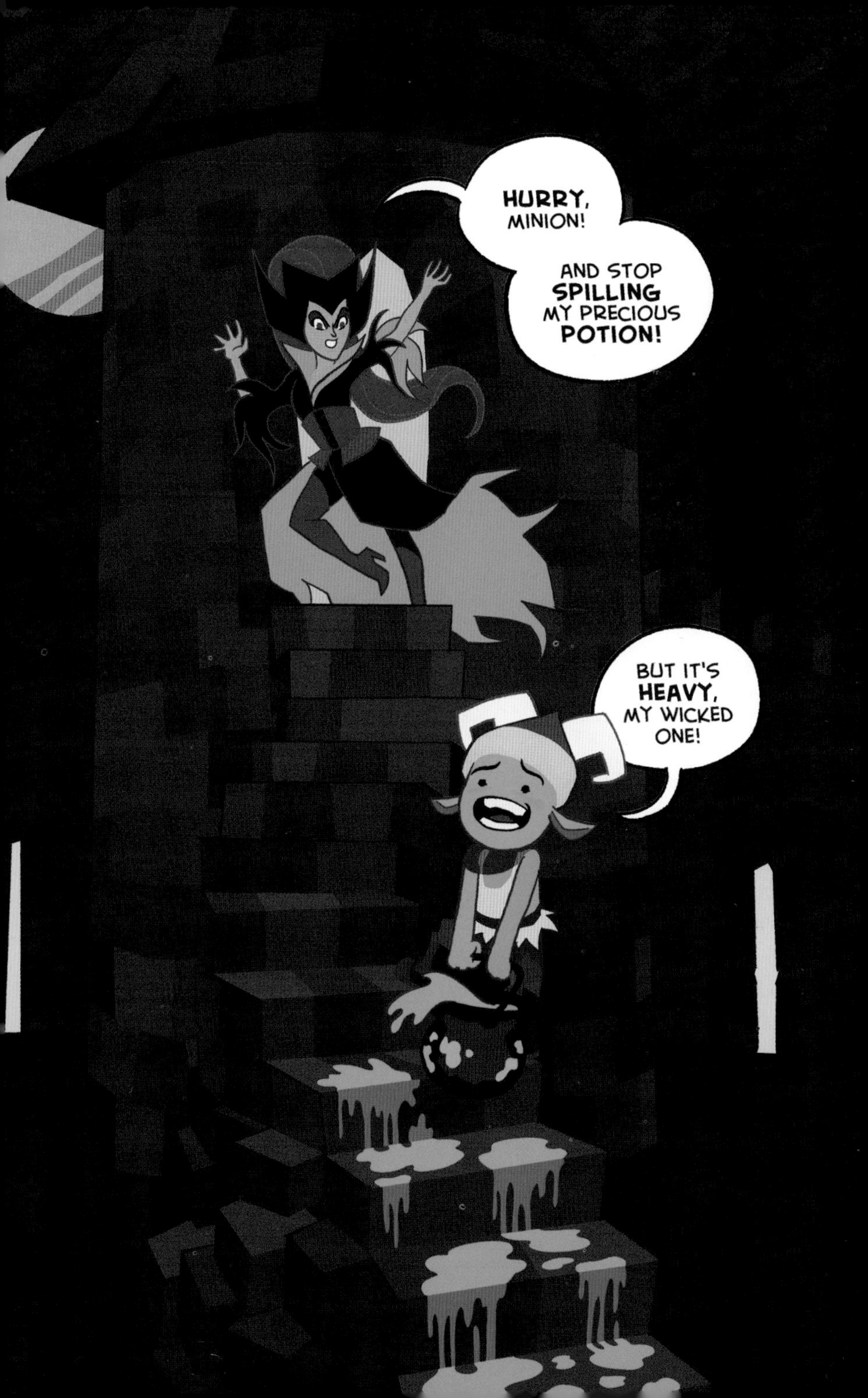
HURRY, MINION!
AND STOP SPILLING MY PRECIOUS POTION!
BUT IT'S HEAVY, MY WICKED ONE!

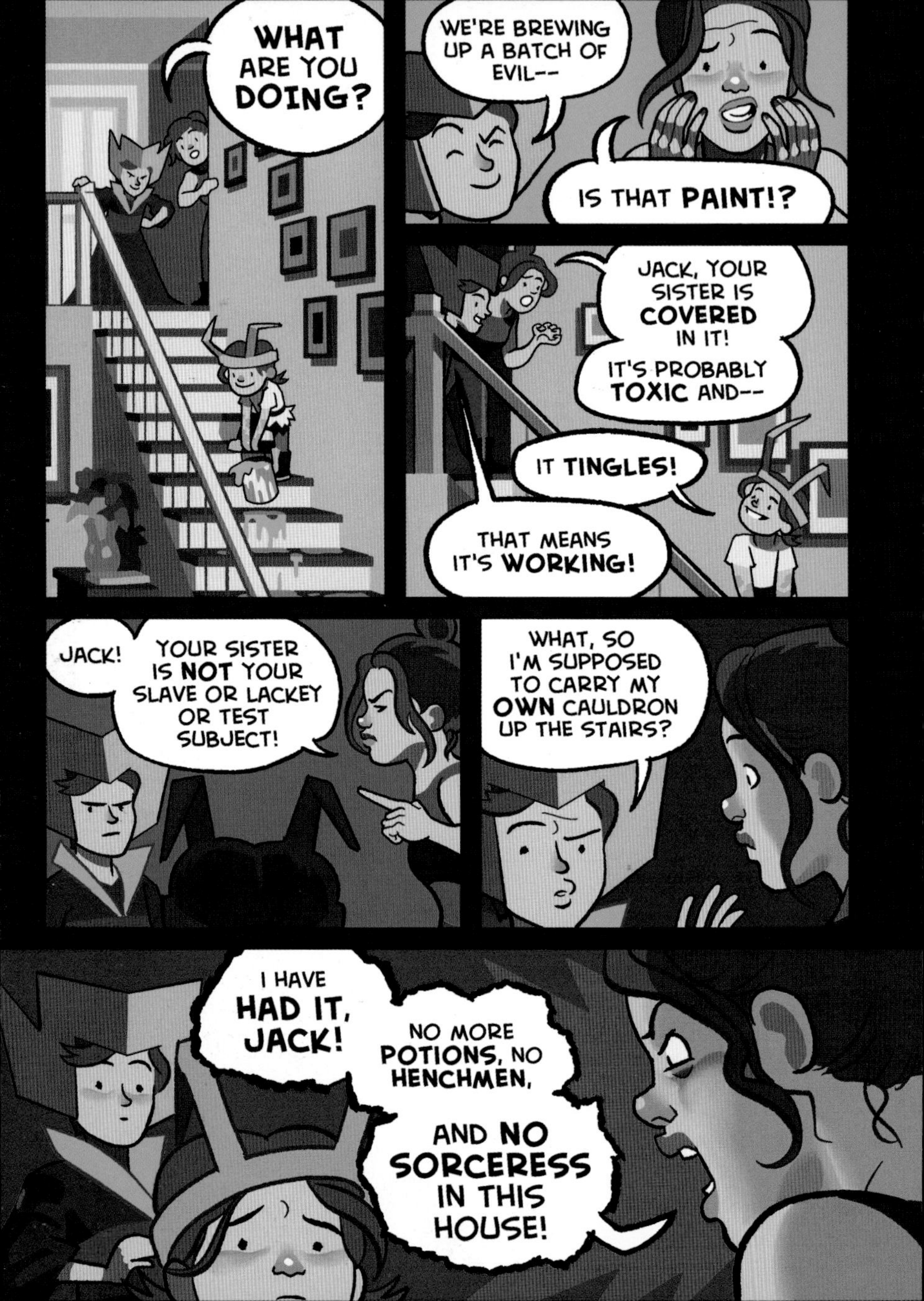
WHAT ARE YOU DOING?
WE'RE BREWING UP A BATCH OF EVIL--
IS THAT PAINT!?
JACK, YOUR SISTER IS COVERED IN IT! IT'S PROBABLY TOXIC AND--
IT TINGLES!
THAT MEANS IT'S WORKING!
JACK!
YOUR SISTER IS NOT YOUR SLAVE OR LACKEY OR TEST SUBJECT!
WHAT, SO I'M SUPPOSED TO CARRY MY OWN CAULDRON UP THE STAIRS?
I HAVE HAD IT, JACK!
NO MORE POTIONS, NO HENCHMEN,
AND NO SORCERESS IN THIS HOUSE!

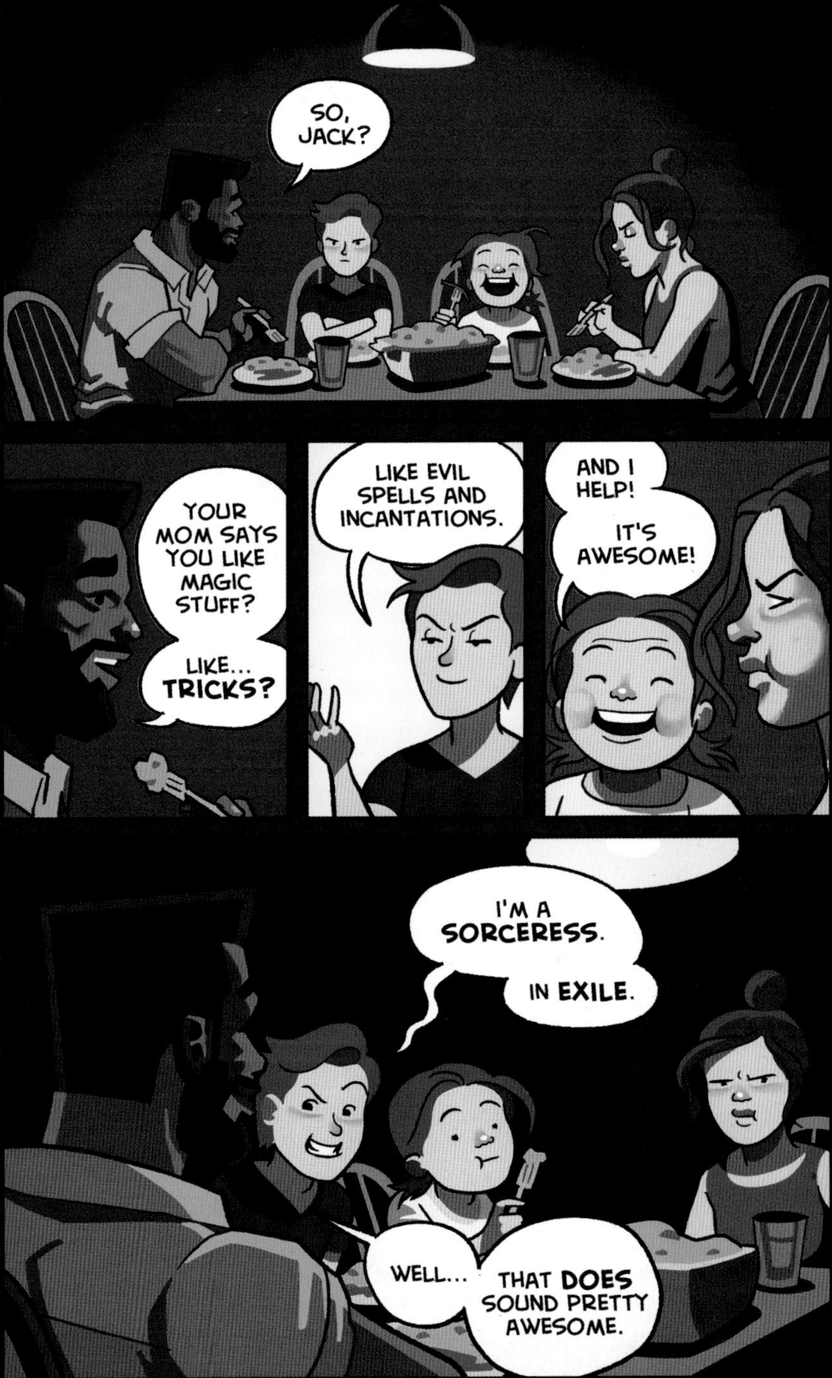
SO, JACK?
YOUR MOM SAYS YOU LIKE MAGIC STUFF?
LIKE... **TRICKS?**
LIKE EVIL SPELLS AND INCANTATIONS.
AND I HELP!
IT'S AWESOME!
I'M A **SORCERESS**.
IN **EXILE**.
WELL...
THAT **DOES** SOUND PRETTY AWESOME.

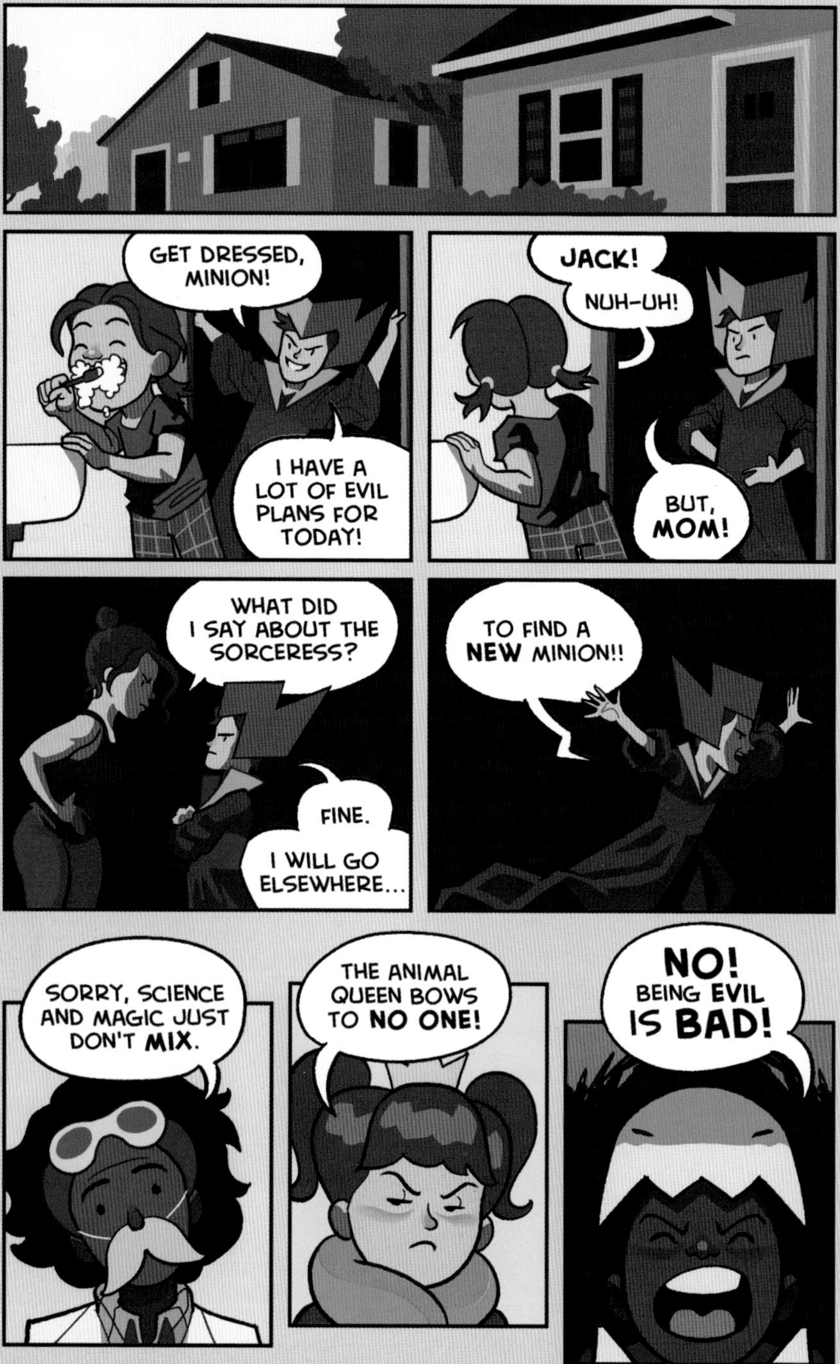
GET DRESSED, MINION!
I HAVE A LOT OF EVIL PLANS FOR TODAY!
JACK!
NUH-UH!
BUT, MOM!
WHAT DID I SAY ABOUT THE SORCERESS?
FINE.
I WILL GO ELSEWHERE...
TO FIND A NEW MINION!!
SORRY, SCIENCE AND MAGIC JUST DON'T MIX.
THE ANIMAL QUEEN BOWS TO NO ONE!
NO! BEING EVIL IS BAD!

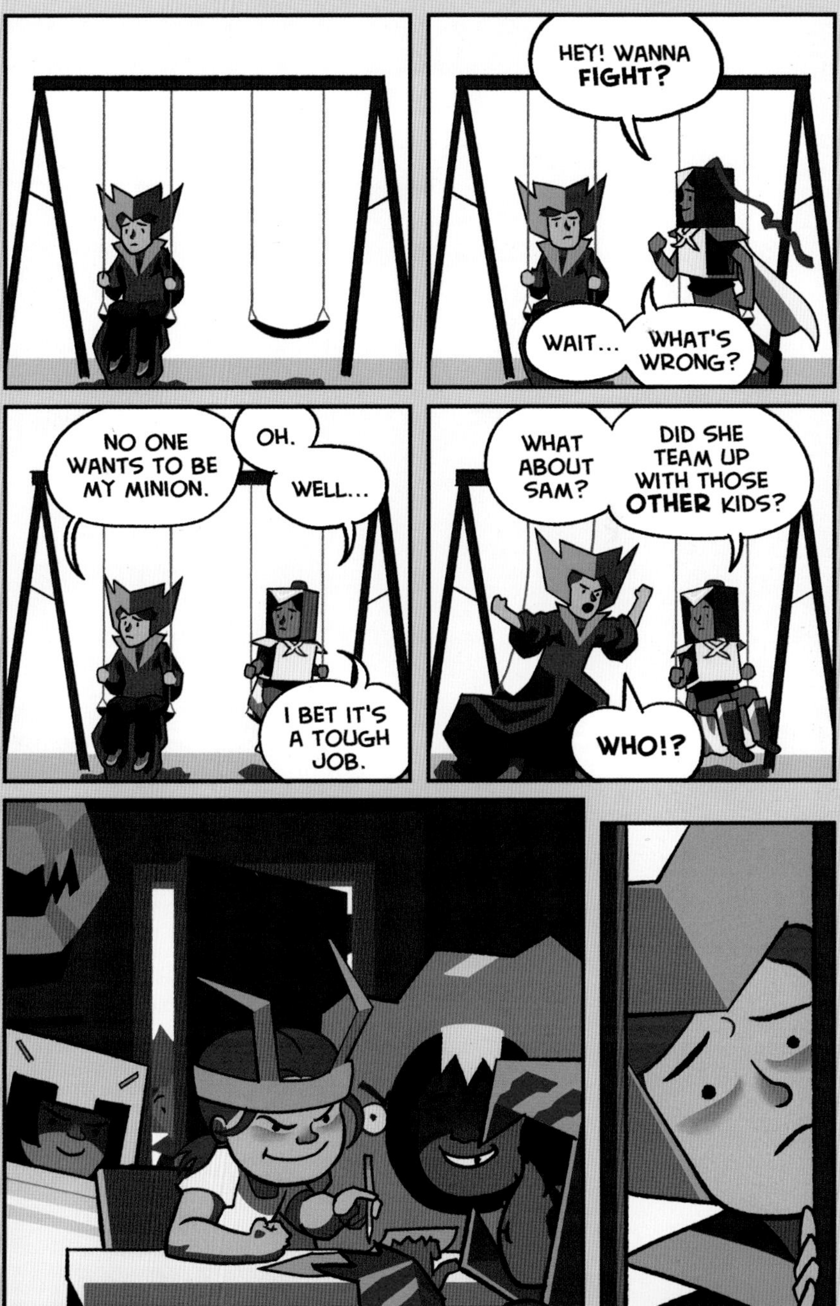
HEY! WANNA FIGHT?
WAIT...
WHAT'S WRONG?
NO ONE WANTS TO BE MY MINION.
OH.
WELL...
I BET IT'S A TOUGH JOB.
WHAT ABOUT SAM?
DID SHE TEAM UP WITH THOSE OTHER KIDS?
WHO!?

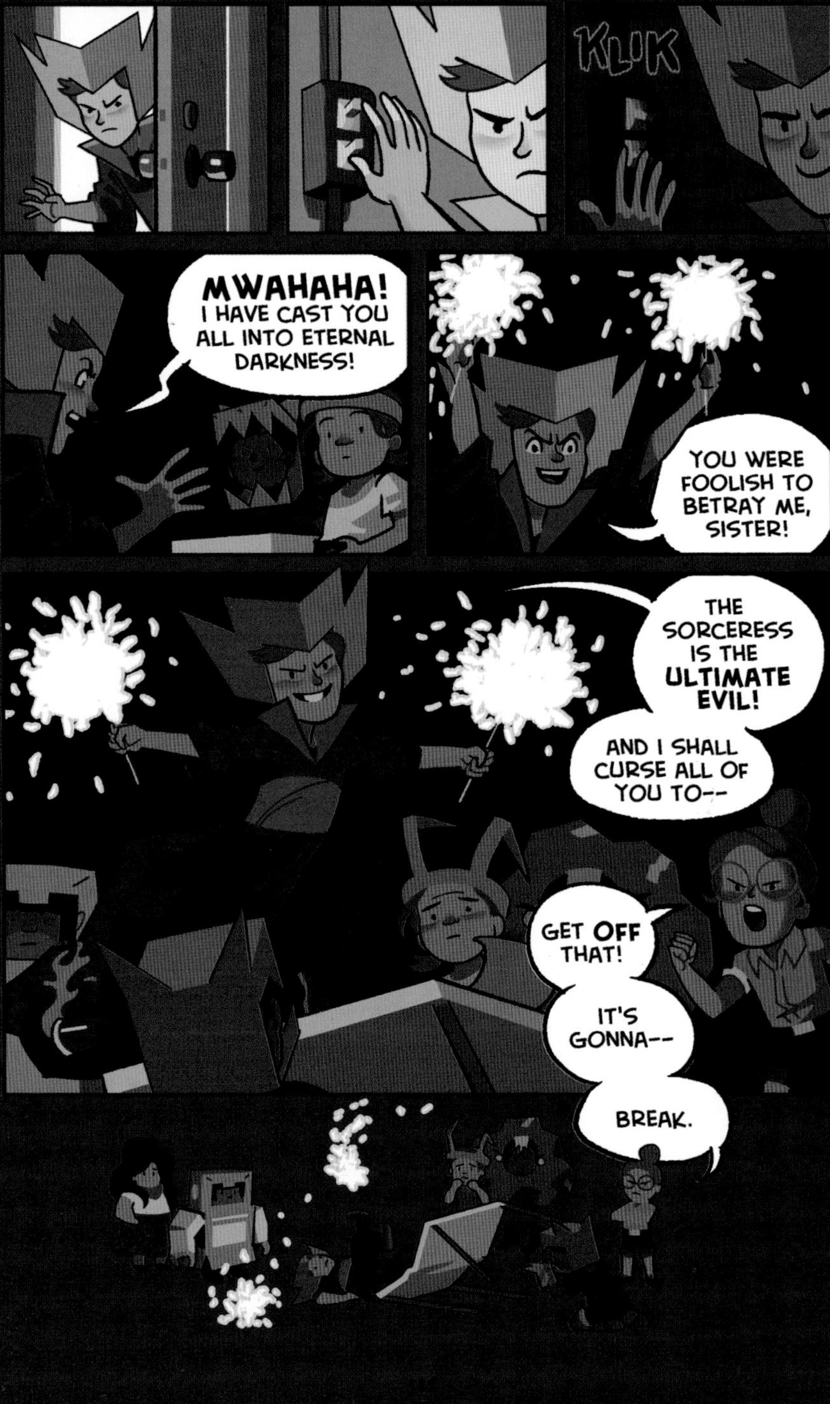
KLIK
MWAHAHA! I HAVE CAST YOU ALL INTO ETERNAL DARKNESS!
YOU WERE FOOLISH TO BETRAY ME, SISTER!
THE SORCERESS IS THE ULTIMATE EVIL!
AND I SHALL CURSE ALL OF YOU TO--
GET OFF THAT!
IT'S GONNA--
BREAK.

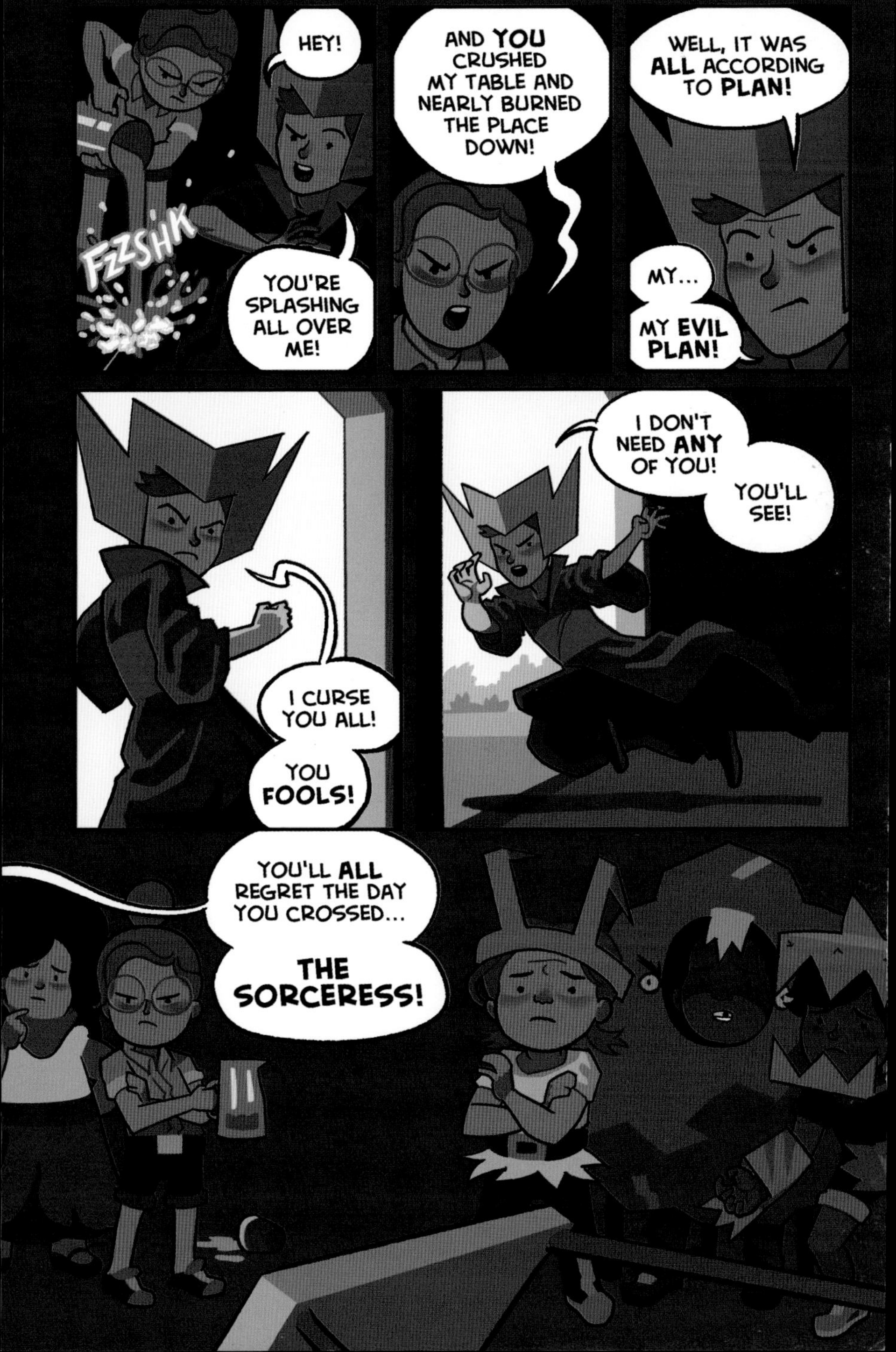
HEY!
FZZSHK
YOU'RE SPLASHING ALL OVER ME!
AND YOU CRUSHED MY TABLE AND NEARLY BURNED THE PLACE DOWN!
WELL, IT WAS ALL ACCORDING TO PLAN!
MY...
MY EVIL PLAN!
I CURSE YOU ALL!
YOU FOOLS!
I DON'T NEED ANY OF YOU!
YOU'LL SEE!
YOU'LL ALL REGRET THE DAY YOU CROSSED...
THE SORCERESS!

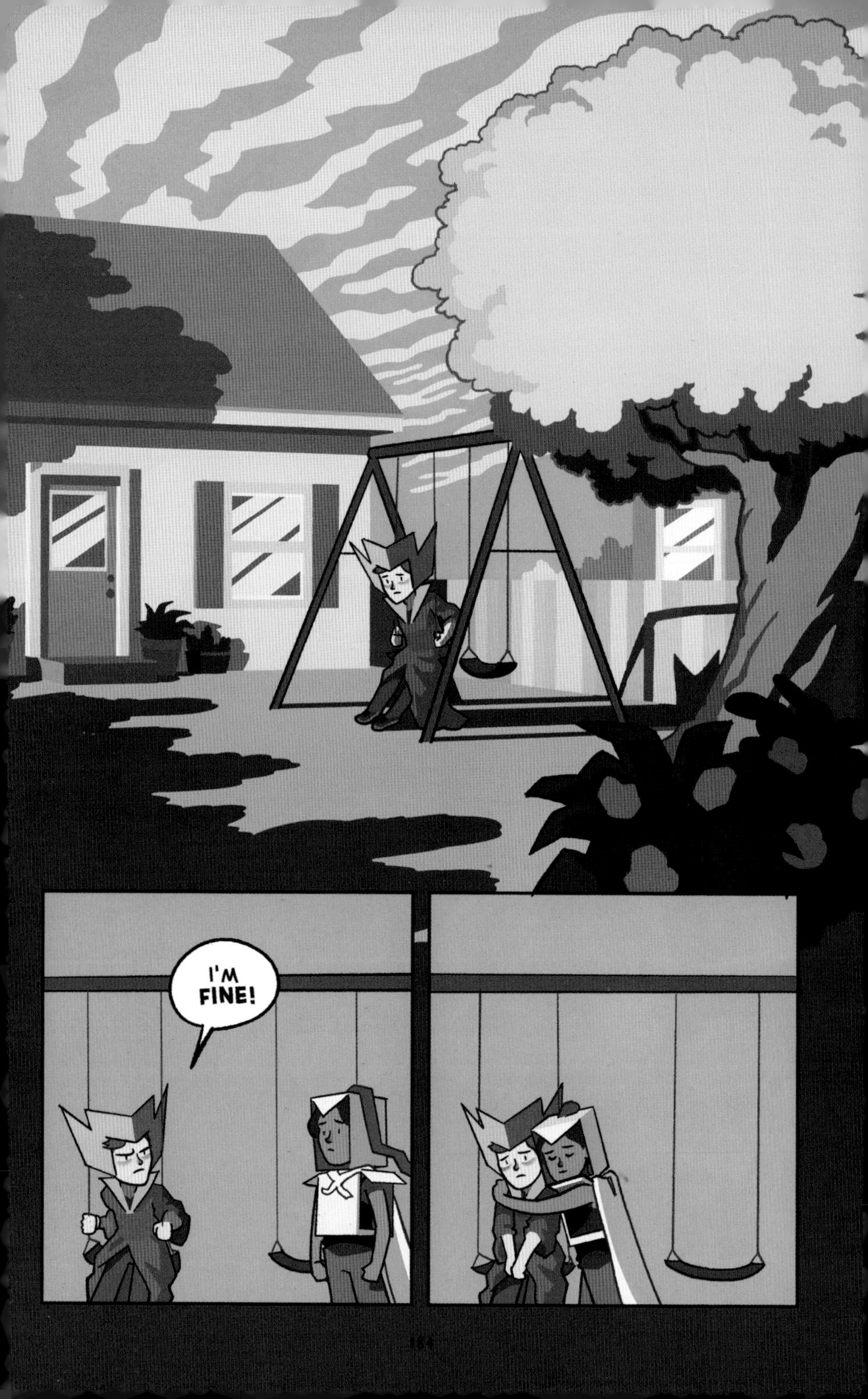
I'M FINE!

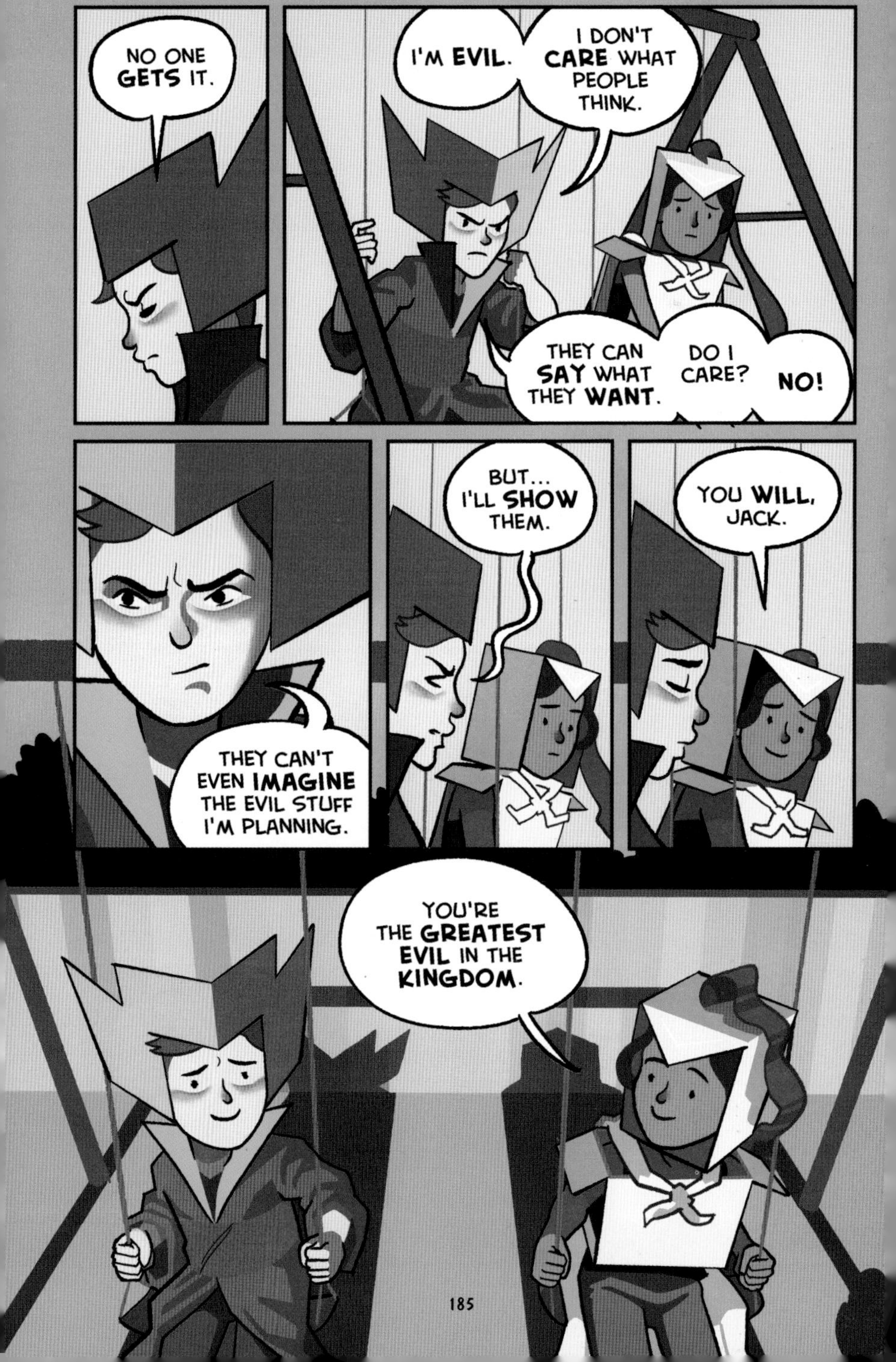
NO ONE GETS IT.
I'M EVIL.
I DON'T CARE WHAT PEOPLE THINK.
THEY CAN SAY WHAT THEY WANT.
DO I CARE?
NO!
THEY CAN'T EVEN IMAGINE THE EVIL STUFF I'M PLANNING.
BUT... I'LL SHOW THEM.
YOU WILL, JACK.
YOU'RE THE GREATEST EVIL IN THE KINGDOM.

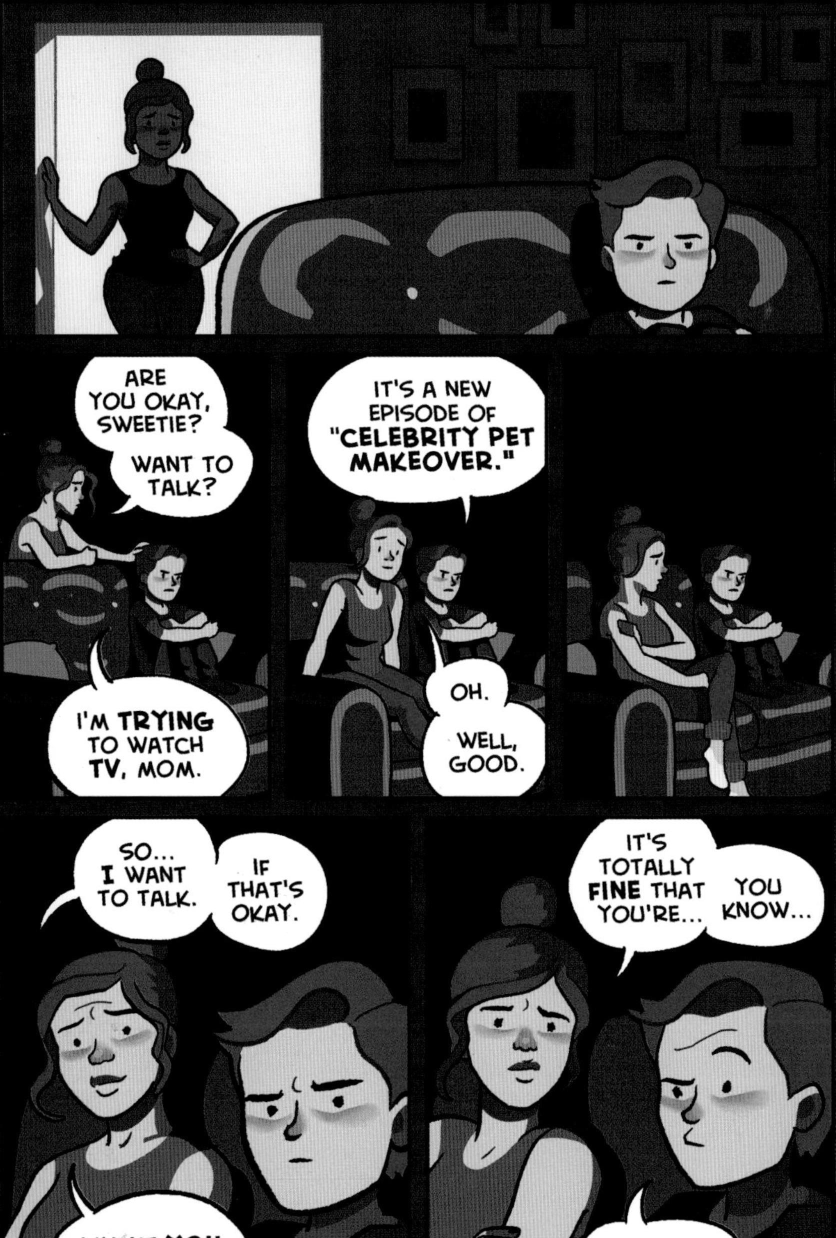
ARE YOU OKAY, SWEETIE?
WANT TO TALK?
I'M TRYING TO WATCH TV, MOM.
IT'S A NEW EPISODE OF "CELEBRITY PET MAKEOVER."
OH.
WELL, GOOD.
SO... I WANT TO TALK.
IF THAT'S OKAY.
I WANT YOU TO KNOW THAT I'M OKAY WITH IT.
IT'S TOTALLY FINE THAT YOU'RE...
YOU KNOW...
WHAT?
EVIL?

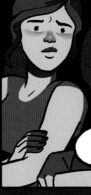

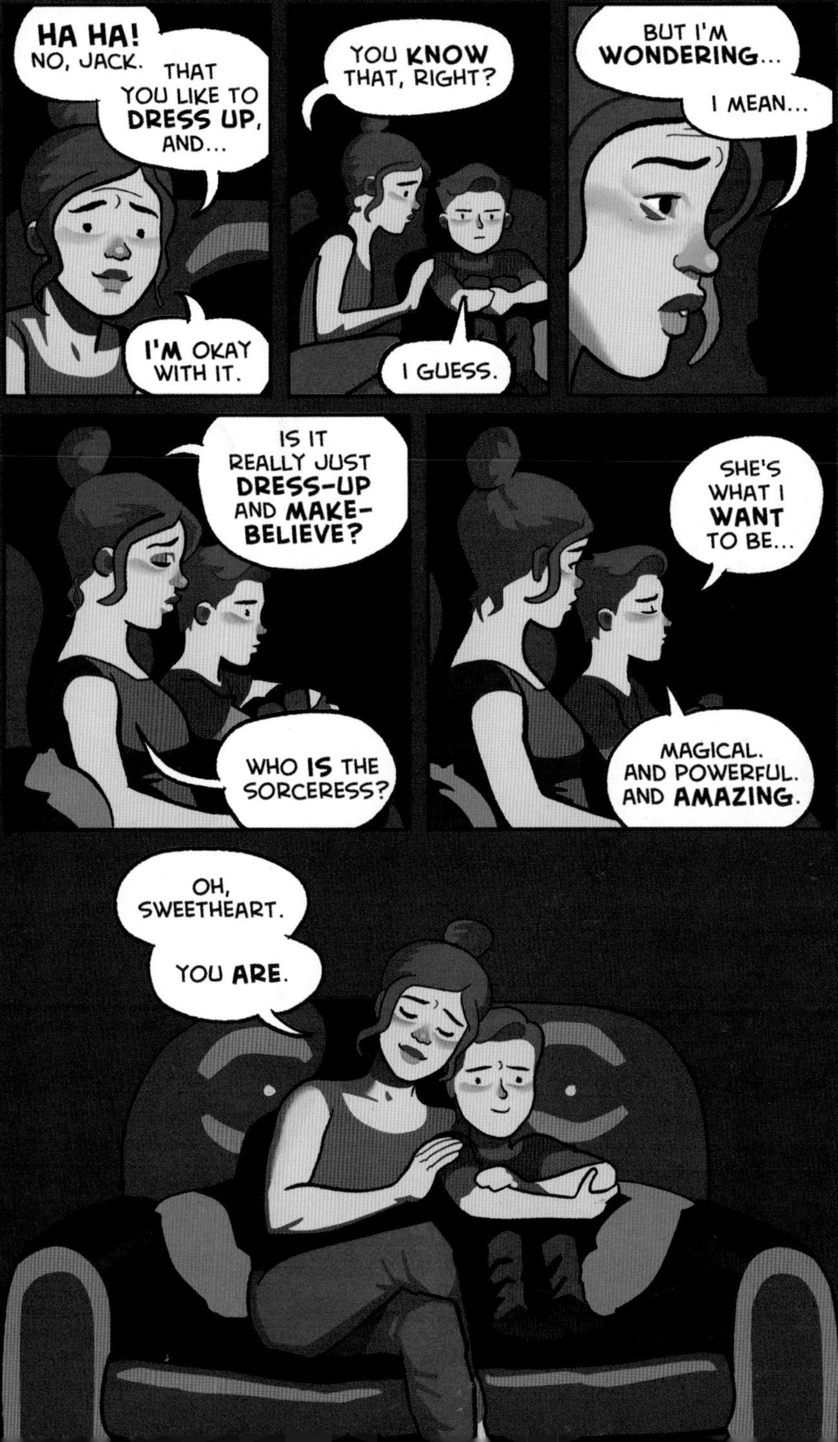
HA HA! NO, JACK.
THAT YOU LIKE TO DRESS UP, AND...
I'M OKAY WITH IT.
YOU KNOW THAT, RIGHT?
I GUESS.
BUT I'M WONDERING...
I MEAN...
IS IT REALLY JUST DRESS-UP AND MAKE-BELIEVE?
WHO IS THE SORCERESS?
SHE'S WHAT I WANT TO BE...
MAGICAL. AND POWERFUL. AND AMAZING.
OH, SWEETHEART.
YOU ARE.

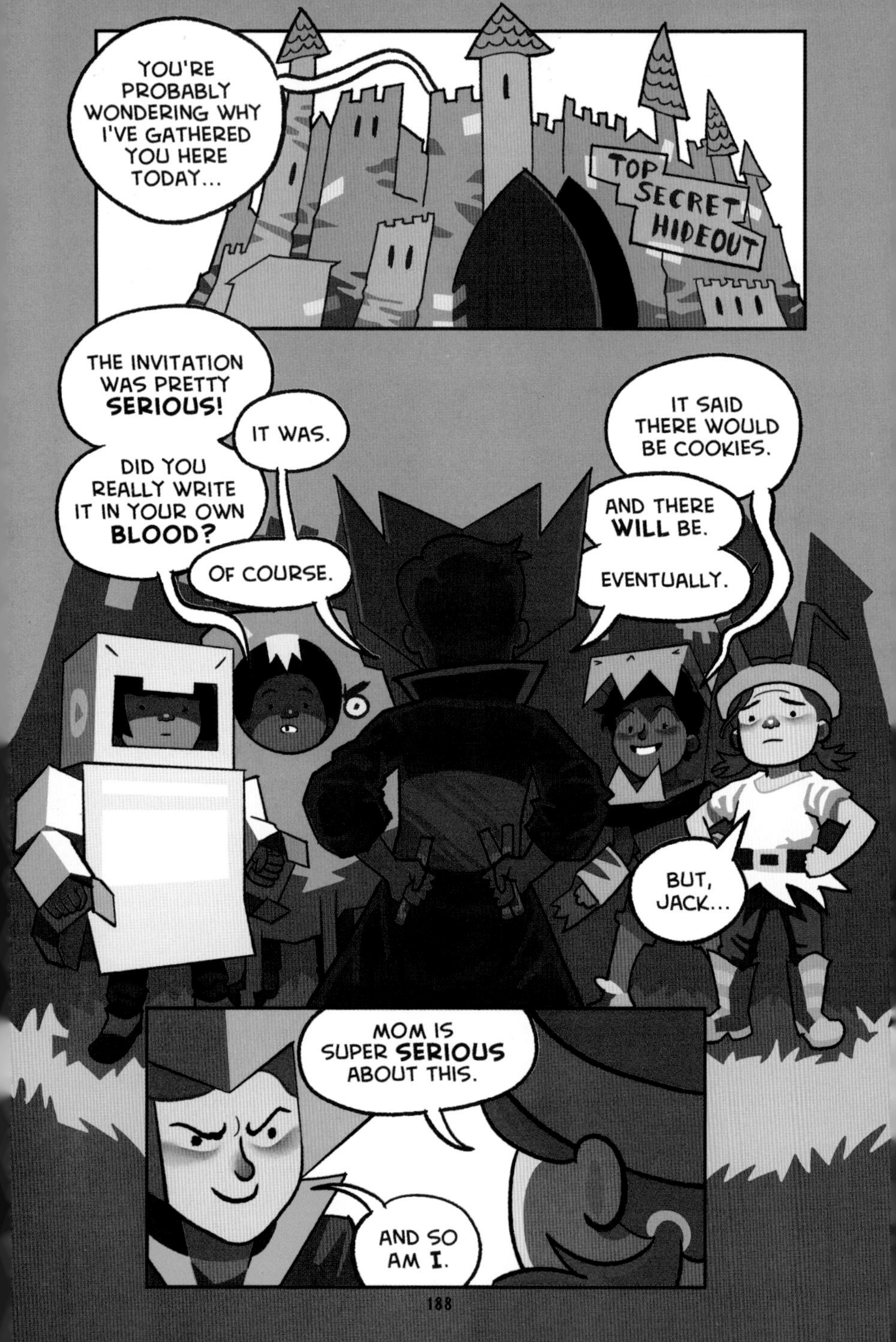
YOU'RE PROBABLY WONDERING WHY I'VE GATHERED YOU HERE TODAY...
TOP SECRET HIDEOUT
THE INVITATION WAS PRETTY **SERIOUS!**
DID YOU REALLY WRITE IT IN YOUR OWN **BLOOD?**
IT WAS.
OF COURSE.
IT SAID THERE WOULD BE COOKIES.
AND THERE **WILL** BE.
EVENTUALLY.
BUT, JACK...
MOM IS SUPER **SERIOUS** ABOUT THIS.
AND SO AM **I**.

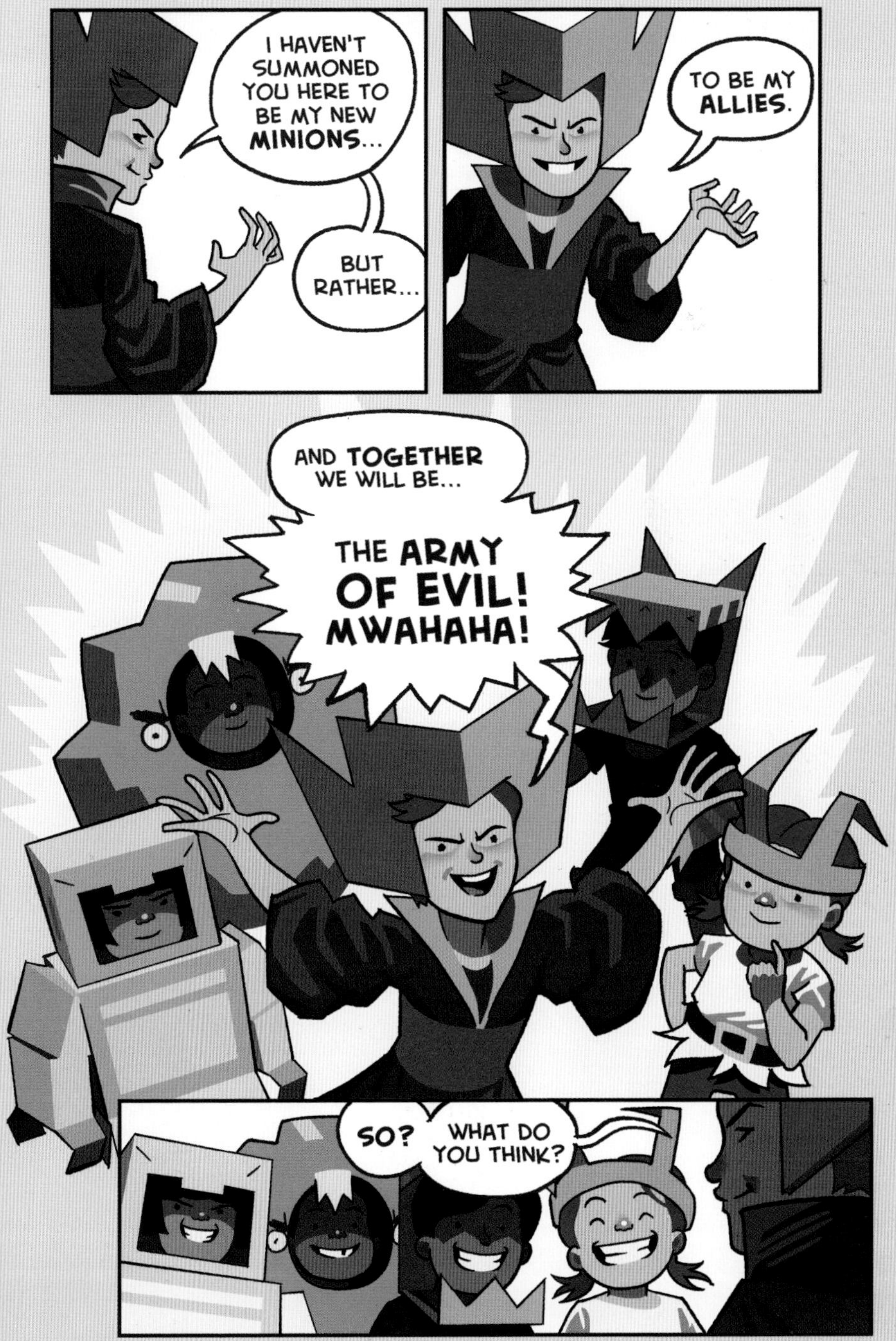
I HAVEN'T SUMMONED YOU HERE TO BE MY NEW MINIONS...
BUT RATHER...
TO BE MY ALLIES.
AND TOGETHER WE WILL BE...
THE ARMY OF EVIL! MWAHAHA!
SO?
WHAT DO YOU THINK?

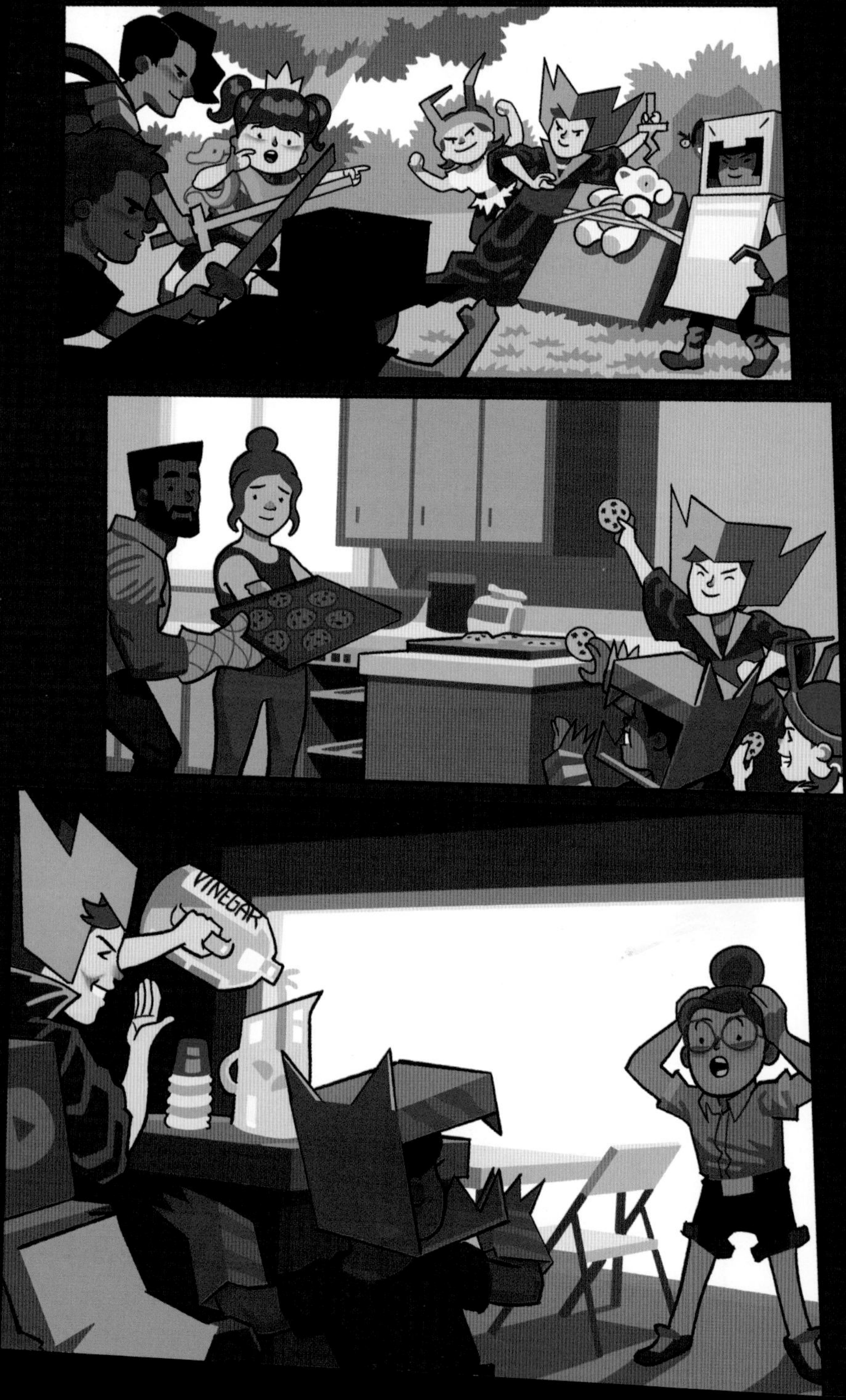
VINEGAR

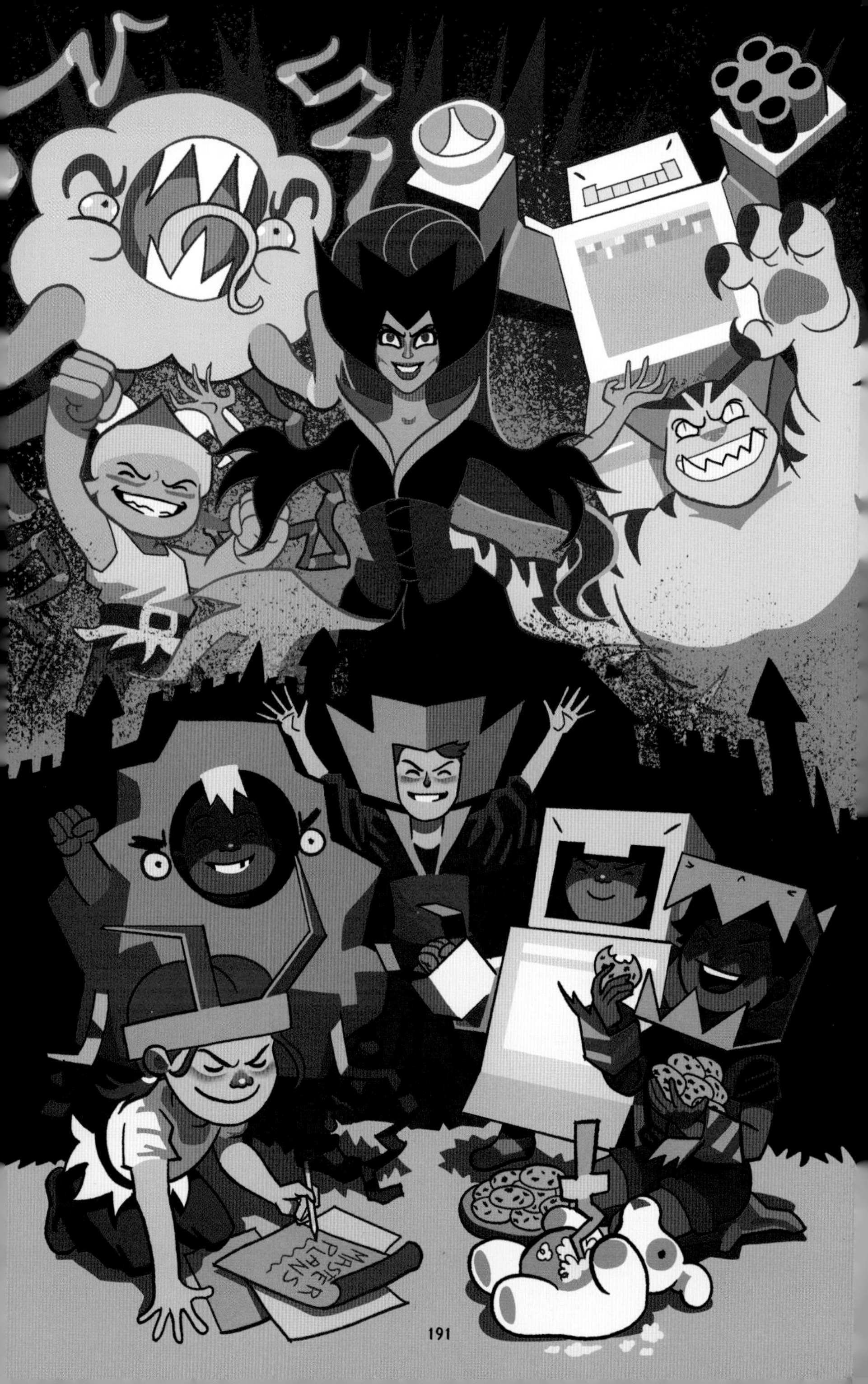
MASTER PLANS

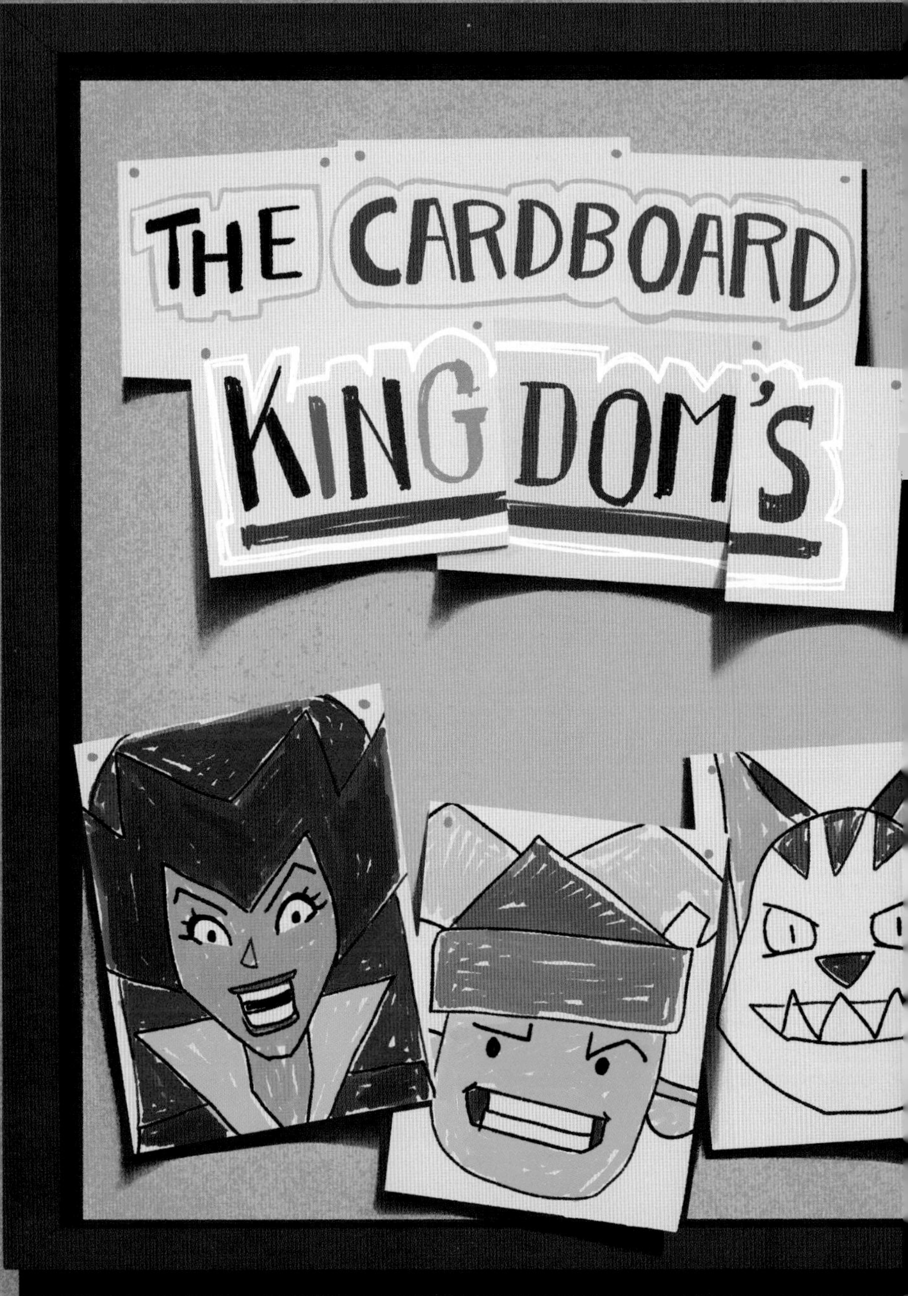
THE CARDBOARD
KINGDOM'S

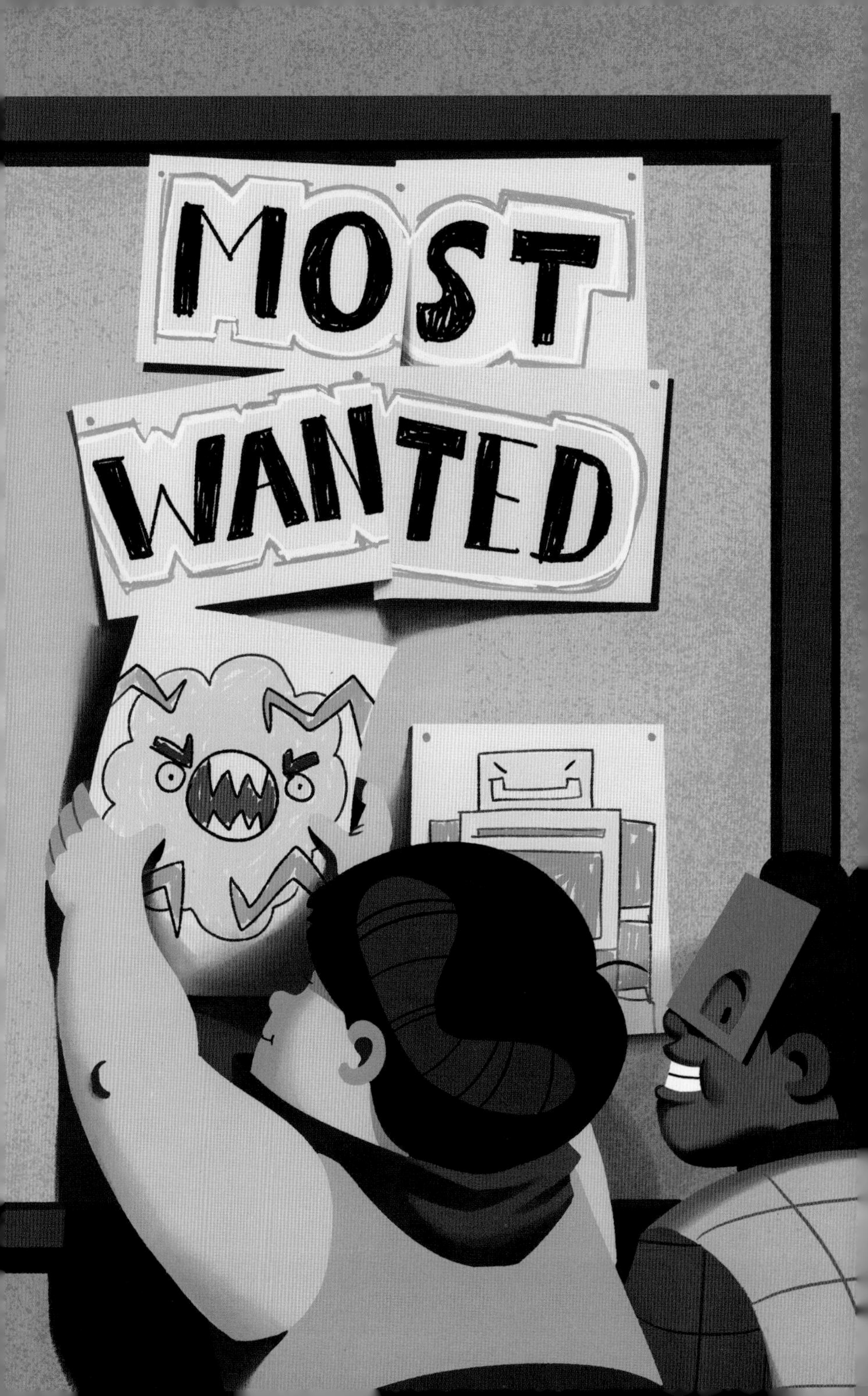
MOST
WANTED

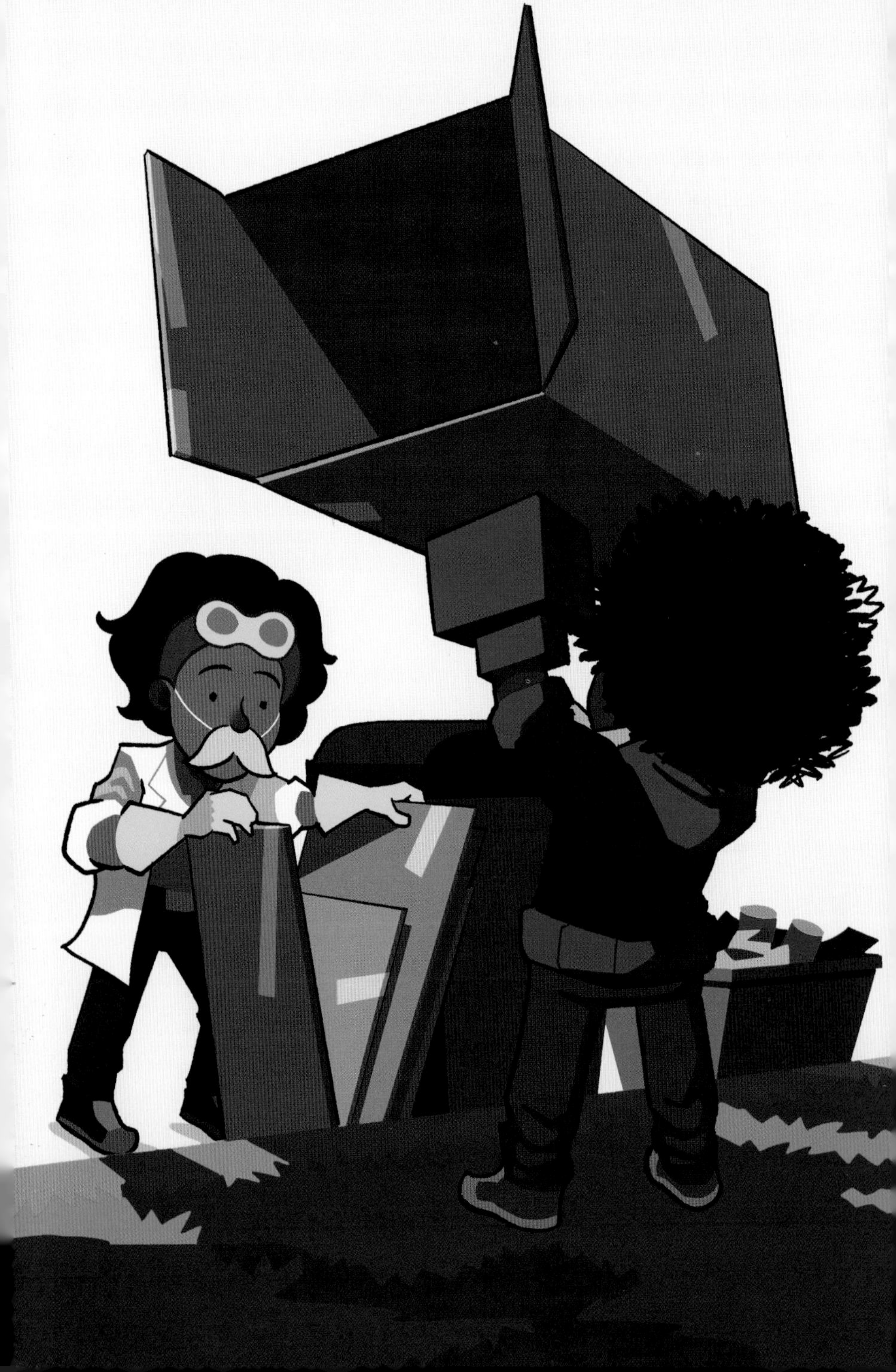

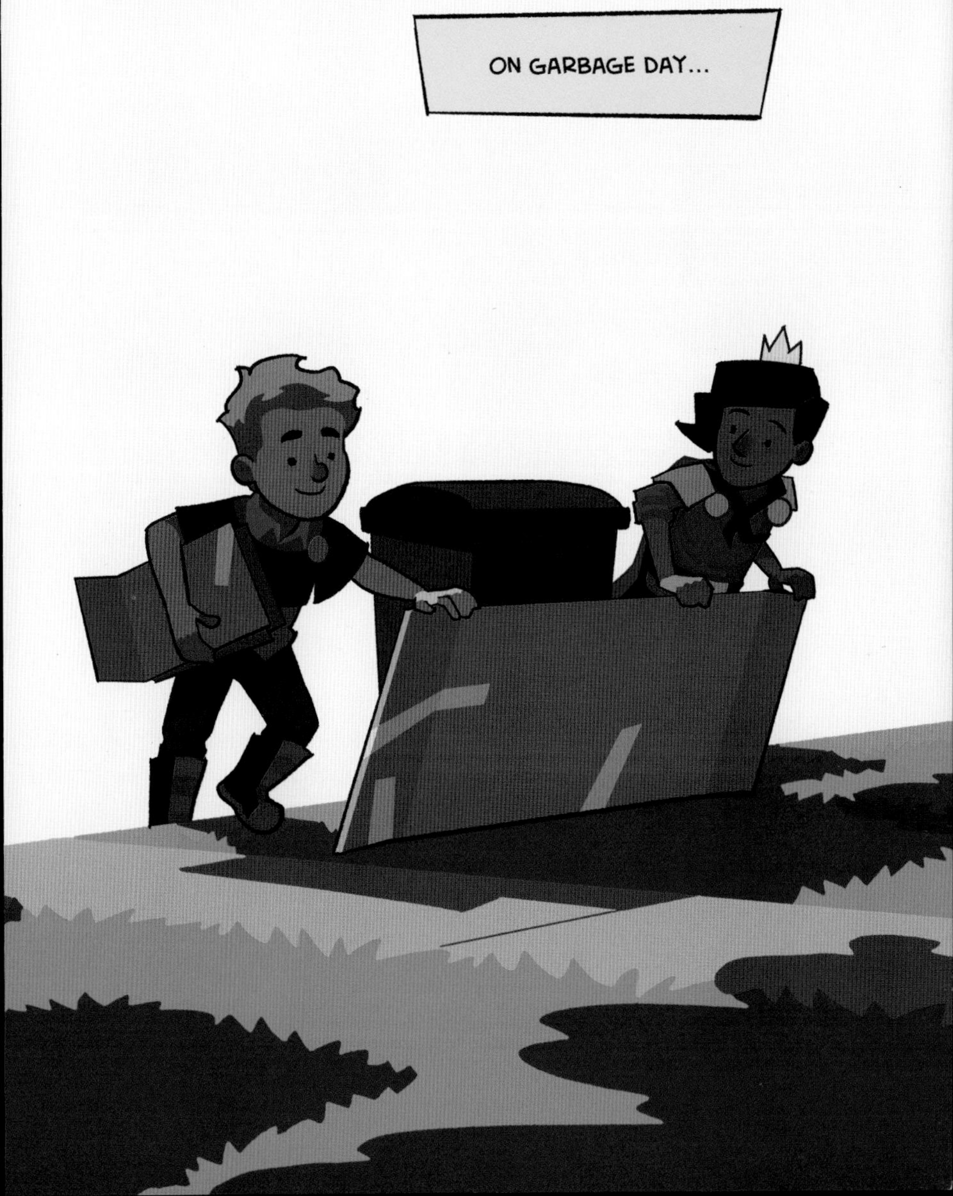
ON GARBAGE DAY...

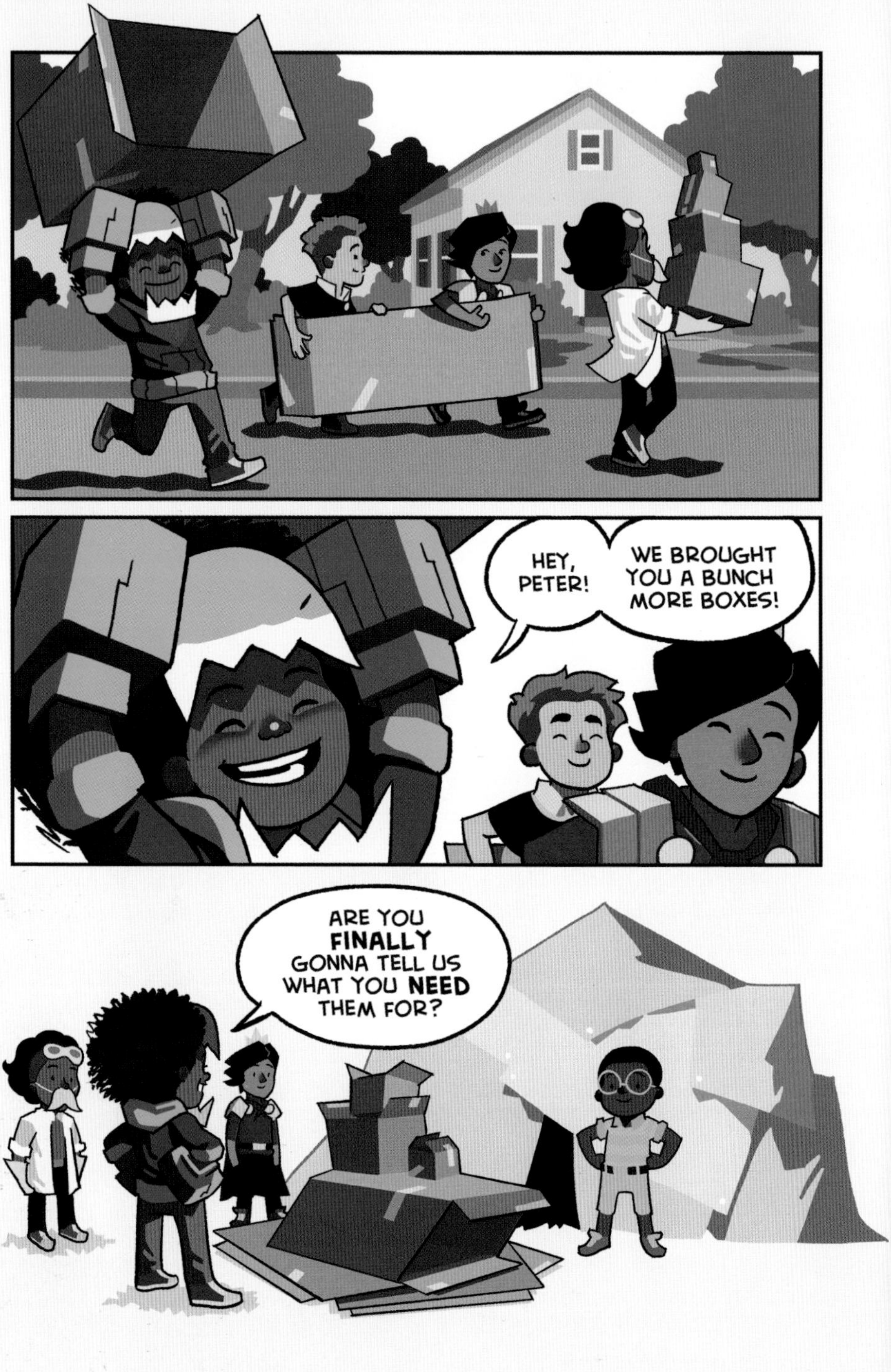
HEY, PETER!
WE BROUGHT YOU A BUNCH MORE BOXES!
ARE YOU **FINALLY** GONNA TELL US WHAT YOU **NEED** THEM FOR?

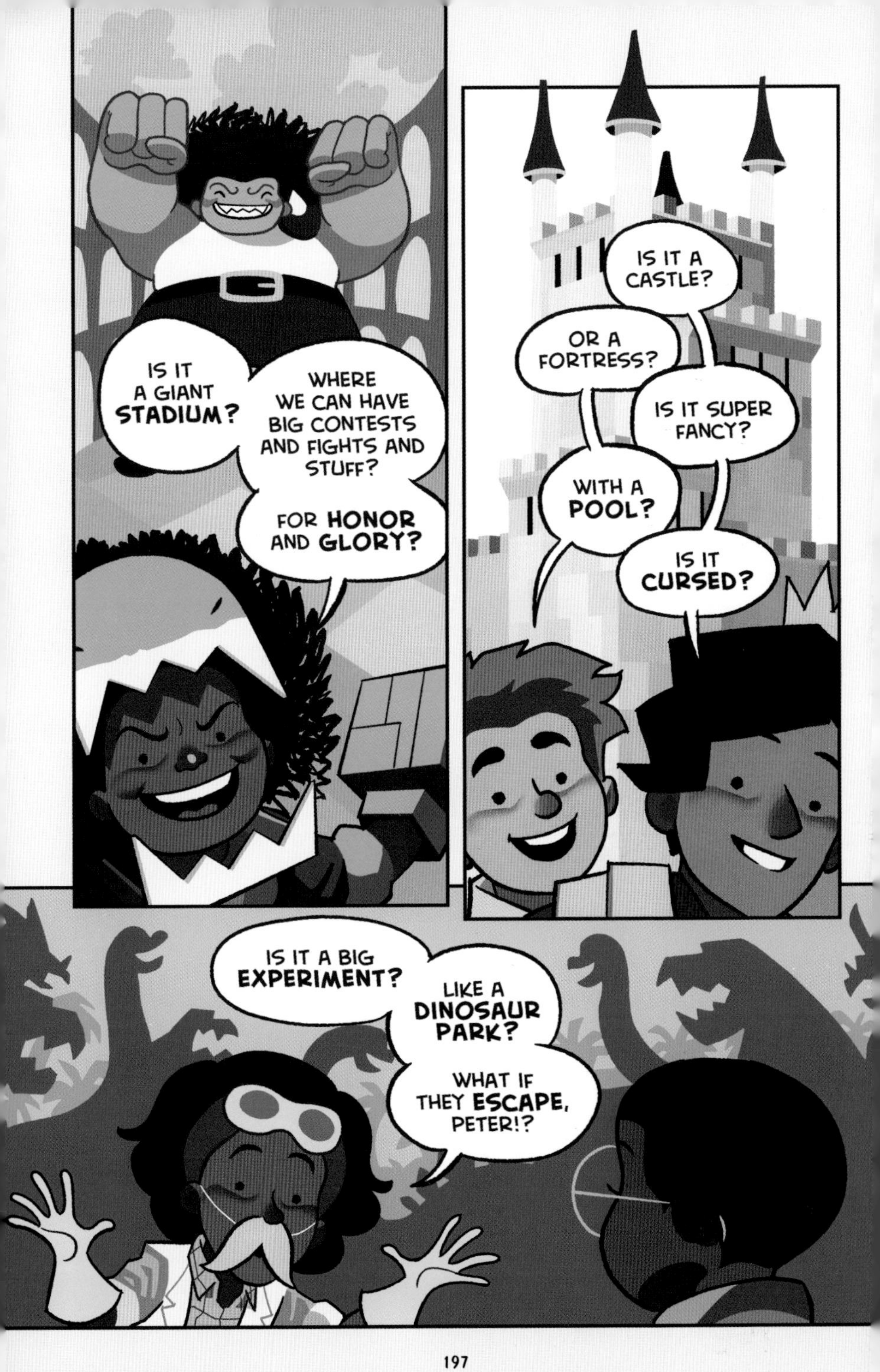
IS IT A GIANT STADIUM?
WHERE WE CAN HAVE BIG CONTESTS AND FIGHTS AND STUFF?
FOR HONOR AND GLORY?
IS IT A CASTLE?
OR A FORTRESS?
IS IT SUPER FANCY?
WITH A POOL?
IS IT CURSED?
IS IT A BIG EXPERIMENT?
LIKE A DINOSAUR PARK?
WHAT IF THEY ESCAPE, PETER!?

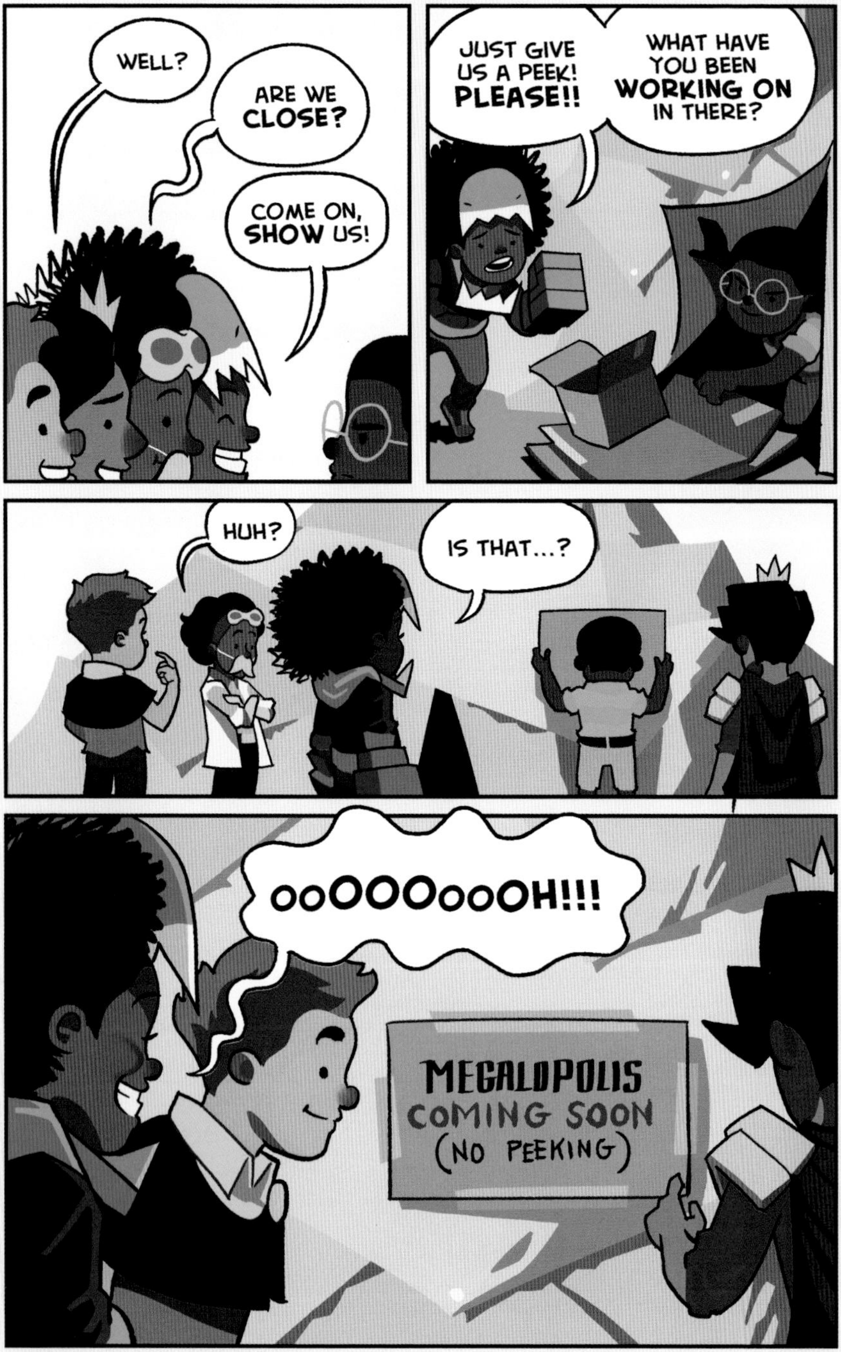
WELL?
ARE WE CLOSE?
COME ON, SHOW US!
JUST GIVE US A PEEK! PLEASE!!
WHAT HAVE YOU BEEN WORKING ON IN THERE?
HUH?
IS THAT...?
ooOOOoooOH!!!
MEGALOPOLIS
COMING SOON
(NO PEEKING)

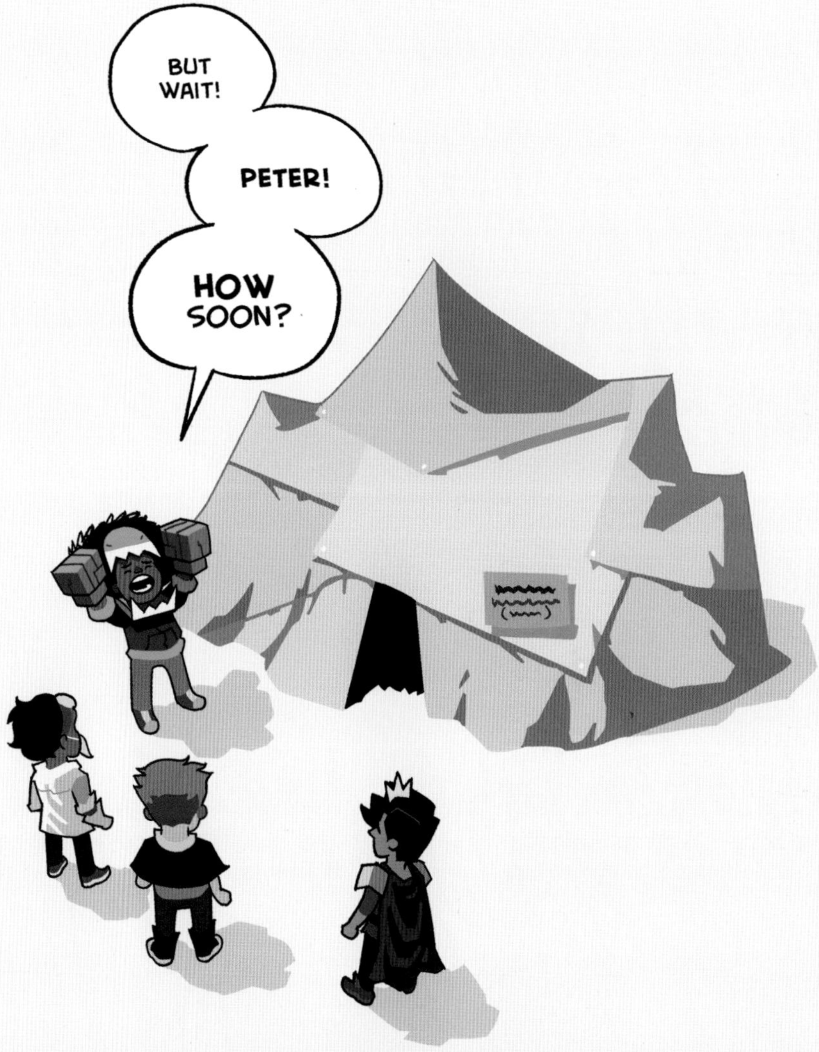
BUT WAIT!
PETER!
HOW SOON?

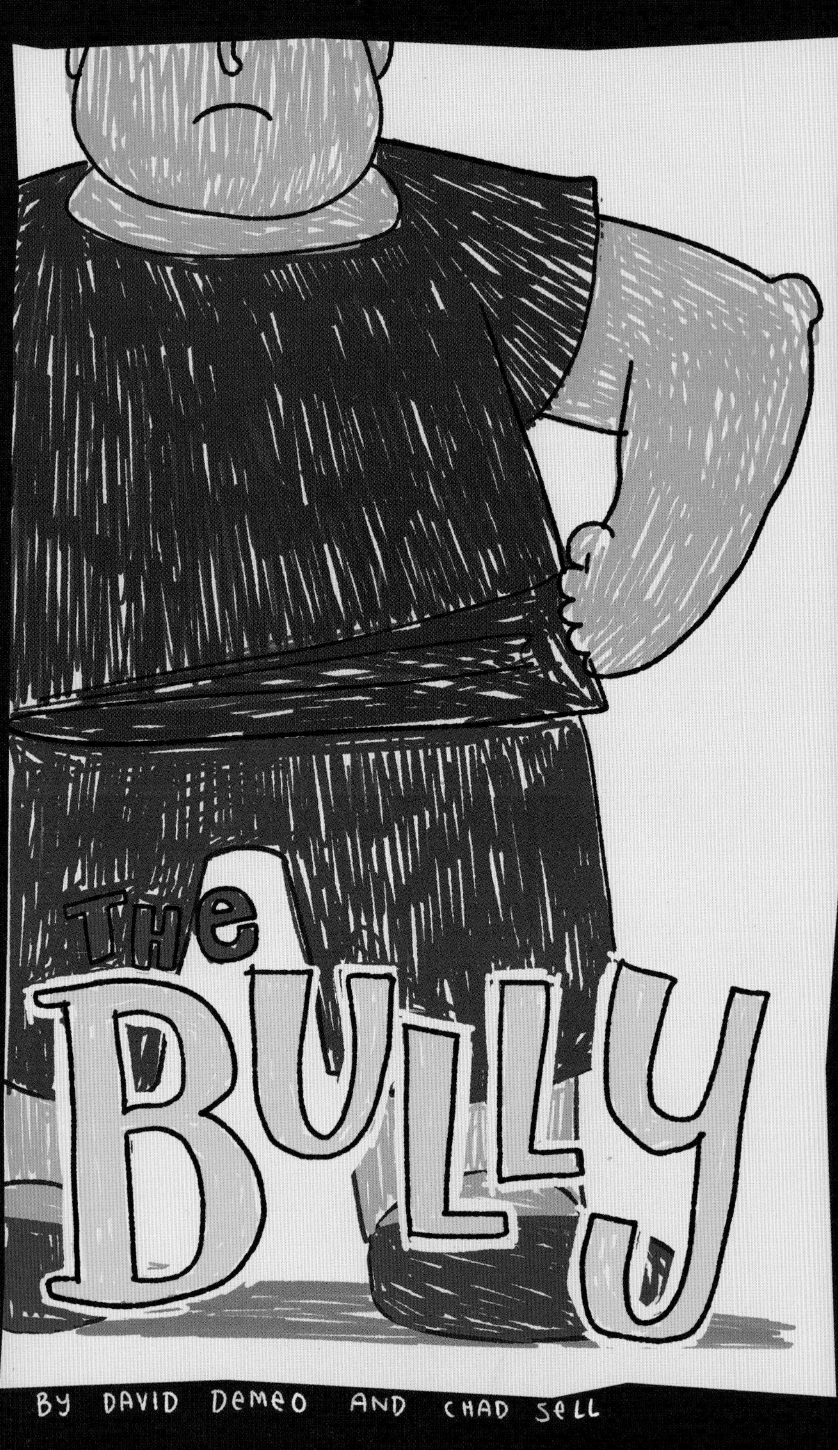
THE BULLY
BY DAVID DEMEO AND CHAD SELL

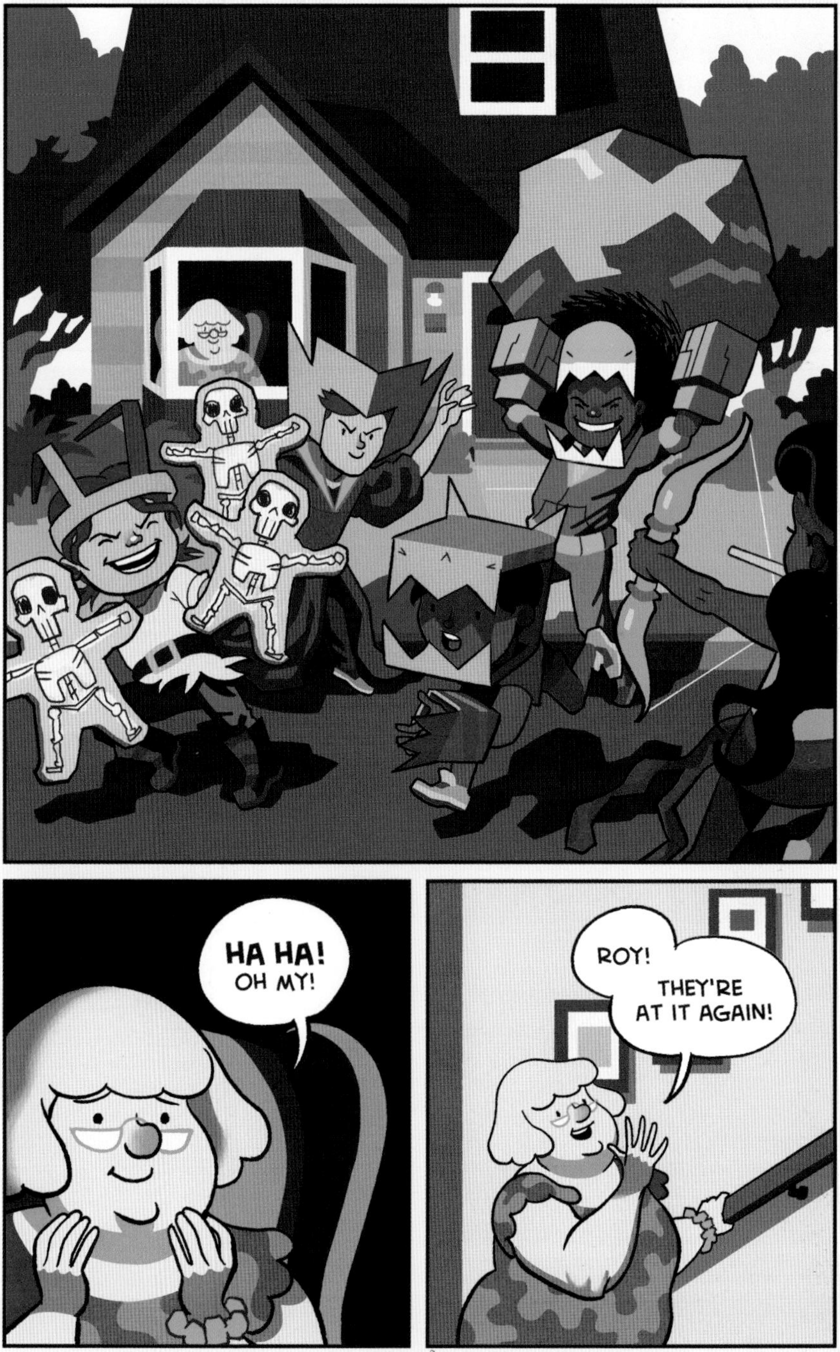
HA HA!
OH MY!
ROY!
THEY'RE AT IT AGAIN!

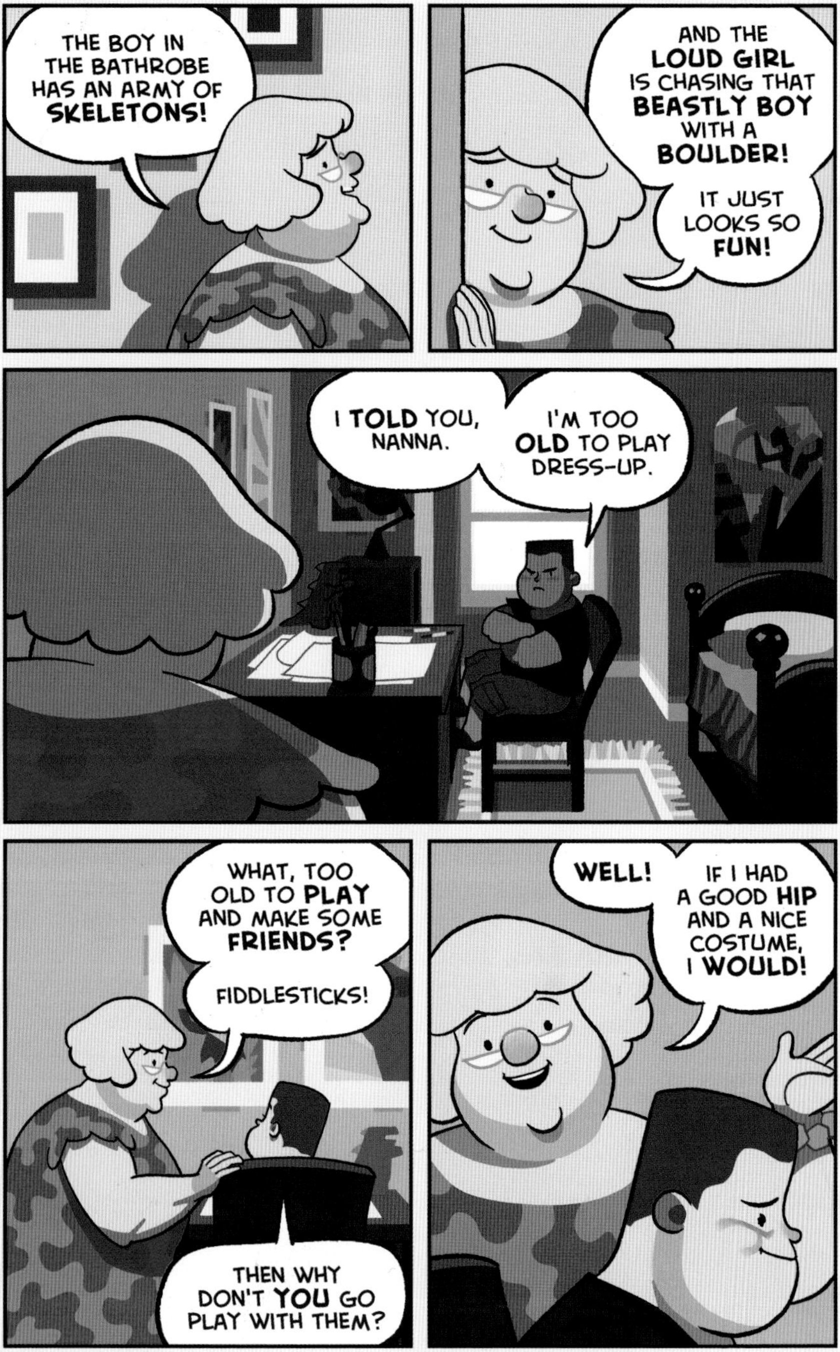
THE BOY IN THE BATHROBE HAS AN ARMY OF SKELETONS!
AND THE LOUD GIRL IS CHASING THAT BEASTLY BOY WITH A BOULDER!
IT JUST LOOKS SO FUN!
I TOLD YOU, NANNA.
I'M TOO OLD TO PLAY DRESS-UP.
WHAT, TOO OLD TO PLAY AND MAKE SOME FRIENDS?
FIDDLESTICKS!
THEN WHY DON'T YOU GO PLAY WITH THEM?
WELL!
IF I HAD A GOOD HIP AND A NICE COSTUME, I WOULD!

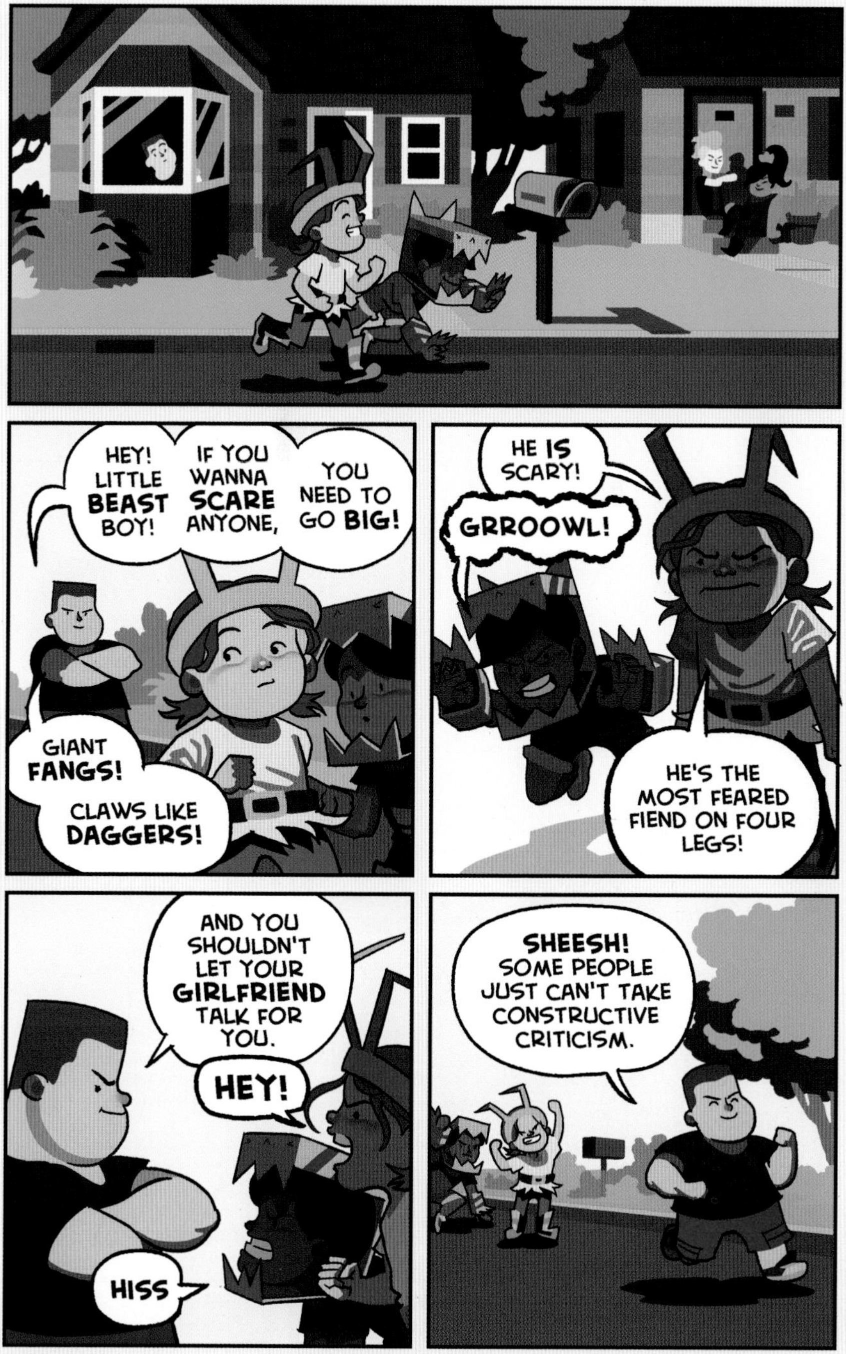

HEY! LITTLE BEAST BOY!
IF YOU WANNA SCARE ANYONE,
YOU NEED TO GO BIG!
GIANT FANGS!
CLAWS LIKE DAGGERS!
HE IS SCARY!
GRROOWL!
HE'S THE MOST FEARED FIEND ON FOUR LEGS!
AND YOU SHOULDN'T LET YOUR GIRLFRIEND TALK FOR YOU.
HEY!
HISS
SHEESH! SOME PEOPLE JUST CAN'T TAKE CONSTRUCTIVE CRITICISM.

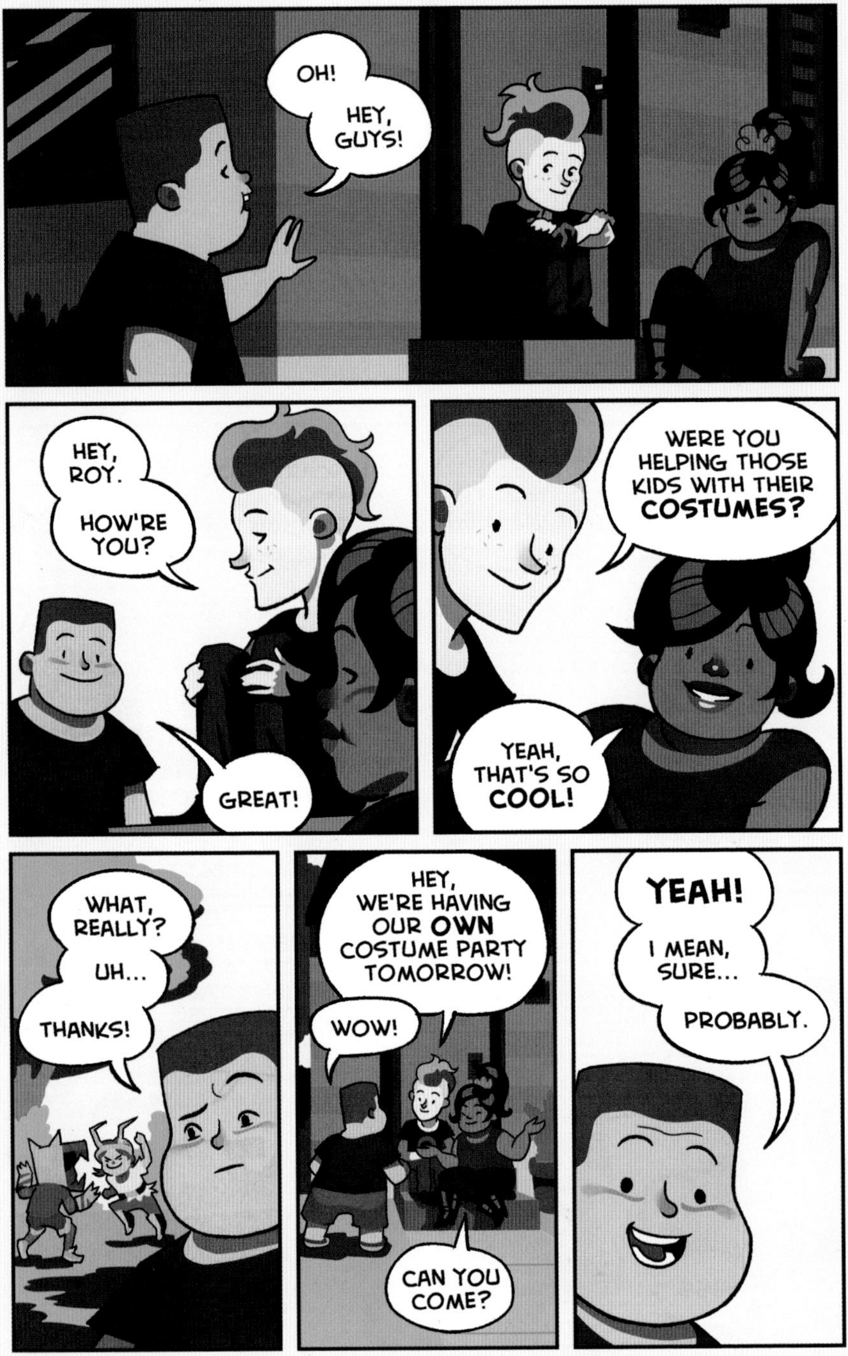
OH!
HEY, GUYS!
HEY, ROY.
HOW'RE YOU?
GREAT!
WERE YOU HELPING THOSE KIDS WITH THEIR COSTUMES?
YEAH, THAT'S SO COOL!
WHAT, REALLY?
UH...
THANKS!
HEY, WE'RE HAVING OUR OWN COSTUME PARTY TOMORROW!
WOW!
CAN YOU COME?
YEAH!
I MEAN, SURE...
PROBABLY.

THE NEXT DAY...

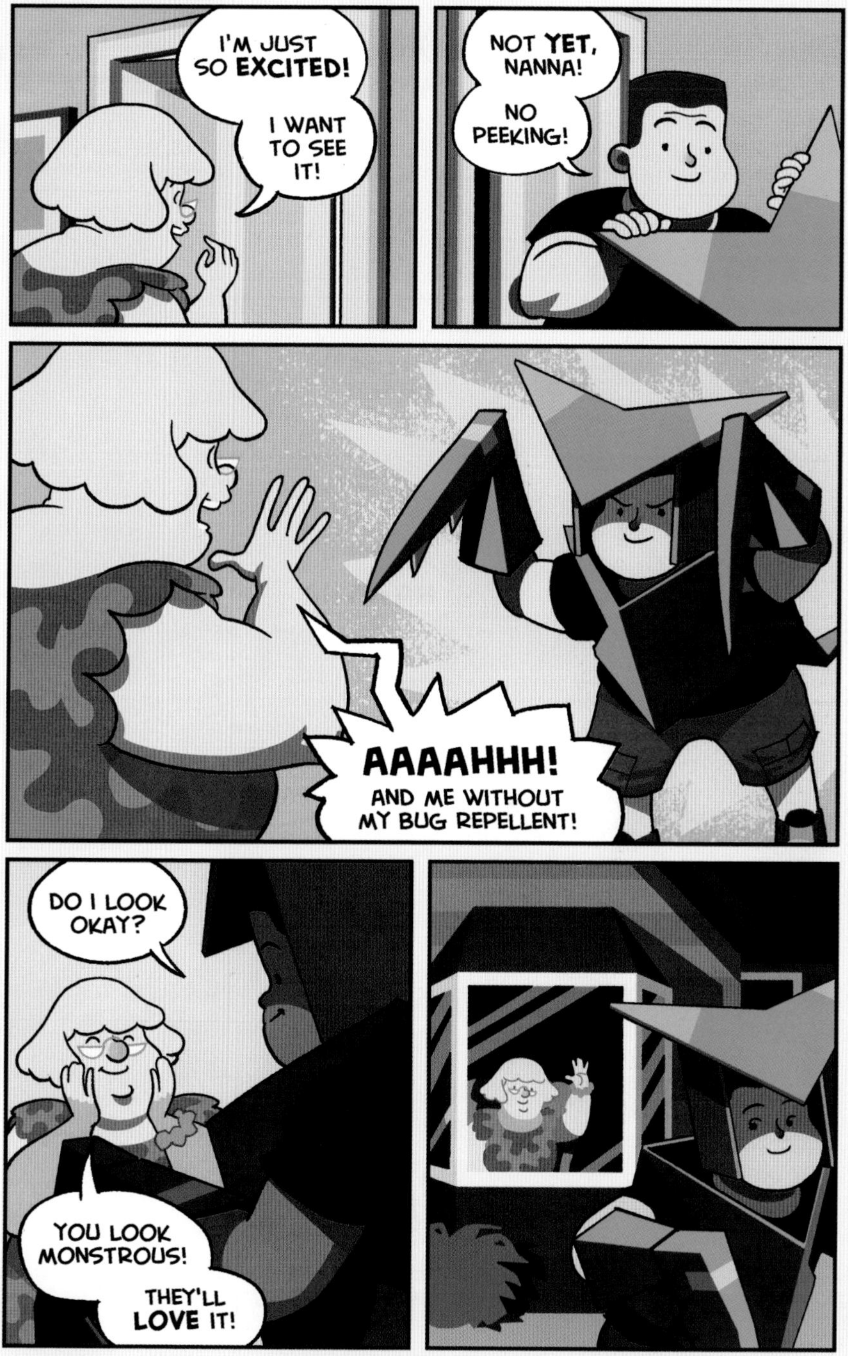
I'M JUST SO **EXCITED**!
I WANT TO SEE IT!
NOT **YET**, NANNA!
NO PEEKING!
AAAAHHH!
AND ME WITHOUT MY BUG REPELLENT!
DO I LOOK OKAY?
YOU LOOK MONSTROUS!
THEY'LL **LOVE** IT!

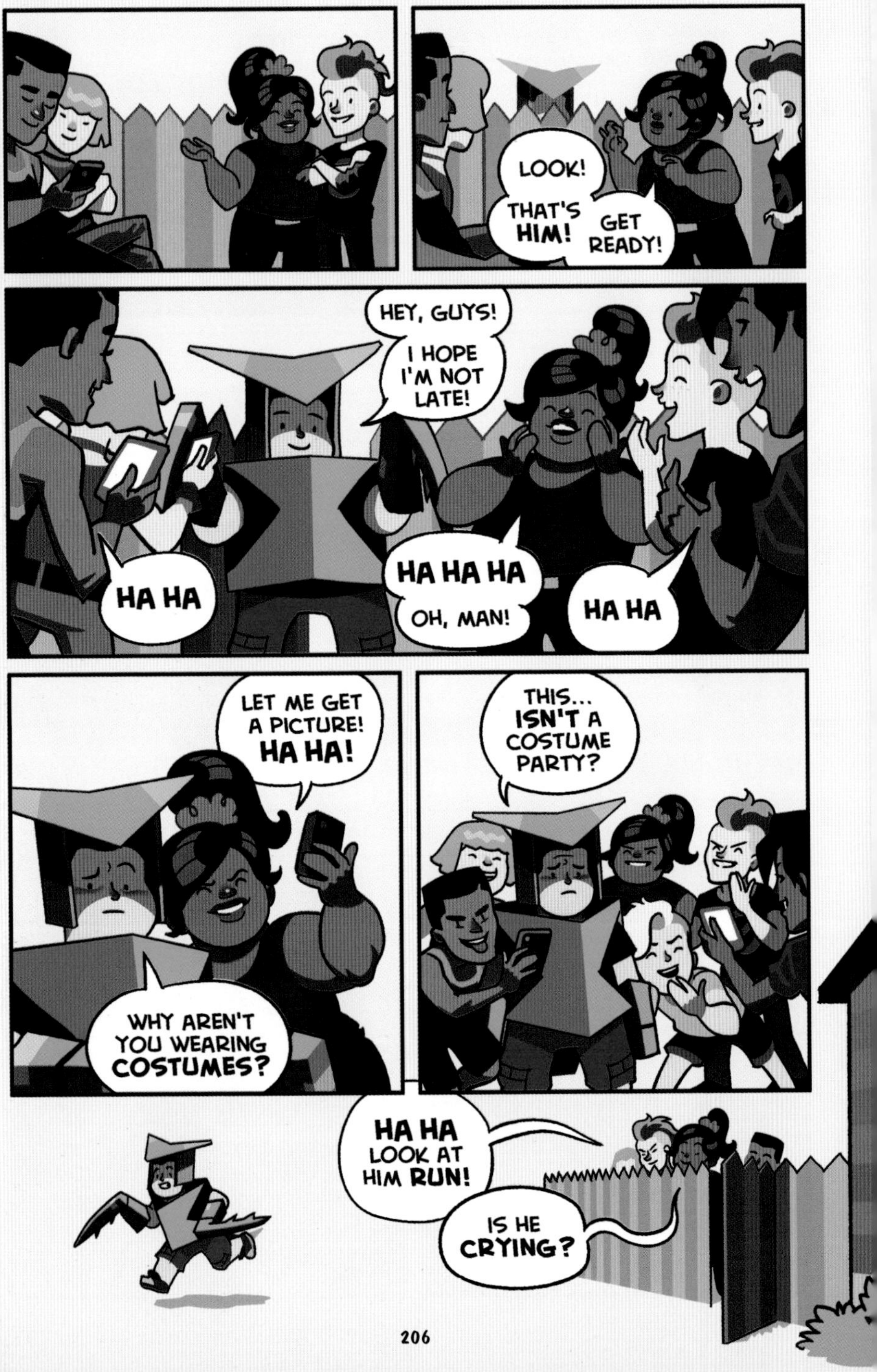
LOOK!
THAT'S HIM!
GET READY!
HEY, GUYS!
I HOPE I'M NOT LATE!
HA HA
HA HA HA
OH, MAN!
HA HA
LET ME GET A PICTURE! HA HA!
WHY AREN'T YOU WEARING COSTUMES?
THIS... ISN'T A COSTUME PARTY?
HA HA LOOK AT HIM RUN!
IS HE CRYING?

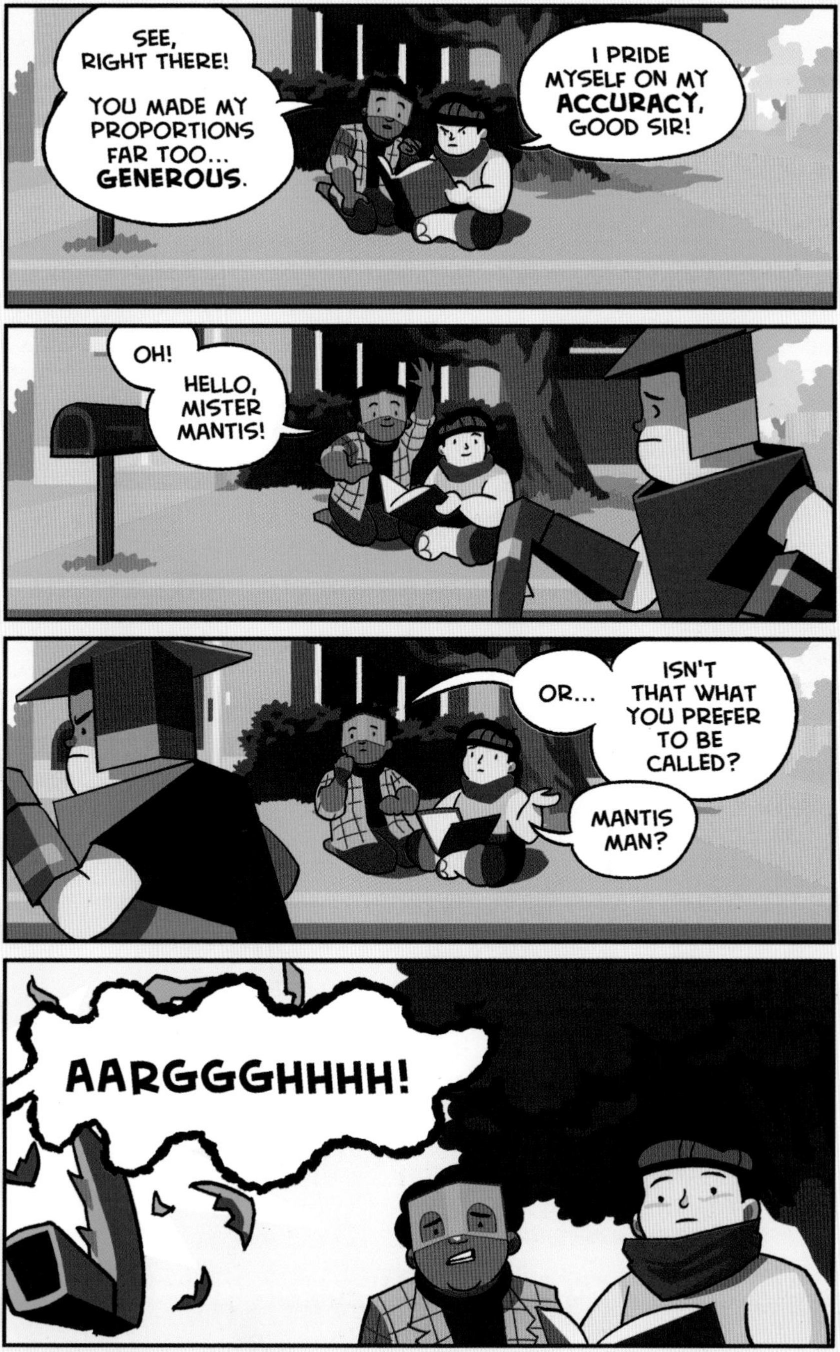
SEE, RIGHT THERE!
YOU MADE MY PROPORTIONS FAR TOO... GENEROUS.
I PRIDE MYSELF ON MY ACCURACY, GOOD SIR!
OH!
HELLO, MISTER MANTIS!
OR...
ISN'T THAT WHAT YOU PREFER TO BE CALLED?
MANTIS MAN?
AARGGGHHHH!

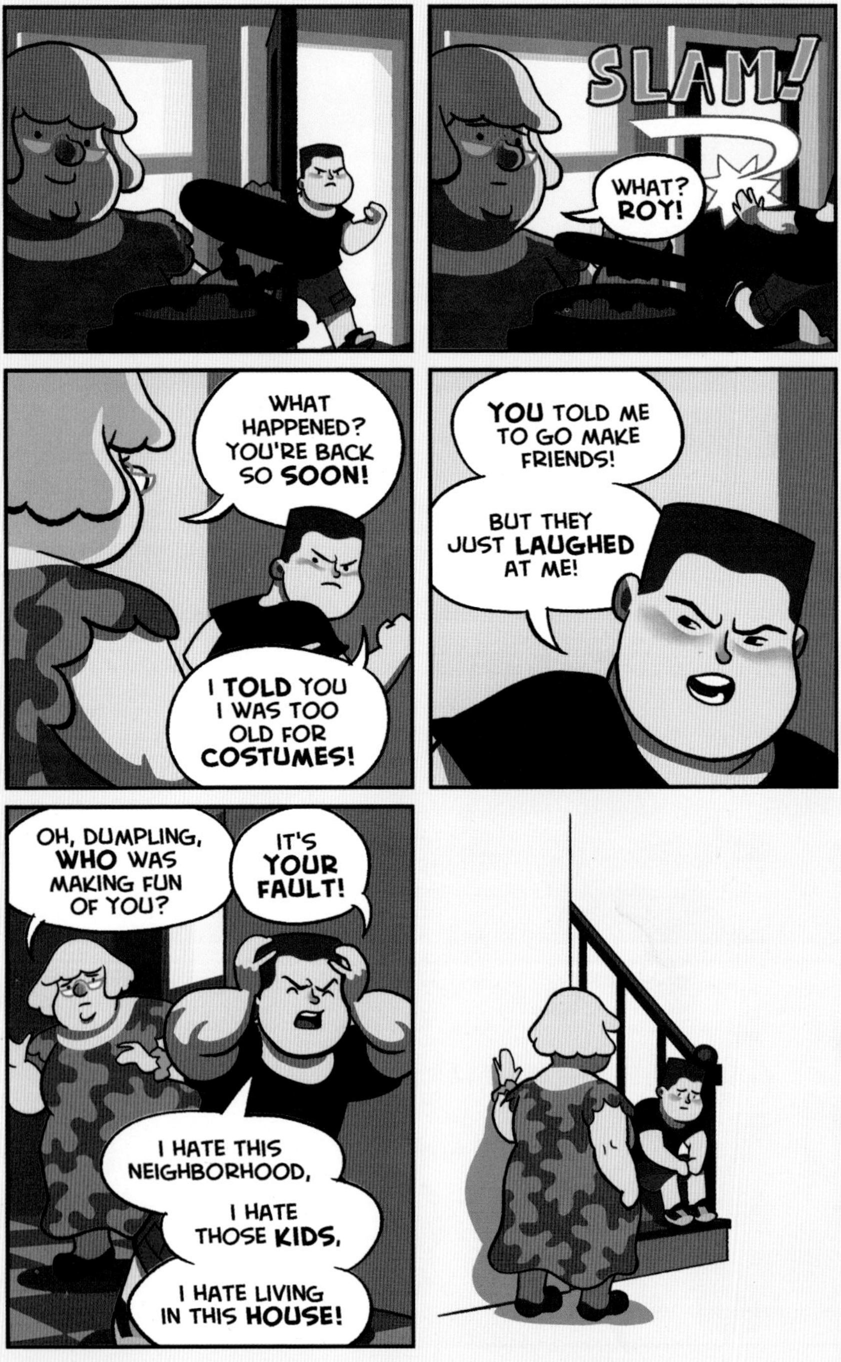
SLAM!
WHAT? ROY!
WHAT HAPPENED? YOU'RE BACK SO SOON!
I TOLD YOU I WAS TOO OLD FOR COSTUMES!
YOU TOLD ME TO GO MAKE FRIENDS!
BUT THEY JUST LAUGHED AT ME!
OH, DUMPLING, WHO WAS MAKING FUN OF YOU?
IT'S YOUR FAULT!
I HATE THIS NEIGHBORHOOD,
I HATE THOSE KIDS,
I HATE LIVING IN THIS HOUSE!

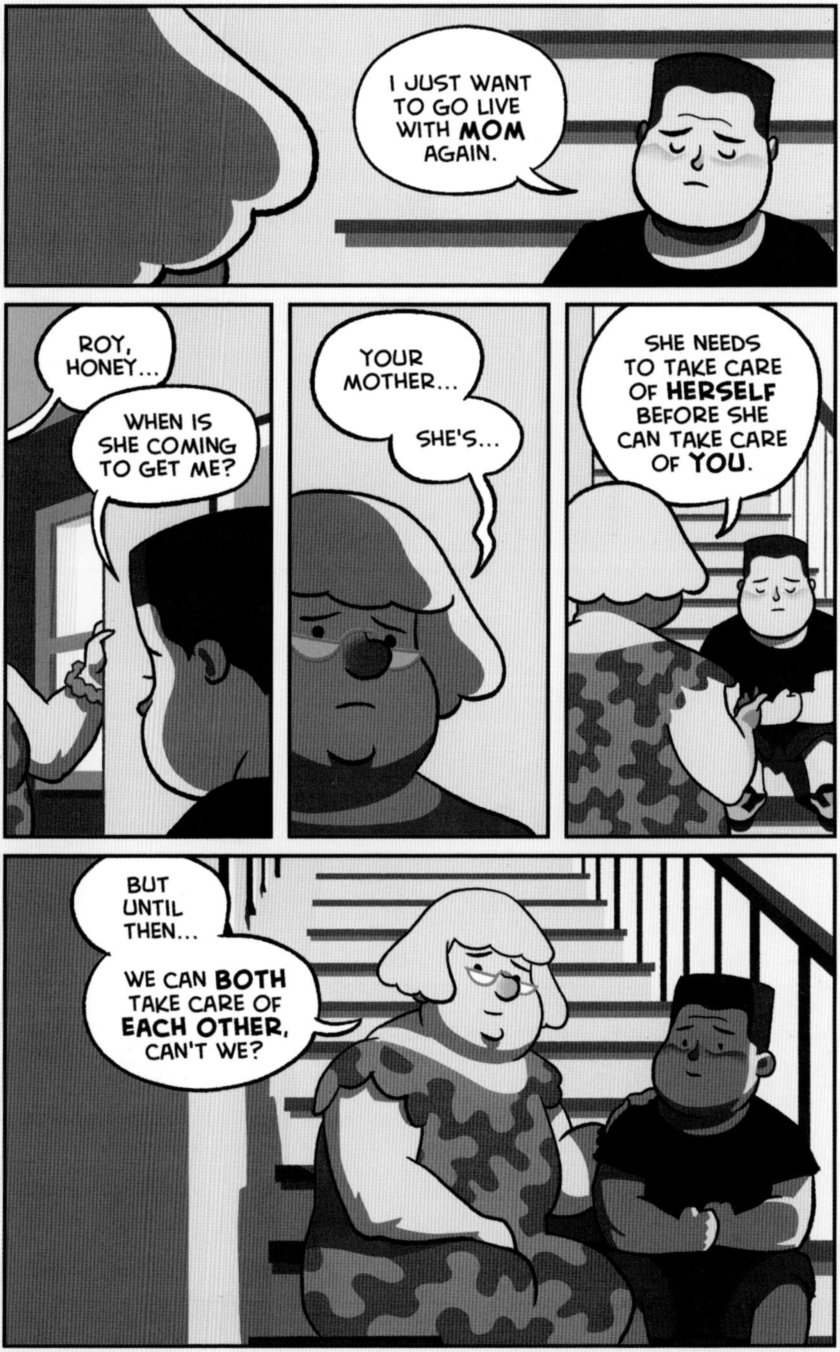
I JUST WANT TO GO LIVE WITH MOM AGAIN.
ROY, HONEY...
WHEN IS SHE COMING TO GET ME?
YOUR MOTHER...
SHE'S...
SHE NEEDS TO TAKE CARE OF HERSELF BEFORE SHE CAN TAKE CARE OF YOU.
BUT UNTIL THEN...
WE CAN BOTH TAKE CARE OF EACH OTHER, CAN'T WE?

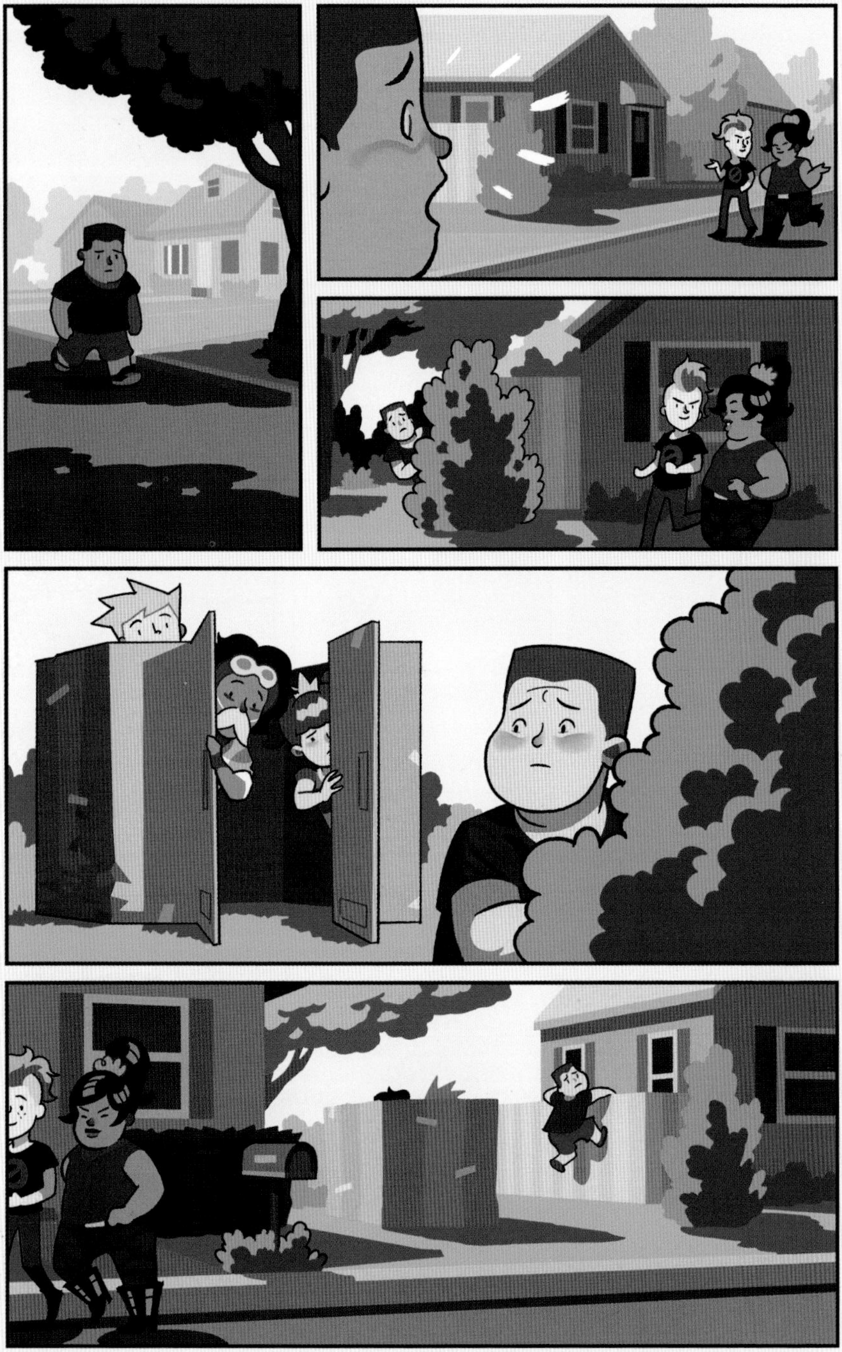

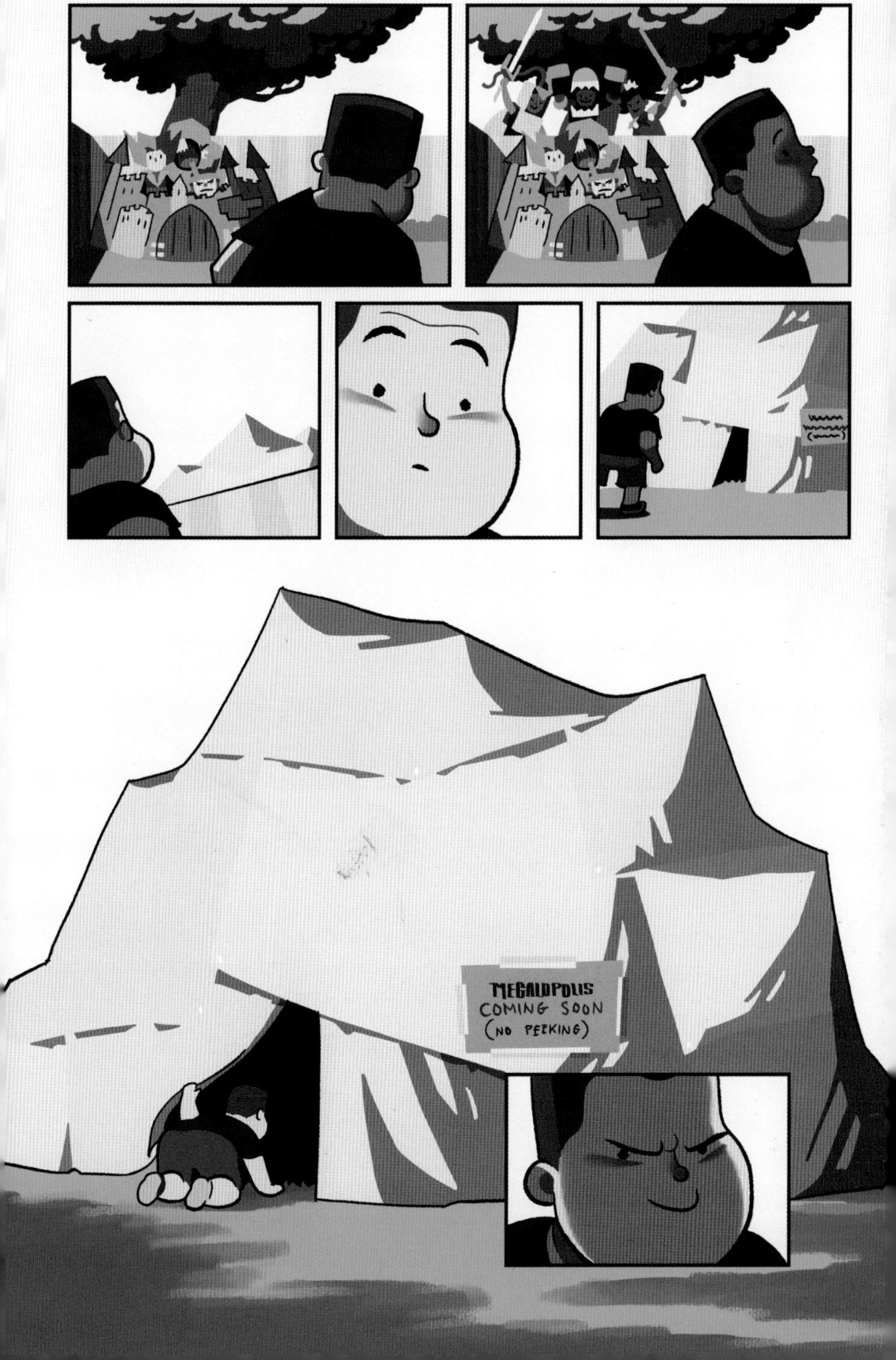
MEGALOPOLIS
COMING SOON
(NO PEEKING)

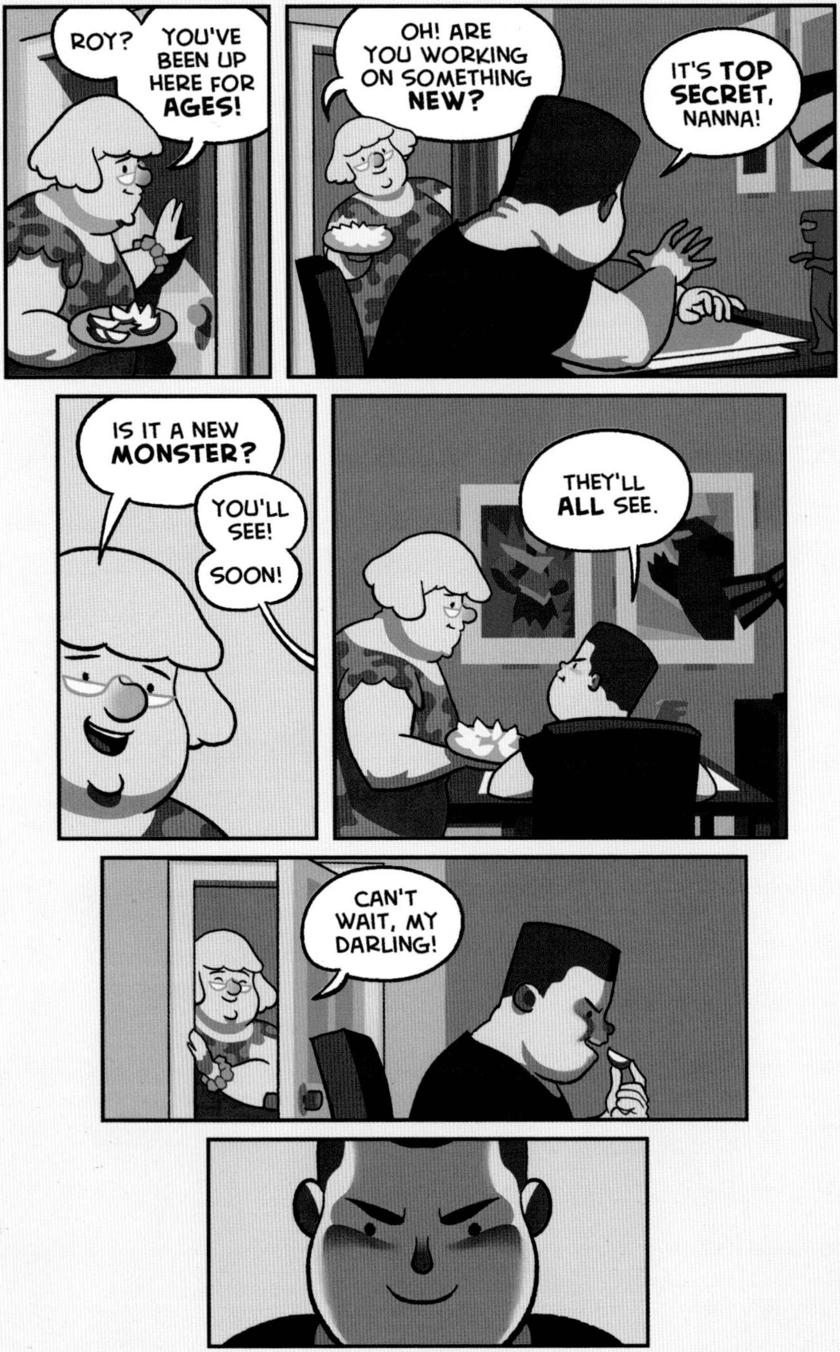
ROY?
YOU'VE BEEN UP HERE FOR AGES!
OH! ARE YOU WORKING ON SOMETHING NEW?
IT'S TOP SECRET, NANNA!
IS IT A NEW MONSTER?
YOU'LL SEE!
SOON!
THEY'LL ALL SEE.
CAN'T WAIT, MY DARLING!

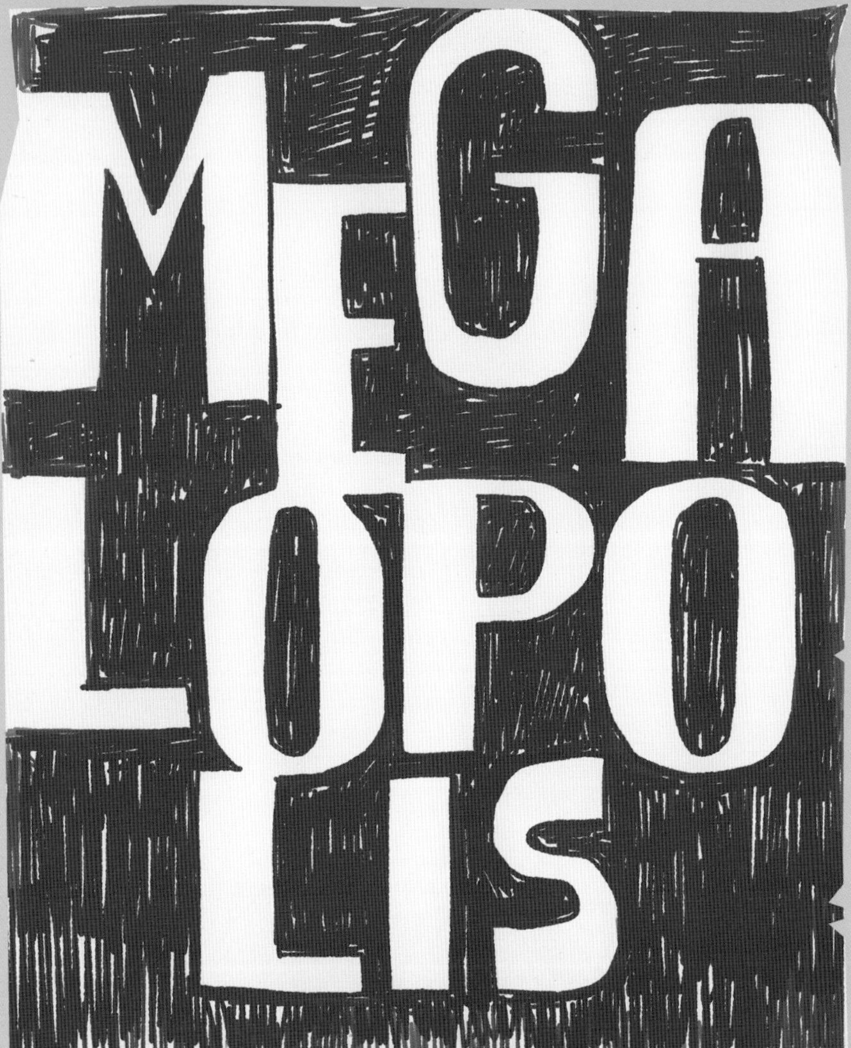
MEGA
LOPO
LIS

BY JAY FULLER AND CHAD SELL

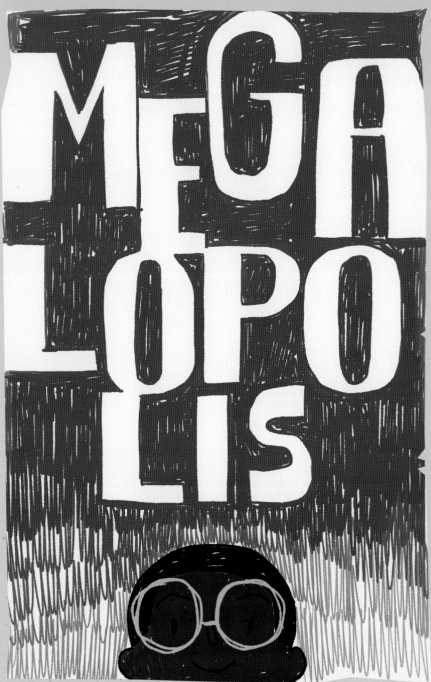

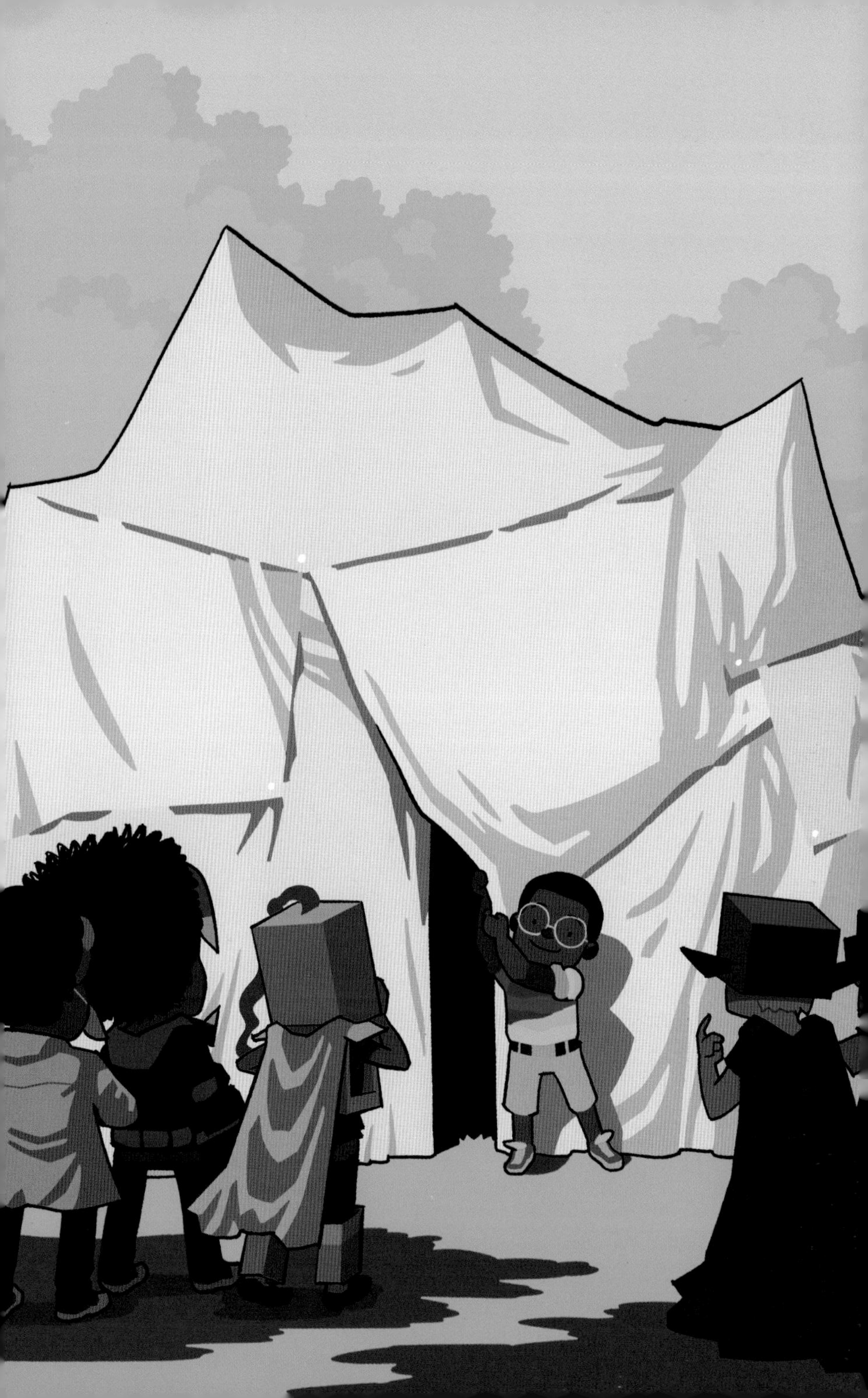

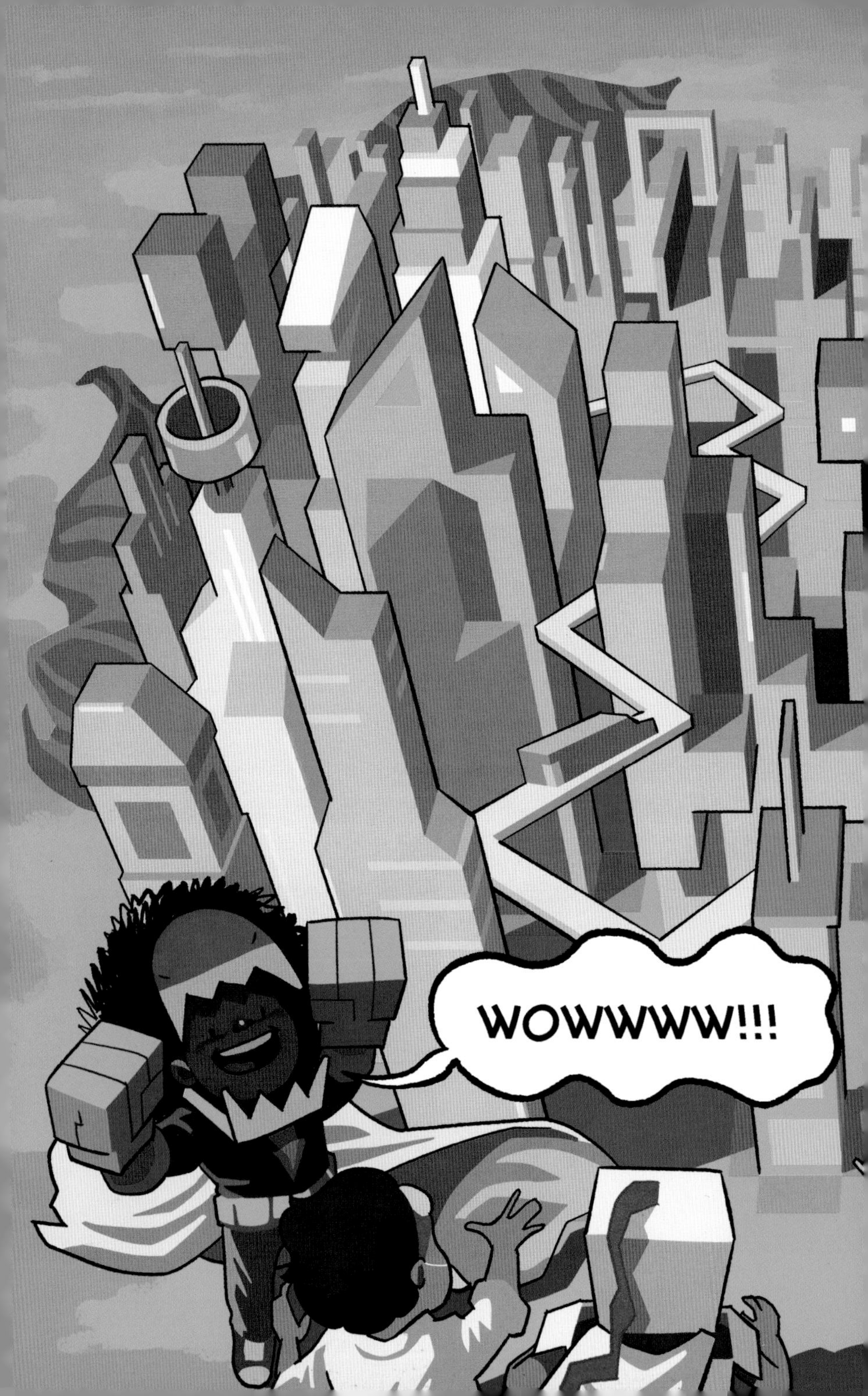
WOWWWW!!!

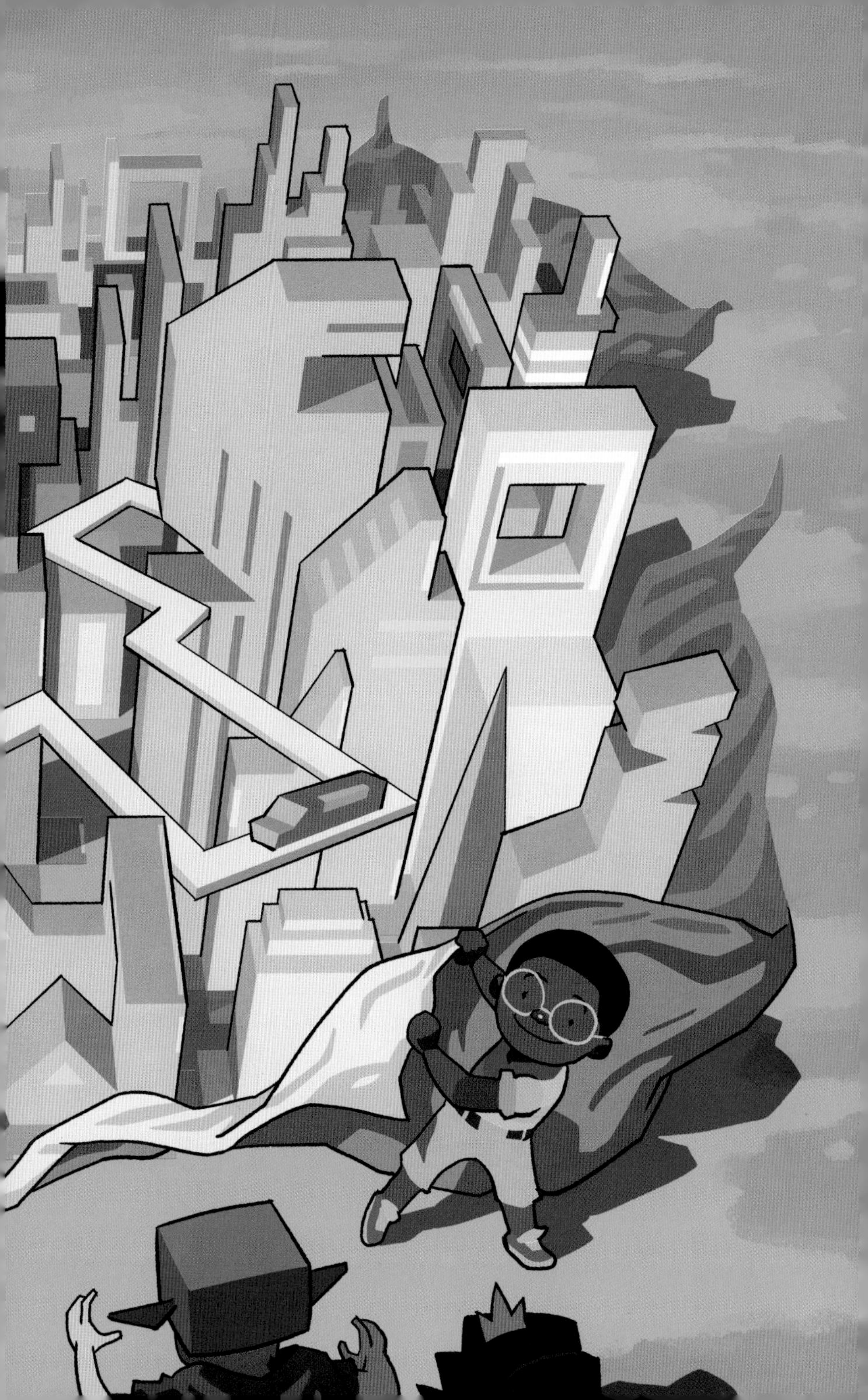

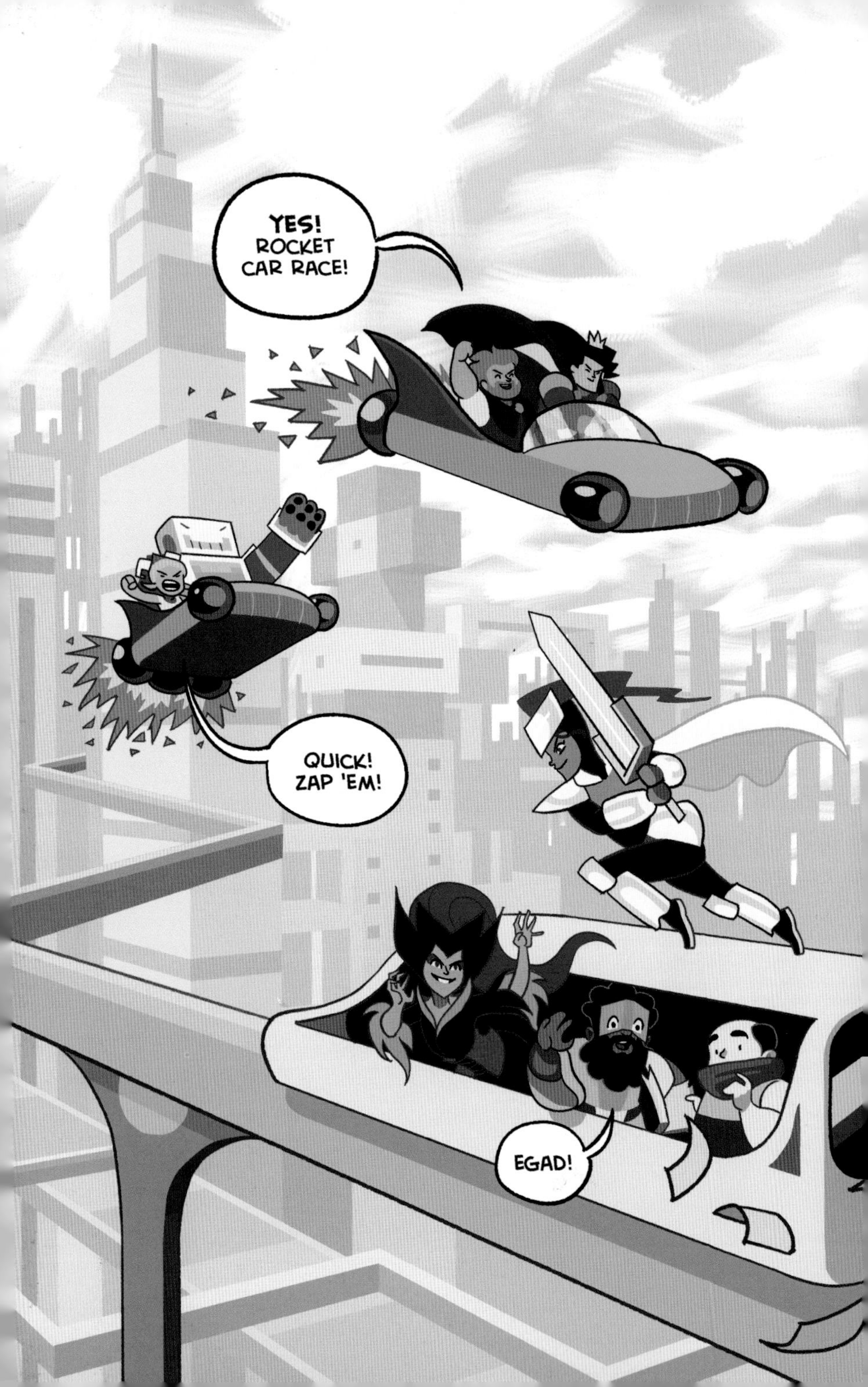
YES! ROCKET CAR RACE!
QUICK! ZAP 'EM!
EGAD!

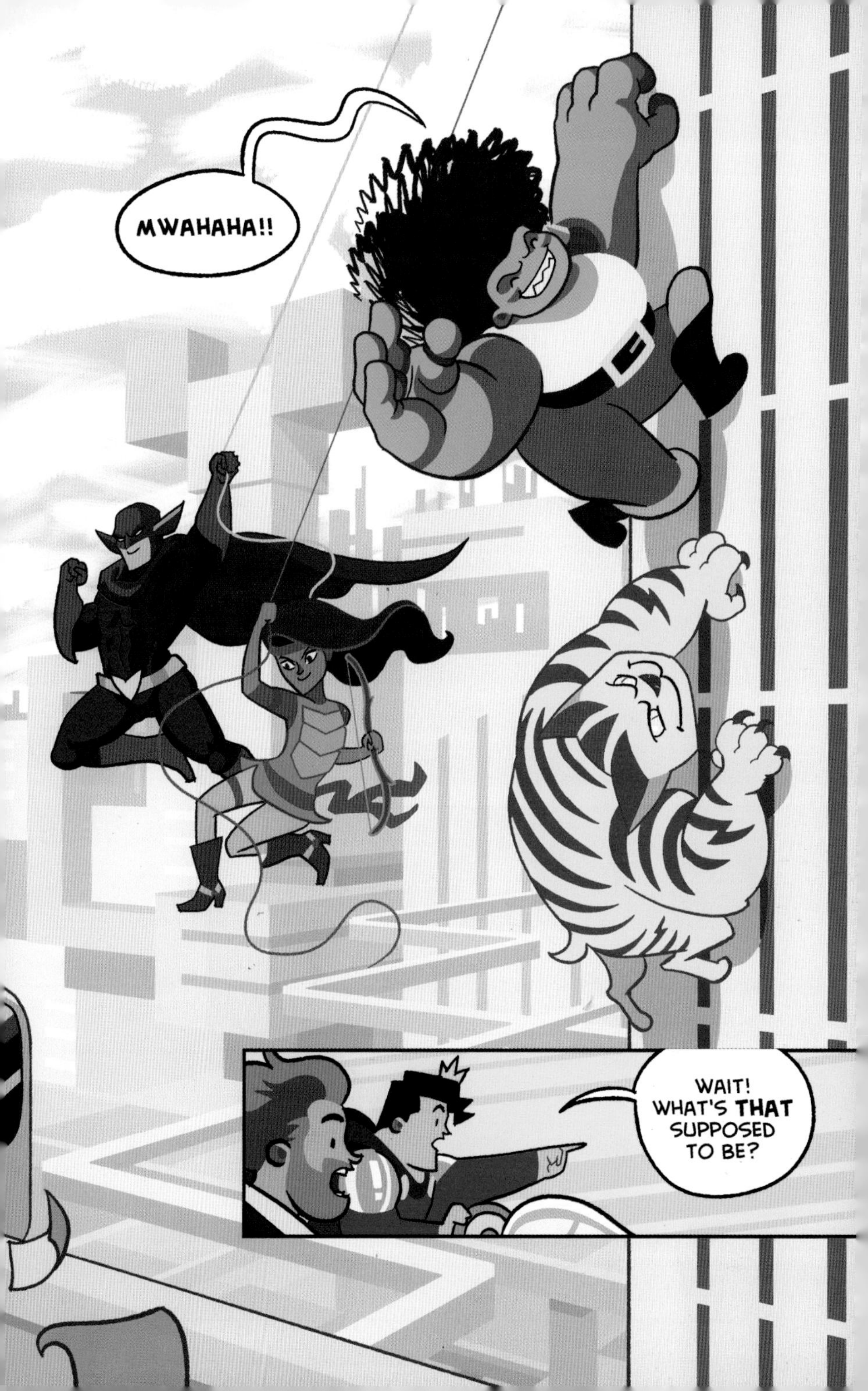
MWAHAHA!!
WAIT! WHAT'S THAT SUPPOSED TO BE?

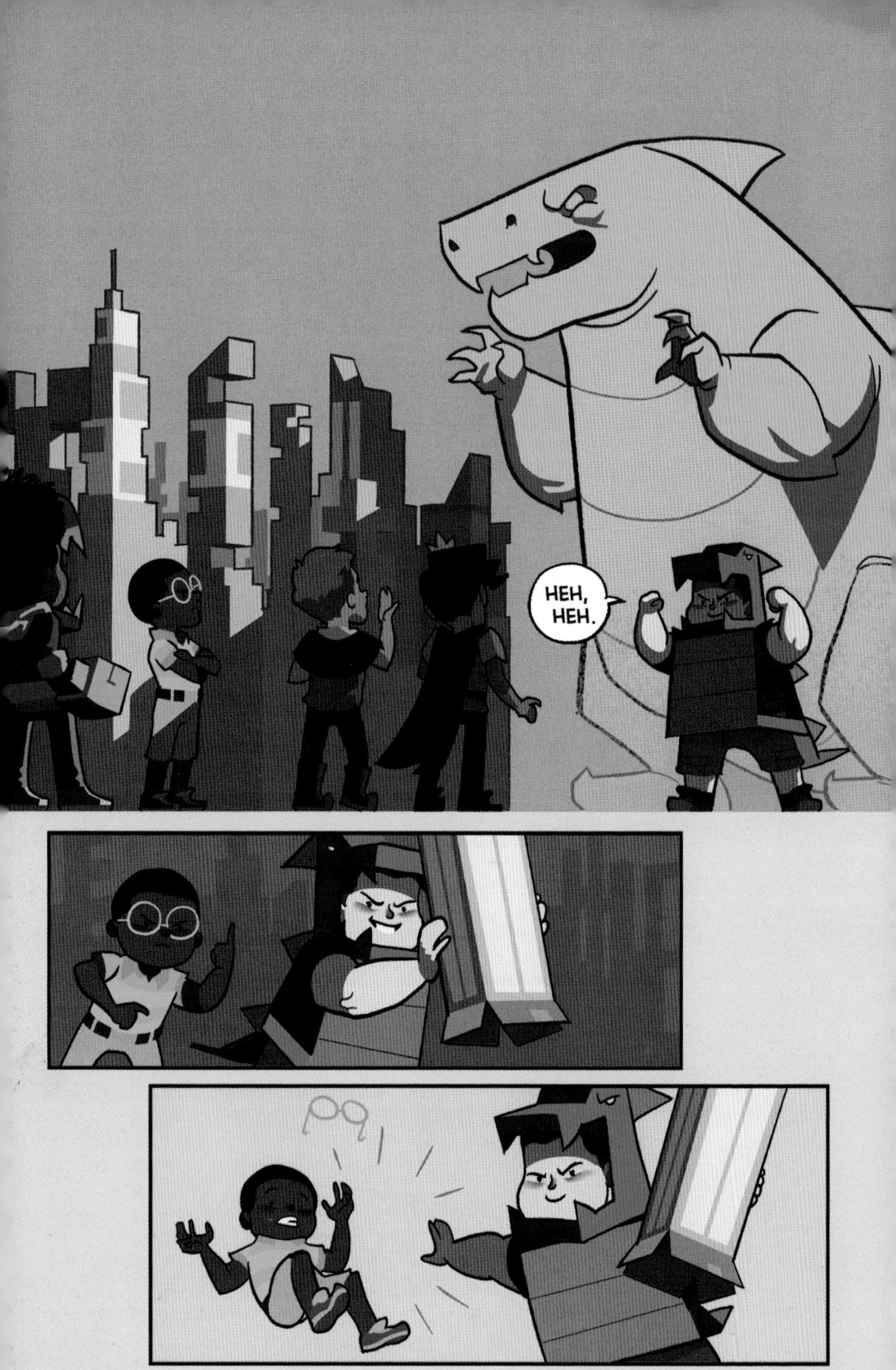
HEH, HEH.

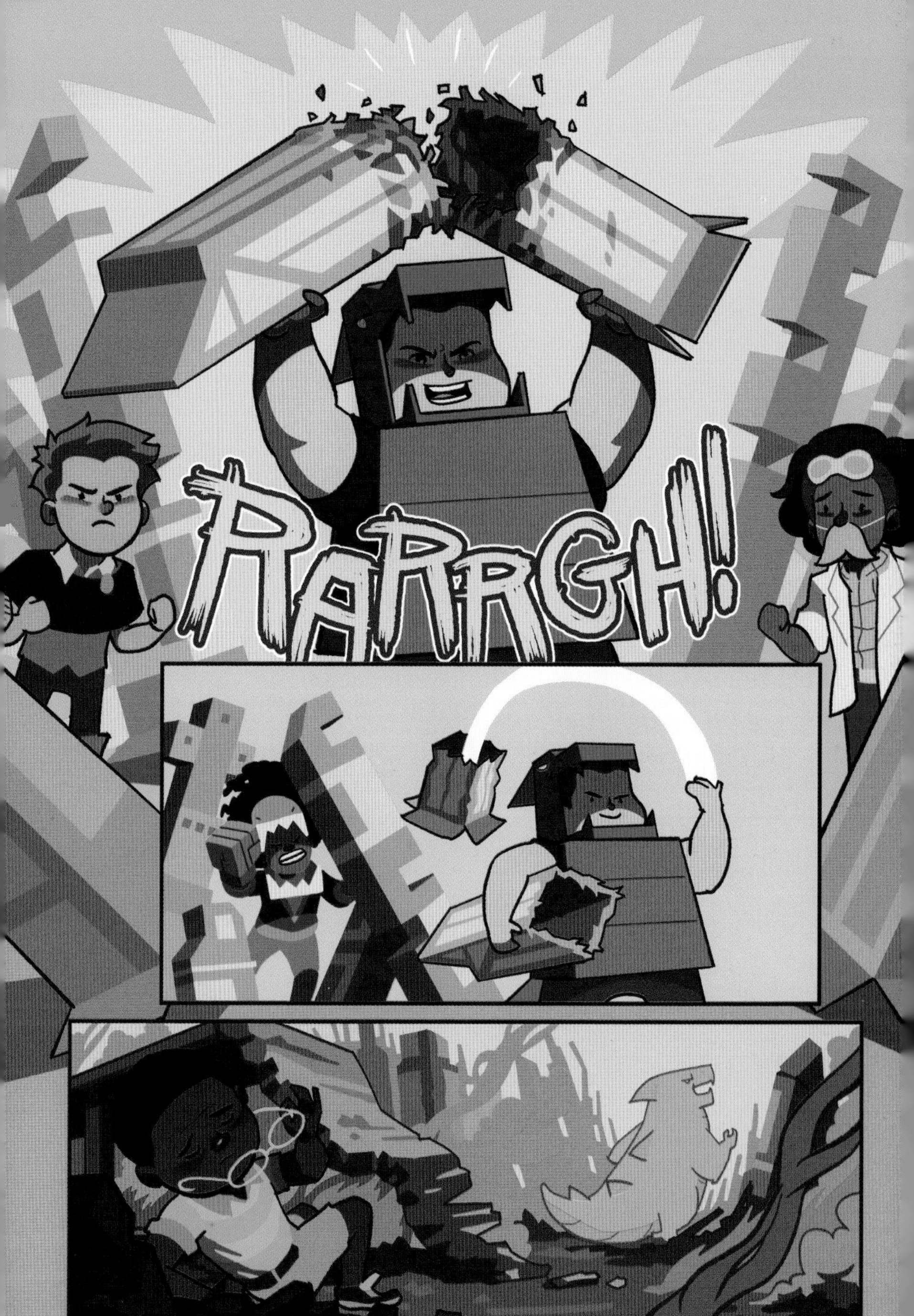
RARRGH!

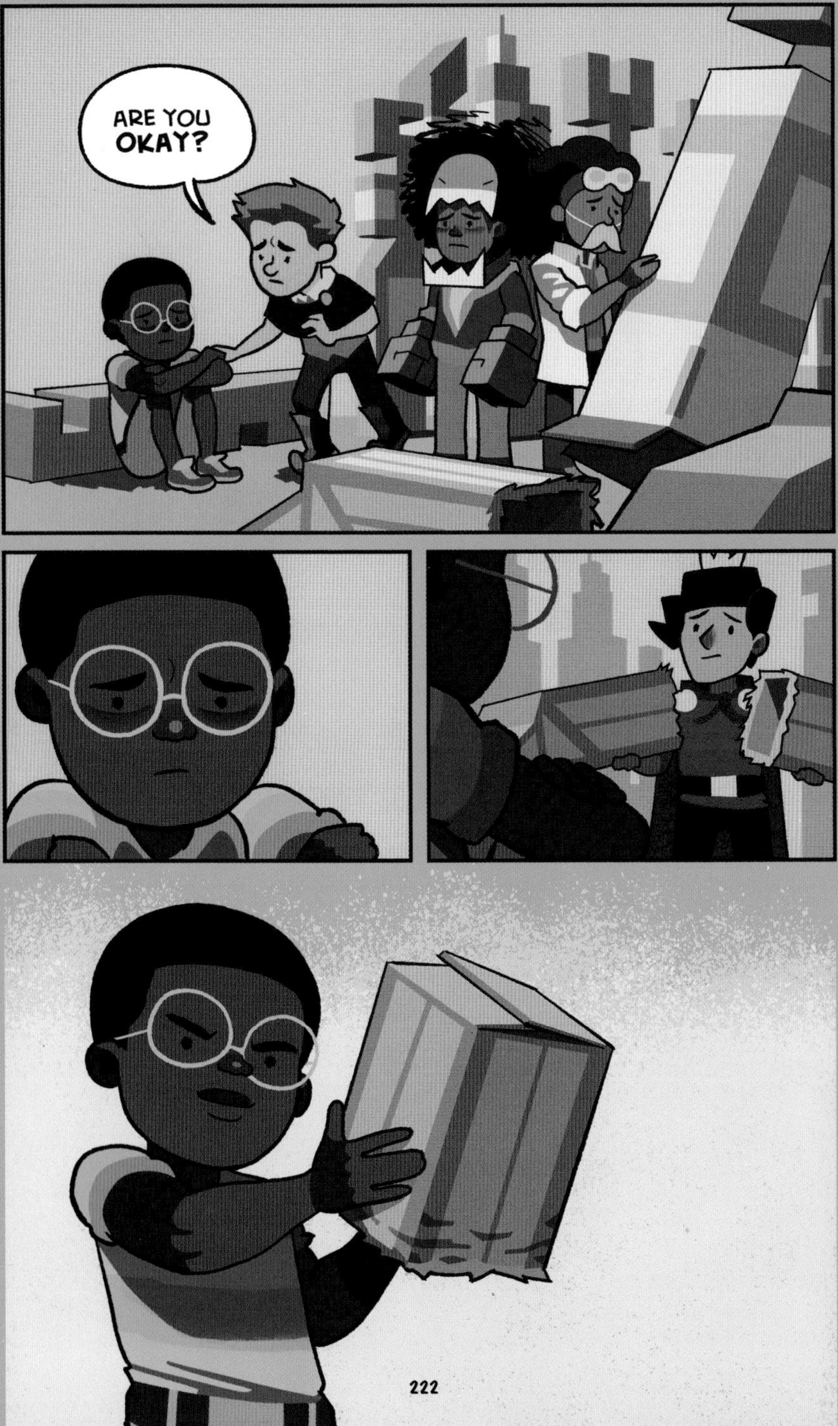
ARE YOU OKAY?

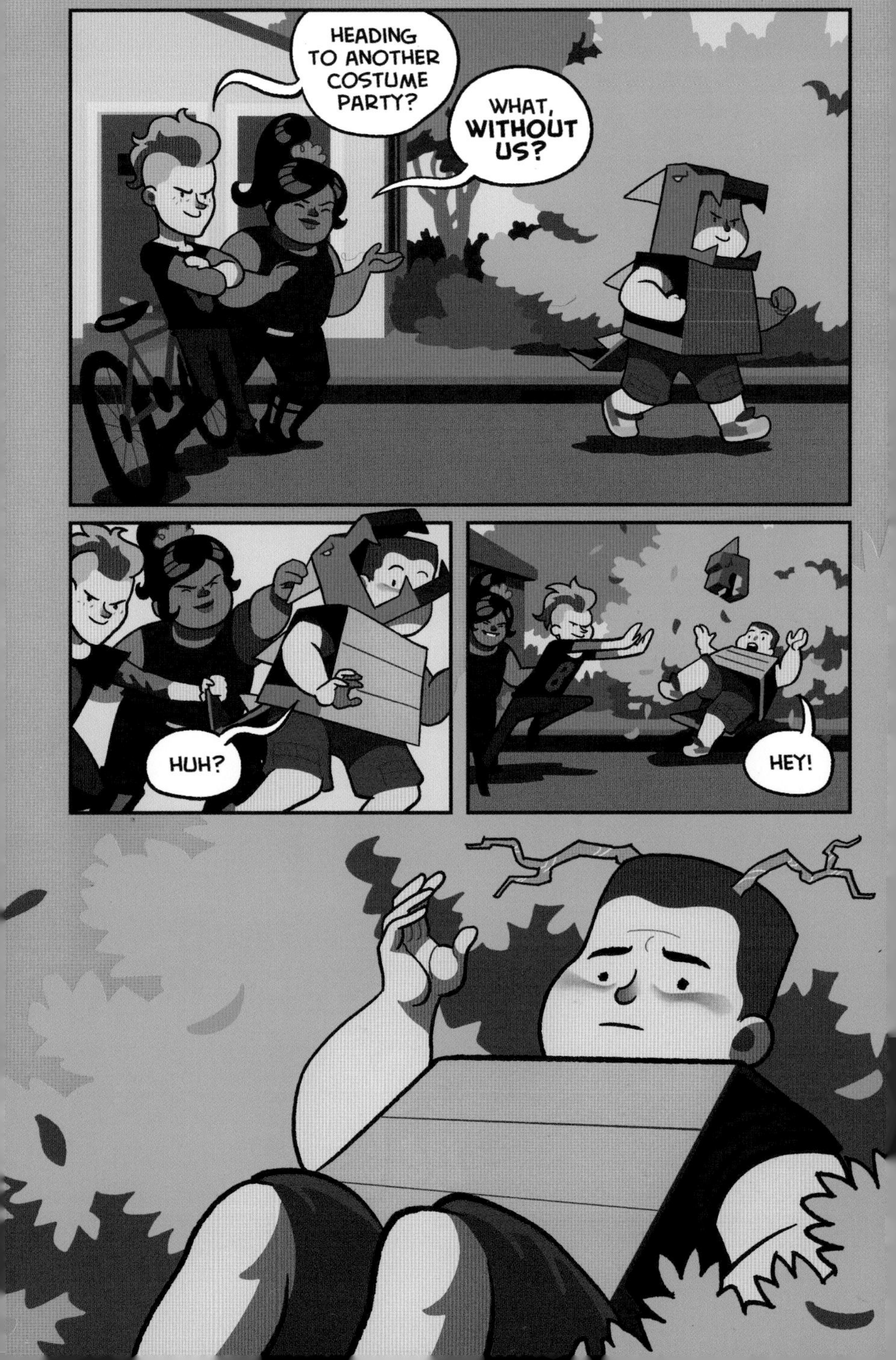
HEADING TO ANOTHER COSTUME PARTY?
WHAT, WITHOUT US?
HUH?
HEY!

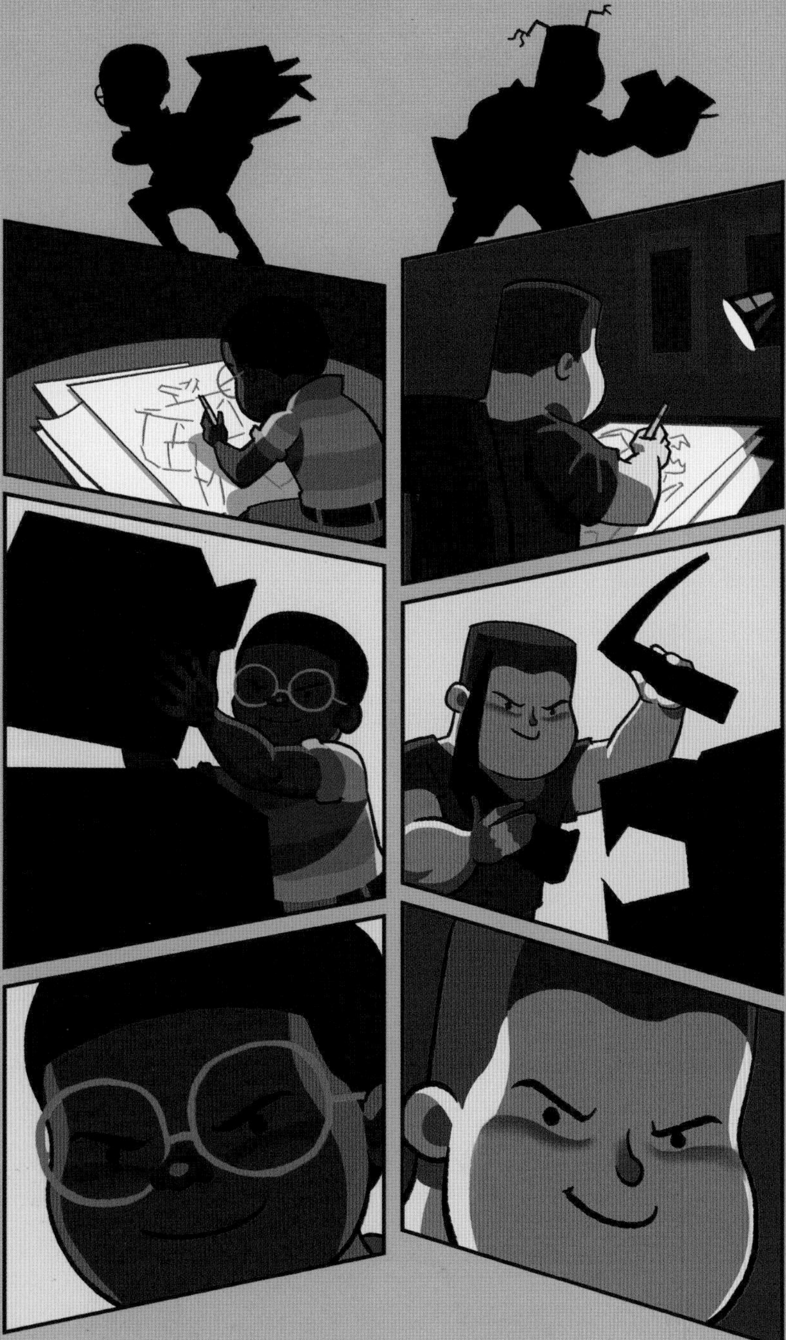

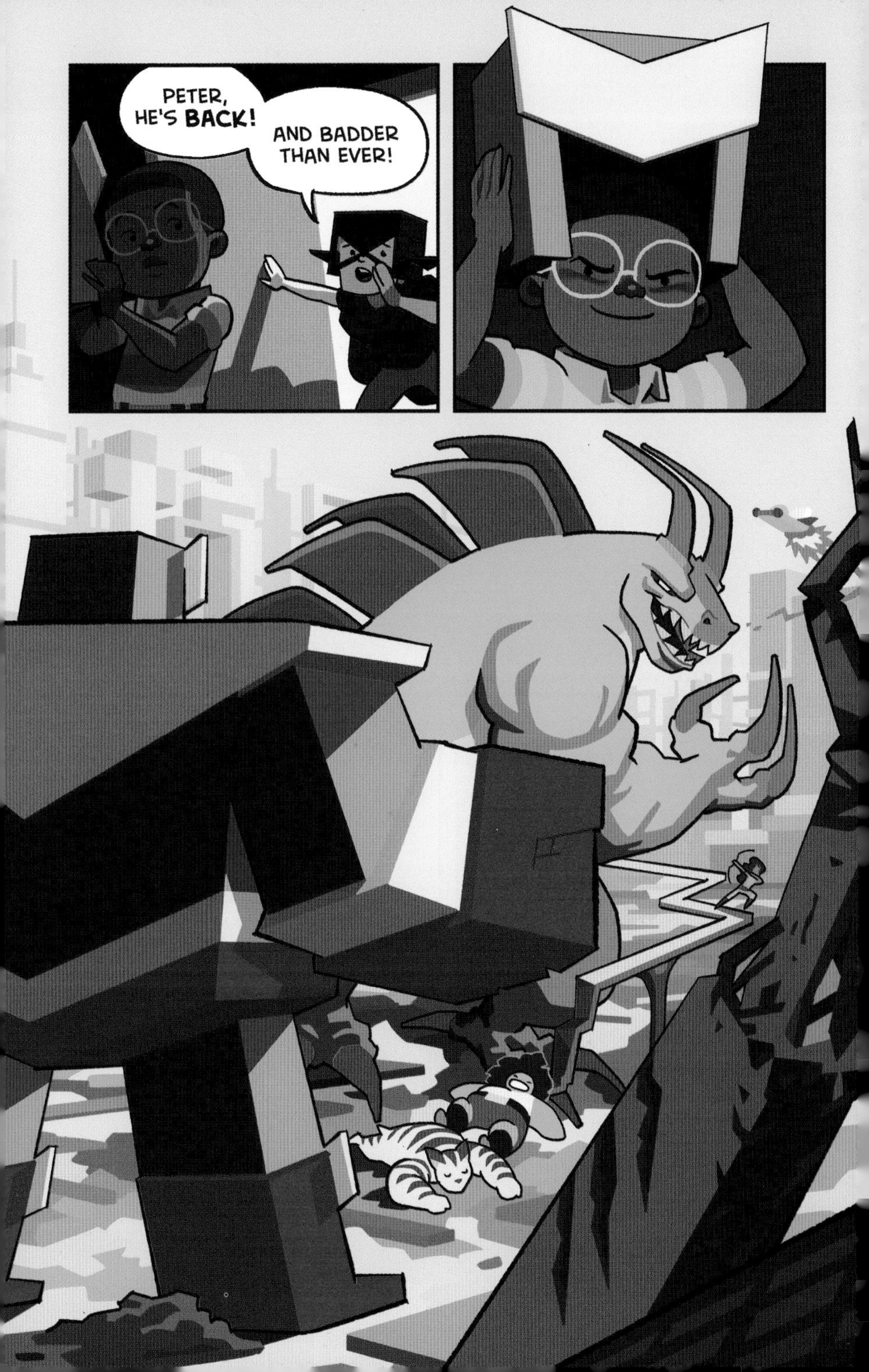
PETER, HE'S BACK!
AND BADDER THAN EVER!

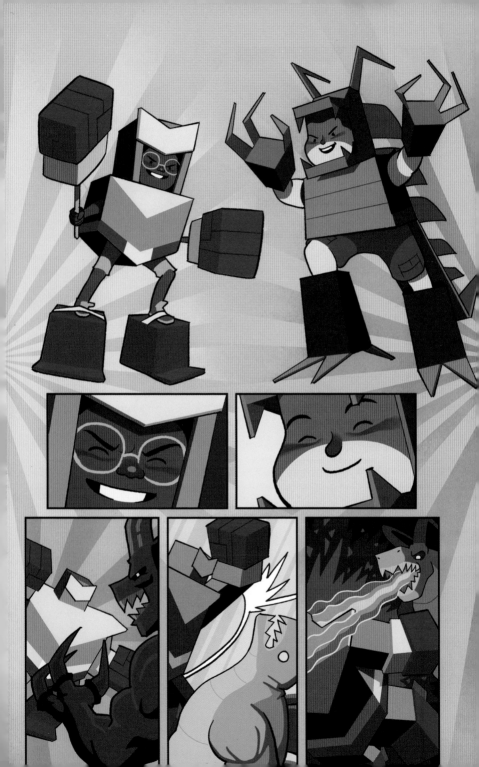

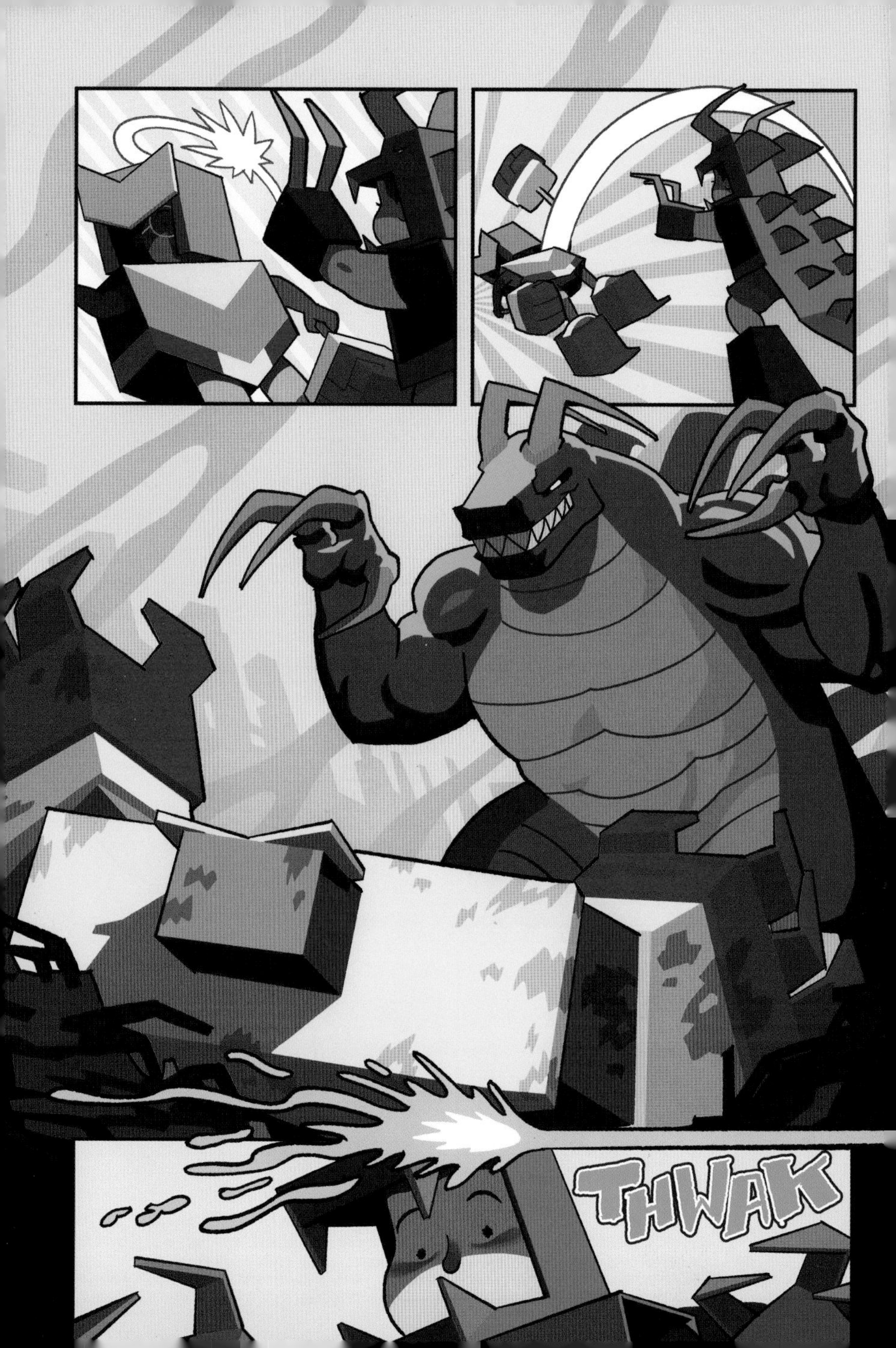
THWAK

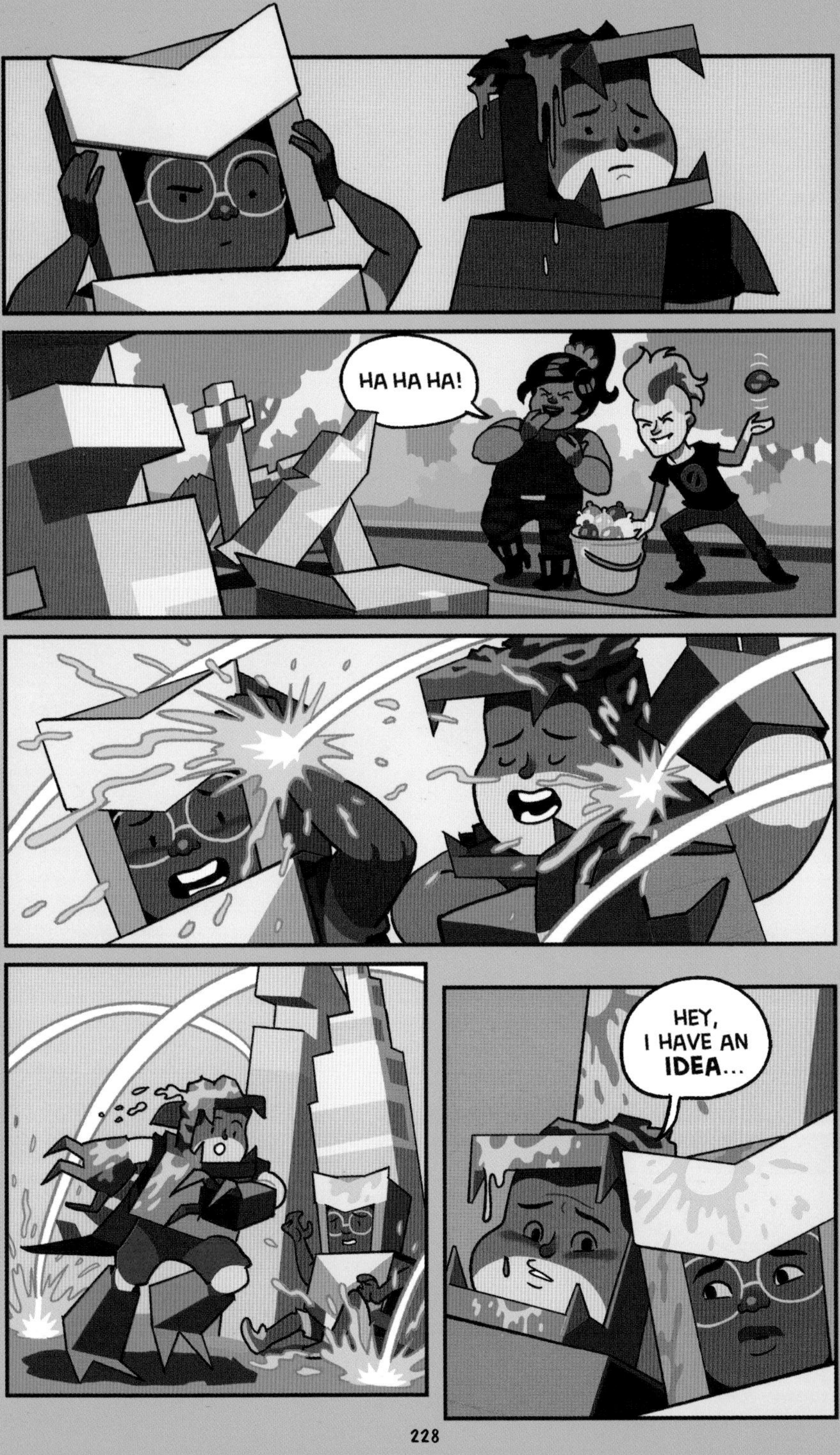
HA HA HA!
HEY, I HAVE AN IDEA...

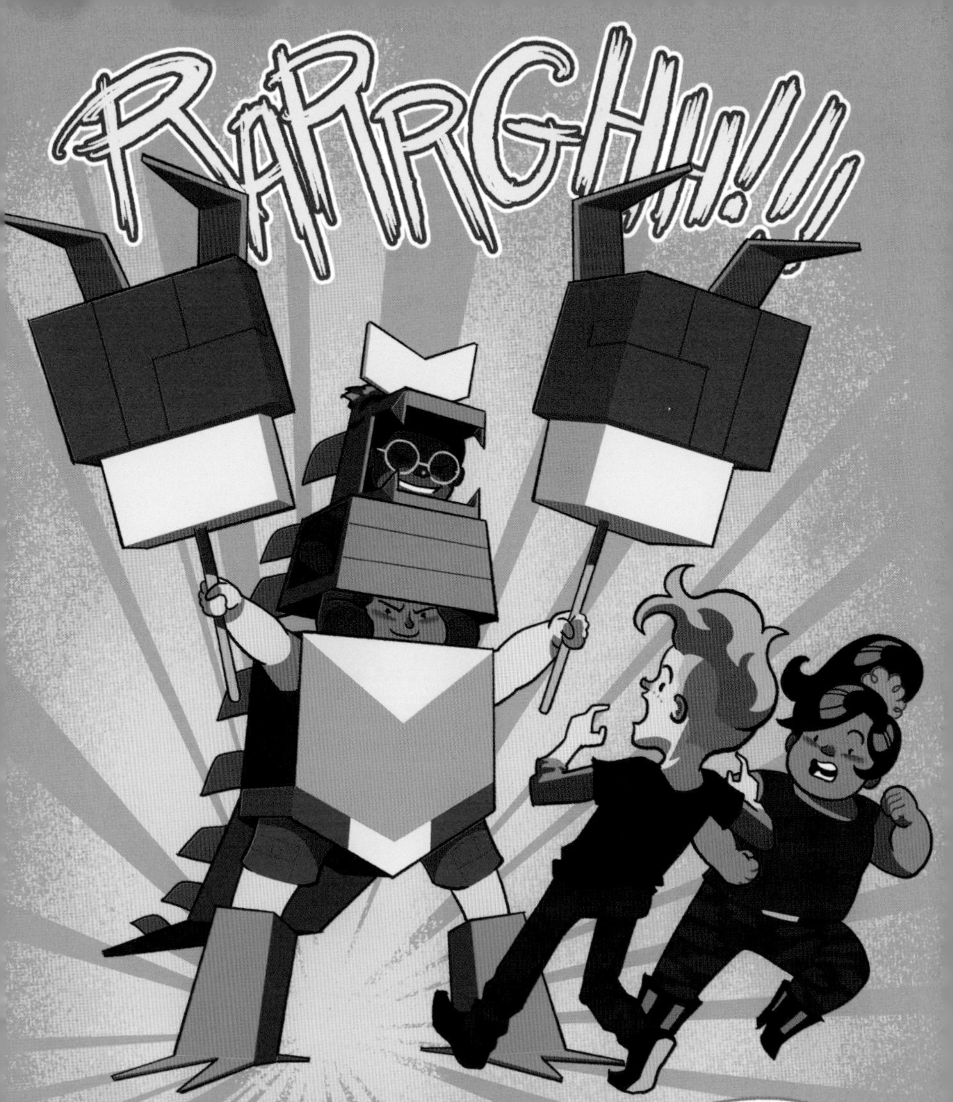
RARRGHH!!!

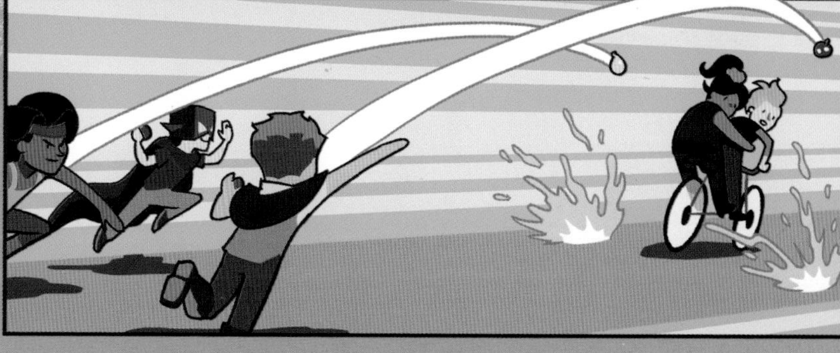

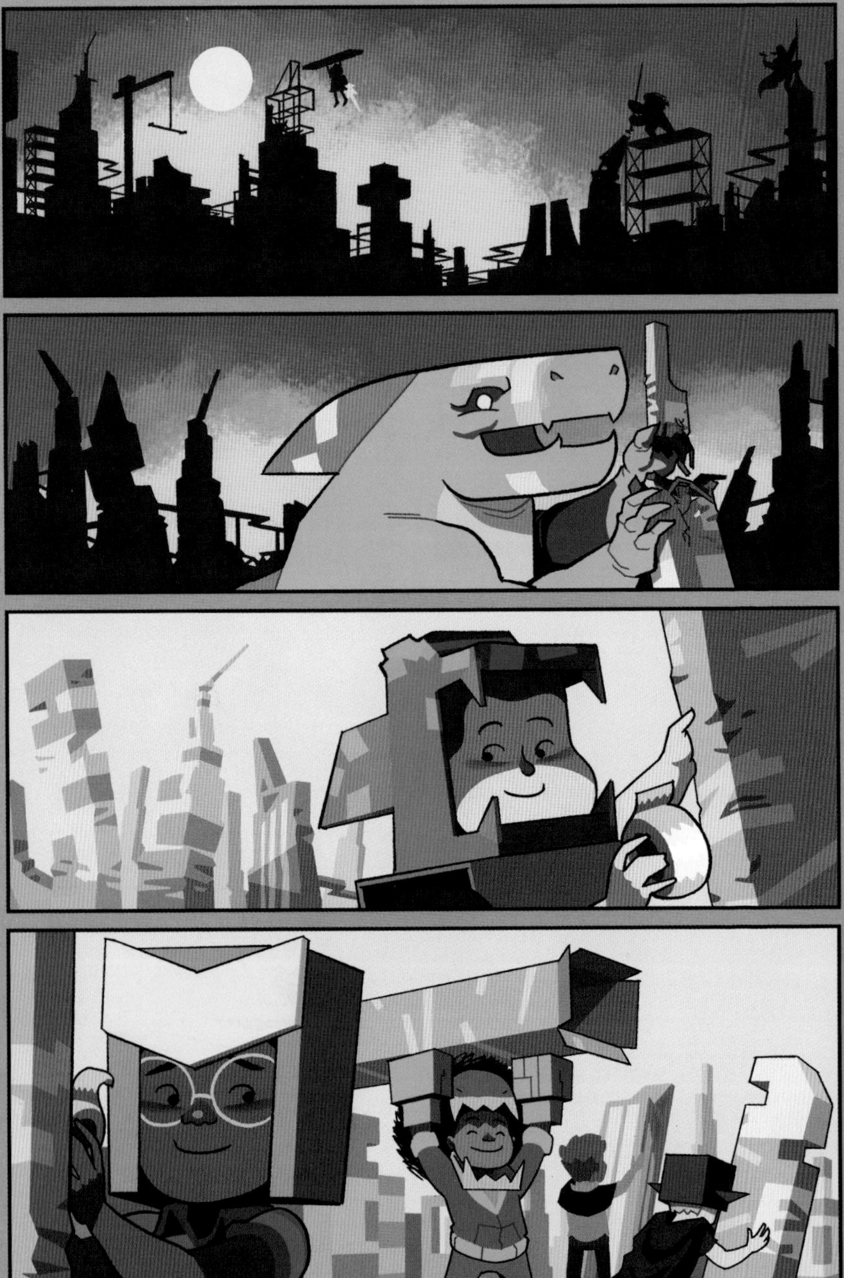

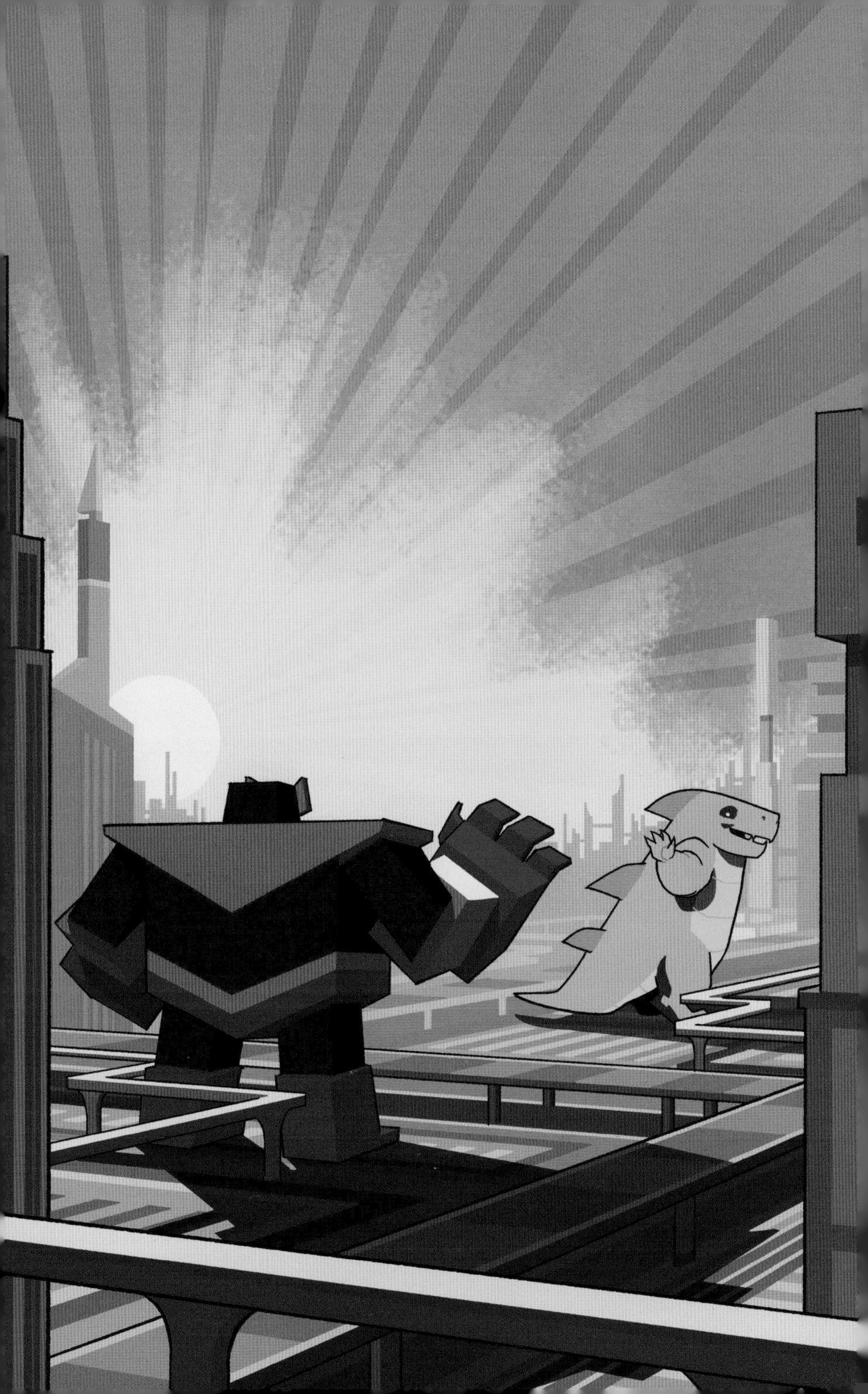

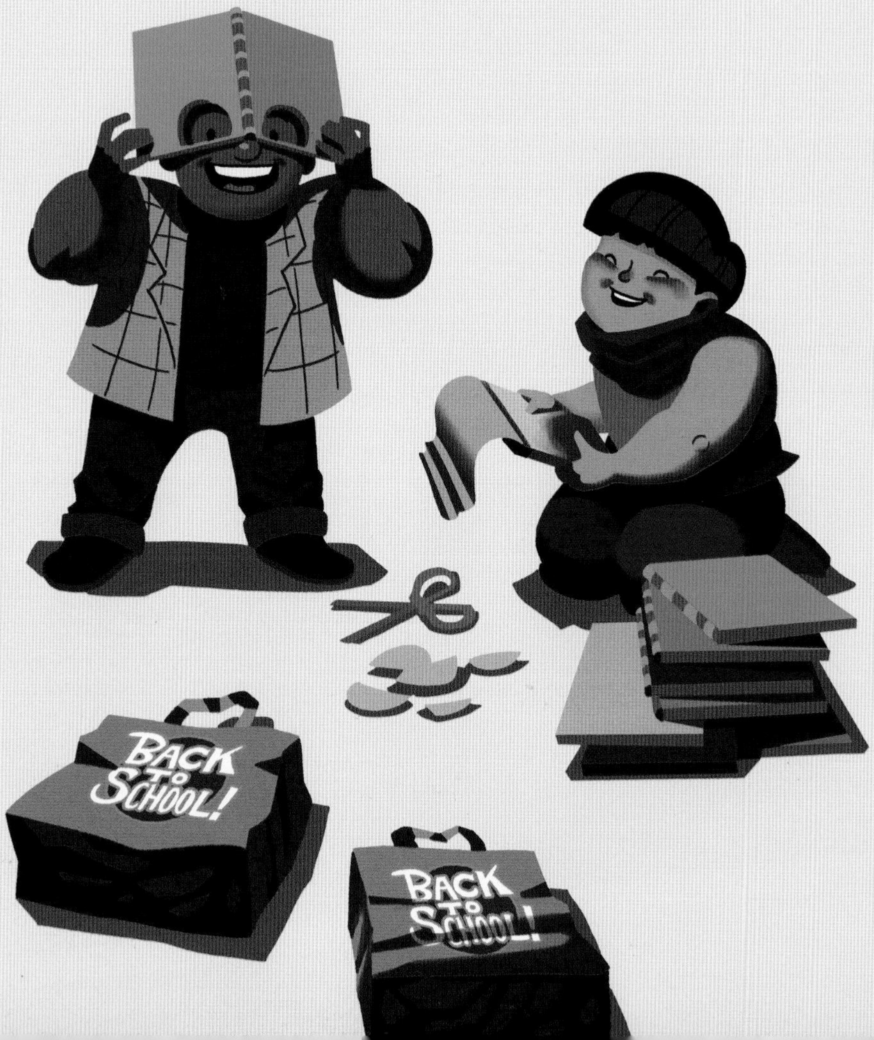
BACK TO SCHOOL!
BACK TO SCHOOL!

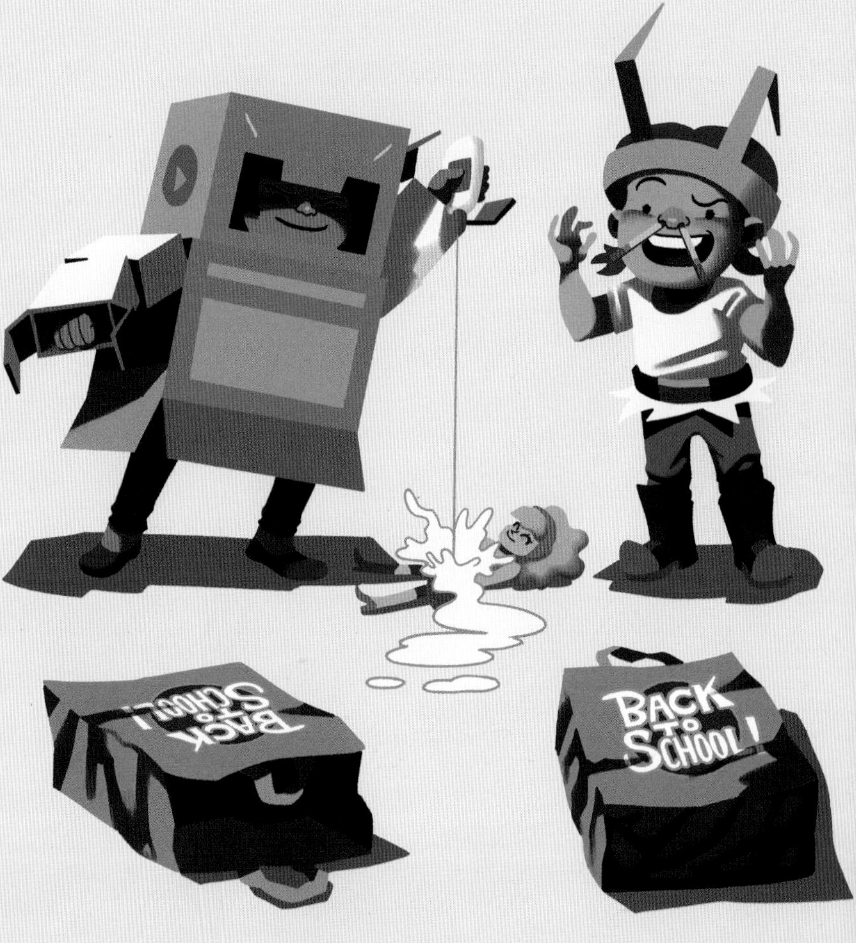
BACK
To
SCHOOL!

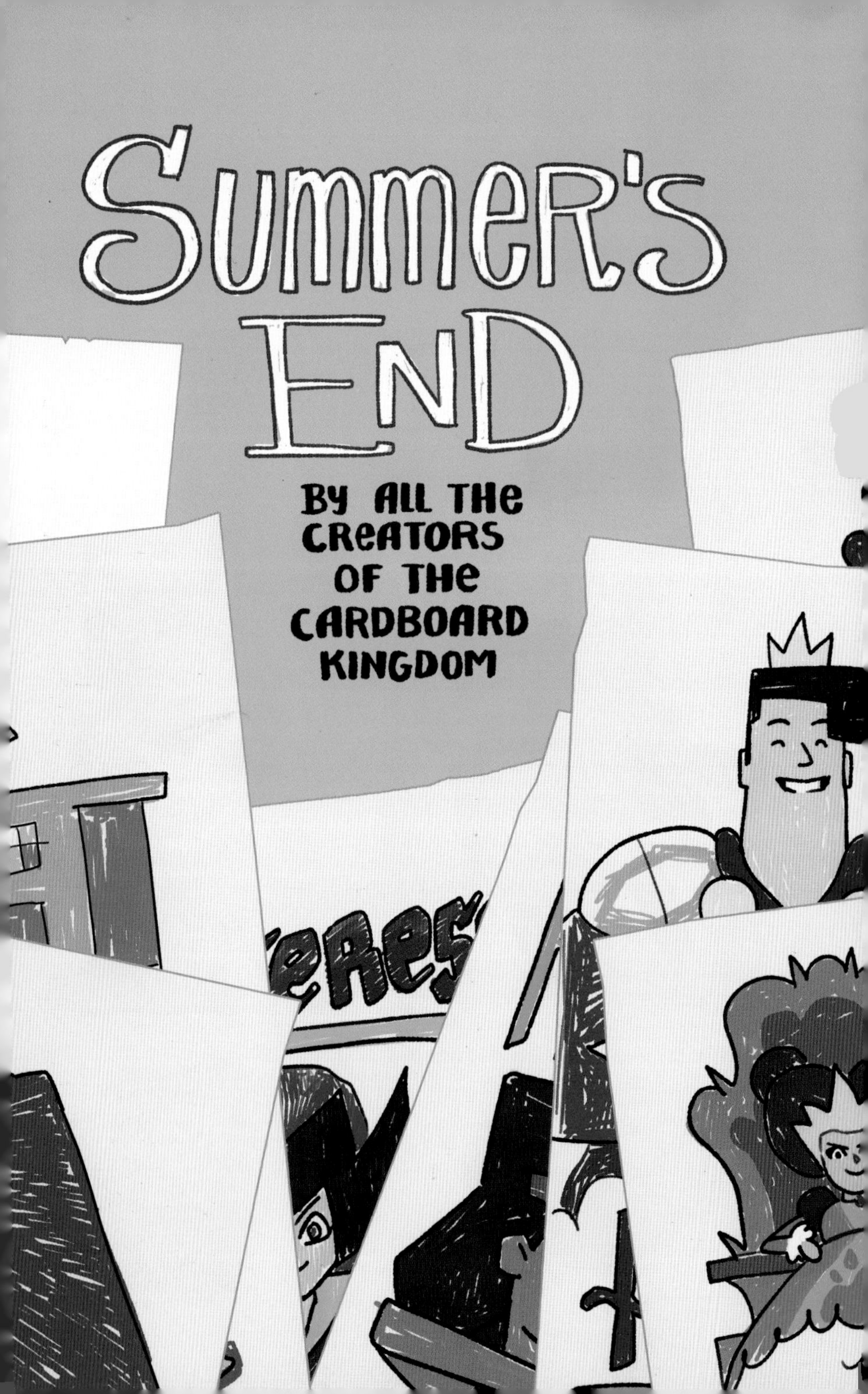
SUMMER'S END
BY ALL THE CREATORS OF THE CARDBOARD KINGDOM

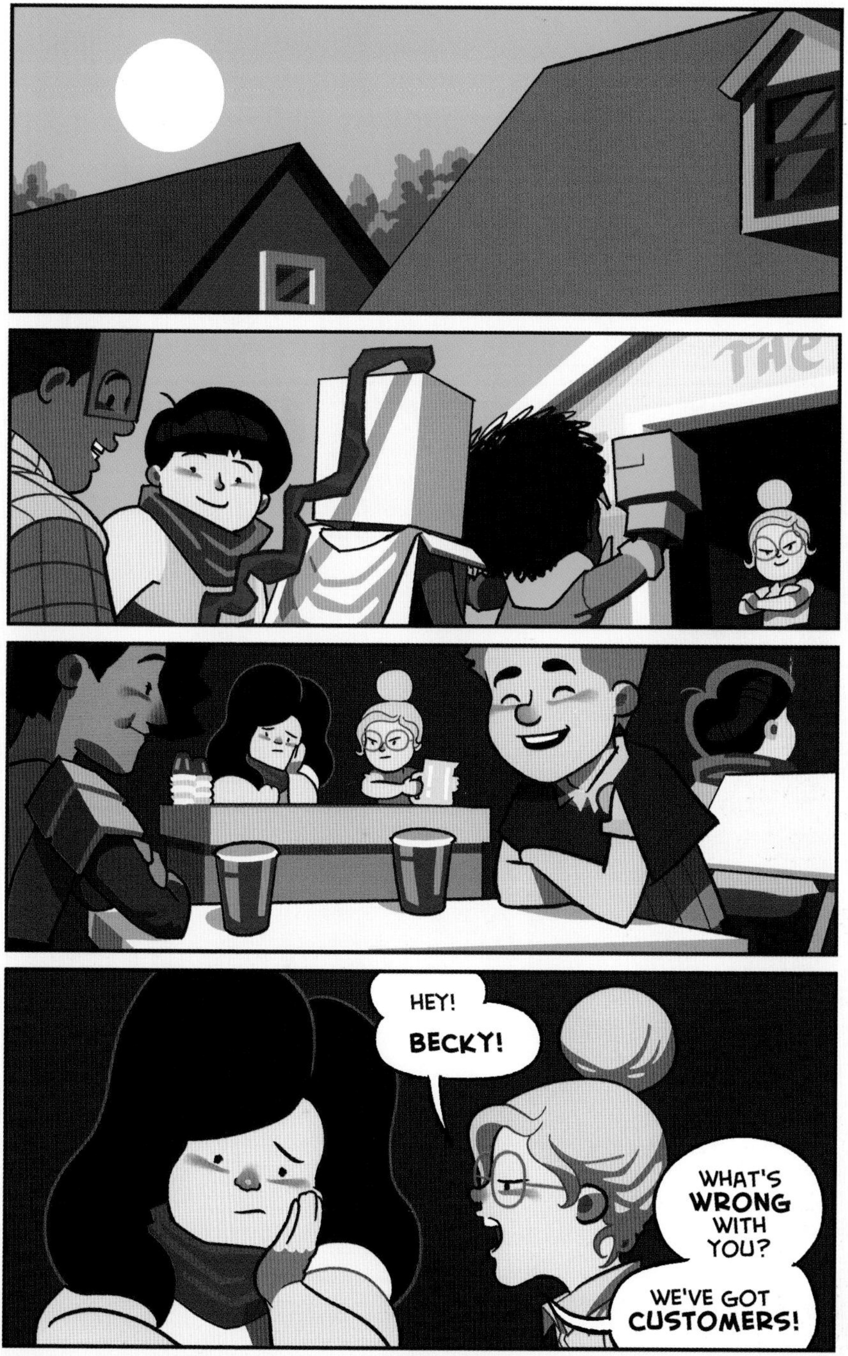
HEY! BECKY!
WHAT'S WRONG WITH YOU?
WE'VE GOT CUSTOMERS!

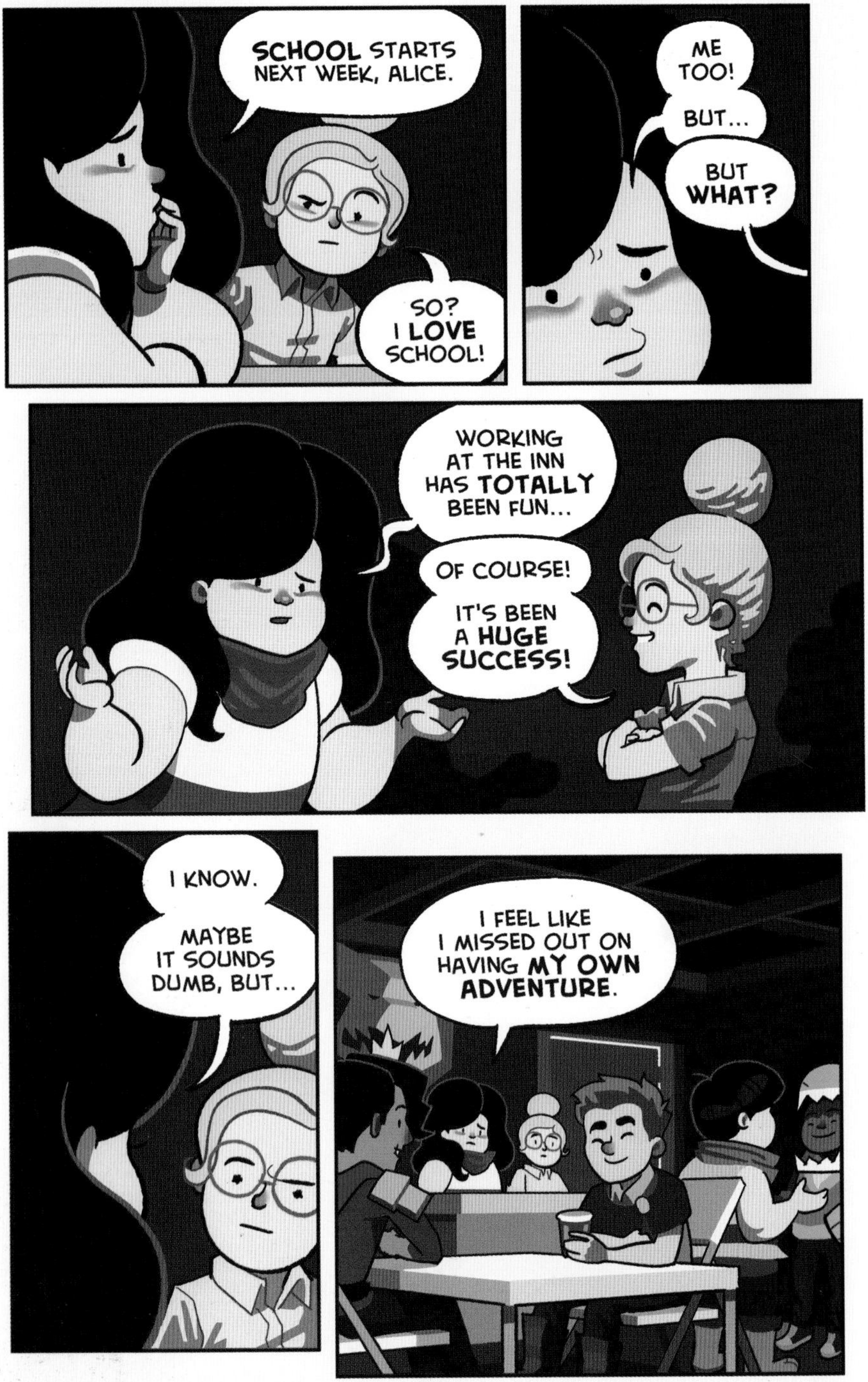
SCHOOL STARTS NEXT WEEK, ALICE.
SO? I LOVE SCHOOL!
ME TOO!
BUT...
BUT WHAT?
WORKING AT THE INN HAS TOTALLY BEEN FUN...
OF COURSE!
IT'S BEEN A HUGE SUCCESS!
I KNOW.
MAYBE IT SOUNDS DUMB, BUT...
I FEEL LIKE I MISSED OUT ON HAVING MY OWN ADVENTURE.

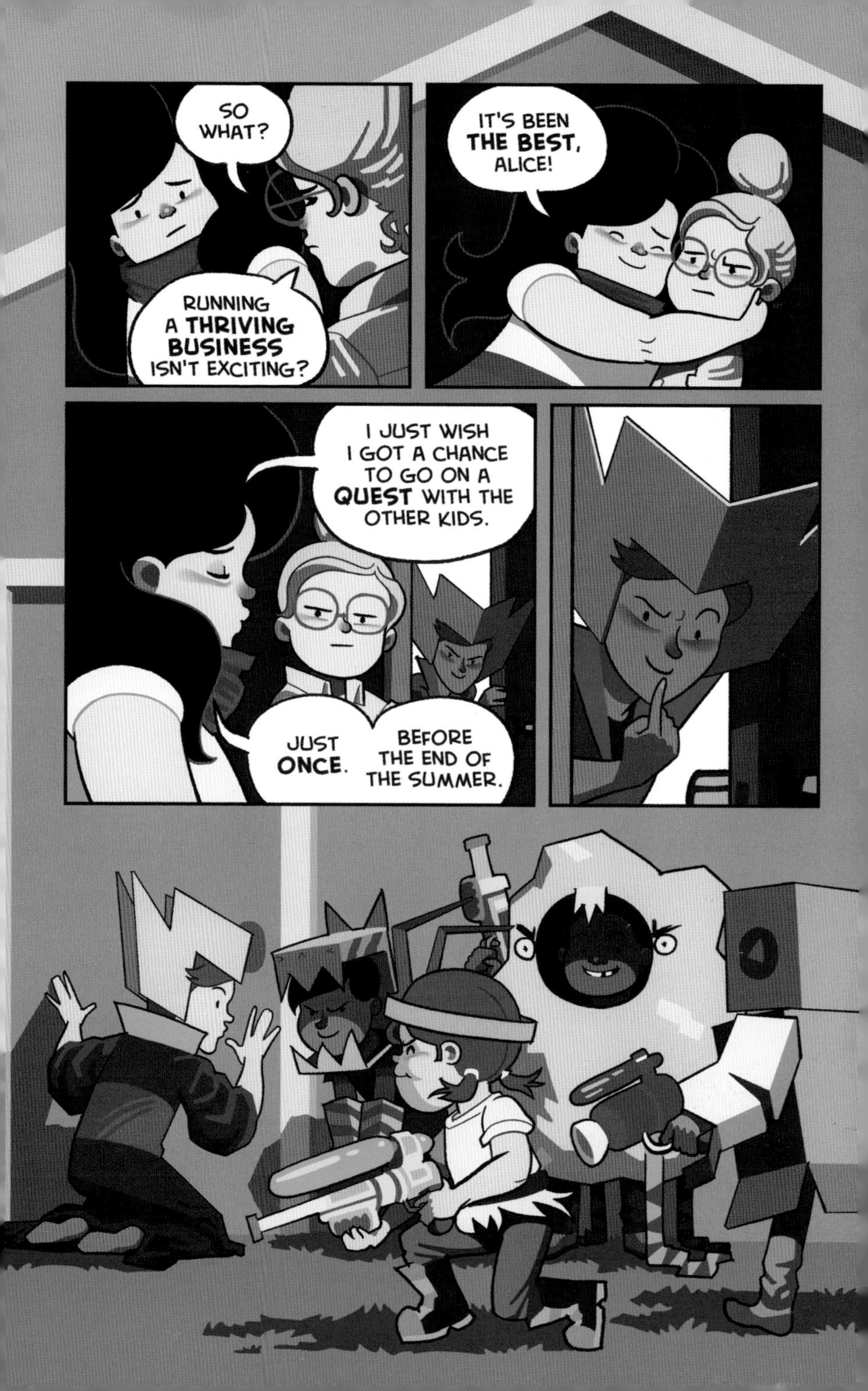
SO WHAT?
RUNNING A THRIVING BUSINESS ISN'T EXCITING?
IT'S BEEN THE BEST, ALICE!
I JUST WISH I GOT A CHANCE TO GO ON A QUEST WITH THE OTHER KIDS.
JUST ONCE.
BEFORE THE END OF THE SUMMER.

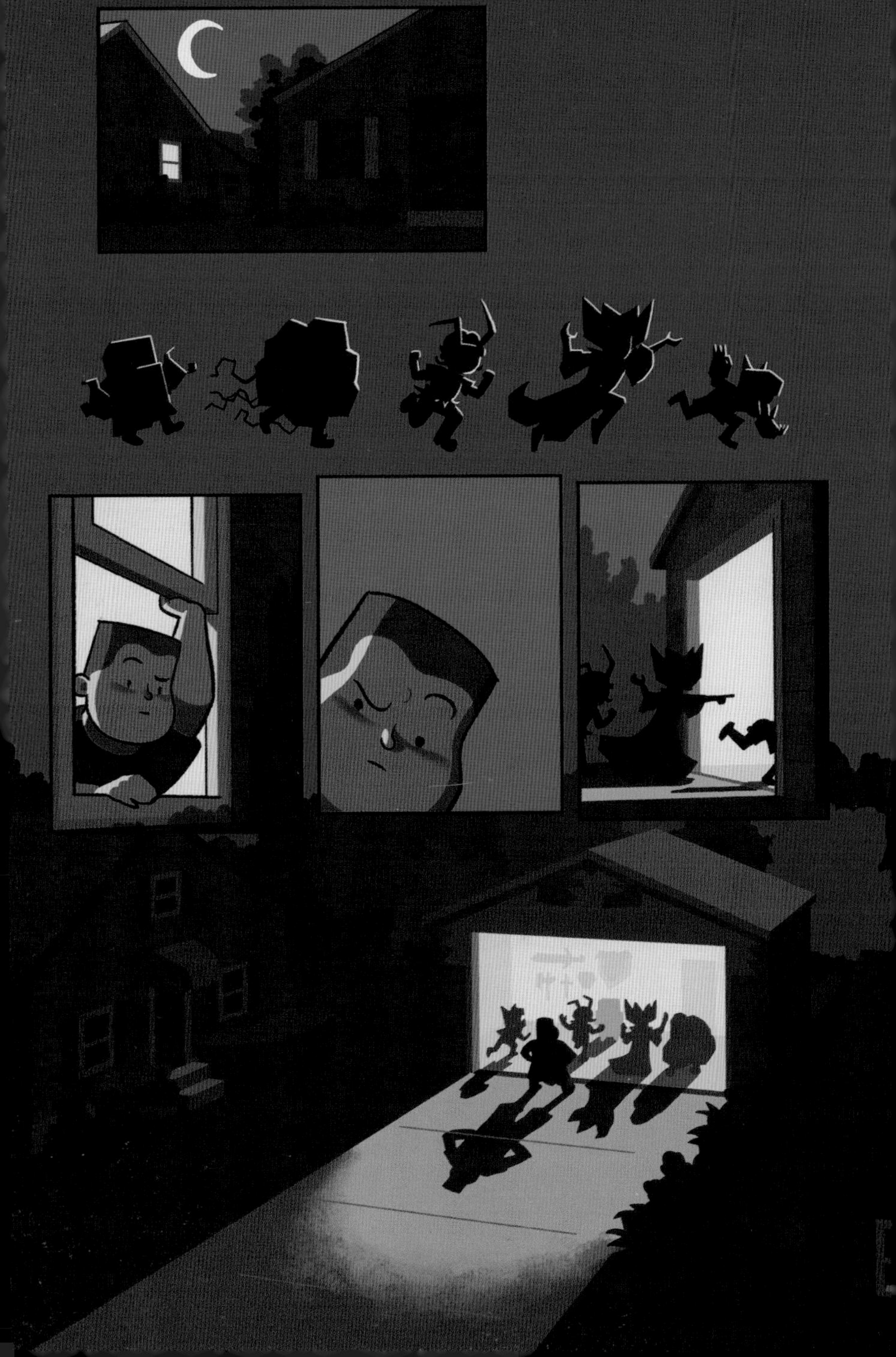

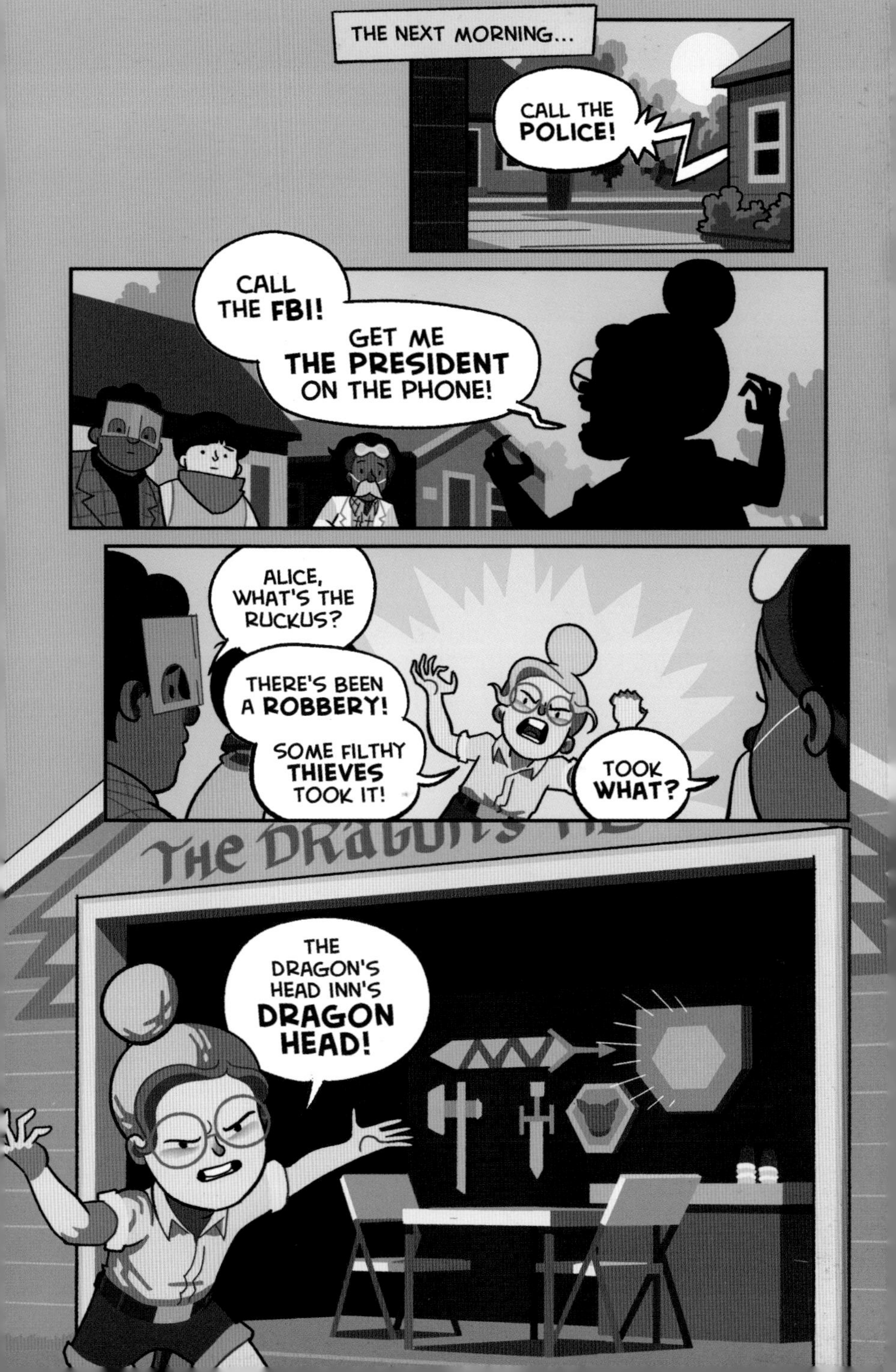
THE NEXT MORNING...
CALL THE POLICE!
CALL THE FBI!
GET ME THE PRESIDENT ON THE PHONE!
ALICE, WHAT'S THE RUCKUS?
THERE'S BEEN A ROBBERY!
SOME FILTHY THIEVES TOOK IT!
TOOK WHAT?
THE DRAGON'S HEAD INN'S DRAGON HEAD!

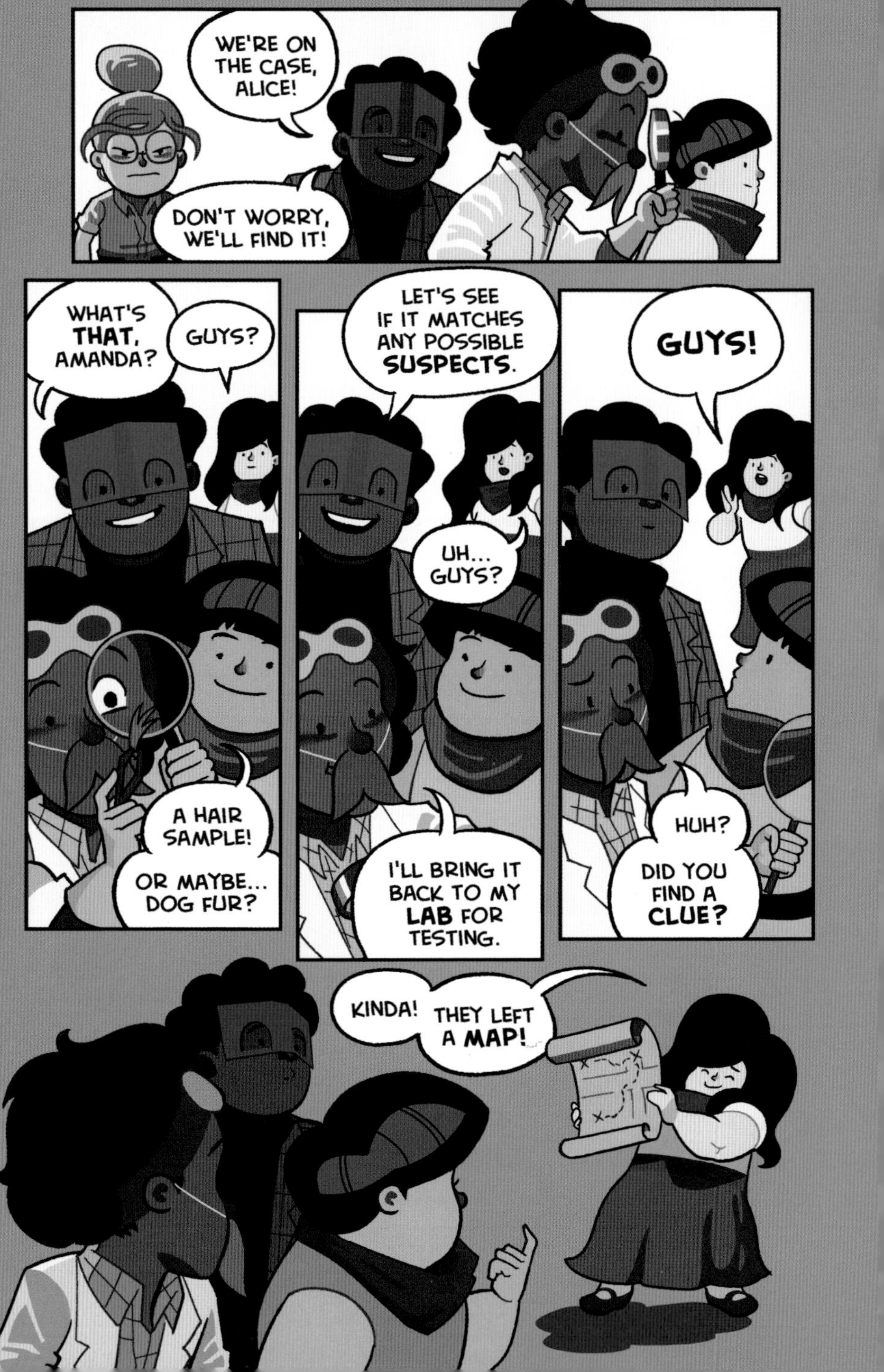
WE'RE ON THE CASE, ALICE!
DON'T WORRY, WE'LL FIND IT!
WHAT'S **THAT**, AMANDA?
GUYS?
A HAIR SAMPLE!
OR MAYBE... DOG FUR?
LET'S SEE IF IT MATCHES ANY POSSIBLE **SUSPECTS**.
UH... GUYS?
I'LL BRING IT BACK TO MY **LAB** FOR TESTING.
GUYS!
HUH?
DID YOU FIND A **CLUE?**
KINDA!
THEY LEFT A **MAP!**

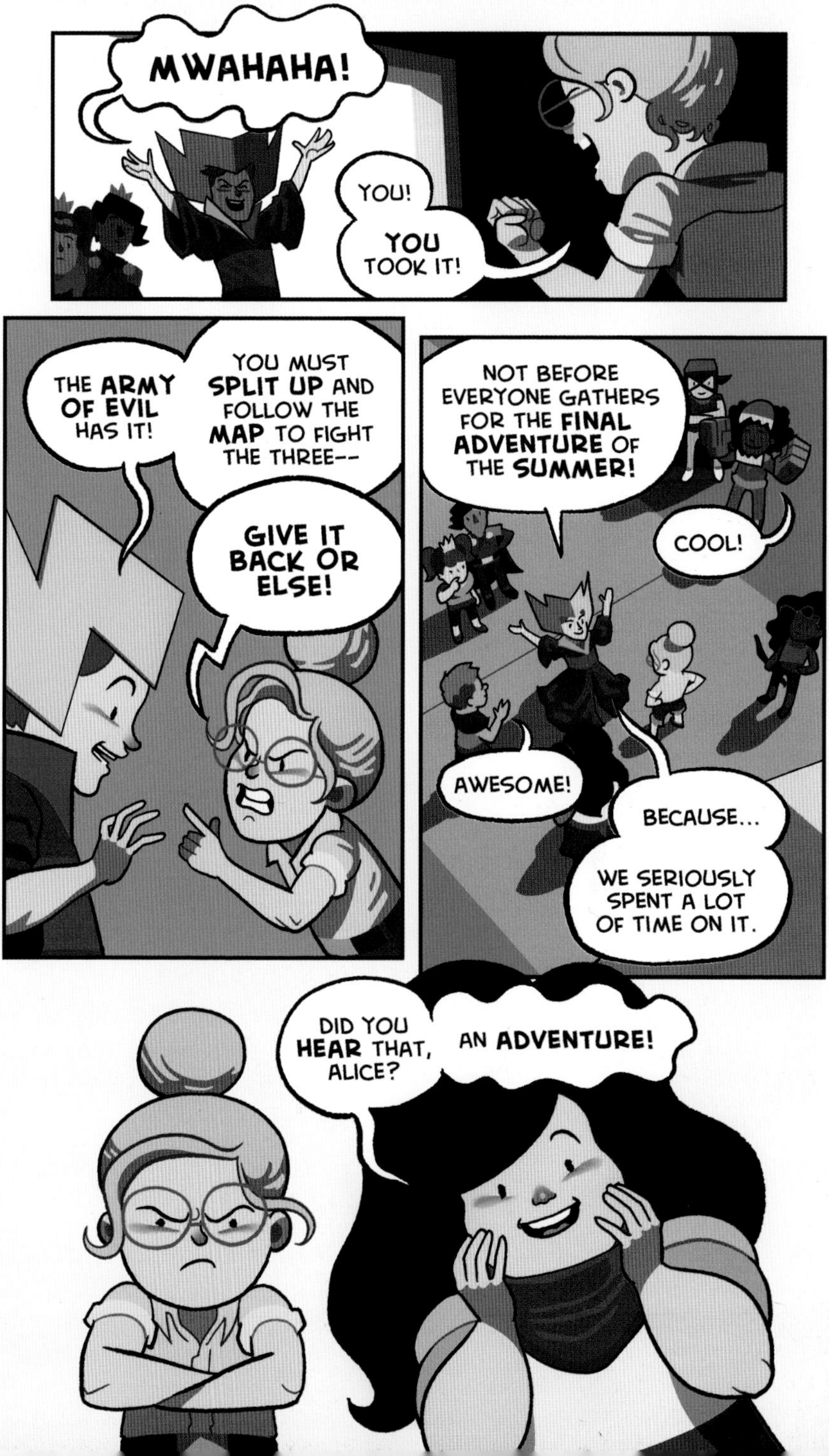
MWAHAHA!
YOU! YOU TOOK IT!
THE ARMY OF EVIL HAS IT!
YOU MUST SPLIT UP AND FOLLOW THE MAP TO FIGHT THE THREE--
GIVE IT BACK OR ELSE!
NOT BEFORE EVERYONE GATHERS FOR THE FINAL ADVENTURE OF THE SUMMER!
COOL!
AWESOME!
BECAUSE...
WE SERIOUSLY SPENT A LOT OF TIME ON IT.
DID YOU HEAR THAT, ALICE?
AN ADVENTURE!

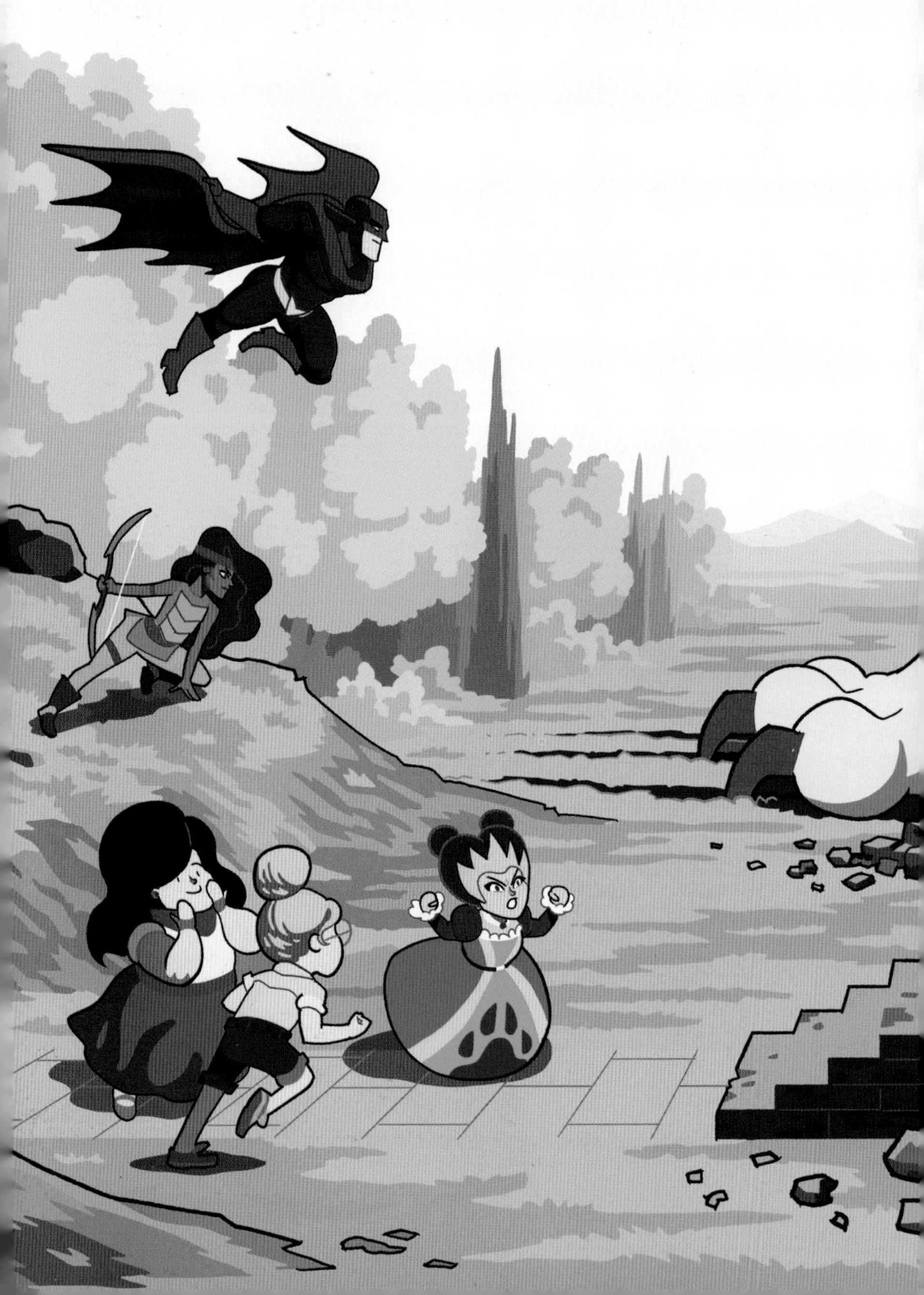

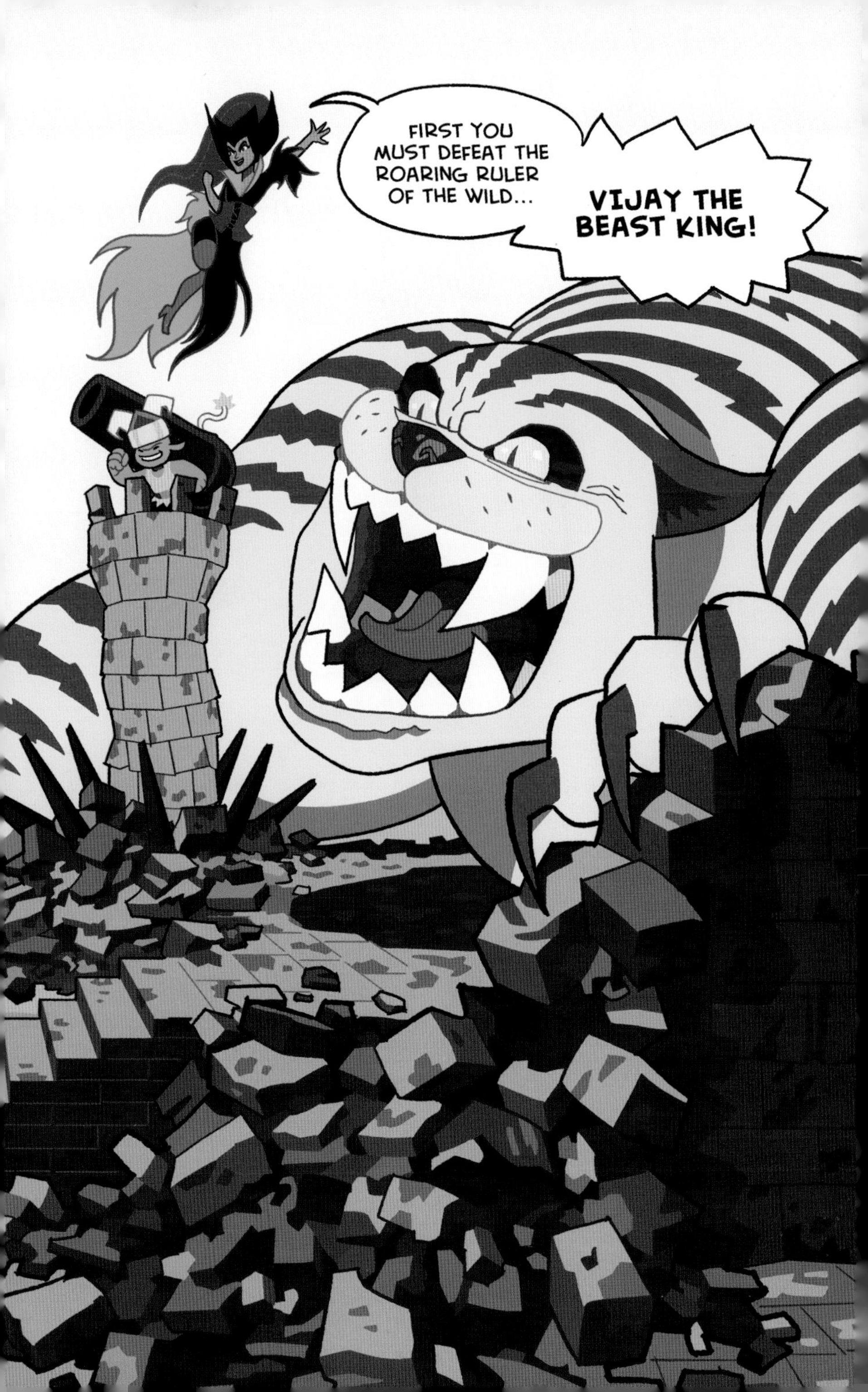
FIRST YOU MUST DEFEAT THE ROARING RULER OF THE WILD...
VIJAY THE BEAST KING!

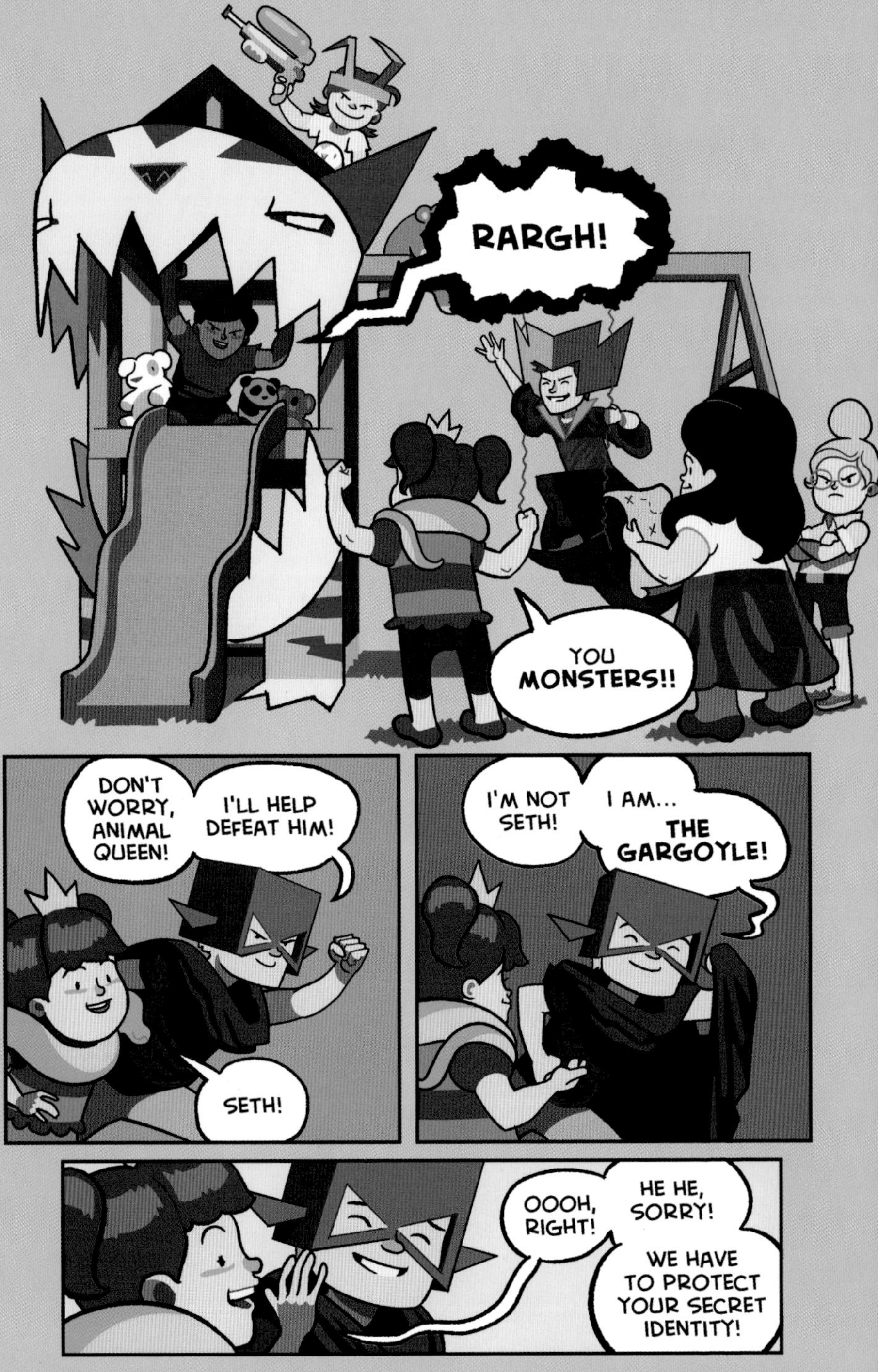
RARGH!
YOU MONSTERS!!
DON'T WORRY, ANIMAL QUEEN!
I'LL HELP DEFEAT HIM!
SETH!
I'M NOT SETH!
I AM... THE GARGOYLE!
OOOH, RIGHT!
HE HE, SORRY!
WE HAVE TO PROTECT YOUR SECRET IDENTITY!

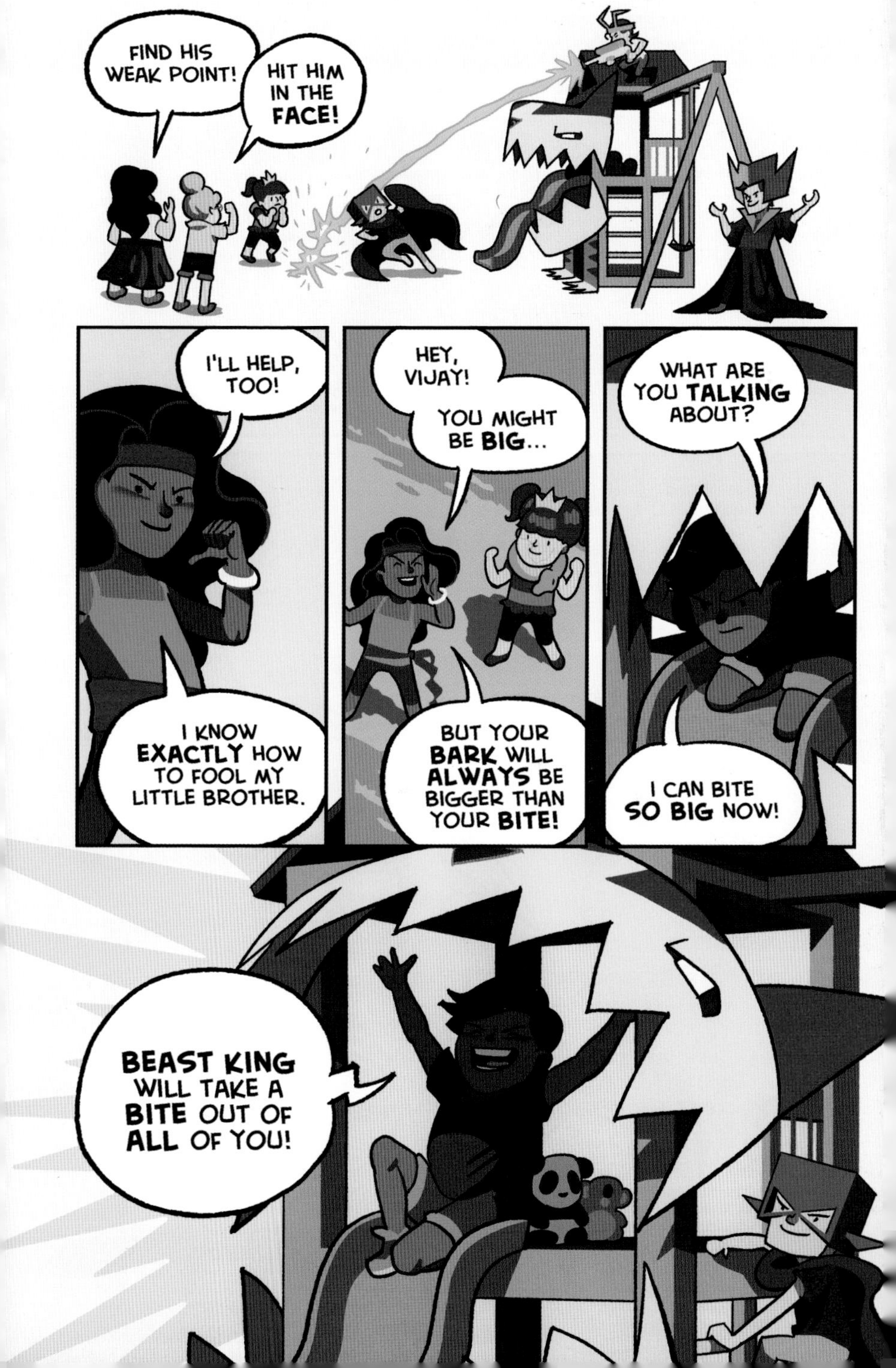
FIND HIS WEAK POINT!
HIT HIM IN THE FACE!
I'LL HELP, TOO!
I KNOW EXACTLY HOW TO FOOL MY LITTLE BROTHER.
HEY, VIJAY!
YOU MIGHT BE BIG...
BUT YOUR BARK WILL ALWAYS BE BIGGER THAN YOUR BITE!
WHAT ARE YOU TALKING ABOUT?
I CAN BITE SO BIG NOW!
BEAST KING WILL TAKE A BITE OUT OF ALL OF YOU!

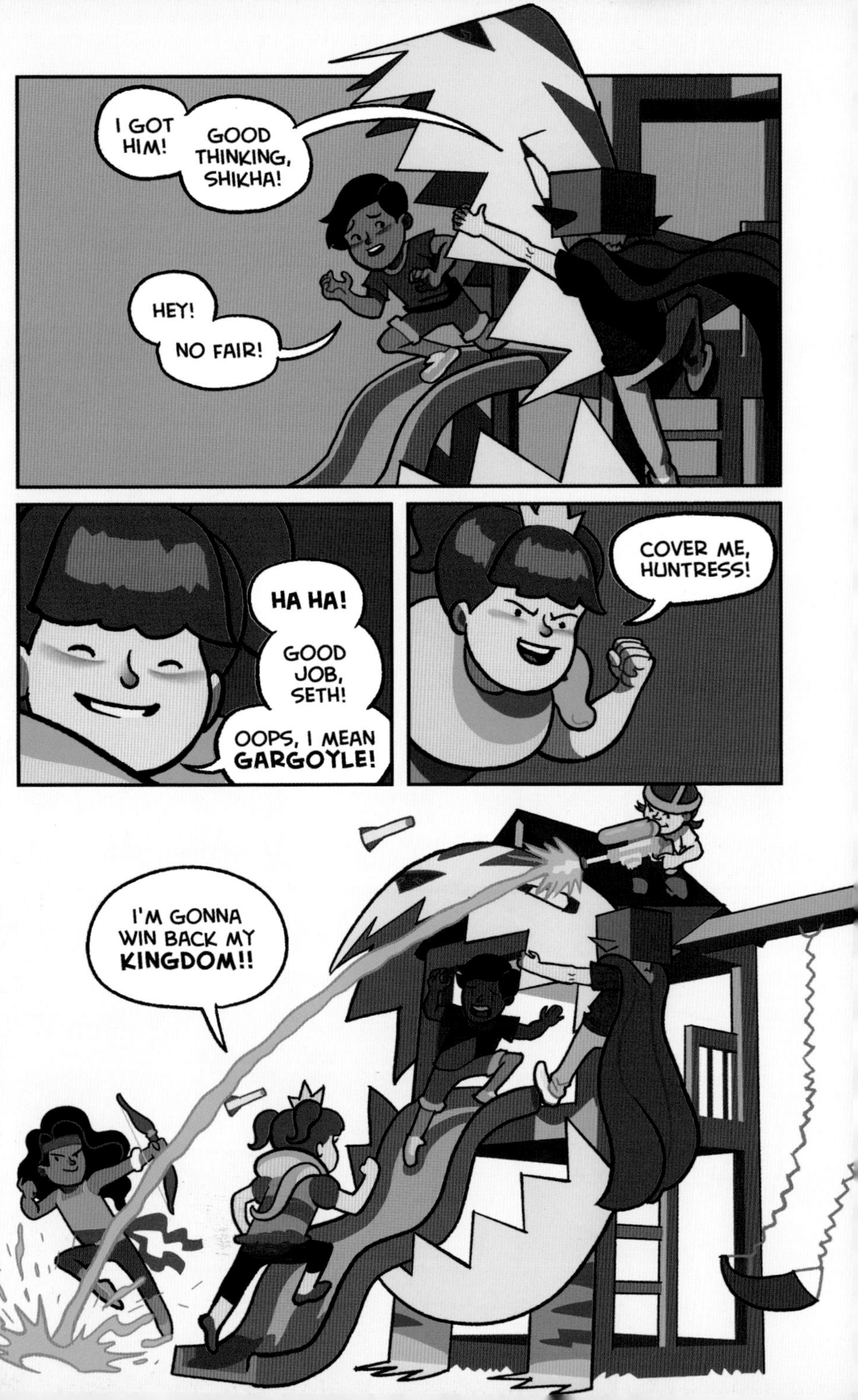
I GOT HIM!
GOOD THINKING, SHIKHA!
HEY!
NO FAIR!
HA HA!
GOOD JOB, SETH!
OOPS, I MEAN **GARGOYLE!**
COVER ME, HUNTRESS!
I'M GONNA WIN BACK MY **KINGDOM!!**

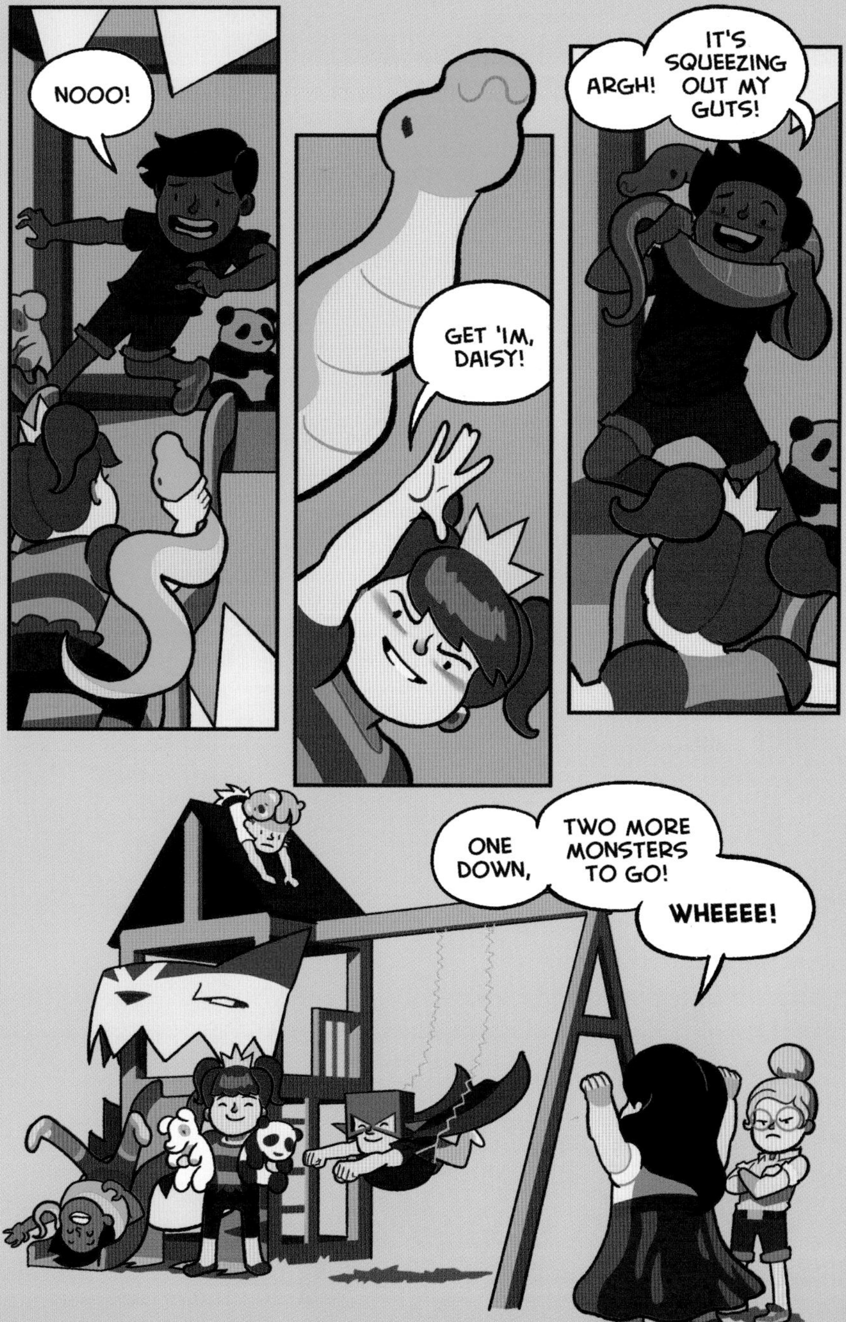
NOOO!
GET 'IM, DAISY!
ARGH!
IT'S SQUEEZING OUT MY GUTS!
ONE DOWN,
TWO MORE MONSTERS TO GO!
WHEEEE!

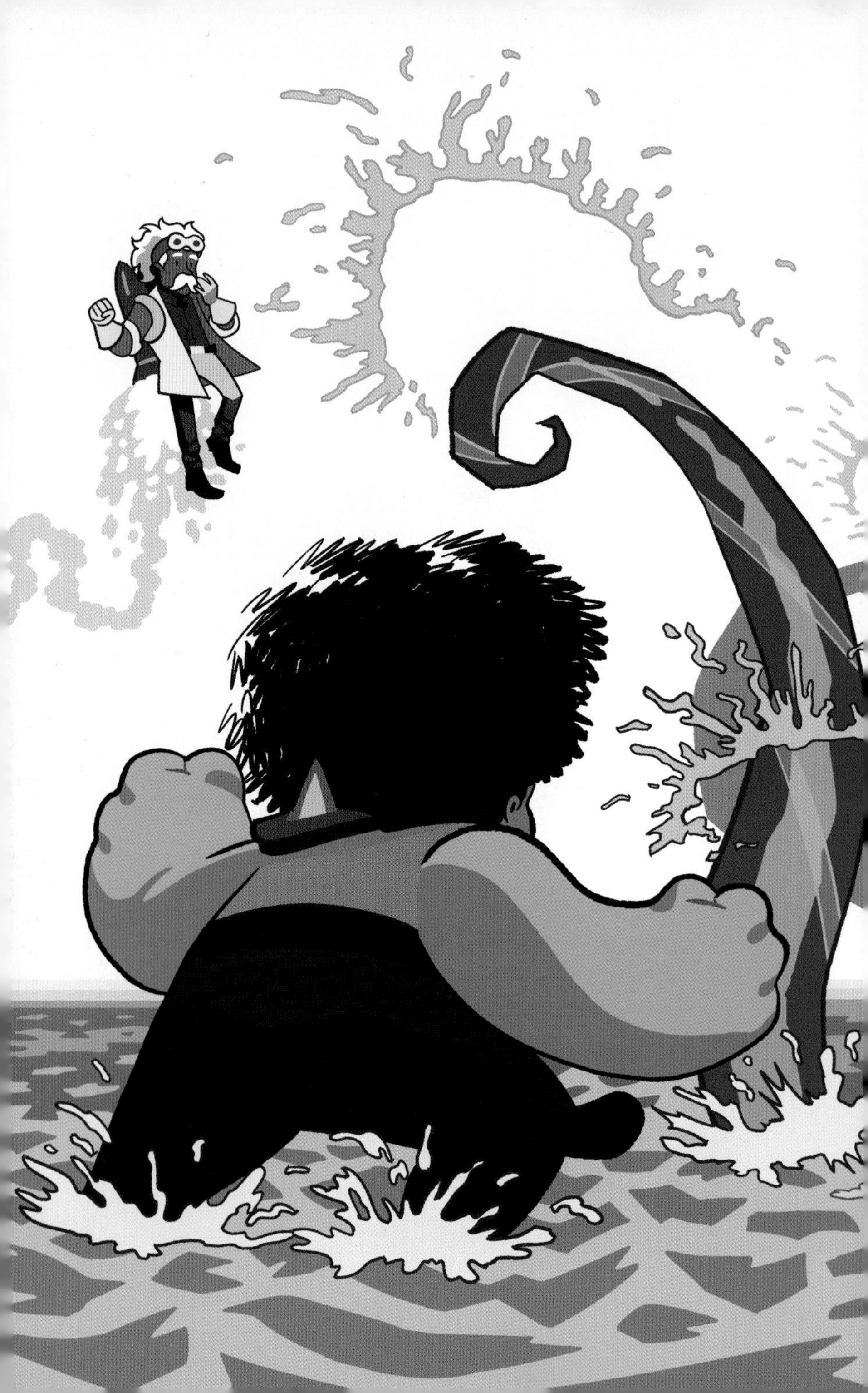

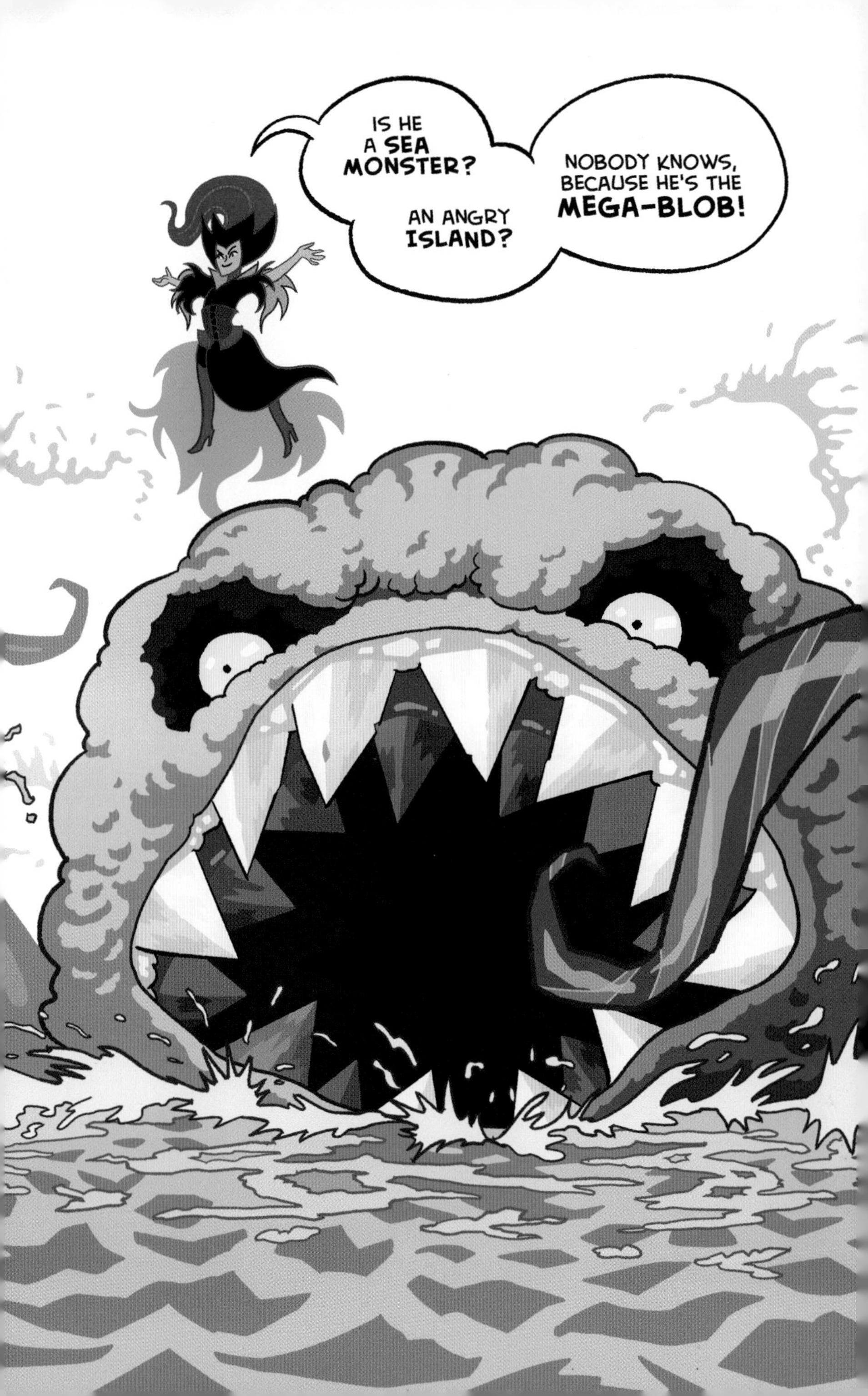
IS HE A SEA MONSTER?
AN ANGRY ISLAND?
NOBODY KNOWS, BECAUSE HE'S THE MEGA-BLOB!

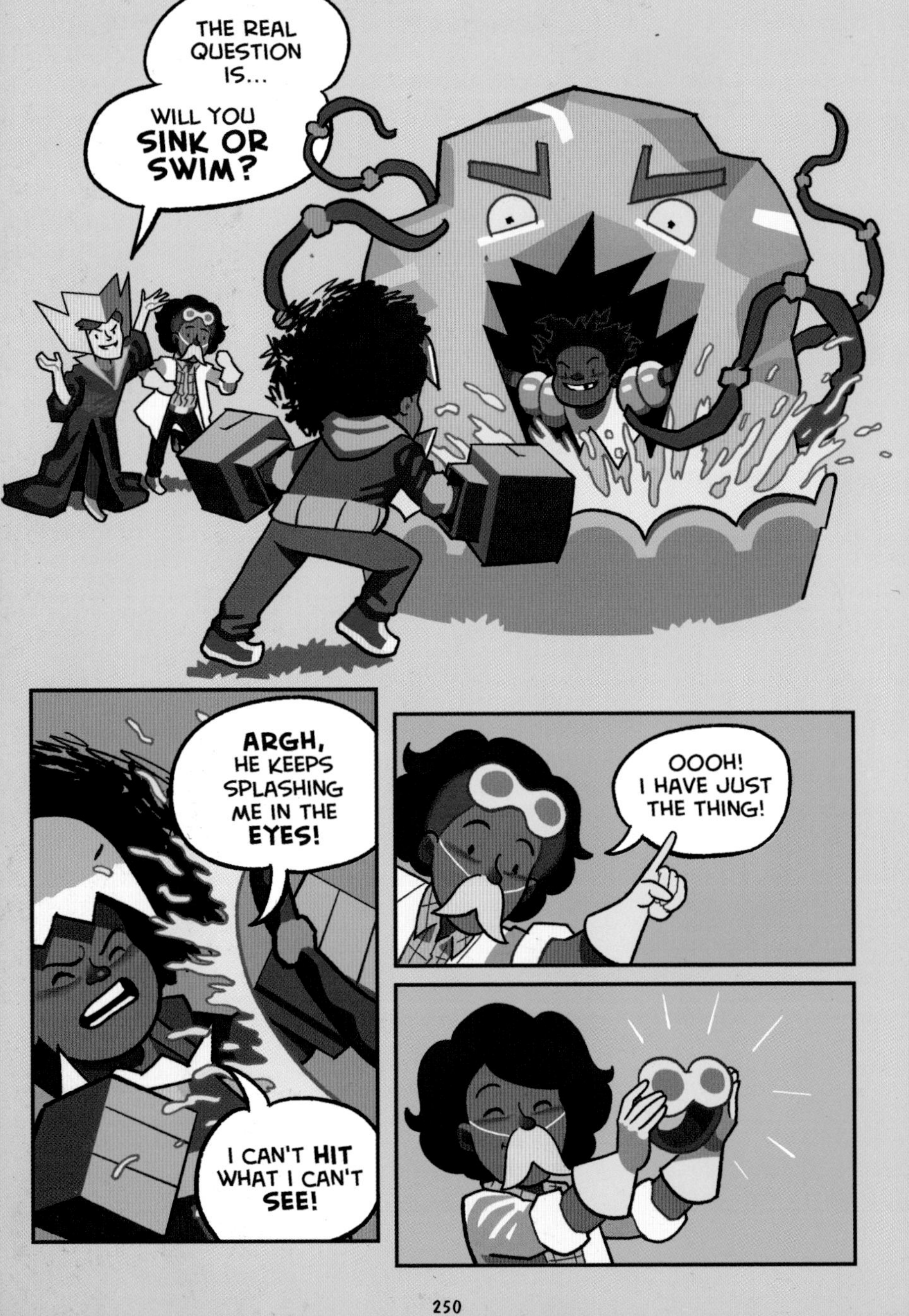
THE REAL QUESTION IS...
WILL YOU **SINK OR SWIM?**
ARGH, HE KEEPS SPLASHING ME IN THE **EYES!**
I CAN'T **HIT** WHAT I CAN'T **SEE!**
OOOH! I HAVE JUST THE THING!

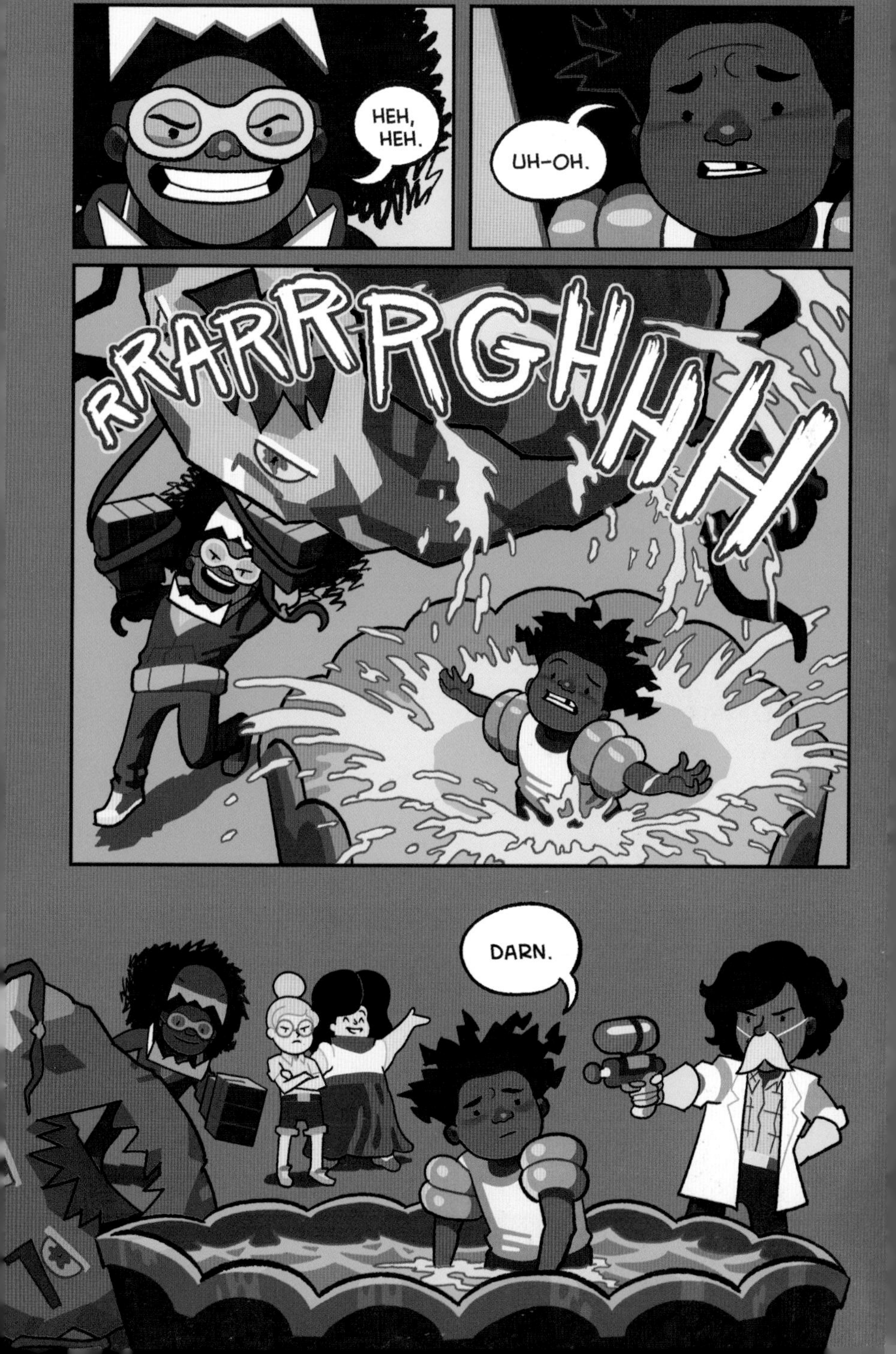
HEH, HEH.
UH-OH.
RRARRRGHHHH
DARN.

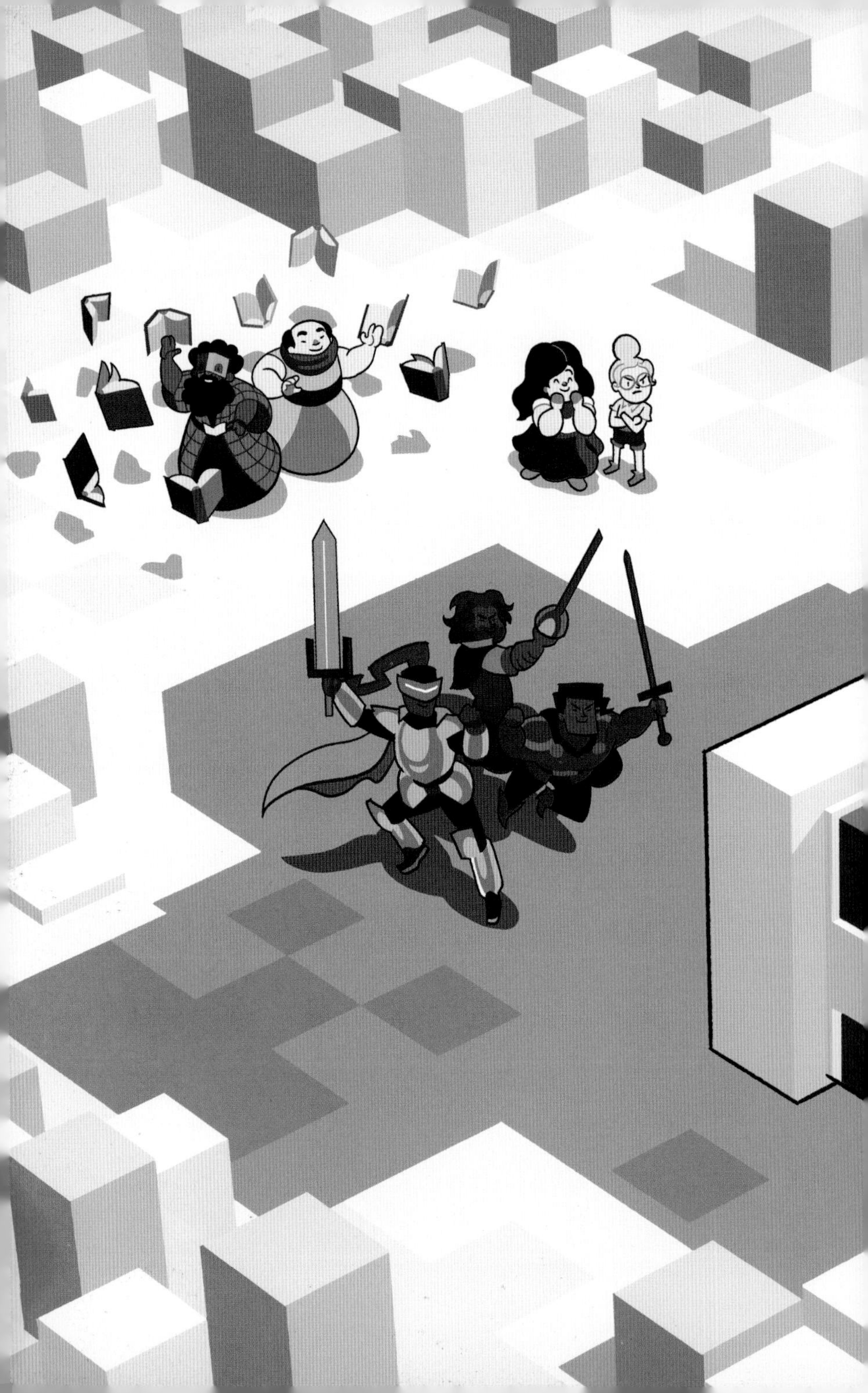

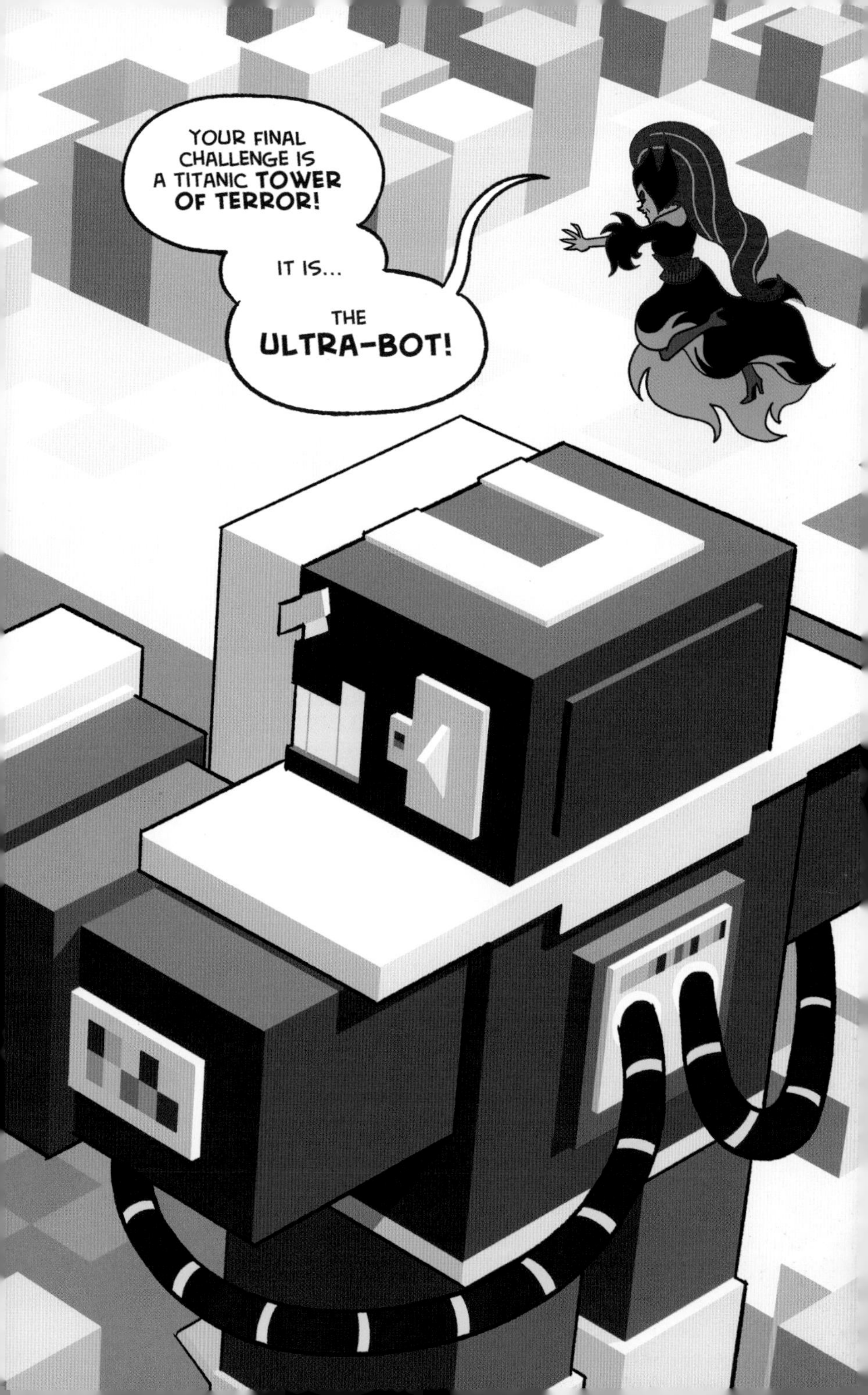
YOUR FINAL CHALLENGE IS A TITANIC **TOWER OF TERROR!**
IT IS...
THE **ULTRA-BOT!**

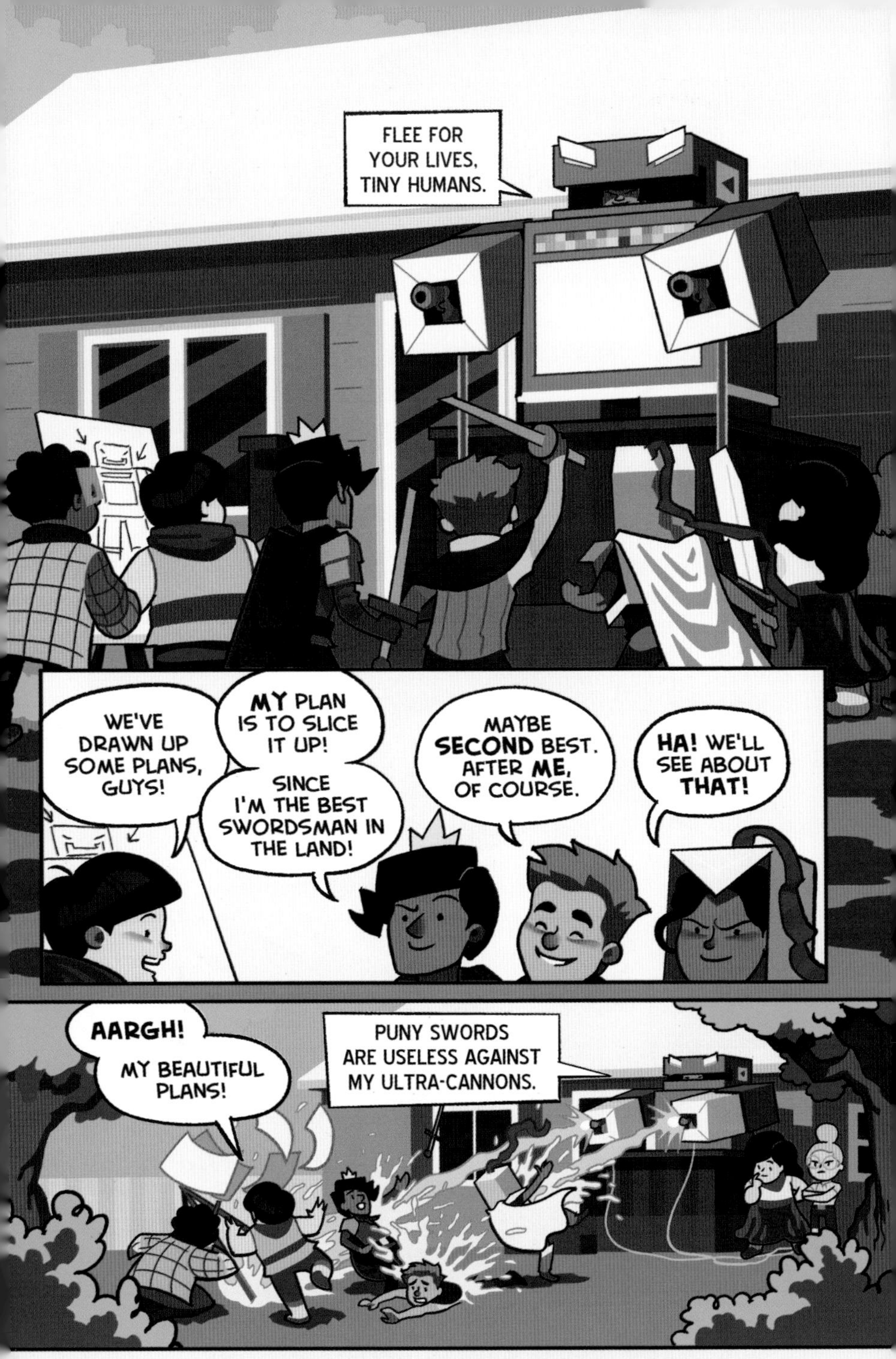
FLEE FOR YOUR LIVES, TINY HUMANS.
WE'VE DRAWN UP SOME PLANS, GUYS!
MY PLAN IS TO SLICE IT UP!
SINCE I'M THE BEST SWORDSMAN IN THE LAND!
MAYBE SECOND BEST. AFTER ME, OF COURSE.
HA! WE'LL SEE ABOUT THAT!
AARGH!
MY BEAUTIFUL PLANS!
PUNY SWORDS ARE USELESS AGAINST MY ULTRA-CANNONS.

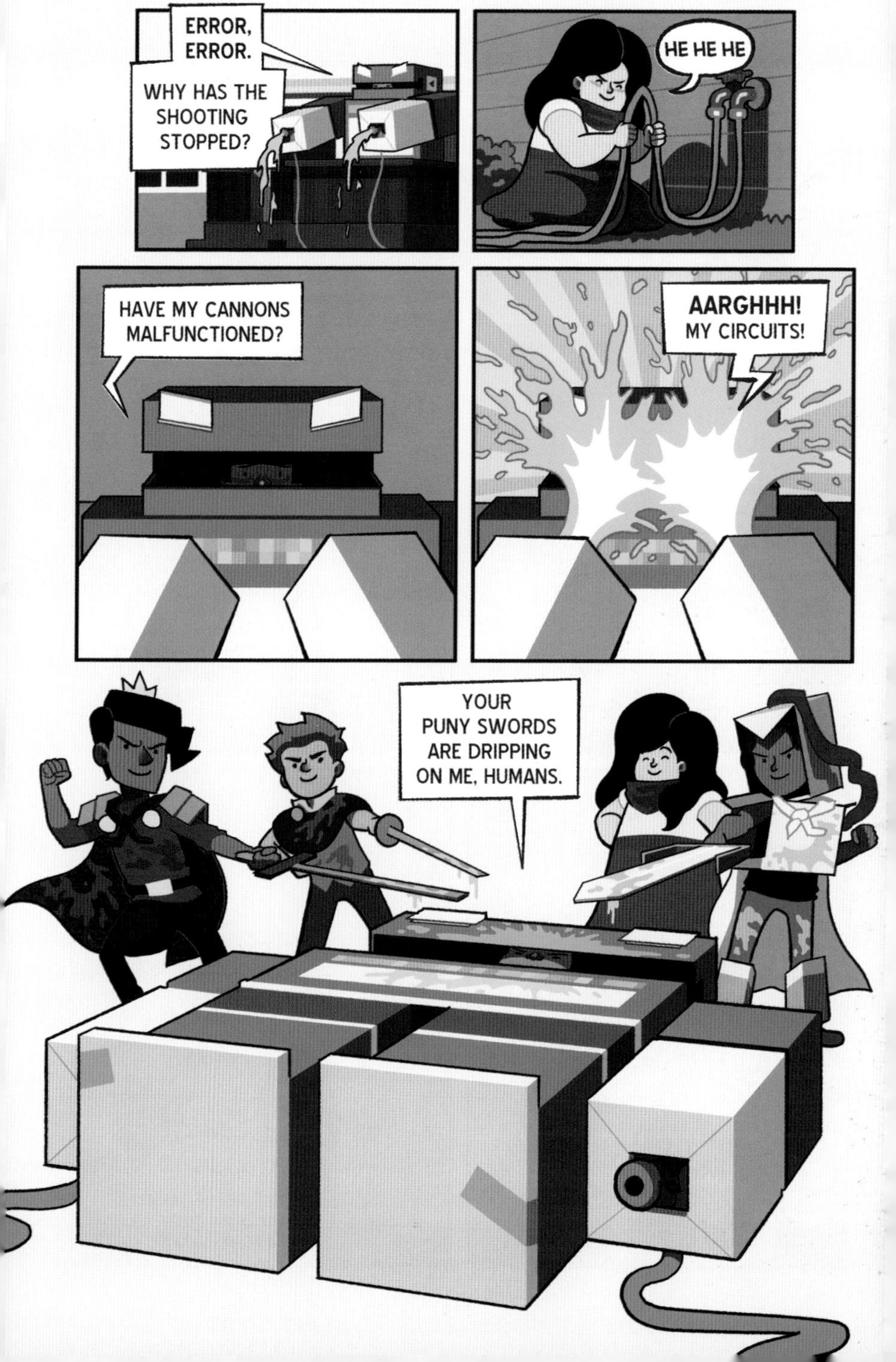
ERROR, ERROR.
WHY HAS THE SHOOTING STOPPED?
HE HE HE
HAVE MY CANNONS MALFUNCTIONED?
AARGHHH! MY CIRCUITS!
YOUR PUNY SWORDS ARE DRIPPING ON ME, HUMANS.

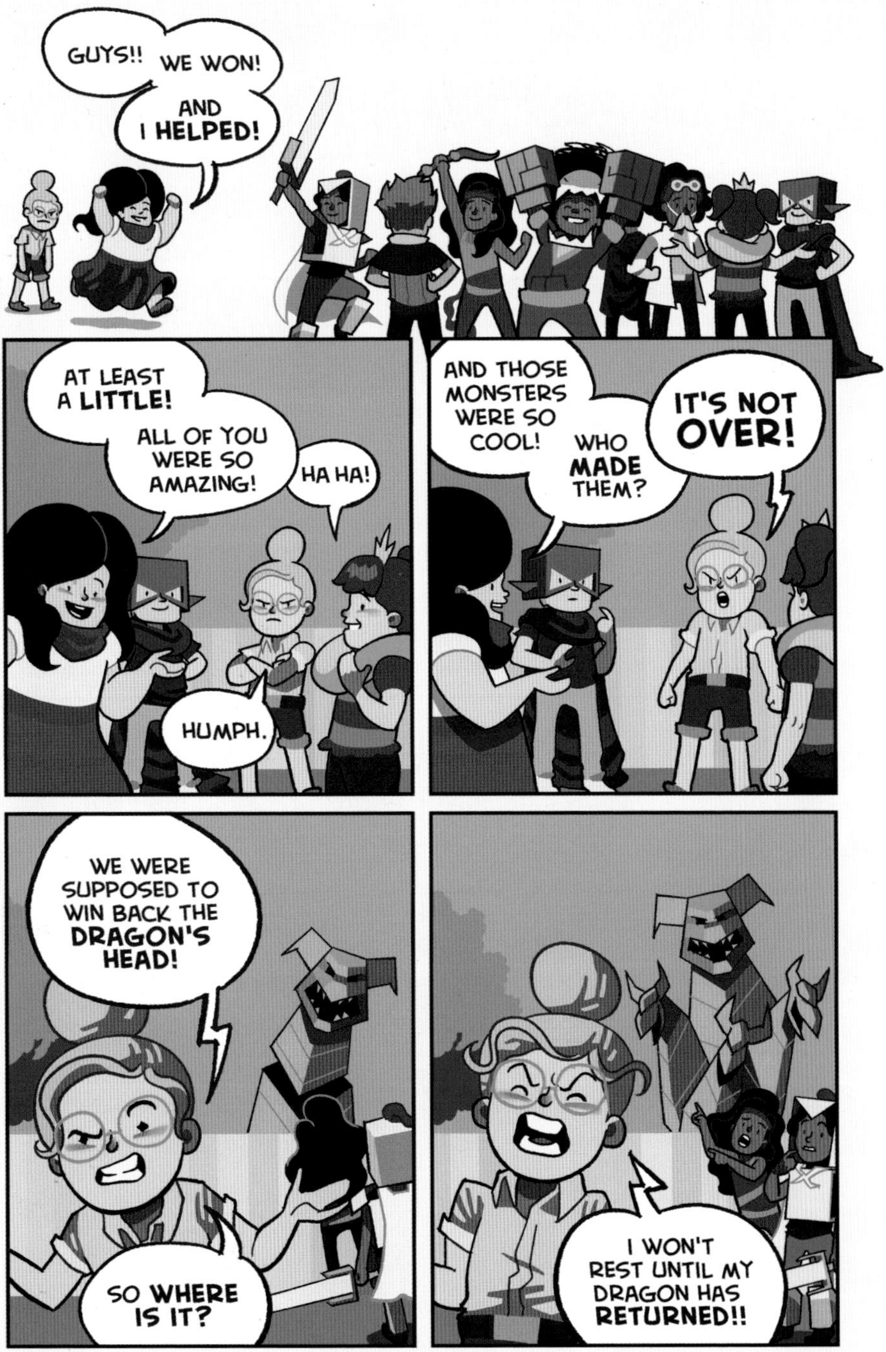
GUYS!! WE WON!
AND I HELPED!
AT LEAST A LITTLE!
ALL OF YOU WERE SO AMAZING!
HA HA!
HUMPH.
AND THOSE MONSTERS WERE SO COOL!
WHO MADE THEM?
IT'S NOT OVER!
WE WERE SUPPOSED TO WIN BACK THE DRAGON'S HEAD!
SO WHERE IS IT?
I WON'T REST UNTIL MY DRAGON HAS RETURNED!!

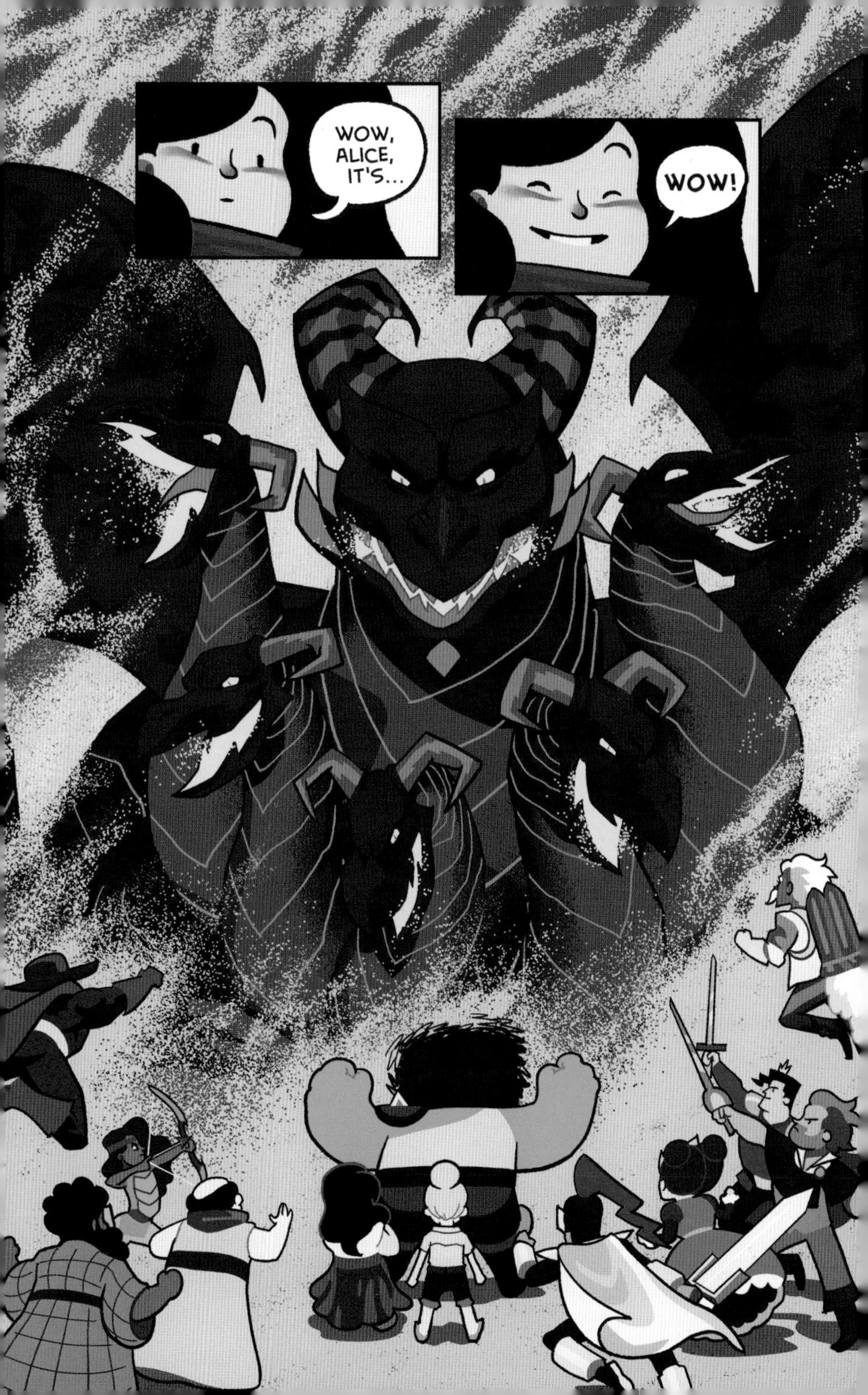
WOW, ALICE, IT'S...
WOW!

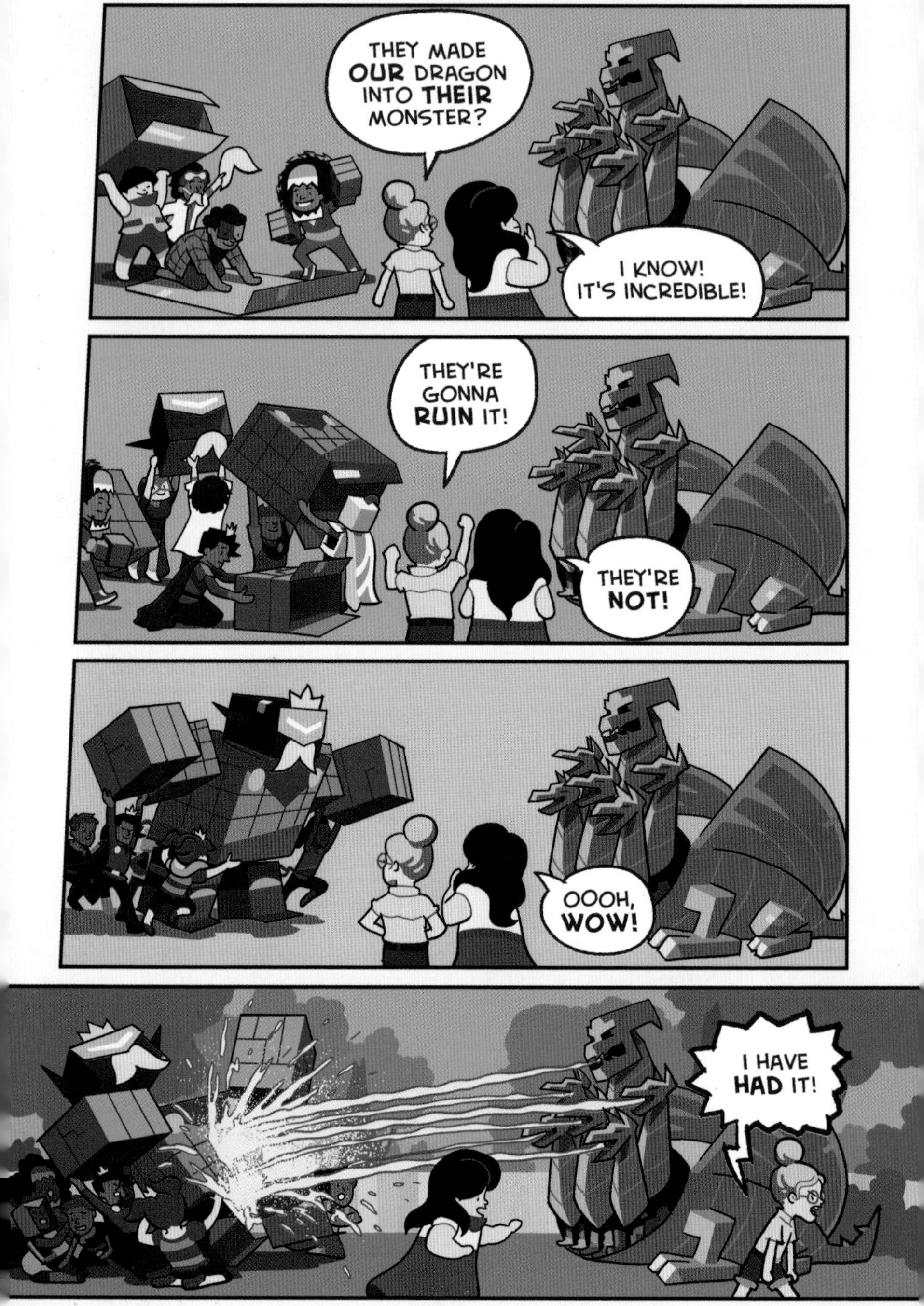
THEY MADE OUR DRAGON INTO THEIR MONSTER?
I KNOW! IT'S INCREDIBLE!
THEY'RE GONNA RUIN IT!
THEY'RE NOT!
OOOH, WOW!
I HAVE HAD IT!

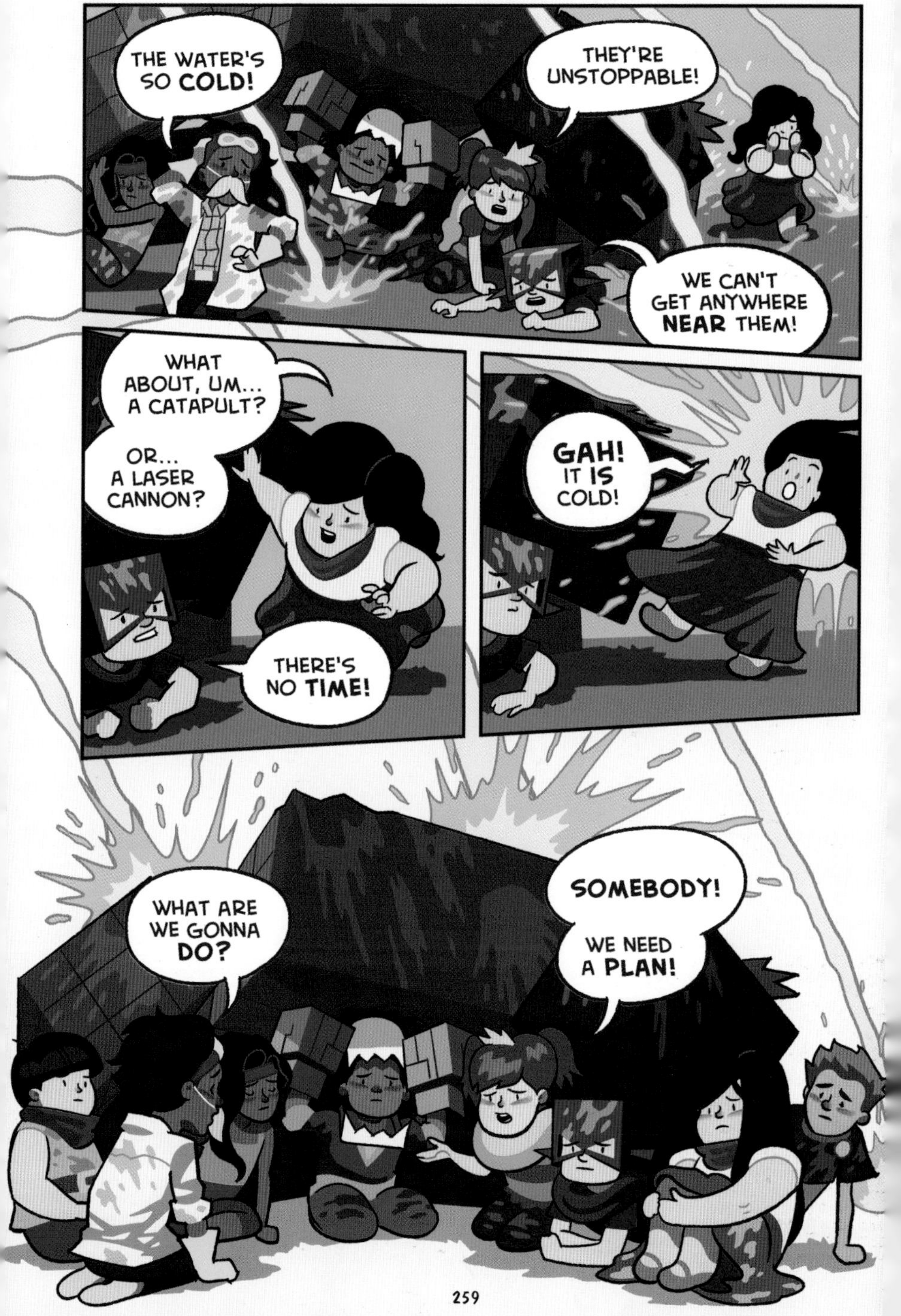
THE WATER'S SO COLD!
THEY'RE UNSTOPPABLE!
WE CAN'T GET ANYWHERE NEAR THEM!
WHAT ABOUT, UM... A CATAPULT?
OR... A LASER CANNON?
THERE'S NO TIME!
GAH! IT IS COLD!
WHAT ARE WE GONNA DO?
SOMEBODY!
WE NEED A PLAN!

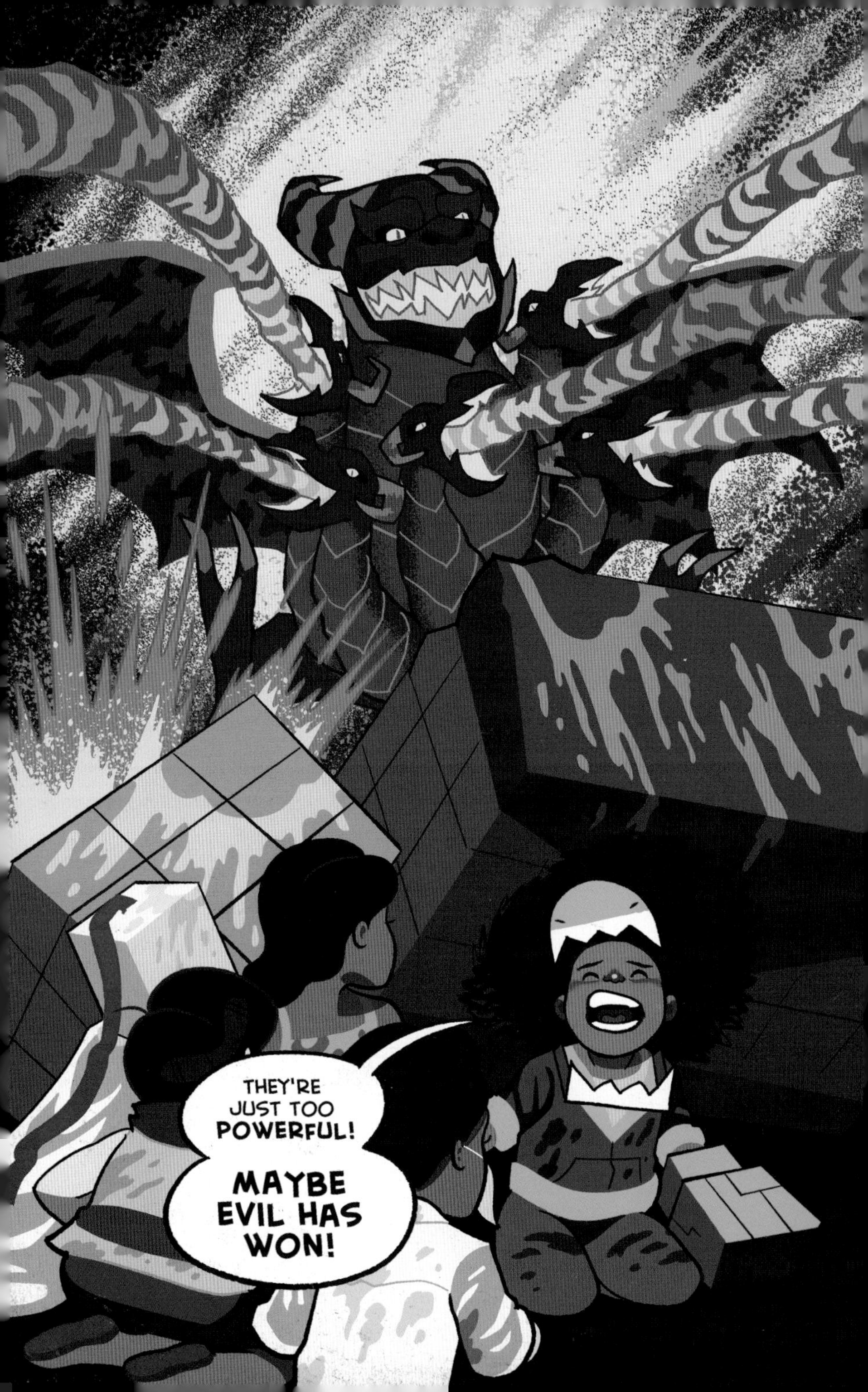
THEY'RE JUST TOO POWERFUL!
MAYBE EVIL HAS WON!

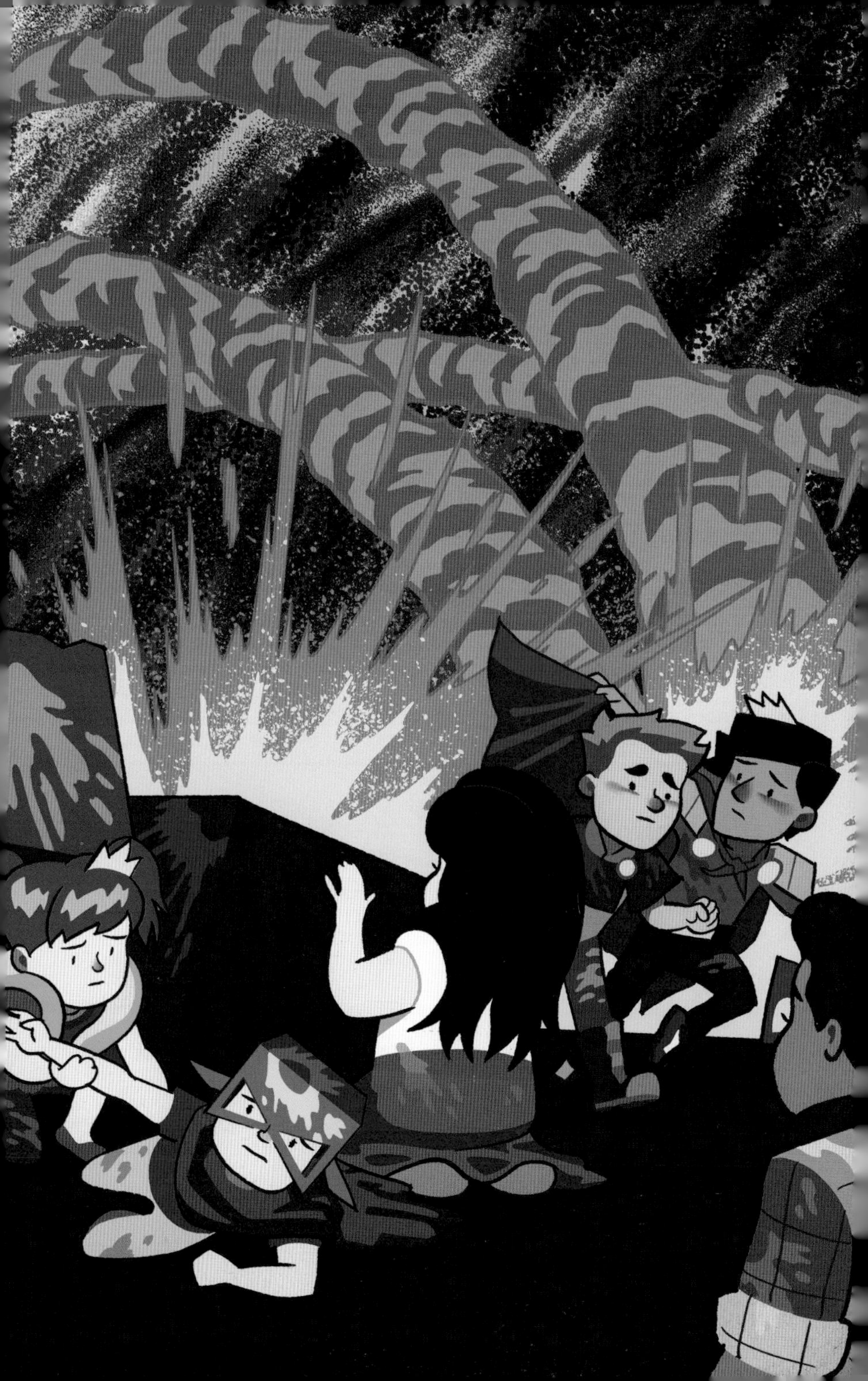

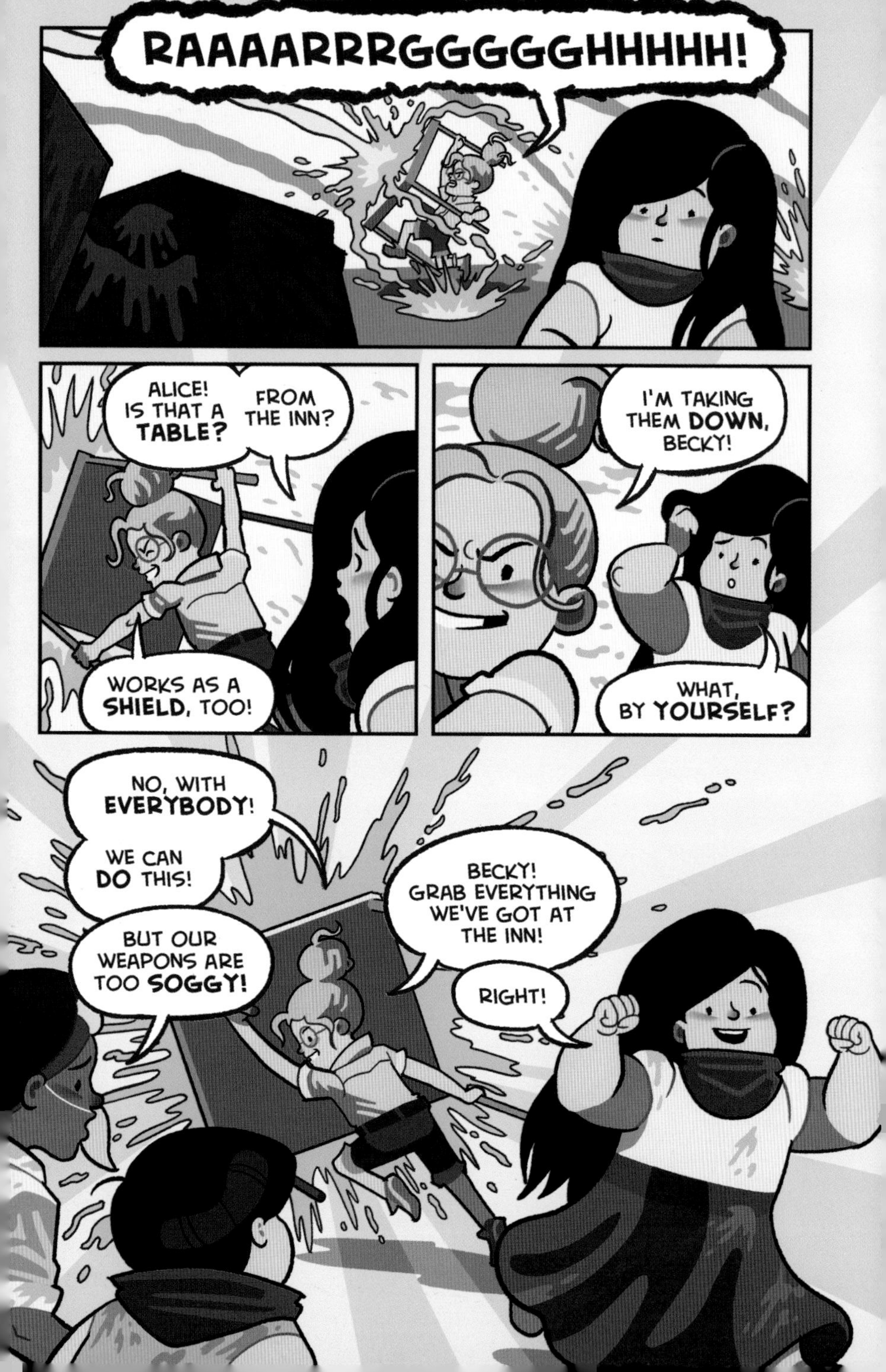
RAAAARRRGGGGGHHHHH!
ALICE! IS THAT A TABLE?
FROM THE INN?
WORKS AS A SHIELD, TOO!
I'M TAKING THEM DOWN, BECKY!
WHAT, BY YOURSELF?
NO, WITH EVERYBODY!
WE CAN DO THIS!
BUT OUR WEAPONS ARE TOO SOGGY!
BECKY! GRAB EVERYTHING WE'VE GOT AT THE INN!
RIGHT!

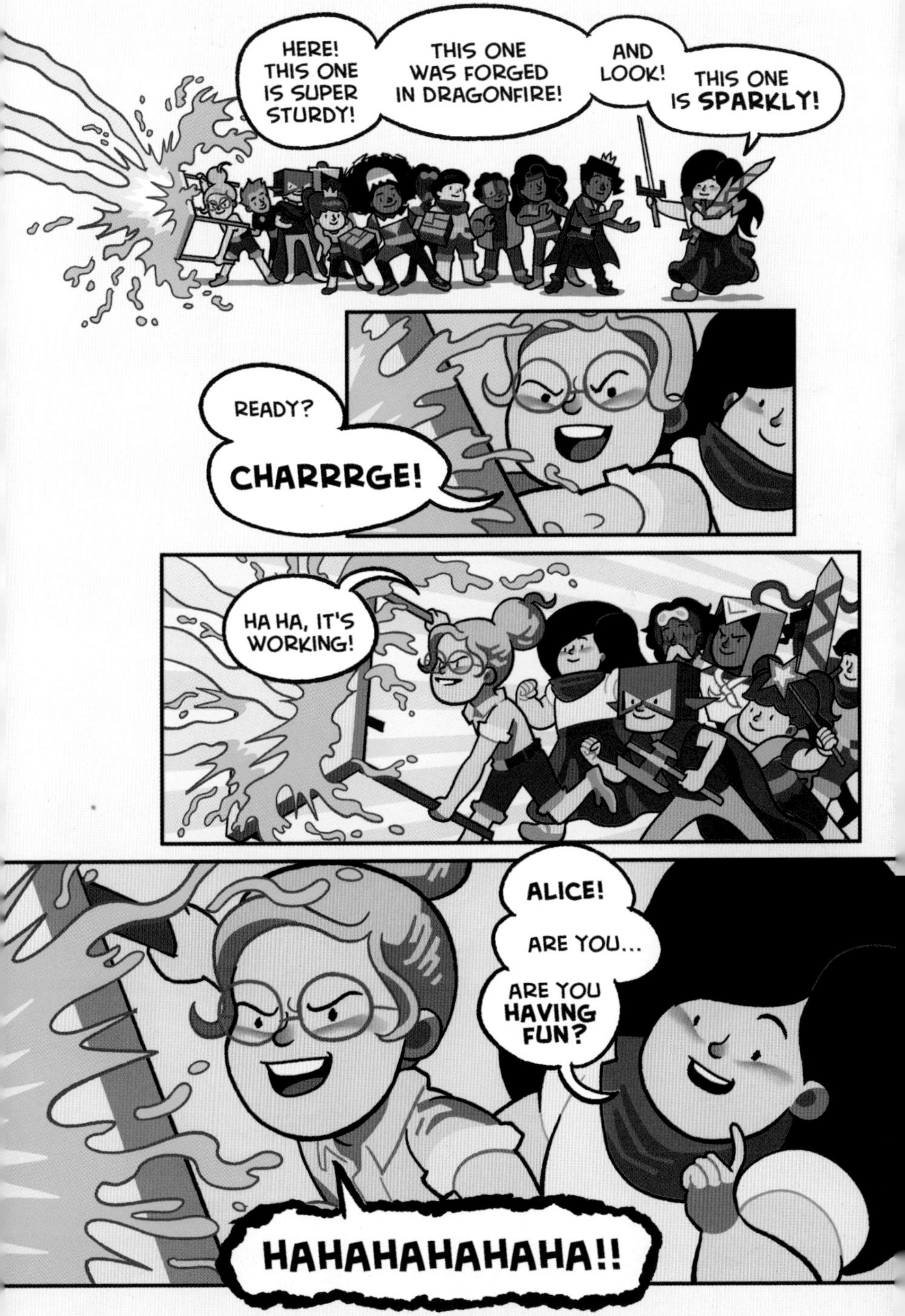

HERE! THIS ONE IS SUPER STURDY!
THIS ONE WAS FORGED IN DRAGONFIRE!
AND LOOK!
THIS ONE IS **SPARKLY**!
READY?
CHARRRGE!
HA HA, IT'S WORKING!
ALICE!
ARE YOU...
ARE YOU HAVING FUN?
HAHAHAHAHAHA!!

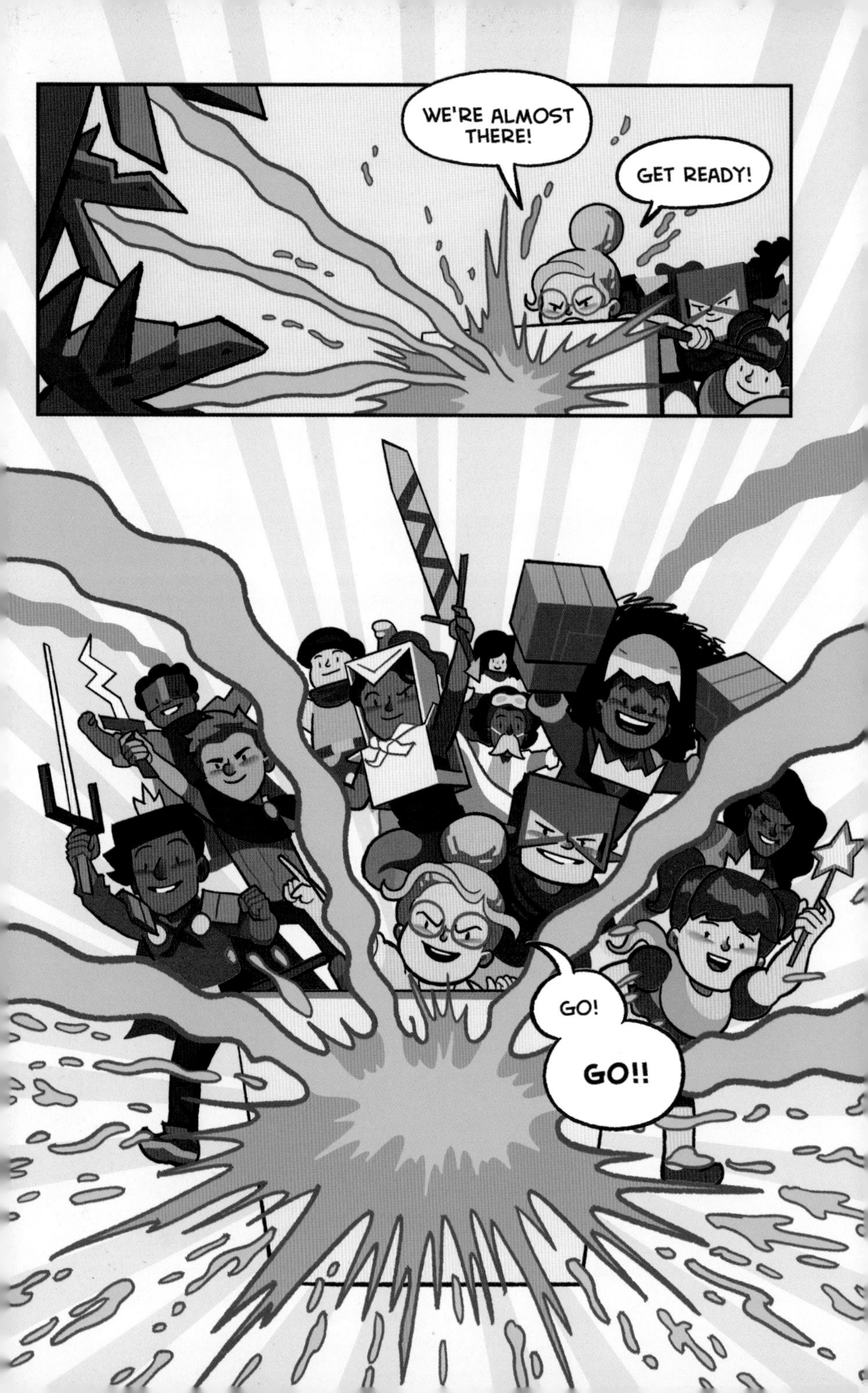
WE'RE ALMOST THERE!
GET READY!
GO!
GO!!

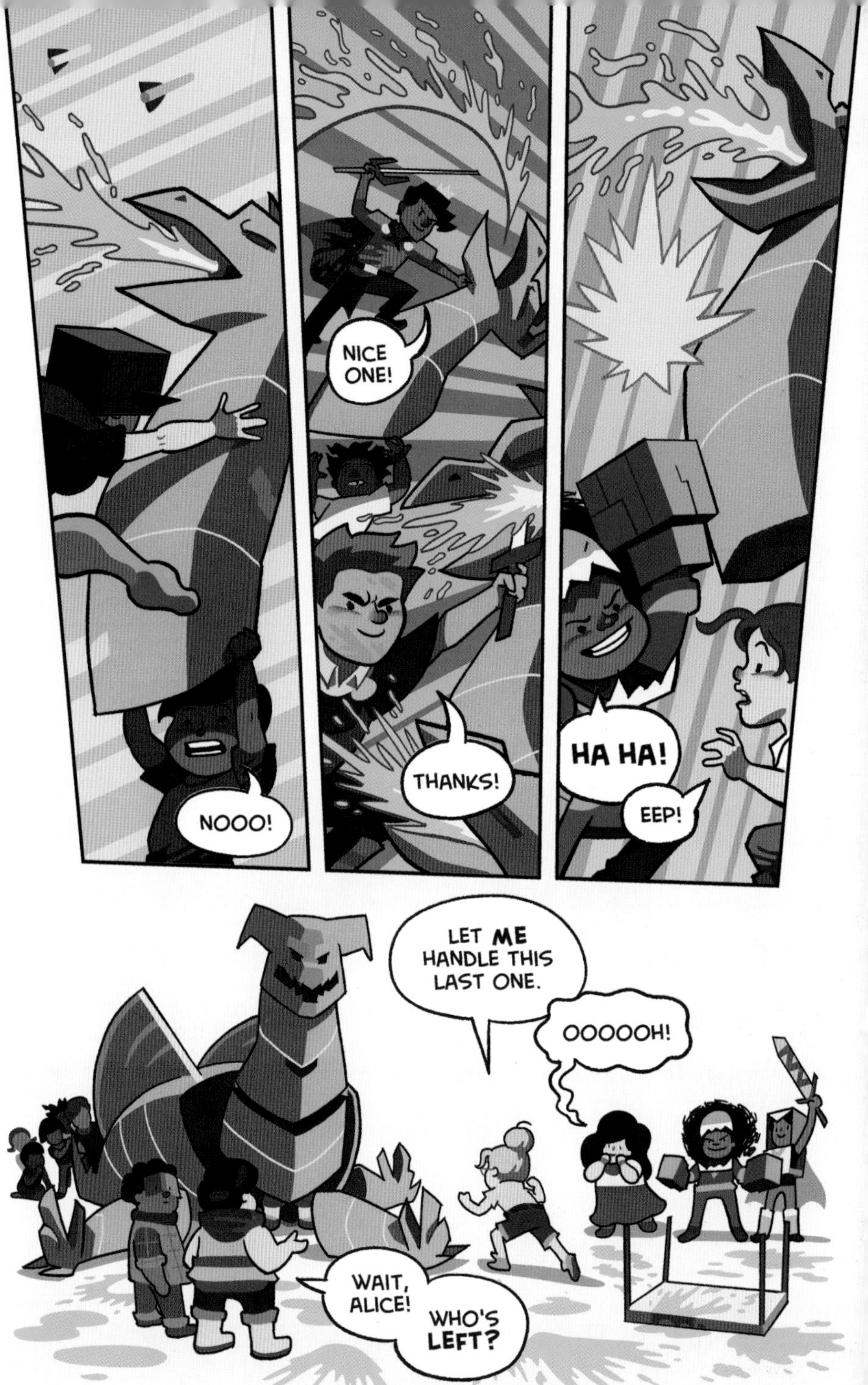
NOOO!
NICE ONE!
THANKS!
HA HA!
EEP!
LET ME HANDLE THIS LAST ONE.
OOOOOH!
WAIT, ALICE!
WHO'S LEFT?

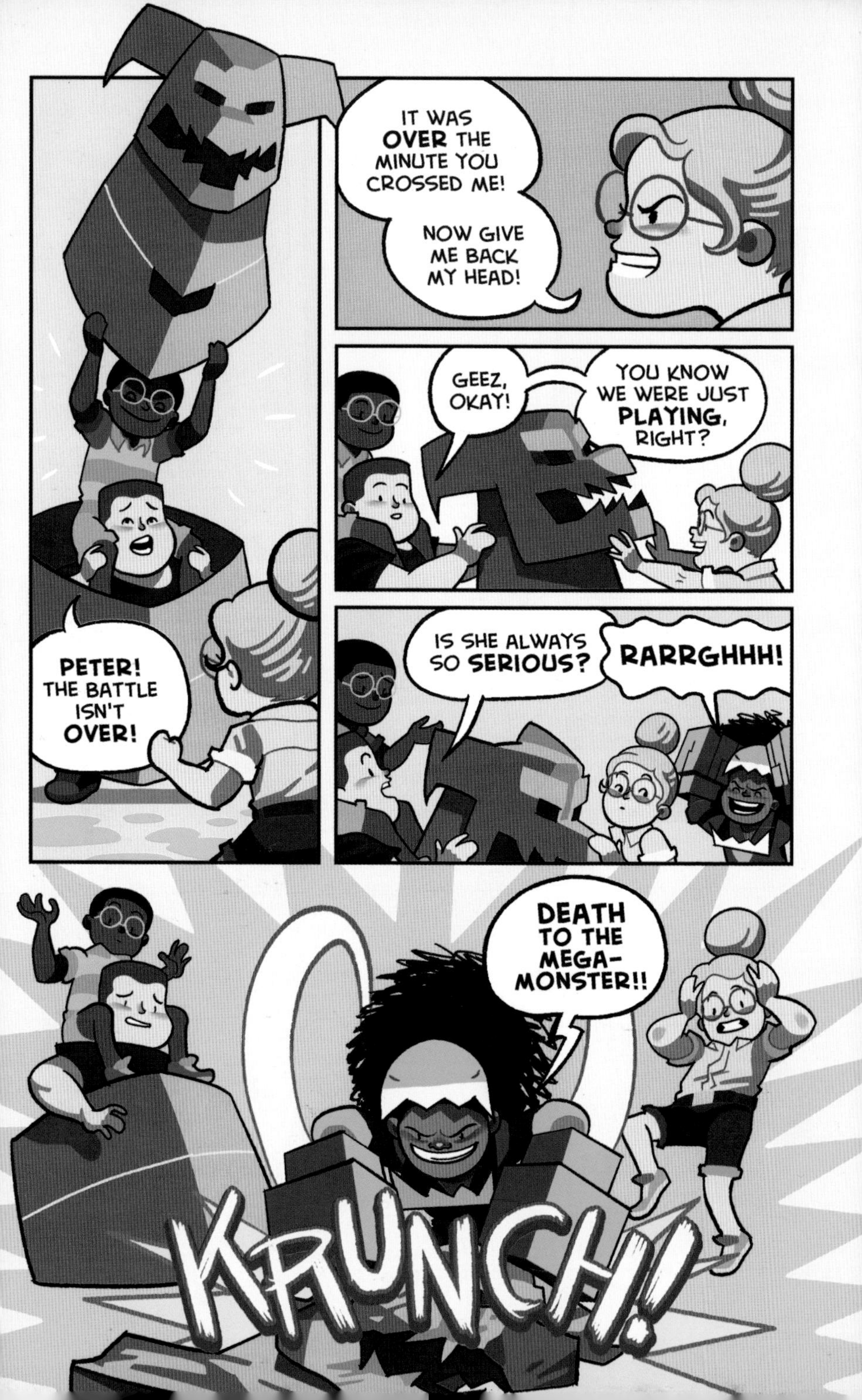
IT WAS OVER THE MINUTE YOU CROSSED ME!
NOW GIVE ME BACK MY HEAD!
GEEZ, OKAY!
YOU KNOW WE WERE JUST PLAYING, RIGHT?
PETER! THE BATTLE ISN'T OVER!
IS SHE ALWAYS SO SERIOUS?
RARRGHHH!
DEATH TO THE MEGA-MONSTER!!
KRUNCH!!

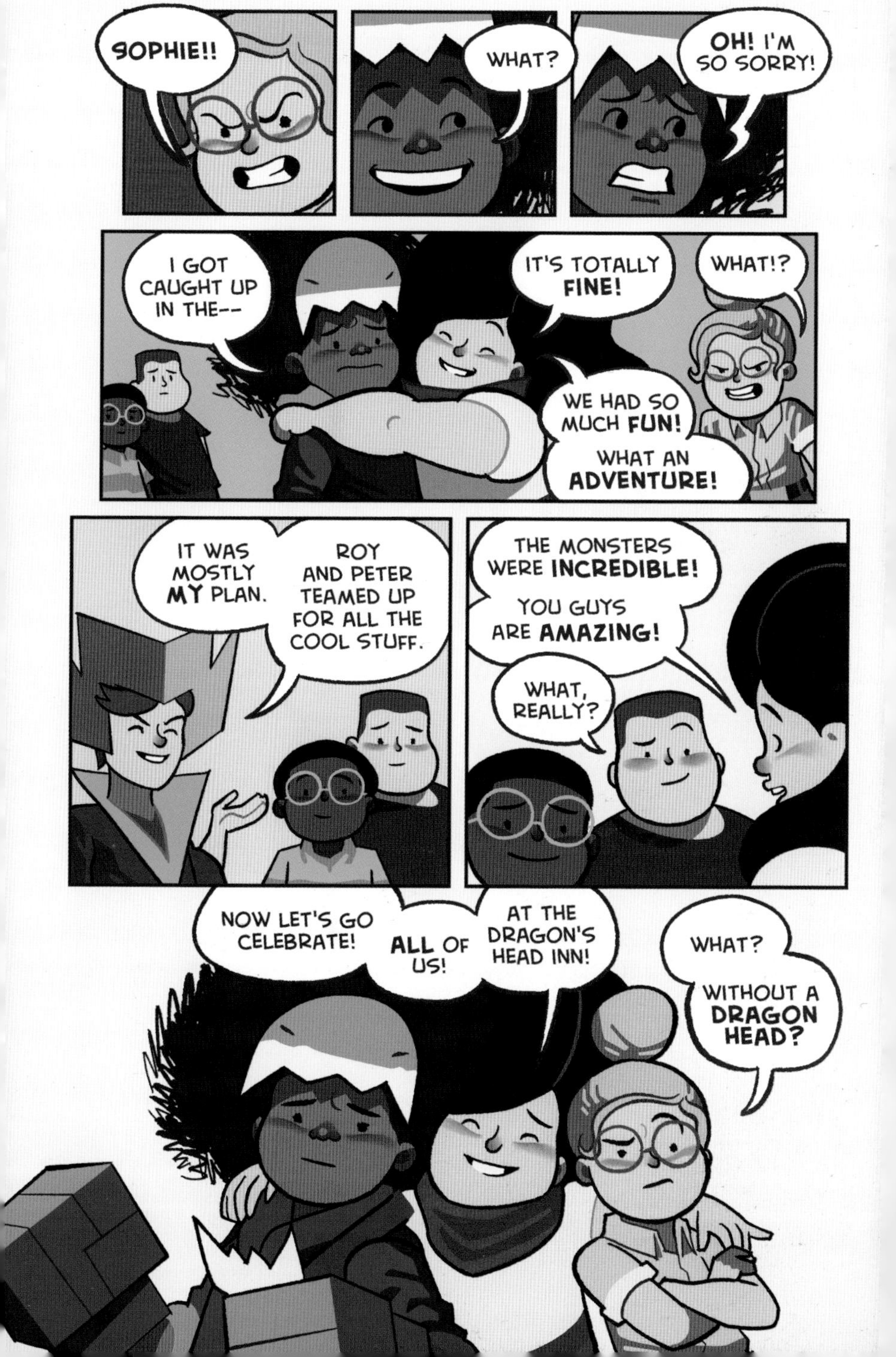
SOPHIE!!
WHAT?
OH! I'M SO SORRY!
I GOT CAUGHT UP IN THE--
IT'S TOTALLY **FINE**!
WHAT!?
WE HAD SO MUCH **FUN**!
WHAT AN **ADVENTURE**!
IT WAS MOSTLY **MY** PLAN.
ROY AND PETER TEAMED UP FOR ALL THE COOL STUFF.
THE MONSTERS WERE **INCREDIBLE**!
YOU GUYS ARE **AMAZING**!
WHAT, REALLY?
NOW LET'S GO CELEBRATE!
ALL OF US!
AT THE DRAGON'S HEAD INN!
WHAT?
WITHOUT A **DRAGON HEAD**?

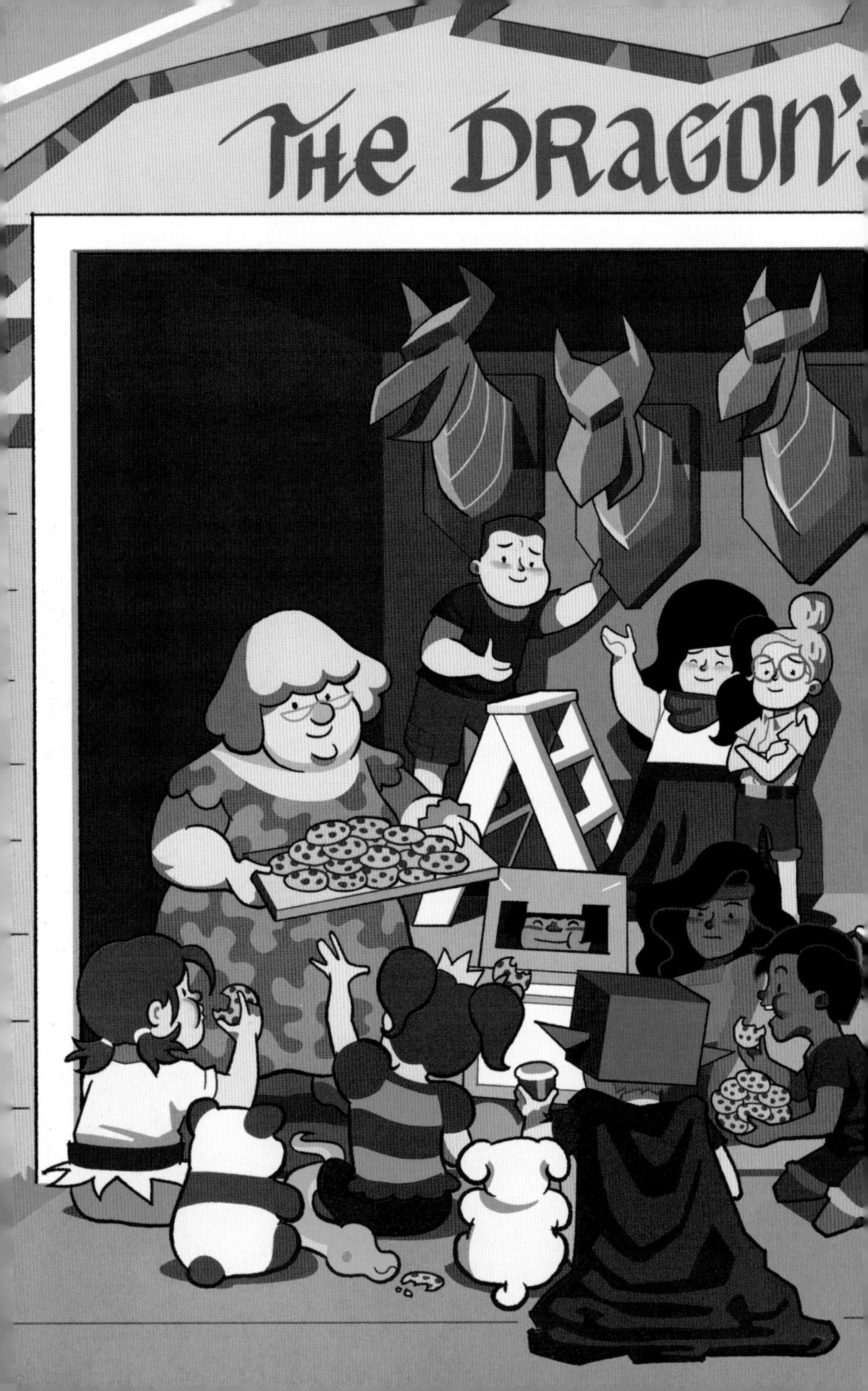
THE DRAGON'S

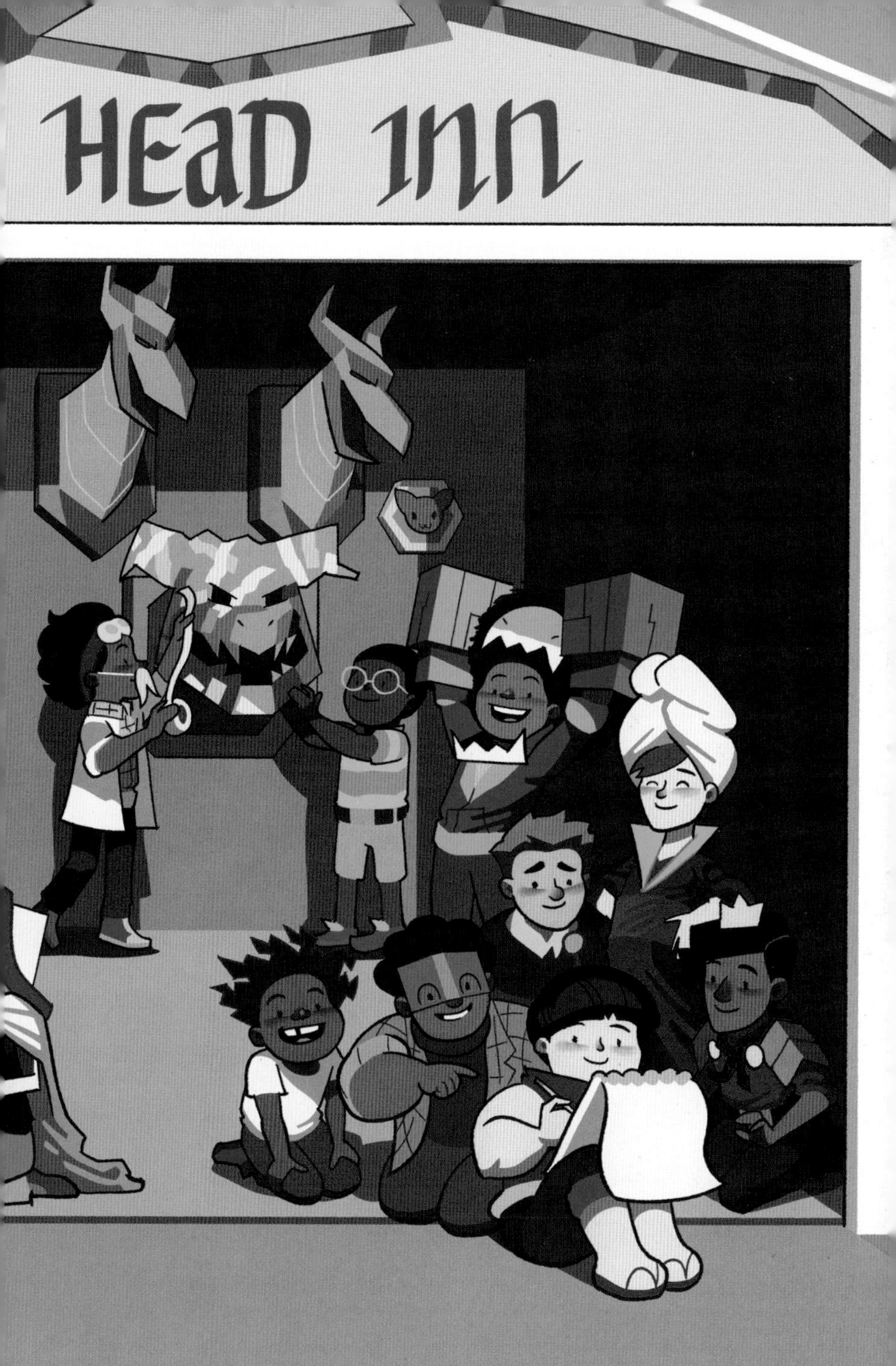
HEAD INN

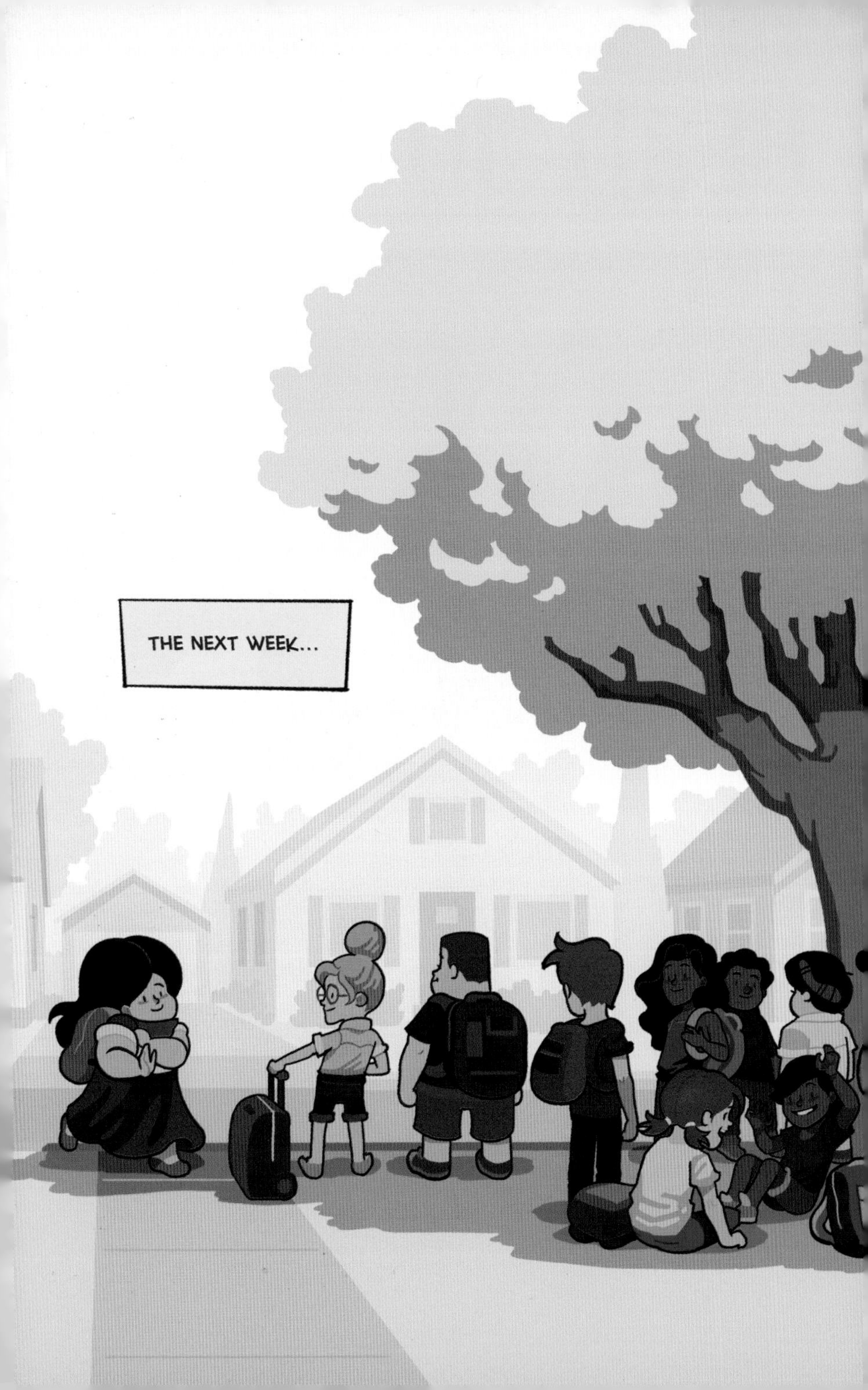
THE NEXT WEEK...

THE CARDBOARD KINGDOM
THE CARDBOARD

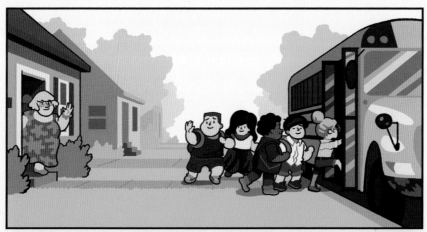

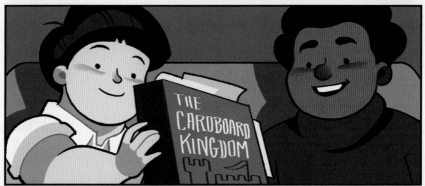

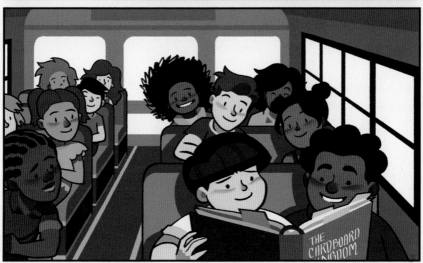

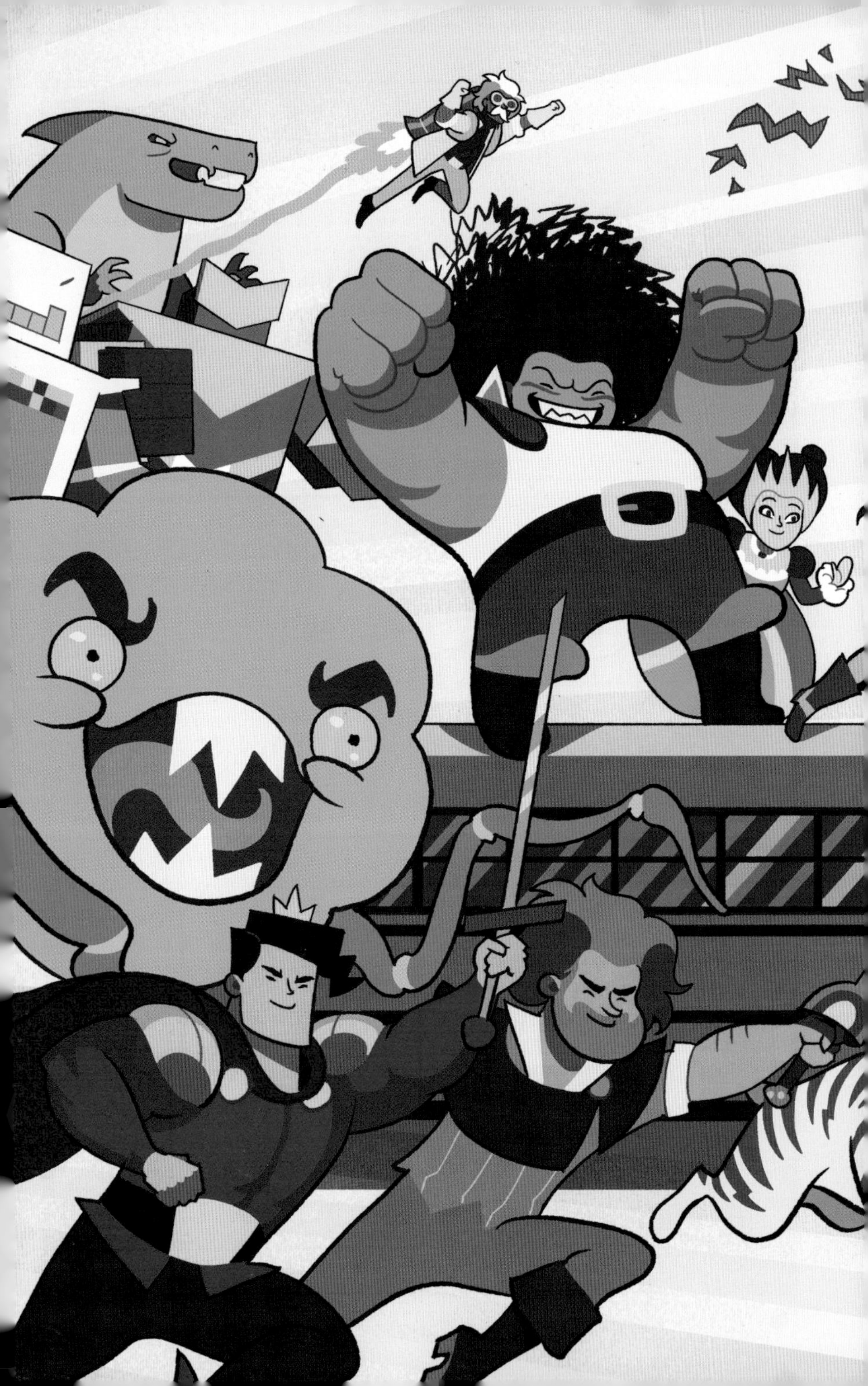

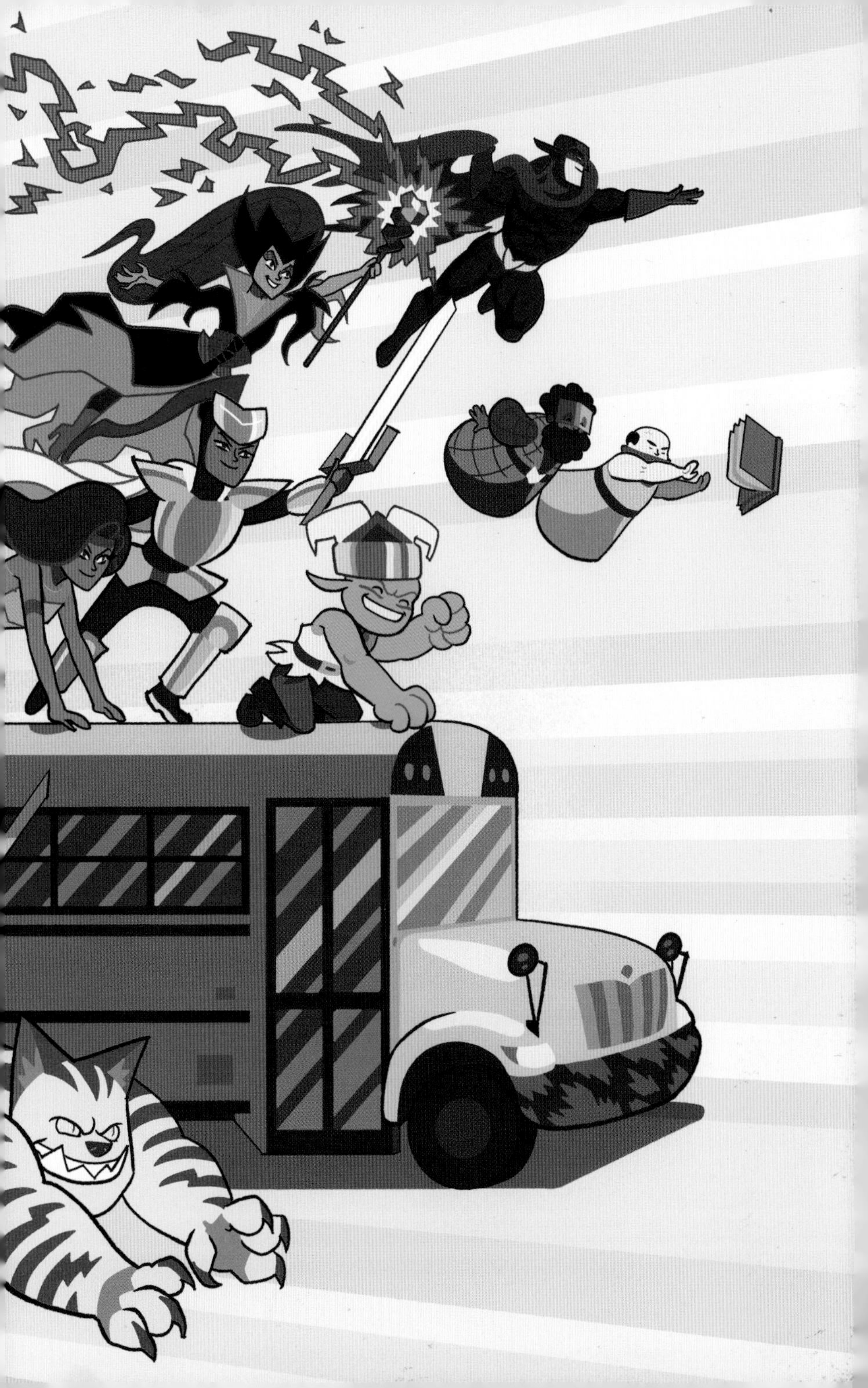

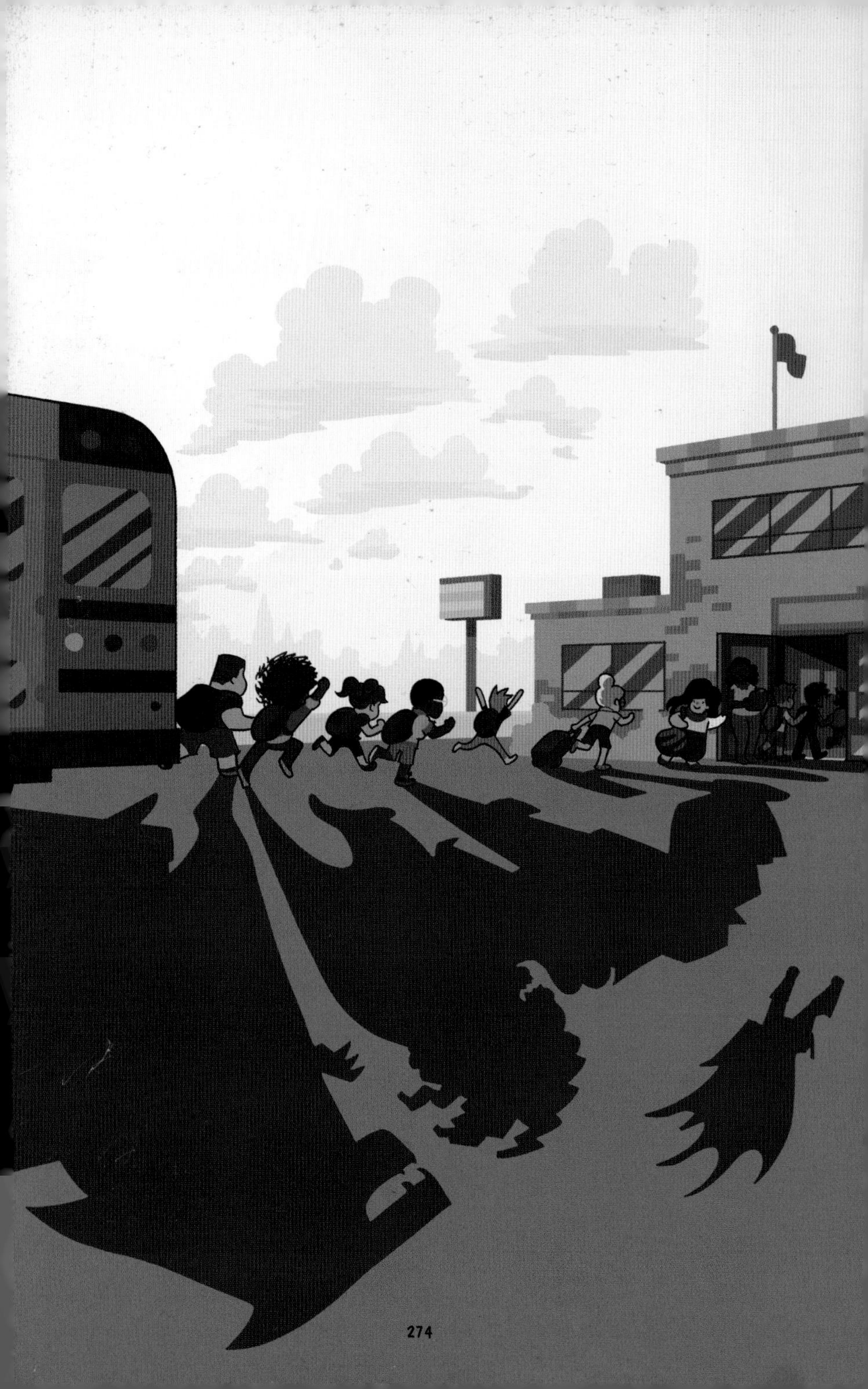

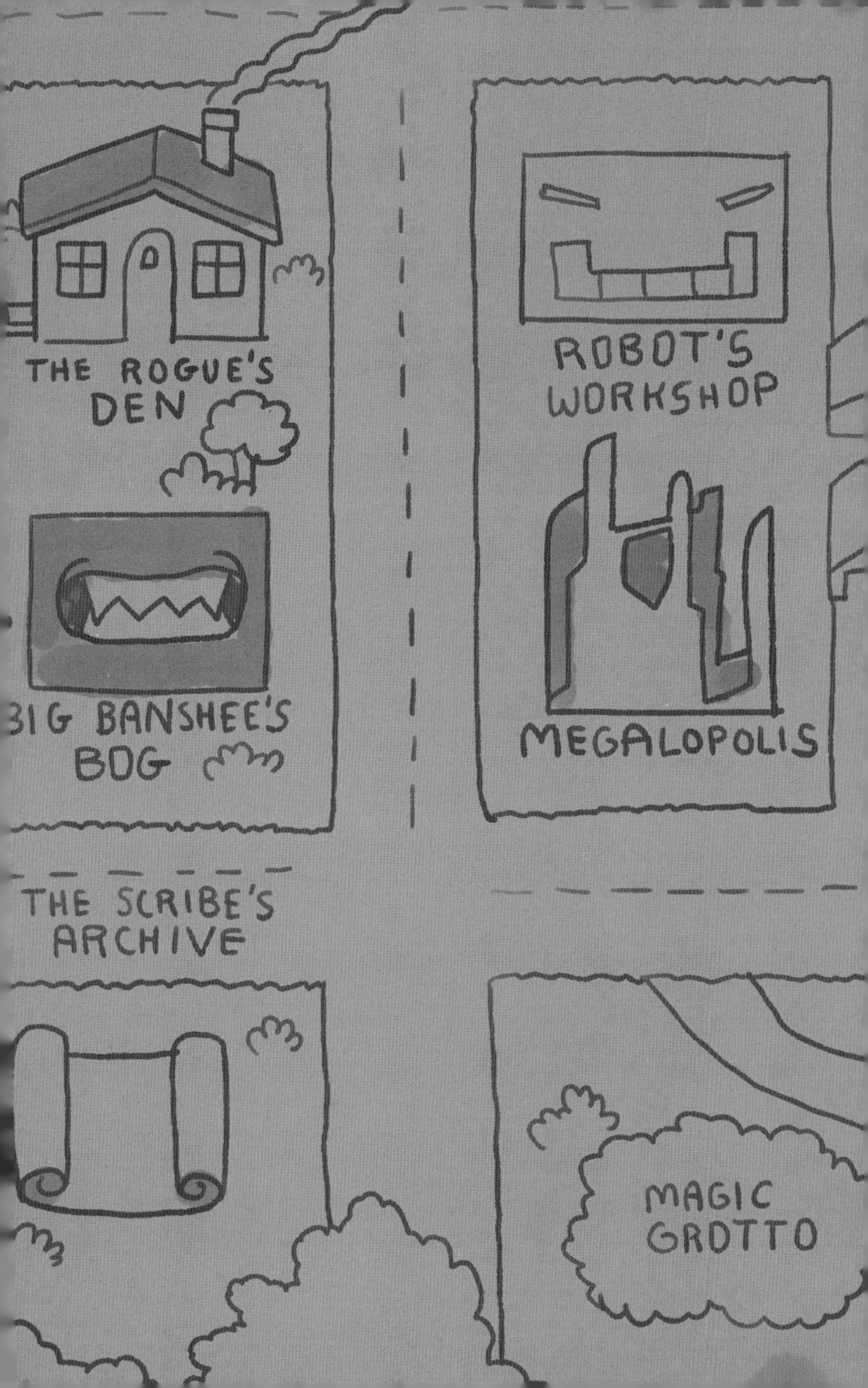
THE ROGUE'S DEN
ROBOT'S WORKSHOP
BIG BANSHEE'S BOG
MEGALOPOLIS
THE SCRIBE'S ARCHIVE
MAGIC GROTTO

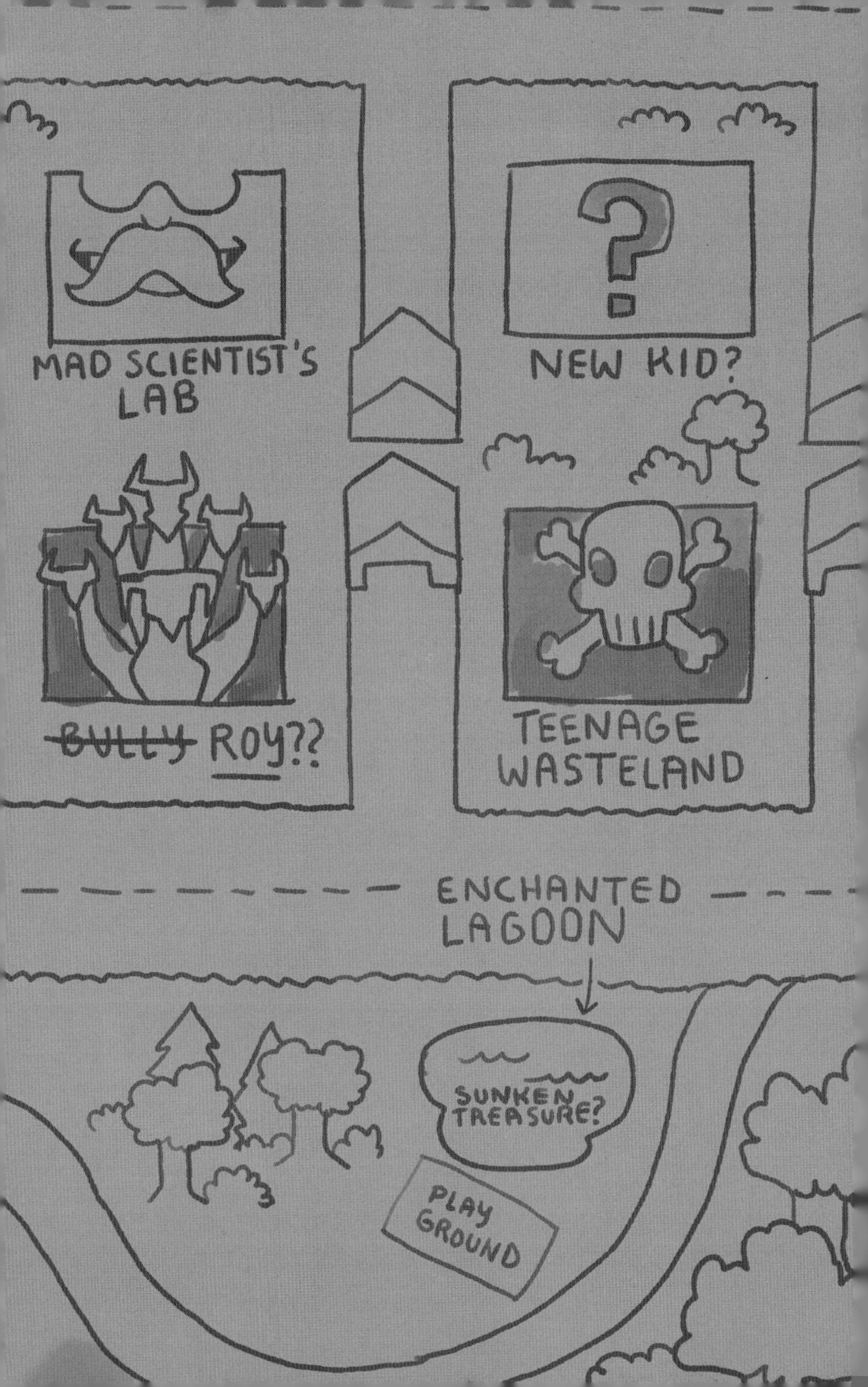
MAD SCIENTIST'S LAB
NEW KID?
~~BULLY~~ ROY??
TEENAGE WASTELAND
ENCHANTED LAGOON
SUNKEN TREASURE?
PLAY GROUND

HOW WE BUILT THE KINGDOM

It all began with the mysterious and bewitching magic of the Sorceress! Chad Sell developed her story with his friend Jay Fuller, which became the first chapter of this book. But like the humble Scribe character from the pages within, Chad sought to chronicle the stories of *all* heroes of the realm. So he asked for other writers to join forces and help fill the Cardboard Kingdom with the charismatic, courageous, and magical characters you've met in this book.

JAY FULLER

The Sorceress & Megalopolis

Jay is a cartoonist living in Brooklyn, New York, with his husband, Kevin, and their little corgi pup. He writes and illustrates his comic, *The Boy in Pink Earmuffs*. Megalopolis was inspired by Japanese monster movies and the little cardboard dioramas Jay used to make as a kid.

DAVID DEMEO

The Huntress & The Bully

David is a bald jewelry designer with a large variety of hats. His favorite holiday is Halloween, and even though he is supposedly a grown-up now, he still makes his own costumes and dresses up every year. David lives in Caldwell, New Jersey. The Huntress was based on David's babysitting responsibilities as the oldest of three beast brothers.

KATIE SCHENKEL

The Big Banshee

Katie lives in Chicago with her partner, Madison, and she wants to be Batgirl when she grows up. In the meantime, she's written comics like *Moonlighters* and *100 Light Years of Solitude*. The Big Banshee was inspired by Katie's memories of being the girl who "talked too much."

MANUEL BETANCOURT

The Prince

Manuel spends his days in New York City writing, baking, and watching way too many movies. He has a PhD but doesn't like to brag about it. The Prince was inspired by the many (many!) childhood crushes Manuel had on several animated fairy-tale heroes. He's happy to have finally written the story he wished he'd had while growing up.

MOLLY MULDOON

The Animal Queen

Molly is a writer, editor, and newly minted librarian who's always on the move with her pawtner-in-crime, Jamie McKitten. At the moment, they live in Portland, Oregon. The Animal Queen was inspired by Molly's childhood menagerie of stuffed animals.

VID ALLIGER

The Blob & The Robot

Vid is an aspiring writer and illustrator living in upstate New York. He's still figuring things out, and that's okay. The Blob was inspired by Vid's constant desire as a child to tag along with his older brothers, who were usually kind enough to let him play, too.

CLOUD JACOBS

Professor Everything

Cloud is a fifth-grade teacher in Stuttgart, Arkansas. When he's not reading and writing comics, he's working his way through every Star Wars book he can get his hands on. Professor Everything was based on Cloud's awkward childhood, when he would usually be reading while the other kids were playing football.

MICHAEL COLE

The Gargoyle

Michael teaches English literature at Wichita State University, where he also works as an accessibility technologist and is pursuing a master's degree in creative writing. In his free time, he can be found with his three dogs, playing *Breath of the Wild*. The Gargoyle was loosely based on Michael's childhood experiences, but if he had been a superhero, he would rather have been Jean Grey, not a gargoyle!

BARBARA PEREZ MARQUEZ

The Mad Scientist

Barbara is a Dominican American writer. She lives in Baltimore and has been writing since she was in seventh grade. Just like Amanda, Barbara was born and raised in the Dominican Republic, loves mustaches, and believes we can all experiment a little more in life!

In Memory of

KRIS MOORE

Kris grew up in the suburbs of Detroit and lived there with his partner, Weston. As a kid, all he ever wanted to do was write comics, and as an adult, he did just that with his comic anthology, *Saturday Morning Snack Attack!*, and all-ages series, *Science Girl.*

His characters, Becky and Alice, were inspired by the girls he grew up with, who were some of the most ruthless entrepreneurs ever to run a Kool-Aid stand.

His boundless creativity and unforgettable characters were essential in making this book—we couldn't have built this kingdom without him.

To my parents, who gave me a childhood full of love,
encouragement, and creativity
—C.S.

"The Sorceress" text copyright © 2018 by Chad Sell and Jay Fuller
"The Huntress" text copyright © 2018 by Chad Sell and David DeMeo
"The Big Banshee" text copyright © 2018 by Chad Sell and Katie Schenkel
"The Alchemist and the Blacksmith" text copyright © 2018 by Chad Sell and Kris Moore
"The Prince" text copyright © 2018 by Chad Sell and Manuel Betancourt
"The Animal Queen" text copyright © 2018 by Chad Sell and Molly Muldoon
"The Blob" text copyright © 2018 by Chad Sell and Vid Alliger
"Professor Everything" text copyright © 2018 by Chad Sell and Cloud Jacobs
"The Gargoyle" text copyright © 2018 by Chad Sell and Michael Cole
"The Mad Scientist" text copyright © 2018 by Chad Sell and Barbara Perez Marquez
"The Robot" text copyright © 2018 by Chad Sell and Vid Alliger
"The Army of Evil" text copyright © 2018 by Chad Sell
"The Bully" text copyright © 2018 by Chad Sell and David DeMeo
"Megalopolis" text copyright © 2018 by Chad Sell and Jay Fuller
"Summer's End" text copyright © 2018 by Chad Sell, Jay Fuller, David DeMeo, Katie Schenkel, Kris Moore, Manuel Betancourt, Molly Muldoon, Vid Alliger, Cloud Jacobs, Michael Cole, and Barbara Perez Marquez
Art copyright © 2018 by Chad Sell

All rights reserved. Published in the United States by Alfred A. Knopf, an imprint of Random House Children's Books, a division of Penguin Random House LLC, New York.

Knopf, Borzoi Books, and the colophon are registered trademarks of Penguin Random House LLC.

Visit us on the Web! rhcbooks.com

Educators and librarians, for a variety of teaching tools, visit us at RHTeachersLibrarians.com

Library of Congress Cataloging-in-Publication Data is available upon request.

ISBN 978-1-5247-1937-1 (trade) — ISBN 978-1-5247-1938-8 (pbk.) —
ISBN 978-1-5247-1939-5 (ebook)

The illustrations in this book were created using Clip Studio Paint.
MANUFACTURED IN CHINA
June 2018
10 9 8 7
First Edition

Random House Children's Books supports the First Amendment
and celebrates the right to read.